Intrigue

Intrigue

Anne Schulman

POOLBEG

Published in 1994 by
Poolbeg,
A division of Poolbeg Enterprises Ltd,
Knocksedan House,
123 Baldoyle Industrial Estate,
Dublin 13, Ireland
Reprinted in 1994

A catalogue record for this book is available from the British Library.

ISBN 1 85371 336 8

Cover photograph by Gillian Buckley
Cover design by Poolbeg Group Services Ltd
Set by Poolbeg Group Services Ltd in Garamond 10/11.5
Printed by Cox & Wyman Ltd, Reading, Berks.

*Dedicated with love to Bea Woolfe
whose friendship is unconditional*

Acknowledgements

Patricia Scanlan, the most generous and supportive friend.

My editor, Kate Cruise O'Brien, who, with tact and humour, taught me that 'less is more.'

Lynda, my daughter, who read each chapter and spurred me on. My son-in-law Pat who, with great patience showed me not only how to put the material into the computer but also how to get it out again.

I am most grateful for the shared wisdom and expertise of Maurice Abrahamson, Don Buchalter, Elaine Kennedy, Dr. Patricia Quinlan, Noirin Scully, Hilda Simon, Dr. Gerry Tolkin – and Ed Vincent, who has always been there for us.

To my family and friends who patiently suffered the slings and arrows of my outrageous fortune, thank you sincerely. And lastly, my husband David, endlessly loving and encouraging and without whom life would be the poorer.

PROLOGUE

Claude examined the gleaming red Ferrari and flicked an invisible speck of dust from its bonnet. He crossed the short stretch of garden from the car port to the terrace and inspected the table with a practised eye. He straightened an already perfectly positioned fork and with rare smugness allowed his mind to wander back over the last fifteen years - fifteen years of blood, sweat and fears. The Château d'Albion, his almost perfect hotel.

The sound of women's laughter and the tap tap of high heels clicking along the path nudged him back to the present. Gaby O'Neill and Laura Bingham stepped onto the terrace where Claude was waiting to greet them. They could hear the distant sound of a bell through the open doors of his drawing-room.

"Signor Eduardo Conti," the waiter announced, leading a slim, young-faced man with prematurely greying hair towards them. Both girls sized up the new arrival.

What a fine-looking man, Gaby silently admired.

"You're leering!" Laura whispered.

"Welcome," Claude smiled, no flicker of recognition in his eyes.

As he made the introductions they were again interrupted by the doorbell. Claude nodded to the waiter to serve the drinks and excused himself. Drinking their champagne from delicate Baccarat flutes the three of them glanced expectantly towards the open doors. Claude returned with the most stunning woman Laura had ever seen.

"Rachel Hunt," Claude smiled, noting the spark of interest in Eduardo Conti's eyes.

She was simply dressed in white, her olive skin and shining black hair glowed in the candlelight but the most arresting feature of her beautiful face were her huge, almond-shaped brown eyes.

"Now *you're* staring," Gaby retaliated, as she nudged Laura.

❋ ❋ ❋

Claude beamed as Rachel complimented him.

"It was a wonderful meal, Claude," Gaby agreed.

"And those wines..." Eduardo Conti smiled with appreciation.

"Perfect," Laura added, shyly.

Cocooned by the warm, sweet night air, they sipped their coffee and liqueurs as Eduardo told them an amusing tale of a large, florid lady and his new Panama hat. They didn't hear the end of the story nor did they notice the masked figure, dressed from head to toe in black, who slipped silently along the bushes at the edge of the candle-lit terrace. A shot rang out on the scented evening breeze.

The animated group froze. The intruder, lowering his gun, faced them.

"Don't anyone move, don't even breathe," he instructed harshly. "I'm here for just one of you - one of you is going to die."

Shocked into silence they sat, each of them guilty. Remembering. Regretting. Terrified. None of them wanted to die.

Book One

Gaby

CHAPTER ONE

"**P**retentious cow," Gaby O'Neill thought to herself as she listened to Aideen Connor's sycophantic voice shrilling down the phone. Who the hell invites anyone to a soirée these days? More to the point - who the hell was Aideen Connor?

Gaby O'Neill lay in bed with her eyes firmly closed and her head pounding. She allowed the voice with its affected accent and stomach-turning compliments to wash over her. Through the mists of sleep she struggled to put a face to the voice. Another monumental hangover.

"We would love you and your father to join us," the voice gushed. "If the date isn't suitable we can change it."

Gaby racked her muzzy brain. Triumphantly she recalled the ambitious wife of an eager advertising executive. They had met at a party the previous week. Gaby had become adept, even expert, at dealing with unwanted invitations. With her eyes still tightly closed, Gaby declined regretfully. She dropped the receiver somewhere in the vicinity of its base. Gingerly and slowly she prepared to open one eye. The dreaded shaft of light attacked. Groaning, she pulled the sheet over her head. She felt a bit sheepish - normally she wouldn't have reacted so uncharitably.

It was fully two more minutes before she groped for the phone and asked for room service. "Orange juice, toast, a pot of coffee, and," she stressed, "something for a headache."

"Certainly, Miss O'Neill," a quiet voice responded. "She has a hangover again," the grinning receptionist informed the kitchen staff. No one needed to ask who *she* was; indulgent smiles were the only response.

Gaby and her father, John O'Neill, had been regular guests at the Berkeley Court Hotel since it had opened. They were popular, liked by all the staff. With the exception of her school, the hotel was the nearest thing to a home that Gaby could remember.

The tablets had begun to work their magic. Her pounding headache subsided. She sipped her coffee and smiled in anticipation of the lunch-time appointment with her two closest friends. She'd been looking forward to it for days. The three girls had formed a bond from their first night at school when, as timid ten-year-olds, they tried to hide their tears from each other. Their sniffles had ended in laughter. Tucked away at the foot of the Wicklow mountains, the school, with its sprawling white buildings and extensive grounds, was welcoming and homely. Gaby had been nervous and shy when her father took her to see it for the first time but soon she was "oohing" and "aahing" as she discovered the tennis courts, the newly built swimming pool and the "pupil-scaped" flower gardens. She'd never seen so many girls gathered in one place before; they were everywhere. The hustle and bustle, the noise and sounds of screeching laughter appealed to her fun-loving nature. John O'Neill was content with his choice. Gaby's enthusiasm set his mind at rest.

After their initial homesickness, the trio settled down into a happy existence. Their hair-raising escapades won admiration from other more timid pupils. Not for those three were the usual childish pranks. They had instead removed bicycle chains the night before a cycling-picnic, emptied the swimming-pool the morning of the annual swimming gala and, with the aid of two of their friends, they'd lugged the sports master's motorcycle up three flights of stairs to their room. With muffled snorts of laughter they hid in an alcove on the ground floor and waited. The coach, despite his physical fitness, puffed and panted with exertion as he bumped the heavy vehicle down the stairs. The noise had brought two of the staff running into the corridor. Without any prompting they knew exactly where the blame lay, who the culprits were.

"Gabrielle O'Neill, Jacqueline Maher, Jill Riordan! Come here immediately!" an angry voice commanded.

"Here we go. Trouble!" Jill grinned.

"How do they always know where to find us?" groaned Gaby, totally perplexed.

"We make so much noise that's why," reasoned Jacqui, always the most practical of the three. Over the years they'd accepted their many punishments with good grace. Gaby attributed her love of gardening to the weeding and digging of flower beds that was their usual penalty following one of their capers.

The trio presented a startling contrast in appearance. Gaby with her silvery-blonde hair and green eyes was the tallest of the three. Her love of sweets and chocolates had earned her the nickname of *Flabby Gaby*. Her constant diets usually ended the day they began. She dwarfed the flame haired and diminutive Jacqui by at least six inches. Jacqui, who longed to be taller, had tried everything. At one stage, in sheer desperation, she demanded that Gaby and Jill grip her feet and arms and pull with all their might. After four days of exertion on their part and a strained shoulder on hers, she resigned herself to her fate and remained a dainty figure. The middleman, as they referred to Jill, was the darkest of the girls. Her black hair gleamed like silk and her grey-blue eyes with their long lashes were the envy of everyone who knew her.

Giggling aloud, Gaby remembered asking permission to visit the local chemist.

"For what reason, Gaby?" the cautious teacher enquired.

"On compassionate grounds," she answered. She'd read that in a book somewhere and liked it.

The teacher's lips twitched. "That won't do, Gaby."

Blushing, Gaby confessed that she and Jacqui wanted to buy some almond oil that they were convinced would make their eyelashes grow as long as Jill's.

Religously they applied the liquid. Every day for two weeks. Their only reward was stinging, blurred eyes, greasy faces and oily exercise books. One of Gaby's essays became so spattered with drops from the "magic oil" that it had to be rewritten. With great ceremony and mock greasy tears they'd poured the rest of the liquid from the slippery bottle down the sink. They finally accepted that they were forever doomed to have normal eyelashes just like other mortals.

A discreet tapping at her bedroom interrupted Gaby's reflections. She glanced at her watch as the waiter removed the breakfast trolley, he moved silently across the thickly carpeted floor. Gaby chided herself for day-dreaming and gently edged herself out of bed. The room lurched slightly. She steadied herself and frowned as she noticed the skirt of her elegant Chanel suit lying crumpled on a chair. The previous evening, when she was dressing to go to dinner, the button at the waist had refused to do its job and had flown off into space and disappeared from sight.

"The diet begins as of now!" she told herself sternly as she began her search for the missing button.

CHAPTER TWO

Twice John O'Neill knocked on his daughter's door but failed to get any response. "Gaby?" he called loudly.

"Ouch!" he heard her yelp. "Come in."

He pushed the door open and laughed as he saw the truncated body of his daughter with her satin-pyjammed bottom and long legs, wriggling from under the bed.

"You gave me a fright," Gaby said rubbing her head.

"What on earth were you doing?" her father asked.

"Looking for a button and trying to get rid of a hangover - so speak quietly," she warned, holding her hands over her ears.

He frowned - but hid his disquiet. He'd heard that all too often lately. A wave of guilt swept over him. Her nomadic lifestyle; living in hotels, eating rich restaurant food and drinking more than was good for her. It was always a worry, a cause for concern. Over and over again he'd promised himself that they would buy a permanent home. With Gaby away at school it had been all too easy to allow himself to become a workaholic with little or no social life. During the holidays she'd joined him on his travels. She adored the exotic countries which his work took him to.

His gift of three computers to the school had been a stroke of genius. And not entirely altruistic. Reluctantly at first Gaby agreed to enrol in the computer classes. It was the lesser of two evils. The alternative was the home economy sessions which she'd never liked. Her lack of dexterity with pots and pans was legendary - her teacher frequently remarked that Gaby was the only person she'd ever met who could burn a boiled egg while she watched it. The only pupil who could make a loaf of bread which was an inch deep in the middle and a foot high at the sides.

"Never mind," Gaby said with equal frequency, "I can always eat at Jacqui's."

To her surprise Gaby found computers fascinating. She soon became adept at programming and she enjoyed using the machines.

To John O'Neill, his daughter was the most important thing in his life. Even when she was a young teenager he had taken her with him to meetings and introduced her to clients. Afterwards he had patiently explained what was happening and answered her questions in detail.

Gaby found herself watching people's reactions and had been proud when, at the age of fifteen, John had shaken her hand and said solemnly, "Welcome partner."

She had sat quietly beside her father as he talked to a client. They arranged to meet the following day and when the man left Gaby asked her father, "Why did he tap his foot when you asked him some questions?"

"What do you mean, Gaby?"

"When you asked him about his figures, he tapped his foot. When you asked about annual profits he did it again. Then you asked to see audits and he tapped faster than ever."

"Are you sure?" John hadn't noticed the tapping routine.

"Absolutely. I watched him."

"We've had a lucky escape," John told her a few days later. "Your observation saved the day." In his trouble-shooting business people relied on his judgement and so far he'd made few mistakes.

When the three girls finished school John O'Neill took his life in his hands and brought them to Paris. He was ready for that drink at the end of each exhausting day. He'd always considered himself to be energetic but having tramped from one end of Paris to the other he gave in and admitted he was no match for those three live wires. It was in the evenings at dinner that he enjoyed their company most. How many times had he told himself that Gaby was blessed to have such wonderful friends? They were as close as sisters if not closer. John rarely missed one of Gaby's birthdays or a school holiday but, if it was really difficult for him to get back to Ireland, he knew she was welcome and happy at either of their homes. Gaby's sunny nature delighted most people. Her charm had often proved to be an asset to John. Clients relaxed in her wide-eyed company and often she would learn more about them in ten minutes than he could in a week. He came to rely on her intuition. When Gaby became his travelling-assistant they maintained their wandering lifestyle.

Gaby knew that her father spoilt her. He

encouraged her to buy beautiful clothes and had never disapproved when she made a mistake and wore something outlandish. Eventually she found her own style and stuck to it. He had big cupboards built for her on the top floor of their office in Dublin and she had the only key. She began to buy small ornaments on their travels. These she carefully wrapped and stored in the office waiting for the day when they finally had a home again.

Gaby never came back to Dublin without a gift for Jill and Jacqui; perfume, the latest make-up or glamorous tights from the States, unusual foods from France for Jacqui and gorgeous silk scarves for Jill. When Jacqui and Colin had their first baby, Gaby haunted the toy shops in every city that she visited. After all, she reasoned, I am one of his godmothers. Jill, of course, was the other. Gaby missed the girls when she travelled but her friendly manner and ready smile drew people to her like a magnet. Soon she had quite a number of young people she could contact in most European or American cities. John watched her blossom from an awkward teenager into a most attractive young woman. He was proud of his daughter. She was so like her mother it tugged at his heart.

"You're meeting the girls for lunch?" John asked as he opened the door to leave.

"Downstairs in the lounge at twelve thirty," replied Gaby. "It will be great to see them again. It's been ages since the three of us have been able to get together."

"I'll try to say hello if I get time after my meeting."

Anne Schulman

laughter and, unable to contain themselves any longer at the sight of the bedraggled victim, they screamed with unrestrained laughter. Janine's face was puce with fury.

The stern-faced head had approached the three "known criminals". Their laughter had been tinged with fear, fear that Janine might take legal action. The dressing-down they received in the head-mistress's study made them both frightened and ashamed. They'd gone too far this time. "It was irresponsible and dangerous...," Mary Doherty was unable to continue the lecture. A vision of the dumbstruck Janine, staring like a zombie at the fallen hair, came into her mind. She tried desperately not to give in to the laughter welling in her throat, but she was lost. Great snorts of helpless mirth filled the silent room. "Go to bed!" she half-sobbed.

The following morning they apologised and to their relief Janine made no mention of suing them.

Even now the two of them, sophisticated young women that they were, roared with laughter at the memory. People at nearby tables smiled indulgently at the pretty girls' obvious enjoyment.

"Listen, Gaby," Jill said wiping her eyes, "to get serious for a moment, I'm concerned about Jacqui. She doesn't seem to be her usual self; she's... sort of distracted and vague."

"Odd you should say that - when I spoke to her yesterday she was quite brusque. No time for a chat. She rang off with hardly a goodbye, most unlike her."

Their varied lifestyles and frequent separations

hadn't changed their concern for each other. Their friendship was as solid as it ever was.

Jacqui rushed up to where they were sitting and flopped into the empty chair. There were dark circles under her eyes and she looked exhausted.

"Sorry to be so late," she panted, "I got held up..." They waited for her to go on but instead she picked up the menu and gave it her full attention.

Jill and Gaby glanced questioningly at each other.

"What are you going to have?" Gaby attempted brightly. "I, of course, am on a diet."

They both grinned at her. "Well, I am!" she defended.

A waitress hovered by their side as they made their choice. "Sandwiches and coffee OK? A selection of sandwiches will be fine," Jill confirmed, returning the card to the glass-topped table.

"Gaby was telling me about Kevin, they had dinner last night," Jill said, filling Jacqui in on their conversation.

"How was he?" Jacqui enquired, "I haven't spoken to him for ages."

"Not a happy soul unfortunately. Madam is adding to his problems. She's spending money like it's going out of fashion," Gaby said, making no effort to hide her antipathy towards Janine. She'd always felt a twinge of guilt, it was she who'd introduced them in the first place.

"You don't know the half of it," Jill added, "she's put a deposit on one of those new houses in Foxrock."

"Kevin didn't tell me that," Gaby said,

surprised.

"Kevin doesn't know yet!"

"How did you find out?" Gaby demanded.

"One of my clients was interested in the new development and he asked me to phone the agent for details. I did of course, and while we were talking he mentioned that Janine Dowd had paid a deposit on one of the larger corner sites," Jill explained.

"Not very ethical," Jacqui remarked.

"He'd sell his own mother to clinch a deal," Jill replied. As the proprietor of a small but thriving estate agency Jill heard a lot of gossip. She'd often heard snippets of useful information which she stored in her mental filing cabinet for future use.

In her inimitable witty manner Gaby told them of the phone call from Aideen Connor. Jill frowned, she'd heard of the couple - vaguely. Jacqui's face was white as chalk.

"Jacqui, are you all right?" Gaby fretted, "you look so pale."

Before Jacqui had a chance to reply, Jill interrupted. "Here's Uncle John." John O'Neill was scanning the spacious room with his eyes - searching for their table. He smiled as he saw the attractive group in the corner by the piano. His dark-suited figure showed none of the excesses of executive living. His rugged face was transformed with pleasure when he saw "his three girls". The streak of white in his hair added a look of distinction to his square-jawed face, and the smile which creased his lips brought a softness to his dark eyes. Jacqui and Jill hugged him and rushed to draw up an extra chair.

"I wish I could join you," he said regretfully, "but I have a one o'clock lunch meeting."

There was so little time these days, he thought ruefully; he missed their bright company. There was so little time for anything but work.

His workaholic life had been easy when Gaby was in school. It had earned him a small fortune, but the money became less important than the need to keep his mind occupied every hour of his waking day - and most of the night.

"Gaby'll fill me in later with your news. Next time we're in Dublin we'll have dinner together and you can shock me with your wicked antics."

"I *do* miss seeing him," Jacqui added wistfully, as he disappeared through the adjoining bar towards the dining-room. Her own father had died when she was only three and John O'Neill had filled that role whenever she needed advice. He had nudged her towards her successful goal; joining two other girls, equally dedicated, in opening their own small catering firm. He had proved his confidence in her by recommending them to several friends and business associates. Before long they were tearing around from one executive dining-room to another - with bookings months in advance.

Jill ordered fresh coffee. Surreptitiously Gaby watched Jacqui's face, rosy-cheeked again. But something was wrong, Gaby was sure of it. She half-listened to Jill's praise of her father. Both girls adored John O'Neill. From their schooldays onwards he had taken as much interest in them as he had in Gaby.

Without much persuasion on Gaby's part, Jill had joined her friend in the computer classes.

Jacqui was totally content to remain in the cookery class where she was earning a reputation for herself as a talented and natural cook. When they left school Jill enrolled in a secretarial course, then found a job as a secretary with a small firm of estate agents. Within months her efficiency and ability were noticed. She was asked to show properties to prospective buyers and her honest evaluations had led to further recommendations. John O'Neill became their most valued client.

She remembered the day when he'd phoned and asked her to attend an important meeting. It was reassuring that Gaby would be there. Her nervousness soon vanished as she understood the requirements of the multi-national company's representative. She and Gaby were totally professional, John O'Neill noted proudly. An idea began to form in his head.

"Do you have time for lunch, Jill?" he asked.

"Say yes," Gaby urged. They'd seen little of each other for the past few months. "Only dieters and shoppers skip lunch," she announced, perkily.

Jill had no urgent appointments. "I'd be delighted." She smiled at her friend's exuberance.

"Let's go back to the hotel," John suggested, "it's quiet there and we can talk."

Jill's mind raced. Talk about what? Uncle John looked very serious. Had she said something wrong?

When they were settled in the deep comfortable sofas in the drawing-room of their suite, John put his thoughts into words.

"You're totally capable of running your own

agency," he began, "without prying, I imagine that you must generate a lot of your company's business. It's time, Jill, to start out on your own. Start your own agency."

Both girls stared at him, Gaby as stunned by his suggestion as Jill was. Finally Jill spoke. "It's a wonderful idea but utterly impossible. My parents couldn't pay for me to set up an agency and I've very little money of my own."

"I've thought of that. I will pay all your expenses and when you're fully established you can repay me. It's the most practical way of dealing with the matter," he said, brooking no argument.

"And if I fail to make it work?" Jill queried.

"That'll be my loss, won't it? You'll have to find out exactly what it takes to open an agency, locate the right premises, hire staff and then launch the firm. Maybe you couldn't cope with all that?" he challenged.

Jill was undaunted, her response was as he'd expected. "Of course I can," she assured him, unaware of his devious method of nudging her towards a decision. He dismissed her counter-suggestion of a partnership.

"It must be your company and yours alone."

Finding premises had been the least difficult of her tasks. Hiring the right person to help her had taken longer; her girl-Monday-to-Friday. The launch party hadn't cost her a thought; she'd left that in Jacqui's capable hands. The licence was granted and the expensive bond paid. Six months to the day following John O'Neill's heady challenge, Jill Maher and Company, Ltd., opened its doors for business.

"More coffee anyone?" Gaby enquired.

Jill started, dragging herself back from her memories.

"Not for me," Jacqui answered, "I have to go now. I... " Her voice trailed off.

Gaby looked at the gold-braceleted watch on her wrist. "It's only two o'clock," she said, disappointed.

"I'll see you tomorrow night, about eight? We'll have plenty of time to chat then," Jacqui said, gathering up her coat and handbag. Promising to phone Jill the following week she walked quickly away from the table.

"There *is* something wrong," Jill frowned as she watched their departing friend.

"Did you notice how white her face was just as Dad came in? I'll talk to her tomorrow night. Even that's odd, now that I think of it - she never mentions a time. I always get there before the children go to bed," Gaby mused aloud. "What a shame you're going to London tomorrow."

"I'm really excited about this trip; a new client. I must admit that this has taken the gloss off it a bit. I'll phone you tomorrow - about midnight and you can clue me in. I suppose I'd better make tracks too, I've a three o'clock appointment and must check my paperwork beforehand. What are you going to do, Gaby?" she asked.

"I'm going to buy my usual present for Aunt Mary's birthday," she replied. They both laughed, remembering the years Gaby had agonised about gifts for her only relative. They'd been accepted with thanks but little interest. One year, in desperation, she gave her aunt a generous gift voucher from Brown Thomas. Although her aunt wouldn't admit it she had thoroughly enjoyed her day in Dublin. She loved the train journey, browsing round the shops and her visit to the store to choose her own present.

Gaby stood under the hotel awning sheltering from the drizzle. The hotel doorman, in his black and gold-braided uniform, drew up in her hired car and, warning her to drive carefully, handed her the keys.

"I will," she promised, smiling at him and hopped into the driver's seat. She usually had a chat with Peter but a queue of taxis was forming, waiting to unload their passengers.

She made her way out of the carpark and edged into the untidy stream of traffic heading towards the city. As she waited for the lights to change her troubled thoughts strayed back to Jacqui. Turning right she drove along the busy car-lined street. Without any warning, the lightly-dressed figure of a young girl darted into the road in front of her car. Gaby swerved to avoid her. The thud jolted through her body.

Why was her tongue so swollen, her mouth so dry? She could only breathe in gasps. Who was this woman leading her from the car? Why was she sitting on a tiny stone wall? All round her people were asking questions. A siren wailed in the distance, followed by another one with a different tone. There were people in the road, so many people. The traffic had stopped, someone was sobbing - why did they cry so loudly?

"Gaby..., Gaby!" She heard her name. Her father's voice? She stared at him blankly. Someone put a tube in her mouth. She was *trying* to blow hard, couldn't they tell? The siren wailed again. "What's happening?" she asked vaguely. She recognised her father, he was talking to a tall man in a black uniform. Was it Peter, from the hotel? He always wore a black uniform. There were other people talking to him too. He was writing in a notebook. She was cold. Trembling. She wanted to sleep.

CHAPTER THREE

John O'Neill tiptoed away from his sedated daughter's bedside and closed the door. He poured himself a drink from the decanter and slumped into one of the softly-cushioned chairs in the drawing-room of their suite. The roller-coasting day had left him totally enervated. He blessed the honesty of the three people who had witnessed the accident and their generosity in becoming involved. Their detailed statements to the police had exonerated Gaby completely.

His paralysed brain had ceased to function when the news of the accident reached him. Stephen Drake, his spectacled face as bloodless as his own, had moved into action and within four minutes of hearing the bad tidings they'd reached the scene of the accident. That vision of the crumpled figure, covered only by a short jacket, would remain imprinted on his mind forever. On one outstretched hand, a ruby and diamond ring glinted in the afternoon sun. His worst fears were allayed when he saw his daughter sitting on a little stone wall, apparently unhurt. The garda on duty steered him away from the crowd that had gathered round the hapless girl, lying in the centre of the road like a discarded rag doll.

"Is she badly hurt? Alive?" John O'Neill asked the policeman who was attempting to move people aside.

"Barely," he responded, his mournful face

offering little hope.

John was rigid with tension as Gaby blew into the tube of the breathalyser. The test proved negative and the relief that flooded through his veins almost caused his knees to buckle.

Dr Gerry Oscar arrived at the hotel in less than half an hour.

"You must have had a dreadful fright Gaby," he said soothingly, satisfied that she wasn't hurt.

"Yes?" Gaby wasn't sure what he'd said.

"I'm going to give you an injection, it'll make you sleep. You'll feel a lot better then, OK?"

Gaby nodded silently, her eyes dull and unfocused.

"She's suffering from shock," Gerry Oscar told John. "Don't worry if it lasts for some time, that's to be expected."

"Thanks for getting here so quickly, Gerry. I must admit when I heard the news that she'd been involved in an accident I thought the worst."

"I don't blame you, I was scared myself when I heard Stephen's voice."

The two men had been friends for years, ever since Gaby was a newborn baby. It was Gerry Oscar who'd helped John to recover from the shock of his young wife's death. Gaby loved him. They missed his company terribly when he left Wexford to open a practice in Dublin but they'd never lost touch. John had missed their weekly dinners and chess games. Gaby missed his bear hugs and his presents. He always brought her chocolate or ice cream. If she was very good she was allowed to watch the game with its kings and queens and prawns, as she called them. For a long time they didn't have the heart to correct her.

"I'm at the end of the phone if you're worried," Gerry Oscar reassured John. "I'll pop in on my way to surgery in the morning and have a look at her. Pour yourself a good stiff whiskey, John, you could do with it."

Gaby stirred restlessly, private demons chased through her misty sleep. She could feel the thud as the girl hit the car but then the image faded as the swirling clouds of sleep claimed her. They were all there with her, Róisín and her father, Uncle Gerry and Jill, Jacqui. They were in France, swimming in the warm water. Róisín warned her not to swim out too far, it was dangerous. Gaby loved Róisín, she'd been like a mother to her. She cried out, cried as she had when she heard that Róisín was going to marry Seán and had to move away. There was that girl again, swimming towards her in the blue water. They collided. Gaby screamed out in her sleep.

"Gaby, Gaby. It's all right," her father's voice said. The dream faded.

She was late for her meeting. She kept on running but her feet wouldn't move. The man at the other side of the desk was angry. She smiled at him but he glowered back at her, annoyed. The heat of his face created half-moons of cloudiness above the lower rim of his steel-framed spectacles. Gaby sorted out her papers but on every page there was a blurred photograph of the girl in the cotton dress. She must ignore that, be professional.

Gaby's eyes fluttered open. The room was dark except for a thin line of light under the door. The black shadow was beside her and the torment began again. Was the girl alive? She tried to call out but her voice made no sound. Could she have avoided her? It had all happened so fast, she tried to stop, but the girl was moving too fast. It was just a dream it would be gone tomorrow, I just need to sleep, she thought.

John O'Neill thought he heard Gaby call out. Quickly he went into the room but there was only the sound of her even breathing. He was determined now that they should have a proper home. He loaded himself with guilt. Thank goodness she hadn't had a drink at lunch-time. He shuddered to think what would have happened if she'd been over the limit, or even near it.

The telephone startled him out of his reverie. It was Jill. She'd forgotten the name of the perfume that Gaby had suggested she should buy at the duty free. Briefly he told her of the tragic accident and for a minute she was silent.

"I'm so sorry. I'll phone you tomorrow," she promised in a strangled voice. "I'll come over the second I get home. Does Jacqui know?"

"No, I'll tell her tomorrow, there's nothing she can do now. With a bit of luck Gaby should sleep through the night, she's well sedated."

"Goodnight Uncle John, please give her my love when she wakes. You look after yourself too."

"I will, goodnight Jill, have a safe trip."

It was still dark when Gaby woke. Something was worrying her, gnawing at her, it was something bad. "Oh no," she cried aloud as the horror of the accident came back to her semiconscious mind. Was she dreaming or was it real? She struggled to clear her muzzy head but nothing was clear. She had to know what had happened to the girl. The room was so quiet.

"Dad," she called, "are you there?"

He was at her side almost before she finished speaking.

"The girl? What happened to her?"

"Sh! Don't worry, go back to sleep Gaby." He couldn't tell her now, it was too soon. It must wait till morning.

"What time is it?"

"Three o'clock. Try and sleep."

Her eyelids drooped as she tried to fight her tiredness. "I want to know..." Mercifully the injection was still working and Gaby slept.

She was sitting on her father's knee looking into his face. "Tell me 'bout Patrick and Amanda," she said poking a tiny finger into her nose.

"Which one, Patrick or Amanda?" John asked pulling her hand away gently.

"Amanda," the little girl decided.

"She worked in the same office as I did. The first day I met her she had loads of coloured pencils stuck in her hair..."

"And she looked like a hedgehog," Gaby said, laughing as she always did. "Tell me about my mummy."

Her father's face looked sad. "She was lovely, just like you. She died a long time ago and left me my little girl as a present."

"And we lived in the cottage with Róisín happily ever after?"

"That's right."

"And Seán and the garden and Matthew and

Gerry and… and… and…"

Gaby fought to stay in her dream but the tiny sunbursts of light which shone through the top of the curtains woke her. The nightmare was real. She had injured, maybe killed another human being. Tears squeezed through her closed eyes and trickled into her ears and her mouth. Had the drink from the night before made her sluggish? She vaguely remembered someone telling her to blow into a tube. The girl had darted out without looking, but could she have braked more quickly? She wasn't a fast driver and she certainly hadn't been speeding.

Gaby lay on her damp pillow torturing herself, searching for the answers that she could never hope to find.

CHAPTER FOUR

Gerry Oscar's prognosis was correct. Dull-eyed and listless Gaby failed to respond to anything. When she finally awoke from her drug induced sleep she immediately demanded news of the girl. Was she all right? Was she badly hurt? They avoided her questions and painstakingly explained to her that she had not been responsible for the accident and that there'd been three witnesses, all willing to testify if necessary. She had been blameless. Gaby sensed the terrible truth and sought refuge in silence, refusing to talk to her father or to Gerry Oscar. Nothing they said or did could rouse Gaby from her deepening depression. No tablets eased her torment.

John O'Neill cancelled his travel plans. He arranged to transfer them from the smaller suite into the magnificent duplex Penthouse Suite. It was expensive but ideal for their temporary use. Its seven thousand five hundred square feet of space was divided into two floors giving Gaby the complete silence and isolation that she craved. Under normal circumstances Gaby would have loved the luxury of the duplex with its own butler and valet service, but these were not normal circumstances.

The black and white marble-floored entrance-hall furnished with its precious antiques gave way to a carpeted area opening on to an airy, pillared sitting-room. Chairs and couches were grouped round low coffee tables. On the antique tables there were soft-shaded lamps and delicate flower arrangements. A grand piano in one corner was dwarfed by the sheer spaciousness of the room and on one wall was a functional marble fireplace. John and Stephen used the leather-furnished mahogany-panelled study as an office. The fully equipped room with all its modern technology kept them in constant contact with their clients. The kitchen staff tried to arouse Gaby's interest in food but the trays were returned to the kitchens almost untouched. Gerry Oscar referred Gaby to a psychiatrist who changed her tablets and recommended counselling for post-traumatic shock. He was confident that she would recover in time.

Jill and Jacqui spent all their free time with Gaby. The three of them sat on the large, beautifully draped, canopied bed just as they used to sit on beds in their schooldays. She barely noticed their teasing. She listened to their chatter without comment. They racked their brains for things to say that might bring some response. They explored the glamorous marble bathroom adjoining her sunny bedroom. A television was concealed behind the mirrors surrounding the Jacuzzi at one end of the long room. A Chinese lacquered screen reflected its own beauty in the mirrored walls. An array of elegant bottles and jars preened themselves on the shelves above the vanity unit which held twin washhand basins. Waterford glass tooth mugs stood alongside the cotton buds and cotton wool balls. Tissues and pretty soaps nestled in delicate porcelain containers and luxurious fluffy bathrobes hung outside the marble-tiled shower cabinet.

"I could live with this," Jacqui stated, modelling one of the robes.

"I could suffer it too," Jill answered, slavering her hands with a perfumed cream.

"You can have the other bath, Jill," Jacqui said loftily, as she formed two circles around her eyes with her fingers. "My binoculars are steaming up, but it's down there at the other end of the room. I shall make the ultimate sacrifice and use the Jacuzzi."

"You're too kind," Jill bowed.

Their light-hearted banter failed to bring even the ghost of a smile to Gaby's lips. Her dulled blonde hair hung limply round her shoulders. Her normally glowing skin was pale because she refused to leave the safety of the flower-filled bedroom. Patrick and Amanda came to visit her and were shocked by her appearance. Gaby had become almost skeletal. Róisín left her busy life for the day to visit her "baby". She cradled Gaby in her arms but that brought no reward, just a bout of weeping.

"Sad isn't it?" Jill sighed, as she played some almost forgotten scales on the mellow piano in the living-room. "Gaby would have so enjoyed the fun of living it up here, and being slim, but none of it even touches her."

"There must be some way to jolt her out of this depression. Could we persuade her to take some exercise, to swim perhaps?" Jacqui said in desperation.

Jill nodded. "Anything is worth a try, if the medicos agree," she said looking at her friend. Her attention lately had been so deeply concentrated on Gaby that she'd failed to notice Jacqui's haggard appearance.

"Are you all right Jacqui? You look a bit frazzled?"

"Fine, I'm just worried about Gaby," she said dismissing Jill's query.

The two girls made their suggestion to Gerry Oscar.

"It's an excellent idea but it'll probably take all your powers of persuasion," he warned.

As he predicted, it had taken days of coaxing to cajole Gaby to agree to their scheme. Finally she gave in for the sake of peace but without any enthusiasm. The two girls were getting frustrated, they just wished she'd pull herself together a little and help them.

John O'Neill contacted one of his clients who was more than happy to let them use his swimming-pool. The therapeutic outings brought no more than a slight response. One or other of the girls continued to collect her each day for the rest of the week. A slight chink in Gaby's armour appeared the following week when Jill accidentally flopped off the low diving-board with an almighty splash. For the first time in over two months the vestige of a smile appeared on Gaby's solemn face.

Jill insisted on taking Gaby to her hairdresser in Molesworth Lane. The attractive salon was bright with plants and lively music played through hidden speakers. The owner of the salon, Paul, quietly snipped away at Gaby's lack-lustre hair and, as the wisps fell to the floor, Jill noticed Gaby's foot tapping in time to the music. Gaby stared at herself in the mirror as if seeing a stranger. Her eyes were enormous in her thin face and, as she turned her head from side to side, the bouncing waves softened the gaunt hollows of her cheek bones and minimised the slenderness of her neck.

"Unfair, isn't it?" she said to Jill, "after all my attempts at dieting it took something so horrible to make me slim. Now I'm too thin." It was the first time that Gaby had even referred to the accident. A good sign? Jill chose to think so.

Gaby opened one of the double doors that led into the foyer of the suite. Her footsteps attracted John's attention. He called to her from the open drawing-room. A stranger sat opposite her father, a man whom she presumed was a new client.

"Gaby, let me introduce you to Myles Richards."

The serious-faced man rose to his feet and politely held out his hand.

"How nice to meet you," he said in a well-modulated voice.

Gaby gave him a watery smile and gestured that he should return to his chair. She perched on the padded arm of her father's seat and paid little attention to their conversation. Richards was anxious to acquire a ship-breaking company and needed John O'Neill's expertise in finding the right one. The location was not important. They talked about the budget available and, satisfied that they had gone as far as they could at this stage, arranged to meet again in a few days. John O'Neill ended the formal discussion and poured drinks for Myles Richards and himself. Their conversation became general. Gaby studied the man more from habit than interest. He exuded an aura of composed assurance. His luxuriant straight brown hair fell across his forehead to one side almost hiding his eyebrow. His serious eyes were almost the same colour as his hair. The long straight nose lent an air of arrogance to his face and when he smiled it revealed perfect teeth. Almost to be expected, Gaby decided. A determined jaw hinted at stubbornness and the only feature which softened his face was a dimpled chin. Certainly he would not have looked out of place on the cover of a magazine. Gaby flushed slightly as she realised that she'd been staring at him.

John O'Neill excused himself as the telephone rang and Myles Richards turned the full charm of his attention on Gaby.

"I understand from your father that you're his assistant," he said pleasantly.

"Yes, I travel with him, but Stephen Drake is his home-based secretary and organiser," she replied in a flat voice.

As she spoke his eyes assessed the pale-skinned girl. Five foot ten he judged; she was a beauty but too thin. Her oval, saucer-like green eyes were expressionless in her wide-planed face. The tautly stretched skin over her high cheekbones created deep hollows in an otherwise lovely face. Gaby shifted uncomfortably under his gaze. Making an effort to divert his stare she questioned him about his hobbies.

"I don't have too much spare time but I enjoy the theatre and the cinema. I read a lot. Whenever I can I train at a gym; swimming, weight-training and tennis mostly. There are so many more places providing these facilities now as you probably know."

Who cares, Gaby thought, unkindly.

"I use the Riverview Club when I'm in Dublin," he continued, "Usually I try to get there by six-thirty in the morning. I train or swim - both if time allows, and then have breakfast. By nine o'clock I'm ready for my first appointment."

Gaby made no effort to respond.

"What do you do with yourself in your free time?"

"Travelling seems to take up most of my free time too. If I'm here I spend time with my friends. We too go to a theatre or a film or sometimes have a meal together. We have friends in most places we visit. I play chess with my father - mostly on the long plane journeys, or just read," she finished, lamely.

"Do you play tennis or swim?" he asked, trying to prolong the difficult conversation.

"I've been swimming a bit recently." Gaby replied, mechanically.

"Maybe you'd care to join me one day at Riverview? They have a lovely pool, it's all very relaxing and informal."

The vestige of a wry smile crossed Gaby's lips. "Thank you, but I'm afraid six-thirty is too early for me."

He smiled, "I agree. Lunch-time perhaps?"

"Maybe," she said, ungraciously.

"Maybe, what?" enquired John O'Neill.

"I've suggested that perhaps Gaby would care to have a lunch-time swim at the Riverview."

"What a lovely idea, Gaby. I understand that it's one of the best equipped sports clubs anywhere."

"Please, come and see for yourselves, both of you. You must be my guests."

So magnanimous, Gaby thought, sarcastically. I really am becoming such a bitch, this isn't like me, he's only trying to be polite.

John O'Neill glanced at his daughter's face. He could detect no flicker of animation in her expression.

"That would be delightful," John accepted, ignoring Gaby's mute look of appeal.

"Perhaps we could meet there tomorrow, twelve-thirty if that's OK? You can do the tour and then we can have lunch." Myles Richards awarded them one of his rare smiles.

Mentally rearranging his calendar, John O'Neill agreed, speaking for both of them.

It would be an excellent opportunity for Gaby. Not by the slightest hint or gesture had Gaby's two stalwarts begrudged the hours, days, and weeks they'd spent with her. It must have been difficult for them. Jill's constant support must be eating into a tremendous part of her valuable time. Jacqui, too, had been a constant crutch. She'd been quiet lately. The easy relationship he shared with the girls had been lost in the trauma of the past months. He must try to find a quiet moment to have a chat with Jacqui, he sensed that she had a problem.

Myles Richards waited for them in the entrance to the club. Sportily dressed in a navy blue and white track suit his six-foot-two frame was lithe and athletic. Enthusiastically he showed them round the tennis-courts, full at this time of the day with white-clad figures. The attractive indoor pool had its share of members too, some lazily chatting, others dedicated to swimming a number of laps. The all-weather indoor tennis-courts were almost empty, the fine day had drawn players outside into the warm summer air. They climbed the stairs to the second floor and explored the gymnasium. Amongst the fitness machines there were treadmills for walking, cycles with monitoring meters and powerful weights for able-bodied lifters. In the centre of the room was a square carpeted area, its four corners supported by slim columns.

"That's reserved for limbering up before exercising," Myles explained, noting their look of puzzlement. Gaby peeped inside the hairdressing salon and beauty room. They had a serene atmosphere.

"There are rooms in which guests can stay, usually out-of-towners or visiting athletes," Myles said leading them back to the ground floor.

"I wonder if he has shares in the place," Gaby muttered to herself under her breath.

They chose their lunch from the buffet in the restaurant and carried their plates outside. Myles had reserved a table by the tennis-courts. As they ate they watched the energetic players bounding and leaping, enjoying the run and chase of the game.

"Well Gaby, what do you think?" Myles Richards asked. He noticed that Gaby did little more than toy with the food on her plate.

"It's very nice," Gaby said, cautiously.

"Would you like to join me for a swim tomorrow evening? Maybe we could have dinner afterwards?" Myles persisted.

"I don't think so," Gaby answered laconically.

John O'Neill frowned. "You'd enjoy it, Gaby. It'd be easier for you and the girls than going to Egan's pool." Turning to Myles, he explained. "A friend of ours in Blackrock has kindly given Gaby and her friends the use of his pool."

"OK, then," Gaby sighed with resignation. She knew she was acting like a spoiled brat.

"That's settled then. Tomorrow at five-thirty," Myles agreed cheerfully refusing to take offence at her apathy.

"I'm afraid I don't drive," Gaby added quickly. This could be a get-out for her.

"That's no problem. I'll collect you - five-thirty at the front door."

"He's stampeding me." Gaby complained to her father on their way back to the hotel.

"He just wants to take you swimming; after all, you're a very attractive young lady."

"Attractive my eye. I look like a bag of bones."

"When your appetite comes back you'll be complaining you need to diet again," her father teased but his ribbing failed to bring the normal spirited reply from his daughter.

"Gaby, if it's possible to arrange it, how would you like to go to France with the girls - to the Château d'Albion? Just for a week. The sunshine would do you good."

Gaby shrugged. He hadn't expected her to jump at the chance. Trying again, he added, "It would be a nice way to thank them for their kindness - a break for you all."

Gaby looked at her father with a cynical eye. "Nice try Dad! Blackmail."

John O'Neill's spirits rose, this was the kind of

response that had been missing for so long. "Leave it to me, I'll try to arrange it."

She had no doubt that he would.

"I'll phone Claude d'Albion and see if there are any rooms vacant, and then we can liaise with the girls. There's no point in discussing it with them until we're sure of a booking."

She waited at the front door of the hotel, John was on duty today. As they stood talking a car swung through the gates and drew up in front of them, Myles Richards hopped out. He opened the passenger door and took her small bag, containing a swimsuit, towel and her make-up, and threw it on the back seat.

Despite her earlier misgivings, Gaby enjoyed her swim. Myles had given her a head start. "One complete lap. Best of ten," he challenged.

He'd beaten her by two lengths of the pool and breathlessly she assured him that she was just out of practice.

"Prove it next time," he provoked. Gaby felt exhilarated by her effort. She dried her hair and added some light make-up. She changed back into her attractive red silk outfit. The only one she owned with an elasticised waistband, the only one that fitted her slim body without falling into endless folds or, worse still, slipping off her slim hips on to the floor.

She joined him in the open lounge where he'd ordered tea. "Would you prefer a cold drink?" He was solicitous and polite.

"I hope you don't mind, but I've taken the liberty of booking a table for dinner," he smiled, disarmingly.

A look of alarm crossed her face. She was not

ready to go out for dinner, not ready for company.

"It's not compulsory, just a suggestion," Myles pointed out astutely, sensing her mood.

Her panic subsided. He must think I'm a terrible fool, she thought, or at best as thick as a plank.

"I'd like that," she replied, and attempted a half-smile.

He parked the car outside a small restaurant in Camden Street and rang the bell at the entrance. The door was opened by the *padrone*. He greeted Myles warmly and shook hands with Gaby. When they were seated at the table Gaby gazed at the walls of the restaurant with interest. Scattered with cushions the high-backed pew seats reached halfway up the walls. From thick beams rows of decorative jugs hung and every inch of the remaining walls was concealed by brightly-coloured hanging plates.

"They come from every corner of the world. Some are gifts from regular customers, others the family have collected themselves." Myles pointed to one of the plates over his head on which a small mountain deer posed. "That is a kapriol, found in the Alps between Italy and Yugoslavia. It's the animal which the restaurant is named for."

They studied the menu. "I can recommend the pasta, it's home-made and the best in Dublin," Myles suggested helpfully. "The Prawns Kapriol are wonderful too, the speciality of the house."

Gaby settled for a delicate pasta dish with crisp, lightly-battered courgettes.

"What wine do you prefer, red or white?" Myles asked.

"Ballygowan please. I don't drink," she answered, a trifle sharply. They discussed the theatre and books, their travels, the latest films and television. She even managed to make a dent in the delicious pasta.

"Do you travel a lot?" Myles queried.

"We cover quite a bit of territory in a year," Gaby admitted.

"Do you enjoy it?"

"Yes, mostly. Sometimes I feel it'd be nice to have a permanent home, but I love being with Dad. My mother died when I was born. I was looked after by a wonderful person called Róisín and, when she left to get married, we gave up our cottage in Wicklow and I went to boarding school. We've collected quite a bit of bric-a-brac and small antiques over the years. It's all stored along with our clothes and the books we want to keep, in specially built cabinets on the top floor of our offices."

Myles nodded his head understandingly. "It must be difficult to live out of a suitcase. Strange not to have mementoes, photographs, books and all the personal paraphernalia of life," he said thoughtfully.

"You get used to it. One day we'll have a home again but things have always been so hectic that we've just never got around to doing anything about it."

They ordered coffee. Gaby told him about her friends, particularly Jill and Jacqui, but she didn't mention the events of the past few months.

"Tell me about your childhood," he prompted.

"That would take all night," she laughed.

"We have all the time in the world."

He watched her as she spoke, her green eyes shining with mischief. "We were a real scourge, I'm sure if we'd lived in the days of flogging in schools the three of us would've been the perfect candidates. It was wonderful to have three lots of parents too. Jill's family, my own and Jacqui's. When Dad was away at half-term or for a part of the holidays I went to stay with one of the girls. The other one came along too so's not to miss the fun. We've had some great times abroad together. That was Dad's way of repaying Jill's parents and Jacqui's mother for their kindness." Gaby smiled as she thought of Jacqui's wonderful, crazy mother.

"Why the smile?" Myles prompted.

"I was thinking about Jacqui's mother. She's an artist and tears round everywhere at breakneck speed on a huge Harley Davidson. She was wonderful to me and I adored visiting their home. No routine, no order, just do as you please."

"Sounds good. You were saying that your father…"

Gaby nodded. "He took the three of us to Stratford-on-Avon - to the theatre; not that we appreciated that at the time. We went to London and to Wimbledon to see a tennis final. Then he risked his health and his sanity and took us all to Paris after we finished school. And so on…" She stopped abruptly, embarrassed at her own garrulousness.

Myles frowned, "Why did you stop?"

"Sorry, I've been rambling on. I know nothing about you, tell me more about you," she said.

"We'll leave me for another time," he said. "It's

been very... enlightening."

Myles signalled for the bill and when she glanced at her little gold watch, Gaby discovered that it was almost midnight. She'd enjoyed the evening and, for the first time in ages, she'd felt a part of the world. Myles was a charming man, kind and thoughtful. Handsome too - especially when he smiled.

"Don't forget we have a re-match at the pool," he reminded her, "I'll phone you in a day or two. Six-thirty a.m. booking suit you?" he teased.

The following morning an exquisite spray of Singapore orchids arranged in a delicate glass vase was delivered to the suite. "I wonder if they're for me?" John O'Neill asked with a grin.

Gaby wrinkled her nose at her father, a flush rising to her cheeks. They certainly were exotic and she felt an unexpected wave of pleasure as she read the note:

Thank you for a lovely evening. These flowers remind me of you. M.

"Ridiculous," she snorted.

The buzzing of the intercom announced the arrival of Jacqui and Jill.

"Wow! Who's your secret admirer?" Jacqui whistled as she saw the vase of exotic blooms which Gaby was clutching.

Gaby surreptitiously slipped the note into the pocket of her jeans.

"Not so fast, Gaby O'Neill." Jill said, making a grab for the pocket.

Gaby ducked her friend's grasp but Jacqui, standing behind her, was quicker. Deftly she removed the message from its hiding place and she read it aloud. Both girls demanded to know all about the mysterious "M".

"Before you begin the Irish Inquisition, ladies, I want to talk to you." John O'Neill held up his hand in a gesture of peace. "How would a week at the Château d'Albion appeal to you?"

Even though it was high season, his old friend and proprietor of the château, Claude d'Albion, had been sympathetic about Gaby's experience.

"*Tragique,*" he'd exclaimed, and promised to book two double rooms for them - the only ones he had free, he regretted.

The girls had often heard Gaby talk in glowing terms of the hotel just outside Beaulieu, a jewel amongst a strings of gems on the French Riviera. Their short birthday visit to the beautiful Côte d'Azur had been spent in Cannes which John thought at the time would be more lively for the boisterous trio.

"I could certainly take a week off," Jill said.

Jacqui looked more doubtful. "It sounds like heaven, but I don't think it's possible," she said, ruefully.

"Surely someone would help Colin to look after the children?" Jill pleaded. "Wouldn't your mother take them for a few days? It would be great, a whole week. Think of it, all that sun and all that wonderful food."

"It would be terrific but I really don't want to leave Colin with all the responsibility; he has a lot on his plate just now."

"Why not phone him and discuss it?" John O'Neill urged gently.

"I'll ask him tonight," Jacqui answered, her eyes avoiding his.

"Let me know later this evening, I'll need to book the flights."

CHAPTER FIVE

The heat enveloped them like a blanket as they stepped from the plane. Joseph was waiting with the limousine to whisk them in comfort along the busy auto route to the château. Gaby enjoyed their sighs of contentment and delight. The weather was heavenly, as soothing as a warm bath; and for a week they relaxed by the pool, ate the wonderful food and read copious amounts of books.

Every day flowers signed with the familiar "M" arrived for Gaby. She flourished in the sunshine. Her eyes recovered their sparkle and under Claude d'Albion's paternal eye she regained a little of the lost weight. Gaby had won his heart when she was a little girl. He'd asked her what she wanted to do when she grew up. With great solemnity she considered the question then smiled her beautiful smile and replied, "I want to be a business typhoon like my daddy."

They made an attractive trio as they swam in the pool, sat in the tree-shaded gardens and entered the dining-room each evening; cool and sophisticated one minute, laughing and giggling the next. In the relaxed atmosphere of the colourful gardens, Jacqui finally told them the reason for her recent mysterious detachment. Colin had been made redundant. The recession had taken its cruel toll on his firm and, as the most junior member of the team, he was the one who'd been fired. To add to Jacqui's worries,

Aideen Connor had been hanging around Colin, encouraging him to play golf with her and her empty-headed cronies. Jacqui had gone back full-time to her former job at the catering firm. She still had a financial interest in it, and it was the money from this that was keeping their heads above water until he found a new position.

As Jacqui talked, Gaby remembered Jacqui's ashen face when she told them about Aideen's pretentious phone call - that fatal day in the lounge at the Berkeley Court. No wonder she'd been upset. An involuntary shiver ran down Gaby's spine as the memory of the awful accident came back. Come on now, she silently scolded herself squaring her shoulders, no getting in to that now.

"Colin would never take any notice of a wagon like Aideen Connor," Jill said vehemently. "She's always been horrible, even her imaginary childhood friend committed suicide!"

Jill's remark made them laugh and relieved Jacqui's tension.

"She's a real air-head," Gaby added her own insult. "He's devoted to you and the children. You might be blind to your charms but Colin isn't."

"I did tackle him about her - the night we talked about this holiday," she confessed, shamefacedly. "At first he was amazed that I thought he could have any interest in her. He'd refused all the invitations to join her and her friends for golf. He preferred to play on his own. Then he was furious with me. Furious that, while I was working so hard, I thought he was chatting up a nitwit whose greatest problem was what she'd wear that night."

"You're on velvet with that man," Jill insisted.

Gaby would mention Colin's redundancy to her father tonight when she spoke to him. Although she'd lost touch with the networking world, John O'Neill hadn't. He constantly updated a "people" list - fitting square pegs into square holes whenever needed.

Myles Richards telephoned early the day after Gaby returned. John O'Neill was happy to see the return of the old Gaby, her exuberance as she talked on the phone. "Yes, I'd love to go to Wexford. No, no plans. An hour? Sure, that's fine. See you then. Bye!"

Replacing the receiver she asked, "You don't mind if I spend the day with Myles, do you Dad?"

"Of course not, I've loads of work to catch up on. Plenty to keep me occupied for the day. I think I've found just the company that Myles is looking for. I'll tell you about it later."

Hugging her father, Gaby rushed up the wood-panelled stairs two at a time.

Myles Richards was astounded by the change that one week in the sun had made to Gaby's appearance. Her golden skin glowed with health, the subtle colours of her silk blouse flattered her sun-bleached hair and luminous green eyes.

He drove steadily and easily along the quiet roads while she told him about their holiday. They turned off the main Wicklow road and travelled for about a mile and stopped outside a mellow old stone house.

"I won't be a minute, just some documents I have to collect," Myles said.

He didn't tell her where they were going for

lunch and she was happy to be surprised.

They continued their journey until they arrived at tall metal gates leading into a tree-lined drive.

"Did you notice the finials on the gates - the wrought-metal pineapples?" Myles asked.

"Not really," Gaby confessed.

"They show that the house originally belonged to a judge."

"Remind me to take a proper look on the way out," she said, anxious to be agreeable.

Myles parked the car opposite the entrance to the house and crossed over the tiny bridge which led to the front door and the spacious circular foyer of Marlfield House. Mary Bowe, the owner of the pretty country house hotel came to greet them. She and Myles were old friends. They admired the new extension with its elegant reception table and marble fireplace. Gaby was fascinated by the chimney breast above the fireplace. Over it there was a window through which she could see the tall trees that grew in the garden. The softly carpeted corridor lit by Waterford glass chandeliers led to spacious rooms. It was lined with exquisite satinwood antique bookcases, antique tables and large porcelain vases. They admired the new suites on the ground floor.

The conservatory dining room was attractive. Geraniums in hanging baskets made a bright splash of colour.

"Sunday lunches are always popular," Myles said, tucking into featherlight blinis with sour cream and caviar topping. The tiny lamb cutlets were delicious and, though Gaby claimed that she couldn't eat another thing, she succumbed to a delicious portion of tarte au citron. She did, however, stick fast to her preference for "designer water".

"Three days of this wonderful food and I'd put on a stone in weight," Gaby groaned.

"You'd look marvellous at any weight," Myles replied. He watched her colour heighten at the compliment. I'm behaving like a schoolgirl, Gaby reproached herself.

"You promised to tell me about yourself, I know so little about you," she said curiously.

He told her a bit about his life in London, his friends and about his business - mainly to do with shipping. "Like you I spend a considerable time abroad each year. I've very few close friends. Travelling so much has made it difficult to widen my circle and like so many others born in Ireland I found it necessary to emigrate in order to find work. I'm longing to return to Wicklow, that's where I was born and raised. I want to set up a permanent base and enjoy an easier way of life. The documents that I collected this morning are in fact the plans of the house," he confided. "If everything's in order, I hope to buy the house and restore it. I'm now in the happy position of having a small office in London and I can commute from here whenever it's necessary." His intense serious eyes reflected his dreams. Gaby totally understood his feelings, she too had often yearned for a more normal life.

After lunch they strolled round the gardens and inspected the herbs and vegetables which supplied most of the hotel's needs. Gaby laughingly told him about her gardening punishments at school. "I was never sure whether or not the teachers knew that I really liked working in the garden. But I always moaned and groaned about it, just in case."

They enjoyed the leisurely drive back on almost deserted roads. It was still too early in the afternoon for the traffic jams of returning weekend commuters.

John O'Neill felt sure that he'd found the right company for Myles Richards. It was in Castellón, about an hour's drive north of Valencia in Spain. He'd made arrangements for them to visit the site and meet the owners. It would take about two weeks to complete his investigations, he reckoned, three to be on the safe side. Much to his delight Gaby agreed to accompany them. That solved the problem of leaving her on her own, he was still loath to do that. Her counselling had finally ended and her doctor was satisfied that a relapse into depression would be unlikely.

Gaby and Myles spent most of their evenings together. They were an eye-catching couple as they made their entrance at theatres and attended the openings of exhibitions in all the smart art galleries. He accompanied her to obligatory cocktail parties and to business dinners. His reserved manner intrigued her. Myles had often kissed her but he'd made no attempt to lure her into his bed - not that she minded. When she was nineteen she had lost her virginity. At a party on a beautiful moonlit night in Rome. The host had been a client of theirs. And when John successfully concluded a very lucrative deal for him, he'd thrown a lavish party in their honour. The son of the house, sophisticated beyond his years, had followed Gaby around all evening. He plied her with pink champagne. Tipsy from the heady bubbles, Gaby allowed him to lure her to a secluded part of the garden. He had gorgeous melting brown eyes and flattered her extravagantly. Their lovemaking had been swift and disappointing. Vowing to love her forever, this young Romeo had dashed off to fetch them both yet another glass of champagne. He vaulted a small well-clipped hedge which hid the tiny secret garden from the main grounds, and disappeared from her life forever.

There'd been few men in her life to whom she'd been seriously attracted; certainly none who compared to Myles. He enjoyed surprising her with flowers or tiny gifts, and often refused to divulge their destination in advance.

"Life should be full of mystery," he laughed. Life with Myles would never be dull. Suddenly the realisation dawned. Gradually and without warning, she'd fallen in love with her "quiet man". Despite his urbane manner he was a thoughtful, kind, reserved man.

They collected the hire car at Valencia Airport and drove to a small hotel in Castellón near the beach in a totally unspoilt part of the country. It had little to attract the casual tourist other than a golf course. Gaby declined their offer to accompany them to the breaker's yard in the port. She preferred to remain at the pool and soak up the sun. John and Myles returned late in the afternoon and reported that everything was going smoothly. They should more or less conclude their business the following day and planned to return to Dublin in a few days. At

night they ate in the local restaurants, fresh
sardines grilled on open fires, salads of lettuce,
tomatoes and the sweetest onions they'd ever
tasted. They enjoyed the showmanship of the
waiters when they presented them with complete
spirals of perfectly-peeled skin from sweet juicy
Valencia oranges. Myles promised that he'd take
them for a day's outing that they'd really enjoy.
As usual he refused to elaborate. Two days later
he and Gaby left the hotel and headed for the
mountains above the port. John begged off the
excursion. He wanted to sit and relax, read and
doze in the sun.

The road wound up the mountainside. They
passed farms with stepped plateaux of almond
trees, the earth beneath baked brown from the
hot sun. The mountain air was comparatively
cool as they made their way into the taberna
which slept lazily in the midday sun. In the dimly
lit mountain inn with its wooden floors and time-
worn tables several weather beaten local farmers
nursed their glasses. Their rapid-fire speech
echoed around the tavern. Placing an arm on her
shoulder, Myles guided Gaby towards the middle
of the room which was dominated by the bar.
They sat on stools at the broad wooden counter.
Her attention was drawn to a number of short,
evil-looking sharp knives which rested on
battered plates beside dishes of oil-slicked green
and black olives, shellfish and thinly sliced tortilla
with fillings of cod and potatoes.

"Look up," he instructed. Dangling from
hooks, attached by strings, were an astounding
variety of salamis. Short stubby sausages, studded
with peppers, hung beside long thin black sticks

with checker-board patterns of white fat. Red garlic-perfumed cylinders tempted the eager tapas aficionados. Gaby counted a total of twenty-two different shapes, sizes and colours. She watched as the initiated stood on the sturdy bottom rungs of their stools and reached with the cruel knives to cut a chunk off the salami they fancied. They joined the pre-lunch sport and were soon hacking and cutting with aplomb.

They moved on to the next leg of their expedition. They climbed past lush olive groves, their trees studded with oval green fruits ripening in the hot sun. Myles stopped briefly at a tiny house nestling in the hillside. He smiled enigmatically promising not to be more than a moment. In a small courtyard adjoining the house two men were turning a huge wooden barrel which lay on its side. They rocked it backwards and forwards between them. Myles called to them as he left the farmhouse carrying a parcel.

"What's that?" Gaby asked, her curiosity piqued.

"Wait and see," he retorted, as he wedged the mysterious article tightly into the back seat.

"What were the men doing with the barrel? At least you can tell me that," Gaby laughed.

"They're preparing it. Several litres of rough brandy are poured into it then they're swilled around to season it. After a time the brandy is poured away and then it's ready to store wine."

Gaby could see an austere whitewashed farmhouse as they rounded the final bend of their upward-climb. As she looked back the view was breathtaking. A picture of serenity as the land gracefully undulated towards the sea. The stepped plateaux of almond and olive groves were interspersed with the houses of the fincas, the farms.

"The owner of this farm was a friend of mine, a young Englishman who died. For sentimental rather than practical reasons his parents chose to keep it even though it isn't productive any more. Three or four times a year they invite guests to lunch - it helps to keep the place alive. You'll meet them and a few friends who are villa and apartment owners, golfing regulars," he said.

A stolid, red-faced man stood in the doorway waiting to greet them. He was joined almost immediately by a large athletic woman who pumped Gaby's hand with such a firm grasp she was sure her arm had loosened in its socket. The couple led them into a spacious white-painted room its dimness contrasting sharply with the blinding sunlight of the exterior. They introduced Myles and Gaby to the other two couples who were having a sherry before lunch. The room was sparsely furnished. The shutters on the windows were open and a narrow column of sunlight shone on a long wooden table like a theatre spotlight. Attractively twisted ornaments made of black wrought-metal helped to relieve the starkness of the walls.

"Local craft-work," their host said, as he observed Gaby's appreciative scrutiny.

Their hostess clapped her powerful hands and asked them to be seated. As the rough wooden door opened, a man with his back turned towards them slowly and carefully made his way into the room. He was followed by a large red-faced woman and between them they carried the

most enormous shallow pan of paella that Gaby
had ever seen. The guests applauded.

"It's as big as a table," Gaby whispered to
Myles.

"The cooks come to the farm at eight o'clock
in the morning to begin the cooking," the host
explained for Gaby's benefit.

It tasted wonderful. Saffron perfumed rice
blended with delicate shellfish and chicken and
freshly picked vegetables offered a contrast in
taste and colour. Bottles of light local wine added
to the rustic meal. A while later the couple
returned carrying plates, knives and a tall loaf of
freshly made marzipan. Gaby recognised it as the
mystery parcel which Myles had collected earlier.
They helped themselves to the marzipan which
tasted better than any she'd ever eaten before.

Gaby's attention strayed from the conversation.
Her thoughts drifted to the young man who had
owned the farm. He too had been robbed of the
chance to live his life. She felt tears begin to
prick her eyes and she knew it would take only
seconds before they brimmed over and ran down
her cheeks. She excused herself and left the
room. Gaby walked away from the house and
she sat on a small patch of grass hidden from the
building by parked cars. Bitterly she wept for the
two young people. She sobbed as she hadn't
done for months, crying her Kleenex into a pulp.
Myles quietly handed her a handkerchief as he
sat down beside her. He didn't speak. She blew
her nose hard and apologised for her hasty
retreat.

"Why are you so sad, Gaby? Do you want to
tell me about it?"

In a torrent, the words flowed as she told him about the accident and of the terrible feeling of guilt.

"Despite what the witnesses or the coroner said, I'll never be able to forgive myself. I still ask myself if I could've seen her sooner, yanked the wheel harder." The tears flowed again and he held her hand loosely in his own. The tranquillity of the mountain was broken by Gaby's racking sobs.

He tightened his grip on her hand and through the misty eyes she saw her pain mirrored in his eyes. His face was rigid. They sat quietly, words were unnecessary.

"I love you so much Myles," Gaby said with honest simplicity. "You brought me out of my gloom-filled world, I thought I'd never leave it again. You're the one who gave me back my reason for living."

"Gaby, will you marry me?" he asked.

His proposal came like a bolt from the blue.

"Yes Myles," she answered, laughing and crying all at once. "I'll never forget today as long as I live," she said hugging him.

"Nor I," he agreed, holding her tightly in his arms.

John O'Neill was overjoyed to hear their news. Gaby deserved to be happy, to have a home and a loving husband. Long training in the dog-eat-dog world of business had taught John to tread warily. Quietly he'd sought information about Myles Richards. He was unmarried, successful and hard-working, respected and straight in his dealings. John's mind was at ease.

Gaby sat on the floor her head resting against

Myles' knees. She chattered twenty to the dozen about their plans, the wedding, the arrangements. Both men smiled and threw their eyes up to heaven.

"Gaby, how would you feel about a honeymoon in the Far East? Singapore, Hong Kong and Thailand?" Myles interrupted her excited flow.

"Wonderful, but I don't care if we go to Tralee or Tibet," she admitted.

"Hear me out before you get carried away," he cautioned. "I've already planned a business trip to the Far East leaving three weeks tomorrow. It should take about a month altogether. Rather than be separated for all that time it struck me that we could combine the trip with a honeymoon. It may be rushing things a bit, but the sooner the better for me." Myles smiled at her affectionately. With raised eyebrows Gaby looked at her father.

"Why not?" he answered.

CHAPTER SIX

"To your last night as a single woman," John O'Neill toasted his daughter.

"But not my last night as your daughter," Gaby assured him hastily. She had seen the look of sadness on his handsome face. "I'll always be your little girl, even when I'm old and grey."

During the days of their short engagement, she'd assured John every hour on the hour, that their home would be his home. He was touched by her vehemence.

"Gaby, I want you to have this," he said, handing her a bulky package. "This is a portfolio of shares which I started for you soon after you were born. Patrick's father looked after it in the early years and then Patrick took over. It's time now for you to manage your own finances."

Gaby stared at the big folder, there was something so final about it, like cutting a cord. Tears of love sprang to her eyes for the man she adored, the father who had loved and protected her no matter what. Suddenly panic seized her, was she doing the right thing? Did she really know Myles well enough to spend the rest of her life with him or had she been blinded by his charm and good looks?

Sensing her mood, John covered her hand with his own. "Everyone gets nervous, Gaby," he said, "pre-wedding jitters."

"Did you?" she queried, instantly sorry she'd asked. Gaby didn't talk about her mother any more. The sadness in her father's eyes when she did, tore at her heart. Now that she and Myles were so happy together she wished that her father could meet someone special, someone he could love.

"I suppose so," John said untruthfully. He'd never had a moment's doubt where his love for his bride was concerned. "It's all so long ago I can't remember. Now, I want to give you your wedding present. Open it, " he urged.

Gaby gazed at the beautiful necklace resting on a bed of black velvet. Pearls the colour of palest cream were curled around a jewelled clasp.

Gaby flung her arms around her father hugging him till they were both breathless.

"Come on," he said, his voice hoarse with emotion, "let's see how they look."

Gaby walked to the mirror and carefully fastened the strand of creamy beads round her neck. "The pearls are beautiful and I love the clasp," she said.

"You can wind them round your neck a few times if you want to shorten them. Now, this is the last time I can say it - it's late Gaby, go to bed!" John said with mock severity. "We don't want you looking anything but your beautiful best tomorrow."

She clung to her father until he gently pushed her away. "Sleep well and have a happy life, darling."

The sounds of laughter could be clearly heard coming from the luxurious main bedroom of the Penthouse Suite. Gaby's bridesmaid, Jill, and matron-of-honour, Jacqui, had arrived early to supervise the dressing of the bride. Jacqui, as *a married woman of vast experience* according to her, directed operations. Jill obeyed orders. Gaby, totally unperturbed, read the morning paper and drank coffee as they fussed and fretted. Paul, her hairdresser, arrived. An hour later he left mopping his brow, relieved to escape the chaos. At last they were ready.

John O'Neill stood nervously in the square foyer and watched his daughter come down the stairs. She took his breath away. Her silk organza dress was blindingly white and exquisite in its simplicity. The fine silk fell straight and narrow from a high draped neck to an asymmetrical line just below her narrow right hip then fanned out into hundreds of fine, sharp pleats which swayed and rippled as she moved. The long narrow sleeves ended in points at her wrists with the same tiny pleating. Two camellias were pinned to her shining hair with a pearl clip. And around her neck were the pearls; their clasp the only touch of colour.

She smiled at her father, her eyes shone with happiness. He couldn't trust himself to speak. His little blonde scamp, his tomboy teenager, his high-spirited business companion had turned into this beautiful, elegant young woman. These might be the last few minutes in which she would look to him for help or advice. Probably the last time she would cling to him. He had to let go but he didn't want to.

The staff were gathered in the foyer and waited to see the bride and wish her luck. Gaby and her father had a quick peek into the ballroom. The heady perfume of fresh flowers greeted them. The tables were ready for the reception. The limousine was waiting. They arrived at the church as the clock struck noon. Stephen Drake was waiting for them and he smiled longingly as he handed Gaby a tiny sprig of white heather. She kissed his cheek and slipped the good luck offering into her simple bouquet. A motorcyclist roared to a halt alongside them.

As he approached the wedding party he removed his helmet. "Gaby O'Neill?" he enquired.

"That's me," she smiled. He handed her a white envelope and returned to his sputtering machine then roared off into the traffic.

She tore open the envelope and read the note inside. As she collapsed into a cloud of fanned pleats the note fluttered from her hand on to the pavement.

For a few seconds no one moved. John O'Neill knelt beside his daughter as Stephen Drake bent down to retrieve the discarded note. Had the excitement been too much for her?

"John, you'd better read this," Stephen urged, placing a warning hand on his arm.

Gaby,

When I engineered our meeting you had no will to exist. But, by your own admission, I gave you a reason to live. You were responsible for killing my fiancée. She was my reason for living, she was my life. Now I hope that you experience all the heartbreak of losing someone that you love just as I have done. Someone to whom I should have been married this very day.

Myles Richards.

Edward

CHAPTER SEVEN

Sooner or later they all sat at the bar; the big gamblers, the tourists, the losers and the winners, the ones with the infallible systems. Edward knew them all. They flashed their eyes and their money. They discussed their problems and they shared their successes. It was always the same, always different.

"It's all so exciting, isn't it?"

Edward smiled at the woman facing him, she reminded him of his mother.

"We won this holiday in a magazine you know," she confided, "Daddy, my husband I mean, didn't want to come here - but for once I insisted. Take it or leave it, I said, we'll never get a chance like this again and I'm going, no matter what."

She was plain but pleasing... frizzy permed hair, wobbling chins and all, she looked like a nice woman.

"The people are so interesting, aren't they? Such glamorous women, such handsome men." She blushed slightly as if she'd violated her marriage vows. "Daddy" was not difficult to spot in the surging crowds of the *grand salon* of the casino, the plume of blue smoke from his pipe wouldn't have gone amiss in an old western film. He watched the punters throwing away their hard-earned cash on the spin of a wheel or the turn of a card.

"Daft, that's what Daddy said when we came

here first," the woman told Edward. "'It's not your money,' I told him. Usually I agree with his opinions for the sake of peace. I might even have a flutter myself. 'Have you taken leave of your senses, Mother?' he asked me." She stopped to take a sip of her drink.

"'What's wrong with a flutter?' I said. 'After all it is a casino - one of the most famous casinos in the world.' And then I left him standing there with his mouth open."

Edward nodded sympathetically.

Sensing that she was losing her listener, she swallowed the last of her rum and coke and clumsily climbed down from the high bar stool. Edward smiled at the plump little revolutionary with her red and white flowered polyester dress and colour-matched shoes as she tottered towards the nearest of the roulette tables. Her progress was slow, made uncomfortable by the sandals which, because of her swollen feet, were embedded into her flesh, causing her ankles to hang like tiny pelmets over the wounding straps. None of that seemed to worry her, the light of battle and determination was bright in her flushed cheeks. Edward hoped she would win a few francs, but win or lose she'd have more enjoyment than most of the gamblers at the tables at this early hour.

"Fresh orange juice, and lots of it. Glasses, he insists, no jugs." The waiter cocked an eyebrow towards a stocky red-faced man moving rapidly between three of the roulette tables.

"Who's he?" Edward asked, as he lined up several glasses.

"Italian, judging by his accent. He's with his

brother, I think." The waiter shrugged and left with his tray bearing the glasses of juice which he placed on a little table by one of the pillars which rose towards the ceiling. Fascinated, Edward watched the demented gambler running from table to table. He played the same numbers at each one, he threw down thousands of francs at each spin of the wheel, stopping only to down another glass of orange juice. One of the ladies-of-the-night, the *filles de joie* who frequented the casino every evening, latched on to him. She stayed at one of the tables guarding his winnings. Edward filled another three glasses and continued to watch the fevered player dashing around in his relentless pattern. Edward's eye returned to the girl as, slyly and with great dexterity, she slipped a large square chip from the bottom of the pile. Dropping it down the front of her skin-tight dress she shimmied out of sight towards the ladies' room.

Edward was so engrossed in the whole episode that the head barman had to tug at his arm to gain his attention. He waited with bated breath to see if the marathon gambler would notice that his pile of winnings had diminished. The attractive girl had returned to the table but the Italian just nodded at her without seeing her. She pushed the pile of plastic money towards him and he handed her a small chip, drank another glass of juice in a single gulp and continued on his crazed path. Edward's attention was claimed by two bored wives whose husbands were firmly entrenched at the baccarat table. He filled their order and by the time he was ready to watch him again, the Italian's play had settled into a losing streak.

The girl had become bored standing at the

table and propped herself on to the bar stool,
smiling disarmingly at Edward.

"Whisky," she requested. He was embarrassed,
feeling guilty at being a party to her secret. The
whole idea of the girls touting for business
amongst the available and encouraging men had
shocked him at first. These aloof, attractive
women, were a fixture, part of the casino scene.
When they sat at the bar just chatting, their
hauteur and mystique vanished and they became
normal friendly people, workmates just like the
waiters and barmen. In just over a year of turmoil
and change Edward had come a long way from
his quiet Wicklow town.

"Bon soir, mon ami."

"Bon soir, Henri, ça va?"

The bulky man with his long hair - half blond,
half grey - aquiline nose and sensitive face
heaved himself on to his usual stool at the
extreme left of the bar. It was an excellent
vantage point. From there he could see the plush
room, and smell a blend of a hundred different
perfumes. The chandeliers shed a kindly light on
the glamorous women and the immaculately
dressed men. There was always an air of
expectancy, an excitement in the ever moving
throng. Pulling out his cigarettes and flame-
thrower lighter, a small pad and several pencils
from his copious jacket pockets, Henri placed
them carefully on the counter in front of him. He
was one of Edward's favourite customers and had
become a good friend to him in his lonely exile.
Nursing a drink for hours, Henri would sketch
anyone of interest to him; maybe just a nose,
sometimes the bend of an elbow or even a

stance, but rarely a whole person. His wicked sense of humour, and running commentary on one and all, kept the barmen amused. No detail escaped his eye or his razor-sharp wit.

Edward had often visited Henri's studio and had been struck by the variety of his artwork. "Why not, my friend? I am one of the best forgers in the world." Henri was unhampered by modesty.

Edward had been stunned into silence - a real life, self-confessed forger? Henri Ducroix lived in a garret just two streets away from Edward's flat. The garret was a well lit, luxurious apartment-cum-studio which ran the full length of a large house. Henri didn't starve there. He aged and stressed the Old Masters and Impressionist works of hour-old art in a multi-locked shed at the back of the house. Forging and copying were rewarding. Edward, seated amongst the oil paints and half-finished canvases, received an education.

"These sunflowers would have put a smile on Van Gogh's face," Henri said. He added his own indistinguishable signature with a flourish. "This is for someone who wants a copy, not a forgery."

A painting of a Spanish gentleman with a fierce swarthy face was propped against the foot of an easel, ready for the ageing process. "He would have intimidated even Velazquez," Henri laughed. Edward understood that the loss of Henri's own particular style and his natural ability was his worst punishment. He'd been questioned by the police and had once served a week in jail during their enquiries.

"They could not prove anything," he said smugly, and had shrugged it off and returned to his vocation. One or two art dealers retained his services. Henri would give them his opinion as to whether the paintings were authentic or not.

"I am an expert in spotting fakes," he informed Edward with his usual humility.

Whenever he could Edward made his way to the harbour - the sea was his first and greatest love. As a small boy in Wicklow he had hung around the boats and earned himself many a clip on the ear when he got in the way. But, as he grew and made himself useful to the fishermen, they took him for granted. He was as much a part of the scene as the circling seagulls.

His parents lost a baby at birth and they'd long given up hope of ever having another child. They had greeted his arrival with ecstasy. On the lonely farm where they lived there had been little to distract him from his schoolwork. He had been a good student. His mother and father had watched as he packed his bags to go to university in Dublin to study law. They'd saved and scrimped for that. They wanted him to study law far more than he wanted it for himself. He'd enjoyed the company in college but missed the boats. Law was interesting and challenging but he longed for the smell of the sea.

At the end of term in his third year, he joined in a boozy evening with his classmates. The evening had ended up in a private gambling house. Poker was second nature to him and many a matchstick had found its way into his pocket. He'd won them with pride from hardened fishermen. Edward sat at a table, one that accepted small stakes, and he had played for an hour, winning steadily. Stud poker was the game he enjoyed best and, as the evening wore

on, the smoky room filled with late-comers
anxious to play a few hands. People queued
behind the tables waiting for an opportunity to
join the game. There was a buzz of talk and
occasional raucous laughter. Edward waited for
the dealer to finish the deal, two cards face
downwards and one face up. This would be his
last hand. He didn't particularly like the man
who'd joined the table in the last half hour. His
face was cruel, with hooded eyes, a reddened
bulbous nose and fleshy cheeks. He was pushing
the stakes higher and higher.

Edward looked at his two concealed cards, a
pair of aces. His heart gave a lurch, his open card
was an ace too. The man opened the betting and
Edward immediately raised it. Two of the players
threw in their cards. The dealer read the fourth
card of the deal, "Ten to the jack, seven to the
king, a pair of aces, six to the nine and a pair of
threes." A dream hand, four beautiful aces.
Edward steadied his trembling hands by clasping
them firmly together on the table. He doubled
the stakes and the man with the ten and jack of
hearts raised again. Three more players folded
their cards. That left just the two of them. A pulse
throbbed at the side of Edward's head. He
looked around for his friends to share his
excitement. But they'd drifted to the bar in the
alcove at the far end of the room. He turned his
attention back to the game. He concentrated as
the fifth card was dealt.

"Possible straight flush," the dealer said in a
bored voice throwing a queen of hearts on the
ten and jack.

"No chance," Edward mumbled under his
breath. He checked his concealed cards again -

the same pair of aces stared back at him.

"A five to the pair of aces."

The five made no difference to his four aces.

"Double," Edward said as calmly as he could.

"I will see your double and double again."

"And I will double that," Edward said, his face passive.

The man looked at Edward then, nodding through his haze of cigar smoke, he pushed the stake to the centre of the table. "And double once again," he said.

A noisy bunch of students passed behind the table. They'd obviously had too much to drink. They laughed and bumped into people as they bulldozed their way from the room. Edward smoothed the back of his hair with his hand, slightly jostled by their noisy exit. He acknowledged the bet. "I'll see that and raise another hundred."

"Are you good for it, I don't see the cash?" the man asked, placing his whiskey glass on the baize cover. His nose had become even redder from the whiskey.

"Of course," Edward said pulling his cheque-book from his pocket. There were three hundred pounds in his account and he was still short of two hundred and fifty pounds on the table. He could write a cheque for a million pounds with this hand. A crowd, sensing the tension, had gathered closer round the table. The malevolent-faced man thought. He looked at his concealed cards, examined the ten, jack, queen of hearts open on the table and, he leaned forward to look at Edward and said, "Let's make this a game. How about another five hundred pounds, a nice round figure?"

Edward pretended to consider the offer. "Why not? Better still let's make it an even rounder figure, a thousand pounds." He could smell a bluff a mile off.

"That's the limit bet, gentlemen," the dealer warned.

"Done. Write your cheque," Edward bit back a smile and wrote the cheque. At the end of this hand he'd be rolling in money.

"Call," the malicious-faced man said.

"Four aces," Edward said triumphantly.

"Not good enough. I have a straight flush." The man turned his cards.

Edward stared at the king and nine of hearts. He was struck dumb. It could not be. Blood was pounding in his head.

"Sorry, son," the man said, without the slightest trace of sincerity. "Time for me to go." He lumbered to his feet, his large hand scooping up the pile of money and Edward's cheques. "I hope these cheques are good. I won't be pleased if they're not, not one bit pleased." His tone was menacing. He stopped as he reached Edward and grabbed one of his lapels, almost lifting him off the ground. His breath smelt of stale whiskey. "Listen you little creep! Birds can't fly on one wing, horses don't run on three legs so it's God help you if these cheques bounce. Still it won't be a worry to you. You won't live to tell the tale."

There was no mistaking the real threat in his voice.

"Edward, come on, let's go."

He pushed his friend's arm away and stood there looking at the cards lying on the table.

The full horror of what he had done hit him in

the stomach with the force of a physical punch. That last cheque would have more bounce than a pebble skimming the waves. He was helpless, broke and worse still, in debt to a man who would at best kill him.

By eleven-thirty the following morning he was sitting in his mother's kitchen eating an enormous breakfast. He had hitched a lift from a van driver. Saying little, the kindly man had made a detour, dropping Edward at the gate of his farm. Edward didn't doubt that the evil man who, in his mind's eye, had grown horns by then, would be as good as his word. Luckily the taciturn van driver had left him with plenty of time to think and work out his salvation. By ten o'clock that night he was a foot passenger on the Rosslare ferry and on his way to France.

Edward hated lying to his parents. He told them he was going to work in France to learn the language. It wasn't far from the truth. His father had pushed a small wad of notes into his hand before Edward boarded the boat and Edward felt he had hit an all time low. But he desperately needed the money. He'd make it up to them somehow.

It had taken him three days to reach the southern coast of France. By far the most dangerous section of his journey had been in a little silver sports car driven by a sex-mad girl named Marie-France. She drove at breakneck speed round bends, up hills and through terrifying traffic, with one hand on his knee. He supposed it wasn't a bad way to die, but die he was sure he would. He'd escaped death by running away and here he was again. This time death was imminent. They broke the hair-raising journey at a little hotel near Avignon and made love with such ferocity that he was positive he'd be safe from her advances the next day. But it was worse. Her hands roamed all over him and she gave him loving glances. Prayers he hadn't said for years came to him with clarity, his hands were constantly ready to grab the wheel. As suddenly as she had entered his life, she left it; she was travelling west. Waving weakly from the comparative safety of the grass verge of the road with its thundering traffic, he vowed to avoid attractive girls in the future - girl-drivers anyhow.

His last journey had been in a broken-down truck with no doors which had puttered sedately southwards through the French countryside. It was a relief after his previous experience. Reeking of garlic and talking twenty to the dozen, the driver spoke to Edward as an equal. Edward tried desperately to remember his schoolboy French, but he succeeded in understanding only one word in ten. He nodded knowingly whenever there was a lull in the conversation. Even with the natural air-conditioning of the doorless, rickety truck, Edward's cotton shirt was soaking wet and sweat poured down his face from the unaccustomed heat. The further south they travelled the hotter he'd become. Noticing his passenger's discomfort the Frenchman produced a half-full bottle of water and pushed it into Edward's hands. The lukewarm liquid helped a little but the bottle tasted of garlic.

They had struck a rapport. Shaking hands warmly Edward left the truck clutching a soiled piece of paper bearing the address of the driver's sister who sometimes had rooms to let.

CHAPTER EIGHT

Cannes lay before him shimmering in the heat of afternoon sunshine. Edward had never seen a sky so achingly blue. It hadn't taken him long to find the address that the truck driver had given him but he'd been totally unprepared for the beauty of his surroundings. He pushed open a large rusty metal gate and stepped into an ancient courtyard. The riot of colour tumbling from the crumbling, honey-stoned buildings almost took his breath away. Wisteria cascaded from high walls, gnarled and twisted branches almost invisible in a confusion of blue flowers. A guard of honour on either side of the stone steps which led to a faded door on the first floor was formed by dozens of terracotta pots crammed with white, pink and red geraniums. Carefully wired pots hung on the metal window grilles and, in the centre of the courtyard, a time-worn octagonal marble fountain held ferns and delicate grasses. It was watched over by the chipped, noseless marble bust of a young woman. As he stood mesmerised by the colours and fragrance a small woman, carrying a battered watering-can, appeared from a doorway in one of the buildings and eyed him suspiciously. Hastily he produced the crumpled note the driver had given him.

The room was spotless but spartan. The whitewashed walls were bare. A brass bed was tucked into a corner with a well-worn chair standing beside it. A scratched, lovingly polished wardrobe held drawers and hanging space, more than enough for his needs. At the furthest end of the room a faded Chinese papier mâché screen masked the tiny kitchen which contained a chipped sink, one draining board and a small cupboard on which stood a two-ringed cooking stove. Two folding chairs were propped against a drop-leaf table. A vase of sweet scented white jasmine was the room's only concession to decor. The rent had been surprisingly reasonable, the only proviso being that he had to water both the pots on his windowsill and those attached to the metal grille outside, every morning and evening. Edward readily accepted her terms and paid his first week's rent in advance. He unpacked his small case.

Edward made his way to the harbour to look for work and his eyes snapped open as he discovered a whole new world. Opulence beyond his wildest dreams lay before him in the shape of the yachts that were berthed in this playground of the rich. The boats, large and small, gleamed against the backdrop of the tideless Mediterranean Sea and the cloudless azure sky. It didn't take him too long to pick up an occasional job which earned him just enough to keep his head above water and his feet firmly placed on the decks.

The people fascinated him as much as the boats. The cafés scattered around the harbour area were melting pots - owners, crews, locals and tourists. Before long he found that there was usually someone with a friendly face with whom he could have a drink and pass the time of day.

His French improved in leaps and bounds. A tip-off from one of his new found friends had led him to the Casino and, after rigorous interviews, he had secured his bartending job. It was a real bonus to be able to combine his love of the sea with his working hours which didn't begin until the late afternoon. After a while, the threat of being pursued by his debtor and the dishonoured cheque had faded from his mind.

On Sundays, sometimes, he joined his landlady and her family for lunch in the small garden behind the house. Another tiny courtyard held the garden's only tree, an acacia. Madame Claire vowed that when it blossomed in spring, it was the best in all of France. A bare wooden table stood in its shade and held a few plates and wine glasses. Crunchy bread and a huge salad always accompanied the iron cauldron containing the main course. Pungent with fresh herbs and garlic, the rustic pot of beef or lamb stew was washed down with fresh-tasting wine. On special occasions coq au vin was the great treat and he laughed at the childrens' delight as they scrabbled around in the pot with a long handled spoon searching for tiny onions. Fruit and cheese ended the meal, the sweet smell of peaches or melons lingering on the warm air. The adults would sit and talk while the children scampered away to play. Those lazy afternoons in the perfumed courtyard were the nearest thing to family life he'd known in his adopted country. He told them about his life in Ireland but he didn't mention his last traumatic night in Dublin.

Edward was polishing the glasses until they gleamed when his attention was drawn to a row that had broken out at the roulette table nearest the bar. A tall bronzed man, American probably - Edward liked playing guessing games - was heatedly pointing out to the croupier just where he had placed his winning chips. They were being claimed by a beetle-browed Frenchwoman dressed totally in black, with claw-like hands and black-varnished, chipped nails. Play stopped as the two of them argued. A manager quickly appeared at the croupier's side. The garrulous woman won the argument and the angry loser left the table and approached the bar.

"Bourbon, please." He pointed to the bottle behind Edward's shoulder.

He downed his drink in one swig pushing his glass forward for another.

"I've just been conned by a woman twice my age and half my size," he said in amazement. "That couldn't happen in Las Vegas."

So he was right, the man was an American. "Why's that?" Edward asked politely - the poor man was still purple with anger.

"The chips are different colours and each player has his own colour, that's why."

"Good idea. A tip for you; if you want to place a bet, give it to the croupier and then there'll be no argument." Edward was sympathetic. He was willing to believe that the little habitué had indeed seized her opportunity to cheat. He'd seen her type before, a couple of times in the last year.

"Have you ever been to Vegas?" His customer was calmer now.

"No, this is the only place I've been to outside Ireland."

The American's family had all come from Ireland although some of his father's ancestors were Scottish, he said, as Edward half-listened, a skill he had acquired since working behind the bar.

The following night was particularly busy, a gala night always brought people flocking to the tables. The famous stood shoulder to shoulder with the tourists who were usually more interested in the celebrities than the gambling. Jewels sparkled under the great chandeliers and Edward was as guilty of rubbernecking as anyone else. The head barman and his friend Henri pointed out the famous and infamous, bandying names and titles as if they were on a first name basis. Exquisitely dressed women moved restlessly around the room, winning admiring glances from tanned, expensively groomed men, and earning envious looks from other women. The hum of conversation mingled with the croupiers' calls as the salon became more and more crowded. A flurry of people preceded the entrance of a slightly plump, middle-aged woman with black hair and a still beautiful face. Never had Edward seen such wonderful eyes.

"Who is she?" he asked the barman beside him.

"Deposed royalty?" the barman said vaguely, "She was married to one of the crowned heads of somewhere or other."

Three exuberant girls diverted his attention. They perched at the polished counter and discussed what they should order.

"Céad míle fáilte," Edward said, grinning.

They stopped talking and looked at him as if

he had two heads.

"It's OK," he laughed, "I heard your accents."

"Where are you from?" the tall blonde asked, smiling broadly.

"Wicklow," he answered delighted to hear native voices. "What are you going to have to drink?"

"We don't know, what do you suggest?"

"Is it a celebration?"

"Yes, joint twenty-firsts," one of the trio answered.

"Champagne, the only drink for such an event," he agreed.

"Perfect." A handsome man with a white streak in his dark hair had joined them.

"What's your name?" the blonde asked Edward.

"Edward."

"Mine's Gaby O'Neill, and this is Jacqui and Jill. This devilishly handsome man is my father, John O'Neill."

Edward shook each of their hands solemnly and then expertly removed the cork from the bottle holding it out to Gaby to take as a souvenir. He poured the fizzing drink into the fluted glasses and listened to the familiar Irish banter.

"These three ladies are running me ragged, I need this," John O'Neill said, feigning exasperation.

"Happy birthday to you all, have fun." Suddenly, Edward felt older than his twenty-four years.

"Oh please, join us," Gaby O'Neill insisted. They laughed and chattered as each of them added their initials to the cork.

"It's time to break the bank," they chorused.

"Wrong town," John O'Neill corrected them.

"Did someone really break the bank at Monte Carlo?" Jill asked, looking at Edward.

He nodded his head. "I believe so."

John O'Neill agreed. "It's really more a figure of speech, broken as in one table. A black cloth is put over the table and that means the money for that table has run out and it's closed down for a while."

"Is that all? It would be more dramatic if it was the whole casino," Gaby said, disappointed.

They left to try their hand at breaking the bank. Edward spotted the American who'd been at the bar the previous evening. He was handing his bets to the croupier to place on the busy table. Half an hour later he came to have a drink.

"Whisky please, and whatever you fancy for yourself."

"I saw you at the table - no problems tonight?"

"Nope, no problems," he smiled. "Have you been here long, at the Casino, I mean?"

"This is the beginning of my second summer." Edward paused, "I can't believe it myself now that you ask."

"This doesn't seem to be the life for you," the American said frankly.

"Why do you say that?"

"Call it a hunch."

"I was studying law, but something happened..."

"Short of cash, eh?"

"Short of sense, quite honestly."

"Oh, what happened?" the American asked bluntly.

Edward told him.

"I know the type. Not to be tangled with by the sound of him."

"My sentiments exactly." Edward agreed ruefully.

"Do you still play cards?"

"Never, and I never will again. Ironic isn't it, here I am in a casino. It makes about as much sense as an alcholic working in a brewery!"

"Good therapy. What do you do in the winter when the Casino is closed?"

"I found some work last winter at the harbour on the boats. I love them. With that and the money I earned here in tips I was able to survive quite well. Sometimes when one of the smaller hotels is short of a barman I fill in and that keeps me going, but the best time for earning some extra money is the week of the Film Festival. Cannes and all the towns round here are packed. You wouldn't believe how crazy people are that week; I've had tips from a few centimes up to five hundred dollars."

"Lucky hit on the wheel?" the American guessed.

"No, a lucky deal by an agent. A lot of agreements are signed right here at the bar and the victors can be generous." Edward chuckled, remembering one very lucrative tip.

"Share the joke?"

"One producer was chasing a 'money-man' for his film. He ordered a bottle of Dom Perignon and paid his bill plus a tip of one hundred dollars for me. When they finished celebrating and money-bags left the bar the producer sheepishly asked if I'd mind very much returning the tip. He didn't have enough left to pay his hotel bill!"

The American laughed, "I've seen that often enough too. We've had to pay air fares and foot the hotel bill for losers. I own a hotel and casino in Vegas," he added, noticing that Edward was puzzled.

"No wonder you were annoyed last night. Do you gamble in your own casino?" Edward queried.

"Like you, never. It's the rule both for my employees and for myself."

"Sounds sensible."

"It is - believe me! Well, I'm off, all this relaxing is a tiring business. See you tomorrow, no doubt."

"No, not tomorrow. I'm going to Valluris with a friend to see the Picasso panels - La Guerre et la Paix - in the old church and we're going to visit the Madoura potteries."

"Sounds interesting, I'm into sculpture myself." The big man yawned. "See you round," he smiled as he left the bar.

Edward had leapt at the chance to accompany Henri to the quaint village. Several times over the past months they'd visited museums in the surrounding areas.

"It is important to see the original works, to refresh one's eye all the time," Henri explained.

Edward thought Henri's paintings looked just like the real thing. "Can you learn anything new on these visits?" he'd asked the first time he'd stood silently at Henri's side.

"Always," Henri said pointing to a large canvas. "Maybe just a stroke of the brush, the pose of a hand and the light, always the light.

Intrigue

That is the most revealing mistake of forgers."

They sat in an open air café under a shady awning sipping Pernod. Away from the seething masses of the Boulevard de la Croisette, the sweet air and comparative peace of the little side street café in Valluris was soporific. Henri's head was beginning to nod and even Edward's energy had flagged.

"Do you know where all your ... eh, works are?" Edward didn't like to use the word *forgeries*. If he didn't talk he would fall asleep.

"Forgeries, copies?" asked Henri. "Some yes, some no. There are many collectors boasting Manets, Picassos and Constables which are, of course, mine. One famous forger promised that when he died he'd leave a list of his fakes in his will, but he didn't. And before you ask, no, I wouldn't leave any list either."

After a lunch of succulent lamb, cheese and fruit, two bottles of wine and bitter espresso coffee, they lazily made their way towards the pottery where Edward bought a brightly coloured bowl for Madame Claire. It would be a splash of colour for the wooden table in the courtyard. Sometimes he bought a plant or two to add to her enormous collection which she accepted without fuss. He couldn't warm to the family despite their kindness in including him in their Sunday lunches. Madame Claire's husband didn't talk very much and though the children were friendly, they were uninterested in the gently mannered Irlandais.

There were times when he felt so lonely that he was tempted to pack up and go back home. But those moments soon passed. He had Henri's company after all. Edward smiled fondly at the big man plodding beside him, grateful for his friendship. "One day I'll buy a villa in the mountains and then you can come and teach me to paint."

"Why should I put myself out of business?" Henri laughed.

"I'll commission you instead. A couple of Rembrandts maybe, a Picasso naturally, a Chagall or two and a Renoir. You can choose the artists," said Edward magnanimously.

"You're too kind, *patron*." Henri made a sweeping bow.

"Think nothing of it." Edward returned the salute.

CHAPTER NINE

The air in the large salon was stifling. People were packed round the bar. Edward was selling as many soft drinks as alcohol. He longed for the cool of the harbour and the even cooler breeze from the sea.

"How was your trip yesterday?" Edward heard a voice ask. He hadn't noticed the American sitting quietly on Henri's usual perch.

"Very interesting, I enjoyed it."

"This heat is really something, isn't it," the American said, mopping his brow with a large spotted handkerchief.

"Surely you must be used to it in Las Vegas? I've heard that it can often be over a hundred degrees there."

"You heard right, but it's a different kind of heat, a dry heat. Not being rude to the French, we're geared for it."

"What do you mean?"

"Everything is air-conditioned, buildings, houses, apartments, cars - you name it. Even some small houses have swimming-pools. In Vegas they're almost a necessity. Why not come and see for yourself?"

The last thing Edward could imagine was taking a holiday in the gambling capital of the world.

"Better still, why not think about coming to Vegas to work? I'll sponsor you, teach you the ropes. Being a dealer there is a very good job, lots of big spenders - you could really make a killing." He seemed to be surprised by his own suggestion and laughed.

"I've never thought about going to the States," Edward admitted. "It was a shock to the system to find myself here, as you know."

"Here's my card. Think about it and let me know. I'm leaving tomorrow but you can write or call me if you decide you'd like to give it a shot. I could use a bright young man like you."

"Thank you, I'll certainly think about it." Edward was touched by David Lock's offer. He looked at the engraved vellum card in his hand. He doubted very much that he would take him up on the offer. But he slipped the card into the pocket of his shirt all the same.

The night appeared to be endless. The bar was busy in patches, the room stuffy and airless. He was not due to end his shift until four a.m. and it wasn't two o'clock yet. David Lock's description of the air-conditioned casino in Las Vegas at this moment sounded most appealing. Suddenly the whole atmosphere of the room, the claustrophobic effect of noisy laughter, the heady aroma of expensive cloying perfume mingling with cigars and aftershave, threatened to choke him. He had a quick word with the other barman and stumbled out to the terrace to breathe the fresh, clean, cool night air.

At the end of August the pavements were visible again, but only just. The beaches were slightly less crowded than at the beginning of the month. It was a standing joke that they were so tightly packed with wall to wall bodies that when one person turned over everyone else had to follow suit. By the middle of September the yachts in the crowded port had thinned out, pulled up anchor and sailed to new harbours. It was possible to get a seat at a café table without elbowing and pushing through throngs of tourists. Autumn was the time to explore mountain villages and wander through each vielle ville - the old towns of Provence, to travel north and sample the wines in their natural regions.

"There are so many wonderful places to discover in France," Claude d'Albion said as he, Henri and Edward sat enjoying an aperitif one glorious September day. Edward had met the dapper owner of the fabled Château d'Albion once before and listened attentively to what he had to say. "The Loire valley is an endless adventure. Many of the châteaux are open to the public now and it's the best time to see them, also of course, there are the vineyards."

"A lot of them are built right on the river," Henri added. He knew Edward loved water.

"And Paris. You must visit Paris. You must cast your eyes upwards to the wonderful roof tops," Claude said, straightening the little mat under his glass.

They planned Edward's journey, interrupting each other as names and places of interest tripped off their tongues.

"It'll take years to see everything you suggest," Edward groaned as the list of "musts" grew longer and longer.

The two men laughed. "You do a little each year," Claude d'Albion advised as he called the waiter for the bill. *"Au revoir mes amis,* I'm going to see if my hotel is still there."

CHAPTER TEN

January was very cold that year. The courtyard, denuded of its rampaging foliage, looked forlorn. After two months of travelling Edward had returned to his tiny apartment and it too seemed cheerless. There was very little mail waiting for him. A couple of bills, a letter from his mother and, to his great disappointment, a letter from Henri, dated January 4th. He was spending two or three months in an old palazzo in Italy making replicas of paintings. Reading between the lines Edward gathered that Henri was making copies to replace the masterpieces which were to be sent to the international salesrooms.

The harbour was quiet and there was no work. He stared at the grey waves and shivered in the chill of the morning. The café was empty. The owner sat behind his counter reading the paper and looking bored. He was pleased to see Edward who ordered a cup of hot chocolate and they spent a pleasant hour talking together. Very little of interest had happened over the two months Edward was away. The *patron* told Edward that Henri was not expected to return until March or April.

"What did you think of Paris?"

"It's a wonderful city," Edward said, tapping the worn-down heel of his shoe. "I think I must have walked around every one of the twenty arrondissements. There was so much to see, so much to do - but it was very expensive. I could have spent months there."

"It's true, I lived in Paris all my life before I settled here in Cannes, I didn't see a quarter of it."

"It would have been more fun to have had company, someone to share it with, but I enjoyed it just the same."

"Paris in the spring: now that's a sight."

"It must be wonderful but I'll never forget standing at night by the Arc de Triomphe and looking along the Champs Elysées. The trees twinkled with Christmas lights. Fountains sparkled with silver decorations, it looked like fairyland. A magical sight. That must be hard to beat even in spring. The shops were so elegant and I loved watching the chic Parisian women strolling by. I splurged and bought a silk scarf for my mother and a silk tie for my dad. They'll probably stay in their coloured tissue paper. They'll only bring them out to show the neighbours." Edward smiled fondly. He'd missed being at home for Christmas. "You could see your breath freezing in the cold air and the smell of hot chocolate wafting ... I went on a bateau mouche at night and from the river the floodlit buildings were magnificent. I'd love to visit Paris again. With a girlfriend. Even in winter Paris is a city for lovers," Edward sighed.

"Yes, Paris can be a lonely place; I prefer the friendliness here. By the way, I almost forgot - Claude d'Albion was looking for you the other day."

"Did he say why?"

"No, not really, but there's a conference, some multinational company I think, and he's opening the hotel earlier this year, so I think he must need extra staff."

The luxury and hospitality of the Château d'Albion was legendary in Riviera circles. The staff at the château rarely changed and only on very special occasions did Claude d'Albion recruit extra help. Edward liked the idea of working there, if only for a short time.

The café proprietor was right. The château was fully booked for the conference and Claude d'Albion needed an extra barman. Edward would be expected to train for a couple of days before it began. As a fully experienced barman this made him smile, but Claude d'Albion never left anything to chance.

The château just outside Beaulieu was all that he had heard about and more. It was smooth, sumptuous and lavish. Set in beautiful grounds and total privacy, the quiet luxury of the château, catering for its guests' every need, was impressive. Claude was everywhere at once watching every detail from the food in the immaculate kitchens to the linen in the graciously furnished suites. The hours were long. The bar stayed open until the last guest had gone to bed and Edward was back on duty when they appeared in the morning. Only one customer made use of the service before noon.

The delegates at the conference were as sophisticated as their surroundings. They had no difficulty in talking to each other even though they came from all corners of the globe. They spoke easily in French or English. They dressed beautifully and their manners were faultless but impersonal. Edward felt invisible, just part of the scenery.

His loneliness grew. He divided his time between reading and drinking coffee in the couple of deserted harbour-side cafés that stayed open during the quiet winter months. The Paris trip had been costly. His bank balance was perilously low. Time to move on. But where, and to what? He could, he supposed, return to his studies but somehow the idea of those law books had lost its appeal. Long weeks and months of learning and exams. No, law was out, he couldn't face it again. If he went back to Ireland there was still a chance that he might bump into that threatening old devil. He certainly didn't fancy flying on that one wing. He thought of David Lock and his offer of work in Las Vegas. Maybe this was the time to consider it. Would David Lock remember his suggestion, would he even remember me? Edward wondered.

"Leave it to me," David instructed, "I'll send you the fare and all the forms."

His voice was so brisk and business-like on the phone that Edward began to have second thoughts. "Don't be a fool," he chided himself, "you're just going to work for the man, not marry him and, anyway, what better offers have you had?"

Five weeks later he found himself nervously boarding a plane at Nice Airport on the first leg of his journey to America. Madame Claire had accepted the news of his leaving without emotion and he was glad he'd made the decision. Her husband, whose name Edward never discovered, shook hands politely and the children gave him an embarrassed kiss on both cheeks and scampered off to play. The two café owners wished him *bonne chance* and, as quietly as he had arrived in France, he left it.

CHAPTER ELEVEN

The stretch limo waiting for him at the door of the arrivals building was as long as the Dublin-to-Wicklow bus. Half asleep and half awake Edward stared through the darkened windows. He hesitated before pushing one of the buttons on the door - probably an ejector seat. Nothing in this block-long limo, not even that, would surprise him. Success! The window glided down silently.

"We're coming to the strip," the driver said, "you can see the lights up ahead."

"I can see the lights in the sky," Edward yawned.

"Where do you come from?"

"Ireland originally, France today - yesterday." Edward laughed uneasily.

He was dazed from travelling.

"Folks tell me Ireland is beautiful, very green."

"It is. A thousand shades of green. I suppose you don't appreciate how beautiful it is there until you've left it," Edward said, looking at what passed for scenery outside the moving car.

It was as bright as daylight, brighter than daylight. Millions of light bulbs flashed their seductive welcome to the hopeful gamblers who arrived daily in search of fun, fortune and fulfilment. The driver slowed to give Edward a chance to see the famous hotels. Entertainers, film stars, singers, their names were all there on enormous hoardings which winked and blinked their messages.

"That's the MGM building: it went on fire one day and over eighty people died," the driver said.

Edward recognised Caesars Palace, its driveway lined with white pillars and mock-Roman statuary. On the opposite side to Caesars was the Sands Hotel and many other famous names he knew from his cinema visits. New hotels were being built, hoardings with their immense notices announced opening dates, and even they had festoons of showy bulbs.

"That hotel, the one that looks like a tent is Circus Circus. It's the first hotel in Vegas to cater for all the family. The second floor is like a circus, acrobats on trapezes a fairground with all the attractions. It's reasonably priced and they have almost a hundred-per-cent occupancy. Parents can leave the kids to wander around the various attractions while they spend their time in the casino."

"Are my eyes playing tricks or is that tent moving?"

The driver laughed, "No, that's the lighting - neat, ain't it?"

"How long is the strip?" Edward asked, totally dazzled by the lights.

"Two-and-a-half miles, maybe."

Downtown was even brighter still. Casinos promising million-dollar jackpots, free food and drinks vied with each other for attention. A sixty-foot-high figure of a cowboy winked and blinked his welcome. The Golden Nugget, the Horseshoe and the Freemont. You could read the telephone book in these lights.

The driver's face was wreathed in smiles as he

watched Edward's reactions. Normally his passengers were the big players, weekend gamblers or midweek junketeers whose minds were concentrated on the turn of a card rather than the turn of a corner. Those who said little and saw less. He turned the limousine and returned to the Strip and Locks Hotel.

David Lock was waiting for Edward in the lobby of the hotel when the limousine pulled up to the entrance. The glass doors parted and a deafening wave of noise assaulted his ears. The sound of slot-machine handles chunking back into place, laughter, whooping and hollering from players at the crap tables, the public address system paging guests and snatched sounds of blaring music from a lounge whenever its door opened or closed. So this was the glitz and glamour of Las Vegas. For a split second he wanted to turn tail and run. The French casino was silent compared to this racket.

"Welcome to Las Vegas." David Lock smiled at Edward's bewilderment. He put an arm under Edward's elbow and led him through the circular casino to the bank of elevators. They were swished upwards to a cushioned stop. Stepping out of the mirrored elevator David led the way to some double doors a little way along the quiet corridor.

"This is my home," he announced, stepping aside to let Edward pass.

The tiny square entrance hall opened onto a vast circular, modern room. Its walls were almost entirely lined with soft, creamy-coloured drapes. David pressed a switch inside the door and the room was illuminated by restful peach-shaded lamps. The hardwood floor, covered with cream and peach-coloured rugs, was a perfect background for the sofas and chairs upholstered in apricot fabric and stacked high with cushions which matched the curtains. Modern sculptures, some as tall as David himself, were placed at irregular intervals along the perimeter of the draped walls and on glass-topped tables spread throughout the room. David picked up a little black box, and pressed a button. A small section of the drapes at the furthest end of the room opened to reveal a dining area with chairs and a table set for two people.

"You must be hungry," said David.

"I've lost count of the number of those plastic trays of food I tackled." Edward grinned, ruefully remembering the half-frozen bread rolls and the pieces of chicken with nondescript sauces. "One of the plastic knives snapped in two when I tried to cut a steak!"

"I hope we can promise you better," David said, as the meal arrived.

"Turf an' surf," David explained as the waiter placed the huge plates in front of them. "Steak and lobster. You'll get used to that here in the States."

The steak was as good as it looked. The lobster was a tiny bit rubbery compared to the French seafood he'd treated himself to once in a while at one of the harbour side restaurants. A crispy salad with croutons and a large baked potato came with the meal which was washed down by ice-filled glasses of coke and pots of hot coffee. Edward began to feel human again.

"That was good," he declared, sitting back in his chair.

David lit a cigar and they talked for a while about Las Vegas. The crazy hours and the peculiar effect of living without clocks - something that no hotel or casino ever displayed. "Tomorrow I'll give you the grand tour and we'll talk about what I have in mind for you. Sleep as long as you like and call me when you're ready. Here's a key to your room," he said to Edward, who could barely keep his eyes open. "Room 412, press the fourth floor button, you'll find your baggage there. Sleep well."

Edward woke up at one-thirty next afternoon. The droning of the planes' engines had finally ceased and he felt better, excited at the prospect of his new life.

CHAPTER TWELVE

They met at the reception desk in the lobby. Dressed in a quiet checked grey sports jacket, open-necked shirt and black trousers, David Lock made a handsome figure as he walked to the amply staffed reception area. "We don't waste any time here with check-ins, time spent here is time spent away from the tables!"

Edward laughed but as he looked at David's serious face he realised the man wasn't joking. "It's as much a part of the plan as having no clocks."

The casino area dominated the circular building. Restaurants, bars, banks of elevators, were reached by the carpeted corridors which criss-crossed it.

"I suppose this encourages people to stop and gamble," Edward said.

"Absolutely. It works," David Lock assured him.

A group of dealers were making their way to breakfast. It was almost three o'clock in the afternoon.

"You'll get used to the odd hours," David smiled, and opened the door of an enormous tiered room furnished with banquette seats and tables. "This is our showroom, our theatre. We book only top names in the entertainment business. Two shows a night, the earlier one with dinner."

"Room three hundred, room three hundred

please, contact reception," the public address system boomed.

"That's the call for security. Look, over there; someone's creating a hassle," he said, pointing at a poker table. A player had overturned his chair and was shouting at the dealer.

They stood against the ornamental, wrought-iron balustrade and watched. Two burly guards, their holsters bulging with guns, approached the table. The dealer was making his point to one of the pit-bosses and a manager. The irate gambler danced up and down trying to out-talk him. The manager nodded to the two guards and, one on each side of the trouble-maker, they propelled him unceremoniously to the door. The dealer changed shifts and the game went on. David Lock caught the eye of the dealer and introduced Edward.

"What's the problem?" David asked the dealer.

"He said I was cheating, dealing the cards to the man beside him. He'd been playing for hours and losing, of course." They'd seen it all before.

"Can anyone wander in and out of the casino without ID?" Edward asked. There was a system of rigid passport control in French casinos.

"Yup, but we know the troublemakers and there are lists of *no-no's*. Security men in this town have good memories."

The attractive green and white cafeteria was doing a brisk late-lunch trade. Most of the people at the tables were playing a numbers game. Pretty girls in green and white striped dresses collected the cards.

"Keno," David said, "they're betting on numbers, like a lottery. The girls are called runners."

Intrigue

Edward said nothing. Talk about seizing opportunities.

The hotel wasn't large by Las Vegas standards but it had everything that was necessary to keep its two hundred rooms and suites busy all year round. The pool and garden area were well equipped with loungers and umbrellas. The poolside restaurant was cool and shady, not everyone wanted to broil in the sun. A television set and a fully stocked bar made the place a welcome hideaway. Edward felt the heat he'd expected the night before. The glare of the relentless sun made him grope blindly in his shirt pocket for his sunglasses.

"In the summer you can't walk more than a couple of steps without sweating. There's a lifeguard on duty full-time when the pool is in use," David said, pointing at a raised seat at one end of the pool. "A few drinks too many, too little sleep... and bingo."

Edward wasn't quite sure what David Lock wanted him to do. He'd expected to be trained as a dealer and croupier. But the three-hour tour of the hotel and all the details about how it was run surprised him. He'd been given management tips that had nothing to do with being a croupier.

He'd been delighted with David's invitation to join him for dinner and a show at Caesars Palace and was looking forward to seeing the famous hotel and even more excited that the entertainer that week was Sammy Davis Jr., his childhood idol.

Edward and David were shown to a table for six in the front of the theatre. A few minutes later they were joined by two women. The women spoke very little English.

"Spain... *España*," the older of the two explained. Neither of the men spoke Spanish so they just smiled and nodded. Edward loved the buzz in the theatre. He was no stranger to celebrities - he'd seen dozens of them in Cannes. But Sammy Davis Jr. in the flesh! A young couple both dressed in white were led to their table. The girl's hair was sprinkled with confetti. Edward smiled at the youngsters. They were touchingly awkward.

"When did you come here?" he asked.

"This afternoon. We were just married an hour ago."

"Congratulations," David said.

"From me too," Edward added, thinking how sad it was that they were sharing their great day with total strangers. The Spanish women smiled and muttered something incomprehensible. David called a waiter who appeared a couple of minutes later with two bottles of champagne and six glasses.

"At least they'll have something to remember the day by," David said, then added in a cynical whisper, "before the divorce."

Edward flinched as the sound of an alarm bell rang through the noisy casino.

"It's OK, someone's hit a jackpot." David pointed to a crush of people attracted by the bells to one of the huge slot machines. "The slots make up about half the profit in a casino."

"Do you want to try a hand of poker?" David asked.

"No." Edward was adamant.

He wasn't sure but he thought he detected a

look of satisfaction in David's eyes.

"Let's eat and talk," David said.

"I've been thinking about my original offer," David began. "You seem to pick up on things very quickly. I'd say you're on track to be a manager. I'll pay you well. You'll have a great apartment with a pool, of course, and all the fringe benefits that go with the job."

So that's what the extended tour was all about. A testing ground. He'd been right.

"Sounds good to me. I am, as you say, a fast learner and I'd certainly like to learn the business."

"Great. You start tomorrow; the sooner the better."

The apartment was light and airy. The small kitchen was thoroughly modern. The living-room was furnished with big, comfortable chairs, matching ottomans and occasional tables. A large-screen television dominated one corner and pleasant pictures covered a small section of the walls. The bedroom with its walk-in closet was huge. Another television faced a king-sized bed. The headboard was quilted to match the brightly coloured bedspread. Edward opened one of the bedside cupboards and discovered a miniature refrigerator complete with ice-trays. A far cry from the spartan whitewashed room he'd called home in France.

CHAPTER THIRTEEN

Everyone at Locks Hotel went out of their way to make Edward feel at home. He liked the friendliness of his American co-workers, the informality of their ways. Most of them were from other states and they became each others' family. They shortened his name to Ed and then nicknamed him *Sure and Begorrah*. They never tired of listening to his Irish accent. Edward's story of his flight to France was regarded amongst them as hilarious and it made him quite a hero. He was never lonely. He heard through the grapevine that David Lock was pleased with him and he'd found it an interesting job. The months of his training flew by and he was happier than he'd been for years.

The galleried area around the casino was bustling with life as Edward made his way to the smallest of the hotel's bars. The message on his walkie-talkie had sounded urgent.

"Congratulations," their voices all shouted as one.

Completely taken aback, Edward stood in the doorway and stared at the crowd of people gathered in the small room. Someone pushed a glass into his hand and shouted for silence.

"Quiet, please! Let's make a toast to our new manager."

"Good luck, Ed."

"Well done, welcome to the team."

"Thank you," he managed to stammer. The

blur of faces came into focus as he looked from one to another. Three of his fellow managers, four of the tall showgirls from the hotel's chorus line and several dealers. One by one they came towards him, the men pumped his hand and the girls gave him a peck on the cheek.

Sitting quietly at one of the small round tables, the willowy girl watched the young man's look of confusion change to one of appreciation. It was good to see someone who was not blasé these days. She judged him to be about her own height, perhaps slightly taller. She noticed his tanned face with its strong and even features. Edward's slim frame had filled out. Using the pool each day for exercise had built his muscle power. Height was very important to Nicole. It had governed her life and ruined her ambitions. Edward suddenly noticed the lovely girl alone at the table. He looked questioningly at one of the dancers.

"Sorry Ed. Should have introduced you." Dragging him to the table she said, "This is Nicole. She's replacing Terry in the line, starting tomorrow. Ed is our new manager."

She was lovely. Blonde hair tumbled around her face in waves and her eyes were the colour of violets. Even in the darkness of the bar the graceful curves of her body with her long dancer's legs were clearly discernible.

"I hope you'll be happy at Locks." he said, returning her smile.

"Thank you, I hope so too," she answered, without enthusiasm.

He looked at her quizzically but she wouldn't look at him. Edward glanced at his watch and reluctantly said goodbye to the three remaining girls. "Can't get fired on my first day as manager. See you later, and thanks again."

They were busy in the hotel. It was two days before he found time to stand at the back of the showroom and watch the line of scantily dressed dancers. Those headdresses had always fascinated him, structures of wired art in feathery plumes and gauzy fabrics which nodded and waved as the girls kicked their legs high in the air and danced their way across the stage. Nicole was no taller than the other girls but she had a rhythm and grace which made her outstanding. He'd like to get to know her, maybe take her out to dinner and a show when they both had a free night. Edward made his way backstage and he ran into girls straggling back to their dressing-rooms.

She said yes to his invitation to dinner but preferred not see a show, "Too much like work," she said.

Sitting over their coffee they swapped life stories. Edward made her laugh as he told her of the man who had lifted him "out of his standing", the man who'd made him flee to France. "It seems so long ago now, but I can still picture that man's face as if it was yesterday." A shiver ran down his spine. "What about you? How did you get involved in show biz?" Edward asked. He was a little embarrassed. He'd done all the talking.

Her expression hardened, the violet eyes were suddenly cold. She spoke hesitantly at first. "Ballet is my great passion. Ever since I was three. I spent every waking moment practising and training for my career as a prima ballerina. My parents encouraged me and they enrolled me in one of the best dancing academies in Paris. When we emigrated to the States, the first thing they did, even before they found somewhere to live, was to find a dancing school for me in Los Angeles. When I was ten I was chosen to play a small role in a film. When I was twelve I suddenly started to grow. But by the time I was sixteen I was six feet tall in my bare feet. My dreams were shattered. No male dancer wanted to lift a six-footer gracefully into his arms. I was told to give up. I was disgusted. I left dance school and enrolled with an agency which specialised in movie parts. But the film world was no different. Few actors wanted to work with an actress who towered over them. My agent said modern dance would be ideal for me."

Edward could hear the bitterness in her voice. "You are a terrific dancer," he said, hoping a bit of flattery would help.

"Big deal. I turned down one offer of chorus work after another. There were no movie roles. My agent took my name off his list. He wouldn't answer my calls. I quarrelled with my parents. I suppose I blamed them for the genes which made me so tall. I moved to New York, did sleazy, tawdry shows and even worked a stint as a stripper to pay the rent, but the customers' groping hands made me sick. One of the girls gave me the name of an agent who booked dance acts. I accepted his first offer - as a dancer in the chorus line of a Broadway musical. That job lasted for three years and, when the show closed, the agency scouted around and

Anne Schulman

found me this opening at Locks. I'd *love* to have gone back to France," Nicole said longingly, "but I couldn't get anything there."

Edward understood her frustration. "I suppose being here isn't ideal but you could do a lot worse."

Nicole didn't answer him. She was tired of hearing how lucky she was.

CHAPTER FOURTEEN

David Lock was still in his sweat suit, a towel wrapped loosely round his neck. Signalling to Edward to take a seat he listened to the caller on the phone, nodding and taking notes. "Right, right, fine, OK." Dropping the receiver on its cradle he pulled the towel free and rubbed his damp hair. "Everything happens at once here." He scowled but didn't look too unhappy.

"What's up?" Edward asked.

"Pour some coffee, will you, just give me a minute to shower and I'll tell you."

Edward uncapped the vacuum jug which stood on a small table near David's desk.

Taking the china coffee mug in his hand he prowled around the room examining the sculptures and ornaments which he admired so much. With the drapes open the room appeared even larger. He tried to peer through the smoked-glass windows which overlooked the pool and the gardens. At this time of the day the padded sun-loungers around the pool would all be occupied. He could visualise the pool waitresses taking orders for drinks, warning the guests to keep oiling their skins as protection from the gruelling dry desert heat.

"Sorry about that." David Lock's voice startled Edward. Picking up the coffee mug David joined Edward at the window. "We've got a big player coming in today from Canada, million dollar limit."

"Another one?" Edward whistled. "It never rains but it pours. I see what you mean now."

"Can you hear me complaining?" David Lock laughed, "I want you to act as host for this one."

"Sure, but where's Tom?"

"Tom's been player-hunted." David accepted it without rancour.

Edward shrugged; it happened sometimes. Every hotel had its hosts. He would have to take care of his *special* from the moment the stretch limo appeared at the front door until, win or lose, the player left the hotel. The hosts built up their connections and were sometimes lured away by large sums of money to other hotels wanting their share of the big spenders.

These high rollers with their huge credit rating were always guests of the hotel. They were wined and dined, every whim catered for.

"Do you know anything about this guy?" Edward asked. It was important that a host knew the foibles of these players.

"Very little. He's in import-export. Of course we've checked his credit with his bank."

Very few players arrived carrying that sort of cash.

Edward waited just inside the lobby doors for the limousine to arrive. The blast of hot air hit him with a punch as he stepped outside to greet his player.

He shook hands and introduced himself to a small, rotund, florid-faced man who was reaching into his pocket for a handkerchief to mop his perspiring brow.

"Alan Cruise, call me Al. My god, it's hotter 'an hell out there." He scuttled inside the building as the driver opened the trunk of the car to remove the baggage. Edward whisked him up to his suite on the fifth floor. A jug of freshly squeezed orange juice sat cooling in a large ice-bucket. Quickly he poured a glass and handed it to the profusely sweating man.

"That's better. I must grab a shower before I melt."

A light tap on the door announced the arrival of the bags and Edward waited patiently while the Canadian disappeared into the marble-tiled bathroom to have his shower.

"How about lunch?" Edward asked, "you can have room service or maybe you'd prefer to eat in one of the restaurants, or at the pool bar?"

"Not the pool bar, the heat would kill me," Al grimaced, "let's have a look at the restaurants."

There were three restaurants inside the hotel. The grill room, the huge coffee shop and a gourmet restaurant boasting one of the best chefs in Vegas. Every hotel had its draw and the exorbitant amount of money that David Lock paid his chef reaped its own rewards at the gaming tables.

"Join me?" Al Cruise asked reading the menu Edward produced from the Le Gourmet restaurant.

A flurry of waiters greeted Al Cruise by name. He obviously enjoyed that. Most guests liked fuss and attention. That had worried Edward in the past. He wasn't schmaltzy and flattering like some of the hosts. During his years at the hotel he'd lost a lot of his shyness and had gained confidence. He knew he'd always been a good listener.

David Lock joined Edward and Al for a few minutes. "If there's anything, anything at all..." he stressed, "please, don't hesitate to ask. Enjoy your stay and good luck at the tables."

Edward had fine-tuned the story of how he'd come to be in Vegas; they all asked about that sooner or later. He made it sound amusing and daring and he always drew a laugh. Al Cruise asked questions about Edward. But he didn't talk about himself. He ate the beautifully cooked meal without comment and refused coffee.

A sheet of noise hit them the second they stepped out of the restaurant. Chunk click the machines sang, bells rang discordantly as they paid out their jackpots. Music blared over the strident shouts of the players at the craps tables but lost. There was no escaping the noise.

One of the poker tables was almost empty, just two men, one woman and a dealer. The woman was a plant, she worked for the hotel. Her job was to swell the number of players at a quiet table. As soon as people drifted towards it and started to play she would wander away and find another table with a similar need.

"I'll leave you in Gerry's capable hands," Edward nodded to the dealer. "Here's my bleeper number Al, just call if you need me, I'll be in the hotel."

Nicole didn't bother to hide her disappointment when Edward called to cancel their date.

"How many nights does he expect you to work?" she sulked.

"This is a special customer, Nicole, I'm filling in as host as long as he stays. You know how it works by now."

Not bothering to say goodbye she dropped the receiver and the phone went dead in his hand. Edward shrugged his shoulders and went back to the casino to see how Al was getting on at the baccarat table. Edward stood quietly watching the game. Al was betting twenty thousand dollars a time, losing steadily by the looks of it. The cards drawn from the "shoe", a long box containing eight decks of well shuffled cards, were passed to him and, noticing Edward standing behind him, he gave a rueful grin. "This is my last hand," he said. Losing again he threw in his cards and left the table.

"I've spent more profitable nights," Al grinned, his losses obviously not worrying him. Al Cruise was plain, almost ugly, but he was a pleasant man, undemanding and easy to please. He'd lost steadily for the last few days and the word at the tables was that he'd dropped almost half a million dollars. If he was hurting, it didn't show.

"Do you have a girlfriend?" he asked Edward. They were having a drink before the show.

"Yes, she's in the show here at the hotel."

"You'd better point her out, I don't want to tread on your toes." Al laughed uproariously at himself, his five-foot-three frame heaving with merriment.

Nicole wasn't enjoying her night off. She'd looked forward to seeing Edward, and maybe they'd go to a movie after dinner. The heat had made her hair limp and one of her arms was red from the sun. She'd fallen asleep under the umbrella at the pool. She avoided the sun, it wasn't kind to her fair skin. Now she would have

to use make-up on her arm for weeks. She spent
two hours at the gym every day. Her body was
lithe and supple - the training of years was hard
to break. She hated the dead-end job in the
chorus line and if she hadn't met Edward she'd
have left Las Vegas ages ago. He asked her to
move in with him but she resisted, she liked her
independence. "One day," she sighed, jabbing a
pin into a hair roller, "one day I'll get out of here,
have my own ballet school and my own pupils.
Not in Las Vegas."

Edward and Nicole waited for Al Cruise in the
bar. Al had asked to meet Nicole and she had
agreed.

"There you are!" Al smiled, holding out his
hand to Nicole who towered over him. "A good
night for a change. I'd begun to think there was a
plot afoot where I was meant to lose everything."
He rolled his eyes in horror and flopped into the
club chair opposite them. "Well young lady, it's
real nice to meet you at last. I warned Edward to
watch out, I might lure you away from him."

Nicole laughed, then checked herself, she
didn't want to insult the casino's guest. She liked
his direct manner and cheeky grin.

Looking at Edward, Al said. "I'm leaving
tomorrow and I wanted to thank you for your
company. He makes an excellent nursemaid." He
winked at Nicole.

"It's been a pleasure." Edward meant it; he
liked the man. The hosts had often complained
bitterly about their charges, the unreasonable
demands, one guy even suffered a beating from a
sore loser. An enormous sum of compensation
was paid by the casino to the battered host to

keep him sweet.

Edward stood in the early morning sunlight and watched the stretch-limo as it edged its way into the traffic. The temperature was soaring. His shirt was clinging to his back. He stopped at the desk to phone David Lock and the cashier handed him an envelope. Its contents made his eyes open in amazement. A note on hotel paper, four casino chips, each one worth ten thousand dollars. The note from Al Cruise was short, *Just a thank you for your kindness. Al.*

"What did you do to deserve that?" David Lock whistled at the size of the gift.

"Search me. He was easy company. Fun," Edward said.

"Nice work all the same. I haven't heard of any guest being that generous."

"I wouldn't say no to a few more like him," Edward grinned.

"Anyone new in today? I haven't seen the bookings."

"Two couples from New York and a guy from Laughlin."

Laughlin was on the border between Nevada and Arizona. It was a miniature edition of Vegas, under-developed but it attracted its fair share of gamblers. Several of the big hotels were looking at the small town with a view to opening there and over the last few years it had created considerable interest amongst casino owners. David Lock himself had toyed with the idea of opening a second hotel there but he'd changed his mind at the last minute. "Locks, Las Vegas" was enough for him to cope with. He preferred to remain a little fish in a big pond.

CHAPTER FIFTEEN

Crowds were gathered outside The Mirage, Las Vegas' newest and most costly hotel. Edward held on to Nicole's hand as they were jostled by people wanting the best view of the erupting volcano. In the night light, the conical mound with its open top spitting fire, burst into life. White steam, followed by orange red flames, shot up into the air and cascaded down the sides of the volcano. Flames changed to white and erupted again. Edward had been told that this display cost a cool thirty million dollars.

"They're talking telephone numbers," he'd said as he read the breakdown costs of opening a hotel of this size with its three thousand plus rooms. Leaving the fascinated crowds Nicole and Edward made their way into the lobby of the hotel. Running the length of the wall behind the check-in desk was an enormous aquarium packed with colourful tropical fish. It was an awesome display but nothing compared to the tropical rain forest through which everyone passed to enter the casino. Steamy green plants and flowering trees flourished under a high glass atrium, a curtain of green foliage creeping and winding along its path. The clinking and whirring of the slot machines combined with music and laughter was deafening. Was everyone in Vegas crowded into the huge casino? No escaping the noise. Nicole settled herself in front of a poker machine and Edward wandered round the public rooms of the new building. Impressive.

Edward ordered a drink and sat at one of the small tables in the bar away from the noise and the crowds.

"Quite something, isn't it?" the man sitting at the next table remarked.

"Certainly is," Edward admitted.

"Are you visiting at the Mirage?" he asked.

"No, I work in Vegas, at Locks Hotel further along the strip."

"That's where I'm staying. I prefer a smaller hotel - more intimate. Smaller the hotel the less the noise."

They both laughed. "Everyone should be given earplugs when they enter Vegas," the man said.

Edward looked at his watch. "I'll have to collect my girlfriend. I have an early start tomorrow."

"Maybe we can have a drink together at Locks some time."

"I'd like that," Edward said, reaching into his credit card case and handed him his engraved card. "Give me a call when you're free."

"Oh, excuse me," Edward apologised. He'd been reading a memo and he hadn't seen the man standing at the notice-board in the lobby.

"Hello again, Edward," the man said. Edward struggled to remember where they'd met. "I'm Tony Berry. The Mirage - at the bar?" the man prompted.

"Of course. Long day, sorry." Edward smiled disarmingly.

"Do you have time for a drink? I'm celebrating."

"Sure, we can use the Keyhole Bar."

"Bourbon and branch for me, what will you have?" Tony Berry asked Edward.

"I'll have a glass of white wine; put this on my tab, Lorraine." Edward smiled at the pretty waitress and she returned his smile with a wink.

"You look pleased with yourself. What do you play?" Edward raised his glass in salute.

"Cheers. I am pleased, but it's nothing to do with gambling." He sipped the drink.

Edward waited.

"I'm in real estate. I've just closed a deal on a big lot in Laughlin. A big deal and a big lot," he said emphasising the word *big*. "All my life I've made money for other people, finding lots for developers who have made fortunes, supplying information to buyers and sellers, whoever is in the market, putting deals together and watching everyone else get rich. Oh sure, I've made a few bucks but everyone else cleaned up. Now it's my turn. This time next year I'll be the owner of a fine hotel and casino in Laughlin." His chest puffed up with pride. His eyes shone with fervour.

"Sounds great, good luck." Edward found the man's grin infectious.

"Thanks. I'm going to make my own good luck. Luck is earned. It doesn't happen by accident. That's my philosophy. What's your line here?"

"I'm a manager, sometimes a host. Whatever," Edward rolled his eyes.

"What do you earn a year?" Berry asked bluntly.

Edward didn't mind those questions any more. When he'd come to Las Vegas he'd been stunned by forthright inquisitors. He'd clammed up tighter than a fresh mussel. Soon he discovered that they were equally frank in return. It had all been so long ago, he couldn't believe he had been in this tinsel town for over five years. Five years of constant night and perennial summer.

"Come and work for me and I'll double your salary plus a car and your rent thrown in," Tony stated baldly.

Edward had had many tempting offers over the years, but this was the best yet. He looked frankly at his companion. There was nothing flashy in his dress nor his demeanour; he looked back at Edward gravely and appeared to be serious and sober.

"Not your average conversation between strangers," Edward laughed. "Besides you don't know anything about me."

"I go with my gut feeling, and it tells me you're an OK guy. I'll check you out, don't worry. Tell you what, to sweeten the pot, why not take a stock option, a nominal amount - a hundred grand say?" Tony Berry said thoughtfully.

Tony had bought the site for the new hotel years ago, one of the few lots he'd held on to. The funding was available from the bank but, he insisted, the project was to be privately funded with the stockholders taking an active interest in the running of the hotel. Edward listened to his reasoning. He wasn't the first person to seek private funding and there was no shortage of people willing to invest in a sure thing.

"Can I think about this?" Edward responded, his mind reeling with questions and doubts, elation and optimism.

He needed time to think, to sort out his head. Making his way to the pool bar, he ordered breakfast and sat under the cooling fan. Living in Vegas had been a breeze financially. He had few expenses other than his clothes and an infrequent meal, many of the hotels waived the bill. There was no need for a car, he used the hotel shuttle or grabbed a cab. Everything at Locks was paid for and his savings, plus the often generous gifts he'd received, had mounted up. He could invest the money and there was no doubt in his mind it would pay handsome dividends, but it would take every penny he had. Niggling doubts manifested themselves in his mind. Nicole, he was sure, would not be happy to move to Laughlin, there would be even less scope for her there than in Vegas. Then there was David Lock. He had been good to Edward; leaving Locks would be like betrayal.

"More coffee?" The girl smiled. Edward looked at his cup; he hadn't realised he'd drunk the first one.

"Thanks, yes."

"You look very serious. Problems?"

"Sort of, decisions more than problems."

"You know I'm here for you." She smiled, knowing it was a waste of time. The girls all liked the good-looking Irishman but he was well and truly hooked by that haughty French girl in the show.

"I'll remember that," he winked. How simple it would have been if he could have fallen for someone like her. She seemed to be uncomplicated and up-front, no hang-ups. The most difficult people were always the most challenging, he supposed. Nicole certainly fitted that bill at times.

They lolled in Edward's huge bed, the tray with the remains of the Danish pastries and coffee resting precariously between them. Her hair tumbled wildly around her heart-shaped face, he traced a wave with his finger. Pushing the tray out of the way with her foot she moved closer to him winding her long legs around his. He responded instantly to her caresses, slipping the thin straps of her nightdress from her silky shoulders. "Mm. You smell good," he said burying his face in her silky mane, "if you played your cards right, you could do this every day." She slapped his arm playfully, breaking the mood.

Edward turned over on his back, placing his hands behind his head. It was not in his nature to miss any opportunity to make love to this gorgeous creature but he needed to talk to her about Tony Berry's offer. He had bided his time not wanting to spoil their night out together. Still she resisted his pleas for them to live together and he had more or less accepted that.

Her jaw dropped as he outlined Tony Berry's plan. "You're crazy! How could you even consider it?" Edward had not expected such a violent reaction.

"In five years we could retire. You could open your own school of dance, maybe go back to France?"

She was unmoved. "If you go to Laughlin, you go alone." She dragged the sheet off the bed and, wrapping it round her, headed for the shower slamming the glass door behind her. There was no doubt that she meant what she said; being honest he hadn't expected to find it easy to persuade her, but now he had to face the thought of going it alone.

He didn't want to lose her. The apartment suddenly felt empty and silent. The aroma of Nicole's perfume lingered in the air. He wished that Nicole would marry him, he'd asked her often enough. But her reply was always the same. "I need more time."

Edward picked up the phone and dialled the agency they used sometimes to check out the guests. Within half an hour they returned his call. Yes, Tony Berry did indeed own the lot and had presented plans for a new hotel and, yes, he had been granted his gaming licence. Edward showered and dressed, his thoughts twisting and conflicting. This could be the opportunity of a lifetime. A chance to earn big money and leave tinsel town. Life had been good to him here. He had been accepted with friendliness, never a moment when he needed to be lonely. Meeting and loving Nicole had filled his life with purpose and yet, he wanted more. Not just the crumbs - he wanted the whole loaf. There were only two days left in which to make up his mind. Maybe he could broach the subject again, later, after she had given it some more thought.

Tony's face fell when Edward gave him his decision. "You're missing out on a hell of a good deal."

"Don't I know it," Edward said, miserably. "My girlfriend flatly refuses to budge from here. And she's not that crazy about Vegas either." There were the odd moments when Edward resented his dependence on Nicole and this was one of them.

"OK, your decision. You've just lost a great chance."

"Don't rub it in. Besides Nicole, there's David Lock. He's been very good to me and I do have a conscience where he's concerned too."

Tony Berry cocked his head on one side. "I like a guy who's loyal. Tell you what I'll do, I'll cut you in anyway. Naturally your share will be small, but even so you'll make a handsome return on your money."

Edward was taken aback by Tony's offer. The unexpected gesture reduced him to silence. This was like having your cake and eating it. "That's a very generous offer," he said, beginning to wonder what the catch was.

"Not really." Tony answered quickly, his eyes narrowing. "It'll keep your interest alive. You may change your mind - call it an investment."

The stock certificates were delivered and Edward wrote his cheque. Nicole laughingly offered to buy him a drink as he was broke. "You'll have to do better than that, I'll need to be a kept man for a while." He laughed, hugging her. At least he had her support in this venture.

CHAPTER SIXTEEN

The Christmas lull was over and the New Year's rush had begun. It was the busiest time of the year in the hotel when Las Vegas became one big party. Feeling smug having carried out family duties the big players rolled into town on a wave of self-indulgence. There wasn't a room to be had anywhere. Hotels phoned each other trying to place valued guests. Sometimes they lost one of their players to another establishment but they gained others – it was all business.

Edward was looking forward to February and a week in New York. It would be bitterly cold, maybe even snowing, but that would be a welcome change after the incessant sunshine. It had been a hectic few months. He and Nicole had had little time free to spend together. Nicole thought of little else but their winter break. She planned where they would go and what she'd buy.

The highlight of the last year for Edward had been his mother's visit. He'd asked her constantly to come to Vegas but his father was ill and she wouldn't leave him. A great wave of melancholy swept over Edward when he heard that his father had died. Sadness for himself and for his mother and father who had done so much for him. David Lock saw Edward's grief and suggested that he send her an open ticket.

"On the tab," he insisted. Edward was glad he

hadn't accepted Tony Berry's offer to work in Loughlin and felt guilty for even having considered it; there weren't too many David Locks around.

"Edward, look here." The security man called him to the bank of screens which scanned every inch of the casino floor.

Edward roared with laughter as they watched a woman, clutching a little white plastic pot of coins, surreptitiously looking left and right. She walked towards one of the machines, put her glasses on and read the instructions. Looking around again she gingerly chose one of the coins, changed her mind and picked another one, her hand moving in slow motion. She placed the coin in the slot and jumped back as if expecting to be electrocuted by the monster. Motionless, she watched quietly as the wheels moved into place. She practically danced as a handful of coins tumbled into the tray. Scooping them up carefully she added them to the others in the pot and moved to the next machine.

Again her hand went hesitantly to the coin slot and it gobbled her money. This time nothing happened. She pulled a face and moved to the next vacant one along the bank. Quicker now to place her coin, she still stepped back, waiting. The wheels stopped and she looked at the three identical windows, puzzled. The machine spewed out the money until the tray was full. One of the change-girls passing by handed her a larger pot, the size of a miniature bucket. She emptied the smaller pot into the big one then carefully gathered up everyone of her ill-gotten gains, feeling along the tray for any missed coins. The two men smiled with amusement as they watched her progress around the floor. She never played any machine more than once. Good fortune had smiled on her and they watched the sheer delight on her face as she cashed in her winnings, and stashed them in the purse hidden under her cardigan.

"A gambler is born. Thanks, Pete." Edward laughed as he went to join his mother for lunch.

At first she refused to have anything to do with the casino. She loved the shows, blushed at the scantily clad girls and formed an affinity with the odd pina colada or two. "It's the taste of coconut I like," she said defensively, drawing up the last drops of liquid with a straw.

"I see you've taken to evil ways. Gambling, are we?" Edward teased as they waited for lunch.

She looked startled. "What do you mean?" she stammered, her face turning the colour of beetroot.

"I have my spies," he said mysteriously.

She looked around as if expecting to find a slouch-hatted man with a smoking gun.

"Well, I had a good teacher," she said tartly but her eyes were twinkling.

"What do you mean? What teacher?"

Now she was enjoying his confusion. "A certain gentleman of the gambling fraternity was enquiring for you after you left for France. Several times in fact. He had a cheque with your name on it."

Edward was rooted to the chair, his fork midway to his mouth.

"Put your fork down, son, you know I taught you better manners than that. And close your mouth, you'll catch cold."

Edward stared at her lost for words. She stared too, not at Edward, but at the foot-high sandwich and the heaped bowl of salad that the waitress placed in front of her and which was one portion. "You could feed the whole of Wicklow with this." She laughed digging in with gusto.

"What did you tell him?" Edward finally found his voice, it came out as a croak.

"Tell who, what, dear?" she asked innocently, spearing a piece of tomato.

"The man, the man with the cheque." He stopped, realising she knew exactly who and what.

"I paid him," she said simply.

"You what?" He almost roared.

"Paid him."

"How?"

"With money, of course," she looked at him, "what else?"

Taking pity on him she explained. "I didn't want your father to find out. I arranged to pay him a little each week until the debt was cleared. At first he refused but I told him that I had no obligation to pay him anything, nor did you; gambling debts aren't enforceable by law. He accepted my offer and that was that. By the way, are gambling debts legal here?"

Edward nodded his head. He felt as if he was seeing her for the first time. How did she know about gambling debts? Had she always had a sense of humour? And why had he never noticed it before? His heart swelled with love for the amazing person sitting opposite him chewing contentedly. Her slightly faded grey eyes sparkled, her cheeks with their tiny broken veins were naturally rosy. He got up and went around the table to give her a hug. She pushed him away gently. "Edward, stop," she said sternly, but her face creased with pleasure.

"Make an honest man of him," Edward's mother said, kissing Nicole goodbye. She'd enjoyed every second of her stay in the wicked city. But now she was ready to go home. She'd allowed herself to be dragged to a local women's association and she'd made a lot of new friends.

"Of course I miss your father terribly," she said, her eyes misting over, "but we must get on with life."

Settled in the back seat she eyed the huge car sardonically. "If we walk to the front of it we'll be at the airport; it has no need to leave the hotel at all."

❋ ❋ ❋

Nicole crossed the lobby waving a newspaper. She rarely came to the hotel this early and he noticed that she wasn't wearing any make-up.

"Look at this," she demanded pushing the paper into his hand.

IMPOSTER HITS THE JACKPOT, the headlines screamed. Underneath was a photograph, the hunched but unmistakable figure of Tony Berry, alias Al Brown. Edward took Nicole into the empty bar near the lobby and with shaking hands spread the paper on the table.

Brown as a Berry, the sub-heading read.

The only tan Al Brown acquired was a bar-room tan. He worked his way around Las Vegas conning unsuspecting gamblers out of large sums of money. Armed with correct information and false stock certificates he raised two million dollars. An astute investigator checking on hotel occupants accidentally uncovered his clever scam.

Irate investors screamed for a return of their money. In a three-week spree in Reno and Atlantic City, Brown managed to lose the lot. This was confirmed by smiling casino owners in both resorts.

The article described how Al Brown had latched on to big players in the private rooms, gambling large sums spasmodically to gain their confidence. The dates reported in the paper were all after the time that Edward had signed away his cheque. Feeling sick he realised his "meagre" investment had bank-rolled the scam, giving the con-man playing money. He'd lost everything, years of work, of heat, noise and sweat. Years of polite interest covering agonising boredom, unable to distinguish night from day, summer from spring: all for nothing. Misery washed over him, sucking him down into its depths. Anger welled in his throat threatening to choke him. He had not felt this hopeless and despairing since the night in Dublin when he had stared at the straight flush lying on the table.

Rachel

CHAPTER SEVENTEEN

Twice she passed the stylish shop with its white awning and twice she lost her nerve and kept on walking until she found a window that reflected her image.

Her long black hair hung straight and silky. A neat little red jacket added a fashionable splash of colour to her short black skirt, opaque tights and trendy flat shoes. She removed two tortoiseshell combs from her luxuriant mane, and deftly folded the shiny cascade into a pleat, jabbing the combs into her hair to hold it in place. Ignoring the amused stares of the customers and staff watching her through the reflective window, she drew a deep breath and purposefully retraced her footsteps. Rachel stepped into the subtly perfumed interior and came to a halt in the centre of the thickly carpeted floor.

"May I be of help?" enquired a you-can't-afford-to-buy-here voice.

"I'm applying for the position of assistant," Rachel answered pointing to the miniature gilt easel with its thick white card in a corner of the window.

Assistant wanted.
Expert needlework required.

"I'm Meg Adams, manageress of the boutique. Have you had experience in this sort of work before? It's a testing and very responsible position," the stern-faced woman said, expertly appraising every detail of Rachel's appearance with a single sweep of her experienced eye. "How old are you?"

"I'm twenty-one," lied Rachel, who was a month short of her twentieth birthday. She took stock of the skeletal woman, noting her tired face accentuated by thin black pencil-drawn eyebrows and scarlet mouth. She must put on her make-up with a trowel, Rachel reckoned but her criticism was short-lived as her eyes were drawn to the exquisite cream silk suit with its navy blue contrasting blouse. Creamy-coloured leather shoes and a perfectly matched two-tone scarf completed the outfit.

Recognising Rachel's admiration Meg Adams's glance softened slightly. "The new season's stock."

"It's beautiful, such wonderful raw silk," Rachel said. "May I?" She gently touched the edge of a sleeve.

"At least she knows her fabrics, that's a help," Meg Adams thought. She pressed a buzzer and locked the front door, barring casual intruders.

"Come into my office," she said, leading the way towards a softly draped lemon curtain at the end of the boutique. She moved a straight-backed chair away from the large table that served as a desk, Rachel watched the prickly, efficient woman pour coffee from a percolator into pale grey and lemon china cups.

"Tell me about yourself," she urged.

"I've been studying fashion and design at the Winnward College in Washington," Rachel said. She hoped to make an impact by mentioning the famous school. "I was taught to sew by the nuns at school and I went to Winnward two years ago."

Meg Adams excused herself for a moment and returned carrying a small piece of black material and a needle trailing a long stream of white thread. "Hem this while we're talking," she instructed, handing them to Rachel.

"Isn't Winnward a three-year course?" she asked, watching Rachel's needle flashing in and out in the light of the lamp that was poised over the fabric.

No flies on her, Rachel noted silently.

"Yes it is, but I don't have the money for the tuition fees so I have to drop out," Rachel answered truthfully. "My mother paid my school bills and I helped by doing alterations but she has, er..., I must get a full-time job."

She passed the finished sewing to Meg Adams. The stitching was almost invisible. The hem, even without pins, was perfectly straight.

"Yes. This is good, very good." The manageress nodded, her tone slightly grudging.

"What do you know about Caprice and its reputation?"

"It's one of the best shops in Georgetown - maybe on the East coast. The clothes are top quality and expensive. I've often seen the name mentioned in the fashion magazines and I know that you have a lot of famous clients, rich clients."

"Do you realise what hard work it is running a boutique like this? It takes long hours. Everything promised must be ready on time, often altered in an hour. We make sure that no two people buy the same garment if they move in the same circle.

We have to be available at odd hours for special customers, ready to fit in wives of visiting diplomats who often don't speak English. We advise the 'new woman' what's the right dress for which function. We change our window displays daily. We check clothes for make-up marks and jewellery snags before they are returned to their hangers. The boutique must be spotless. No pins left on the carpets, coffee and tea available at all times, and newspapers and magazines freshly stocked daily."

"I'm not scared of hard work," Rachel assured her.

"If Winnward give you a good recommendation ...when can you start?"

"Today - tomorrow, as soon as you like, I told the college that I have to leave."

"Leave your number, I'll get back to you tonight."

Rachel left the boutique with a buoyant step, a lighter heart. Caprice was so elegant and the clothes were a dream even if the price tags made her gasp. Accessories costing more than her whole year's wardrobe were laid casually on dainty antique display tables. Belts, some as pricey as blouses, expensive earrings with bracelets to match, a king's ransom in her eyes but she had been smart enough to keep quiet.

The bustling Georgetown street was alive with shoppers and browsers. She loved the smart little shops, the art galleries and the "in" restaurants with black limousines outside waiting patiently for their occupants. It was the place to see and be seen - bright and inviting, lively and alert.

Rachel smiled to herself as she remembered

the trips she and her friends had made as soon as
they'd been old enough to go out
unaccompanied. The four of them had drooled
over the beautiful clothes in the smart boutiques,
envied the sophisticated women strolling
nonchalantly towards the glamorous restaurants.

"I'll drink nothing but champagne when I'm
older," Sandi said. "No more coke."

"My clothes will all have designer labels,"
Rachel ventured pulling at the worn sleeve of her
baggy sweater. Only Sandi and Rachel still lived
in Washington though their paths led in different
directions. Sandi had been bitten by the teaching
bug. She was putting herself through college,
working at night, studying by day. They stayed in
touch but the carefree hours they'd spent
together had been supplanted by snatched phone
calls and an occasional night out.

Today she would dip into her meagre purse
and treat herself to lunch in anticipatory
celebration. There was no reason why she
shouldn't get a good recommendation from the
famous school. She was quick to learn. That
would make up for her lack of experience.

Turning off Wisconsin Avenue towards M.
Street, Rachel felt more optimistic than she had in
a long time. Her mother (and her sleazy, beer
swilling boyfriend) had disappeared from her life
leaving her $300 in cash, a two months rent- paid
apartment, and nothing else. The swiftness of
their departure had stung almost as much the
unfairness of it.

On this beautiful Spring day she couldn't allow
herself to be drawn back into the endless
searching for reason or understanding. Today
was a day about which songs were written, she

mused as she drained her coffee cup. Smiling inwardly at her poetic frame of mind she left the noisy cafe with its multi-coloured chairs and, with unprecedented extravagance, hailed a passing cab.

Every Spring as far back as she could remember she and her mother had made a trip to the Tidal Basin to marvel at the blossoms that crowned the flowering cherry trees. The white lace-petalled trees with their slim stems were always the first to burst into bloom and she had squealed with delight if the tiny flowers, caught by a sudden gust of wind, swirled into the air and then fell like dainty snowflakes onto the ground at her feet. The man-made lake with its thousands of trees attracted visitors and Washingtonians alike. She stood amongst the appreciative tourists and drank in the beauty of the cotton wool clouds of cherry blossom rising from their slim stems. When she was a little girl she loved to watch the lighting of the stone lantern among the trees that heralded the start of the Cherry Blossom Festival. When she was seven she cried as she heard a man explaining to his children that, when Pearl Harbour was attacked, some angry residents took buzz-saws and chopped down several of the Japanese cherry trees. The memory of that day once again caused tears to flow down her cheeks. Not for the poor, sad broken trees but tears for herself, for her gullible mother who could not stand the competition of her daughter's beauty and tears for the weeks of pain that she'd endured, lonely and unsure. If only Sandi had been there she would have had a shoulder to cry on, a sympathetic ear.

CHAPTER EIGHTEEN

Rachel knelt on a little grey velvet cushion pinning the hem of a dress. The customer standing on the dais tapped Rachel's hand and raised her eyebrows in silent question. Meg Adams had spent a considerable time talking the nervous-faced, plump woman into this unsuitable puff-sleeved, full-skirted dress. It had been a long day, and considering her hard sell successful, Meg Adams left them to the alterations while she relaxed in the tiny office to take a breather and make up the sales slip. The woman fidgeted from one foot to the other, making Rachel's task harder. She bent down and touched Rachel's hand, pulled a face and whispered, "Do you really like it?" Glancing towards the curtain that separated the spacious fitting room from the boutique, Rachel put her finger to her lips, wrinkled her nose and shook her head. The browbeaten woman understood. "Which one?" she mouthed.

"The black one," Rachel whispered.

"I've changed my mind," the intimidated customer announced in a loud voice. "I'd prefer the black dress." Rachel gave her the thumbs-up sign.

Sighing, Meg Adams dropped her pen on the table in exasperation - the black dress was three hundred dollars cheaper. That meant less commission for her. That white dress had been rejected by everyone who'd tried it on. Just when she thought she'd unloaded it...

Rachel sat back on her heels, her face expressionless. If she was found out she'd certainly be fired. Carrying the black dress in front of her, Meg Adams, a pained smile on her face, showed it to the nervous woman. "This one?" she enquired in a strangled voice.

"That one," the newly confident customer confirmed, bolstered by Rachel's approval.

Rachel helped her to remove the billowing extravaganza. In her opinion it was suitable only for a reed-slim, seventeen-year-old debutante. She quickly pinned the hem of the second garment on the contented customer. It made her look slimmer, smarter and taller. The only thing Rachel really disliked about her work was Meg Adams's insistence that they must sell clothes whether they suited a client or not. Once she had argued with Meg that, if customers were able to rely on good advice instead of insincere flattery, surely it would make them return all the quicker? Meg's warning glare had been enough to make her retreat to her workroom and she had never broached the subject again.

Ushering the pleasant woman to the door, Meg Adams practically banged it shut on her rear. Accusingly she turned to Rachel who was removing pins from the offending dress. "Why did she change her mind?" she demanded, suspiciously.

"I haven't a clue. I was pinning the hem when suddenly she said the dress wasn't right for her." Rachel's gaze was innocent and unwavering, but her heart pumped uncomfortably in her chest.

Rachel went on taking out pins as she listened

to Meg stamping back to her bolthole. She could hear the tearing of paper - the rejected sales slip, no doubt.

Despite Meg's mercurial temperament and her own low salary, Rachel loved working in the boutique. The seven weeks she had spent there had taken the edge off her traumatic introduction to the world of luxury shopping - she no longer mumbled the prices or blushed in apology. Her fear of sticking a pin into the wife of a senator or cutting too deeply into a seam of a suit for the vice-president's wife, soon disappeared as she confidently went about her alterations.

The buzzer sounded constantly announcing the arrival of the famous and the infamous, wives and mistresses, career-shoppers, wealthy socialites and time-rationed working women. Commoners and royalty exchanged pleasantries. Enemies acknowledged each other frigidly. Gossips and journalists fuelled the fires of rumour or distorted truth. It was never dull; always a challenge, exciting and absorbing.

Meg Adams was pleased with her assistant. The beautiful almond-eyed girl with her model figure had proved to be a hard worker, tactful and pleasant, popular even with more difficult clients. Rachel's instinctive feel for fashion, and her confidence in her own needlework, had convinced several hesitant customers that an ill-fitting ball gown or trousers would look perfect by the time she was finished. If she could just teach Rachel to push harder with the more expensive garments she would be content. After all, that was what she was here for - to sell.

"Mrs Abadi will be collecting her gown soon,

Rachel, is it ready?" Meg called.

Rachel was bent over the ironing-board. She didn't hear the question, she was steaming a difficult bias seam and lost in her own worry-world. She had nine days to find another apartment. She couldn't possibly afford the rent that her mother had worked hard to meet each month. The search for an apartment had taken her only to the drug-ridden areas of downtown Washington. She'd been terrified to go into some of the buildings, she was afraid of the gangs of bored youths, the glazed-eyed stares of spaced-out heroin freaks. There had to be somewhere less frightening, less threatening. The familiar resentment welled up - how could her mother have chosen that lazy, no-good creep instead of her? She had avoided his lust-filled eyes with an icy coldness and her method had proved successful until that last day - the day that her mother had called to say she'd be home late. She couldn't leave her patient. The relief nurse had been delayed. In private nursing there was no team to take over. Rachel prepared the evening meal ignoring his pleas to watch television with him. On the floor around him empty beer cans had leaked their last frothy dregs leaving dark wet patches on the worn carpet.

"I need to wash my hair," she had responded coldly moving towards the bathroom.

"Snooty, aren't we?" he goaded. "Who are you saving yourself for, you cold bitch?"

The noise of the hairdrier had drowned his approach, she hadn't heard his footsteps behind her and screamed with fright as his sweaty hands began caressing her almost bare back. With one

arm tightly round her small waist he fumbled
with the catch of her bra, pulling at the small
hook. In an involuntary motion she turned. His
disgusting shirtless body was right beside her, his
bleary eyes stared into her own. With her full
strength she'd smashed the hairdrier into his face.
Blood poured from his forehead into his eyes
giving her a split second in which to grab a robe
and run half-naked into the corridor. Zigzagging
along the narrow passage she hammered on
doors hoping that someone would help her. She
heard bolts and chains being checked, sliding
into place. No one wanted to get involved.
Looking back over her shoulder she could see his
lumbering form at the doorway of the apartment.
Blindly she ran round the corner and crashed
into an approaching figure. Sobbing hysterically
and begging for help she found herself in her
mother's comforting arms.

When she woke up next morning the
apartment was empty, the closets bare except for
some wire hangers drunkenly lopsided on the
empty rail. The double bed was stripped down to
the mattress. Missing photographs and ornaments
were conspicuous by their absence leaving dust-
free spaces on the surface of the chest of
drawers. Rachel ran from the bedroom to the
living-room and back again checking the empty
closets. Surely she'd wake up soon and find that
this was all a bad dream.

Uncomprehendingly she read and re-read the
short letter while the crumpled dollar bills lay
unheeded on the floor. She was sure that her
mother with her sunny smile and warm Irish
charm would be back. She didn't leave the

apartment. Five days of waiting turned her hurt to anger then to fear. She wept uncontrollably alternating between despair and hope. She became light-headed and weak. Why had Sandi chosen that six month teacher's training exchange? "I need you here, now," she wailed.

"Rachel!" Meg Adams' raised voice reached her subconscious.

"Oh! Did you say something?"

"What's the matter, Rachel? I've been trying to get through to you for the last two minutes."

Rachel fought hard not to cry but it was useless.

Meg Adams had made a conscious decision never to become involved on a personal level with any employee. She had enough problems of her own, enough complications. Pleasant but aloof was her code. That last over-smart little cookie she'd tangled with had almost ruined her by poking her nose into things which didn't concern her. After Meg fired her she vowed she'd always keep her distance, keep it strictly business. But there was something vulnerable about the troubled girl who stood with her head bowed, something that touched her.

"What's the matter, Rachel?" she asked. Her tone was harsher than she intended.

Rachel too had made a vow but she sobbed out her helplessness for the first time. Strangely, she felt better; cleansed somehow, as the awkwardly sympathetic listener offered her a tissue. Rachel didn't think of Meg Adams as kind.

"You mustn't blame your mother too much," she counselled. "The love between a man and a woman is often unreasonable. I'm sure that your mother didn't mean to hurt you." Men, she thought inwardly, they're all the same. You can never do enough to please them, she should know.

"Keep looking in the classifieds, you'll find something," she said, her voice falsely cheerful but Meg felt guilty. Her own four room apartment was costing an arm and a leg, what chance did Rachel have on her salary? Why had she asked the question, why couldn't she stay out of it as she'd sworn she would?

"Mrs Abadi will be here soon, we'd better make sure we're ready for her. Her reception starts at six-thirty," she reminded the red-eyed girl.

Rachel nodded miserably and began padding the sleeves of the delicate dress with wads of tissue paper. Mrs Abadi, safe in her country's embassy, would never know how close her beautiful gown had come to being ruined by tears.

Friday was the busiest day Rachel had known since she'd started at Caprice. It was almost two-thirty before she could leave the elegant lemon and grey boutique to buy sandwiches for their lunch. One of the pre-lunch moochers, as Meg had christened them, spent an hour and a half trying on everything in the shop and left without buying a thing. Meg showed her frustration with the lift of one black-pencilled eyebrow. Passing Rachel she whispered, "You watch, she'll leave at exactly five minutes to one."

She was spot-on in her prediction but, before she could vent her spleen, the buzzer sounded again.

"How may I assist you?" Meg Adams asked without much enthusiasm. Automatically she assessed the vivacious young woman with a glance. Neatly dressed - not much flair, probably looking for a belt for her mother's birthday.

"I'd like to see some casual wear and a couple of evening gowns." Her cornflower-blue eyes were friendly, her smile genuine and her figure trim.

After "Minnie-the-moocher" who had just left, this one was a dream. Meg's irritation vanished as blouses and trousers, Bermudas and cotton sweaters, light sarong skirts with matching tops and two sexy but elegant evening dresses were bundled into Rachel's waiting arms for wrapping.

"Cash or charge?" Meg enquired.

"Cash, please."

"Thank you, Lord," Meg prayed.

Everything was neatly tissued and boxed and the whole operation took less than three-quarters of an hour.

"Mind if I wait for my car?"

"Of course. Make yourself comfortable here," Meg said pointing to the yellow silk chaise-longue. "Would you like some coffee or tea?" she asked, piling up the boxes beside her.

"Coffee would be great. I have to be back at my desk by two o'clock, no time for lunch today," she confided.

"Let me help you," Rachel offered as a black limousine drew up in front of the shop a couple of minutes later. The pretty girl hurriedly gathered her cumbersome boxes.

"No, no, I'm fine," she insisted, dropping two of the boxes on the grey carpet. Bending to retrieve them Rachel followed her outside to the waiting car.

An attractive man with smooth dark hair sat in the back of the smoked-windowed limo. He smiled fondly at the laden girl and rewarded Rachel with a look of thanks. The driver took the girl's parcels. She flopped on the seat and leant over to kiss her waiting companion. Rachel almost forgot the boxes she was clutching as she stared enviously at the loving couple.

Meg disappeared into her office behind the draped doorway leaving Rachel to put the discarded clothes back on their padded hangers. She stroked the fabrics, marvelling again at the elegance of their designs. She felt sad that she would never be able to afford anything as luxurious as these - even at sale prices. What a handsome man he was, what a lovely young woman - no airs and no graces, she'd been thrilled with everything she'd chosen.

"Rachel!" She heard Meg calling her name. Irritated at the constant interruptions, she put the delicate chiffon dress that she was trying to shorten on to a white sheet and went into the fitting-room.

"This is Rachel."

"I'm Debrah Whitney Lloyd," the horsy-faced woman introduced herself. "I understand you're looking for an apartment?"

Rachel nodded, she doubted very much if anything this "old money" establishment woman could offer would be affordable.

"I don't have an apartment but I do have a proposition. Meg tells me you're a quiet girl, respectable and trustworthy?"

"Yes," Rachel answered, unsure of what was to follow.

"My mother lives in Georgetown - though heaven knows why - and the family feel that because her eyesight is failing she should have a companion in the evenings to read to her or just keep her company. In exchange we can offer a comfortable room and your meals. She's a cantankerous woman, I warn you, and not crazy about our idea but she's changed her mind before. At the weekends you'd be free to do what you like. Do you think you'd be interested?"

"I don't know, ... yes, it's all ... a bit of a surprise. But if your mother is against it ..." Rachel's voice trailed away.

The beaded formal evening gown looked all wrong on the raw-boned woman. Jodhpurs and a riding crop maybe. Rachel knew that no-nonsense type. The kind that thought no plan of hers could be less than perfect. "I'll leave you Mother's address, go and see her after work. I'll tell her to expect you."

Before Rachel could reply Debrah Whitney Lloyd smiled dismissively and returned to the job of choosing a suitable dress. Meg's raised eyebrow warned Rachel to ask no questions. Meg's eyebrows spoke volumes at times and Rachel had quickly learned to understand every quirky movement.

CHAPTER NINETEEN

The tree-lined street with its cobbles and fine houses was a thousand miles away from what Rachel had expected. It was a real place, a home.

The front door of the house was reached by a gently curving double set of steps, guarded by black iron railings. Rachel resisted the urge to climb up one side and run down the other. Instead she stood under a narrow pillared portico and waited for her ring to be answered. An elderly white-haired man opened the gleaming front door and shuffled aside a little to let her pass.

"Miz Whitney is expecting you, Miss, follow me please," he wheezed.

Rachel followed him, shortening her step in order to stay behind him.

The room was almost dark, its furniture outlined in the shadows. A voice from the depths of a chair spoke her name. Rachel walked towards it.

"Let me look at you," the voice commanded.

Just as Rachel wondered how she could see anything in that half-light, the tiny figure switched on a lamp beside her and the room was illuminated with diffused light.

A bird-like woman with silver hair, an alert face and soft brown eyes sat in a wing chair, almost swallowed by its size.

The brown rheumy eyes searched Rachel's face.

"Come nearer. Hmm, very pretty, quite a beauty in fact," she said bluntly. "I suppose that daughter of mine told you I was an incapable old lady? Well, I'm not."

"No Ma'am, she felt you might enjoy some company, someone to read to you, maybe?" Rachel felt her chance of living in this mellow old brick house slipping away. In the few short minutes that she had stood in front of the intimidating, diminutive woman her eyes had become accustomed to the gloom of the room. French tapestry covered chairs, ormolu and porcelain jardinieres with their light-starved plants were scattered about the room. Tables were barely visible under a plethora of photographs. As her gaze dropped to her feet she guessed that the faded carpet beneath them was very old but valuable, its exquisite design was still discernible. The paintings on the wall were difficult to distinguish in the semi-darkness. One directly above the lamp looked like a Canaletto, but she must be wrong, pictures like that were found only in museums.

Harriet Whitney stared hard at the girl, "That's my favourite picture. Do you know anything about art?" she quizzed.

"Very little really but I often visit the art museums. It reminds me of Canaletto - the canals of Venice?"

"It is a Canaletto." Her eyes grew dreamy and far away.

"Why did you agree to consider my daughter's offer?" the woman asked.

"I need somewhere to live, my present apartment is too expensive. Besides, I'd like to have company too," Rachel added, hoping that she didn't sound cheeky - she had nothing to lose at this stage. There were only three days left before she must leave her apartment. The only miserable alternative was a fourth floor walk-up at the edge of the drug-ridden area which she had fought so hard to avoid.

"Do you want to spend every night shut up with a crotchety old lady?"

"I'm sure you're not that bad!" Rachel laughed.

"You're not that bad either. Mrs Saunders will show you the room. If you like it we can take each other on trial for a month. If it doesn't work out you're free to go and vice versa. Come back before you leave," she said, pulling a cord hanging by her left hand.

A plump woman with a rounded face appeared at the door and waited for Rachel to follow her up the staircase to the second floor. The bedroom was the prettiest room Rachel had ever seen. White and pink flower-sprigged material covered the four-poster bed and the two night tables, whose covers flowed gracefully to the floor in soft pleats. Fine nets billowed out from the partly opened sash windows as if in greeting. A satinwood bookcase, fronted by delicately traced crossed banding, was crammed with books and there was a semi-circular desk with inlaid flowers and intricate drawers with minuscule brass handles. On the huge expanse of softly shaded pink carpet two padded armchairs and a round table huddled together companionably. Facing them was a satinwood cabinet.

"This was adapted to conceal a television set,"

Mrs Saunders told Rachel. The slim pliable panels of the door slid into its interior displaying the screen.

"It's a lovely room, isn't it? My favourite one in the house," said the housekeeper. "The bathroom is over there." She indicated a closed door with a workworn hand.

Rachel peeped in. It was as pretty as the bedroom, its colours harmonised perfectly.

"Did you like the room?" Mrs Whitney asked as Rachel returned to the gloom of the heavily velvet draped living-room.

"It's perfect, so dainty and feminine," Rachel replied.

"That's settled then. We eat at seven o'clock each evening. These days I don't get up till noon and when you want breakfast Mrs Saunders will look after you." Harriet Whitney peered at her. "When do you wish to join us?"

"Sunday, if that's all right?"

"Can you manage to move your things on your own?"

There was very little to manage Rachel admitted. Just clothes, a couple of mementoes and some photographs. The thought of the long line of louvered doors stretching the full length of one of the bedroom walls made her smile wryly. Harriet Whitney closed her eyes. Time for Rachel to leave.

She looked back at the house from the footpath and then she gave into temptation. She ran up the steps on one side and down the other.

CHAPTER TWENTY

Meg Adams took a $100 bill from her purse and propped it against the glass. Glancing at her sleeping husband she picked up her shoes and silently left the apartment.

"Please don't give me any trouble today," she prayed aloud as she put the key in the car's ignition. The engine coughed and than growled into life.

"Thank you," she said looking skyward and wondered when, if ever, she'd be able to replace the dying vehicle. Maybe today her tousle-haired, handsome husband would be lucky and find himself some work. Ken had tried so hard. He came home each day his eyes dull with disappointment, breath smelling faintly of liquor. He needed walking-around money, cash to take prospective employers to lunch or dinner and to buy them drinks. Several nights over the last few weeks he'd come home exhausted and had been angry with her if she asked any questions. He had to be smartly dressed too, wearing the best suits and silk shirts with the latest ties. She agreed he must look the part but it was a tremendous drain on their resources.

Rachel had transformed the day's windows with a tempting softly coloured array of chiffons and silks; filmy evening gowns that would float in the warm summer breeze, diaphanous fabrics that flattered tanned skins on the balmy, open-air nights of unceasing parties. Satisfied with her efforts she sprayed a piece of neatly cut white cotton with some jasmine essence and attached it to the small fan hidden in a corner. Slowly a subtle aroma permeated the salon, a light summery perfume. Stepping outside she examined the two windows critically, first the smaller one on the side street then the more important showcase on the main street.

She smiled at the man walking painfully with the aid of a stick. He was late today. Usually they waved to each other through the window when she was still dressing it.

"Good morning." He paused, leaning on the silver-handled cane. Joining her he studied the effects of her work. "Summer in all its green glory! I can picture those dresses swishing on patios and lawns, beautiful ladies preening themselves like peacocks."

Rachel beamed at him, his lyrical words proving that she'd achieved her goal. He continued his slow progress along the street, his cashmere-coated back stiffly erect but his limp more pronounced than usual.

Meg told Rachel that she didn't want to be disturbed. She spread out all her account sheets on the capacious table in front of her and set about checking the figures. Unlocking the drawer of her desk she pulled out an envelope and examined its contents. Everything was in order. She kicked off her shoes and lay back against the chair and closed her eyes. She let her mind drift. Even now after six years of working at Caprice she still did not know who the owners were nor, more irritatingly, who was responsible for the buying. Reluctantly she granted the buyer was good, up to the minute - even ahead - of world fashion, but, as she did the selling, she should do the buying. She was the one who should be swanning off to Paris, being hosted and toasted as she spent hundreds and thousands of dollars. She should spend a few days in the luxury of the Riviera before going to the trade shows in Italy. She'd like to spend large sums of money in top fashion houses and knitwear factories. Ken would enjoy that too - after all, why shouldn't her husband travel with her? They could visit the silk factories in Hong Kong and the incredible fabric houses in Switzerland. Custom-made clothes would be a major part of the business if she had her way, but she had no say. Her only contact was a flinty-eyed accountant she gave a report to every quarter. Female figures were of little interest to him, just the numerical ones, the figures of profit and loss.

Stretching her back she put the sheets back in their folders and her shoes on her feet. She checked her scarlet lipstick in her little handbag mirror and got ready to leave for lunch. It was only twelve o'clock, plenty of time to have a browse around the opposition and to eat a proper lunch. She couldn't face sandwiches again today. She stepped into the perfumed air of the shop and her discontent reared again. Everything was neatly in its place, the hangers with their costly garments hung uniformly in their allotted space, magazines and papers were separated into tidy piles. Glass shone in the display cases filled with artfully arranged belts and costume jewellery. The salon was tranquil. Dammit, she ran the place efficiently and well. She deserved better. She'd treat herself to a new blouse when she got back. The fact that Rachel had been responsible for the artistic displays and shining order didn't trouble her conscience at all.

Rachel slipped the cotton cover over the dress, it was ready for collection. It had been a quiet morning and she was up to date with all her alterations. She poured a cup of coffee and leafed through the latest journals which were ready to be arranged on the long low table in the airy boutique; political journals, antiques magazines, architectural digests, business publications and fashion glossies galore. They replaced *The Washington Post* and *The Wall Street Journal* daily, a small price to pay. It prevented bored men from leaving their wives or girlfriends for the sanity of the streets.

Her attention wandered as she thought of the feisty little lady with the soft tired eyes. They'd fallen into an easy pattern, Rachel kept her amused with tales of her daily routine in the boutique but she never named names. That was one of Meg Adams' explicit instructions. "Confidentiality at all times Rachel," she had repeated pompously many times.

On Monday nights they had abandoned reading altogether because Harriet Whitney wanted to hear every detail of Rachel's lacklustre weekend adventures. Rachel regretted that they consisted mainly of lone visits to one of the Mall's museums or art galleries. She took long walks by the capital's cool waterways as spring turned to summer and temperatures soared. Tonight she'd have something more exciting to report.

Intrigue

By six o'clock Rachel had showered, changed into a cool T-shirt and shorts and was sitting at a corner of the table in the kitchen sipping an ice-cold drink. She chatted amiably as Mrs Saunders expertly mixed the ingredients for the stuffing. Mrs Saunders felt that Rachel had breathed new life into the quiet house. Not that she was pushy or noisy in any way, just lively and even-tempered. Rachel always had a smile. It did Mrs Saunders' heart good to see her mistress's face brighten as the door opened at the end of the day; she didn't complain about the food the way she used to. Even Saunders' grouchy demeanour softened as the pretty girl teased him, tactfully lightening his burden whenever she could.

Enid Saunders had sometimes wondered if marrying this man over twenty years her senior in order to have some security had been a wise move. She had been a young girl when she had first gone to work in the busy Whitney household and she'd been in awe of the man she had married years later and who, to this day, she addressed only by his last name. Spooning stuffing into the cavity of the chicken she nodded mechanically at something Rachel said but she hadn't been paying attention.

"Good, I'm glad you agree."

"Sorry honey, I was concentrating on the chicken, what did I agree with?"

"Eating on the patio in the garden."

"Sorry, you've lost me."

"Wouldn't it be nice for Mrs Whitney to have dinner outside on the patio for a change? I can set up the table."

"You'll never get her to agree to that."

Anne Schulman

"We can give it our best shot," Rachel said optimistically.

"OK by me, but I'll bet fifty cents it won't work."

"Done." Rachel put out her hand to seal the wager.

Wiping her big hand on her apron Enid slapped her open palm onto Rachel's.

"Certainly not," Harriet Whitney snapped at the suggestion.

"It's such a great evening, you'd love it."

"You know we eat in the dining-room," she said irritably.

"Please change your mind," Rachel coaxed. Changing tactics, she added, "I've been indoors all day and I'd love some fresh air."

"Maybe we'll have coffee outside." Harriet relented slightly. Even this would be breaking the habit of years.

Rachel returned to the kitchen and paid her fifty cents.

"Told you, didn't I," Enid Saunders said slipping the coins into her pocket.

"We're going to have coffee outside," Rachel smiled skittishly.

Digging into her apron, Enid solemnly took out a quarter and handed it back to Rachel.

"You're entitled to half the bet." They both laughed.

"I think we'll stay inside," Harriet Whitney said as she prepared to return to her chair after dinner.

"Let's make a deal - try it tonight and if you don't like it I won't try to persuade you again."

"Oh all right, but just this once," she grumbled,

162

resignedly.

Rachel helped her into a padded wicker chair and placed a little table beside her as they waited for Mrs Saunders to bring the coffee cups. The walled garden was sweet with the aroma of honeysuckle and roses.

"It is pleasant," Harriet Whitney grudgingly admitted settling herself comfortably in the still, warm air of the summer night.

"Mrs Whitney, may I ask you something?"

"Depends what it is." She enjoyed being cagey.

"That painting - the Canaletto. It's very special isn't it?" Rachel queried.

"You're very observant, young lady."

"There's always a dreamy look in your eyes when you gaze at it. I didn't mean to pry."

For a few minutes there was silence in the scent filled garden.

"Oh, what the hell. I don't suppose that it matters now, it's all so long ago." Harriet Whitney closed her eyes and began to speak in a quiet voice. "My husband was a powerful man in politics. It took up all his time and then some. He spent very little time with his family. Apart from state occasions, diplomatic parties and Christmas, we rarely saw him. One night at a ball at the White House we were introduced to the French Ambassador and his wife. We all sat together during dinner and apart from being a cultured man the Ambassador was unbelievably charming, a diplomat to his fingertips. His voice was mesmerising and I have to admit that I rudely ignored everyone else around me in order to listen to him. We met several times at various dinners and parties. He always made a point of coming to talk to me. I was flattered, slowly falling under his spell. He invited me to have lunch with him. That was utterly scandalous in those days." She laughed. "Naturally, I couldn't accept. But he refused to take no for an answer. We met at official functions and accidentally on purpose at exhibitions. We met walking in the park, at musical recitals and we met at the ballet. It was entirely by accident that we bumped into one another one day in Virginia. I'd gone to pay my respects to a friend whose husband had died and I was just leaving as he arrived. He begged me to wait for a few moments and of course, I did. By then we were hopelessly in love. After that we walked for miles in quiet parks and out of the way places talking and holding hands. He begged me to leave my husband. He said he'd leave his wife. We'd go away together and live in Venice, *'living 'appily ever after'*, that's what he said." She paused, with a sigh.

"What happened then?" Rachel prompted.

"I suppose by today's standards it sounds very tame. A few kisses, a touching of hands when no one was looking, but maybe that made it all the more precious," she continued. "I needed time to think, this was against all my principles, all my upbringing. But more importantly it would cost him his career - a lifetime's work. He certainly couldn't have stayed in the diplomatic corps. We met again a few days later, this time by design. It took every ounce of courage and strength that I had to stay in a loveless marriage. I wanted to throw myself into his arms, I really wanted that. But I walked away instead. I left the only true love I'd ever had. Three days later I learnt that he had left Washington for personal reasons. I locked myself in my room for days. My husband was far too busy to notice, the children were taken care of by their nanny. It was hard that he'd left without even a goodbye but I presumed that he'd accepted our last meeting as final. The tears that I cried would have filled a small lake. After a week even my husband began to notice. I suppose that was because his friends were asking questions. I didn't think he missed my company. I pulled myself together and went about my duties like a zombie. About three weeks later a large parcel arrived for me. I ripped open the envelope attached to it and read the note inside.

Dear Mrs Whitney,

We are delighted to inform you that your charitable bid for the enclosed painting was successful and we hope it will afford you much pleasure.

The signature was indistinguishable and there was no address on the note. The painting was, of course, the Canaletto, the view as you quite rightly recognised, Venice. I was so confused. I didn't want to share the beautiful picture with anyone. I waited until the children went out for a walk with their nanny. Then I climbed up into the attic and hid the painting behind a lot of old furniture. It stayed there until a year after my husband's death and then I hung it above my chair. My family think it's a copy and that's the way it will remain."

Rachel felt privileged, as if she had looked into Harriet Whitney's very soul.

"You're the first person I ever told - and probably the last. I hope one day, unlike me, you'll find happiness with the *right* man."

Rachel leaned over and clasped Harriet's trembling hand.

"That's enough about me," Harriet said firmly, ending the discussion. "How did you spend your time at the weekend?"

Rachel was astonished by Mrs Whitney's revelation. But she tried hard to concentrate on the little details that she knew the old lady loved to hear. On Saturday she'd been driven indoors by the heat wave to the cool interior of the National Gallery of Art, the "East Wing", the modern art section of the gallery. The soaring beauty of its rose-white marble structure had always enchanted her. It was much more beautiful in her opinion than some of its contents. The light-filled atrium fascinated her. A temporary exhibition by a Russian artist filled two of the rooms. The pictures painted by the artist as a young man were filled with hope but as the dates in the bottom right hand side of the canvases progressed they became filled with despair and sadness. It was a visual diary of a life that began in Russia and ended in the United States. The last of the pictures; a self-portrait of the cadaverous artist on his death-bed, was depressing; his brush-strokes had grown unsure, almost blurred.

"Real miserable end, wasn't it?" The blue-jeaned figure standing beside her was frowning at the portrait. "The earlier ones were fine."

Rachel shivered as she tore her gaze away from the picture to look at the speaker. He was impossibly good-looking with huge round brown untroubled eyes, a perfectly formed nose and, below his smiling mouth, a dimpled chin. At first glance he reminded her of a Greek god with his soft curling hair, all that was missing was the laurel wreath.

"I'm splitting, going to grab a coke at the Cascade Café. I need to cheer myself up. If you feel like checking out of all this…," he indicated waving his arm at the room in general.

"Sure, why not?" Rachel shrugged casually, hiding her enthusiasm.

They chose a table near the picture window and watched the waterfall which cascaded gracefully down the outside wall and burbled to a gentle frothing in the narrow stone-filled gully that ran the full length of the restaurant.

She'd been embarrassed when he clumsily compared her hair to the waterfall, she was unused to compliments.

Roberto Maroni had spotted the lovely girl as she walked through the rooms of the gallery and, biding his time, he waited until she reached the last painting before casually making his approach. Way to go, Roberto, he congratulated himself. Close up she was even better than she'd looked from a distance. His guess had been right - she was friendly, an easy target for his charm. They usually were here. Besides he had a couple of hours to kill.

Roberto was funny and entertaining, around her age she guessed - maybe a year or two older. He was so handsome but she wished that this curly-haired charmer would stop calling her "girl".

"I have to go," he announced suddenly. "It's been great talking with you, girl. Maybe we can get together again, how about that?"

"OK with me," Rachel said, waiting for his suggestion as to where and when.

"Tomorrow? We could go swimming."

"That'd be great." There was just enough time to get to a store before closing time. She didn't own a swimsuit.

The next day was even hotter. The early morning temperature climbed quickly to the high nineties. Rachel's thin shirt stuck to her back and she'd almost given up waiting for him to show up when he appeared at her side.

"Hey, girl. I got delayed, some unexpected business."

They lazed in the cool but crowded pool.

"*Every husband and wife and their two-point-four children are here today,*" Roberto grumbled as he turned sideways to avoid the flailing arms of a water-winged child.

He'd heard someone using that expression and he liked it.

"I'm starving, let's get some stuff for a picnic," Rachel suggested. "We can go to the park and sit under the willow trees."

The world and his wife and their statistical children obviously had the same idea. Noticing his irritability, Rachel, before she could stop herself, heard her own voice say, "Next time we'll find somewhere quieter."

He mumbled a vague yeah and lobbed a wayward frisbee back at its innocent-faced owner with a lot more force than was necessary. "How about going back to your place? This sucks, " he said throwing a disgusted look at the picnicking crowds.

"I'm afraid we can't," Rachel replied, without elaborating.

"How about a movie then?"

The air-conditioned cinema was cool and they sat closely together, his arm around her shoulder. As he kissed her he could feel her trembling in his arms. Inexperienced too, he thought, but that just made her all the more attractive.

It was almost seven o'clock when she returned to the quiet house exhilarated from her day's outing, on tenterhooks until he'd made a date for the following Saturday.

Harriet Whitney closed her eyes. She could just see it all. She felt sad that such a lovely girl spent so much time on her own but her new companion had certainly put a sparkle in her eyes.

CHAPTER TWENTY-ONE

The two women trampled the boxes as flat as they could. Meg's pointed heels punctured the corrugated cardboard. Sheets of protective plastic lay all around them on the floor and caused their feet to slither and slide.

"It looks like an explosion in a wrapping factory. Why so many ballgowns?" Rachel questioned.

"When the new administration comes to power, there'll be dozens of inaugural dances and parties. Personally I hope it will be the 'Hill-Billy' partnership. A young First Lady would get fashion moving again."

Rachel responded to the impatient buzzer. A hard-faced, well-dressed woman in her late thirties strode past her. She kicked aside the remaining plastic covers and rummaged through the rails pulling and pushing roughly at the garments.

"This is creased," she said, sharply, holding up a white crepe dress to the light.

"They've just been unpacked, a minute ago," Rachel apologised watching Meg Adam's eyebrows disappearing deep into her hairline as she left the shop on one of her quarterly visits to the accountants.

"Do you have anything else besides evening gowns?" The woman's tone was sarcastic. "Where is your daywear or do you expect people to wear these during the day too?"

Intrigue

"These are just the first of the deliveries, may I suggest you come back next week? Most of our stock will have arrived by then."

"Hmmph!" she snorted, handing Rachel a white dress. "I'll try this on."

Glancing through the window as she waited, Rachel thought she saw Roberto walking arm in arm with a laughing tow-haired girl about his own height. She must be mistaken, Roberto's hair was shorter. It had been almost four weeks since she'd seen him. She was sure he'd get in touch with her today.

"Ouch! I'm caught in the zipper." She heard the customer call from behind the curtain.

Rachel slipped into the fitting room. The cruel teeth of the metal fastener had caught a little nip of flesh in her side. "Ow! Be careful," she shrieked, squirming as Rachel tried to part the skin from the zipper.

Serves her right Rachel thought, giving a sharp and successful tug, the dress is two sizes too small. The woman flinched rubbing her liberated skin.

Covering the distance between Caprice and the house in record time, she sorted eagerly through the mail on the table but not one of the letters was for her. Absurdly she longed to see her mother's looped writing. She chided herself for her foolishness. Her mother didn't even know where she lived now. She trudged upstairs to her room and opened the card that Sandi had given her weeks before her birthday. The card with its affectionate message was the only one this miserable day, her twenty-first birthday. Roberto had forgotten too.

Anne Schulman

At seven o'clock she dragged herself into the drawing-room but Harriet Whitney wasn't there. Puzzled, Rachel opened the door to the dining-room but the table bore only its tired dried flower arrangement and was not set up for dinner. Alarmed, she ran to the kitchen but it too was empty with just the aroma of cooking wafting from the oven. Rachel's mouth was dry. Something terrible must have happened to Mrs. Whitney. Saunders and his wife were always in the kitchen at this hour. It was almost dusk.

She ran back to the living-room with its partially closed drapes. She sat on the arm of a chair and wondered whether she should call one of Harriet Whitney's daughters. Staring idly into the darkened garden she noticed a flicker of light, uneven and swaying. Crossing to the window she peered through it, but in the half light she could not see properly. She opened the patio doors and a shout of "Happy Birthday" greeted her ears. Rachel jumped with astonishment. The patio lights were switched on, revealing a wonderland of balloons and flowers. In the middle of the patio a small round table was set for two with a beautiful antique lace cloth, gleaming silver and sparkling glass reflecting the lights of the candles which she had seen through the window moments before. A second table held an ice bucket with a gold topped bottle nesting in a bed of ice. Piled neatly beside the serving spoons and plates was a small mound of packages to which more floating balloons were attached.

Saunders came forward, his hand outstretched but as he reached Rachel, he changed his mind and kissed her on the cheek. His wife held out her two plump arms and warmly hugged the startled girl. Running to hug Harriet Whitney, Rachel burst into tears. Harriet held the sobbing girl tightly in her tiny arms for a couple of minutes. She understood her feelings. "This is a happy day, Rachel. Come on, dry your tears and open your gifts."

Laughing and crying all at once Rachel sat on one of the latticed metal chairs with its festoon of silver balloons. Ceremoniously Enid Saunders placed the parcels in front of her and, one by one, she tore open their pretty gift wrap exclaiming with delight at their contents. A large box of eyeshadows with several brushes and a delicate white-on-white embroidered blouse had been Enid Saunders' choice. A card bearing Saunders' shaky writing came with his gifts, a matching hat and scarf for the cold winter mornings and three paperback books. Rachel gave them both a hug of gratitude. They smiled indulgently as Rachel immediately donned the tea-cosy shaped hat, pulling it well down over her ears.

"How beautiful she is," Harriet Whitney thought to herself, her eyes slightly narrowed in the evening light.

"Three left to go." Rachel, now beaming with joy, pulled at the decorative bow on the largest of the parcels. A magnificently illustrated book of art rested on its colourful wrapping, the cover illustration a Venetian scene. Not trusting herself to speak she smiled at Harriet and, leaning over, put a hand on her arm. They understood the gesture and one another perfectly.

"Leave the little one till last," Harriet Whitney

prompted.

In the middle of her unwrapping, Rachel stopped. She had told no one except Roberto about her birthday and that had only been in passing as they'd compared star signs.

"How did you know it was my birthday?" She looked puzzled.

Harriet Whitney tapped the side of her nose.

"Tell me," Rachel begged.

"The locket you gave me to look after... it has your date of birth on the back."

Rachel had totally forgotten the tiny gold locket on its slim gold chain. It had been a christening gift from her uncle and suitable only for a little girl. She had looked after it carefully in the hope that it would be passed on to her daughter if she had one.

Enid Saunders said that dinner would be spoilt if they didn't hurry. Quickly she opened the last two gifts. She gasped as she unfolded an exquisite lace and satin nightdress. "Oh! It's gorgeous. It's a wonderful birthday." Finally she came to the last package and she felt like crying as she stared at the glittering little brooch. A perfectly formed flower of tiny sapphires and diamonds twinkled in its cotton wool nest.

"I don't know what to say," Rachel stammered.

"Say that you're hungry, I am," Harriet Whitney said, gruffly. This tears business was catching. Walking around the table Rachel knelt down and put her two hands in Harriet's. "Thank you with all my heart. I'll treasure this all my life," she said simply.

Tearing himself away Saunders slowly led the retreat to the kitchen. Enid Saunders had carefully prepared all Rachel's favourite dishes and she quickly set about serving the chilled asparagus mousse.

"It's wonderful to hear the two of them laughing," Enid Saunders remarked to her husband.

To the best of her knowledge there had been only one difficult moment since Rachel came to stay with them. Rachel had heard two of her customers discussing a brilliant new ophthalmic surgeon. She asked them for the name of this miracle worker. She begged Harriet to make an appointment with the eye specialist but Harriet gave her a flat no.

"The subject is taboo, Rachel. I really must insist that you don't bring it up again."

"Please," Rachel tried again, "if only for me."

"Rachel, I must ask you to leave me alone. Please leave the room." Harriet's voice was cold and angry and Rachel felt like a naughty schoolgirl. She'd left the obstinate lady to her own devices. They hardly spoke for two days. Tension hung between them like an invisible barrier.

The tiny cutlets were perfectly cooked.

"This is delicious isn't it?" Rachel said, appreciatively chewing a bone.

Harriet Whitney nodded pushing her plate away.

"Well, Miss Insistence, I've got some news that will please you."

Rachel stopped chewing and waited.

"You've won your argument. I've made an appointment with that ophthalmic surgeon you recommended."

Anne Schulman

"I'm very pleased to hear it," said Rachel. They looked at each other and burst out laughing. Enid Saunders came out to the patio, joining in the laughter without knowing why. The feather-light chocolate cake she carried was lit by sparklers. Saunders followed his wife at his own pace, and led a rousing version of "Happy Birthday" - entirely off-key.

CHAPTER TWENTY-TWO

Sitting back on her heels, her mouth full of pins, Rachel waved to her early-morning friend. He stopped to assess the display and he gave her a thumbs-up sign. He was walking more slowly recently, Rachel considered, as she artistically knotted a scarf around the neckline of a dress. Why was he disabled? He was a good-looking man, probably in his late fifties, she reckoned. His finely drawn features were marked by premature ageing lines around his mouth. His hazel eyes, flecked with gold, narrowed slightly with each painful step he took.

Meg Adams startled her as she crashed through the door like a whirling dervish. "Mornin'," she grunted as she slammed through the curtain, rattling its brass rings. Rachel heeded the warning signs and went on with her window-dressing, ignoring the crashing and banging from the office.

"Goddamn you to hell. Open!" Meg yelled, kicking viciously at the stubborn drawer. Her eyes were black-rimmed. Her mouth drooped downwards with worry and lack of sleep. It had been daylight when Ken had finally stumbled into their apartment. Giggling, he undressed. As he flung his Georgio Armani suit towards a chair she'd sat up in bed waiting for an explanation.

"Sweetheart, you're not asleep yet. Wonderful," he said, dropping on the bed beside her as he tried to pull her into his arms.

Anne Schulman

"Where the hell have you been?" she demanded, pushing him away.

"Out," he gurgled, laughing hysterically. Leaning over to kiss her he missed and fell on his face into the pillows. There was no smell of liquor on his breath. If he hadn't been drinking this sort of high could have just one explanation - he was smoking, sniffing or snorting something..

"What are you using, Ken? What are you on?" she clenched her teeth, scared of his reply.

"On the bed, on the wonderful floating boat-bed. Floaty, flying bed. Whoosh! Up she goes."

She was calm. Calm with a hopelessness she had never experienced before. Face it, she told herself, you're married to a bum. A well-dressed and expensively shod, absolutely useless, bum. Layers of self-deception finally fell away. Questions that she'd stifled too often in recent months were answered as she finally acknowledged the truth. She'd been afraid of being lonely and that had kept her on a blinkered path. She loved this handsome husband-stranger who lay beside her. She'd taken dreadful risks in order to please him. The acid of fury burned her stomach. Totally drained she wanted to get into her car and drive it into a wall. But the way things were going the car would probably break down, she thought bitterly.

Meg stormed out of the lemon and grey boutique just as irritably as she had stormed in, barking orders to lock up if she didn't get back in time. Rachel sighed with relief as the door banged shut and ran to the office to answer the telephone. She sat on the table swinging her foot,

178

one shoe falling to the floor. She propped the phone firmly under her chin and bent sideways at a dangerous angle in an attempt to retrieve the flat pump. Scooping it up she noticed a sheet of paper which had lodged itself between the grey silk wastepaper basket and the table. She picked it up and dropped it on a pile of papers as she noted the requirements of the client. Replacing the receiver she checked her notes and then sat idly for a moment. Her eyes strayed to the sheet of paper. *Rachel,* it was headed, *Commissions on sales @ 5%.* Commissions, what commissions? She received a weekly salary but nothing more. Scanning the list she recognised all the items that *she* had sold in the past six months. Should she have had extra money on each of those sales?

Peering cautiously through the open doorway towards the curtain she plugged the calculator into the electric socket and fed it with all the figures which 5% represented. The total amounted to a staggering three thousand two hundred and twenty dollars. More money than she'd ever had at one time in her life. A dull flush swept up her neck to her cheeks. What should she do, return the piece of paper to its hiding place? There had to be a rational explanation. Her inclination was to confront Meg as soon as possible, but veiled hints of her predecessor's dismissal for meddling in things that were none of her business tempered her decision. The figures danced in front of her eyes like puppets jerking on strings.

Meg Adams reappeared ten minutes before closing time. Rachel took a deep breath, summoned up her courage, and resolutely approached the grim-faced woman, almost colliding with her.

"I'll see you tomorrow, Rachel. Lock up please." Meg stayed less than a minute. That put paid to any discussion for the moment. Maybe it was just as well considering Meg's black mood and bristling body language. Rachel fought the urge to check if the paper was still there, and lost the battle. The list had vanished.

The door-buzzer broke into her whirling thoughts. Irritably punching the curtain aside - she could rattle brass rings too - she saw Roberto's smiling face. Her spirits rose. He'd never called at the boutique before. She was so relieved to see him that she instantly forgave him her previous disappointment. It had been almost a month since she'd heard from him.

"Hi, girl," he said, kissing her until she struggled for breath.

"I thought you'd forgotten me," she reproached.

"Hey! Would I?" He looked hurt at her suggestion.

Unusually for him, he apologised for his absence. "I've been looking for an apartment, trouble with the ... er... fumigators," he finished lamely.

"Did you get fixed up?"

"No, that's why I'm here. I have to leave - split-city. I don't even have anywhere to sleep tonight." He stared at her with round, soulful eyes. Cunningly he watched as compassion filled her tender face. She was such an easy target. Sighing loudly he turned his head away. "See you round, sweet girl," he said, giving the final twist to the screw.

"No, wait," Rachel pleaded, thinking fast. "Look, you can sleep in the shop if you like, but just for tonight."

He pretended to consider the offer; she'd reacted on cue. The cops wouldn't look for him here, it would be the ideal hiding place for a few days.

Rachel phoned the house to say she would be a little late. Enid Saunders assured her there was no rush, Harriet had been sneezing all day and had gone to bed early.

"I might go to a movie in that case. You're sure she's OK?"

"Oh yes, it's just a precaution. Enjoy yourself, honey, see you in the morning."

Hand in hand they strolled along the busy streets. Rachel loved the jostling bustle of Georgetown nightlife, oddballs rubbing shoulders with conformists, torn jeans mingling with formal suits, students in deep discussion with their professors - a cavalcade of contrasts. They jumped apart as a teenager wearing an umbrella-shaped hat and shorts roller-skated past them, a walkman securely fastened to his bare chest with sticky tape.

"Let's eat, I'm starving," Roberto said suddenly. Music blared from the brightly lit student-crowded café. Roberto liked that, he pushed his way through the crowd and elbowed his way to a vacant table. Rachel didn't bother to tell him that she hated anchovies on her pizza, she was just happy to be with him. They were joined at the postage stamp-sized table by a couple of rowdy university students calling to friends behind them. Roberto's acerbic comments were amusing, his own peculiar form of jealousy. Rachel looked at him wolfing a large piece of pizza and smiled her beautiful smile. Her heart was filled with love for him. It never even entered her head to question why the fumigation of his apartment was a reason to leave town.

They went back to the shop and moved around in the dark. They didn't want to draw attention to themselves by putting on the lights. The street lights cast a faint glow into the stylish salon and Roberto took Rachel in his arms and kissed her. The sheer sensual delight of his caresses left her weak. Every fibre of her being was given up to his touch. Her nervous resistance crumbled. Never had she imagined that she could be so happy. Rachel was sure Roberto loved her.

Rachel promised to come back at seven-thirty next morning. She locked up the boutique. Roberto aroused in her a passion she hadn't suspected that she possessed. Funny, she didn't even know what he did for a living. "You know, girl, a bit of this and that," he had said quelling her curiosity with kisses.

By six-thirty the following morning, after a night of shallow sleep and vivid dreams, she was pacing up and down the spacious bedroom. The problem sheet of figures returned to taunt her, but her plan to discuss it with Harriet Whitney would have to be shelved until later. Instinctively she felt she could not talk to Roberto about it but couldn't explain that feeling to herself. Grabbing a cup of coffee and claiming that she was behind in her work she left the house and ran most of the short journey to the shop. Roberto was perched on the edge of the very feminine chaise-longue, drinking coffee. Discarded magazines were scattered all around him on the floor. It had been quite a shock to him when he recognised several of the faces smiling from the society and diplomatic columns of the elite journals. They probably wouldn't recognise him, just the little white packages he sold which they needed so badly.

The photographs could be useful in the future so he had ripped out the pages and stuffed them in his pocket.

"Please, Roberto, you must leave," Rachel urged nervously. "There'll be hell to pay if Meg Adams arrives early." These days Rachel was never sure what time the fiery manageress would appear.

"Hey! Relax girl, it's cool."

"Please don't call me 'girl', I hate it," Rachel begged.

"Make some fresh coffee and then I'll split."

She took the empty percolator to the sink in her workroom and removed the filter and replaced it with a fresh one. Listening carefully to the sound of running water, he quickly opened her purse and removed a ten-dollar bill. He couldn't risk returning to his apartment even if the cops weren't looking for him already, not for a few days anyway. It was a good job that he'd removed every trace of his identity from his meagre room. He wouldn't get far on a lousy ten bucks, he'd tap that blonde from the University for some dough. He'd earned it - she couldn't keep her hands off him, couldn't get enough of him. At least Rachel had been a challenge, still

Anne Schulman

was - despite last night. There were always so many girls, women, only too eager for his boyish good looks and the charm of his sleepy brown eyes. All suckers for a good-looking guy. The married ones were the best bet when cash ran out, as it often did. They were generous with gifts too.

They drank their coffee, Rachel sat on the floor by the table. She found herself telling him how she had come to live with Harriet Whitney. She couldn't believe she had been talking non-stop for a whole hour.

Nervously insisting that he stood back in the shadows, Rachel began her morning chores, starting with the windows. "Here comes my favourite critic," Rachel said as the limping man approached the window. She waved to him, wrinkling her nose; there was little to approve or disapprove of so far today.

"Who's he?" Roberto questioned.

"I don't know, he comes by every day and inspects the window display."

At his usual position in front of the large window the elegantly suited man cocked his handsome head in question. Rachel laughed at his comical stance, she mouthed that she was late today. He nodded his understanding, and waved in salutation and continued on his way.

"Holy shit, did you see that watch? It must be worth thousands," Roberto said standing at her shoulder.

"I didn't notice." She was trying to balance the clothes-model that was wobbling precariously on its base.

"Please keep back," she begged, but she was

talking to air. In a flash Roberto had darted out of the shop. He looked both ways, and ran silently after the limping figure, his sneakers making no sound in the empty street. With frozen horror Rachel watched as he grabbed the man's arm from behind. In the surprise of the attack the startled man, unable to maintain his balance, crashed forward on to the unyielding concrete, and cracked his forehead on the sidewalk. Rachel was rooted to the spot as Roberto turned and fled down the side street beside the shop without as much as a backward glance. In a spilt second he has disappeared from sight.

Rachel ran to the immobile figure lying on the ground. There was blood on his face and head and he was deathly pale. Her heart was thumping in her throat as she ran back to the shop and dialled *emergency*, shouting for help. She grabbed one of the little silk cushions from the chaise-longue and ran back into the street where a couple of people were bending over the unconscious man. Very gently she lifted his injured head and slid the pillow under it. "Don't move him," one of the onlookers advised. As she rubbed his white hand she heard the scream of a police siren.

A car screeched to a halt and two burly uniformed policemen, night-sticks in hand, stepped out and made their way to her side. Rachel felt a wave of relief as they took over, she gladly took their advice to move away.

Searching the man's jacket for identification or any medical alert, the stockier of the two men whistled with surprise as he examined the man's wallet. He showed it to his fellow officer.

"Daniel Hunt!" he read aloud.

Rachel vaguely remembered hearing the name. An ambulance arrived minutes later followed by another police car. Suddenly the street was swarming with people. Daniel Hunt was still unconscious, his silver-topped cane lay beside him. She bent to pick it up and held it tightly in her hands, willing him to open his eyes. Working quickly the paramedic team strapped him on to a stretcher and the ambulance, its siren echoing in the comparative quiet of the street, disappeared as swiftly as it had arrived. Rachel was now shaking uncontrollably as the taller of the two policemen led her back to the shop. He poured her a cup of the lukewarm coffee and added three teaspoons of sugar to it.

"That better?" he asked pulling a note-pad and pen from his pocket. "I need to ask you some questions."

The coffee was sickly sweet and at the sight of the official note-pad she felt the blood drain from her face. She breathed deeply as the police officer instructed. Gradually she recovered her composure.

"You OK? Did you see what happened?" he asked, pen poised over the empty page.

She shook her head. She had to lie, to save herself and to protect Roberto. She was frightened for them both. If he were caught she would be implicated too. Anger complicated her feelings. She had committed no crime. What did they call it, guilt by association?

The police officer seemed satisfied with the answers to his questions. She said she'd found the man lying there as she had stepped up on to the little platform that separated the shop from its windows. No, she'd seen no one, heard no sound. Anyone suspicious hanging around? No, she hadn't noticed anything unusual.

Finally he left the boutique to join his unsmiling partner waiting in the car outside, promising that the department would let her know if they caught the perpetrator. She prayed that this would be one of the city's unsolved crimes. This was one secret that she couldn't share with Harriet Whitney or anyone else. What had come over Roberto? Her Roberto - a common mugger.

CHAPTER TWENTY-THREE

Meg Adams arrived at Caprice to find Rachel badly shaken after her ordeal.

"What a terrible experience for you," she sympathised, when she heard Rachel's censored version of the horrible occurrence.

Rachel agreed. Her mind was in turmoil. "Who's Daniel Hunt anyway? The cops seemed to know him."

"Is that who was mugged?" Meg whistled just as the policeman had done. "He's a big noise, mega-rich, with interests in everything from A to Zee. You name it and he's involved in it. Railroads, shipping, property development, construction, everything. Are you OK? You look very pale."

"Just give me a few minutes, I'll be fine."

"Sure, let's make some fresh coffee."

The cane lay discarded on the table. It needed to be returned, but where?

Each day she had waited for the police to return and arrest her, but they hadn't come back and neither had Roberto. Not a call, not a word. Instead, a week later an enormous bouquet of flowers arrived at the shop. Meg Adams signed for it and carried it into the workroom to Rachel.

"Wow, who's your admirer? That's some flower-power."

The enclosed note was written in a shaky hand and bore the address of an expensive clinic. It was signed, *Daniel F. Hunt*. Rachel felt wretched, she'd liked to have trashed the innocent blooms but that would have looked suspicious. Instead she divided them and gave a large bunch to Meg Adams to take home with her. She split the rest into three large bunches. She gave one to Enid Saunders, another she placed in Harriet Whitney's room and she stuffed the third bunch into a vase on the hall table. They would wither soon, the sooner the better and then she would be able to forget about them.

"Will you visit him?" Harriet asked as they sat finishing their dessert.

"I didn't think about it. Do I need to?" Rachel paled.

"I'm sure you don't *need* to. I thought you might like to see him. Besides don't you still have his cane?"

Rachel nodded, her expression remote. Would this awful guilt never go away?

"I suppose I could go tomorrow. But I'll telephone first." She hoped in her heart that her offer to visit would be refused. She was dismayed by the pleasant voice of the clinic's director - "He'd be delighted to see you," she said after a short delay.

The room was large and cheerful. Apart from labelled outlets for oxygen and other emergency machines it was indistinguishable from a hotel bedroom - a luxurious one at that. Thick carpets muffled the sounds of the nurses quietly performing their tasks. Two comfortable couches were pushed against the walls and a high-seated chair, with its footstool, was placed by the window overlooking well-tended gardens. Daniel Hunt was dozing when Rachel arrived and she hesitantly placed the cane, to which she had taped a single red carnation, on the mobile bed-table. He stirred and opened his eyes. "How nice of you to visit me, I do appreciate it. The police have been here too," he said.

"Have they discovered who mugged you?" She could hardly speak her throat was so dry.

"Not yet."

"Thank you for sending the beautiful flowers, it really wasn't necessary." She knew she sounded ungracious. "I mean, well, anyone would have done the same ..."

What a distinguished looking man he is, Rachel thought. His dark hair was, as always, immaculate, highlighted at the temples by a peppering of silver. His hazel flecked eyes were bright and the Roman nose perfect in proportion to his pale face. It was only his mouth, slightly down-turned at the sides, which gave any indication of the pain which he was suffering.

"How are you feeling?" She had forgotten to enquire.

"A little battered and bruised," he laughed, making light of the pain.

She felt awkward. She didn't know what to say. Sensing her difficulty, Daniel Hunt gently quizzed her about her job. Enthusiasm untied her tongue. She found herself telling him all about her work and how happy she was living in the lovely Georgetown house with Harriet Whitney. Daniel was glad to talk to her without the barrier of a glass window. As she talked he listened to the lovely girl, delighting in her expressive face with its exotic almond-shaped eyes. Her vulnerable mouth with generous red lips emphasised her flawless creamy skin.

To Rachel's surprise almost three-quarters of an hour had passed. She got up quickly and apologised for staying too long.

"I've really enjoyed your visit," he assured her, "I'd be delighted to see you any time. I'll be here for several weeks."

A frown creased her brow. "Are you that badly hurt?" Embarrassed at the directness of her question she fidgeted with the tassel of her belt. "Sorry, please excuse me, I mean ... I hope that you're not badly injured."

"I have a problem, a back injury which hasn't been helped by the punk who mugged me."

This was the first time he'd said anything about the attack. She wanted to run away.

"Did you get a look at the ... , the person who knocked you down?" Please say no, she begged silently.

"He attacked me from behind, I guess it was a man by the force that threw me down. I blacked out. Judging from the bump it was my head that broke my fall!" he said with an attempt at humour.

Her knees threatened to buckle with relief.

"The police are doing all they can, but they don't hold out much hope. The street was empty at that hour - as you know - so there were no witnesses. Unless they catch him fencing the watch he'll probably get away scot-free."

She'd forgotten about the watch.

That thought brought back the niggling worry about the sheet of commissions. She still hadn't discussed it with anyone.

Anne Schulman

"Penny for them."

"Excuse me?"

"You look positively fierce," he teased.

"Forgive me, it's just a problem I have to work out," she murmured, a smile lighting her lovely face.

As soon as she had left the room Daniel Hunt pressed the bell for the nurse. The pain was unbearable. He'd told the nurse not to give him his injection until he called for it. He'd been looking forward to Rachel's visit and he wanted to remain alert and awake. The medication made him drowsy, the pain subsided as he drifted into a twilight sleep. Rachel's face floated through his dreams, she was carrying a tray with an enormous hypodermic wreathed in flowers. She was smiling and skipping, whirling the syringe with its trailing ribbons above her head like a dancer. Her beautiful eyes smiled as she rubbed his arm and, as the needle pierced the skin a smell of mushroom assailed his nostrils. Her voice was gentle as she spoke, "Dinner, Mr Hunt, dinner." Opening his eyes to look into Rachel's face he saw instead the starched uniform of his nurse. A bowl of mushroom soup sat on a tray, Rachel was long gone.

There was something compelling about Daniel Hunt. He had a quality which Rachel could not understand, a presence. The following weekend, Rachel found herself drawn back to the clinic again. She had spent one of her lunch breaks searching for a suitable gift to take to Daniel Hunt. She had no idea what he'd like so she'd finally chosen a newly published book of short stories. His face brightened when he saw her. He opened her gift and told her that she couldn't have made a better choice. His attention span was short at the moment. It would be ideal to pick up and put down.

This time she stayed longer. Daniel excused himself after a little while and he reached for the phone and made a call. He wanted some papers which needed signing. How dedicated he is, Rachel thought.

"I have twin sons," he told her, "totally unalike in looks. They're both married but only one of them has a child."

He didn't mention a wife. This time there were no difficult silences. They found no shortage of common interests; literature, art and music. Rachel had discovered an absolute treasure trove of classics and modern literature in the pretty bookcase in her room. They were both fascinated by architecture, the wide streets of Washington and the cosmopolitan air of Georgetown and Alexandria. He loved Paris, hated New York. "My favourite places of all are the beautiful old villages of England and the incredibly green countryside of Ireland."

"I have never been out of the State of DC.," Rachel admitted. "But my mother came from Ireland." It was the first time she had been able to speak of her mother without bitterness.

He resisted an extraordinary urge to tell her that he'd take her to all those places one day, and thought the drugs he was taking must have affected his mind.

During the week he lived and worked in Georgetown, combining home and office in a lovely old house in a leafy tree-lined cul-de-sac not too far distant from Harriet Whitney's house. At weekends and holidays he went back to his home in the nearby hills of Virginia. Rachel told him how Mrs Whitney's daughters would have preferred their mother to live there but that she had refused to leave her red brick home. She found herself telling him about how she'd come to live with the lady of whom she had grown so fond, and about her own mother's overnight flit. Had she imagined the look of pain in his eyes?

There was a discreet tap at the door and a powerfully built man carrying a grey folder came in.

"Thank you, Gates," Daniel said as he took the folder. "Would you mind waiting for this young lady and taking her back to Georgetown?" It was a polite order, not a question.

"Certainly Mr Hunt," he said closing the door quietly.

"Maybe I should leave now," Rachel suggested, she didn't want to keep the man hanging around.

"Gates is used to waiting, it's part of his job." Daniel's voice was firm. "What were we talking about?"

"You were telling me about your homes."

"Oh yes. I'm afraid the medication is taking its toll." He laughed.

"What about your wife?" There, she'd said it.

"She's dead." His response was curt, unexpectedly sharp and a sixth sense warned Rachel not to ask any more questions. Instead she told him stories about her customers.

"You're tired," she said, "I'll leave you to rest." She approached his bed and impulsively bent down to kiss his brow, blushing slightly at her daring.

"Thank you." He touched her hand, slim fingers.

"I'll come to see you next Sunday," she promised.

"That'd be nice. Tell you what, why don't you come at lunch-time and we can eat together?" He waited for her reply.

"I'd like that," Rachel agreed.

The car was smooth and quiet, it was the first time she had ridden in a limousine. Daniel Hunt was a pleasant man and, even in his injured condition, exuded an air of authority. Inexplicably she felt protected and cherished in his company,

Stop being ridiculous, she admonished herself, you hardly know the man. She was looking forward to Sunday just the same.

closed his eyes and relaxed into
ly plumped pillows. The injection
woul do its soothing work and patiently
he wan d for the pain to recede. He thought
about Rachel. She had brought a freshness to his
life with her visits, her bright smiling face and
soft voice were the only compensation for this
whole nasty business.

It's ridiculous, he reasoned, she's young
enough to be my daughter. But he knew he
wasn't thinking of her as a daughter, but as an
attractive young woman full of spirit and
compassion, without guile, honest and forthright.
He tried to think of something that irritated him
about her but failed. She was refreshingly
different from anyone he'd ever met. This was
nonsense, if he didn't stop thinking like this he'd
end up like those men who fell for younger
women, men with trophy wives. "Wife? What's
the matter with me?" he wondered aloud. "I must
be hallucinating."

When he was just a young man he'd inherited
a modest fortune and devoted himself to turning
it into a vast one. He'd worked all hours of the
day and night. It hadn't been difficult to throw
himself into the business after the twins' mother
had ... gone. Even now he couldn't face the
truth. After thirty-five years he still couldn't bring
himself to accept the fact that she had chosen to

run away from her responsibilities. His love and their beautiful twin babies hadn't been enough for her. That had wounded him as surely as the blow of an axe. He found it difficult to trust any woman after that. Difficult to form a permanent relationship. Within one week he'd packed up and left New York to begin a new life in Washington where no one knew anything about his private life. For thirty years he had retained the services of a detective who had reported to him on his ex-wife's whereabouts and changing fortunes. When she'd died, impoverished and alone, it had given him no feeling of peace or satisfaction.

He told no one about his marriage and the twins had grown up in total ignorance of their mother's existence. They believed she had died when they were babies. He kept a low profile and encouraged his sons to do the same. They rarely questioned the wisdom of their father whom they loved and respected. His sons graduated from Harvard and joined their father in his business. Their wealth spiralled upwards as the business expanded. The team of three worked in harmony. They complemented each others' skills and settled into a quiet pattern of life until the day they had discovered a copy of *Fortune* magazine, listing Daniel Hunt as one of the most affluent men in the country. He'd ignored all publicity and refused to give magazine interviews. He hired a valet-cum-bodyguard for himself and armed chauffeurs for his sons, their wives and his grandson.

Now he regretted that he had taken his walk

Anne Schulman

alone each day, though he doubted that his
attack was anything more than an everyday run-
of-the-mill mugging.

Suddenly he had an urge to telephone Rachel.
He stretched out his arm to dial her number but
changed his mind. His thoughts wandered back
to the earlier days of his empire building as he
was lulled into a pain-free sleep.

CHAPTER TWENTY-FIVE

Rachel took great pains with her appearance. The red dress flattered her creamy skin and black hair. It had taken her weeks of painstaking work to make the dress and she had to admit she was pleased with the result. She added a pair of heavily twisted silver earrings and a matching ring and went to join Saunders and his wife in the kitchen for a cup of coffee.

"Hi honey, you look lovely to-day. You've done yourself proud with that dress," Enid said admiringly.

"It's finally finished, and I'm quite pleased with it," Rachel said without conceit.

"There was a phone call for you from Mr Hunt's driver. He'll collect you at twelve o'clock to take you to the clinic."

Rachel was glad, it was a messy journey involving two buses. "I'm getting used to the luxury of limousines now," she admitted.

The drive through the Virginia hills was soothing. The autumn leaves were showing their full colours in a magnificent green, rust and gold display. It must be lovely to watch the trees come into bud then into leaf and finally into this spectacular display before winter, she thought.

Daniel was sitting in the chair by the window watching like a schoolboy for the limousine and his visitor.

"How utterly childish, you're behaving like a young fool instead of a fifty-eight year old man of the world," he chastised himself and grinned as he glimpsed his car snaking around the contours of the winding drive.

Rachel was delighted to find him out of bed, sitting on the upright chair and able to enjoy the view of the grounds with its majestic trees.

"I've ordered lunch from my favourite restaurant," Daniel said, as Gates carried in a pile of boxes and a bottle of wine. "We can have a picnic here at the table."

Gates spread the meal in front of them and discreetly vanished, leaving them together. They munched crispy bread sticks, dipping them into a wonderful mayonnaise and garlic dip flavoured with basil. They ate spicy chicken legs with their fingers but Rachel noticed that Daniel only picked at his food. Her eyes sparkled from the light fruity wine and all feelings of diffidence or shyness she had felt meeting him again floated away.

"I like your dress and your earrings," he complimented.

"I went to Alexandria yesterday and bought the earrings and the ring at the Torpedo Factory."

"I used to love wandering around the old Torpedo Factory. Do they still have craftworkers there?"

"Oh yes, artists, sculptors and jewellers, about eighty-five different studios. They're so talented. I wish…"

"What do you wish?"

"Oh nothing, just a thought."

"Tell me," Daniel smiled, encouraging her gently.

"I wish Caprice sold some locally made

jewellery instead of importing it all. Look at this wonderful workmanship," she said, pulling one of the earrings free and placing it in his hand.

"They're certainly beautiful. Have you suggested it to your manageress?" He turned the earring over to examine the back.

"No point. Meg Adams really has no say in the buying."

"I see. What else would you change?"

"Meg Adams." She laughed bitterly.

He frowned with surprise at her hard-bitten tone.

"How come?"

"I'm just kidding, I didn't really mean that."

"Rachel, that didn't sound like a joke."

She felt she could trust him. She told him about the piece of paper and her suspicions. After the shock of the Roberto episode she'd pushed this other worry to the back of her mind and hadn't found the courage since then to approach Meg Adams. Daniel closed his eyes as he listened to her. When she stopped speaking he sat quietly, digesting her words.

"It strikes me that your suspicions may be well-founded. What other explanation can there be? You'll have to tackle her, Rachel, and ask her point blank exactly what that sheet of paper meant. After all, if she's not paying you your commission what's she doing with the money?"

"I know you're right, but I don't want to lose my job. She fired the last girl who worked there for meddling."

"Maybe so, but if you ask me I'd say that this *is* your concern."

Rachel sighed but firmly resolved to speak to

Meg Adams the following day. Daniel refilled her glass and handed it to her. "A toast," he said cheerfully, "to my homecoming on Wednesday."

"That's terrific news, I'm so happy for you." Rachel beamed.

"I can't pretend I'll be sorry, but maybe I won't see you any more - except through your morning windows. And that won't be for a while."

"Of course you will," she said hurriedly, then blushed.

He laughed heartily at her confusion but was ridiculously pleased with himself.

"Tell me about your twins," she demanded, considerably cheered.

He smiled with affection as he talked about them. As they had grown they had lost their identical looks and developed different personalities. Despite seeing each other every working day they were very close and each had found his own particular niche in the company. Both were married and Jonah, the elder by two minutes, had one son. The other twin, Nicholas and his wife hadn't been able to have children. Jonah was tall, slim and intense; Nicholas was roly-poly and easy-going with a fun-loving nature and a wicked sense of humour.

"What about their wives?" Rachel was curious about Daniel Hunt's daughters-in-law.

"Ah! Well, Caroline, Jonah's wife, is a cool, very sophisticated lady, a most efficient wife and hostess. Jenny - Jennifer - is a warm, very sweet person, she hides her light under a bushel. You'll meet them and you can make up your own mind."

Rachel found herself looking forward to the

meeting but she was even more pleased that her friendship with Daniel would continue.

"May I ask you something personal?" she ventured timidly.

"That depends how personal," he teased.

"What happened to cause you such pain? I've often wondered."

"You mean before the mugging?"

She nodded.

"It's an old sports injury to my hip and back, a disc lesion, and now arthritis has complicated things even more. The doctors say that it won't really get any better, but medication keeps the pain under control." He grimaced.

A wave of guilt silenced Rachel for a minute or two. How could Roberto have picked on such a helpless man? The immorality of his actions sickened her heart. Good riddance to him with his good looks and winning ways. She suddenly remembered the missing ten dollar bill. Had he taken that too?

Daniel's voice interrupted her suspicious thoughts. "You aren't still worrying about tackling Meg Adams are you?"

"No. Sorry, I drifted away."

"I enjoyed the book you bought me," he said. One of the stories had really grabbed his attention he told her. He gave her a short synopsis of it and she became totally engrossed in what he was saying.

"It reminds me of when I was a young man at college. What romantic entanglements we got ourselves into. Sometimes I wonder how any of us graduated!"

"Where did you go to college?" Rachel asked.

"Harvard, the same as the twins - after I graduated I joined my father in his business. Sadly, just a year later Dad died but I kept going, trying to build it up a little." Daniel said modestly. "After that I married. When my wife was no longer with us we moved to Washington and struggled along there."

Obviously Daniel was still not going to talk about his wife, Rachel thought. She began to wonder if Meg Adams had exaggerated his great wealth.

They were interrupted when his nurse arrived and insisted he go back to bed. "Time for your fix," she said humorously, waving the hypodermic.

"Can you excuse us for a moment?" She dimpled at the pretty girl who had put a smile on her patient's face.

"I should leave, you must be tired." But Daniel Hunt refused to let her go.

"Wait for two minutes until I get rid of my dragon here," he grinned disarmingly at the waiting nurse. "Please don't leave yet, Rachel."

Rachel prowled the quiet corridor, her feelings in turmoil. She was enjoying herself immensely. Daniel Hunt was an extraordinarily fascinating man. He made her feel entirely at ease. He listened to everything she said. He explained things simply and was never sarcastic or patronising if she asked questions. *Pygmalion* sprang to her mind. He was so much older than she was and she couldn't imagine how such a worldly man could be interested in her and her mundane life. She'd miss his company terribly. He wouldn't be able to take his walks for a while. He had said she'd meet his family, so he must mean to keep up their friendship.

A pleasant-faced man nodded as he passed her and made his way along the corridor, stopping as he reached Daniel's door. A moment later the nurse left the room beckoning to Rachel to return.

"This is my son, Nicholas." Daniel introduced Rachel.

Nicholas smiled at the lovely girl, his plump face showed no surprise. Nicholas and his father didn't look alike but they had the same gold-flecked hazel eyes. "Oh! So you're the mysterious young lady who helped my father. No wonder he kept you a secret! Seriously, we're very grateful to you; the police told Dad you acted quickly and very efficiently. It doesn't bear thinking about - what could have happened if you hadn't been there. He was a lucky man to have found such a lovely saviour." Nicholas's words were teasing but sincere.

Again the flush rose to Rachel's cheeks, "I did very little," she said, hiding her face from them both by walking to one of the sofas.

As he sat talking to his father, Nicholas's face became more serious. His unruly hair fell forward over his unwrinkled brow and curled towards his ears. He pushed his glasses upwards on his short nose. His generous smiling mouth and round cheeks gave him a cherubic appearance. Daniel looked fondly at his son as he spoke and Rachel shifted uneasily, feeling that she was eavesdropping on a private conversation. Daniel included Rachel in a more general conversation which allowed Nicholas to study his father's visitor. Difficult to guess her age, early twenties he guessed. She was a stunning girl with that jet-black hair and wonderful velvety, almond-shaped eyes.

He knew now why his father had been so enthusiastic about his rescuer. He didn't blame him. Nicholas knew his wife would want to hear all about her when he returned home so he tried to take in all the details of her appearance. He was sure this would be more than a "thank-you" relationship. Pleading a heavy workload, Nicholas excused himself. He thanked Rachel once more and said he hoped that they'd meet again.

"Will you have dinner with me the week after next?" Daniel heard himself ask after Nicholas had gone.

"Thank you, I'd love that. It'd have to be Saturday or Sunday though, I spend all my week nights with Mrs Whitney."

"Perfect. I'll call you to make arrangements."

Rachel insisted that she had overstayed her welcome and this time Daniel, who was tired, didn't argue. As she had done on her last visit, she bent and gently kissed his forehead, bringing a smile to his drawn face.

CHAPTER TWENTY-SIX

As they sat together by the fire Rachel gave Harriet Whitney a blow-by-blow description of her visit to Daniel Hunt the previous day. The wily old woman read more into Rachel's account than appeared on the surface. Her fondness for Rachel had transcended the bounds of friendship and she felt as fiercely protective of her as she did towards her own daughters. She had been sorry for Rachel when Roberto moved away from Washington. He'd really put a sparkle in her eye.

Harriet had gleaned information about Daniel Hunt from her family. He'd been widowed young, had twin sons and he'd made a huge fortune. His companies were privately owned, his dealings sharp but fair. His eldest daughter-in-law acted as hostess for him and she was a "tough cookie". Most people who knew her disliked her. The younger daughter-in-law was far more popular. But she was shy and had been overshadowed by her sister-in-law. Daniel Hunt was in his late fifties, Rachel wasn't yet twenty-two. That worried Harriet; after all, she'd made that mistake, she'd married a man much older than herself, and she didn't want to see Rachel do the same thing.

"Do you have anything in common?" she probed gently.

"Oh yes! Lots of things. He is so knowledgeable it's wonderful to talk to him," she enthused.

Harriet's frown deepened. Mind your own business, she admonished herself. "Maybe I could meet him some time, he sounds a most interesting person," she ventured, casually.

"I'm sure he'd love to meet you too, he knows you well by now," Rachel laughed.

"Hrpmh," Harriet growled, "I'm sure that would be enough to put him off."

"Stop fishing for compliments," Rachel teased, but she was very pleased. They'd like each other, she was sure.

"When he's able to get about again you must invite him to dinner."

Rachel could not have wished for more. Harriet made her feel as if she were part of a family again, a feeling she had missed so much since her mother's hasty flight. Her own experience with Roberto had made her more tolerant. It taught her how easy it was to be taken in by a man.

"In all the upset of the last few weeks I forgot to tell you one piece of news," Rachel said, as she told Harriet about the discovery of the commission list.

"Why on earth didn't you say something before now?" Harriet snapped.

"To be honest I meant to tell you but then, with the attack on Daniel, I forgot. The more I thought about it the more nervous I got, I didn't want to lose my job. I do so love working there," she finished, lamely.

"But Rachel, if this is true, you must stand up for yourself. You're paid a very low salary and that's probably the reason why, it's supposed to be made up by commissions on your sales."

Miserably Rachel agreed. She'd had no opportunity during the day to talk it out with Meg; tomorrow she'd tackle her.

She waited quietly in the little workroom, her heart pounding uncomfortably. Even though she had rehearsed her lines a dozen times, no matter which way she phrased them they sounded accusatory. Maybe she should let the matter drop. The sound of the door buzzer made her jump. She peered through the curtain, and she noted the weary tread of her employer crossing the soft silence of the grey carpet.

"Good morning, Rachel," Meg's voice was flat.

"Hi, Meg. Do you think I could have a word with you?"

"Is it important, Rachel? I'm not in the mood for problems."

Rachel's instinct was to leave it alone, but having finally plucked up courage she ploughed on. "It's important to me, Meg." She'd set the ball rolling and there was no turning back.

"All right, what is it?" Meg sighed impatiently.

"A couple of weeks ago I noticed a piece of paper on the floor of the office and, when I picked it up, I saw my name on it headed by *commissions*." Her voice wavered with nervousness. It sounded all wrong. Meg Adam's mouth had formed into a thin, grim line. Her forehead creased in a deep frown.

"What were you doing snooping in my office?" she demanded.

"Answering the telephone, *not* snooping." Rachel's tone was icy.

"Well, for your information, Miss, that's merely a form of accounting, nothing to do with you at all. I warned you before, I will not tolerate meddlesome employees. In my book, this comes under the heading of meddling therefore you are fired. You may finish your week here and you'll be paid one month's salary. You may go now, you have work to finish."

Aghast, Rachel stumbled from the office with tears stinging her eyes. There was no arguing with Meg Adams, she was like a block of stone. Clenching and unclenching her fists in sheer frustration, Rachel couldn't imagine a worse fate than leaving this boutique that she loved so much. She knew that this was unfair and now she was positive that her suspicions had been right.

Mechanically she went on with her chores. Meg Adams totally ignored her. Rachel pulled the protective curtaining across the rails of clothes, her mood swinging between anger and despair. She couldn't think.

Her melancholy mood persisted all day and into the evening. Harriet was furious at the way Meg Adams had treated Rachel and she tried everything in her power to cheer the miserable girl, while her own mind was churning to find a solution. Maybe it *was* a genuine accounting move on the part of the company, although she doubted it. The following day brought no change in Meg Adams' attitude. She spoke to Rachel only when necessary, her stony heart unmoved by the girl's miserable face.

Rachel looked around the elegant salon for the last time and closed the door. She was almost blinded by tears as she began the short walk home. Meg Adams cursed her ill fortune. Rachel had been ideal for Caprice. However, no matter how perfect she had been, she could not afford to take the risk that Rachel might become even more suspicious and discover the extent of her complicated cover-up. The cash sales that she had regularly pocketed were represented as "sale-time" purchases, giving her two-thirds of the money involved. Her arrangement with certain customers to "borrow" clothes for a reasonable sum and then return them to stock provided her with a lucrative income. The fictitious shop-lifting losses were exaggerated to their limit. All this, with her own commission of ten per cent, to which an assistant's five per cent was added, had netted her tens of thousands of dollars each year and there was no way she could afford to lose it. When she had stubbornly refused to give Ken any more money he had finally admitted to having developed a "slight habit" but didn't seem worried about it.

"Everyone does drugs," he said truculently. She didn't kid herself, it was only her constant source of ready cash that kept him at her side; she was on a merry-go-round and didn't know how to get off.

Rachel left the boutique quietly without saying goodbye and unreasonably, it hurt.

Five minutes later Meg dragged herself to her feet and followed in Rachel's footsteps. She crossed the empty salon and locked the door steeling herself for the long weekend of loneliness and waiting.

"Mrs Adams, I wonder if I may have a word with you?"

She turned to face the man whose voice she

recognised instantly: the voice of her nightmares, Caprice's chief accountant. He placed a restraining hand on her shoulder and he stood to one side leaving her no option but to retrace her steps.

"Let's go into your office, Mrs Adams. I would like to see the account books, *all* of the account books this time."

Claude

CHAPTER TWENTY-SEVEN

Claude d'Albion won his first major battle at the age of four. The youngest of seven boys, he was the last of the brothers to wear the washed-out T-shirts and shorts. The last to be served with a meal and the last to have a bath in the big tin wash tub. With serious brown eyes and a silver tongue he persuaded his weary mother that, because he was the smallest of the boys, he was the cleanest therefore he should have the first bath. That way the water stayed cleaner. She would never admit to anyone but herself that her youngest son with his helpful ways and sweet nature was her favourite. Whether she believed his logic or not, she agreed he was right.

He hated the rough and tumble of his brothers but he was clever enough not to show it. The tiny house, halfway down the steep hill, was bursting at the seams. If a row erupted between any of the brothers, they had to move outside to fight it out. Their father barely scratched a living. He worked as a part-time gardener and odd-job man at a magnificent villa high above their own house and the glittering resort of Cannes. As far as Claude could tell, his father had only two topics of conversation, politics and his liver. His father talked but no one listened. He spent every moment that he could with his friends at the local bar drinking his favourite bière. His sons had little time for him, going their own stubborn ways. That suited him very well. With the exception of Claude none of them took any notice of their mother either, speaking only to demand their meals, their washing, or both. Claude stood at her side carefully drying the rough pottery plates. "When I'm older," he said, "you won't have to wash dishes, cook our dinners or iron our clothes. I'll look after you."

She believed that her serious-faced little champion meant every word he uttered.

Claude hung onto a rail of the open-sided truck for dear life. His neatly combed hair flew in the breeze. His brown eyes stung from the wind as the truck bumped and banged along. It almost turned on its side as his eldest brother negotiated the hairpin bends. At last Claude was old enough to leave the house on the mountainside and wander around on his own, a few centimes rattling in his pocket. He was almost sick with excitement .

"Be back in the square at six o'clock or you'll have to go home on your own," his brother warned, barely stopping to let him jump down.

Claude nodded, he'd be there.

Dressed in spotless shorts and a T-shirt, both so faded that it was impossible to guess their original colour, he walked for two hours just staring at the people. They were dressed in elegant, colourful clothes which he never dreamt existed. They were beautiful beyond belief to his childish eyes. If he put out his hand he could touch them, but he didn't dare. The fragrance of their expensive perfume lingered in the air as they passed the quiet little boy who breathed in deeply as if trying to capture the scent in his

nose. Claude didn't know which way to look
first. The beaches were crowded, each one had
its own distinctive coloured umbrellas and
matching sun-loungers. From the awning-
protected beach bars and restaurants, an aromatic
wave of garlic and herbs blended with the smell
of sun creams and Gitanes. Immaculate hotels
stood blindingly white in the sun. Their gardens
were a blaze of ordered colour. He stopped to
watch as smart uniformed doormen opened and
closed the shining glass doors for exotic guests.
The outdoor cafés were crowded with people
seeing and being seen. The fragrance of espresso
coffee blended with the aroma of costly cigars.
His stomach rumbled as a waiter brushed past
him carrying a large platter of freshly cooked
seafood.

Coming to a corner he turned off the Croisette
and walked along the shaded pavement of the
little sidestreet until he came to a bakery. The
array of breads and rolls was astounding. Placing
his few coins on the counter he asked the baker
what he should buy. The dour-faced man stared
at the eager youngster and, without bothering to
answer him, took two sweet rolls and a croissant
from a big flat basket. He put them on a sheet of
waxed paper and deftly twisted it and handed it
to Claude. Nibbling slowly at the second of the
sweet rolls, Claude walked along the Rue
d'Antibes staring in the shop windows - the
croissant he would keep for his mother. Every
window was an adventure, every shop a
wonderland.

He walked backwards bumping into people as
he stared at the tanned men and women

sauntering along casually. He loved the big shiny bags they carried, the names of the shops printed in bold letters. For ages he stood and stared at the window of a shop which specialised in a magical display of crystallised fruits. Arranged on silver doilies were apricots, figs, mandarins, peaches and chestnuts which spiralled into impossibly complicated and artistic designs. This definitely was his favourite shop. He glanced at a clock. It was almost quarter to six. He ran as fast as his legs could carry him, and arrived at the square at exactly one minute to six, his heart threatening to burst right out of his bony little chest. Gratefully he sank down at the side of an empty building and waited for the truck with his brothers to return. They snatched the little twist of waxed paper from him and between them ate the croissant in two bites.

His mother sat in the old rocking-chair and listened to her youngest child. Closing her eyes she tried to visualise every little detail. She could picture the beautiful people, smell the wonderful aromas and imagine the glorious windows in the Rue d'Antibes. She envied him the enthusiasm of youth and she knew without a doubt that she'd lost her son that day to the town of which she would never be a part.

CHAPTER TWENTY-EIGHT

The neat, shabbily dressed youngster became a familiar sight to the doormen and hotel owners. He ran errands for them, earning a few francs each week. But, better still, he felt he was a part of the glamorous resort town. Claude was no longer dependent on his brothers. He either walked or hitched a lift from a passing motorist or a workman. He spent every free moment of his time doing the rounds of the hotels and *pensions*. As his confidence grew he approached the doormen enquiring politely if they had any jobs that needed doing. Even the most cynical of them would invent errands or minor tasks for him, paying him from their own well-lined pockets. They earned their tips more easily than he did. He walked wayward dogs who yapped on their jewelled leads. He washed mud off the wheels of the expensive cars parked in the forecourts of the smartest hotels.

Once he had been escorted from a smart boutique where he had been sent to collect a parcel for a hotel guest. Using his initiative, he'd approached a customer who was about to enter the boutique and asked her to give the assistant a note bearing the monogram of one of the leading hotels. Although she was surprised at the unusual request she readily agreed. A moment later the same snooty assistant opened the door and handed him a large box - warning him to deliver it straight to its owner at the hotel. Taking the parcel without a word of thanks, he threw her a look of scorn that could shrivel mountains.

The long summer holidays were the best time of all. Cannes was packed with holidaymakers and his services were constantly sought after. He'd become a regular customer at the bakery that he'd patronised on his first visit. More often than not he would stop at the nearby fruit shop to buy bruised and overripe fruit and, on great occasions, some weeping Brie. That he ate sitting in the shade of a small fountain he'd discovered at the end of a quiet little cul-de-sac. Unable to bear the sticky juice of the fruit and the tiny particles of soft cheese that stuck to his hands, he dipped them in the flowing water of the fountain and dried them on a small, well-worn handkerchief.

One hot July afternoon as he was making his way to the bakery and fruit shop he was stopped in his tracks by the sound of a piercing whistle. He turned and saw the sweating figure of Pierre Thibault beckoning to him. Retracing his steps he reached the distracted man in a few strides. "You must help me," the man insisted, "my wife has had to leave in a hurry and there is no one to collect the bread for the evening meal." He pushed a bundle of francs into Claude's hand and urged him to hurry. "They know what I need. Be quick, please."

Claude ran as fast as the afternoon heat would permit. He stopped only to buy himself a slightly bruised pear and, in less than five minutes, he placed a big armful of hot baguettes on the cluttered table in the kitchen of Pierre Thibault's *pension*. He stuffed his own brioche into the back pocket of his shorts. He'd never seen such a mess. Dirty dishes were piled high on the white stone sink. Vegetables sat in bundles waiting to be peeled and chopped. And a stack of tablecloths and napkins sat discarded in an untidy heap on the floor. In the middle of the chaos Pierre Thibault sat, his head in his hands, forlorn and unmoving.

Claude stared at the morose man, normally so garrulous and bombastic. He crossed to the sink, filled it with hot water and attacked the pile of dirty dishes. He stacked them in neat piles according to their size. With a dangerously sharp knife he peeled the vegetables, dicing them finely the way he had seen his mother do. He carefully peeled and removed the eyes from the potatoes then put them in a pail of cold water to stop them turning black. He wiped the sink thoroughly then scooped up the cloths and the napkins and put them in to soak. Sitting opposite the silent man he took his roll from its bag and wolfed it down. Everything was in order in the hot kitchen. "Where can I hang the dish-cloths to dry?" he asked, his voice almost a whisper.

"In the garden, there is a line," the big man answered, slowly lumbering to his feet. He looked at the kitchen as if for the first time. "You've done a good job. I must pay you." He searched through his pockets for some change then stopped and asked Claude. "Can you stay for a while? I need some help with the evening meal."

Claude nodded, he would stay forever if necessary, he assured Pierre Thibault. Leading the way into the dining-room the *pension* owner showed him how to set up a table. The cutlery must be polished and the glasses examined for fingermarks. Claude followed his instructions; smoothing the cloths, carefully folding the napkins and placing the cutlery neatly on the tables. He looked around with satisfaction then returned to the kitchen where onions and garlic were gently sizzling in a huge pan. Pointing to the bread, Pierre told him how to cut it. Soon the baskets were piled high with crusty baguettes. In what seemed like minutes the dining-room had filled and Claude, a big white apron wrapped around his skinny body, was hurrying to and fro from the dining-room carrying bowls of soup piquant with herbs. He mixed up an order or two but no one seemed to mind. As suddenly as the rush had started it was all over. He was weak with hunger. The piles of dishes waiting to be washed were even higher than before. Timidly, as his stomach growled, he asked Pierre if he might have a bowl of soup.

Quickly he ladled out a bowl of soup for each of them. They sat facing each other at the kitchen table, a basket of bread between them. The soup was as good as Claude imagined it would be. Pierre Thibault put two well-covered plates of thinly sliced veal on the table. Then he put a dish of finely chopped vegetables and a tureen-sized bowl of puréed potatoes on the scrubbed wooden surface. Carefully he spooned a rich white sauce over the meat, uncorked a bottle of wine and opened a bottle of mineral water. They ate their meal in troubled silence. Claude had never tasted anything so good. He wondered if it would be polite to ask M Thibault how the sauce was made?

Intrigue

Trudging the last few steps in the darkness Claude knew without a shadow of a doubt that working in a *pension* or a hotel was how he wanted to spend his life. His mother had been relieved when he finally stumbled through the door. There were black circles of exhaustion under his eyes.

"I'll be leaving early in the morning," he announced importantly, "I have a job to do. Don't worry if I'm late home, we'll be very busy."

At six o'clock the next morning he left the house with its terracotta roof and dusty little garden where only weeds grew. An empty clothes-line waited in the dawn light for the day's washing. Somewhere in the distance a cock crowed and the birds trilled their dawn chorus. A van clanked its way down the winding road behind him and stopped with a squeal as Claude waved to his neighbour. "I have a job now and I must be there early," he said proudly.

It took him barely five minutes from where he was dropped to reach the *pension*. Pierre Thibault had more or less cleared the piles of dirty pots from the previous evening and his face lit up as Claude entered the kitchen. Again Claude was sent to the bakery on the corner, this time with a large wicker basket on wheels. The baker filled it with freshly baked bread placing the rolls and croissants on top. The tables were ready for breakfast by the time he returned and he busied himself filling individual baskets from the large one. At eight o'clock the young girl who made the beds and cleaned the rooms arrived. Collecting her mops and buckets she threw Claude a questioning look which he didn't understand. He attacked the washing-up and, when he had finished, Pierre Thibault made him a huge wide cup of frothy steaming chocolate into which he dipped several of the freshly-baked croissants.

"What's to be done next?" Claude asked, ready for anything.

"You could help Jeanne with the laundry, she'll show you what to do."

Climbing two flights of stairs he heard the sound of singing coming from an open door. Jeanne jumped as he called her name.

"You startled me."

"I'm sorry. I've come to help with the laundry."

"Shh! Close the door," she instructed.

He did as he was bid. "What did M Thibault tell you?" she whispered, her eyes on the closed door.

"Tell me about what?" She was a strange girl.

"About his wife and Jean-Paul of course."

Claude looked at her blankly. "Nothing. I don't know what you're talking about."

Pulling him away from the door, she said nervously, "There was a huge row yesterday and before anyone knew it, Madame Thibault and her little boy rushed out of the hotel followed by Jean-Paul. M Thibault ran into the street after her begging her not to leave. I watched them through the window. They stopped a taxi, climbed in and disappeared from sight." She paused, eyeing the door again. "The Monsieur was crying and cursing Jean-Paul for stealing his wife and his little son."

Claude's mind was racing, now he understood why the big man with his wispy hair and heavily jowled face was so upset, so quiet, and it also explained the terrible mess in the kitchen.

"How sad," he said, sympathetically. "His wife

running away, stolen by the horrible Jean-Paul."

She snorted derisively. "Horrible he wasn't. He was very handsome and she was very pretty." Jeanne had been very upset by the whole affair, after all Jean-Paul always found time to kiss and cuddle *her*. She'd been convinced that he was going to invite her out on a proper date and then, who knew what would follow? Now he'd gone, taking Madame with him. Jeanne's eyes were bright with unshed tears of disappointment. Claude listened to her and assumed he'd replaced Jean-Paul.

Claude worked unceasingly, falling into bed at night exhausted. The *pension* was fully booked for the August holidays and after a week he plucked up courage to ask Pierre Thibault if it would be possible for him to use the tiny attic room under the eaves.

"Why not?" Pierre shrugged, "it's empty." Jeanne said it was the room Jean-Paul used. The only thing that Claude hated about his work was the long trek home at night. There were few lifts available at that hour on the dark mountain roads.

His mother would miss him, he was sure. They rarely saw each other these days. Since Claude had started working she'd sometimes found little treats at her place at the kitchen table. A tiny bag containing a candied fruit, a pretty blue comb for her hair or a bar of Swiss milk chocolate - a real luxury. He was the only one who'd ever bought her a present and often in the quiet of the morning she'd wept tears of gratitude for these beautiful gifts. Selfish for once, she hid them in the back of a cupboard and shared them with no one.

CHAPTER TWENTY-NINE

On the morning that he was due to move into the *pension* Claude arrived early. A handsome little blue-eyed, blond-haired boy of about three was sitting on the floor outside the kitchen door. He was playing with some tiny model cars, running them up and down the worn patch of carpet; making engine noises as they moved. Stepping carefully over the cars, Claude joined Pierre Thibault in his kitchen. The change in the man was amazing. He hummed as he rushed around preparing breakfast, throwing a pile of bread baskets to Claude in a playful manner.

They had established a routine and the child barely disturbed it. Thierry was a good-natured little boy and Claude, despite being so young himself, took a fatherly interest in his wellbeing. He held Thierry's hand as they walked to the bakery for the evening's bread. Claude often bought him a little cake or a small bar of chocolate.

"You'll spoil him," Pierre Thibault said with mock severity.

Jeanne thought Monsieur didn't care that his wife had left, not now that his son was back. Neither she nor Claude knew how or why Thierry had reappeared, they were just glad for Pierre Thibault's sake.

Tiny though it was, Claude loved his little room and kept it as neat as a new pin. There was no one to disturb him or his meagre possessions. As September approached he feared he would have to return to school, but although M Thibault must have realised he was still very young, neither of them broached the subject. As September slid in to October, Claude made no move to return to his home or to school. That summer the three eldest boys had left home to seek their fortunes in Paris. Claude's father, greatly relieved by his diminished burden, had talked less and drunk more. Claude missed his mother and conscientiously wrote to her once a fortnight but she never replied; at least she'd know that he was well. Once he'd considered enclosing some money in the envelope. But, knowing that his brothers might take it for themselves, he thought better of it. For over a month he'd lived in fear that one of them would arrive to drag him back to school, but when they didn't appear he relaxed. His formal education was over.

"Madame Garnier arrives today," Pierre said, checking the big black diary which held all the bookings. "We must make sure that everything is just as she likes it. Three pillows, Jeanne, and a carafe of mineral water by the bed."

"Who's Madame Garnier?" Claude asked, as they prepared the vegetables.

"She's one of our oldest guests. She's been coming here for fifteen years now, right back to my father's time. Every October she spends a month in Cannes. She dislikes the summer crowds. Unfortunately she suffers from bronchitis and has to be careful with her health. She can be a ferocious lady, but that's only on the outside,"

Pierre Thibault laughed.

Claude carried her cases upstairs. He smiled as he thought of Pierre's description, there was nothing fierce about her. She was all pink and white, dainty as a china doll with merry eyes and a surprisingly throaty laugh. Pierre fussed over her as she sat at her favourite window table in the dining-room. "I like to see life without making too much effort," she explained to Claude. Each morning, well wrapped up, she walked along the Croisette, stopping at the same café at exactly eleven o'clock for a cup of hot chocolate.

One rain-lashed morning Claude found her sitting at the drawing-room staring through the window at the downpour. "I'd intended visiting the library this morning. But the rain won't stop its ridiculous showing off," she grumbled. "One rainy day is like a week when you are on holiday."

Claude laughed at her description. "Maybe I could go to the library for you - after lunch when we're quiet?"

"That's kind of you. If it doesn't stop, I'd be delighted. I've run out of books to read." She pouted prettily.

"How will I know what to get for you?" he asked; he'd heard about libraries overflowing with books, but he'd never been in one.

"Don't worry, I'll give you a list and you can give it to the librarian." She smiled at the earnest-faced youngster, he was such a serious, well-intentioned boy.

Claude handed the big sheet of paper to the grim-faced woman behind the tall library desk.

Intrigue

She vanished amongst the shelves and returned a few minutes later carrying three books. Carefully he refolded the list and put it in his pocket with Mme Garnier's ticket. He glanced at the big clock above the counter and allowed himself a few minutes to browse amongst the vast collection of books. He liked the big books with their coloured illustrations, geographical books with maps, travel books and books on art and literature. Returning to the hotel he saw a smile of delight cross Madame Garnier's face. "Wonderful, I am happy now. Do you read?" she queried.

"No," Claude answered honestly.

"You must. If you have a book you have a friend, if you have a good book you have a good friend."

Claude considered this piece of information. "Could I join the library?" he asked.

"Of course you can. I'll take you there myself. In the meantime you think about what kind of books you'd like to read."

She kept her word. The following week he walked along beside her carrying three books of hers and three of his own. He felt quite excited, it would be nice to have something to read in the quiet evenings ahead. Madame Garnier was the first guest he'd talked to at any length. And this had been the first month that the pension hadn't been packed to capacity. Judging by the advance bookings it would be fairly quiet until Christmas. It was almost four months since that fateful day since he had walked past the pension. He'd loved every minute of the time, tirelessly doing the work of two men.

Claude had been an able but uninterested pupil in school, easily bored. He liked history and literature but hated maths. He'd enjoyed the challenge of learning English but had found the words strange, especially the ones that were spelt the same but pronounced differently. Now he would learn from the library books, but this time, just things he wanted to know.

"You can travel the world in a book without moving from your chair," Madame Garnier observed as she examined his choice. She winked conspiratorially at the librarian who appeared friendlier and less forbidding today. "Look after him," she whispered to the woman who managed something that passed for a smile.

They did everything in their power to make Madame Garnier's stay a happy one. Claude sometimes joined her in the drawing room with its deep tub chairs and lace embroidered chair-backs. It was not a particularly cheerful room but it was homely and comfortable. Innocuous flower prints hung on the beige papered walls and there was always a vase of fresh daisies or chrysanthemums on the low table in the centre of the square room. It was warm in winter and cool in summer. The original fireplace remained, but it had been blocked up and replaced with an electric heater that did its best to imitate the flames of a fire. He begged her to tell him about her life in Paris. "It is quiet now," she said her face sad. " I don't go out much since my husband died. I own a factory that manufactures plastic piping. I manage it well enough, I suppose, and am learning as I go along."

Claude told her about his tiny mountainside home.

"My brothers have always fought and argued a lot. They had to go outside to fight in comfort. They rolled around on the red sandy ground until they ended up the same colour as the earth."

She spoke to him as an equal, the age gap made no difference. Claude was sorry when the time came for her to leave - she had become his first real friend.

Pierre Thibault sat contentedly smoking his pipe in front of the small electric fire in his bedroom. November was one of his favourite months, the quiet month after the hectic season. Bitterness clouded his thoughts as he remembered the sickening moment he had discovered his wife lying half-naked on one of the beds, kissing Jean-Paul. Jean-Paul had always been a liability, a ladies' man with roving hands. To lose his wife had been terrible but to have lost his son - he was sure it would have killed him. He remembered that night when an urgent hammering on the door had brought him rushing down the stairs. His wife had thrust the child into his arms and left immediately in the waiting taxi without uttering a single word.

Pierre believed that good came from bad and that his loss had been rewarded by the arrival of Claude. The boy was a wonder, working without ceasing from the day he'd arrived. Pierre relied on him totally, although he did feel a twinge of guilt that he hadn't encouraged him to return and finish his schooling. Still, he paid well. A man's wage for a boy. He'd give him a good bonus at Christmas, he deserved it. He'd hate to lose Claude. It would be many years before his son was old enough to take over the running of the *pension*. Thierry would have a proper training. Switzerland maybe. He'd heard that the Swiss were the best teachers for hotel management. Yes, he would make enquiries and then enrol him in the finest school and he would become the greatest hotel manager in France. Pierre's head nodded as he dreamed of his son's glorious future.

In his room, sitting at the small table, Claude opened his new hard-backed notebook and, using one of his library books as a ruler, he drew three columns on the page. Neatly he headed each one. The guest's name, their likes, dislikes and in the last and narrowest of the spaces - whether he liked them or not. He had no problem in filling the first two sections, but the third was slightly more difficult. Madame Garnier had been a model guest, he thought, shutting the book and putting it away in the drawer.

CHAPTER THIRTY

It had taken Claude four years to pluck up his courage and stroll into the bar at the Carlton Hotel for a drink. His eyes stood out on stalks as he surveyed the hotel's opulence, its long corridors with showcases of beautiful clothes, bijoux and tempting baubles. The ornate plasterwork was magnificent and the plush furnishings and soft silk curtains were a joy to the eye and touch. The price of a drink was double that of their *pension*. But, as far as he could see, nobody appeared to object. There was a constant pop of champagne corks, laughter and glamour such as he'd never seen in the daytime. The sound of American voices reached his ears. He watched the elegantly gowned women and immaculately attired men enjoying a drink before leaving for their evening's entertainment. The casino was holding a gala night, possibly that was why everyone was dressed so beautifully, he thought. After his second visit to the hotel, he realised that this elegance was normal.

Pierre Thibault had insisted that at least once a fortnight, high season or not, Claude must take a night off from the *pension*. Claude used this freedom to visit every one of the luxurious hotels. He noted how things were run, examined the embossed printed menus and took in every detail. For some time plans had begun to take shape in his head, but first he must make sure he knew all the answers.

One extravagance he allowed himself each year was a new outfit, suit, tie, shirts and a pair of shoes. He was fastidiously neat in his appearance and he'd built up a nice wardrobe of immaculately pressed suits, impeccably ironed shirts and shiny polished shoes. He had stopped growing when he was sixteen, and when he reached his full height - five feet six inches - the clothes in which he had invested remained a perfect fit. He spent money on little else. He'd never forgotten the promise he'd made to himself, that he would take care of his mother. Regardless of the risk, he sent a small sum of money to her every couple of months hoping it wouldn't end up in his brothers' pockets.

It had been a bit of a struggle for Claude to persuade Pierre to take on extra staff, but he finally won the day. After two false starts he'd found an energetic sixteen-year old boy and was training him to be as particular as he was himself. This allowed Pierre more time for Thierry, his son.

"You must have time off too," Claude admonished, "it is not fair to the child to be cooped up here all day."

Any argument in his son's favour was popular.

Claude's bank balance was building up nicely. His working uniforms, black trousers and white shirts, were paid for by Pierre.

He no longer made the morning trip to the bakery, leaving that task to his protégé, Joseph. But he did enjoy leaving the heat of the kitchen in the late afternoon. He strolled along the street, baguettes tucked firmly under his arm. He liked to break bits of crust from a loaf and nibble it, just as he had done ever since he was a child.

On his way back he stopped to watch two men tacking up a board on the *pension* next door. He stared at the notice and a wild idea began to form in his mind. Instead of just modernising the *pension* they could double the space by adding the next door *pension*.

He and Pierre sat together after the evening meal was finished. Thierry was safely tucked up in bed. Nervously, Claude broached the subject of the next door *pension*.

"... and just imagine what you could do with double the rooms. You turn people away in the summer and that wouldn't happen if you had more space," Claude reasoned.

Pierre stared at him, scandalised by his suggestion. It would cost a fortune to refurbish the *pension* next door, let alone buy it. It was the most ridiculous suggestion he had ever heard!

Claude sipped his wine. He waited quietly, allowing Pierre time to digest the notion.

The big man shook his head, what an idea. It was hard enough running an establishment of this size, he didn't need the headache of a hotel - that would double the work. He pulled himself up. *Hotel*, he thought, not *pension*.

Claude, timing it correctly, played his trump card, his ace. "Just think how good it would be for Thierry, a hotel to manage after his expert training."

Pierre's refusal to entertain the concept died on his lips. It would certainly be more prestigious than a *pension* for his son. *Thibault et fils,* that sounded good, no maybe not, *Hotel Thibault* - that had an impressive ring to it.

"Who knows what kind of price they're asking for it?" he said, speculatively.

"M and Mme Flaubert have done very little to improve the building," said Claude. "And, judging from what I've seen, it shouldn't be too expensive. It would be worth a phone call to find out."

"I suppose so," Pierre agreed reluctantly.

Pierre Thibault was the third generation owner of the *pension*. His grandmother had rented out rooms to gentlefolk seeking sunshine and the prestige of holidaying in the exclusive resort. So successful was the tiny venture that her son, Pierre's father, had moved their own living quarters to the cramped attic rooms offering a further two rooms at reasonable rates. They added two more bedrooms and hired a local young man with a flair for cooking as their chef. The building, not two minutes walk from the sea, had become a fully-fledged *pension,* open all year round and well patronised.

Pierre was not a man to be rushed. In his own slow-thinking way he decided that Claude could possibly be right. It would be progress, his legacy to his beloved son.

They stood in the hallway of the neighbouring building as the first hammer blow struck the wall. When they broke through the wall the two buildings would become one. The builder in his blue overalls dropped the tool of destruction on the floor with a loud clatter. He reached into his worn canvas bag and produced a bottle of wine and a battered corkscrew. "We drink to success, to the Hotel Thibault, *salut*," he announced, taking a healthy swig. Ceremoniously he passed the bottle to Pierre and then to Claude who wiped it surreptitiously with a handkerchief concealed in his hand. The sale had been completed at the best possible time of the year, January. This would allow them to complete the work in time for spring, the official opening of the holiday season - at least that's what they thought. The builder was a man of action. He never refused an offer of work, and divided his time equally between them and goodness knows how many others. Claude watched him constantly and, if he spotted the overalled figure so much as open the front door, he blocked his exit. One year and a lake of wine later, the Hotel Thibault was ready for business.

Pierre stood in the smart foyer, a poor but happy man. He had almost lost his reason and his guests as the dust flew and the bills piled up. The builder nonchalantly toasted every step of the work. No detail escaped Claude's vigilant eyes. They battled daily over what Pierre considered was profligate spending.

"Those carpets are fit for a palace and cost a king's ransom," he groaned, his head in his hands.

"The better the quality, the longer they last. Don't worry, they will pay for themselves," Claude said soothingly.

"Then why am I writing a cheque?" Pierre reasoned.

There were now twenty-one bedrooms, several small bathrooms, a large sunny living room, a cool shaded dining-room and a smart foyer in the Hotel Thibault. The menu of the day, written in Claude's neat script, stood importantly on a gilded easel outside the dining-room door. Pierre had to admit it looked very grand. It needed to be - at those prices. The new prices had been a bone of contention. Claude insisted that with better facilities they were entitled to charge more. He produced menus and wine lists that he'd secretly pocketed on his visits to the big smart hotels along the seafront. Pierre had been astounded as he studied the printed sheets. "This is twenty francs a bottle more than ours." He stabbed the list with a stubby finger.

Claude nodded, he'd won the battle but the war still raged. "We must employ a good chef. Not for a second am I suggesting that *you* are not a good chef," he added hastily, seeing the hurt look in Pierre's eyes. "It's far too much for one man to cope with on his own."

"I can manage," Pierre said, stubbornly.

"Of course you can, but why should you?"

No immediate reason came to Pierre's mind.

"And also," Claude continued, "we must have two more women to help with the cleaning. Jeanne can't manage as well as you can," he added craftily.

A compromise was struck. Two more cleaners and a trainee chef were employed! For the moment Claude was satisfied.

CHAPTER THIRTY-ONE

Claude clasped his hands behind his neck and arched his back. He turned and looked at the ornate jewelled clock beside his bed. It was his most prized possession and his only one of any value. He smiled as he thought of Madame Garnier's arrival the following day. It was ten years since they'd first met - where had the time gone?

He closed the black book and put it in the drawer with the other three. Yawning, he prepared for bed. He owed a lot to Madame Garnier - his thirst for knowledge, her wise advice and the little clock, which she'd given to him the previous year.

"I want you to have this," she'd said unceremoniously on her last visit. "My apartment was burgled recently and a lot of my treasures stolen. At first I was very upset but after a time I no longer cared. Everything was insured and at least now there is little more left for any thief to take. Please accept it. I know you'll look after it well and it will probably be a lot safer here than in Paris."

Claude stuttered his thanks, holding the clock carefully in his hands. He was so touched by her gesture that he was lost for words. He sensed that it was a token of friendship and that pleased him and made it all the more valuable.

Each Christmas for the past six years they'd exchanged cards and small gifts. Claude had chosen her presents with care. He wrapped them neatly taking them to the post office himself. It was exciting to establish a link with the capital city.

Working at the desk in the foyer he kept an eye on the door waiting for Madame Garnier's taxi to arrive from the station. She preferred to take the train and usually arrived at the hotel in time for tea. He'd planned that one night during her stay he would take her to dinner at Chez Félix, a smart restaurant on the seafront which was renowned for its good food. A treat which they would both enjoy.

Claude kissed Mme Garnier and led her into the drawing-room where a small tray was ready. A young waiter arrived with the tea, hot and strong the way she liked it. Claude smiled affectionately at his friend, noticing a new weariness in her eyes.

"Everything is ready for you in your room, I'm sure you'd like to rest until dinner."

She pushed open the door of the room - number 16 as always. It was like coming home. Claude had done wonders for the hotel - how it had changed since he had bludgeoned Pierre into buying that second *pension!* As she unpacked her case she let her mind drift back to the first time she had met the diffident young boy. So bright and anxious to please. That hadn't changed. But each year she saw a new assurance in him, the confidence of a job well done. If only I'd had a son like Claude, she sighed. Come on, you silly woman, she rebuked herself, don't waste time on ifs-and-buts.

The living-room with its soft lamps was cosy at

night. A few couples sat having a drink and Claude hurried to finish his work so that he could join Mme Garnier. He sat down for the first time that day and poured a glass of cognac for each of them.

"So tell me, what has been happening in my absence?" she asked, settling herself comfortably into the down-filled cushions of the big chair. Claude smiled. "I'll tell you that in a few days." He put his finger to his lips.

Madame Garnier's eyes sparkled, she loved intrigue and that's what Claude's tone implied.

"We've been packed all season as usual." His voice returned to its normal pitch. "Sometimes I think the whole world descends on our little town all at once," he laughed.

"And the library, what have you found to read now?"

Claude's visits to the library each week had become a standing joke between them. Having been bitten by the reading bug he'd pick a subject of interest to him and read everything he could find about it.

"Cookery," he answered briefly.

"Recipe books?" she queried.

"Everything to do with cookery. The history of food, the art of cookery, recipes and, most of all, the works of the great chefs. The book I'm reading now is a history of famous banquets. You wouldn't believe the number of courses they served; the best meats, fish and game dishes were placed at the top of the table, the poorer ones towards the end. One of the banquets in honour of an English king had over a hundred different dishes." He shuddered. What a thought!

"Now you'll have to travel to all the great restaurants and sample their food," she said mischievously. "You must start in Paris."

Claude had never considered travelling. Paris was as foreign to him as Timbuktu, yet her casual remark set his mind wondering.

She was delighted to accept Claude's invitation. "It's a long time since a young man invited me to dinner," she laughed. "I'll have to wear my best dress."

They arrived at the restaurant and were seated by the *patron* himself. It was too cold to sit outside as Claude had done in the summer. He was now respected by the restaurateurs and hotel managers as something of a wonder. News travelled fast in the small hotel and restaurant circle and he was welcomed everywhere.

They took their time, nibbling on olives, anchovies and crusty rolls. They chose their meal with care.

"Monsieur will look after the wine," the waiter said, relaying the *patron's* message.

Claude looked admiringly at Madame Garnier. How chic she looked in her black wool crêpe dress, a choker of creamy pearls relieving its severity. Her silvery hair shone in the light and her soft blue eyes glowed with appreciation. What a beautiful woman she must have been, he thought, still was.

Savouring one of the light, crisp pommes de terre soufflées, Claude unfolded his latest concept for the hotel.

"Have you noticed that big wall next door to the hotel?"

"No, I can't say I have," she admitted.

"I'm not surprised. I've passed it every day for years. It's just a wall like any other. One day it struck me that it had no entrance, no break in its surface. Curiosity got the better of me so I borrowed a long ladder and climbed up to have a look." He paused to take a sip of the mellow wine. "There was nothing there except weeds and briars. It's an overgrown derelict garden."

Mme. Garnier's expression didn't change. Is he planning to extend the hotel again? she wondered.

"I know what you're thinking," he laughed, his brown eyes dancing with mischief.

"Go on, M Télépathie, read my mind," she challenged.

"That I would like to buy it and add even more rooms to the hotel."

"You're right," she confessed.

"And you're right too, at least half-right. I do want to buy it, but not for the reason you supposed. I want to turn it into a garden and install a small swimming-pool."

Her blue eyes opened in astonishment. She thought about it for a moment and it was an excellent idea. The hotel didn't have a sea view.

"I think it would be lovely to sit in a quiet shady garden. I'd love to be able to splash in the cool water of a swimming-pool." Her admiration for Claude - this bright young man - grew even more. He'd been right about the business every time. She cast her mind back over the years and the changes she'd seen. She knew that this idea would be as successful as all the others.

"You're very quiet," Claude smiled.

"I was just thinking about your plan."

Claude was gratified by her instant approval, she was the first person he'd shared his secret with. "Of course, I still have to find out who owns it and then persuade them to sell it."

"Does Pierre know about this yet?" she enquired, guessing the answer.

"How well you know me," he laughed.

"How are you going to go about finding the owner?" She frowned.

"That took me a while to work out and then it struck me. It probably was a part of the Flaubert's *pension* originally. Tomorrow I have an appointment with M and Mme Flaubert's lawyer, he may be able to help me."

"Claude, you have a great future in front of you."

"Thank you, Mme Garnier." He flushed with pleasure at the compliment, he had a great regard for the little lady who'd always treated him with interest and respect.

"We've known each other for a long time, don't you think that you should call me Lisette? Madame Garnier is so formal."

"Lisette," he repeated. "*Salut*, I drink to your health."

"Thank you, but I think we should drink to Pierre's health - he'll need it more when you land your latest bombshell. A new shock to his health and his wealth."

Claude looked at her affectionately. It was strange, the older he grew, the younger she appeared. Tonight she looked younger than ever.

"Why are you smiling? " Her elegant head inclined questioningly.

Claude thought a moment before replying. "I

was thinking how well you look … "

"And?" she prompted.

"And how young you look. To be truthful, when I first met you I thought you were quite old, but of course, now I realise that you are not."

She threw back her head and laughed. "The jaundiced eye of youth?"

They walked slowly back to the hotel enjoying the cool air. "Show me the wall," she demanded, walking past the hotel. "It's a good length," she admitted. "You'll tell me tomorrow what happened?"

"Of course, but it must remain our secret for the moment. You know that if all goes well and everything falls into place this will put the hotel into a higher category?" Claude reminded her.

"No, I hadn't thought of that. Pierre Thibault would be a fool if he passes up such an opportunity."

"Would you like a nightcap?" he asked as they entered the hotel.

"I shouldn't - but why not? It's not every night I go out to dinner with a handsome man."

Claude left her in the *salon* and went to fetch a bottle of cognac. As he poured the golden liquid into the glasses he could sense her eyes watching him.

"Forgive a nosy old woman, Claude, but you should have some life outside the hotel. How are you going to meet a pretty girl if you're stuck here all the time?"

The thought had never occurred to him. This was all the life he needed. Jeanne had often suggested that it would be pleasant to spend an evening together but he'd ignored her veiled hints. At times she irritated him with her flamboyance, touching his arm or shoulder at every opportunity. Once he'd been quite blunt and asked her not to do it. She had sulked for a week but then, seeing that it failed to upset him, she returned to her usual talkative ways. The young girls who were guests at the hotel didn't interest him in the least, he treated them with courtesy but that was all.

Lisette feared that she had overstepped the bounds of friendship and hastily apologised for intruding into his private life.

"No, not at all," he assured her. "I have no time for silly girls, there is so much work to be done."

"Oh, *c'est triste*," she admonished. "That is very sad. There should always be time for love."

Claude was not handsome in the strictest sense of the word. He had beautiful almost soulful eyes, a nose that was slightly crooked and a jutting, stubborn chin. It had taken her a long time to fathom what made him so special and she decided that apart from his charming manner it was his immaculate grooming that set him apart. She'd never known such a fastidious man. She'd never seen a crease in his trousers that wasn't as sharp as a knife nor a wrinkle in a jacket. His shirts were always so perfect that they could have come straight out of their boxes. His shoes could have doubled as mirrors.

"Thank you for a wonderful evening, Claude. I can't remember when I enjoyed myself so much. Now I must go to bed before I fall asleep right here, then you'd have to carry me up the stairs."

Kissing him on both cheeks and then on the first one again, she wished him goodnight.

Claude poured himself another drink, sat back in the chair and relaxed. There was no one in the room so he kicked off his shoes and tucked his feet underneath him.

He surveyed the room with its soft colours and rich fabrics. How different it was now, so different from the room it had been - nondescript and dull. Admittedly it was twice the size but now it had elegance and lightness. It was also warm and inviting. He took a mental stroll through the hotel. Each room in both buildings had been greatly improved.

How many hours, days and weeks had he poured into his dream? He rarely slept more than five hours. He was the first downstairs in the morning, the last to go to bed at night. Certainly Pierre paid him well, very well indeed. He was more than just an employee, he was the one who'd breathed life into the place, giving it a name that was respected. Pierre was now able to make more time for his son who was growing up into a fine boy. Thierry was now almost the same age as Claude had been when he first came to the *pension*. Over ten years he'd been here. His every waking thought was given to the improvement and smooth running of Pierre's hotel. He didn't expect praise and rarely received it. But suddenly, Claude needed to know that his position in the hotel was secure. He wasn't being vain, but without his energy and high standards it would probably return to its original mediocrity. A partnership, that was the answer. An interest that was tangible - a recognition for all his hard work in the past, security for the years to come.

Claude's guesswork had been inspired. The Flauberts' lawyers had established that the couple owned the derelict site.

"It was a separate property," they pointed out. "They may indeed be interested in selling it if the price is right."

"What do you think they would consider a *fair* price?" Claude interrogated.

The lawyer was an experienced negotiator. The Flauberts, left to their own devices, would probably sell it for a paltry sum. He eyed Claude warily, and named his price.

"Thank you for your time," Claude said, pushing himself away from the desk. "We're worlds apart I'm afraid, there is no point in proceeding further."

"You can build a lot of rooms in a space like that," the chubby-faced man commented.

"That was not my intention," Claude explained. The flirtation of bidding had commenced. "It was for use as a garden. Some of our guests prefer not to sit on a beach. Just an idea," he finished, casually.

"The idea is charming, but such valuable space..."

"Useful only to us, far too small for an independent hotel, of course."

They finally agreed a price. Claude was pleased with the results of his dealing, so too was the lawyer. He'd enjoyed the challenge. And now to convince Pierre.

With the air of a man pulled by stronger forces than he was capable of handling, Pierre conceded that Claude's notion might be possible.

He rejected Claude's proposal to share the cost of the site.

"We can discuss a partnership later," he muttered.

There was no use denying that Claude was responsible for this fine hotel. But it was Thierry's legacy - the fourth generation of Thibaults to run the establishment.

A feeling of disquiet gripped Pierre as he mechanically set about preparing the evening meal. He was certain that he couldn't manage the hotel without Claude. True, he still did most of the cooking himself but now he had a young chef to help him. Pounding the veal for schnitzels Pierre puzzled as to how best he could avoid the situation. To lose Claude would be a tragedy. He must offer him an attractive alternative. An increase in salary? A generous bonus? He would give the matter careful thought and surprise Claude, but there would be no partnership.

CHAPTER THIRTY-TWO

Claude sacrificed the luxury of fruit and vegetable deliveries in favour of visiting the market each morning. *Fresh, fresh, fresh* stressed the written works of the great chefs. No menu should be decided before seeing what was available that day. The books all seemed to agree on that. Claude studied them avidly, accepting as gospel the many hints and tips generously shared between their covers. Pierre shrugged in resignation; if Claude wished to get up at some ungodly hour it was all right with him. Secretly he thought it was crazy.

Today's market had been particularly rewarding. Claude could almost taste the dishes as he read his own neat writing on the menu card. He placed it on its decorative easel outside the dining-room and made his hungry way to the kitchen. Only a few of the lunch-time diners remained and by now the chef would have prepared Claude's lunch. As he opened the kitchen door the chef scooped a piece of lightly grilled liver from the floor, wiped it on his apron, and slapped it on to a waiting plate which he slid under the grill.

Claude had always prided himself on keeping his temper under control. The man had obviously not heard him come into the kitchen so he'd had no opportunity to get rid of the cigarette dangling from the corner of his mouth. The two men faced each other without speaking. They'd never liked each other. The chef thought that Claude was far too demanding. Claude knew that the chef was sloppy and lazy.

"Is that my lunch?" Claude enquired calmly.

The chef nodded his head, grateful that this eagle-eyed fusspot hadn't noticed his little accident.

Quietly Claude picked up the plate and, pressing the pedal on the large refuse bin in the corner, emptied its contents into the plastic sack. With quiet deliberation he walked towards the chef and with a quick flick yanked the cigarette from his mouth and threw it into the sink.

"Please collect your belongings and leave immediately." There was no mistaking the menace in Claude's voice.

"I am employed by M Thibault," the chef answered, looking at Claude with an insolent stare. "M Thibault hired me and I don't have to answer to you."

"You do and you will. I do not like violence, but if I am forced … " Claude actively avoided any form of physical confrontation. He hoped that his steady-eyed stare would be intimidating enough to convince the man that if he remained, he'd be in mortal danger.

The problem was solved for him. Pierre Thibault came back early from his son's school. Anxious to share the news of Thierry's good progress he had gone straight to the kitchen where the chef was emptying the contents of the huge stock pot on to the floor. Threatening and screaming the chef was escorted from the treacherously slippy kitchen by Pierre and Claude. Pierre, as an insurance policy, had taken the precaution of arming himself with a large rolling-pin.

"Now, tell me exactly what happened."

Pierre listened avidly to Claude's explanation. His faith in Claude was total. But then slowly he realised that he would have to struggle along on his own for the moment.

Claude read his mood. "Don't worry, I'll find someone else for you. Until then I'll help you myself."

Somewhat mollified, Pierre set about the mopping up operation while Claude altered the menu. The soup was off for today.

They worked well together. Claude introduced many new dishes to their repertoire, his months of reading hadn't been in vain. Several people applied for the post as trainee chef, but Claude turned them all down. Pierre, exasperated, would have been content with any one of them. But Claude was determined that, this time, they were going to employ the services of a dedicated cook.

"Too slapdash," he said to Pierre as he surveyed the messy plate the first chef had prepared. "Too untidy," he noted, picking at the badly cut vegetables presented by the second. "They wouldn't cook evenly."

The third and fourth were no better. "Overcooked," he pronounced, "not fit for human consumption," he fretted, as his knife refused to cut a piece of steak.

Pierre concealed his irritation. Claude was right, but then he usually was. Perfection was hard to find and Pierre's feet ached with the long hours of standing.

Claude found the answer to his dilemma quite

by accident. He'd been on nodding acquaintance with a young man at the library for several weeks. He left loaded with armfuls of cookery books just as Claude did. When they both reached for the same book it broke their silence.

"You take it if you wish," Claude said. "I've plenty to keep me busy for the moment."

"No please, I have three books here. They'll last me for a couple of days. Besides, I've nothing else to do at present so I can visit the library as often as I like."

"You obviously have a great interest in cooking. Is it a hobby?"

"For the moment, yes, but now that I have finished my schooling I intend to become a chef - a great chef." The young man's voice was full of conviction.

"Have you been formally trained?" Claude's interest was aroused.

"No, unfortunately my family can't afford that. I worked in a couple of restaurants during the holidays. I help my mother sometimes. She cooks for a family in one of the big châteaux. If there are guests or a party I go along. So far there have been no complaints," he smiled.

"What sort of cooking do you do?" asked Claude.

Enthusiastically he catalogued his abilities. The librarian awarded Claude with one of her best watery smiles. She gave him a neat square of paper on which he wrote the address of the hotel.

"Come and see me tomorrow morning," Claude instructed. "We may be able to help you."

He just knew that this raw recruit could be

their answer.

Three hours after his arrival, Marc Tissot became a full-time employee of Hotel Thibault. Claude was unstinting in his praise and Pierre Thibault heaved a sigh of relief. Marc was a talented cook and nothing fazed him as he worked. The staff, including the contract gardeners, paid frequent visits to the kitchen on some pretext or other, eager for a sample of Marc's experimentation.

The foundations for the swimming-pool had been excavated. It was small but attractively shaped. The next step was to create the patios, lawns and flower-beds. Claude haunted the library once more. With typical thoroughness, Claude swapped recipe books for gardening books. Pierre Thibault spent a lot of time with his head in his hands - but he signed the cheques regardless. Claude ordered the best of everything. He had, after all, offered to share the expenses.

By the following spring the derelict, overgrown site had vanished and in its place a garden flourished. Claude designed separate little paved areas; nooks and crannies each contrived for maximum privacy. They had chosen smart sun-loungers and umbrellas and he and Pierre waited impatiently for the first of the sunshine. Pergolas planted with spiky climbing roses and wisteria were springing to life alongside tiny, splashing water features. It would be beautiful. But the seeds sown in the garden grew with the seeds of discontent in Claude's mind.

Pierre Thibault doubled Claude's salary. He gave him carte blanche in the kitchen. News spread like a forest fire; Hotel Thibault was in line for a Michelin star. Marc's genius was nurtured and encouraged. Pierre Thibault reversed his role. Now he did the preparation and basic chores; a willing disciple at the guru's bidding.

Thierry sulkily refused to spend any time in the kitchen. He had discovered girls. With his blond hair and good looks, the teenager was in constant demand with the giggling youthful beauties.

"He's young." Pierre fondly excused the light of his life.

"Never too young to learn," Claude replied acidly, not bothering to hide his annoyance.

"He has plenty of time. Don't forget he'll have a first class training when he goes to Switzerland," his father defended.

Pierre sat in his comfortable sitting-room; this was his favourite time of the evening. The hotel was quiet, the guests no doubt were enjoying a flutter at the Casino or having an after-dinner drink in one of the open-air cafés, or just promenading along the Croisette. Pierre filled his smoke-blackened pipe and thought about the situation. Claude was becoming difficult to handle, obsessive almost. How could he complain about Claude's dedication? There wasn't a room free until the beginning of November. They had to turn diners away every night. He'd welcomed Claude's suggestion that they should extend the dining area onto the patio. An awning could be added to protect guests from the blazing lunch-time sun and the odd rainy evening.

The night they were awarded the coveted star,

a bottle of Roderer Crystal champagne sat in an
ice bucket at every table. It was hard to tell
which of them was most excited by the honour;
Pierre beamed expansively, Marc burst into tears
and Claude silently congratulated himself on his
gifted find. It was difficult for a classically trained
chef to reach such dizzy heights, but for an
amateur, it was almost impossible. Marc was
amazing.

CHAPTER THIRTY-THREE

The man waiting in the foyer examined his fingernails. Dressed in a navy blue suit, with a dazzling white shirt and subtly patterned silk tie, he looked totally at ease with himself as he sat patiently.

"*Bonjour.* Monsieur Claude d'Albion?" Claude nodded, extending a hand.

"I wonder if we could speak in private?"

He followed Claude into the empty salon and they sat facing one another on the striped sofas. "I am afraid I have some sad news," he said nervously. "Your mother has passed away."

A cold wave passed through Claude's body and he shivered despite the warmth of the room. When he'd received word of his father's death, Claude felt no grief. He'd always been a stranger to his son. The news had reached him weeks after the event in the only letter that his mother had ever written to him. Now that there was no one left in the little house on the mountain road, she wrote, she was moving to Grasse to live with her widowed sister. Each month after that Claude had sent her a larger sum of money, happy in the knowledge that he was able to help a little. He turned his head away from the compassionate stranger as he felt tears welling in his eyes. "Please accept my sympathy." The man looked genuinely sorry. "The reason I'm here is to inform you that your mother has left you her house and a sum of money."

Anne Schulman

His words took Claude by surprise. The tiny house would of course be hers, but the money? "I hadn't realised," he muttered.

Snapping open the lock on the expensive document case the man brought out a sheaf of papers. Claude was puzzled. Why should such a trivial matter not be dealt with by post? He stared blankly at the typewritten sheets.

Pushing his hair back from his forehead, the man spread the sheets into two piles on the polished coffee table. "I represent the firm of Jacquet et cie.," he explained.

Claude vaguely remembered the name.

"Before your mother left to live in Grasse she entrusted us with the deeds of her house. She had no wish to sell it although she received several good offers."

He couldn't be hearing correctly. That tiny little house with its shabby garden? There must be some mistake.

"This letter is for you. On your mother's instruction it was to be given to you after her death," he said.

The cramped, laboured writing brought the tears coursing down his cheeks. The paper was torn from an exercise book. The misspelled and crossed out words tugged at his heart. As he read the letter a feeling of respect blotted out his previous feelings of pity. The land above the house had been purchased by an oil-rich sheikh. The house was of little value but it was an eyesore and spoiled the view from his luxurious villa. Their neighbours had been seduced by the generous prices offered, but his mother had not. This was all she had. She was determined to leave it to her beloved son. He could do with it as he saw fit. She had finally admitted that he had been her most loved child and the page blurred as the words became spattered with his tears. She had saved all the money that he'd sent her. It had been so good to know it was there if she needed it, but her pension had been enough. For several minutes Claude sat still letting the tears heal him.

"Would you like a drink? Forgive me, it's been a shock."

"Some coffee, please." That would give d'Albion time to collect himself, the notaire judged shrewdly.

Claude poured strong coffee into the two cups, and noticed that his hand was shaking slightly.

"It was very good of you to bring me the letter. Is there anything for me to sign?" he queried.

"Yes, but before you do I have a proposition."

He repeated more or less what Claude's mother had written in her letter. Tactfully he didn't say that the house was an ugly blot on the sheikh's landscape. The figure he mentioned staggered Claude and he struggled not to show his astonishment.

"I think it's a generous offer but it *is* my family home, it's not just a matter of money."

The lawyer's eyes hardened; shock or no shock this was going to be a battle of wits. There was little doubt in his mind that it would be for sale this time. He'd been told he could pay three times the starting price he'd offered Claude. There was more at stake here than a simple house. His valuable client would be grateful if he were successful. What a feather in his cap it would be if he could add the sheikh to their permanent list.

"I would like to visit it again," Claude said, it would be foolish to close the door on his offer at this stage.

They climbed the steep hill in the air-cooled luxury of the lawyer's Mercedes. The ruts and potholes were a memory from Claude's past. He stared without sentiment at the broken-down house, shabby beyond repair. Weeds grew rampant. One pole from the old clothes-line peeked through the tangled mess. Looking above the roof with its broken slates he saw a glorious pink villa rising against the azure sky, columns of narrow cypresses pointed upwards in perfect symmetry. No wonder the sheikh was anxious to demolish this monstrosity, Claude thought - I would if I were him.

Claude assured the anxious notaire that he would give the matter some thought. I'll let him stew for a while, thought Claude. Three weeks later he refused an increased offer, saying again that he could not bear to part with his home. One week later the offer was increased again, and refused. Claude worried that he had become too greedy. A month passed and he'd heard nothing further. He would wait. A final offer arrived in writing after another nerve-racking month. This time he accepted. His bank manager congratulated him on his good fortune, adding the sum to Claude's healthy account.

Surprised as he had been at his unexpected windfall he was stunned and speechless when a letter arrived from Paris asking him to attend the reading of Lisette Garnier's will. She had been subdued on her last visit and Claude had been deeply concerned at her listlessness and apathy. The old spark was nowhere to be seen. Claude had begged her to visit a doctor and she had broken down and admitted to him that she was suffering from a weak heart. There was little she or the doctors could do. All she could do was to take her medication. She had already sold the factory. Poor Lisette, his beloved friend and mentor. Claude had lost the only two people who truly mattered in his life within the space of eighteen months.

He was dazed as he watched the Paris traffic roaring all around him. He marvelled at the wide boulevards, the elegant buildings with their differing rooftops - no two were the same. How he wished he could paint! Towering churches, so familiar from the photographs he had seen. The surly taxi driver screamed at a car which cut across his path and tore around the Place de la Concorde like a man possessed. If this lunatic didn't slow down Claude would be the third person to meet his end. He shot out of the taxi the second it stopped, grateful to plant his feet on firm ground.

Claude really couldn't grasp any of the details. They were just figures. *Sole beneficiary…. beloved friend…. trust your instincts and follow your dreams…* The solicitor's words were disjointed, unreal. Claude remembered shaking his hand and walking into the street in a daze. Walking and walking, seeing street names that he recognised but which didn't register.

He was rich - for him, rich beyond words. No

relatives, he remembered them saying, yes, that was it, Lisette had no relations. Suddenly he was starving, he hadn't eaten for hours. Looking around he saw a café, the Café de Flore, and his interest revived. Here he was in Paris and he could eat anywhere he fancied, he could well afford it now. The croque-monsieur was delicious and he made a mental note to add it to their own luncheon menu.

All around him people were enjoying a late lunch, their city attire formal and elegant. He stared at them just as he had stared in awe at the casually dressed people strolling along the Croisette and the Rue d'Antibes when he was a little boy. The smell of Paris, the ambience, was exciting. Suddenly he wished he had more time to explore it all - to climb the Eiffel Tower, to meander through the Latin Quarter, to savour the sights and sounds of the city. His summons to Paris had come as such a shock that he hadn't taken time to think about a holiday. He had never enjoyed more than a day's break before. The realisation hit him; from now on he would take a little time off each year. See some of the places which he'd visited only in his library books. He would travel.

With great extravagance he made up his mind to buy two new suits, one of those luxurious cashmere overcoats that seemed to surround him and, maybe some silk shirts and ties. Handmade shoes? Was that going too far? Why not, it would be a mere drop in his new ocean of wealth. How casual and nonchalant they were, the coffee drinkers and diners at nearby tables. How warmly they kissed cheeks or shook hands.

Claude suddenly felt lonely, a foreigner in the energetic, crackling city.

Pierre Thibault had been genuinely delighted to learn that Madame Garnier had remembered Claude in her will.

"There's no need to hurry back, why not spend a couple of days in Paris?" Pierre suggested.

Claude replaced the phone and walked along the Champs Elysées. He had been sparing with the truth when he spoke to Pierre. Guiltily he intended keeping the full details of his unexpected bequest between his bank manager and himself. He booked himself into the deluxe Georges Cinq Hotel, excusing his new-found extravagance as a fact-finding mission.

Bathrobes, he mused, that was an excellent idea providing their guests didn't take them to the beach or to their homes. He showered and shaved and dressed in one of his new suits. The dapper image that stared back at him from the cheval mirror pleased him. He checked his wallet and left his luxurious room. The lift swished silently to the ground floor. Should he risk life and limb again by taking a taxi to the Tour d'Argent? He'd dreamt about visiting the restaurant for years. This was his big chance. It was a good job that he'd thought to bring his cheque-book. On second thoughts maybe not. He had enough cash. He returned to his room and hid the cheque-book carefully between the side of the drawer and the body of the sturdy little writing desk.

Claude was not disappointed. The meal was excellent and he surreptitiously made notes in the slim notebook with a rolled gold pencil, a gift to himself. The prices shocked him, but it was all in the line of business. The wine list was impressive. Quite blatantly now he wrote down the vintages and their cost in his leather-bound paper companion. Claude smiled. Pierre would be horrified by the prices.

Through the windows of the bateau mouche, the glass fronted boats named after singers, Claude watched as the beautiful, floodlit buildings glided past. For one ridiculous moment he felt that the boat was stationary and the buildings were moving. The great cathedral of Notre Dame rose majestically above the water. He listened attentively to the guide explaining their surroundings in several different languages.

It was too early to go to bed. Paris was alive and pulsating. As he walked he could see shadowy figures moving about in the houses. Chandeliers glittered, lighting the interiors of rooms, flowers in their vases sat like contented cats surveying life outside through the safety of their unshuttered windows. He wished he could see right inside, see the people and their homes. The forbidding, austere buildings were so deceptive from the street. Claude could hear music and laughter coming from a bar, he would have a nightcap before returning to his hotel. The bar counter was hidden by the throng of people surrounding it. Finally he attracted the eye of one of the barmen who waved in acknowledgement. Claude shouted over the din and his drink was passed back to him by willing hands. The handsome young man standing beside him remarked that he hadn't seen Claude there before.

Intrigue

"No, this is my first visit to Paris," Claude acknowledged.

The well-dressed stranger welcomed him to Paris and insisted on buying him a drink. Claude looked around. There were so many well-turned-out men there and, strangely enough, not many women. In the dim light he imagined that people were staring at him. Had that man really winked or had he had drunk too much wine with dinner?

"My name is Marcel."

"Claude," he answered, a little uncomfortable under the scrutiny of so many watching eyes. "Do I imagine it or are people staring at me?"

"Everyone watches everyone here," Marcel shrugged. "Does that make you feel strange?"

"Yes, a bit."

Marcel casually draped his arm around Claude's shoulder and smiled into his eyes. A shiver of excitement ran through Claude's body and the hairs at the back of his neck stood on end.

"Would you prefer to leave this noise and come back to my appartement?" Marcel asked, his fingers caressing the back of Claude's neck.

Mesmerised, Claude followed him from the bar and they strolled along the street. A strange tingle made his legs weak, it was a feeling that he'd never experienced before, a cross between fear and anticipation. As if on an invisible lead he followed Marcel up three flights of stairs and found himself in a plainly furnished room.

"Let me get you a drink," Marcel offered lazily.

The glass was chipped so Claude turned it around and tossed the contents back in one gulp.

Without asking Marcel refilled Claude's glass.

"Take off your coat, I'll hang it up for you," he instructed. They sat side by side on the sofa and Marcel smiled disarmingly at him. "Do you have many friends? Special friends?" he asked in a soft voice.

Dumbly Claude shook his head. Marcel's arm was again round his neck, stroking it in a slow movement. The room was stifling and perspiration beaded Claude's forehead.

"Why not take off your jacket, you'll feel more comfortable." With shaking hands Claude folded his jacket neatly over the back of a chair. He felt as if he were moving through quicksand. Marcel was watching him with soulful eyes. Claude's hands were clammy; his mouth, despite the drink, was dry.

"Do you have a bathroom?" he asked, his voice sounding odd to his own ears.

"Yes, second door on the left."

Claude bolted the door and leant against the basin. Was this why he'd never formed an attachment to any girl? The reason he had found Jeanne's touch anathema? His fate was in his own hands. Splashing cold water on his sweating face, he rejected the grubby towel hanging on the rail and used his neatly pressed handkerchief instead. Claude took a deep breath and unlocked the door. He retraced his steps. Hesitantly he opened the door. The room was empty. He breathed a sigh of relief then sat down on the sofa again. There was still time to leave, but he made no move to go. After five minutes he wandered to the door and called to Marcel. There was no response. He called again. Claude eyes wandered around the shabby room. His heart missed a beat as he stared at the empty peg on the door where his coat had been. Alarmed, he reached for his jacket and plunged his hand into the pocket - his wallet had gone too.

The small appartement had no personal belongings, no identification as to who the owner might be. He was sure that if he returned to the bar Marcel would be long gone. Then he would suffer not only indignity but loss of face too.

Claude lay in the safety of his bed, his mind in turmoil. It had taken him two hours in the chill wind to reach his hotel. Thank goodness he still had his cheque-book. Never again would he succumb to this kind of temptation. He'd found Marcel's embraces exciting - but he'd been frightened. Frightened by his feelings and emotions, frightened to admit even to himself that the young man had aroused him more than any girl had ever done. But how could he have taken such a risk? He could have been injured or disappeared without trace. Would Pierre have searched for him or would he be just another missing person? Was there anyone to care, anyone to worry about him? In the dark and silent room he felt alone, desolate. He needed roots, needed to belong. More than ever he needed to be part of the hotel. He would try talking to Pierre again when he returned to Cannes. Still cursing himself for his stupidity he fell into an exhausted dreamless sleep.

CHAPTER THIRTY-FOUR

Never had Claude been so pleased to see the Hotel Thibault. Pierre was waiting for him, anxious to hear all his news. Claude gave him a highly censored version of his trip: Madame Garnier had left him a small sum of money and his wallet had been stolen in a bar. There was no need to divulge anything else. Claude was deliberately vague. He gave Pierre the silk tie which he'd bought in one of the most fashionable shops in the city. Then he went to find Marc who was delighted with the illustrated cookery book which Claude knew he'd wanted.

Claude informed his bank manager that a large sum of money would soon be placed in his account. Once again Claude approached the subject of a partnership. Pierre squirmed and wriggled but the outcome was the same, "We'll discuss it again at the end of the year. When things are quiet," he promised.

"October will never be the same again," Claude said to Marc as they waited for the butter to melt.

"You'll miss Mme Garnier." He threw the finely chopped onions into the foaming butter tossing them round the pan with a smooth action.

"She was a good friend, and a wise one." If only he knew how good, Claude thought smugly.

Marc nodded, adding the garlic. The aroma filled the kitchen as medallions of beef sizzled temptingly in the pan. Removing them, Marc added some wine, allowing it to reduce. "Now for the magic sauce," he laughed, adding his secret ingredients.

Claude wouldn't spoil Marc's surprise with questions. It had become an unspoken rule that first Claude tasted a dish and then they discussed the recipe.

Taking a knife and fork, Claude cut one of the pink medallions, scooping up a little of the sauce. It was delicious, unusual too.

"A tiny spoon of curry, some crème fraîche and the grated zest of a lemon," Marc revealed.

Claude knew Marc was holding something back, omitting to tell him one of the ingredients, he always did.

Pierre came rushing into the kitchen and beckoned to Claude. Pierre's face was unusually animated. He checked that there was no one lurking in the foyer, then told Claude his news.

"There's an old château for sale on the coast, near Beaulieu. It's been empty for some time and not many people are aware of its existence. I was thinking what a wonderful opportunity it would be to buy it. The Hotel Thibault should fetch a good price now and with a loan from the bank the château could be restored. With your management and Marc's cooking we could have a superb hotel, maybe get our second star?" Pierre waited for his news to take effect.

Claude had never seen Pierre so enthusiastic. Up to now Claude had always had to bludgeon Pierre into making any changes and here he was suggesting that he should buy a new hotel. Claude was astounded.

"Let's go and see it this afternoon," Pierre urged.

Claude's brain was working overtime. This was the perfect opportunity to seek his partnership, once and for all.

"What's wrong?" Pierre frowned, it was not like Claude to impede the march of progress.

"If it's right I'll back you fully but on one condition. Either I become a partner or you must manage alone."

Merde! He might have known that the question of a partnership would rear its ugly head again. Certainly without Claude the task would be impossible.

"All right, you win," Pierre sighed.

"I'm quite willing to invest some money in the venture," Claude volunteered.

"No, no, you save your money. I'll speak to the bank and arrange a loan if necessary."

They hired a taxi to take them along the coast road to the château. Claude had seen few of the towns along the route and Pierre even fewer. He had rarely ventured outside Cannes. Pierre refused to discuss any more details about the château until they'd seen it for themselves.

The gates of the château were badly rusted. With the help of the driver and a tyre lever, they finally managed to prise them open. Carefully Pierre shut the rusty gates behind them. They bumped along the pitted road, overgrown on all sides by a hopeless tangle of trees and briars. Claude could see the blue-green of the sea as the car rounded a bend. A creamy-coloured building with circular turrets lay sleeping in the sun like a great unawakened giant. They stood side by side on the broken concrete flags that formed the path, each lost in his own thoughts. If there was an ideal setting for a hotel, this was it, Claude had no doubt. He could feel a curl of excitement begin to stir. What a challenge. The uneven roof heights gave the building enormous charm, the grounds could be easily restored - the garden they had created at the Hotel Thibault had been just as bad when they'd bought it. This was larger and much more beautiful in spite of its overgrown vegetation. Pierre produced the key of the front door and they spent an hour exploring every inch of the château's cool interior. The rooms were large and dark.

"Certainly there would have to be windows added," Claude maintained. Pierre agreed. Claude glanced at him shrewdly. Pierre would probably agree to anything now, then throw a fit later when the bills started pouring in. It would need a fortune spent on it. Especially with the ideas already forming in Claude's mind.

Apart from the solid, thick walls the building would have to be totally gutted. Bathrooms would need to be added to each bedroom, kitchens installed, the gardens started from scratch - everything. These dungeons would provide ideal space for wine cellars - what a stock they could accumulate and store here. As the thought struck him, Pierre called his attention to bottles lying in a dark corner of the stone floor.

"Pity we have no proper light," Claude remarked, squinting at the cobweb-covered labels. "These look good, maybe we've made a great discovery."

Pierre smiled. Claude and his dreams.

"Now! Tell me about it," Claude demanded

when they'd ended their tour.

"The château has been left to a family who have no interest in retaining it. It will be sold to the highest bidder - by tender. The couple who own it now are quite elderly. They have no children to leave it to and want to rid themselves of it."

Claude whistled his surprise. "What do you think of it?" he queried.

"Perfect. A wonderful place for a hotel." Pierre's eyes glittered with enthusiasm.

They shivered slightly in the afternoon warmth as they surveyed the rolling carpet of weeds which sloped towards the sea. The afternoon sun was low in the sky casting a golden glow over the creamy stone. It is ideal. If only I can buy it, Pierre thought. There would be no problem in selling the hotel.

He could barely wait for Thierry to come home in order to show it to him, but that was still a month away. By then it could be theirs, his and Thierry's. He owed something to his son, he deserved it. He had indulged him slightly, he admitted, but then he'd had to be both father and mother to him. Claude had always been good to Thierry, especially when he was a small child. A frown creased his forehead, lately Claude hadn't had as much patience with Thierry. A boy needed to grow up, stretch his wings a little. They would all work well together, Pierre could see it all. Claude would forget this partnership nonsense especially when he was the manager of this wonderful château.

CHAPTER THIRTY-FIVE

"Everything moves so slowly," Pierre grumbled as they waited impatiently for the architect's report.

It was three weeks since they'd first visited the château. Thierry would be home in two days and Pierre was disappointed that they had made so little progress.

"Patience," Claude counselled, "we must wait for the report before you commit yourself." How often Pierre had curbed Claude's impatience during the building of the Hotel Thibault's annexe.

"I suppose so," Pierre agreed.

Thierry bounded through the door calling his father, Claude, anyone! Pierre rushed from the dining-room and hugged his son. "Welcome home," he beamed. Claude followed and shook Thierry's hand. Thierry had changed in the last six months. His boyish frame had filled out and, if anything, he was more spirited and attractive. Thierry rushed upstairs shouting to Jeanne who hugged him and kissed him until he was breathless. She'd known him since birth and here he was, a fine, young, strong nineteen year old, living and working in Switzerland, the future owner of the Hotel Thibault.

Thierry threw his case onto the bed in his room and went to join his father and Claude in the kitchen. Marc had cooked brioches and croissants especially for his arrival and they sat companionably round the table, drinking steaming cups of café au lait and eating the warm, sweet bread.

"I must give you *our* recipe for brioche," Thierry said, pulling one of the feather-light sweet buns apart. "The recipe *we* use is excellent."

Marc left the table to check the coq au vin which was simmering more gently than he was.

"It smells good," Claude said, watching Marc's scowling face.

Thierry joined Marc at the stove and tasted the chicken dish with his finger. Claude hid his disapproving look.

"It could do with a dash more salt."

Marc's face flamed with annoyance; six months training and Thierry considered himself an expert. In Switzerland we do this, in Switzerland we do that. Finally, unable to bear the pained expression on Marc's face, Claude distracted Thierry's attention by insisting that he must see the improvements to the garden.

"I have no interest in gardens," he told Claude. "When I take over the running of the hotel I'll leave you to see to that." Thierry was anxious to contact his friends and, bored to distraction, he left Claude to his "precious flowers."

His patronising attitude made Claude uneasy. Thierry would be extremely difficult to work with. Maybe the years would soften him, make him more mature. He pulled out a couple of weeds and threw them into a dustbin.

Claude made his way upstairs to the attic room. He still loved his room under the eaves, furnished now to his taste with rugs and a big easy chair. This was where he loved to do all his reading. He smiled as he heard voices coming from the partially open door of Thierry's room. Pierre was never happier than when he was with his precious son.

"A partnership?" Thierry's raised voice demanded angrily.

"Shh! Don't worry. I had to agree to it in order to keep him with us. I'll keep stalling the arrangement until you're ready to take over, or at least until the château is ready. You must understand that no one has Claude's drive or his energy. Without him it just wouldn't be possible."

Claude stopped dead on the stairs. Pierre? Would he do such a dreadful thing to him? Such an underhanded trick. Claude couldn't believe his own ears. Noisily he trod on the stairs and their conversation ceased immediately. He must go to his room and think. He couldn't confront them until he had sorted out his thoughts.

Claude propped the menu on its ornamental stand and made his way to the kitchen.

"What will you eat?" Marc enquired. He enjoyed the companionable lunches that he and Claude shared after the daily rush was over.

"I'm not hungry, just a cup of coffee."

Marc peered at him, "What's wrong, Claude?" he demanded.

Claude shook his head in reply, afraid that if he spoke he would break his own rule and lose his temper. This situation called for a clear head, and at the moment his only clear thought was that he'd been taken for a fool.

Pierre glanced at Claude's impassive face, he was very quiet this morning.

"Anything troubling you, Claude?" his tone was tentative.

Claude shook his head, busying himself clearing some dishes. The young waiter, who had all the skill of a juggler, could manage them in one journey, but Claude needed to keep himself busy. The waiter had become another of Claude's excellent additions to the hotel's growing staff. Now that Pierre came to think about it, apart from Jeanne and himself, Claude had been responsible for choosing everyone employed there. Jeanne had been given the job of supervising the linens whilst he himself had been made almost redundant by Marc's expertise. An energetic team of cleaners arrived each morning and by noon the whole place was sparkling. One of the team remained behind each day for any unexpected little tasks which could crop up. The porter was efficient and amiable; he carried the luggage, ran errands for the guests, doubled as a waiter when someone was absent for any reason and generally made himself available wherever he was needed.

At Claude's insistence the staff all wore immaculate uniforms provided by the hotel; an extra expense of which he hadn't approved but, as always, had been bullied into accepting. He smiled, recalling the day Claude had banished a waitress from the dining-room because she'd spilt cream on her skirt. Wearing a pair of Claude's trousers she'd been sent to the dry cleaners and instructed to wait for the offending skirt to be laundered. The Hotel Thibault certainly could *not* do without Claude d'Albion, Pierre thought. He must tread warily.

Intrigue

Joseph, smartly dressed in his porter's uniform, carried the letter which Pierre had waited for so impatiently. Eagerly Pierre devoured its contents. With a whoop of delight he deposited it on the table in front of Claude.

"This is good," Claude observed as he read the report. It agreed with his own opinion. The château had a solid impenetrable shell which would outlast them all, but the interior needed total rebuilding. "No surprises then," he noted acidly.

"We must contact the lawyers and make our bid." Pierre's face shone with happiness. In his mind it was already his, the Château Thibault.

The kitchen table, home to so many of their dramas, was covered with sheets of scribbled figures. It had taken the two men several hours to arrive at their final decision. "It was much simpler when we bought the pension, at least we had a price, a guide to follow," Pierre grumbled, conveniently forgetting his stubborn resistance to their previous transactions.

"That is your final offer?" Claude asked.

"Positively," Pierre nodded. "Will you notify them of my bid immediately?"

My bid, not *our* bid, Claude noted bitterly. You may have made your bed Pierre, but if I have my way, you will never get to lie in it.

CHAPTER THIRTY-SIX

That afternoon, as Pierre and Thierry Thibault bowled along the coast in Thierry's little sports car, Claude assembled the entire staff of the hotel around the wooden kitchen table.

His preoccupied silence the last few days was most unlike him. The secrecy surrounding the meeting he'd called was even more so. They waited, intrigued.

Every waking moment since he'd overheard the conversation between the two Thibaults had been devoted to solving his problem. At first he thought he had the answer - he would buy the Hotel Thibault from Pierre. But if he left Pierre, there would *be* no hotel for sale. Pierre couldn't supervise the rebuilding of the château on his own nor could he buy the château without selling the hotel. Several times during the building of the annexe Pierre had shown how impractical he was and how easily he'd become irritated. Several times he'd stormed out leaving Claude to soothe the ruffled workmen and temperamental builders. Pierre could not do it alone.

The worries of Claude's days spilled over into his sleep. Turrets dominated his dreams, multi-coloured roof tiles pierced his subconscious like lasers, weeds in the garden wrapped themselves around his body. One night he'd woken sweating and distressed to discover it was barely two o'clock. He'd padded quietly down the stairs and put a pan of milk on the empty stove to make himself a cup of hot chocolate. The little pot was like himself, small and alone. As he sat in the silence a phrase that the notaire had read from Lisette Garnier's will echoed in his head... *trust your instincts, follow your dreams...* What were his dreams? He hardly dared voice them, to own and run a hotel - the château near Beaulieu. He sat bolt upright on the chair. The truth was, Pierre Thibault needed him but he didn't need Pierre Thibault. He was sure he could hear Lisette Garnier's voice guiding him, see her benevolent face smiling her encouragement.

"Thank you," he whispered aloud in the quiet kitchen.

The chocolate grew cold and formed a wrinkled skin as he made plans.

"I must ask you to treat what I'm about to tell you in confidence." They all nodded their silent agreement.

"I have been duped, taken for a fool," he began, looking around at their expectant faces. Slowly and deliberately he unfolded the news of the château. He told them about the conversation he'd overheard and how it had shaken him to the core. The deceitfulness of Pierre and Thierry. Their expressions changed, became sympathetic. They all regarded Claude as a fair and understanding man. A hard taskmaster, yes, but he'd given them a sense of purpose and of self-worth. They were part of a team and were proud of it. Anyone not measuring up to his exacting standards was despatched firmly, but fairly, to other less demanding jobs. Claude had been the one who'd fought for higher than average wages for them. He'd remembered their birthdays, sympathised with their problems. They looked upon him as their champion.

"It isn't in my nature to be disloyal to my employer," he continued. "But he obviously doesn't find it in his heart to feel the same way about me, so I intend to beat him at his own game. I have put in my own bid for the château. A higher bid than his."

Nobody spoke. Despite the gravity of the matter Claude almost laughed at the astonished looks on their faces as they digested the information he'd sprung on them.

"I'm sure we all feel the same," Marc finally said. "We are truly sorry. It won't be the same without you..."

"I won't *stay* here without you," Joseph interrupted.

"Nor me," two of the cleaning staff spoke as one.

Jeanne's mouth was set in a grim line. "After all you've done for M Thibault," she said, "it's disgusting." Her support pleased Claude; she was the one person he thought might side with Pierre. Even if she had chosen to reveal his scheme to Pierre, the bid had been made.

"That brings me to my next point. If my plan works there are large quarters behind the château. They would make excellent staff quarters and my intention is to turn them into comfortable rooms and add a large sitting-room. Every one of you will be welcome, that is, if you care to stay with me."

"Count me in," Marc said with relief. One by one they echoed his sentiments.

"I must talk to my boyfriend. He works in the bar at the Majestic Hotel - it's a very good job," one of the waitresses said.

"I understand. I'll need a good barman myself."

"Would you consider him if he was interested?" she queried, her mind racing ahead.

"Certainly, but you know the rules," he cautioned.

"What about gardeners?" Claudine, a shy little waitress asked.

"That's imperative; the château has large grounds, we'll need more than one."

"Then I know just the person for you, my father. He's an expert on plants and flowers."

"We must have a drink to celebrate," Marc interrupted.

"It's a kind thought but a bit premature I think," Claude remarked wryly.

"Nonsense," Jeanne said indignantly. "You can do anything you put your mind to."

Claude smiled his thanks. "Tell me about your father," he prompted Claudine.

"He's employed as head gardener to the lady who owns the Villa Des Fleurs at Haute-de-Cagnes. It's a ridiculous name considering that she won't permit any flowers to be planted. All the grounds are just grass and gravel now, they were magnificent gardens. When she and her husband divorced, she was awarded the villa. Her first instruction to Papa was to pull out every one of the prize-winning blooms and plants and burn them. Any member of the staff caught taking as much as a petal would be instantly fired."

"I wonder why she keeps that name?" Joseph asked.

Claudine shrugged. "Sentiment or spite? Who knows? No one would dare ask."

They raised their glasses, "*Bonne chance*," they chorused. Claude was dangerously close to tears. This small group had become like a family to him and, if everything worked out, they wouldn't be separated.

"If things go right you'll be fully paid from the day I take possession of the château. It'll take some time before your apartments are ready. Some time before you'll be needed. But you'll be paid regardless. If you care to take other jobs in the meantime, feel free to earn some extra cash," he offered generously. "You may prefer to remain here until we are ready to open."

"You'll need help at the château," insisted Jeanne. She wrinkled her nose with distaste at the idea of remaining at the hotel.

"I appreciate your loyalty more than I can say," Claude assured them. "Now we must wait."

Claude continued to go about his work quietly. He knew that he'd taken a risk telling them about his plans. But there was no turning back now. They hadn't betrayed his confidence, instead they showed their support in unobtrusive little ways. The waiting was nerve-racking.

Pierre was on tenterhooks. Every morning he stood on the doorstep waiting for the post. He scrabbled through the stack of correspondence and scratched his head in puzzlement. At long last it had arrived. He looked at the letter from the firm of solicitors who was handling the sale of the château. It was addressed to Claude d'Albion.

Laura

CHAPTER THIRTY-SEVEN

Laura leant on the fence and enviously watched the horses as they splashed in the waters of the therapeutic pool. "Bloody marvellous," she whinged to herself for the hundredth time, "they have all the luck - and all the luxury."

She tried to ignore the clanging bell which echoed in the morning stillness but knew it would be just a matter of minutes before she answered it. Kicking at the gravel with her dusty boots, she slowly trudged towards the big stone house. Even in the morning sunshine it looked grey and dingy. The windows, rotting in their frames, needed replacing and the heavy black painted door had faded with age. The broken fanlight window had been blocked with cardboard to prevent draughts. Laura had long given up suggesting to her mother that everything was in need of repair. Now it was too late. A bonfire is the only suitable place for most of it now, she considered grimly. Funny, it's my home and I feel nothing for it, but then she'd thought this for as long as she could remember.

She crossed the chipped marble flags and threw her riding crop on the scratched table which stood in the centre of the light-filled hall. Picking up the post she glanced through it briefly. As she expected there was nothing addressed to her, just the normal clutter of letters, receipts and bills for her mother. The roar of a motor-bike halted her at the bottom of the stairs.

"Package for Mrs Bingham," the helmeted rider mumbled, pushing a clipboard and chewed pencil at her. "Sign here, please."

"What is it?" she asked the visored alien, wondering if there was a face under the black helmet.

"Dunno," he muttered, his speech muffled. He handed her a large brown envelope and crunched his way back across the gravel to his powerful machine. He revved his engine and disappeared round the corner of the drive in a spray of tiny pebbles.

Laura walked up the stairs, deliberately sliding her feet forward to the back of each step. She liked the hollow thud that her boots made as they came into contact with the tarnished brass stair rods. Hesitating for a moment, she took a deep breath and opened the door to her mother's room. "Post's here," she said, putting the pile of letters on the bedside table; the big brown envelope she put on the bed. "This one came by courier. What's in it?"

"Nothing to worry you," her mother replied tartly, without opening it. "I rang the bell ages ago, where were you?"

"Helping Tony with the horses," she lied glibly. So what if she stole some free time, she had little enough of it. Laura's days were divided between helping Mrs Oz and doing the typing and bookkeeping for her mother. She deserved some leisure.

"I'm uncomfortable, please move me," her mother said, trying to move onto her side.

"Hang on, I'll get Mrs Oz and we can remake the bed. You'll be more comfortable then."

"Hurry up, I've been waiting..."

Laura pulled a face. "...

"five minutes if that."

Mrs Oz, alias Miss Loretta O'Sullivan, was re-christened by the two Bingham children when they were tiny - her real name was too much of a mouthful for them. As a young girl in her late teens she'd committed the unpardonable sin of having a child out of wedlock. When she refused to give the baby up for adoption, her father had thrown her out of the house. She had answered every advertisement she could, finally finding work and a home for herself and her son with the newly-wed Binghams. Being called "Mrs" was the only favour she'd asked of her employers. They were delighted with the pleasant hard-working girl and had respected her wishes. To this day no one else had known the truth. Also there was no one else to call her by her pet name, Lally.

"Here we are. Oh! you poor dear, are you stiff and sore?" Mrs Oz smiled as she bustled into the room. Laura marvelled at the woman's patience and kindly nature. There was no sign of impatience in her manner. She was a happy soul, always singing or humming as she went about her work. Laura had never seen as much as a frown on her cheerful face as she constantly answered the demanding bell. Time had blurred her girlish figure and had added a few grey hairs to her auburn locks, but her twinkling brown eyes and every-ready smile hadn't changed.

They pulled the sheet free from under Olivia Bingham. In two minutes the bed was freshly made and her mother, her faced creased with

...ed for her medicine.

"...w then, that's more comfortable, isn't it?" ...ked Mrs Oz, soothingly. She gathered up the discarded bedding and an empty glass and left them to their morning's work, humming as she went.

Laura sat at the battered desk, her bitten fingernails tapping irritably on the wood. Slowly and awkwardly, Olivia Bingham inserted the letter-opener into an envelope and pulled a jagged tear across its top.

"We must pay this by the twenty-third, it's a bill for the new harnesses."

"Hm! We must not let the harnesses get worn," Laura said, with quiet sarcasm.

"Did you say something, Laura?" her mother questioned.

"Nothing really, just that harnesses must be worn."

Her mother looked at her pouting daughter. She really is very plain, Olivia thought, she should do something with that straggly hair. Why does she insist on wearing those baggy shapeless sweaters? They make her look like a lumpy sack of potatoes tied in the middle. Her jeans were sagging at the knees and her leather riding-boots were worn down at the heels.

Olivia Bingham, ill though she was, still made a pretty picture lying against the neatly repaired lace pillows. Her blonde pageboy hairstyle, unchanged since she was a girl, was neatly held in place by a velvet headband. The fair skin stretched across her high cheek bones was translucent in the shadowed light of the room. Telltale lines around her grey-blue eyes told the story of her painful illness. Laura had seen photographs of her mother when she was a young girl and she'd been a real beauty. Slim as a reed with dainty patrician features. Like all the county set Olivia had ridden horses and hunted, attended hunt balls and bloodstock sales. Like all her contemporaries she kept two wary eyes open for a suitable husband. He had appeared from out of the blue or, more correctly, from out of the sky, arriving by helicopter for the sales; a daring young man just missing the treetops as the whirling blades of his helicopter descended. Within minutes the attractive man with his slight air of arrogance became fair game for the single girls. William Bingham, the eldest son of a merchant banker, had been sent by his father to Ireland to replenish their stock of brood mares. He fell in love with the unhurried lifestyle, the soft air and peaceful Kildare countryside. He had found his niche. He left the City of London and the family bank to cope without him. Olivia was first past the winning post when six months later they walked hand-in-hand down the aisle.

The couple shared a great love. Not for each other nor, sadly, for their children, but for horses. They lived and breathed horses and started their own stud farm, breeding horses for racing, hunting and for polo. Reluctantly they agreed they should have a family - if only to carry on the family name - and a year later their son Charles was born. Almost as soon as he could sit up on his own they bought him a tiny pony which he loathed, yelling and shrieking every time he saw it. His parents were terrified when he screamed himself blue in the face. They were never quite sure if it was caused by fear or by temper. Gratefully, they handed him over to Mrs Oz. For the first eight years of his life Charles and Mrs Oz's son, Billy, grew up as brothers while Olivia and William got on with their own busy lives.

When William Bingham's father died, the family bank continued to run smoothly with his younger brother Anthony as chairman. Much to William's relief their lives remained unaltered. As the eldest son he'd inherited a considerable fortune. Part of it he put to use extending the stables and increasing the breeding stock. Under his brother's watchful eye his dividends from the bank and the remainder of his trust fund along with the income from the stud were wisely invested. He was relieved to leave his complicated financial affairs in his brother's capable hands.

Their social life was hectic. They threw big parties at the drop of a hat, recruiting extra help from the village to help with the catering for the constant stream of people coming and going at all hours of the night or day. The big house was lively and, at night, lights shone in every room and the sound of music and laughter floated on the breeze through the open windows. The Horse Show, held each year at the Royal Dublin Society, was the busiest week of their year. All the houses in the area were crammed to bursting with guests and there was a non-stop round of dances, dinners and parties. Charles and Billy used to love to sit at the top of the stairs and watch the flow of chattering people moving from room to room. Mrs Oz, no matter how busy, always took two plates of party food to the youngsters warning them not to get caught out of bed. More than once, tired and excited, they fell asleep on the stairs.

The stud flourished under the Binghams' careful supervision. They fast earned a reputation for being one of the best breeding establishments in the county. They extended the stables again and became busier still.

When he was nine years old, Charles was removed kicking and screaming from Mrs Oz's loving care and, like his father and grandfather before him, he was sent to Eton. The year that Laura was born.

She was a wiry little mite and showed no objection to being jolted along on the back of a pony grabbing it firmly by the mane. The first word she uttered was "Oz" which put a beaming smile on the housekeeper's perky face. As the business expanded Olivia and William Bingham travelled more and more, leaving Laura with Mrs Oz and her son Billy. He adored the little girl, treating her like a piece of delicate china. But she was a tomboy, forever scratching and scraping herself climbing trees or scrambling through the brambly hedges in search of blackberries or some small animal. Billy scampered after her, afraid she would hurt herself. When Charles came home for the school holidays, Laura clung to Billy. She didn't like the serious-faced stranger who was her brother.

The Curragh, Phoenix Park, Newmarket, Cheltenham, Ascot, were all names that Laura had grown up with. She owned more jodhpurs than dresses, more riding-boots than shoes. As a little girl she'd ridden ponies and fallen off, then she rode horses and fell off those too. Gymkhanas and horse shows - she could take them or leave them, always a little jealous that the horses got more attention from her parents than she did. She consistently refused her parents' offer of a pony or a horse of her own. She was content to ride whatever horse was available in the stables at the time.

"Poor little thing," Mrs Oz said, cuddling Laura to her.

"What's wrong, Mrs Oz? Why are you crying?"

"Don't worry my pet, you'll be all right, don't you fret."

Laura was puzzled. Billy looked sad too. She'd never seen Mrs Oz cry before, she always laughed.

Two weeks later her Uncle Anthony came to stay. Laura liked him. He didn't smell of horses but of some tangy aftershave that remained in a room long after he'd left it. With a kind look on his serious face he sat her beside him on the sofa in front of the fire and awkwardly broke the news to her.

"When your parents were travelling from London to a race meeting at Cheltenham, the helicopter they were flying in crashed. Your father was…killed and your mother was injured. But don't worry, she'll be all right, she'll be home soon."

The impact of the news had little effect on Laura. She sat quietly listening to her uncle, she was glad that it wasn't Mrs Oz who'd been hurt. Laura still blushed whenever she remembered her shameful reaction. Two months later her mother was brought home by ambulance strapped to a back-board, almost totally paralysed. She had never left her room or her bed since. At first a nurse came to bath her and help her with her exercises every day. Then she came every second day. Mrs Oz looked after her the rest of the time and when Laura grew older and stronger she helped too.

Her mother had shown a stubborn determination to continue running the stud. With the help of a manager, as devoted to horses as she was, it thrived. She issued instructions that the derelict cottage in the grounds was to be restored for him. When it was finished, in Laura's opinion, it was a little palace. Olivia Bingham updated the stables, enlarged the tack room, installed the latest feeding methods and finally built the large therapeutic pool which, to Laura's utter disgust, cost a fortune.

Her brother rarely came home anymore. He preferred the lively company of his cousins and school-friends in England. It was understood that when he came down from university he'd take his place in the family bank. Unlike her brother Laura attended the local school and then went on to a secretarial college. After she qualified she was awarded the job of unpaid secretary to her mother. She'd begged to be allowed to do part-time work but her suggestion had met with her mother's firm refusal.

"There's more than enough to keep you busy here," Olivia insisted.

It had been a terrible blow to Olivia Bingham when the stud manager was spirited away by one of their biggest customers. Billy took over some of the work, helping the stable lads whenever he could. The house had become shabby. But Olivia, who never left her big sunny bedroom, felt it was unnecessary to waste any money decorating it especially as nobody visited any more. The silk curtains were rotting with age on their blackened brass poles. The carpets were threadbare from the rough-and-cut of riding boots. The chintz patterns on the sofas and chairs were so faded that their patterns were barely discernible. The central heating became temperamental, always choosing the coldest days and nights to break down. When Mrs Oz had suffered a really bad cold which threatened to turn to pneumonia, Olivia agreed to have the heating repaired, but the system was obsolete and parts were no longer obtainable. Reluctantly she'd allowed Laura to buy some paraffin heaters. The kitchen was shabby and worn. There were holes in the linoleum and, no matter how hard Laura or Mrs Oz scrubbed, it remained scarred and marked after more than twenty years of wear.

"The place is falling apart," Laura grumbled to her mother. "Mrs Oz nearly died from that cold." Laura liked to exaggerate, always punching home her point - but this time it backfired.

Her mother listened to her daughter's grumbles. My limbs might not work but my brain does, she thought, seeing through Laura's ploy.

"Right, I have the answer," Olivia said, her eyes narrowing in concentration.

Laura brightened visibly.

"Mrs Oz can have the cottage," Olivia announced triumphantly. "It's empty now."

"But Mother, I'll be here all on my own," Laura wailed.

"Nonsense," her mother snapped, "I'm here."

Serves me right, Laura thought, now I'm really sunk. I won't be able to go to a film at night or even have a drink at the pub. No one will drive up here in winter, they'd freeze to death. But that hardly mattered, most of her friends had left Kildare to work in Dublin or in England. Laura could feel the grip of loneliness tightening around her like a vice.

Mrs Oz was thrilled with the lovely cottage, her first real home. She'd plant some flowers in the tiny garden, maybe some roses, they could be trained against the walls.

"You'll always be welcome, darling," she assured Laura. "And I'll come over any night to look after your mother if you want to go out." She knew the girl would miss her company in the house and would be lonely. It was a shame, a youngster like that - she should be out and about laughing, dancing and enjoying herself instead of reading her eyes sore with all those books. She should be experiencing life not just reading about it. Such a terrible pity that Mrs Bingham was so sour towards her daughter. Still it must be miserable lying there year after year in pain. Thank goodness she has her horses, they keep her mind busy. The television was a great thing, at least she was able to watch the racing.

CHAPTER THIRTY-EIGHT

"Damn and blast it!" Laura said, slamming her fist on the jumbled keys.

"Laura! Please don't bang the typewriter like that, and don't curse and swear," her mother said peevishly.

"I refuse to type one more word on this antiquated machine. Look at this letter." She ripped the page from the roller and pushed it under her mother's nose. "Look at this mess. The top of the 'e' is solid, the bottom of the 'y' is missing, it looks like a 'v' without a tail and the keys stick. We need a new typewriter."

"The keys have always stuck like that, ever since I first used it," her mother scowled. Despite its minor faults *she'd* managed it very well. But now she found it too painful to use. She left all the typing to Laura. Her daughter was constantly nagging her to spend money; new carpets, new windows, why couldn't she leave well alone? Was she never satisfied?

Laura banged the lid on the typewriter and snapped the lock shut.

"You haven't finished the letters yet."

"No, I haven't, and I'm not going to. Not until we get a proper machine, an electric typewriter with plastic keys not like these metal-rimmed ones that you have to punch with all your might."

Her daughter's face was sullen and suddenly Olivia was too weary to argue.

"You don't need an electric one, an ordinary one would do," Olivia capitulated.

"An electronic one," Laura corrected. "You can see the line you're writing before it's transferred onto the page and it self-corrects." She warmed enthusiastically to her sales pitch.

"Get some catalogues and I'll have a look at them," Olivia sighed in resignation.

"That will take forever; I know exactly which one to buy. If you sign the cheque I'll go and buy it this afternoon. We'll have the rest of these letters finished in an hour." Laura stood defiantly at the foot of the bed until her mother asked for her cheque-book.

"Here you are, and don't waste money, Laura. Now, put this envelope away safely." She removed the key which permanently hung round her neck on a narrow ribbon. Laura unlocked the heavy door and propped the thick brown envelope at the side of the safe beside the sheaf of bank statements. Her mother was so secretive - what harm if she did know what was inside the envelope? She dealt with all the correspondence anyhow, everything except her mother's private bank statements.

Laura knew that they couldn't be poor. Charles, on one of his rare visits home, had roared with laughter when she'd asked him if their mother was broke. "Don't be ridiculous," he'd chortled, but refused to elaborate. He agreed with Laura that things had been allowed to get a little out of hand and even his half-hearted attempt to persuade Olivia to do some repairs had fallen on deaf ears.

"Why should you be so concerned?" his

mother snapped, "you're rarely here anyway."

He didn't pursue it any further.

"I tried," he told Laura, "but she won't hear of any changes."

Laura had been unimpressed by her brother's detached manner. He'll go back to London to his comfortable life and I'll be stuck here forever. I bet his flat isn't freezing and full of draughty windows. He probably has a modern kitchen with loads of gadgets, she thought. Two days later, she morosely watched the cloud of dust as he drove away in the smart hire car, down the twisting driveway, and out of their lives for goodness knew how long.

"Great, you just look after number one," she snarled with temper as she glared at the back of the speeding car. She crashed the front door of the house so hard it rocked on its hinges.

The old Range Rover noisily covered the winding roads. The leafy lanes and fresh fields with their hedgerows were waking up for Spring. The flat, lush green countryside stretched for miles. Laura drove slowly, savouring every moment of the beautiful sunny afternoon, her spirits lifting. She smiled as she saw the first of the baby lambs huddling close to their mothers. This was her favourite time of the year, the rebirth of nature.

It took her just ten minutes to complete her purchase. As she filled in the cheque for the state-of-the-art machine, she preferred not to think about her mother's reaction. She'd added some extras to the list; backing paper and carbons, a cleaning kit and several spare ribbons which, she knew from experience, didn't last too long. Laura left the shop and walked along the street looking in the other windows. Her jeans were shabby, maybe she'd treat herself to a new pair - possibly a chunky sweater too. It was ages since she had bought herself any clothes. At least she didn't have to rely on her mother's bounty for this. Twice a year she received a cheque from the bank in London, a dividend from the trust fund set up for her by her grandfather. On her twenty-first birthday she'd gain full control of her own finances. Then she could do as she pleased.

The coffee shop was busy. Tourists mixed with the locals, all enjoying a welcome cup of tea. The tourists were easy to spot with their sensible flat shoes and rolled-up raincoats. Some of them had maps sticking out of their pockets or handbags. No one took any notice of the girl as she edged her way round the tables to an empty seat.

"Coffee please and an eclair." Laura smiled at the waitress.

The cake was gooey and oozing with cream, she'd love another one, a meringue this time. So what if she was overweight, who cared? She chased the escaped crumbs of sugary meringue and cream around the plate with her fork. Now she felt a bit sick, but it was worth it. This was like being on holiday. Next stop - the bookshop. Laura browsed for half an hour and selected an armful of books. Pleased with herself she paid the cashier - she'd really done well today.

"*How much*? It cost *how* much?" her mother's voice rose to a screech. Laura stood her ground silently; the shock would pass in a few minutes, she'd expected this reaction.

Lifting the machine from its polystyrene box

she put it on the desk. Her mother eyed it in disbelief. How could a typewriter cost so much, she thought angrily?

"I should never have allowed you to buy it without seeing it first."

"Now then, let's make a start." Laura ignored her mother's histrionics. A few minutes later she presented the first letter to her mother for her signature. Grudgingly Olivia admitted to herself that it did look good, very professional. She painfully added her signature as Laura typed the envelope.

True to her word, by the time that Mrs Oz appeared with her mother's dinner tray, Laura had finished the typing and all the envelopes were stacked ready for posting. Her mother had calmed down at last. Although Olivia wouldn't admit it Laura could see that she was pleased with the results. Why was she so grudging?

Laura awoke early next morning and looked out of the window. She could see Mrs Oz walking along the short path from the cottage. Now that she was in the house, Laura could go riding before breakfast. The stables were almost empty, the horses out on their morning gallops. Mist lingered gently over the fields and in the distance she could see the stable lads with their mounts, ghostly riders on the horizon. The house was lost from view as she cantered along the perimeter of the land. This was the best time of day, the sweet smell of morning dew and the birds chirping their greeting. Mrs Oz would be in the kitchen preparing breakfast which she and Laura always ate together at the table by the old Aga. After that Laura took her mother's breakfast tray upstairs and an hour later they were ready to settle down to the day's work.

Her fingers flew over the keys of the new typewriter, it was such a pleasure to use.

"I must throw the old one out," Laura said, in a lull between letters.

"No, certainly not. Put it in the attic. Who knows how long it'll be before that contraption breaks down." Olivia had no faith in technology except where the horses were concerned - then she was totally convinced that anything new was a miracle of engineering or a brilliant invention.

"Listen to this, it's a letter from Charles," her mother's voice sounded excited.

A letter from Charles! My, my. That in itself was another miracle, Laura thought sourly.

"He's arranged for a stud manager to come over from England for a while. He'll see what needs to be done to get the stud running smoothly again." Olivia carefully studied the enclosed references.

Since their manager had left, taking the best lads with him, things had become difficult and more than a little chaotic. For the first time since the stud had opened Olivia Bingham began to feel that she was losing her grip. It was hard not being able to talk over her problems with someone. Charles was too far away and Laura was uninterested. How different it had been when William was alive. The friends who'd regularly filled the house vanished on the wind after her accident. The big house lay empty with hardly a sound to disturb its quiet existence. Bricks and mortar, just bricks and mortar.

Laura sat on the floor outside the linen

cupboard and sorted through the pile of sheets. They'd become so worn and thin they were almost in holes. A feeling of frustration swept over her. It would be pointless asking her mother to let her buy new ones. That was her problem, let her suffer the embarrassment, Laura could do no more. She picked the best out of the bad lot and dumped the sheets unceremoniously on the bed and then opened the windows of the guest room. If she didn't leave for the airport right away she'd be late.

CHAPTER THIRTY-NINE

Laura watched anxiously as the passengers streamed through the terminal building. It was fun to see the people from earlier flights greeting relatives and friends. One young Asian girl was so excited to be reunited with her parents that she yelled out their names in sheer delight. She was soon wrapped in the safety of their arms. In her excitement she'd forgotten the bottle of duty-free drink that she was carrying and as it hit the floor it smashed into smithereens at her feet.

This must be Terence Harvey, Laura decided. The stocky man with a pipe clenched between his teeth was dressed in a tweed jacket and cords. His eyes searched the waiting crowds at the barrier. Laura approached him tentatively. A smile touched his lips as he walked towards her. Passing her he swooped to kiss a small child who'd wrapped herself around his legs. Feeling foolish she slunk to the back of the diminishing throng and waited for someone who seemed likely. This time she'd be sure.

She heard her name being called over the public address system. A tall sandy-haired young man stood patiently at the desk beside his trolley. As she approached the information desk the young man smiled at her. Oh no! I'm not getting caught that way again, she thought warily, as she responded to the call.

"How do you do?" he said formally, "I'm Terence Harvey, Terry to my friends."

Anne Schulman

"Laura, Laura Bingham." She stuck her hand out awkwardly. "Did you have a good flight?" She wondered how she'd missed him.

He nodded, skilfully manoeuvring the trolley to avoid the moving people. He swung his case into the back of the Range Rover and settled himself in the passenger seat beside her. They didn't speak again until she'd joined the stream of traffic heading towards town. From the corner of his eye he watched her as she concentrated on the merging traffic at the roundabout. She was totally unlike her brother. Her mousy hair half-covered her face and what he could see of her skin had that scrubbed, fresh, outdoor look of someone who didn't bother with make-up. Her manner was friendly but defensive. Charles had said she could be bristly. Like an unbroken filly; she responded to a firm hand, he had warned.

"Charles sends his love," Terry broke the silence, "he hopes to be over in a couple of months."

"If he remembers where we live," Laura said, sarcastically.

"How are things at the stud?" He ignored her bitter tone, he didn't want to get embroiled in family matters.

"All right I suppose - well, a bit hectic. I don't have much to do with it - just help out occasionally. It's fallen off a bit lately." She honked loudly at a car that was trying to squeeze her into the bus lane. "Do you know Charles well?"

"We meet all the time at race meetings and at polo matches. We have several friends in common so we bump into each other at parties too." His tone was light. She liked his accent.

"Why did you agree to come over here?" she asked bluntly.

"You don't mince your words, do you?" he laughed. A flush tinged her cheeks, she resented his rebuke.

"I just wondered," she said lamely, trying to soften her brusque question.

"The stud I worked for amalgamated with two others and I didn't fancy being part of a consortium. Horses are like people, they respond to the personal touch. When there are so many animals to look after, all that gets lost. That's my way of thinking anyway." He paused. "So when I resigned Charles asked me if I would take a look at the stud here while I was waiting for something more permanent."

They drove in companionable silence through the countryside. It had a raw beauty. So flat, he thought.

"Would you like to stop for some lunch? You must be tired," Terry suggested.

"There's a nice pub two miles further up the road, we can stop there," Laura agreed.

He took the key from her and locked the doors of the vehicle. The pub was still quiet - just a few motorists, like themselves, needing a break.

"We have toasted chicken sandwiches or toasted cheese and ham." The red-cheeked waiter shuffled from foot to foot as he waited for their order.

"That will do fine, one of each for me," Laura said, "Do you have any soup?"

"Home-made-vegetable-brot," he said all in one breath.

"What's brot?" Terry whispered, as the waiter wrote on his pad.

"Broth." She giggled.

The waiter's cheeks flamed redder than ever.

"A toasted cheese for me and some soup. Soup for you, Laura?"

"Yes please and a packet of cheese-and-onion crisps. We'll order dessert later."

"I don't know why but I thought that the countryside would be mountainous, rather like Wales." Terry remarked trying to make conversation.

"It is in parts, specially around Wicklow, but we're flat here. It's the nicest part of the country," she defended.

"Just another mile and we're there," Laura said reaching into her bag for a Mars bar.

Terry smiled, she had just walloped through two sandwiches, two bowls of soup, a packet of crisps and an enormous slice of Black Forest gateau, washed down by two glasses of Coke.

"The stud is very modern and well equipped but don't expect too much of the house, my mother doesn't think it's worth spending money on," she warned, changing her mind about a bar of Kit-Kat.

Again he heard the anger in her voice. Surely things weren't that bad.

She honked the horn as she drew the Range Rover to a halt at the front door. Hopping out she grabbed his case from the back and waved to Mrs Oz who stood in the entrance.

"This is Terry Harvey," she smiled fondly at the woman, "and this is Mrs Oz, Mrs O'Sullivan, to be precise. My favourite lady in the world."

He was amazed by the change in her voice.

Terry shook her hand politely, her grip was firm and warm.

"You're very welcome here," she greeted. "Would you like a cup of tea before you meet Mrs Bingham?"

"You'll need it," Laura muttered.

"Thank you, Mrs O'Sullivan, " he smiled.

"Mrs Oz will do just fine," the cheery woman assured him.

Olivia Bingham studied the sandy-haired man. He didn't flinch under her direct gaze. His baritone voice was pleasing to her ear and his green eyes were alert. His big frame dwarfed the chair. He looked every inch the country gentleman, in corded trousers, finely-checked open neck shirt and a green Barbour jacket. He was relaxed and assured.

"Laura, go and give Mrs Oz a hand with dinner," her mother instructed.

Terry avoided looking at the girl, even after such a short acquaintance he could imagine her rebellious glare. It was none of his business, but her mother's tone was harsh - unnecessarily so, he felt.

"My son has informed you of our problems?" she queried, her hand plucking at the frill on the sheet.

"We talked a little, but he wasn't able to shed too much light on the matter. Obviously, until I've looked at the accounts and at the stud itself, I won't be able to make an assessment."

Olivia grimaced inwardly. She hated the thought of a stranger poking through her personal affairs, anyone in fact. Laura needed to know what was going on but that was only because she found that writing for more than a few minutes at a time was painful. Besides, she doubted that Laura was clever enough to think for herself.

"Yes, very well," she frowned, "Laura will show you the account books. I would like you to check them here, please, in my room ... I ... er, you. ... may have some questions." Olivia avoided his eyes.

He was not fooled by her lame reasoning. Charles had stressed that his mother was a very private person. He didn't want to add to her troubles, so Terry agreed to her request. It could be beneficial if he needed any extra information.

He unpacked his case then made his way along the corridor leading to the stairs. Light spilled from the domed skylight on to the dingy carpet with its faded colours. Racing prints and some barely discernible landscapes, blackened with age, hung on the walls. The curving staircase had an elegance of its own, the twisted wooden banisters reminded him of barley sugar sticks. The proportions of the black-and-white flagged square hall were quite magnificent but it was cold and bare save for a scratched table, a tall wooden hallstand with a misty cracked mirror and a boot-shaped umbrella holder full of walking sticks. Terry stopped to look at the lovely old handles of the sticks. Although they were tarnished and pitted from age, that didn't hide the beauty of their design. He selected one at random then pressed a tiny button at the base of the handle and pulled. Slowly it slid apart from its wooden base revealing a badly rusted sword.

He replaced it promising himself that sometime he would oil and clean it, preserve its beauty. He chose another one which also had a tiny spring in its side and gently applied pressure. He smiled as he pulled it free. A slim glass phial for carrying alcohol appeared in his hand. It was still half-full but he resisted the temptation to taste the contents. Laura called to him from an open doorway. "If it's all right with you we'll eat in here, it's warmer." She waved her hand towards the room. A large stone fireplace with bright flames licking its hearth cheered the room.

She added two more logs as thick as miniature trees to the blaze. A shower of sparks flew out onto the rug in front of the hearth and she stamped them out with her feet.

Terry meandered around the room. Despite its shabbiness the room had an air of cosiness with its overstuffed chairs and sofas, their springs poking through at odd angles. Empty plant pot holders and bits of bric-a-brac gave the room a cluttered look. Mistaking his interest for criticism Laura raised her eyes up to heaven in disgust. "Miss Havisham would be at home here, wouldn't she?" she volunteered.

"It has a cosy atmosphere, a room for a cold winter's night with a good book to read," Terry placated.

"It's always a cold winter's night here!" Laura said dourly.

They pulled a small square table up to the fire and Laura unfolded its four triangular flaps. The baize top was dotted with stains caused by years of spillage. Laura threw a cloth over the stains and rummaged around in a glass-fronted cupboard. She found two heavy crystal goblets which she clattered noisily onto the table. He cringed as he recognised the age of the beautiful old glasses which she handled as if they were plastic mugs.

"I'll fetch the meal if you'll drag those chairs over," she instructed pointing to two leather-seated dining chairs pushed into a corner.

He could smell the aroma of fresh bread as Laura kicked open the door with one foot. On the tray she carried were two earthenware bowls of steaming soup, a generous dish of yellow butter and a basket of coarse dark brown bread, still warm from the oven.

Reverently he dusted the cobwebs from the bottle of vintage Burgundy. Judging by the label this should be a bottle to remember.

"Wonderful," he said slavering, as he piled half an inch of butter on to a slice of bread.

"Mrs Oz's speciality," Laura said pushing the almost empty basket towards him.

At that moment Mrs Oz herself came into the room and Terry leant sideways to allow her to put the big cauldron shaped casserole in the centre of the small table.

"That was delicious, Mrs Oz, I've never tasted bread like it."

She beamed as she lifted the lid of the dish, sending a spiral of steam into the air. He sniffed appreciatively. The stew was as good as it looked, full of tender meaty chops, large fluffy potatoes and loads of sweet onions. He spooned a ladle full of the gravy over it all and sighed contentedly. He couldn't remember when he'd last eaten a good home-cooked meal.

"What do you do with yourself in the evenings?" he asked, buttering the last piece of bread - at this rate he'd be as big a house in a week.

"Read mostly, write some letters to my friends. They like news from home but there usually isn't very much to tell them. We have a television but the reception is temperamental. An odd time if one of my friends comes home we go to the pub for a drink. Exciting, isn't it?" Her voice trailed away.

He didn't reply, thinking how her sour expression spoiled her face. She would be quite pretty if she smiled instead of frowning.

"I'll go over to the stables in the morning, would you like to come with me and show me around?"

"Sure." She'd like that. She liked Terry. Liked his smile and his warm green eyes.

"The head stable lad can take him round the stud, I need you here," Olivia Bingham insisted as Laura went to say goodnight. She put the cup of cocoa in her mother's hands and sat in the big chair facing the bed.

"It would be better if a member of the family showed him around," Laura argued.

"Really Laura, Tony can do it - he's quite capable."

Laura's mouth was set in a grim line. She waited for her mother to finish her drink, then she settled her for the night and left the room without speaking.

"Laura! Laura!" she heard her mother calling but she ignored her, slamming the door of her own bedroom where she threw herself on her bed and wept with tears of rage and frustration.

Her mother treated her like an unloved, unpaid interloper.

CHAPTER FORTY

".....and in my opinion that's the only way to make it pay." Terence Harvey sat on the edge of the desk, one long leg crossed over the other.

"But that means getting rid of half the horses." Olivia was aghast.

"Exactly. You wanted my opinion and now that I've seen the stud and looked at the figures, it seems to be the only sensible action. To be totally honest, I suggest that you get out of the racing end of the business and concentrate on the polo ponies and the hunters." Terry had expected that his findings would upset her but, with the recession taking its toll, breeding racehorses that couldn't be sold was an expensive and draining luxury.

She dropped back on her pillows and digested his news.

"Let me leave you to think about it then we can discuss it again tomorrow. Would you mind if I took Laura to the pub for a drink tonight?" His tone was challenging. "Mrs Oz has offered to stay with you."

Olivia's eyes narrowed. Had Laura pressured him into taking her out? She had little choice but to agree. Laura had become more than difficult the last couple of days, since Terry had arrived in fact.

"Apparently it's all arranged." Her tone was accusing but he chose to ignore that. As far as he could judge, Laura was shabbily treated by her

mother, shamefully, he thought, might be a better
description. She was at Olivia's beck and call
night and day. He hadn't once heard Olivia say
please or thank you, she just issued her orders in
a harsh voice. It was no wonder that Laura was
so discontented; if it had been him he would
have packed his bags and left long ago.

Laura ran down the stairs two at a time. He
immediately noticed the change in her
appearance. Her straggly hair had been cut into
the latest short chunky style which flattered the
shape of her face. Her grey eyes, with a touch of
mascara, looked huge and her high cheekbones
were emphasised by the short cap of shining
hair.

"You look great," he admired, turning her
around, "let's see the back."

Laura blushed furiously. It was the first
compliment she'd received from anyone other
than Mrs Oz. She wished the white blouse wasn't
so skimpy and that her bottom didn't stick out
quite so much in the tight blue jeans. She'd have
to stop eating so much chocolate and those
endless packets of crisps.

A singsong was well under way. They could
hear the thump of the piano from outside. They
edged their way to the bar and ordered drinks
then found an empty table in the centre of the
room. Laura was a little self-conscious at first but
soon she entered into the spirit of things as she
added her sweet soprano voice to the chorus.
She smiled at him and he was pleased to see her
relaxed and carefree, her face shining with
happiness for a change. Terry didn't know the
words of the songs but he hummed along to the

music. Looking around he found a real blend of people in the crowded pub. Although it was still early in the year, the tourists were beginning to arrive. Just after ten o'clock a group of six smartly dressed and well-watered visitors made their appearance in the lounge of the bar. Laura was not alone in staring frankly at the noisy bunch.

"Good heavens, Terry! What on earth are you doing here?"

"Jeremy, Alex! This is a surprise."

Terry introduced Laura to the couple who in turn introduced their friends. Laura tugged at the front of her blouse pulling it together with nervous fingers. The women were so elegant she felt dowdy in her jeans which had suddenly acquired a second pair of knees all their own. The newcomers managed to find extra chairs and pulled them over to the table. Terry bought a round of drinks. Laura edged her chair until it was almost behind Terry's. She felt tongue-tied and awkward in their company. Their air of sophistication was intimidating, the men reminded her of her brother.

"Bingham? Bingham, it rings a bell," the woman beside Terry said with a puzzled frown.

"You know, Charles Bingham?" Terry prompted.

"Of course, we met at Lydia … thingy's party last week. Are you related?" she asked, glancing towards Laura in a bored manner.

"My brother," she answered, shortly.

Terry sensed that she was uncomfortable, he knew that they could be a bit much, a bit over the top. "Laura lives here. I'm here to have a look at her family's stud farm."

"You thinking of buying it?" Jeremy frowned.

Terry laughed. "No, merely as an adviser."

"You could do no better than Terry," Jeremy informed Laura, loftily.

"I'm sure you're right, he certainly knows what he's doing," Laura agreed.

"You can say that again!" The dark woman in the short skirt snorted with laughter at her own remark. Terry looked embarrassed.

"Will we see you at the sales?" Alex enquired. Of the three women Laura liked her best. She was more polite, less patronising than the others.

"I doubt it, although it is a possibility. Mrs Bingham is considering whether to give up her stable of racehorses and concentrate on polo ponies. To be honest, she has some exceptionally fine horses which should fetch excellent prices but she still has to decide whether she wants to sell them or not."

"We're here to buy - for the syndicate actually. Any chance of having a look?" Jeremy swallowed the bait.

"Possibly, why don't I give you a ring in the next day or so?" Terry suggested, trying to sound vague. This could be an absolute godsend. The syndicate were notoriously big spenders with more money than horse sense.

Terry drove slowly along the unfamiliar roads. Laura had been relieved when Terry said they must leave. She'd been enjoying herself until they had appeared with their in-jokes and brittle conversation. She might as well have been a Martian for all they had in common. Certainly they were glamorous and glossy, like the women in the magazines groomed to their red-tipped fingernails with tights that didn't wrinkle and dresses that didn't crease. She was fascinated - even after a couple of drinks their lipstick stayed firmly in place and their cheeks didn't redden. She put her hand to her own cheeks which felt like little patches of fire.

"What did you think of them?" Terry broke the silence.

"Not a lot, they neighed like the horses they wanted to buy." Laura said, bitchily.

Terry grinned in the darkness at her retort. His guess had been right, they'd made her self-conscious.

"Alex was the best of the bunch. The one in the red dress was definitely unbalanced - one wheel short of a tricycle." He laughed at her exaggeration, Laura didn't mince her words.

Privately she hoped that they wouldn't come to the stud, or at least not to the house. She could just imagine their smart town houses in Belgravia or their chintzy country houses in Gloucestershire designed by flavour-of-the-month, double-barrelled, interior decorators. When she was much younger she'd stayed in London for a week with her aunt and uncle. The visit left its mark on the impressionable youngster. What she remembered most was the casual hospitality, pre-theatre drinks, elegant dinner parties and unashamed luxury. Laura decided at the time that one day she would live in a house in one of those beautiful London squares. She loved the quiet little side streets, the delightful mews houses with their tubs of perfect miniature bay trees and the window boxes riotous with a profusion of flowers. She'd enthused so much that her mother, fearful of losing her when she grew up, had quietly refused all further invitations for her daughter.

Mrs Oz had dozed off in the chair. Laura called her name softly and she awoke with a start.

"Did you have a good evening?" she asked, pleased to see Laura smiling.

Terry walked Mrs Oz home the few short yards to her cottage. "I'm really pleased you took Laura out. It's a lonely life for her here and she deserves to have some fun." She wasn't sure why but she trusted this man even if she did feel a little disloyal to her mistress. Privately, she thought that Olivia had become utterly selfish where her daughter was concerned.

"Laura looked lovely tonight and, if you'll pardon me saying so, any time you want to go out in the evening I'll be only too happy to stay at the house and look after her mother."

Terry read her message perfectly. She was a delightful lady, full of compassion.

"Thank you, I'll be happy to accept your favour."

By the time he returned Laura had thrown another huge log on the fire and poked it into a blaze. A decanter of brandy, two glasses and a tray of neatly cut sandwiches, which Mrs Oz had prepared, sat on the little square table they'd used for dinner the night he arrived.

"This is cosy, isn't it. Will you have a brandy?" Laura asked, the decanter poised.

"No more for me tonight," Terry said, but seeing the look of disappointment on her face, he relented. "Maybe just a sandwich then, I'm not a great drinker." He felt he owed her something to make up for her spoiled evening. A warning bell sounded in his mind, if he wasn't careful this could get a bit heavy. He was more than happy to brighten her dull evenings and he liked Laura but that was as far as it went. He had no wish to get involved in a relationship with any woman at the moment, particularly one as fettered as Laura.

"Time to hit the sack," he yawned, stretching his arms above his head. He bent down and kissed her forehead. "Thanks for a lovely evening, we'll do it again some time."

Laura sat by the glowing fire too wide awake to go to bed. Life had changed in the short time since Terry had arrived at the stud. It was fun to have someone to share dinner with, someone who really appreciated Mrs Oz's good food too; she'd pulled out all her culinary stops for his benefit. Even her mother seemed to like him and to respect his opinion - at least as far as she knew. During most of their discussions Laura had been banished to the kitchen. The Cinderella syndrome, she giggled, how apt. Her mother would be ideal in the role of an ugly sister, both the ugly sisters. Mrs Oz would be a perfect Buttons. Terry of course fitted the part of the handsome prince. Laura took another swig of the brandy, she was getting really sloshed - but what the heck. Lolling in the chair she pictured herself getting ready to go to the ball, leaving at midnight, her ball gown changing to raggy jeans. Trying on the glass riding boot, which of course would fit perfectly. Terry would rescue her from this terrible prison in a beautiful white Rolls Royce and they would live happily ever after in Mayfair in a tiny mews with flower boxes at every window.

It was almost three o'clock when she woke up, shivering. The fire was dead in the grate and the decanter of brandy was almost empty. Laura struggled to her feet then staggered backwards. Her head ached and her mouth felt as though she had eaten a handful of sawdust. Groaning she lurched up the stairs and collapsed fully dressed on to her bed. Within seconds she was fast asleep.

CHAPTER FORTY-ONE

Olivia Bingham watched the waving shadows of the tree on her bedroom wall. It was her living cinema screen, a barometer of the seasons. How many years was it since she'd been confined to her bed? How many times had she watched the bare winter branches turning to spring buds then blossoming with cloudy flowers? The leaves replaced the blossoms and then completing the cycle they fell, leaving the bare branches to start the process over again. It reminded her of O Henry's story of the young girl who lay dying of pneumonia. She too had watched leaves growing on a vine outside her window, convinced that, when the last ivy leaf dropped, she would die. One stormy wet night her friend, aware of her belief, had in desperation painted a leaf on the wall. When she awoke the following day and saw that the last leaf still clung to the vine, she rallied. Later that day her friend was discovered in his ground-floor apartment lying shivering and soaking wet. His lantern, ladder and paint pot were still in the tiny garden. He was rushed to hospital where he succumbed to a fatal dose of pneumonia.

Stop that, she rebuked herself, you are becoming morbid. Concentrating her mind, she tackled the problem of the stud. Terence Harvey, more than likely, was right. It seemed that every day on the radio racehorse owners were groaning about the recession. She didn't believe the half of it. It had become fashionable to moan.

At every turn someone was urging her to spend money. Laura with her constant nagging about improving the house, Charles always wanting to borrow cash for some business venture or other that couldn't fail. And now, Terence Harvey was suggesting that either they increase the staff or reduce the stables by two-thirds or sell off all her precious thoroughbreds.

When she and William were running things they managed with fewer stable lads than they had now. Typical of today's generation, a bit of hard work and everyone was kicking and screaming.

"I don't have any option, do I?" she said as he waited for her decision.

Terence Harvey refused to influence her one way or the other, leaving the answer in her own hands.

"If we do decide to sell, how do we go about it?" She shifted uncomfortably, wincing with momentary pain.

"Either at auction or, of course, by spreading the word around the private buyers. That's up to you. As a matter of a fact last night at the pub we met some people I know who are members of a large well-funded syndicate. They're here for the sales. When I mentioned that you might be selling some horses, they expressed an interest."

Her eyes narrowed suspiciously. "Quite a coincidence wasn't it - you meeting them accidentally?"

"What are you driving at?" He resented her accusation. "Let's get this straight, Olivia, I was asked to try to get your affairs in order and I'll do so to the best of my ability. But any more remarks like that and I'll be on the next plane out of here. You may treat other people with contempt but *I* won't tolerate it." In his anger he had spoken more bluntly than he'd intended.

She was unused to people answering her with such strong conviction. Most of them deferred to her or, if she was honest, to her disability. "I apologise. Having no control over your own life can be frustrating."

"Now, what have you decided?" His voice was cold.

"I'll take your advice, you'd better put the wheels in motion. We'll sell."

"I'll contact my friends, we don't want to lose them to the auctions." His tone was businesslike. He resented her sharp words.

"Thank you, I'm very grateful," she said, but her feigned humility didn't impress him for a minute.

He didn't exactly bang the door, he closed it firmly, she decided. Why do I always rub people up the wrong way? I'm sure Laura hates me and now Terence has gone off in a huff. Lying here year in and year out is hard but, if I let go of the reins, it will be harder still. The iron hand, that's the only way to keep control. Yes, that's what it is, control, I must keep the control.

Laura, unaware of the contretemps, bounced into the room. "Ready to do the letters?" she questioned cheerfully.

Olivia glanced up from the mess of papers strewn on the bed. Laura looked different with her hair short, better. Her eyes had a shine they didn't normally have.

"Are you wearing make-up, Laura?" She peered at her daughter.

"Yes, a little. The girl who cut my hair said that my eyes needed accentuating so I used some mascara."

"Rubbish! You'll ruin your eyes with that muck."

Laura deflated like a burst balloon. Pleased with the effect of the mascara she'd added a bit of eyeshadow too, carefully copying a model in her magazine.

"I like it," she said, defiantly. "Let's get started, I want to go to the shops this afternoon."

"You went yesterday."

"And I'm going again today."

Olivia sighed, why was everything a confrontation? A knock at her door prevented any further argument.

"May I come in?" Terry stood in the open doorway, his tall frame reaching almost the full height of the lintel. He was still in his outdoor clothes, hands plunged into his jacket pockets, his sandy hair blown from the wind. Although Laura turned her head to the work in front of her, her daughter's half-smile and slight flush didn't escape Olivia's eagle eye.

"Laura, you can leave that for now, we'll do it this afternoon."

"I'm going out this afternoon," she repeated stubbornly. "It will have to wait till tomorrow." She astonished herself with her determination.

"I have made an appointment," Terry said, "the syndicate is very interested in having a look at what we have to offer."

We? Olivia noted, silently. She nodded without speaking.

The Range Rover's wheels crunched on the gravel, spraying it in a wide arc. Honking the horn Laura waved to Terry, who was deep in conversation with one of the grooms. She hummed as she drove towards the town.

There was a parking space right outside the little shop, a good omen. Taking a deep breath and willing herself to be brave she opened the door and strode inside. Up until now she'd never given the shop more than a passing glance. It was like an Aladdin's cave, full of blouses, skirts, suits and dresses, far more cavernous than it appeared from outside. The tall, slim woman was dressed in a grey suit with a crisp white blouse. With a warm smile she encouraged Laura to browse. "If you need any help, just shout," she said, returning to a little table in the front of the window. She watched discreetly until she sensed that Laura was becoming overwhelmed by the large choice, the colours and the sizes. Time to step in, she thought, before the girl loses heart and makes a beeline for the jeans shop. "I'm trying to do the accounts for this lot - it's like a nightmare," she laughed, waving an arm towards the crowded rails.

"Rather you than me. I can't even choose two things that go together." Laura was sorely tempted to pack it in, she really didn't fit in here.

An hour later, soothed by tactful assistance and a welcome cup of tea Laura threw her parcels into the faithful Range Rover and headed for home. She hadn't felt this pleased with herself for years. Sheena O'Loughlin had been a marvel, in no time she put together several outfits that she knew would flatter Laura.

"Come back any time, we'll take them in for you," she said, declaring Laura's need to diet was unnecessary. "You look lovely now so don't starve yourself to death."

Olivia cursed as the paper-knife slipped from her swollen fingers. The room was stiflingly hot and perspiration beaded her upper lip. The breeze blowing through the open window felt pleasantly cool, surely Laura had switched off the fire before she'd left. This cough was irritating.

The high-ceilinged room was unfussy; the bed stood between the two tall windows, shielding Olivia from draughts. On either side of the bed was a table. One held her medicines, a carafe of water and the telephone; the other was cluttered with a bedside light, a radio and her books. Two chairs, covered with faded flowery chintz, filled some of the space on the long wall which she'd privately christened her cinema screen. The battered desk with its typewriter and a small cupboard helped to relieve the boredom of the blank wall opposite. Behind the door was the small wardrobe which held her meagre clothing, mostly nightdresses now. Tucked neatly into the corner of the cupboard stood the compact safe whose key never left its place of safety round Olivia's neck. A circular table with a vase of wild flowers stood between the bed and the door. With its lofty proportions it could have been a lovely room but Olivia Bingham was satisfied with things as they were. Laura thought it was a miserable, bleak room.

CHAPTER FORTY-TWO

"Show Lady Georgina in, please."
Charles Bingham's face was identical in hue to his shirt - white. So this was the crunch. He'd done it now, broken the eleventh commandment - *thou shalt not get caught*. Rumour had it that open prisons weren't so bad.

"Lady Georgina, how lovely to see you." He rushed round to the front of his desk and held the chair for her. She was a formidable lady, imperious and a very rare visitor to the bank. Her unannounced arrival was exceptional.

"Your uncle is too busy to be bothered with me, I understand."

"Not at all, Lady Georgina, he's with a client - a long-standing appointment - and begs to be excused." Charles was telling the truth. On and off for days now his uncle and his cousin had been secreted in his office with a client. This had made Charles even more nervous.

He rested his elbows on his desk, his hands were firmly clenched together under his chin to prevent them from shaking.

"Now, young man, I want you to sell these shares." She pushed a folder across the desk. "Then I want you to buy, and time is of the essence, Treadwell Steel, as many and as quickly as possible."

Charles controlled his trembling as he took the file from her black, lace-gloved hand. Strange to see someone wearing lace gloves these days, he thought. Relief almost paralysed his mind.

The list she handed him was long. The shares were strong, solid even in these days of a wildly fluctuating stock market. A puzzled frown appeared on his forehead.

"Are you sure, Lady Georgina? This is a very sound portfolio, Treadwell Steel is a very minor company."

"I'm positive. Please do as I ask, I have my reasons."

"Yes, of course, but naturally you understand that I'm concerned?"

"My business with the bank is confidential?" She regarded him fiercely.

"Absolutely, Lady Georgina, and highly valued." She should know that by now.

"Very well. I understand there's to be a takeover." She lowered her voice almost to a whisper.

Charles was trembling now even more than before. So that's what it was. He needed to replace her funds immediately. With this information he would have a heaven-sent opportunity of making a killing. He'd have to do some juggling and number-crunching but that was no problem.

"Would you like some tea?" He smiled, his face relaxing slightly.

"No, thank you, I have another appointment."

Resisting his offer to help her from the chair, she walked slowly to the door. "Don't forget, as fast as you can, please," she repeated, pointing her umbrella in his direction.

Charles almost collapsed into his chair. He closed his eyes and, thinking quickly, he worked through a list of possible sources of capital. He was fully aware of the flagrant crime that he'd committed and which he was about to compound with an even bigger sin, insider trading with clients' money.

It had started so innocently, investing his capital in the futures markets. Everything he'd touched had turned to ashes. His costly lifestyle hadn't helped - his flat in Lowndes Square was costing him a fortune and his unsuccessful visits to the races had drained him of everything except his monthly salary. Even his meagre twice-yearly trust fund cheque was already spoken for. He had to pay his racing debts and they had mounted alarmingly.

Resentment welled in his throat. His friends controlled their own destinies while he was supposed to eke out a paltry existence. His mother had refused to give him any more help. She could have got him out of this mess without making the slightest dent in her income. She lived without worry and ran a healthy, profitable business from which he'd never received a penny. And Laura, always moaning and whingeing about the house and the boring life she led. Compared to him she lived the life of Reilly without having to pay for a thing. He was fed up listening to her telling him that he should visit his mother, how could he possibly spare the time? He took enough time off from the bank as it was, for important occasions like The Derby, Ascot, Wimbledon and Cowes week. At the moment he didn't dare to leave the bank for any length of time. Terry Harvey seemed to be running things satisfactorily. Judging by the cheques which were being lodged from the successful sales of the old trout's horses, very satisfactorily indeed. He watched her bank balance grow and that didn't include her accounts in Kildare or the legacy from her own wealthy father. Charles had no access to these. She must be worth millions, he concluded, a sour bile rising in his throat. If only she would help him now instead of leaving it to him in her will - at this rate he would probably be serving a jail sentence anyway. His blood ran cold at the thought and he switched on his computer terminal, pushing the terrifying thought from his mind.

Less than half an hour later he had made his plan. If this didn't work he might as well jump from the window, but it would work - he'd make it work.

CHAPTER FORTY-THREE

The August sun had scorched the grass and dried the stream which ran along the edge of the field before disappearing underground behind the house. Terry swung the picnic basket and Laura carried the old plaid rug. "That's as far as I go," she laughed, dropping on to the grass.

Opening the folds of the rug, Terry shook it until it billowed out and then he laid it on the ground. They sat with the basket between them, the sun beating down on their bare heads.

"This is heaven," Laura sniffed the air, "no rain. I adore picnics."

Terry smiled at her affectionately. She was so candid, so black and white in her likes and dislikes. No grey areas clouded Laura's thinking.

"I'm starving, how about you?" Undoing the peg on the basket she began to put the plates on the rug and examined the contents of the hamper. She found dieting difficult at first but she stuck to it rigidly.

Terry lay back on the rug watching her as she unloaded the food. Tanned from the sun with bare brown arms and slim legs, her hair now streaked with blonde highlights, she made a pretty picture. Her dieting had certainly paid dividends and looking back he could hardly remember the prickly plump girl who'd met him at Dublin Airport four months ago.

"What?" she asked. He was staring at her without realising it.

"Nothing, just dreaming. Let's eat."

They sat in contented silence. Terry ate the delicious chicken sandwiches in Mrs Oz's brown bread - he never tired of it. Laura munched her way through her sandwiches, also chicken, flavoured with lemon juice but rolled in crispy lettuce instead of bread.

"I don't miss the crisps any more," she said, for the fiftieth time.

"So you say, every hour on the hour," Terry teased.

"Yes, I suppose you're right. Still, it's worth it." She waited for him to compliment her on her weight loss. She pulled a face as she drank the slimmers' tonic. She'd kill for a sweet glass of Coke.

"Oh lord, look at the time. I suppose I'll have to be getting back," she moaned, "it's too nice to be indoors." Turning to collect the debris they almost collided with one another, their lips not two inches apart. He put his arms around her and pulled her to him, kissing her lightly and then languorously. She leaned against him until they fell backwards on to the rug. She wound herself around him like a snake. His intention not to get involved was lost and forgotten. Her skin was like silk under his hands, her body supple and pliant. Ripples of pleasure coursed through her body as he caressed her. They murmured loving words as they lay entwined in each other's arms.

Laura ran towards the house as if on winged feet. She dashed up the stairs two at a time. Olivia was irritable and cross. "Where have you been?" she demanded.

Anne Schulman

Laura shivered with pleasure, she could still feel Terry's arms around her, his kisses. An incredible feeling of fulfilment permeated her body. She smiled enigmatically, not bothering to answer her mother. Olivia pulled her mouth into a tight line, suspiciously scrutinising her daughter's dreamy eyes and faraway look.

Terry slowly folded the rug, picked up the basket, and dropped them into the kitchen on his way to the stud. This was the last thing he wanted. He'd fought hard to keep himself from falling for the lovely girl with the open trusting eyes but now he was becoming enmeshed. There was no doubt that Laura thought that she was in love with him but Terry was struggling with his own feelings. He'd been weak and now he'd really complicated the situation. He pushed his misgivings aside and turned his attention to the stable lad, listening attentively to what he had to report.

CHAPTER FORTY-FOUR

Charles was surprised to hear his mother's voice, usually it was Laura who dialled and then put the receiver into her mother's hands.

"What's up, Mother?" he asked.

"Charles, I want Terence Harvey out of here."

"Why?"

"I just do. And as far away as possible."

"What's going on?" Charles demanded to know.

Olivia could see that she was getting nowhere with this conversation. She'd better tell him the truth. "Laura is falling for him and, before things go too far, I want him out of the way - completely out of the way. Far enough away so that she can't get on a plane and follow him, if you understand my meaning."

Charles's mind was working overtime. There were always people in the market for an excellent stud manager. He could certainly put out a few feelers, in fact, one name sprang immediately to mind.

"It'll be expensive." Charles grinned to himself with satisfaction.

"How expensive?" She gritted her teeth.

"Very. If I can persuade someone to take him on there'll be my expenses and the person I have in mind will need some gentle persuasion, if you know what I mean."

"This is pure blackmail," she barked.

"Not at all, it's a business transaction." The

333

man he already had in mind was an Argentinean polo player whose family was as rich as Croesus. He was constantly on the lookout for someone to care for his string of ponies and advise him on future purchases.

"I want Laura to spend a week with you. When she returns, Terence Harvey will have gone."

Even Charles was taken aback at his mother's scheming. "You'll have to find a good reason for her to visit London," she warned. Let him have the worry of that, the blackmailing little sod. How could he do that to his own mother?

Any time now Charles was due to haul in his profits from the takeover. A few thousand pounds from his mother would tide him over and a finder's fee from Alvirez would gild the lily nicely. At long last there was light at the end of the tunnel.

Olivia fretted for two days wondering what was taking Charles so long. She endured the loving glances which passed between Terry and Laura. Now she was positive that they were becoming dangerously close, the sooner he was gone the better.

"Alvirez, my old friend, Charles Bingham speaking."

"Charles, how are you? How did you track me down? I only arrived today."

Charles had been overjoyed to find that Alvirez and his family were expected in England that day for a family holiday. "Can we meet for a drink tomorrow?"

"Well, I promised my wife ... " Alvirez apologised, hesitating.

"This won't take more than a few minutes, I have something to tell you that may be of interest. I promised to speak to Ignacio today but for the sake of friendship I've called you first." Charles was well aware that the very mention of the Brazilian's name was enough to bring Alvirez out in a rash. The fierce competition between the two men was legendary in polo circles.

"Barrett's at one o'clock," Alvirez agreed, his curiosity getting the better of him. If Ignacio was interested then so was he.

Charles pocketed the post-dated cheque, and the two men shook hands on the deal. It had been childishly simple to convince Alvirez that his Brazilian opponent was most anxious to take Terence Harvey into his employ. Signed, sealed and to be delivered - it had taken Charles just ten minutes.

❊ ❊ ❊

Finding an excuse for Laura to visit London had been easy. Her nephew's wedding! Olivia had ignored the invitation. It had been torn up and thrown it in the wastepaper bin with used envelopes and unwanted circulars.

"Of course! I'd forgotten about the wedding." Usually she ignored any correspondence involving family celebrations.

"It's all up to you now," Charles stressed. "How are you going to get rid of him? He's done a good job for you and remember, you mustn't ruin your reputation or his either for that matter."

"You're going to do it for me," Olivia rejoined. "You must telephone him with the offer from your friend and I'll insist he accepts it. When

Laura is with you make sure the telephone in your flat is out of order so that he can't phone her. I suggest that after the wedding you keep Laura in the country until Harvey is out of harm's way."

"And how am I supposed to arrange all that?" Charles could foresee a disastrous mess. It was all too chancy.

Olivia spoke softly into the phone as Mrs Oz closed the windows. Olivia was scared of the big moths which fluttered harmlessly, attracted to the electric lights. Mrs Oz moved quietly about the room. She finished her chores and signalled that she would be back later.

"Don't worry Charles, you just do what I say, I'll see to the rest. I'll speak to you in a couple of days." Without saying goodbye, she replaced the receiver and rubbed her swollen hands. It had taken all her energy to make the call. Whatever the cost, those two must be separated.

Laura glanced through the post as she took it upstairs. Her mother opened the monthly statement from the Bingham bank. It included a handwritten note from her brother-in-law.

"There's a note here from your uncle to remind us about the wedding."

Laura shrugged, what difference, she couldn't go anyway. It didn't bother her particularly. "I suppose I'd better reply. It's rude to ignore it." Laura said, searching in the drawer for some notepaper.

"I think you should go to the wedding." There, she'd said it.

Laura looked at her mother incredulously.

"Pardon?" she said, positive that her mother

had said that she should go to the wedding.

"Have you gone deaf?" Olivia snapped. "I said, I think you should go."

If she went to the local shops Olivia kicked up a fuss, and now she was suggesting that Laura should go to London.

"It's about time we made our presence felt in the family and, as obviously I can't travel, you can represent me. Besides … "

Here it comes, Laura thought, there had to be a reason.

"Besides," Olivia repeated, "there are some papers to be signed at the bank, the second stage of your trust fund." She watched Laura guardedly; had she swallowed the excuse?

Normally Laura would have jumped for joy at the chance to visit London. She hadn't had a holiday for years. Leaving Terry even for a day would be like a lifetime but she wasn't going to look a gift horse in the mouth. Odd, she thought, normally papers like that were sent by registered post.

"Well, what are you waiting for?" Olivia flared, her heart beating fast.

"I suppose I could accept." There was no way she could tell her mother of the reason for her hesitation. And it would be a lovely break. She could visit a theatre, maybe have an evening out with her girlfriends and look round the shops which had never particularly interested her before. She began to feel excited as she picked up the pen to write her reply.

Laura watched the horses grazing in the field as she waited for Terry to come back from a neighbouring stud. He listened to her astonishing news and encouraged her to grab the opportunity. "You'll really enjoy the trip," he said, kissing her forehead tenderly.

"I'll miss you so much," she said as she hooked her arms around his neck.

"I'll be here when you get back," he said.

Laura looked lovingly at his bronzed face. She traced the small crescent-shaped scar at the side of his mouth with her finger and tried hard to remember how things had been before this sandy-haired man with his soft green eyes and rugged face had turned her miserable life around.

Laura sat on the step outside the kitchen and babbled excitedly about her trip to London. She made a list of bits and pieces that she would need for her short holiday. Mrs Oz's expression was grim as she pottered amongst the herbs selecting the best of them for drying. Each year at this time she picked them then tied them into bundles and hung them on old-fashioned meat hooks in the kitchen. She wasn't taking much notice of what Laura was saying, her mind was on the conversation she'd overheard between Olivia Bingham and her son. Unfortunately Laura's sparkling expression when she'd burst into the kitchen garden, had confirmed her suspicions. With a heart of lead she went about her chores, unable to look at the lovely girl sitting excitedly making her notes. How could they do this to her? It was the cruellest thing she'd ever heard. And she was helpless to do or say anything. After all, Olivia Bingham had given her and her son Billy a home and she must never forget that.

Tears of rage and frustration pricked at her

Intrigue

eyes. That poor child, manipulated like a puppet by two greedy unfeeling people. Her own family. Billy had discovered years ago that Charles was an arrogant, difficult and demanding taskmaster. Billy too had gone to England and Charles had given him a job at the bank. But after a short time he left, their childhood friendship came to an abrupt end. At least she knew Billy was happy now. He'd gone back to the work he knew best - working with horses. His last letter had been full of bright news. He was on course to become a manager with one of the biggest trainers in Norfolk and he'd met a lovely local girl.

"What shall I wear to the wedding, Mrs Oz?" Laura repeated.

"Sorry Laura, I was miles away," she said. "I don't really know. Why not treat yourself to something new? Maybe that lady in the shop could help you to choose something."

"Good thinking," Laura replied.

She hoped Mrs Oz's lack of enthusiasm wasn't a reluctance to cope alone.

"Will you be able to manage on your own?" Laura fretted.

"Lord bless you, child. Of course I will, and Mr Terry is here don't forget…" Her voice trailed off. But for how long she wondered?

Packed and ready, Laura went to say goodbye to her mother. "Don't forget your cough medicine," Laura reminded her mother.

"I don't need medicine," Olivia snapped.

In an expansive mood she hugged her mother gently and received a cold peck on the cheek in return. Olivia was not a demonstrative person but that failed to dampen Laura's spirits. Mrs Oz

339

stood by the front door as Terry jumped into the driving seat. "We'll have dinner together when I get back from the airport," he promised.

The car rounded the bend and disappeared from sight. Mrs Oz pulled her apron to her face and wiped away a guilty tear.

CHAPTER FORTY-FIVE

Laura clutched the arms of her seat as the plane hurtled down the runway and rose into the air. A noisy party of football supporters had started their celebrations early, calling to each other with good humour. As the welcome sound of the drinks trolley made itself heard over the drone of the engines the man on her right smiled at her. "Goin' to the match?" he asked.

"I'm playing in it," she answered before she could check herself.

He roared laughing, nudging his red-haired, freckled companion.

"Would ya listen to Lady Di here, she's playin' in the match!"

Leaning forward, the red-headed man grinned at her, his face lighting up with mischief.

"Wha' are you doin' afterwards?"

"Going to listen to some tapped recordings, of course," Laura said straightfaced.

The stewardess interrupted them. Laura ordered a gin and tonic and opened her magazine.

"Would you take a looka' that, she's legs up to her tonsils."

The two men pored over the photograph of a leggy model.

"I saw her on a programme on telly the other day - Linda Evangelical she's called."

"No she's not. Evangelistical, ya eejit."

Laura bit down hard on the inside of her

cheeks to prevent herself from laughing as they discussed the photograph of the gorgeous model, Cindy Crawford.

"Wha'ever she's called I'm free to take her ou' on the town."

"She'd be a big improvement on the dinosaur you'd with you last week."

"Would ya looka who's talkin'? The one you were dancin' wit had a face like a bulldog chewin' a wasp."

Laura closed her magazine. The good-natured repartee between the two was entertainment enough.

Laura said goodbye to her two friends and walked into the bright arrivals hall. She scanned the cardboard name plaques displayed by waiting drivers. Charles had promised to send a car. A fresh-faced man raised his cap politely, somehow it looked all wrong on someone so young. The traffic was heavy and she sat back in the sedate saloon and planned what she'd do with her time. Nadia worked in central London and Laura hoped that they'd be able to spend time together. I should have phoned her from home, she thought, annoyed with herself, I was stupid. Never mind I'll phone her as soon as I get to the flat. Nadia would love Terry. Her heart gave a skip as she thought of his handsome face and the shock of thick hair which fell forward whenever he bent to examine a horse's hoof or pore over stable records. Yes, Nadia would definitely approve. She was going to enjoy this week enormously and Nadia no doubt would round up as many of their other friends as she could.

The car stopped in front of an elegant house.

Intrigue

No peeling paintwork in sight here, Laura noted sourly. She hopped from the car and looked up and down the street with its central grassy park. The period buildings shone with care and attention. And this was Lowndes Square in the heart of Knightsbridge. She envied Charles. Laura tore open the envelope containing the key to Charles's flat and stood aside to let the driver pass. Her suitcase was heavy and she was glad that she didn't have to carry it up the two flights of stairs.

She had imagined the apartment. It would be cosy. All silk-shaded lamps, flower-covered upholstery and antique occasional tables. She smiled her thanks to the driver, then stepped inside and closed the door. Laura clasped her hand to her mouth in amazement. She stared at the stark white, high-ceilinged room with its black furniture relieved only by harsh chrome. Three quarters of the way down the long living-room a four-sided open fireplace acted as a divider between it and the dining area. Fascinated she walked around it. Its gas logs were visible from all angles. She crossed the small hallway to the bedrooms which were equally severe. She chose the smaller of the two.

She slid the mirrored wardrobe door into place, she still wasn't used to the svelte image that confronted her when she came face to face with her reflection. There was a faint resemblance to Princess Di. It was the hair. Laura smiled, remembering her two neighbours on the plane. The kitchen was even more antiseptic than the rest of the flat. Its black granite counters and cupboards were immaculate but cold. She opened the fridge which contained one overripe avocado, three bottles of mineral water, a bottle of champagne and an out-of-date milk carton. She filled the kettle and opened several of the cupboard doors until she found a mug then made herself a cup of coffee. Wandering back to the living-room she placed the mug on a table and rummaged through her bag for her address book. She dialled Nadia's number. It was engaged, then she tried again. The phone seemed to be out of order. She glanced at her watch and realised it would be at least an hour and a half before Charles was home. She picked up her purse and wandered into the warm airless street.

Laura walked along the Square and turned into the Halkin Arcade then sauntered along looking in the shop windows. This was a delightful way to waste time. She was free to meander as the mood took her, no one to think about but herself. She found herself on a small street and went into a mini-market. Although it was full of enticing foods, she kept her shopping to a minimum, some milk and bread, another jar of coffee and a packet of biscuits. The shop assistant didn't speak as she rang up the items on the till. For an instant Laura missed the friendly smiling faces of her shop at home, at home there was always time for a chat and a laugh. But that was there and this is here, she chided herself. She stacked her purchases into the plastic bag and smiled at the girl but received only a cold stare in response. She continued her walk along the smart street with its restaurants and chic boutiques. She noticed that the clothes in the windows of an exclusive dress shop had no price tags. The autumn colours reminded her that, despite the heat, summer was almost over. She might have gone in and looked around but the lack of price tickets made her wary. Instead she crossed the street and bought herself a magazine and a paperback. As she came to the end of the road she realised that she'd walked in a small circle and she started back. In a pretty laneway on the opposite side of the street she saw exactly what she needed, a telephone kiosk.

Nadia was surprised but delighted to hear from her friend. "Of course we can have lunch tomorrow. I'll meet you outside Harvey Nichols. Where are you staying?" she asked.

"Lowndes Square."

"Even better. It's only a two minute walk from there. I'm dying to see you, twelve-thirty OK?"

"Any time, I've only to go to the bank and then the rest of my day is free." Laura rang off, her face creased in a wide smile. She was going to enjoy every minute of her time away from her isolated backwater.

She lay back in the reclining chair and started the book that she'd bought. Charles's key sounded in the lock. Laura swung her legs off the chair on to the white shag-pile carpet.

"Laura?" Charles called from the doorway then came into the room. "Who are ... , Laura? Is that you?" His eyes were unbelieving. The slim attractive girl with the sun-streaked hair who faced him was unrecognisable as his doughy, plain sister with her lumpy sweaters and baggy jeans.

She laughed. Of course, Charles hadn't seen

her for a long time and she was enjoying his confusion.

"My God, Laura. I can't believe you've changed so much, you look, ... you look, ... terrific. What happened?" he blundered, tactlessly continuing to stare at his sister.

"Hello Charles, nice to see you too," she said, looking as aloof as she could manage. She was chuffed by his eye-popping admiration.

"Sorry, I didn't mean to be rude. You look super!"

Laura laughed, letting him off the hook. "That's OK. I suppose I used to look a bit of a disaster."

He threw his jacket on the back of a chair and sat down.

"Would you like a cup of coffee?" Laura asked. He looked whacked.

"No, I think I'd prefer a drink. You?"

Laura shook her head. He went into the kitchen and rattled around opening cupboards and then the fridge. She heard the fizz of a bottle and he called, "Oh good, you've bought bread and stuff. I meant to stop on the way home but I forgot." He dropped back into his chair and sipped his drink appreciatively.

His arrogant face was handsome but the lines around his mouth and his forehead were deeply etched. He'd aged considerably since she'd last seen him, too much for a young man.

Laura shifted in her chair, "By the way, your phone seems to be out of order."

"It's been acting up for a few days now, I've reported it." He ran his finger round the rim of the glass, avoiding her eyes. "Where would you like to eat tonight?"

"I'll leave that up to you - you choose."

"OK. By the way, do you have any plans? We're invited to stay on at Uncle's house after the wedding on Saturday." Charles had no intention of staying buried in the country after the weekend but he wasn't going to tell Laura that. Once he got her there it was going to be difficult for her to leave without a good excuse. He could plead a heavy workload.

"I phoned Nadia, we're meeting for lunch tomorrow." She was disappointed that they were expected to spend time at their uncle's country house. She wanted to be surrounded by concrete and people. "How long do we have to stay in the country?" Her tone was petulant.

"Oh, a few days." Charles dismissed her question nonchalantly. "How did you manage to phone Nadia?"

"There's a call box in the lane at the end of the road. What time do you want me at the bank tomorrow?" Laura asked.

He'd forgotten about the phone box near the flat. But it didn't matter for today. Alvirez wasn't due to phone Terry until tomorrow afternoon. He must make sure that she didn't have easy access to a phone after that.

"Bank? Oh yes, the papers. Any time you like."

The evening was pleasantly cool as they walked along the quiet square. Despite his earlier misgivings he'd actually enjoyed his sister's company. He was proud when heads turned to admire the attractive girl. She had a quick tongue and a welcome sense of humour. That allowed him to forget his worries for most of the evening. A spark of guilt was beginning to ignite, at least for his part in the scheme. If she'd been lucky enough to find someone who was attracted to her, what was the harm? Don't weaken now, he cautioned himself, you need that cheque. The proposed takeover was still in the pipeline but it was taking an inordinately long time. Every week that passed made him more nervous, increasingly anxious. He was living on a knife-edge of worry.

Nadia rushed towards the entrance glancing briefly at Laura as she passed her. "Nadia, come back," Laura called.

The girl in the beige raincoat stopped in her tracks. "Laura?" Her eyes rounded in disbelief.

Laura was really enjoying the reaction to her new appearance. First her brother, now Nadia.

"I don't believe it, you look sensational." Nadia hugged her then pushed her away at arm's length to examine this phenomenon that was Laura.

They ordered lunch and settled in a quiet corner of the buzzing restaurant.

"So *he's* the secret of your success!" Nadia nodded sagely as Laura told her about Terence Harvey. "I must admit your last letter was very chirpy but I'd no idea he'd become such a big part of your life." Secretly she was thrilled - the poor girl lived a dull life but Nadia had never tried to influence Laura to get out and make a life for herself. She was all too aware of Laura's situation. "He must be something special to put that gleam in your eye," she laughed. "What are you doing at the weekend?"

Laura groaned. "Going to a family wedding, deep in the heart of the Gloucestershire countryside. Just what I need, more open fields and horses."

"Never mind, phone me as soon as you're back and I'll round up the girls and we'll have a good night out. Let them have the delight of discovering the 'new Laura' for themselves! How's your mother?" asked Nadia.

"She's OK, bit of a cough, but it's miserable for her lying there." Now that Laura was away her attitude was more charitable.

The hour and a half vanished in a trice. Nadia with her bouncy hair and big open smile hugged her friend again, and rushed to get back to her office. Waiting to pay the bill, Laura thought enviously of her friend's high-powered job at one of London's top estate agencies. The easy casual social life and the hordes of acquaintances and friends. All this could have been hers too. Laura shrugged off her dismal mood. She was determined to make the best of her afternoon, shopping and maybe a film. They were not due to leave London until seven o'clock. By then they should avoid the rush of traffic leaving the capital every Friday.

CHAPTER FORTY-SIX

Charles drove steadily, concentrating on the twisting leafy lanes. Occasionally Laura glimpsed the roof of a sprawling house. Tall gates, thickly planted hedges and trees hid the houses from prying eyes such as hers.

They turned off the main road and pulled to a halt in front of two huge ornamental iron gates and honked the horn. The gates parted in a stately fashion revealing a well-maintained winding drive. Dust rose in a cloud as they made their way along a path just wide enough for two cars. No weeds grew at the edge of the perfectly trimmed lawns and through the open car windows the smell of the newly-mown grass was sweet in the evening air. As the car rounded a bend, she saw a large Tudor house covered in climbing roses. A pond lapped peacefully and ducks glided silently on its glassy surface. The pond was perfectly edged, the grass so green and smooth it would put a bowling-green to shame. How different it was from her own home.

Charles honked the horn again and two young men dressed in tennis shorts and white open-necked shirts appeared at the front door.

"Your cousins," he told her. He'd said very little on their drive, she thought idly, probably he needed to concentrate on the roads.

The two men shook Laura's hand politely, the shorter and younger of the two pecked her briefly on the cheek.

"I'm Andrew, the one for the chop tomorrow," the taller one said, his laughing brown eyes belying his expression of doom.

"And I'm Bertie, the one who's escaped for now."

At first Laura didn't recognise the man who appeared at their side.

"Laura, Charles, good to see you; welcome to Amberhurst." Since she had last seen him, her uncle had put on a lot of weight and his hair was almost grey. Only the twinkling blue eyes and the long remembered fragrance of his aftershave told her who he was.

The brothers carried her cases up the dark-panelled stair-case. Sounds of good-humoured banter echoed behind them. Laura looked around appreciatively. Huge vases of flowers perfumed the air and the windows were thrown open, adding a lightness to the rooms. The heavy furniture was lovingly polished and smelt of beeswax. There were no shabby tables, scratched surfaces or faded coverings. No matted rugs threatened life or limb with their jagged unravelled edges. This was a house that was lived in and loved. Before she could explore any further, a wispy, bewildered woman with a perplexed frown came into the room, her hands outstretched to Laura in greeting. Laura barely remembered her aunt or her cousins. She took an instant liking to the blue-eyed woman whose smile lit up her whole face.

"It's lovely to see you again, we're so thrilled you could come and stay with us." Elenora Bingham's greeting was sincere and warm. "The boys are going out tonight to celebrate Andrew's last night of freedom. I hope you won't mind sharing a quiet evening with your uncle and myself."

"I'd love it," Laura answered quickly, watching the frown disappear from her aunt's worried face.

The chicken salad with honeyed sweet melon and ginger was delicious, the Italian bread studded with olives was as light as a feather. Laura longingly eyed the wonderful chocolate meringue but the battle for her new-found figure was still fresh in her memory. She relaxed in the company of her family. This was something she hadn't enjoyed since she'd been a young child. They weren't the terrible monsters she'd been led to expect, just warm and friendly, entertaining kindly and without fuss.

The rest of the house was just as beautiful. Its age and charm was enhanced by masses of wedding flowers.

Laura and her aunt gazed through the window of Laura's bedroom at the marquee below.

"Why is the wedding being held here?" Laura asked. "I thought it was usually the bride's parents who organised that?"

"You're quite right but Arabella's parents live abroad. All their friends live here and besides, where would you find a better setting for a wedding?"

Laura agreed wholeheartedly. From the huge white tent the sounds of an argument could be heard.

"The caterer and the florist," Elenora grimaced.

"You're not putting your bloody flower stands so near my top table, they're probably full of insects. I don't want them crawling all over the crystal and cloths, thank you."

"Well, where do you suggest that I *do* put them, in my van?" the voice wailed.

"Stick them anywhere you want - I've some good suggestions; but keep them away from my tables, and watch you don't crush those ribbon festoons."

The two men bustled from the tent almost crashing into each other in their fury.

"They've been bickering all day," Elenora said wearily. "Can you imagine how they fight at home?"

Hanging out of the window, Laura laughed heartily as she watched them flouncing towards the house, their scowling faces distorted from above.

"You can laugh, I keep wondering if they'll end up throwing the food over each other before we return from the church." Her aunt suddenly started to giggle with Laura. She turned to her niece and hugged her.

"It's so lovely to have you here. I'm used to being surrounded by men who don't worry about anything. They leave me to do it all for them."

The bride arrived in a flurry of white. Three bridesmaids arranged her veil and her train and three page boys scowled in their satin suits. The service was short and soon they were back in the enormous marquee, complete with insect-free cloths and beautifully arranged flowers. Champagne flowed and voices burbled their greetings. Laura was surrounded by people called Arabella and Regina, Cosima and Caroline, Tarquin and Frederick, even Pogo and Piggy and Twinks. Their surnames were double-barrelled and instantly forgotten. The hats fascinated her. Feathers, straw, birds and flowers collided with each other as their owners kissed air.

She took a glass of champagne and wandered around the marquee. Someone knocked her arm, apologising profusely. "Jeremy!" Laura recognised the man she had met in Kildare, the buyer for the syndicate. Between them they had bought most of the horses. He stared at her blankly, delighted to be accosted by such a pretty girl.

"Laura, Laura Bingham, Kildare? ... Terence Harvey, remember?"

"My goodness I'm sorry, I didn't ... you have," he floundered.

"I know, you didn't recognise me, no one does."

"Alex, come here," he called to his wife. "Do you remember Laura... the stud... in Kildare?

"Nice to see you again," Alex said, politely trying to hide her surprise. "How's Terry?"

"Terry's fine, I'll give him your regards when I get home."

Laura nibbled a tiny sandwich and observed the floating mass of people. They all seemed to know each other. She was quite content to stand on the sidelines quietly watching. Parties and strangers were not her thing. Her mind drifted to Terry and to her mother. If her uncle didn't mind, she'd phone this evening.

The guests slowly dispersed after sending the bride and groom on their way under a hail of rice and confetti. The caterer and the florist appeared to have settled their differences and were sitting on two gilt chairs outside the marquee drinking a well-earned glass of champagne and gossiping like two old women.

Elenora Bingham eased the satin shoes from her feet and collapsed onto a plump sofa, declaring that she would never move again. Laura smiled at her sweet-faced aunt and insisted on making her a good old-fashioned cup of tea. Her uncle, her cousin Bertie and Charles were talking in the garden. Apart from the enormous tent and a few tyre-tracks on the immaculate lawns there were no visible reminders of the day.

Laura went in search of Charles and found him in the study earnestly talking to someone called Alvirez on the phone. As she entered the panelled room with its hammered beams and black oak furniture he suddenly stopped talking, and frowned at her. She left the room closing the door behind her. Maybe it was her imagination but, as she turned the handle, she thought she heard him mention Terry's name.

I must have Terry on the brain, she sighed.

Ten minutes later Charles joined the family in the little conservatory where they indulged in the usual after-wedding gossip. Laura and Elenora discussed the fashions although Laura suspected that was for her benefit as she knew few of the guests. The men discussed business news.

"Johnny Medworth was a happy soul today," Bertie remarked, lolling sideways in the wicker chair, his legs dangling over the arm.

"Poor Georgina Wagstaff won't be," his father replied.

Hearing Lady Georgina's name, Charles sat bolt upright as if he'd been stung. "Why not?" he demanded harshly.

"You remember, she sold most of her portfolio

to buy Treadwell Steel. Didn't you deal with it?"

"Go on," Charles urged.

"The takeover has fallen through and now the banks, learning that the purchasers have backed out, are calling in their loans. Treadwells have gone to the wall. Johnny Medworth has been bought out instead."

Charles's world spun. He fell back in the chair white-faced and faint, the sandwich in his hand pulverised by pressure.

"You all right, Charles?" his uncle asked.

Charles couldn't make his voice reach his throat, it came out as a croak. Pointing to the tray of sandwiches on the wicker table, he coughed.

"Do you want a drink?" Bertie asked.

Charles nodded his head. He fought to bring some sense of reality to his mind. The tens of thousands of pounds that he'd carefully misappropriated from several of the bank's clients, all lost - gone. How long could he keep that hidden? Why had that stupid woman been so certain? His whole life and career were at stake. He had to get out of here and as fast as possible. How soon could he leave without raising suspicion? Wrapped in his own misery he took no further part in their conversation.

The telephone shrilled. "Answer it, Bertie, there's a love," his mother said.

"I'll go," Charles volunteered, anxious to escape his uncle's shrewd gaze.

It was one of the guests thanking them for a lovely afternoon and enquiring if a brooch had been found. Just as he was about to go and ask, the caller's husband shouted that he'd found it. Thinking quickly, Charles returned to the group looking worried. This took no effort on his part. A good friend of his, he lied, had been involved in a car crash and needed Charles' help. He must return to London right away. Laura jumped up offering to pack immediately. "No, you mustn't leave on my account." His tone was insistent. "I'll probably be at the hospital all night."

"You must stay Laura. We've had so little time to get to know you," her aunt pleaded.

Charles kissed his aunt and shook hands with his uncle. He promised to phone Laura and fled as fast as he decently could. Five minutes later they heard the roar of his engine as his car sped down the drive.

CHAPTER FORTY-SEVEN

Terry strode quickly over the cobbles of the courtyard towards the house. This was the first time he'd heard the clanging bell since Laura had left. He bounded up the stairs and knocked lightly on Olivia's door.

"Come in," she called impatiently. "There's a call for you." She handed him the phone and lay on the mound of pillows watching every flicker of his eyes. She listened to the one-sided conversation. Her heart thudded uncomfortably. He was going to turn the job down.

"Ask him to ring back," she mouthed.

Terry replaced the receiver and stood beside her bed. Just in time. She'd prevented him from refusing Alvirez's offer out of hand.

"A job offer, I gather. Before you refuse it I must tell you that I'm seriously thinking of closing the stud. I haven't been feeling well lately." She held out her swollen hands. "I don't know how long I can continue like this. Laura certainly can't manage things." Olivia stopped, searching his face for a reaction. " I'm quite prepared to let you leave. I gather that you'll be needed almost immediately?"

Terry stared at her with unseeing eyes. Argentina. He'd always wanted to travel, and the Alvirez ranch was reputed to be superb. The salary that the Argentinean had offered him was staggering. Laura, what about Laura? Her situation hadn't changed; with her mother's health it would probably get worse. She'd be tied down for years to come. Argentina could be the answer, two years minimum with an option on either side to renew the contract. It was an exciting opportunity, he could even start his book while he was there, something he'd been promising he'd do for years.

"It is a wonderful offer," he admitted after what seemed to be a lifetime of silence to Olivia.

"Very well," Olivia said, decisively. "Phone him back and tell him you accept. When does he want you?"

"Wednesday. He and his family are returning to Argentina and as they're using the family jet, I can travel with them."

"How the other half live," Olivia remarked sourly, through a fit of coughing.

Make the call, she begged silently.

Everything had been agreed and Olivia practically collapsed with relief. He would take an early flight on Wednesday morning and should be in Heathrow in plenty of time to join the Alvirez family on the long flight to Argentina - as far as Olivia was concerned that was a million miles away on the other side of the world, totally out of Laura's reach. For once Charles had done the right thing.

Book Two

Gaby

CHAPTER FORTY-EIGHT

The bedroom she'd left twenty minutes ago bore no telltale signs of the morning's fevered activity. The bed was freshly made and the furniture was polished. Only her two cases - packed and ready in a corner - gave any reality to her nightmare. For one ridiculous moment Gaby wondered if she'd dreamt the whole thing.

"Gaby, I have a cup of tea for you." She recognised Jill's voice through the closed door. Who else was downstairs in the drawing-room of the suite, watching and waiting to see how she reacted? Jilted, what an old-fashioned word; stood up, left in the lurch, dumped - yes, that was it, dumped. Dumped, for all the world to see. *Whisper! whisper! Such a dreadful thing, such a shameful thing to do to poor Gaby. He didn't seem to be the type, did he? What went wrong?*

"Gaby, please open the door," Jill pleaded. "The tea's getting cold."

Kicking a shoe away from her, slowly Gaby walked to the door and unlocked it. Unceremoniously she plumped back down on the side of the bed, her beautiful dress trailing unheeded on the floor around her.

"Drink this, it'll do you good. That sounds so stupid, but I really don't know what else to say." Jill peered at Gaby nervously. She *seemed* calm enough and collected. The only sign of disarray was the satin shoe lying forlornly on its side.

"Talk to me, Gaby, don't bottle it up."

"You mean, don't let it happen again - don't get depressed again?"

"I can't blame you for being angry, but..."

"...but he's not worth it, is that what you were going to say?" Gaby lashed out.

"Well, he's not, he's a cowardly bastard," Jill said vehemently, "unfair and unreasonable."

Gaby looked at her friend for the first time since she had entered the room. Worry is written all over her face, concern for me, and I'm taking it out on her, she thought.

"Jill, please, I'm sorry. It's not your fault."

Jill sat beside her on the bed and took Gaby's hand in her own.

"Who's downstairs?" Gaby asked.

"Your Dad, Stephen Drake, Róisín and Seán, Jacqui and Colin, Patrick and Amanda, Matthew, Gerry Oscar - only close friends."

"I can imagine them all standing around like spectres at the feast."

"That's not fair. We all care about you, all love you. Whatever you may think right now, we're on your side."

Gaby got up and walked over to the mirror. She looked just the same, she could see no difference. She sensed Jill's anxious eyes watching her.

"You look worse than I do," she said, turning to Jill. Suddenly, and without warning, laughter welled up in her throat.

Jill tried not to let her alarm show.

"Look at us, all dressed up and nowhere to go!" Gaby giggled and then the tears came. For ten minutes she cried, great streaming, hot, drenching tears. Jill put her arm round her shoulders and held her friend, making no attempt to stop her.

"It's not fair," Gaby sobbed with rhythmic gulps, "*he* knew I wasn't responsible for that girl's death - the witnesses said so. She ran straight out in front of the car, but he still blamed me."

"*Everyone* knows it wasn't your fault, Gaby. Look at it this way, if there'd been any doubt you'd have been charged, wouldn't you?"

Gaby nodded, wiping her mascara-ed eyes on the hem of her exquisite dress. "I suppose that's true."

"Gaby, can I say something? It seems to me that you're hurting far more from his unfairness than from the fact that he…"

"…dumped me?" Gaby said bluntly.

"Well I wouldn't have put it like that, but OK. Am I right?"

Silences between them were never a problem and Jill continued to sit quietly beside her friend.

"I was crazy about him." The tears flowed again. "But you could be right. It *is* the unfairness of it. Maybe my pride too."

"Can you imagine living with a man like that? God knows what else he might have done. Your father had a fax a few minutes ago. The bastard has cancelled their business deal too - not that your Dad would have gone through with it himself after this."

Afterwards when she thought back to that horrible day it was his treatment of her father that hardened her heart. She simply wouldn't let thoughts of Myles Richards plunge her back into the depths of depression, be sucked back into that black abyss.

"I never want to see this dress again," Gaby said firmly, her chin stubbornly set. "Can you get rid of it for me? And the shoes and this..." She ripped the head-dress from her hair and crushed it in her hand.

"Yes, sure. I don't blame you." Jill detected a new determination in her friend.

"I'm going to change now and then we'll go downstairs."

John O'Neill sat on the arm of a chair talking to Gerry Oscar. Stephen Drake had walked the length of the church aisle and in a calm voice announced, "I'm sorry. There'll be no wedding." He had offered no reason, made no apologies. Then - this was John's idea - Stephen had invited their closest friends back to the hotel. Some of them had travelled a fair distance, the least John could do was to see that they had lunch.

Chefs hurried around the kitchens reorganising the aborted wedding lunch for the reduced number of guests in the Penthouse Suite. As Jill came back downstairs followed by a jeans-clad Gaby, all talk in the room ceased.

Clearing her throat, Gaby faced the silent gathering.

"You all know what happened at the church - please, don't feel badly for me. I can't pretend that I wasn't hurt, still am, but obviously I've had a lucky escape. You're all friends here and I know I have your support. Please try to salvage what's left of the day - there's a lot of food to be eaten up here, so get to work!"

John O'Neill was at his daughter's side in a

couple of short strides. "I'm so proud of you," he said.

"I'll be OK, Dad, don't worry. It'll take a bit of time, but I won't let that creep get the better of us - Jill told me he's backed out of the Spanish deal too."

"That's the last of our worries. As it happens I have someone else who may be interested, but that's unimportant now, forget about it."

"Let's try to forget about everything and enjoy being with our friends." Jill's reprimand had struck home. "We'll talk tonight, OK?"

When their guests left John and Gaby sat in the big living-room. Gaby lolled sideways in the chair, bare feet dangling over the side.

"Can you believe that despite everything, I enjoyed this afternoon?" Gaby said, selecting a dainty sandwich from the platter balanced on her knees.

"Me too. Once I heard what you had to say and saw that you were fighting fit, I relaxed too. After you went to your room, I have to admit that I was worried. I appreciated that you needed to be alone but I must confess I was concerned that you might do something, well - to be honest, to harm yourself."

"No way! I wouldn't give him the satisfaction. But someday, somehow, I'll make him pay for what he's done."

CHAPTER FORTY-NINE

Gaby and Jill sat in their favourite corner of the big lounge in the hotel waiting for Jacqui to join them.

"I've had a good look at what's available on the property market, but I honestly don't see anything that's right at the moment. Something will come up, it always does," Jill said, in a placatory voice.

"It's not a problem, I can stay on here. Dad's altered his plans and he'll be in Dublin for another six weeks at least. We've moved out of the Penthouse Suite now - more's the pity! It's been an expensive few months, well you can imagine," Gaby laughed, rolling her eyes in horror.

"Hi, am I late?" Jacqui asked, smiling at the two girls. "Oh great, you've ordered - I'm famished."

"How are things going with the big job?" Gaby enquired. She'd been delighted when she heard that Jacqui had landed a contract to cater for an important medical conference.

"Not bad, considering. It gets a bit hairy at times, but so far ..." Jacqui crossed two fingers of her right hand.

"You'll do it brilliantly, you always do," said Jill.

"Make that by two," Gaby added, "I'm with her."

"How's the house-hunting going?" Jacqui

asked, smoothing some pâté on a piece of toast.

"Nothing yet, but I'm looking," Jill assured her, more for Gaby's benefit than Jacqui's.

"Now that we're all here, come on Gab, spill the beans, what's your news?"

"I've decided to go to college, to take a proper computer course."

Their faces were a study. Laughing, Gaby said, "Don't look so surprised. I've thought about it all week and this morning I finally took the plunge and enrolled."

"It's a great idea, but how long will it take?" Jill recovered first.

"About a year. There are several courses, some very difficult, some not, but the best for me is a programming course. That'll take a year."

"You'll enjoy it. You've always been good with those ghastly machines. One day I might get you to teach me, but I doubt it!" Jacqui groaned.

"Like me learning to cook?" Gaby retorted. "I've just had a horrible thought, if we do find a house, I'll have to cook. Watch out McDonald's, here I come."

"Now I have news," Jacqui smiled, her timing was perfect. "We're expanding the business and going to do meals for home freezers."

"Brilliant!" Gaby said, "I'll be your best customer. Put it on the list, Jill - there must be plenty of room in the kitchen for a massive freezer, to heck with cupboards."

Jacqui didn't have the heart to tell Gaby that the idea for her new venture had come to her when she had first heard that the O'Neills had decided to buy a home of their own. She'd wondered how they'd exist on Gaby's cooking and then it struck her that there must be other women like Gaby, women who worked full-time, and men on their own.

"Can't you just see me at the head of the table accepting compliments for my exquisite food? 'It's nothing,' I'll say, brushing it aside."

"You wouldn't be the first. At one dinner party I catered, the hostess beamed graciously until she was asked for the recipe, then she stuttered and stammered because she didn't know if the mousse I'd served was made from chicken or fish! Don't you remember the night at Marie's? The night she served the cake from the supermarket and passed it off as her own?"

"I don't remember, what happened?" Jill asked.

"There was a plaster in it."

"Oh yes! I remember now," Jill smirked.

"Warning received and understood," Gaby laughed.

John and Gaby almost simultaneously came to the same decision. It was time for them to have a home. "Wouldn't you prefer to have your own flat?" he offered, hoping that she would decline.

"Positively not." Gaby was adamant. "We've always lived together. We've been happy - besides, what would be the point of your coming home to an empty flat? You might as well live at the Berkeley Court as we've always done. Or, own up, is it the thought of my cooking?"

John laughed, the girls had often regaled him with stories of Gaby's culinary disasters. He could live with that, but he was pleased that they'd stay together. He'd miss her company on their trips but she needed an anchor, a proper home, now more than ever.

Intrigue

"I did tell 'El Soddo' that I might take cookery lessons, but I've been thinking about it and it's not on. I've decided that a computer course would be more my line."

"That's an excellent suggestion. I think it'd be good for you."

"Keep me off the streets, you mean."

"That too," John grinned, marvelling at the speed of Gaby's recovery. She never used Myles Richards' name, instead bestowing on him more disparaging nicknames than John ever imagined existed. It was a harmless way of venting her anger, a safety valve.

CHAPTER FIFTY

She enjoyed the walk from the Berkeley Court to Leeson Street each day. Most of the students were much younger but there were two or three people of her own age too. She slipped into the work with ease, delighted to meet the challenge. Her teacher, a jolly-faced lady with a good sense of humour, knocked the mystique of computing on the head with her down-to-earth approach. The days spent at Keyboard were satisfying, her life had routine and a pattern.

"Is anyone sitting here?" a voice asked.

"No, no one," Gaby answered, looking up from her book.

The pretty girl with the cornflower eyes plonked herself unceremoniously on the seat opposite, disgorging parcels in a heap at her feet. "Haven't I seen you at Keyboard?" she asked frowning. Gaby was far too attractive to go unnoticed, especially in a small college like theirs.

"That's right. And I've seen you, in the hallways."

"You're obviously with Nóirín, I'm in Barbara's class. Would you mind keeping an eye on my things while I summon up the energy to find something to eat?"

"'Course, no problem," Gaby said affably. "The curry's good."

The petite girl wrinkled her nose. "It'll take me all my time to swallow some tea, shopping's not my thing and when I do have to do it, I get bad-tempered for hours afterwards. As for the sales - they make me almost suicidal, give me a computer problem any day."

Gaby laughed and, placing her open book on her knee, she stacked her plates and cup and saucer into a neat pile to make room on the small table.

"At least it's healthy," the girl said, unloading a glass of apple juice and an open sandwich of cottage cheese and sliced peach from the tray. "I'm Mary Anni Elizabeth Jane Brigitte Maguire - in short Janey."

"Gabrielle, blank, blank, blank O'Neill, alias Gaby."

The two girls laughed. "Maybe I should borrow some of your names," Gaby said.

"Be my guest. Did you ever hear anything like them? The only time I use them is at a time like this - you must admit they make a great ice-breaker. Sometimes at night if I can't sleep I repeat them over and over, it's easier than counting sheep!"

Gaby picked up her book and they sat in silence while Janey ate her lunch.

"That went down all right," Janey said, sitting back in her chair. "How long before we have to get back to class?"

Gaby looked at her watch. "Another three quarters of an hour."

"Thank heavens, it'll take me all of that to collect the parcels and get to my feet. As well as having five names I have five brothers and sisters, two parents, one grandmother and two uncles and aunts. It's easier to shop for their

Christmas presents now than on Christmas Eve. That's what I used to do, it was cheaper too. My cousins and I have now made a pact, no gifts."

"I don't envy you - shopping for that mob I mean - not for having all those brothers and sisters. That must be fun - I'm an 'only' myself."

"Yes it is really, except at times like today. It must be strange not to have loads of siblings all nicking your clothes or your notepaper, using all the hot water or laddering your best pair of tights - and that's just my brothers!"

Gaby laughed again. She liked the girl's sense of fun, the impish twinkle in her eyes. Janey's hair was much fairer than her own, straight, almost white and cut in a shiny bob. There was something Slavic about her clear little face. Gaby admired the golden skin, the incredibly blue eyes, the small straight nose, upward-tilting high cheekbones and naturally pink mouth. In fact, Janey was quite simply beautiful.

"You're wondering if that's my natural hair colour?" Janey challenged.

"Yes, I was." If Janey could be honest, so could she.

"It is. My mother is Swedish and as fair as me."

"My hair is aided and abetted by streaks in winter, in summer it takes care of itself," Gaby confided.

"Do you live in Dublin, I mean, all the time?" Janey asked. "My home town is in Meath, but I've a flat here, not far away, Dartmouth Square. It's very handy, just a hop, skip and jump and I'm in Leeson Street."

Before Gaby could answer the question as to where she lived, Janey groaned, "We'd better leg it, or we'll be late."

Carrying half her parcels for her, Gaby slowed her stride to allow Janey's dainty feet to keep up. She's like a porcelain doll, Gaby thought, one puff of wind and she'll blow away. They reached the college and separated at the stairs leading to the first floor. "I enjoyed meeting you," Janey smiled.

"Any time you fancy having a bite, not a 'byte'," Gaby laughed, "you know where I am."

"Gladly. I have lunch out three times a week, that's all the budget will allow."

It was quiet in the drawing-room of the smaller suite, nothing but the tap of keys disturbed the silence. I really miss Dad's company, Gaby thought, it's too quiet here on my own. She got up from the towel-protected inlaid table which served as a desk for her computer and arched her back, then she massaged the stiffness from her neck. Jill was in London and Jacqui was up to her eyes with plans for Ice-Savers, her new company. She and Janey had lunch together at least twice a week, and Gaby had suggested that they might meet one night and go to a film. But Janey had refused. She told Gaby that one night was taken up waitressing in a club and she baby-sat most evenings as well. At weekends she hitched a lift home to Meath from a neighbour who worked in Dublin. "Maybe we could go out on a weekend when I'm not going home?"

Janey was the most blisteringly honest person Gaby had ever met. Gaby had considered that one of her greatest skills was the ability to judge people at a first meeting. As far as Janey was concerned, Gaby freely admitted to herself, she couldn't have been more wrong. The delicately-boned girl, with the *helpless-little-doll* appearance was the most single-minded person she had ever met, with the exception perhaps, she reminded herself, of "Prince Rat".

"You certainly know where you're going," Gaby said, as Janey mapped out her future plans.

"My family says I have tunnel vision, but let's face it, that's better than wandering all over the tracks."

"So you have to study here, then you'll be sponsored by the firm in the States?"

"Bingo! That's why I'm doing systems analysis too, three years altogether. My boyfriend's boss has agreed to sponsor me, all I have to do is get my degree and find the cash to get there. I'll need to have a few bob in my pocket besides the fare. The sooner the better I can tell you, I don't fancy him wandering around Silicone Valley without me. You know those Californian beauties, not a reassuring flaw in sight, and my God, those teeth! I swear they have at least four more than Europeans do."

"Do I detect a hint of jealousy?" Gaby teased.

"Damn right you do. Hugh Breen is the greatest thing since electricity, and if anyone's going to blow their fuse over him it's going to be me."

"I've got the message," Gaby laughed, "you're a real tiger where he's concerned, aren't you?"

Janey growled her assent. "By this time next year I hope to drag him up the aisle, mind you, there'll be no objections from him," she added. "What about you, Gaby? Anyone special in your life?"

Janey had established an image for herself as a tough, no-nonsense girl. But not too far below the surface was a sensitive soul. She saw the dart of pain which crossed Gaby's face.

"Oops! sorry, I've touched a nerve. I didn't mean to upset you."

"You didn't. Maybe I'll tell you all about it sometime, now is too soon."

It was a bitterly cold November. All through the night the snow fell, huge flakes of starry-cold. The paths around the hotel bore the car-tracks of the early movers. Warmly wrapped up, Gaby gathered her papers and opened the door, her taxi would be here in a few minutes. The burring of the telephone brought her scurrying back.

"Gaby, it's Jill. I think I may have found just the thing for you." Her voice sounded excited.

"Fantastic! What? Where?"

"In Monkstown, off the main road. It's a bungalow, but I won't tell you any more about it now. How are you fixed tomorrow? We could go and see it then."

"Tomorrow's fine, the sooner the better, unless we get snowed in."

"Then we'll put snow chains on the car," Jill offered laughingly. "Come and have lunch with me at the flat and then you can drive me there."

"Can't you come here instead?" Gaby pleaded, "you know how I hate to drive now."

"No Gaby, it's awkward, I'll expect you around twelve-thirty. Must rush now, I'm late, see you then, bye." Without giving Gaby time to argue, Jill hung up and sat down to finish her coffee. It was mean of me to do that, she told herself, but it's the only way to encourage her to get behind the wheel of a car again. Uncle John had made her promise that she wouldn't go on being a chauffeuse. He'd asked her to tell Jacqui the same thing. Keyboard was near the hotel and, on the odd bad day, according to her father, Gaby took a taxi. It was vital that she regained her confidence, especially if she was considering living in the suburbs.

Gaby arrived at the flat without mishap but she was a bit shaky. Jill ignored the signs and led the way into the modern kitchen with its tiny table. "I thought you might enjoy one of my new concoctions, no offence taken if you don't!"

"This soup is lovely," said Gaby. She had reached the stage where she was impressed with anything that didn't come out of a packet or a tin. Jill drained the pasta over the sink and with a long-handled spaghetti spoon scooped it onto the plates.

"That's downright professional," Gaby laughed, "watch out Jacqui, here she comes."

"Taste it first, then rave," Jill advised.

The sauce was creamy and tangy. "I can taste basil, garlic?"

Jill nodded. "Keep going."

"Tomatoes, cream and something else. It's really great."

"We can please ourselves what time we go today, but I gather you'd like to leave now," Jill smiled as she drained her cup.

"I'm dying to see it, especially as you won't tell me anything about it. Will you drive? You know the way."

"Listen Gabs, I understand your feelings about driving, really I do. But think, if you like this place or any other for that matter and you move out to the suburbs, you can't rely on taxis or friends. In a little while you'll stop being frightened. You'll be confident again but not if you don't try."

Gaby agreed, but she wasn't happy.

The snow had melted to a mush and Gaby drove slowly, jamming on the brakes whenever a pedestrian threatened to cross the road. Jill ignored the nervous braking and chattered normally.

"Turn left just after the next lamppost, there, the gate on the right."

"Oh Jill, just look at that, it's gorgeous!"

They sat in the car halfway along the curving drive. The bungalow was an old-world cottage complete with a scalloped, thatched roof. Melting snow still clung to the branches of the trees, dripping on to flowers and plants in the raised rockeries. Lawns lay sleeping peacefully under their blanket of white. "Can you imagine all this in summer? Tea on the lawn - with Jacqui's cakes!" They laughed uproariously.

"Barbecues at night…"

"…With Jacqui's burgers," they chorused.

"That's very hurtful," Gaby said, wiping away an invisible tear. "But true!"

She drove the few yards to the oak door at the front entrance.

Jill handed her the key and followed her through the door of the cottage into a square hallway. "Look at those beams, they look like they've been there forever." Gaby pointed to the coved ceiling.

"It's eighteenth century, with twentieth century

additions," Jill explained.

At the end of the hall two glass doors led to the back garden. From where they stood they could see an arch which was formed from the bent boughs of trees. It was still covered with the wintry skeletons of climbing roses.

"Look in here," Jill called as Gaby stood with her nose pressed against the panes of the double glass doors. Gaby paused on the edge of a room which was about twenty-five feet long. She gasped with delight at the spread of windows, two of them deeply curved bays all with tiny panes of diamond-shaped leaded glass.

"Certainly in keeping, aren't they?" Gaby said tracing the pattern of the cold diamonds with her finger. A round dining-table with its chairs fitted neatly into the curve of one of the bays. In the other niche, a window seat heaped with coloured cushions caught the weak afternoon sunshine.

"Can't you just see it?" Gaby enthused. "Sitting here in the sunshine, reading or listening to music? All the furniture seems to be new. Look at those couches and chairs, the fabric is wonderful - cabbage-roses, so right for a cottage."

Empty bookshelves waited for their burden and Gaby ran her fingers along the uneven wood lovingly. She thought of her books, piled up in cupboards on the top floor of the office, and imagined them in the mahogany bookcases in front of her. They'd be perfect here, bright-coloured dust covers properly displayed at last.

"This is the end," Gaby said, standing in the centre of the bedroom floor. Another stretch of windows, broken only by the narrowest of walls, greedily extracted every ounce of winter sunlight.

Most wonderful of all was the door leading straight out to the garden. The double bed, still in its plastic wrapping, stood importantly all on its own. Wardrobes occupied a full wall opposite the windows. A door led to the bathroom, tiled from ceiling to floor with the palest of pink tiles. Even Gaby was impressed by the kitchen with its old-fashioned dresser, concealed ironing-board and white machines, all brand new. There, in all its white glory, was an empty alcove.

"Freezer space!" Jill laughed, "just as you ordered."

"I can't talk, it's all too good to be true." Gaby was entranced.

"Come and see the rest."

They sat on either side of the empty stone fireplace. "OK, what's the suss?" Gaby demanded. "Apart from the age of the building everything looks new."

"It is. It was bought, totally renovated and furnished by a young American couple. They were crazy about it and due to move in this week when, without warning, the husband was given a super promotion, an offer he couldn't refuse. Their problem was that his new position is in London."

"What about the furniture, carpets and everything?"

"All included in the price. These Americans have to leave almost immediately and the ultra-modern flat they've been given is 'designer-fitted' from head to toe. So they decided to sell the cottage as is."

"I wish Dad were here, he'd love this. He'd love the added wing of the cottage. The study is large enough for an office and there's loads of room for a couple of easy chairs, or sofas even, at the fireplace. Sometimes he likes to read and work on his own. Wouldn't that be an ideal room for it? Are there other people interested? There must be, it's so gorgeous," Gaby asked anxiously.

"Luckily I'm the sole agent so naturally I haven't shown it to anyone else yet. My gut feeling told me this was the ideal place for you and Uncle John, not too far from town but with a country air to it."

Slowly this time, they went back through the picturesque cottage, all pinks and creams and greens. Apart from the gardens, the cottage could be easily managed. The division of rooms was ideal - John could have his quiet zone whenever he needed it and at other times he could join Gaby in the main part of the house.

"The answer is yes, I love it." Gaby's green eyes sparkled. "I'll talk to Dad tonight. I can't wait to tell him. The only problem is that he could be away for at least another week."

"Speak to him, see what he says. Now, what are we going to do with ourselves for the rest of the day and night?"

"We're going to commemorate this marvellous find. Let's go and see Jacqui and persuade her to come out with us. We'll book a table and have a super meal. We haven't had a night out together for ages."

Jacqui was lying on the floor on her tummy, her cookery books spread all around in ordered disarray. "Be a pet, answer the door, will you Colin? I'm in the middle of writing a list for this recipe."

Her head lifted from the book as she heard the voices. Before he and Jacqui were married, Colin had worried that Gaby and Jill, still footloose and free, might have had an unsettling effect on his future wife. But his fears were unfounded. The girls had been as good to him as they had to Jacqui. They'd included him, elected him an honorary fourth member of their trio. Gaby's quiet word with her father had succeeded in landing him a far better position with a multinational firm than he could ever have dreamt of. Their financial worries had floated away in an instant. Now they could afford to do all the repairs and additions to their home. Colin could redesign his garden and Jacqui could plant her longed-for herb garden. Just that morning after the children had been whizzed away by friends for a short weekend, they had spread big sheets of graph paper on the kitchen table and started discussing their plans.

"Hey you two, what brings you this way?" Jacqui demanded.

Tripping over her words with excitement, Gaby described the cottage and its garden. "We'll need your help and advice, Colin, you'll freak when you see the garden, overgrown but beautiful; great potential."

"Say no more, I'm all yours."

"Oh no you're not," Jacqui said, slapping him lightly on the leg with her notebook, "my herb garden comes first, sorry Gaby!"

Always glad to have guinea pigs on whom she could try her recipes, Jacqui insisted that they forget about going out and stay to have dinner with her and Colin instead.

"Marks out of ten, please," Jacqui requested when the delicious meal was over.

"Ten," Jill held up the fingers on both hands.

"Ten." Colin followed suit.

"Gaby?"

"One."

"One? Didn't you like it? You ate it all, what was wrong?"

"I loved it. But I'm sulking because you wouldn't give up your chance of a herb garden for me."

"Idiot," Jacqui laughed, throwing her napkin at Gaby.

Gaby waited anxiously for John's call. Before he had a chance to say hello, she launched into an enthusiastic verbal tour of the cottage that would have put Jill's copywriter to shame.

"I gather you're taken with it?" John could imagine Gaby's eyes flashing as she talked.

"You could say that, yes! I'm a bit over the top, aren't I?"

"What's the asking price for this dream cottage?"

He whistled softly as she told him the price. "That's a bit steep, isn't it?"

"It does include all the furniture, carpets and fittings. The only major item that we'd need is a freezer. We *could* manage without one, but it means you'd have to suffer my cooking."

"Sweetheart, the freezer in your case is not a luxury, it's a necessity!"

"Charming! Seriously though, when are you coming home? Jill is quite prepared to hang on till you get back, but the sooner the better."

Intrigue

"What does she think of it?"

"The cottage or the price?"

"Both."

"Now that you mention it, she said very little. I suppose she didn't want to influence me. She does like it enormously, that I do know, and when she first phoned me she said she thought it was just the thing for us."

"OK. If Jill thinks it's good value, then go ahead and start things rolling. Tell her to use all her negotiating powers - and haggle. I should be back within ten days maximum."

As she undressed Gaby hummed a tune, something she hadn't felt like doing for a long time.

CHAPTER FIFTY-ONE

She threw her finished shopping list into the trolley and pushed it towards the checkout. With grim persistence and months of heartbreaking failures, Gaby had finally succeeded in breaking the jinx on her cooking. Slowly she had gathered together a series of simple but tasty dishes. Her failures were a secret between her and her dustbin. Determination drove her to keep on practising until she felt competent enough to invite Jill, Jacqui and Colin to dinner.

Their praise was music to her ears. They would have said it was good no matter what she cooked, but she knew that their compliments were sincere.

"You can come to dinner twice more," she said, " then we go round again."

After she had survived three dinner parties she plucked up courage and invited Janey for the weekend. February had dragged by. She was a bit bored by parts of the computer course. A lot of it she'd done before. Her father's absence made the evenings long and Janey's company would be a tonic. She chopped the vegetables, added them to the softening onions, poured in stock and placed the lid on the saucepan.

The timer would remind her when she needed to put the chicken in the oven.

Gaby smiled as she thought of her phone call to the butcher. "I need a chicken, a really beautiful plump one," she appealed.

"A VIP chicken for Miss O'Neill," he called to his assistant.

She checked that the fire was burning cheerfully and hurried to change into jeans and a comfortable sweater.

Rosy-cheeked from the sharp winter air, Janey pressed the bell.

"What a heavenly cottage!" she said as Gaby opened the door.

"Come in. As my first overnight visitor you're doubly welcome." Gaby took the small hold-all from her and shut out the cold air.

"It's warm as toast here, it's going to freeze out there tonight."

Janey followed Gaby into the kitchen and sniffed appreciatively. "I thought you couldn't cook," she said, lifting the lids off the saucepans.

"I couldn't, but I was determined to learn. This weekend you can suffer the fruits of my labours."

With her timer beside her Gaby sat on the floor near the fire. She had drawn the curtains and the room was bathed in the glow from the lamps and the orange firelight. In the alcove on the table set for two, a pretty bowl of early spring flowers predicted warmer days to come. "It's a shame in a way," Gaby said, when Janey admired the arrangement, "the seasons have melded into one. Strawberries all year round, daffodils in January, salmon in season all the time. We were invited to a wedding in London last December, it was held at the bride's home in a marquee which included the rose garden. Apparently the bride's mother had restrained herself from pruning the bushes. Before the wedding the florists, armed with thousands of roses from buds to full-blown blooms, had wired each one individually on to the bare branches. In the heat of the marquee and with the perfume from the roses it was like a summer's day, June in December."

"I know just what you mean. You can choke on cherry stones all year round now. In June when we were kids we must have used gallons of calamine lotion for our strawberry rashes, even scratching the itch was fun. We always ate far more than was good for us. Then there was a mad scramble to see who could get the cream from the top of the milk. Nowadays it's all irradiated fruits and antihistamines - and when did you last manage to pour any cream out of a carton of milk?"

The soup was flavoursome and hearty. "That was good," Janey said, tipping up her bowl to scoop up the last chunks of vegetables. The chicken, stuffed with apricots and pine nuts, was awarded grunts of appreciation. Gaby relaxed, she'd broken her own rule of trying out something new before springing it on someone else. Jacqui was right, it had been quite foolproof. Only one cut on her finger. She had followed the illustrations assiduously on how to make potato fans and, now that she saw the golden results, she decided that, if they weren't a world record, they were certainly a personal best. The rest was easy. She had picked leaves from the garden and oiled them to make them look glossy. On the leaves she built a pyramid of fresh fruit which to her delight stayed upright as she brought it to the table. Her latest acquisition, a vacuum-plunger jug, fragrant with Bewley's Rich

Roast coffee, stood on the table between them.

"Oh boy, that was the best."

Leaning over, Janey reached into the basket beside her and selected a knobbly log which crackled and hissed when she threw it on to the fire. "I miss having a real fire at the flat. I missed our lunches this week too."

"How *was* the anniversary party?" Gaby asked.

"It was great *craic*. The place was bursting with relations and friends we hadn't seen for years. Our old neighbour next-door wanted to know how I was doing in the city-of-sin. My aunt hinted that, at my age, I should be married and have a pram load of kids. Just for divilment, I told her that as far as I was concerned a pram was for keeping the turf in. That went down well, I can tell you! She muttered something about my having turned into a smart-mouthed-townie and didn't speak to me for the rest of the night. That didn't bother me one bit, but the trouble was, I think it made her more determined than ever not to let my poor cousin, Orla, out of her narrow sight. Mama and Dad loved every second of the fuss; the flowers, the cakes - a two and a five decorated with silver ribbons and horseshoes. My aunt, one of Mama's sisters, and her husband came from Stockholm specially for the night and one of her friends, who'd been their bridesmaid, phoned them from the States. All the boys went up to the North the week before and you never saw so much booze in your life, car loads of it. I don't want to see another bottle of beer as long as I live."

"How did your tights last this time?" Gaby laughed. Janey always complained that her sisters raided them.

"Need you ask? The two youngsters snaffled the lot. I buy them for the girls, although I don't tell them that. It gives them much more pleasure to think they've got away with pinching them. Enough about my lot, what've you been doing with yourself while I was away?"

"A couple of business friends from the US were here on holiday last week. I took them out for dinner one night and to the Abbey, and to a singing pub the next. On Friday Dad's assistant, Stephen Drake, invited me to the ballet."

"He wasn't the one who upset you, was he? You remember, the day when we talked about me and my Hugh."

Gaby, having enjoyed a rare glass of wine with her meal, wondered if she was capable of telling Janey the story of "Genghis-Richards" without blubbering. With Gerry Oscar's approval, occasionally now, if she was at home for the evening or at a special party, she allowed herself a single glass of wine.

"I'll probably dissolve into tears," she warned, "so ignore me."

Janey sat on the floor, her knees tucked under her chin, without saying a word until Gaby brought her sorry tale to a close without dissolving into the expected flood of tears.

"I've never heard anything so rotten in my whole life. It's a real horror story."

Gaby shrugged, "It's over now."

"How you must hate - whatever his name is."

"Myles Richards," she practically spat out the name.

"My God, I know him! He asked me to go out

with him a couple of weeks ago."

"How do *you* know him?"

"The people I baby-sit for, at least the husband, is in marine insurance and as far as I know he does some work for Myles. He called to the house to collect them a couple of weeks ago and that's when I met him first. Last week, before I went home, he invited the family to be his guests at the K Club - that posh golf club in Kildare - and I was invited too. I didn't see any reason to be there, but Beth asked me if I would go in case the children started acting up, so I did."

"And?" Gaby said impatiently.

"And, after lunch, when we were walking about having a look at the place, Myles asked me to have dinner with him. I refused, but he said he'd ring me in case I changed my mind. He must have wangled my address out of Beth and next day he sent.."

"He sent you flowers. Singapore orchids, I'll bet."

"How do you know that?"

"Don't annoy me. Did he follow that up with a 'tasteful flower' each day?"

A dull flush crept into Janey's cheeks and mutely she nodded.

"What happened then, did he phone you?"

"Four days later. Beth and Tim were away - they're the people I work for - so, since I had nothing better to do, I said I'd have dinner with him. I told him about Hugh and my plans to go to the States later this year and he said there was no reason why two friends couldn't enjoy an evening out together. Now I feel so badly, like a traitor - not to Hugh because there's nothing in it, but to you."

"How were you supposed to know? The swine can be very persuasive. Anyway, are you going to see him again? For heaven's sake, Janey, don't get involved with that 'Snake-breath'."

Janey said hesitantly, "Next Tuesday, we're going to the Gate Theatre."

Gaby sat staring unhappily into the flames. Janey nervously justified her actions; if he was willing to waste his money then she might as well take advantage of a couple of nights out; he knew she wasn't available.

"Then by all means take every advantage of him that you can." Gaby's tone was bitter. "After all, you're dealing with the master, the king, El Primo of the advantage-takers."

"It certainly sounds that way, maybe I should make him fall for me - then I can dump *him*. Mind you, after what you've said I don't think I'd want to go out with him again."

They watched a film on television until after midnight.

"I think I'm going to turn in," Gaby said. "Do you have everything you need? Shout if you're in trouble. Sleep well, see you tomorrow."

Janey watched Gaby's tall figure walking from the room. There was a dejected slope to her shoulders - none of the usual spring in her step. It had taken all her credulity to absorb what Gaby had to tell. It was a wonder the girl hadn't fallen apart again, *she* would have. How could anyone be so blind, so stubborn? It was almost as though he needed someone to hang the blame on. Why couldn't he accept it was an accident? Janey believed Gaby. She had no doubts at all that Gaby was innocent.

CHAPTER FIFTY-TWO

Janey sat at the kitchen table reading the paper and drinking a mug of tea.

"Good morning," she said brightly when Gaby, red-eyed from lack of sleep, slithered on to the chair facing her and yawned.

"Cup of tea?" Janey asked.

"Thanks."

"You look mangled, bad night? I kept dreaming all night about your awful story. I didn't know whether I was asleep or awake."

"It's very cold out but would you fancy a walk on the beach?" Gaby suggested as she pottered around tidying the breakfast dishes. "It'll blow our cobwebs away. We could go out for lunch, maybe see a film and then two friends are coming over for a floor-supper tonight."

"Sounds great, but what's a floor-supper?"

"A throw-back to our schooldays when we used to pull a sheet off the bed and spread it on the floor then scoff every bit of food we had by torchlight. I was a real tubby effort in those days. My nickname was *Flabby Gaby*. Every so often we get together still and pig-out. You'll like them - Jill and Jacqui."

They walked along the path above the beach at Sandymount Strand, the icy wind blowing in their faces. Only the hardy regulars had braved the freezing weather. Scarves firmly round their heads with the ends tucked into the raised collars of their coats, they strode out. They reached the end of the path and turned. With the wind to their backs, they slowed to a more leisurely pace.

"Janey, there's something I want to talk to you about but first you must promise me that you'll never breathe a word of what I say to anyone."

"You have my word." Surely there couldn't be more to add to the tale of horror.

"Hear me out, then when I'm finished you can tell me I'm mad. Last night when I was lying awake I felt furious with 'Rasputin Richards' all over again. I thought it was over, out of my system, but seemingly not - I want my revenge, Janey. For a while after it happened I thought up silly ways of getting even, I wanted to kill him, but that was just wishful thinking. Then last night you said something which gave me food for thought, a banquet for thought more like, when you jokingly suggested getting the 'Traitor' to fall for you. Well, that's *exactly* what I want you to do, *make* him fall for you. Mesmerise him. Bait him on your hook and reel him in."

Gaby wasn't sure whether Janey's silence was caused by shock or disbelief. "You hoped to get to the States by the end of June and, you said, you're still well short of your target. So this is what I propose. I'll pay for your ticket and give you five thousand pounds in dollars."

"But Gaby, that's crazy!"

"Wait Janey, listen to the rest of what I have to say. If you decide to go along with this, you mustn't allow yourself to get emotionally involved. If you do, then the deal's off. If you play your cards right I'm sure you should be able to lure him into your web by the end of June and be on your way to Hugh. You'd have to find a

way of getting him to propose to you and
then…"

"… Don't show up for the wedding!" Janey
looked at Gaby with awe.

"That's right," Gaby nodded. "The timing
would be up to you, obviously the quicker the
better from your point of view. At this stage I'd
rather be up front with you. In order to safeguard
myself, on the morning of the proposed wedding
I'll take you to the airport myself and give you
the ticket and cash as you board the flight. If you
don't succeed, we'll come to some other
arrangement - but let's think positive. Now you
can tell me I'm nuts."

They walked on in silence until they ran out of
path again and turned to retrace their steps into
the merciless wind. Gaby didn't look at Janey.
She watched a departing ferry out at sea, a shiver
ran through her. She was glad to be on terra
firma and not being buffeted to and fro on the
undulating waves. Janey hadn't replied. Gaby
began to feel extremely foolish. Was this, she
wondered, the crazed result of a night's lost sleep
or a feasible plan of revenge? Anxiously she
waited.

"I'll do it. It's so far out, so crazy, it might just
work. There's one proviso - I will not go to bed
with him even if it means the whole thing falls
apart."

"Agreed. Actually, that might be a plus, it
could make him keener."

They increased their pace as it began to
drizzle, fine misty spray seeped into their chilled
bones. "Let's go and have lunch, we could do
with something hot," Gaby suggested as they got

into the car. By the time they reached Ailesbury Road with its embassies and fine houses, the car-heater was beginning to do its work. They crossed the lights at Donnybrook and headed for Clonskea, passing the Riverview Club on the way. "That was the first place 'Prince-Bad-News' took me to," she said.

Ashton's, the popular pub on the main road, was beginning to fill up with early weekend diners. They selected their lunch from a long buffet and, still numbed from the cold, Janey ordered a Gaelic coffee before she tackled her plate, piled with rare roast beef and roast potatoes. Gaby refused the offer of a hot whiskey, and contented herself with a bowl of steaming soup. "Sorry, I forgot," Janey apologised.

"Doesn't bother me," Gaby assured her. In low voices they thrashed out their campaign. "I'll have to give up my evening work - the baby-sitting in particular." Janey looked apprehensive.

"The nightclub even more so. Don't forget the object of your exercise was to earn the money for your travel and so on, now you'll have considerably more cash than you could have made by working." Gaby's tone was harsher than she had intended. Once set on the path of Myles' destruction she wanted no obstacles in her way.

"Tell me everything about him, his likes, dislikes, foibles and hobbies. It's painful for you, I know, but it will help enormously."

The young woman sitting at the next table was edging closer to them, their conversation had piqued her interest and with nothing more than a meal for company she was doing her best to eavesdrop.

"Tables have ears," Gaby said sharply and inclined her head in the woman's direction. In a louder tone she continued. "Now, you know Mary from accounts, well, she was a bit short of the readies last month so she popped something in her grandmother's tea and, in half an hour, the old lady was gone."

The woman flushed and sidled back to her original position on the padded seat.

Janey grinned, for a couple of seconds she thought Gaby had gone bananas.

On the way home Gaby stopped to pick up some hot crusty French loaves and another pack of coffee - it would be a long weekend.

CHAPTER FIFTY-THREE

In a capricious mood the four of them sat cross-legged on the floor either side of the folded white bed-sheet. Jacqui had brought a huge dish of vegetable lasagne which smelt divine. Cheeses and olives, smoked trout, crispy French sticks, fish mousses, and salads painstakingly chopped by Gaby were displayed against the background of the fire's leaping flames.

"Posher than we used to be, aren't we?" Jill laughed. "I remember sleeping on currants from your mother's fruit cake for days after our old parties," she said to Jacqui.

"And what awful cake it was too, always tasted slightly of turpentine from her brushes. She is so wonderfully absent-minded," Jacqui explained to Janey, "once she was so engrossed in her art that she poured her painting water into her tea instead of milk and drank it without noticing. Mind you, we were worse, we saw her do it and didn't stop her!"

"At a cocktail party last year Dad and I were talking to someone and he was so involved in what he was saying that he demolished three plastic grapes from a bunch that were sitting in a bowl on the table. You've no idea how hard he had to pull to get them off the stalk!"

That evening was the best Gaby could remember for a long time. They didn't often have the opportunity to revert to their naturally skittish and mischievous personalities but they made sure, as they reminisced, that they didn't exclude Janey who had hilarious tales of her own to tell.

By one-thirty the two girls had finished washing-up and, apart from the wine-stained sheet, all visible signs of the party had vanished.

"What fun they are," Janey remarked, drying the last cup. "You must have had fantastic times together."

"We did. They were the sisters I never had and we're as close as family. I couldn't imagine my life without them."

"Are you going to let them in on what we're planning to do to *you-know-who?*"

"Not till afterwards, no. For once, I'm not sure how they'd react or, maybe I am. My gut instinct tells me they might try to stop me - us. For the moment I think it's better to say nothing."

"Is it too late to start my instruction?" Janey perked her head to one side.

"Let's not spoil a good evening. Last night I tossed and turned so much that frankly I could do with a good night's sleep. Tomorrow we can talk."

"...and basically that's all I can tell you about him," Gaby finished.

"It's difficult now to imagine him as I did when I first met him," Janey frowned. "Now I see him with a forked tail and curved horns either side of his head!"

"Stupid of me Janey, I know, to influence you like that, but I'm so biased I can't give you a dispassionate description."

"There's no need to worry, I have his mark now. I'll put on my best *little-girl-lost* look and see how that works. I'll throw in a few seductive glances followed by some wide-eyed *impressed-sick* intelligent listening. From then on I'll play it by ear, pardon the pun. Kidding aside, Gaby, I wish for your sake it was foolproof - and that's nothing to do with the money. You deserve to be happy again and possibly this will help you. You must promise me that if it does work out you'll write and tell me how he reacted."

"It will be my greatest pleasure," Gaby smiled.

"And that's all I can think of for now. OK, I'll see you at one o'clock today as usual, but let's have lunch on Wednesday instead of Thursday and then I can keep you up to the minute. Don't forget I'm going to the theatre tomorrow night."

"I hadn't forgotten. One last word on the subject. As far as you're concerned, he has no ulterior motive - as in my case - therefore his interest in you is probably a normal one. By now, and obviously I've no way of knowing, he may be ready for a genuine relationship. This could make a big difference, let's wait and see."

CHAPTER FIFTY-FOUR

Janey was ready and waiting when Myles rang the bell. Her outfit, chosen carefully for the occasion, was demure but sophisticated, her fair hair shining.

"Myles, spot on time. I do love punctuality." One point to me, Janey noted his look of approval. Gaby had coached her well.

"I hope you like Michael Medworthy's plays, he's always been a great favourite of mine," Myles smiled.

"I do, very much." Janey had never heard of Michael Medworthy before but she had spent her lunch-time at the library boning up on any information she could find about the playwright. Casually she mentioned two other productions, "her favourites", about which she had read a short synopsis.

For Janey the evening dragged, the play was cleverly produced and deep but she couldn't concentrate on the lines uttered by the talented actors and actresses. Was it really possible that this beautifully-mannered, courteous man could be such an ogre? Now and again, without moving her head, she swivelled her eyes in his direction. He must have sensed her surreptitious glance because he turned towards her and gave her a lazy smile.

"It was excellent, wasn't it?" he enthused as they sat over their coffee and sandwiches.

"Marvellous," Janey agreed falsely. "I liked the

hero even if he was a bad lot. The subtle way in which they introduced the mitigating circumstances of his behaviour was very clever, but then Medworthy has always been a good writer - don't you think?" Yuch! Such pretentious twaddle, she almost laughed out loud. Janey, you are becoming a prize bull-merchant. Gaby will crease herself when she hears this - or will she?

At home in her flat after the weekend with Gaby, Janey had thought long and hard about everything Gaby had said. If this whole set-up backfired Janey worried that it could have disastrous consequences for Gaby, it might even push her over the edge. The thought was chilling. There was still time for her to back out before it was too late. The money was tempting, no getting away from that, but it was not her only motive. She wished there were someone she could discuss the whole thing with but she'd given her word and nothing in the world would make her go back on it. Janey had vacuumed and dusted her flat at a ferocious rate, the furniture gleamed with beeswax. Never had the windows sparkled quite so brightly. Her ironing piled up in record time and, as suddenly as it had appeared, her drive dissipated - her head was clear and her mind made up. Come what may, I must keep my promise.

They walked through Stephen's Green but neither of them paid any attention to their surroundings. Gaby was hungry for information and Janey did her best to repeat exactly what Myles had said and done. "I felt such a fraud," Janey laughed as she related their discussion after the theatre. Gaby smiled wanly, but didn't respond the way Janey had hoped.

"Hey Gaby, lighten up, the high drama was in the theatre!"

This time she did laugh. "I'm too tense, you're right. Neither of us will last through months of this. It's all so strange, I suppose I'm nervous still."

"Try shaking in my shoes, kiddo, I nearly fell over twice." Janey coaxed her out of her jittery state and brightened Gaby's mood by reading her a letter she'd received from her cousin that morning.

"I did her a power of no good when I went home to the party - you remember, being cheeky to my aunt. Now Orla, as you can see, regards herself as a martyr and blames me." Janey grinned remorselessly. "I'm always in trouble."

For the rest of their lunch break they managed to shelve the subject uppermost in their minds and when Gaby returned to her class she felt better than she had since she first thought of this bizarre scheme.

For two days Janey bit her lips, then her nails and finally the sleeve of her sweater. Myles had said he would phone, but the instrument was silent. By Friday morning she was ready to admit defeat. She was gathering her books to leave for Keyboard when he phoned.

"Myles, how nice to hear from you." You pig! she muttered under her breath. She had spent the last quarter of an hour rehearsing how to tell Gaby that her scheme had gone kaput - after only one date.

"Janey, I'm glad I caught you. Sorry I haven't been in touch before now but I had to fly to

London and the operator said there was no number listed for you. In my rush I left my address book in Dublin."

"The phone is under the landlord's name." Looking at her bitten nails she gave him nine out of ten, it was a good excuse.

"I'd like to take you to dinner tomorrow night if you're free. It's a late invitation, I know."

"I'd love to, Myles, but unfortunately I've already made arrangements."

She was paralysed by the silence at the other end of the phone. Oh please let me have done the right thing, she prayed, how am I going to tell Gaby about this little episode? I'll wing it, find some excuse.

"How about Sunday then? Would you like to spend the day in the country?"

Her knees buckled, she had gambled and won. "That would be lovely. What time?"

Replacing the receiver she blessed her luck, how near she had come to throwing away their chances.

"...I don't mind telling you, my hands were shaking and my knees were knocking. I don't know what possessed me, unless it was because I'd waited two days to hear from him." She held out her hand with its bitten nails.

"Poor Janey, imagine if you really fancied him, the other nails would be gone too."

Janey held out her other hand, its chewed partner.

"Would you like another cup of coffee?" Janey asked.

"Yes, we've loads of ti ..."

"Down! Get down." Janey grabbed at Gaby's

hair and pushed her down on the chair.

"Janey, you hurt me," Gaby said, her head missing the wall by an inch.

"Stay down Gaby, he's here, Myles, stay still. He's at the doorway looking around." Janey raised the newspaper to cover her face. Gaby could hear its pages rustling nervously in Janey's hands.

"I can't look," Janey whispered. "If he spots us together that's it, *finito*."

For several minutes neither of them dared to move. Gaby felt ridiculous almost doubled up under the table. "Take a look, I'll faint if I stay like this, the blood's draining out of my head," she whispered.

Half an inch at a time Janey lowered the paper, as it reached her eye level she looked towards the door at precisely the same moment Myles turned his back on the crowded café and started walking towards the street. "It's OK, he's just gone." Janey released her breath.

The two women facing them had ceased all pretence at conversation and were staring at the girls. "Do you think it's Mike Murphy's show - you know, the one with the hidden camera?" One of them, her eyes darting, whispered in a low voice to her companion. Janey smiled at the pair disarmingly. "Reporters," she sighed, "you just can't get away from them." The women's eyes were wide with eagerness. Silently like Tweedledum and Tweedledee, they nodded their heads in unison, sympathetic to the girls' predicament. Taking her lead from Janey, Gaby stared at them and said in tragic tones, "Don't *ever* become famous no matter how much you are tempted, it's not worth it." Gathering their handbags and Janey's disguise they left the table choking with laughter as the women racked their brains to put names to these two film stars.

Light-headed with relief they collapsed onto a bench in Stephen's Green. "That puts paid to our lunches in town, we'll have to be careful in future." Gaby recovered first.

"I couldn't believe my eyes when I saw him standing there. One minute later and I would have stood up to get the coffees and it would have been all over."

"A horrible thought occurred to me as I was losing consciousness, had he set us both up?"

"You're getting paranoid."

"See how well you'd do with your head swimming and your brain defunct."

"We've really got to straighten out," Janey warned.

"If I ever can again." Gaby tottered from the bench and doubled over, groaning and moaning as if in terrible pain. Janey sprang up and swatted her with the rolled-up newspaper. "There's not much good news in it today, but this paper has certainly had its uses."

Laughing, they headed back towards the college.

CHAPTER FIFTY-FIVE

John O'Neill glanced at his daughter as she sat chewing the end of her pencil. "How's it going?" he asked.

"Not bad, but I'm in a bit of a muddle with this flower-bed."

He left his chair and joined her at the table. Not that he could tell a lily from a lilac, nevertheless, he told himself, he must show interest. Gaby had worked hard to establish order in the pretty garden and, with Colin's advice and the aid of a six-foot three semi-professional gardener, she had succeeded in clearing some of the overgrown shrubs and rampant weeds. "Colin said I should draw the rough shape of the garden and then tackle it little by little. The trouble is, I really don't know what goes where."

John smiled helplessly. "I'm not going to be any help, but why not make a list of all the things you like and then hire a horticulturist to plan it out for you, but you've done a very good job so far."

"Brains, father! I'll do just that. Jacqui and Colin have loads of books and they've already offered to lend them to me."

"Is he happy in his new position? It seems like ages since I've seen Jacqui and Colin or Jill."

"He's over the moon and Jacqui is doing brilliantly with her new company. Now that you're here for a couple of weeks why don't I ask them over? How about Saturday if they're free?"

"Perfect, I'd love to see them. Imagine, you making dinner and I don't even wince!"

Gaby stuck her tongue out at him and crossed her eyes, pulling her hand across her throat at the same time. "Don't eat the mushrooms," she warned. They both laughed remembering the joke about the wife who got rid of several husbands by feeding them the poisoned fungi.

"I'll be careful," he promised.

When John saw the cottage for the first time he was captivated by the beauty of the spreading buildings and their thatched roofs.

Gaby dragged him by the arm. "You must see your rooms first," she insisted. Obediently he followed her through the hall and along the little corridor. Throwing open the door to his study she nudged him inside. Painted the colour of fresh cream, the big bright room was as beautifully proportioned as the rest of the house. Honey velvet curtains hung neatly in sections on the narrow dividing walls, emphasising the windows and the door leading to the garden. In all the main rooms the Americans had substituted a sympathetically matching door for one of the windows, allowing access to the garden.

John's desk - a partner's desk with four sets of drawers - had been rescued from the office's top floor. With Stephen Drake's help it had been restored. He and Gaby had found a comfortable brown leather chair with an adjustable seat and swivel base. In the grate a fire burned and on either side of it were two matching velvet couches loaded with bright cushions.

Gaby had scoured the auction rooms and antique shops until she found what she was looking for, a pair of elegant bookcases. John disliked ornate furniture and Gaby was well pleased that their narrow, finely fluted sides were the only ornamentation on the satinwood bookshelves. Throwing caution to the winds, she had bid for an exquisite seventeenth-century Chinese brush-holder, seeing instantly that the delicate apple-green jade container would make a perfect, if wildly extravagant, plant-holder. A glowering look thrown her way by a dealer as she left the auction room confirmed that she had made a good buy. It would be just right on the Pembroke table in a corner of the room. Bright bowls of flowers added colour and gaiety to the study's subdued colouring.

"Gaby, it's wonderful, and just look at my desk! The bookcases, where did they come from? The books, I haven't seen them for years and the jades, how marvellous. That plant-holder, it looks like jade too?" John darted around, touching the books, running his fingers over the polished surface of his desk, he was discovering old friends amongst his belongings.

"The planter, that's my gift to you - the bookshelves too. I know how you hate fussy furniture."

"Thank you, they're perfect, the whole room is."

Gaby beamed with pleasure. "Your bedroom

isn't finished and there are loads of bits and pieces we could add all over the house but they'll come later - bit by bit."

For two days Gaby hardly saw John, except at mealtimes. He had years of catching up to do. Apologetically he withdrew to his study where, in front of the fire, he browsed through the dozens of volumes he'd forgotten over the years. "It's incredible how easily the hours slip by," he said, as they sat in the sunny niche in the drawing-room having lunch.

"Don't apologise. I'm thrilled to see you and the whole point of having your own space is to enjoy it. There's loads for me to do and just to know you're in the house is enough."

Janey had phoned early that morning to report on the previous night's outing. "It was a fabulous meal, we went to Patrick Guilbaud's. My clothes are beginning to get tight with all this dining out in posh places. Anyway, Myles was his usual attentive self. I'm sure he practises being charming in his mirror - especially that slightly crooked smile. Now hear this, he asked me to go away with him next weekend."

"What did you say?" Gaby asked quickly.

"I said no."

"Why? That would have been a great opportunity."

"I don't think so, he's getting more and more interested and I thought that a 'no' now and again would fuel the flames. Trust me, Gaby, I'm sure it was the right thing to do."

"OK. You're the boss."

"He asked me if I'd heard from Hugh lately. I said yes, but that he writes far more often than I do. Then he quirked his eyebrow, you know, the way he does, 'Losing interest in him?' he asked.. I thought he looked pleased but you know how difficult it is to read his face. 'I suppose so, a bit,' I said with my best coy look. What else? Oh yes - he asked when I was going home again, he'd love to meet my family. I brushed that off in a hurry saying I always go home with my neighbour, it's company on the drive for him. He didn't push it, so I hope that's out of the way, and that's all really. The usual kiss goodnight and we're going to an exhibition at the Solomon Gallery on Monday. I'll see you on Tuesday. Give you all the gen, then, hen," she said cheerfully and rang off.

The garden was Gaby's calendar. As the weeks ticked by, new shoots poked their heads cautiously through the loamy soil testing the temperature above their safe winter bed. The girls were cautious too, they chose their meeting places with care; out-of-the-way small cafés near the college or, on the odd day when there were no afternoon classes, suburban coffee shops. They left Keyboard separately and returned separately.

Rushing from college one afternoon Gaby had skidded to a halt at the street door. In the car outside Myles was reading *The Irish Times*. She slammed the door shut and drew back into the depths of the dim hallway until Janey's slim figure emerged from the lecture room.

"Gaby, what's up? You look like you've seen a ghost."

"It's *him*, he's outside. You idiot, why did you tell him you studied here? I almost walked straight into him."

"Did he see you?" Janey's face was puzzled. She couldn't remember telling Myles where she studied.

"No, he was reading the paper. When I recovered my wits I dashed back inside."

Janey tapped an impatient finger on her cheek. "The day we went to the K Club, that's it! We were walking around the grounds and that's when he asked me which college I went to. God, I'd totally forgotten. Maybe he's waiting for someone from another building?"

"No way. He forgets nothing, believe me, his mind is as sharp as a razor and he has an elephant's memory. You'd better go out to him, I'll wait here until you've gone. Phone me tonight, will you?"

Janey ran down the few steps and Myles honked lightly on the horn.

"Hi, what are you doing here?" she demanded, a smile lit up her face.

Leaning over he opened the door. "Hop in," he invited. "I'm glad I caught you. Something has come up - I must go to London later today. Sorry I'll have to break our date."

Janey pouted prettily. "What a shame. I was so looking forward to seeing you."

The tilt of her head and the disappointment that showed in her eyes pleased him. At times she was elusive and distant, then her spirited side would shine through, vibrant, challenging and comical. He really liked the mercurial girl.

"Let's make it Thursday instead. You decide where you'd like to go and I'll book it now." Picking up his mobile phone from the dashboard, he waited for her decision.

"Put it away, Myles, I have a better idea. Why don't I cook dinner for us both? That way you can relax after your trip."

"There's nothing I'd like more. A home-cooked meal would be a real treat."

Janey felt a pang of sadness for him. She adored the glamorous restaurants, the luxury of someone serving delicious food with not a cup to wash up. But, sometimes, after a hectic week of running around from one exotic establishment to another, she was more than content to slouch in her terry-cloth robe in front of the television with an omelette filled to bursting with onions and tomatoes or fried eggs on toast and a mug of hot steaming tea. It was only since she got caught up in this crazy scheme of Gaby's that she had understood Gaby's pleasure in the cottage. A life spent living in hotels had sounded appealing, no chores and no responsibilities, but now, with such a short taste of the good life, she was tired of it already. Yes, suggesting an evening at home to Myles had been a good move.

CHAPTER FIFTY-SIX

Humming to himself Myles Richards stepped from the shower. The swirling waters had washed away the grime of London traffic, the stickiness of air travel too. As he towelled his hair he thought about the trip. Meetings had run smoothly and the eager, hungry young man he'd hired with a view to delegating a goodly section of his work had turned up trumps. But best of all, contracts had been exchanged and the lovely old house in Wicklow would soon be his. Fifteen years of travelling the world had reduced his hunger for adventure and lessened his need for power and money. He was ready to settle down now in a quiet backwater, away from some of the pressures and the tensions of life. It would be foolish and impractical to pretend to himself that he could retire. He liked life in the fast lane - but not that fast. No, he wanted to slow down slightly, but he'd keep a watchful eye on the business.

Unwrapping the short-sleeved blue casual shirt, he pulled it over his head. A bonus, he thought, no formal shirt and tie tonight. He smiled as an image of Janey crossed his mind, that almost white-blonde hair, the ever-changing eyes in her animated face, she reminded him of a butterfly. He was happier than he had been in a long time. He gave Janey credit for lifting him out of the doldrums. All the plotting and activity he had put into that O'Neill girl's comeuppance had left him enervated and miserable. He'd felt none of the elation that he had expected, just loneliness and misery. For months she had been his only reason for living, to destroy the destroyer. He would never forgive her - not if he lived to be a hundred. The bitch. Her carelessness had killed his beautiful little Maria. He should have killed Gaby O'Neill. She'd been so much in love with him and he hoped with all his heart that the pain she had suffered had been as bad as his. In some ways, Janey reminded him of Maria. Was that why he was so attracted to her, he wondered? Comparing them was dangerous, no one could live up to Maria, but she was gone and he had come to terms with it now.

Would Janey be a suitable companion, a wife? He liked her enormously. Did he love her? It was astonishing how much they had in common. For Myles it had been wonderful to find someone who liked the same writers, the same music, enjoyed the same food. Her love of the theatre matched his. They even shared a taste for the more obscure playwrights. Janey was almost his mirror image. He wondered what would happen tonight, just the two of them in her flat? Was it more than just a dinner invitation?

Picking up the bottle of wine he made his way to the car. Take everything slowly, he advised himself, don't rush it.

Comfortably dressed in a black tracksuit, Janey put scented candles in place and sat down to read the morning paper.

It had been a hectic rush but the shepherd's pie was heating in the oven and everything was under control. A quarter-of-an-hour to unwind, Myles was never late.

The bell sounding in the quiet flat startled her, looking at the little mantle-clock she wondered if it was fast or was Myles ten minutes early? Smoothing her hair and smiling she threw open the door in welcome. The bedraggled figure of her cousin Orla stood there. She was red-eyed and she carried a battered suitcase. "I've run away and come to live with you," she announced, tears coursing down her cheeks.

Janey was gobsmacked. "But you can't, you haven't," she stuttered. "You can't stay here."

Of all the moments to pick, this had to be the worst. In less than ten minutes Myles would be standing in Orla's place on the mat. "Come in," she said "for heaven's sake, Orla, you can't run away like this, not to me, not now."

Her cousin's miserable face fell even further. "I've nowhere else to go," she sobbed, "I can't stand Mam bossing me and watching me all the time. I want to work in Dublin and have fun like you."

Janey's mind was working furiously. "Leave your case there and go and wash your face, quickly."

Orla trailed towards the door which Janey pointed out, and frantically Janey dialled Gaby's number. Please be there, don't be out, she willed silently.

"Hello."

"Oh Gaby, thank goodness. Big problems. My cousin Orla, you know the one from home, has just this second landed on my doorstep, bag and baggage. She wants to stay here, how am I going to get rid of her before Myles arrives? I've less than ten minutes."

For a couple of seconds Gaby didn't speak. "Gaby, are you there?"

"Yes, shush a minute and let me think."

Janey stood impatiently as the precious seconds ticked by.

"Right, phone for a taxi and send her over to me. Dad's away and she can sleep here tonight. I'll bring her back to you in the morning."

"Oh great, that'll solve tonight's problem at least. Please Gaby, try and talk some sense into her, baby-sitting her could wreck everything we've done especially if she meets him."

Banging down the phone Janey scrambled for her address book. "Taxi, taxis, oh where are you? Got it," she said, feeling Orla's red eyes boring into her.

"I have a guest coming tonight," she explained to Orla, " you're going to stay with a friend of mine. You'll like her. Tomorrow she'll bring you back here and we'll have a serious talk."

"But Janey, I want to stay with you," she wailed.

"Orla, you can't. If my landlord catches me letting anyone else stay here, I can lose the flat." Good thinking my girl, she congratulated herself.

Reluctantly Orla allowed herself to be propelled to the door. The next five minutes were like an hour but then the black car with its yellow sign pulled up to the flat.

Thrusting the address into the driver's hand, Janey turned to go back inside just as Myles' red sports car rounded the corner.

Composing herself, with a smile of welcome

pasted on her face, she opened the door again.

"Myles, it's you," she said foolishly.

"Help yourself to the crisps," she called through the open kitchen door. She carried in two glasses and a bottle of wine and set them down on the little table between them.

"How was London?" Always appear fascinated by what he has to say, Gaby had advised, even if you're not. It wasn't that she was bored, she hadn't yet recovered from the shock of finding Orla standing on the step.

"...and I'm sure he'll run things well."

Janey dragged her attention back to Myles. "I'm sure you're right." What was he talking about? Pay attention, she chided herself, we can sort Orla out tomorrow.

As it neared midnight, Myles dragged himself out of the comfortable chair. "It's been a great evening, Janey, I've really enjoyed myself. Thanks again for a lovely meal."

She walked the few paces with him to the door. Swiftly he turned and pulled her towards him. His kiss was passionate and, to her surprise, she found herself returning it. It was a long time since she had felt Hugh's arms around her, his lips on hers. Again Gaby's voice rang inside her head, "Don't get involved".

"Goodnight, Myles," she said softly, pushing him away. "I enjoyed the evening too."

Leaning against the frame of the door, Janey felt drained. Myles had been so entertaining she'd forgotten all about her cousin and had listened intently to his amusing stories. He was certainly well-travelled and she could visualise the places he spoke about as if she were there. Only once did she throw him a wary look, when he talked of the Far East. That, she reminded herself, was where he and Gaby were supposed to spend their honeymoon. He encouraged her to talk about her course at Keyboard, he knew about computers and delighted her by solving a problem she'd been working on for days.

"Wonderful, I can stop worrying now," she laughed. "I've been going round in circles with this one for ages. My teacher will be very impressed. No need to tell her I got help."

Myles loved to hear about her family. Once she'd started there was no stopping her.

"When am I going to meet them all? I feel I know them so well."

Janey smiled and covered her confusion by offering to make more coffee.

"Janey, is there some reason you don't want me to meet them? Do they know that I exist, even?"

She should have known he was too astute to be fobbed off with vague answers. Here goes, there's nothing for it but to give him a convincing answer. "Of course they know. Good lord, how could I keep someone like you a secret? The problem is that Hugh and I were childhood sweethearts and the family are extremely upset that I've been bewitched by a sophisticated man of the world. Our parents have been friends for yonks and Hugh is like a son to them. It will take them a while to get used to the fact that Hugh and I are no longer..." Her voice trailed away and her lovely face looked sad. Peeping from under her lashes, she could see a look of understanding softening his face. Well done, she mentally clapped herself on the back, I'm turning into a right little Meryl Streep.

It was too late to phone Gaby now, it would have to wait until she saw her tomorrow. One thing that could be omitted from her report was his goodnight kiss. That was another thing she had enjoyed this evening, she thought, as she got ready for bed. She would have to watch herself, Myles Richards was an attractive and dangerous hobby.

They stood on the platform waving as the train pulled out.

"I don't know how you did it," Janey said, relieved to see a smile on her cousin's pale face.

"She's just kicking a bit against parental discipline, she'll settle down and forget about all this," Gaby said.

"Don't you believe it, you haven't met my aunt. Still, for now we've convinced her, or you have."

"So how did your evening go?" Gaby was consumed with eagerness.

"To be truthful, it wasn't bad at all. He talked about travel, about books and computers. He solved one of my homework questions that I'd been wrestling with for days. You should have seen Barbara's face this morning, she was most impressed - but I digress. Things got a bit dicey, he asked again when he was going to meet the family. Where my answer came from I don't know! You may be interested to learn that both our families are heartbroken now that Hugh and I have broken up. Because all the parents are such close friends they're annoyed with me now that I have become involved with such a suave and sophisticated man, therefore it wouldn't be wise for me to take him home until things have cooled down. How do you like them little apples?"

"Very good, sounds plausible."

"Yes, I thought so. I'm becoming a first-class liar, aren't I?"

Gaby felt guilty as she thought of Janey's subterfuges. Still, that's what they had agreed. "So what's the next move?" Gaby asked.

"Now you mention it, he didn't make any arrangements. I suppose he'll phone."

After a two-day silence on Myles' part they began to get a little anxious. "Don't panic, he'll ring," Janey said, but she was worried.

When he did phone to make a date, she accepted immediately. "Would you like to come and see the house I've bought? We could make a day of it tomorrow," he suggested.

Gaby was relieved to hear from Janey, but the venue for their outing pleased her less. She could still picture the old house that was to have been her home. Don't let it get to you, she warned herself.

Stephen Drake had taken to popping in every couple of weeks and Gaby was grateful for his company. She missed the travelling and the challenge of the business world, his visits kept her in touch with clients she had known well. He never teased her about her cooking, and he brought her plants for her garden and sometimes tickets for the theatre or the cinema. She had a sneaking suspicion that he cared for her more than he allowed to show.

When John O'Neill had asked him to keep in

touch with Gaby he had done so willingly, there was nothing he would rather do. Naturally she was not attracted to him as he was to her, but he accepted that, to be in her company was reward enough for him. John was right, she did seem to be a bit down these days. He racked his brains for something to say that might put back a little of the missing spark but so far he had found no solution. She was, he supposed, still fretting over that fellow Richards but there was nothing he could do about that.

As the term drew to a close, Gaby looked forward to Easter with little interest. Janey was going home for the holidays as Myles would be in Malaysia. Gaby's father had begged her to join him in Germany but for once she had refused. Falsely cheerful, she claimed that she couldn't leave the garden - there was so much to do. She mooched around the cottage, read a great deal and pottered in the garden but she couldn't lift her spirits. Even Jacqui, Colin and the children received fewer visits than usual. Grumbling to herself, Gaby slouched towards the ringing phone.

"Hi, Gaby." Jill's cheery manner didn't help. "What's happening over Easter, anything?"

"Nothing really, I have no plans." Gaby fought bravely to keep from sounding miserable.

"Good. How do you fancy spending a couple of days touring around Ireland, just as the mood takes us?"

"I don't know, I don't think so."

"Oh come on, Gaby, it would be fun, just the two of us."

After a little more coaxing Gaby agreed as

graciously as she could. They fixed the dates and Jill rang off. Gaby threw open the door to the garden and stood staring moodily at her handiwork. Myles was finally winning. He was behind all her misery and now, months later than he had probably planned, he was achieving his aim. She stood for a long time on the brink of despair.

CHAPTER FIFTY-SEVEN

As Jill predicted their short break had been fun. At the start Jill apologised that she had a call to make at a client's house in Kildare before they could begin their holiday proper. She'd made a reservation at the Kildare Club for lunch. The lovely old house which served as a hotel had been beautifully restored and the golf club was alive and buzzing with people. Both girls had heard so much about the place they were anxious to see it for themselves and they weren't disappointed. The meal, which they ate in the busy dining-room of the golf club, was excellent. Before leaving they explored the grounds and decided that, although they were not golfers, they would have a short break there sometime in the future. "Come on, let's go. The quicker we get this call over the sooner we can start our holiday."

Within ten minutes of leaving the elegant surroundings of the club they were lost.

"Look, there's a pub," Gaby said pointing to a lone building. "I'll go and ask for directions, give me the address."

A few seconds later she returned to the car, her face a study. "Never again," she said and started to laugh. Two minutes passed before Jill could get any sense out of her. "I've never been so intimidated in my life. The place was full of locals - all men, drinking their pints and when I came in they stopped talking and stared at me. I walked across to the bar and they shrank back on their stools as if I had the plague. The barman looked at me like I was a disease and I just choked and ran for my life. You could see it written on their faces, 'That one should be at home where she belongs - making the dinner.' Drive on Jill, we'll find it eventually, but that's the last pub I'm going into on my own."

The roof of a house could just be seen from the road. "Your turn," Gaby said, settling deeper into the car seat. Jill was back even faster, pursued by two vicious-looking Dobermans who halted as they reached the end of their rattling chains. Far from being sympathetic, Gaby howled with laughter. "You never ran that fast in school."

When her heart stopped pounding, Jill too saw the funny side of it. Winding round the country lanes they saw a man walking along with his dog. "Ask him," Jill instructed stopping the car. Winding down her window, Gaby asked for directions. The man attempted to lift his cap which appeared to have been surgically grafted to his forehead when he was a boy. Judging by the smell of his breath he had enjoyed a liquid lunch. Putting his head through the window he peered sincerely into Gaby's face and smiled. The one tooth remaining in his mouth was yellow, and the nearer to Jill she moved the further into the car his head came. Scratching his head through the cap he smiled again. Jill was now doubled up, laughing hysterically and Gaby could feel her eyes filling with tears from her own suppressed giggles. By this time the dog had joined in the act. Jumping up and down unsuccessfully it tried to hook its paws on the window, but fell back each time hitting its nose against the door. Snorts came from the driver's seat and Gaby gave her a hefty thump with her elbow but it was no good, Jill was beyond help. Unable to contain herself any longer when the man gave an enormous burp, Gaby started to laugh as hard as Jill. Taken aback at her sudden outburst the man stepped back and Jill, her eyes blurred with tears, slammed the car into gear and screeched down the narrow road like a maniac.

Tidying herself as best she could, Jill crunched over the gravel to meet her client and rang the bell. She avoided Gaby's eyes, it would take very little to start her laughing again. After a moment the door opened and Jill disappeared from sight.

Rubbing her face to remove the smeared mascara, Gaby was gratified that she'd been able to avoid the crisis that had threatened to drag her back into depression. "He won't win, I won't allow him to win," she repeated to herself over and over again. For three days, she'd dug the garden and had exhausted herself physically and mentally. Sheer grit and determination kept her going and, by the end of the third day, she had looked at her newly dug flower-bed with satisfaction. She had survived.

Singing along with the music on the car radio she looked at the big old house. I could do wonders with this, she thought, what a shame the garden is so overgrown. Static distorted the sound and she pressed the switches, changing stations until a clear one emerged from the screeches and crackles. The fresh country air was sweet and before long she dozed lightly, lulled by the soothing music. Jill climbed back into the car, waking her, and they set off down the long drive - giggling again.

✳ ✳ ✳

Gaby dumped the luggage in the hall and switched on the central heating while Jill carried the provisions into the kitchen. The three days meandering as the fancy took them had been refreshing, relaxing too. They still had two more days free, and Jill had promised to spend them at Gaby's cottage. They had stopped several times on the road on the way home to buy free-range eggs and freshly dug potatoes. One of the roadside vendors had told them about a smokehouse nearby boasting the finest smoked salmon in Ireland. Not a hundred yards further on they drew into the courtyard. In a shed sides of salmon hung in neat rows on their hooks, trout and chickens too had just emerged from their wood-smoked bed and neither of them could resist the wonderful oak-smoked goods. "Wait here a minute," the apple-cheeked woman who had served them instructed. "It's still hot," she smiled, giving each of them a round cake of hot brown bread. They had barely driven out of the gate before the aroma of the sweet-smelling bread filled the car.

"It was a wonderful few days," Gaby said, smiling. "I needed a break and that really did the trick."

"Me too," Jill assured her, "I'm almost sorry to have to go back to work."

Gaby was looking forward to getting back to Keyboard. Her course would be finished soon and in September she and her father planned to travel to the States. It would be good to slip back into their old routine for a while, feel the buzz of excitement again, but before that there was the little matter of Myles Richards.

CHAPTER FIFTY-EIGHT

Janey listened as Gaby told her about her traumatic couple of weeks. "I've decided that from now on I would prefer not to hear any more details. Just let me know how you're getting on."

"That sounds a sensible idea. It has to be upsetting for you and all I'll say for now is that things are going well."

They cut back their lunches to once a week and Gaby began her social life again. She contacted friends and acquaintances with whom she had lost touch. Before long she was earning a reputation as a good hostess. The cottage became open house each weekend with people dropping in for a cup of tea or a drink and staying for a pot luck supper - frequently backed up by Jacqui's Ice-Savers freezer selection.

The weather had turned warm and everywhere the signs of an early summer were evident. Heavy coats were discarded, windows were thrown open without fear of cold blasts of air and everything from houses to shop signs sported fresh coats of paint in readiness for the season ahead.

Leaving the lecture room one afternoon Gaby heard Janey's voice calling her.

"I have some news for you. Can we have a coffee somewhere?"

Gaby could see the mischief dancing in Janey's eyes.

"I've cracked it at last. He says he's in love with me." Janey stirred the sugar into her coffee waiting for Gaby's response. It was difficult to know how much to tell Gaby. It was even more difficult to remember that this attractive man with his charming manners and loving nature was the ogre of Gaby's past. Janey could see few faults in him. But then neither had Gaby at the time. Myles had become vulnerable in her eyes. There was no doubt in Janey's mind that he loved her. The time they'd spent together had widened her horizons and she found herself being drawn to him. More than a couple of times lately she'd wondered what would happen if she allowed herself to care for him in return. She was thankful that Gaby didn't want more details, Myles' affection for her was becoming hard to resist.

"Well done, Janey. Has he proposed? I couldn't imagine any man being able to withstand your charms."

"Thank you, kind lady. I would say a proposal is imminent. He's asked me to choose colours for the house - *colours I can live with* if you please. He phones every day, sometimes twice a day and, unless he's away, I see him every night. Last night he talked about his girlfriend - fiancée - for the first time."

"Did he say that I was responsible for her death?" Gaby asked bitterly.

"No," Jill lied, "he just said that she died in an accident." There was no point in telling Gaby that he had blamed the driver of a car for Maria's death. She had sympathised with him. He had swiftly changed the subject, but hadn't mentioned Gaby by name.

"How imminent do you reckon this proposal to be?" Suddenly Gaby wanted it over, finished with.

"Any day now or I'm not the woman I thought I was," Janey grinned wantonly.

Gaby didn't ask any questions and Janey said nothing about Myles when they next met for their weekly lunch. Instead she bombarded Gaby with questions about life in the States.

"Should I buy clothes in Ireland or wait till I get there? Do you think I'll be able to understand the computer terminology there? An apartment? I'm not sure if we should rent or buy one - we'll both be earning good salaries. Yesterday I signed all the relevant documents necessary for my emigration. Hugh's counting the days until my arrival." Janey's queries came so quick and fast that Gaby made no attempt to respond.

Driving home in the heavy traffic on the dual carriageway Gaby thought about the situation. She reckoned that if Janey's predictions were correct Janey should be on her way to America by the end of June as planned.

Those awful weeks of solitude and despair had robbed Gaby of her passion for revenge, leaving in its place a clinically cold need for retaliation. Several times she had considered calling a halt to the charade, but she had detached herself and played a waiting game. Is that what it had become? A game?

On the morning of her birthday Gaby removed the stack of cards from their drawer and armed with a cup of tea she sat on the cushioned window seat in the morning sunshine. Sunday. Blissful, lazy Sunday. She rifled through the pile and picked out an envelope bearing her father's writing. She read the message then, smiling, she put it aside and opened the others. Leaning back against the soft curtains she let her mind drift back to so many other birthdays. The ones at school, shared with Jill and Jacqui. Their trip to London as hysterical teenagers, and, most memorable of all, her twenty-first - spent in the South of France with the three people she loved most in life. Tomorrow night the three of them would celebrate together as they always did. She would miss her father but he'd be home on Tuesday for a week. He'd promised to keep his time strictly for leisure, but Gaby doubted if he could spend a whole week away from the challenge of work he loved so much. John's business was not a chore - it was a way of life.

She raised her head as she heard the sound of a car. A taxi had pulled up outside the gate and Janey, clutching a pink-ribboned bottle of champagne, waved as she ran towards the open window.

Thrusting the bottle into Gaby's hand she climbed athletically through the window and flopped on the birthday card-strewn seat.

"You're up with the lark," Gaby said, giving the panting girl time to recover her breath.

"Happy birthday, Gaby, I'm engaged!" Janey hadn't meant to blurt it out like that but everything she'd planned to say sounded wrong.

Gaby felt no sudden rush of triumph, no elation. Now that the moment had arrived, she felt nothing, empty.

"What's up? Aren't you thrilled we succeeded?"

"It's strange but I don't feel a thing."

"Have you changed your mind?" Janey's own doubt flared.

"I've considered it several times I admit and I don't understand why I feel like this, still the ball is rolling down the hill now and I suppose we can't stop it."

"Come on, cheer up, you can't spend your birthday with a long face. How about a cup of tea for your weary traveller?"

So much for the happy birthday. She flung a tea bag into each of two mugs, and drummed her fingers on the counter top as she waited for the kettle to boil. She wondered how long Janey intended to stay. She pulled herself together and forced a smile on to her face and prepared to be more gracious.

"Gaby, I hate to do this, but we must talk about *the day* - the non-wedding plans. Are you up to it?"

"Sure, fire ahead."

"OK. Myles has two long trips coming up, one at the end of June, the other in July. Problem is, I want to get out of here before then. He suggested August or September, that would allow me to finish at Keyboard and still have plenty of time to organise whatever is involved. All I need is one day to get packed and be off."

"I see what you mean. How about suggesting that you have a registry office wedding, then the real one later."

"Yes, but how would that help the date?"

"You could be married in June and go with Myles on his trip, then have a church wedding later. When we were planning to get married so quickly it was so that I could travel with him to the Far East."

"Do you realise that's the first time you've called Myles by his own name?" Gaby's name-calling had grated on her lately.

"It is, isn't it! I wonder what that tells us. Anyway, back to the drawing board. How does that idea appeal to you?"

"Very much, in fact it's an excellent idea. I'll put it to him tonight and see how he reacts."

By the time Myles arrived at her flat that night, Janey was word-perfect. He kicked the door shut with his foot while kissing her at the same time. It was becoming difficult to escape his embraces. He had accepted her ground rule that she wouldn't make love to any man unless she was married to him and if anything it had pleased him, but those probing kisses and his smooth hands ranging over her slim body were hard to resist. She wondered if Hugh had been faced with temptation too, they'd been separated for a long time.

"You look sad, Janey. Why the long face?"

Janey sighed loudly, turning her face from his. "It's nothing. Well, I am sad I suppose. I hate the idea of being apart from you all those weeks, it'll be awful."

"They'll fly by. You'll be up to your ears with all the arrangements and before you can say *knife*, I'll be back."

She stood on tiptoe and wound her arms around his neck, nuzzling into the warmth of his chest. This part of the plan was becoming far too enjoyable. They stood together, locked in each other's arms as Janey pinched the flesh on one of her own hands, just enough to make a tear sting her eyes. Pulling away from Myles she dashed her hand across her eyes and gave a little sniff.

"Janey, you're crying."

"I'll be all right, just give me a moment." She dabbed her eyes with her handkerchief and then pushed it into the pocket of her jeans. "Let's eat now, it'll make me feel better."

She left him sitting in the deep armchair and went into the kitchen with dragging steps. I should win an Oscar, she thought. Taking more time than was necessary, she pottered about with the plates of cheese, rearranged the slices of bread and dressed the salad. Padding backwards and forwards, her head slightly drooped, she avoided Myles' compassionate stare.

Poor Janey, he hated to leave her but he had no option. Her sunny face had replaced Maria's both in his dreams and waking hours. She had lifted him back to a level of happiness he had thought impossible. Tomorrow he would pick her up at Keyboard and take her to buy her engagement ring, that should perk her up.

"You've hardly eaten anything, you're not coming down with a virus, are you?" Myles asked.

"I'm not hungry. Myles, I have an idea..."

"No Janey, absolutely not. You are going to have a proper wedding, church bells, choir boys - the lot."

Genuine tears oozed from her cornflower eyes. Tears of frustration. How easy it would be to go ahead with their plans.

"Please don't cry, I hate to see you unhappy like this."

Leaving the table, sniffling and blowing her

nose she went into the kitchen and switched on the kettle again. She crammed a buttered slice of bread into her mouth chewing quickly. She was starving.

"Janey, *I* have an idea," Myles called.

Wiping the crumbs from her mouth, she returned to the table carrying a fresh pot of coffee.

"If I made all the wedding arrangements and left you free to do your exams, could you manage everything else by the end of term?"

She felt the excitement of victory curling in her veins. Keep calm, take it easy she cautioned herself. "What do you mean?" If she opened her baby blue eyes any further they would fall on to her plate.

"We could be married before I have to leave for Japan and we could turn it into an extended honeymoon. Would that solve your unhappiness?"

She dashed round the table and flung herself at him hugging and kissing him with squeals of delight.

"Whoa! Hold on there, you'll knock everything flying," Myles laughed, lifting her featherweight body on to his knee like a child. She was so simply pleased, so childlike one minute, so adult the next. The wedding could be organised in a trice, all Janey needed to do was choose a dress, the flowers and the invitations.

"I'm so happy. Oh Myles, you'll never know how happy you've made me."

Janey was happy. Happy that now she could see an end to this charade. Myles was proud that she couldn't hide her emotions from him, he could read her like a book. She hugged and kissed him and jumped from his knee, declaring that she was ravenous. He smiled at her lovingly as she wolfed down hunks of bread and great wedges of cheese.

"What about your parents?" he asked, frowning, "now that we are getting married, shouldn't I meet them?"

Janey stopped in mid-bite. Not that again, more complications. "Oh yes, my parents." Frantically she sought an excuse. "I was thinking about that, maybe the best thing would be to leave it until the day of the wedding. They wouldn't miss my big day for anything and when they see how happy I am they'll relent, I'm sure they will." Would he swallow that?

"I suppose you're right, but what if they don't?"

"Believe me, Myles, nothing will matter after that day." The first truthful words she had spoken all night.

"If you say so. Now, let's decide what to do. What date do you finish college?"

"The twentieth of June."

"I have to leave on the twenty-fourth so how about the twenty-third?"

"Perfect," Janey said.

"You'll want to get married in your own church, of course. Now, where's the best place to hold a reception in Meath?"

Not for a second had she imagined the wedding would be anywhere but Dublin. Her blood ran cold as she thought of the chaos it would cause at home if Myles turned up trying to arrange a wedding. She could see it all. Fighting to speak calmly she said, "If you don't mind, I'd prefer not to get married in Meath. I've always dreamed of having my wedding in Dublin."

There was a stubborn set to her jaw that warned him not to pursue the matter. Presumably she would tell him her reasons when she was ready.

"That would make it easier," he confessed. "You choose a hotel for the reception."

She resisted an urge to say the Berkeley Court Hotel, that would really be pushing it. "How about the Shelbourne?"

"Good choice, I'll phone tomorrow and see if the date is available. You choose the invitations. Make out your guest list and give it to me, I'll have them written for you, that'll save you having to worry."

"Thank you, Myles." Is this was what it was like walking through a mine-field?

"Flowers. I'm sure you would like to order those yourself, your bouquet, the bridesmaids' posies and flowers for the hotel. All I need are buttonholes for myself, the best man and the ushers. That just leaves your dress."

"I'll do it on Tuesday."

Myles was relieved but slightly perplexed by Janey's laid-back attitude to her own wedding. He hadn't even met her sisters, the bridesmaids, yet. It was a far cry from the fussy preparations for his other "wedding".

"I was just about to ring off," Janey said as Gaby breathlessly answered the phone.

"Your idea worked. He wouldn't hear of a registry office though, he wants the whole works. Pity, but what the hell."

"What date did you settle on?"

"June the twenty-third, providing he can book the hotel so, fingers crossed."

"They are, and my toes and my eyes too. When will you know?"

"Tomorrow, possibly after college, he's picking me up. Tell you what, if it's yes, I'll try and dash back in, wait for me at the back of the hall."

"See you then."

So Janey had finally snared him. An image of Myles standing alone outside the church filled her mind. He would feel the pain that she had, the agonising pain of rejection and hurt that she had bottled up for so long. From deep within her a howl of grief escaped. Her scream of anguish echoed around the empty house.

CHAPTER FIFTY-NINE

Gaby left the bank with Janey's traveller's cheques tucked safely inside her pocket. Tomorrow it would be all over. Since the terrible night of her birthday she knew she was no longer in love with Myles Richards. Of that she was positive. Now all that was left was the anger.

She walked along Dawson Street, her long legs covering the distance to Travelwise in a few minutes.

"Hi," she said, smiling at the girl, "my name's O'Neill, I'm here to collect a ticket for a friend, Janey Maguire."

"Here we are, one ticket Dublin, New York, Los Angeles. She knows she needs a visa, doesn't she?"

"Yes, she does." Gaby paid for the ticket and left the travel agency. She would have time to go to Waterstones to see what new books they had before her parking meter ran out. How long had it been since *she* travelled by plane? Slowing her pace she tried to remember. Impulsively she turned and retraced her steps.

"Have you forgotten something?" the girl smiled.

"No, I was wondering if the direct flight to Nice still operate on Saturdays?"

"Yes it does, there's a charter leaving in the afternoon."

"Could you get me one seat for this Saturday?"

"Let me have a look. Yes, that will be fine, we

have a seat."

"Right, book me on it please - Gabrielle O'Neill. Can I confirm it later this afternoon?" Two days to get ready, that would be plenty of time. I'll phone Claude as soon as I get home.

Tomorrow would be a lost day. Her heart gave an involuntary jump as she thought of Janey, winging her way to Hugh, and of Myles, dressed in his wedding finery with that brown hair of his sleekly brushed, waiting to claim his bride. She couldn't bear to think about him, it made her shake with nerves. Taking her mind off the day to come, she began to make a checklist in her head; phone the Château d'Albion, phone Jill and Jacqui - it would be wiser to meet them rather than tell her story on the phone. Her father was going to call tonight from Hong Kong, she'd try and persuade him to join her at the Château d'Albion if he could. Her summer clothes would need pressing and, apart from a few bits and pieces that needed to be bought, she could see no reason why she couldn't be ready by Saturday. The urge to get away had never been stronger.

❋ ❋ ❋

Janey snapped shut the locks on her cases and turned the tiny keys. Looking around to make sure she hadn't missed anything she made one last journey into the bedroom, the bathroom and the kitchen which had been her home for the past three years. She stood twisting the magnificent ruby ring on her finger, by midday it would have to be returned to Myles. She didn't

Anne Schulman

envy Gaby her confrontation with him, but that was her dubious privilege. In order to spare her from the trauma of meeting him, Janey had suggested to Gaby that she should take a leaf out of his book and return the ring and a note by courier. Gaby stubbornly had refused. "This is something I have to do. I must face him, see him miserable, then I can rest easy."

Gaby was early. She had allowed herself plenty of time to get to the airport. In all the months the two of them had spent together their conversation had flowed unceasingly but now, in their last hour together, neither girl was inclined to speak.

Gaby still hadn't decided how to approach Myles or what she was going to say to him. Janey, excited though she was at the thought of being reunited with Hugh, knew she would miss Myles. He was an interesting man. Good company and handsome, physically attractive too. For the last couple of months she hadn't even needed to think for herself. Myles had lavished so much attention and kindness on her that she'd begun to depend on him. She remembered reading about people who'd been kidnapped and held hostage forming a bond with their captors. Sometimes they ended up becoming sympathetic towards them. Was this what had happened to her? Myles wasn't her jailer, but in some ways she'd been a prisoner. In two hours she would be in the air and out of this mess for good.

Out of the corner of her eye Gaby could see Janey twisting and turning the ruby on her finger. In a short while Janey would be winging her way

to the States. Gaby wondered if Janey would tell
her story to others, or would she prefer to forget
it, bury it in her past? That was her prerogative,
she had kept her part of the bargain and in a
very few minutes she would reap her reward.
Janey had made it easy for her. Even yesterday
when they had gone to the bank - Janey signed
the traveller's cheques and, pleading that she was
in a hurry, tactfully left them to Gaby to collect.
Janey had kept her part of the bargain without a
hitch - well, almost without a hitch. There had
been lighter moments, but just now she couldn't
muster even the slightest smile.

The parking area of the terminal building was
busy. Holidaymakers struggled with their
cumbersome luggage, fractiously warning their
children not to wander away.

"Don't come in with me, Gaby, let's say
goodbye here."

Gaby drove to the furthest end of the set-down
zone and switched off her engine. Pulling her
bag from the back seat she opened a zipped
compartment and took out a large envelope. She
held it for a moment as Janey removed the ruby
ring from her finger.

"I hate goodbyes," Janey said, looking straight
ahead.

"I do too, so let's wish each other luck. I'll
write and tell you what happened before I leave
for France, I promise."

"You must! I won't rest until I hear. We're only
spending a couple of days in Los Angeles, as you
know, so by the time we get back to San Jose,
your letter should have arrived. Good luck, Gaby
and, some advice you could do without, get all

this out of your system today and forget it. Concentrate on the rest of your life."

With a quick hug, Janey swung her legs out of the car and, half running to the boot, she pulled it open and dragged her two suitcases to the ground.

Gaby waited until Janey had entered the building and then she locked the car and ran back towards the entrance. Through the heavily tinted windows Gaby could see Janey's neat figure at the check-in desk. She watched as Janey collected her ticket and walked towards the back of the terminal building. It was the first time Gaby had been positive that Janey was actually going.

You're getting paranoid, my girl, she told herself as she got back into her car, checked her rear mirror and pulled out into the stream of slow-moving traffic.

Gaby had fifteen minutes to spare. "Brilliant." She spoke aloud, as a car pulled away allowing her to park not twenty yards from the church gate. Her heart was thumping so much she could hear its every beat in her ears. The ring, wrapped inside a paper tissue, was burning into her palm. "Breathe slowly and steadily, in … and out, in … and out." She remembered receiving that advice sometime. As she sat in her car she recognised a couple walking towards the church from the opposite direction. The woman was clutching at the brim of her hat with a gloved hand. She and Myles had met the couple at an art exhibition one evening and afterwards they had joined them for a snack. Suddenly, Gaby's face burned. Had they known about her? Would he have boasted about his deliberate betrayal, or would he have been too ashamed? Anger pounded in her head keeping time with her heart beats.

A chauffeur-driven black car, bedecked with white ribbons, came to a stop. It was Myles, immaculate in a morning suit. As Myles adjusted his pearl-grey tie, the driver reached inside the car and brought out a top hat. Gaby jumped from her car, slammed the door, and in three long strides she was at his side. Myles gaped at her, his mouth opened and closed without a sound.

"Hello Myles!" Gaby forced herself to keep her voice steady. "Going to a wedding?"

"What are you doing here, are you invited?" asked Myles. Janey had never mentioned this O'Neill bitch and she didn't look as if she was dressed for a wedding...

"No, I'm not invited," she mimicked his tone perfectly. "Are you?"

"Yes, I am." His eyes narrowed. "Not that it is any of your business, it's *my* wedding. My wedding to a girl that I love and who loves me." The venom and spite in his tone acted as the trigger Gaby needed.

"Oh no, Myles, there isn't going to be a wedding, and Janey doesn't love you." Gaby's voice was icy. "What's that expression, Myles? *Do unto others...*"

Opening her hand, slowly and deliberately she unwrapped the tissue. With her forefinger and thumb, she delicately extricated the ruby ring and held it up in front of him.

"As you can see, Myles, there will be no wedding. I engineered the whole thing. How does it feel? It's true, and you're not going to wake up and find that this is all a bad dream. I've just taken Janey to the airport, and in about...." she paused to look at her watch, "ten minutes or so, she'll be on her way to New York. By the way, five thousand pounds and an air ticket was her price."

The blood drained from his tanned face and then a purple anger suffused his handsome good looks. She'd read that somewhere but now it was happening right in front of her eyes.

"You scheming little tramp, you conniving bitch!" he roared at her with such force that she stepped back in fright. "I should have finished you off once and for all, not let you off the hook so lightly."

Gaby was sure he was about to hit her.

"This time you've gone too far. You'll never be able to destroy anyone again. You can count your days because there won't be many of them left."

The driver of Myles' car gawped at the furious bridegroom. Several guests had congregated a few feet away and were staring, horrified.

"Give me that ring," Myles bellowed, moving towards her. A man dashed from the church. "Myles," he said, his voice stopped Myles dead. "What the hell's going on? Bunny just ran into the church and said that the wedding's off."

"It's this bitch, the one who killed Maria."

The man looked at her with alarm. Gaby stared back at him coldly. "I did *not* kill her," she stated emphatically. Throwing the ring at Myles she turned on her heel and walked towards her car.

She could hear the sound of thudding feet, the

arm that grabbed hers was like a vice. As she yelled and struggled to free herself, Myles thrust his face into hers and roared. "You don't know what it is to suffer - yet - this time you won't escape!"

Myles was grabbed from behind by his friend. "You'd better leave," he told Gaby.

"Don't worry, I'm going. I've done what I came to do." With all the dignity she could muster she straightened her blouse, pushed back her hair and climbed into her car. Her trembling hands clutched the wheel tightly as she drove away. She looked frantically for somewhere to park but every space was taken. Some double yellow lines were visible further down the road. Not caring, she pulled in and stopped. Her whole body was shaking uncontrollably. She gasped for breath, deep rasping gulps of life-giving air. After half an hour the trembling finally stopped and Gaby headed for the haven of her cottage.

* * *

"Just don't interrupt until I've finished," said Gaby, as she began the bizarre story of her revenge on Myles. Jill and Jacqui sat in obedient silence. They loved Gaby but this was horrifying and dangerous. They couldn't look at one another - or at Gaby.

"That's the whole story," Gaby finished lamely.

Neither Jill nor Jacqui moved.

"Say something, please," Gaby begged. She hadn't expected them to applaud her actions but their silence was unbearable.

"That has to be the craziest, most dangerous

thing you have ever done." Jill's tone stung.

"I have to agree, Gaby - Jill's right. The mere fact that you never said a word all these months proves that you knew it was wrong. Why didn't you discuss it with one of us first?"

Gaby hung her head.

"Stop play-acting, it won't wash," said Jacqui furiously. "I bet Uncle John doesn't know about this?"

"No, he doesn't."

"What about the police? Don't you think you should tell them? Myles did threaten you and in front of witnesses too."

"He was just angry, that was just the heat of the moment."

"How do you know that? For God's sake, Gaby, he set out to destroy you once, what makes you think he won't do it again, only worse? I'm sorry I snapped at you but I'm scared - we're scared."

Jill nodded her head in agreement. "How did you *think* he'd react?"

Gaby shrugged. "Anger, surprise - I didn't allow myself to think anything, to be honest. It was so - unreal - I suppose. Right up until the last few seconds I didn't even know how I was going to confront him or what I was going to say. All I knew was that I needed to get rid of that terrible hurt. I can see how you feel and I don't blame you."

"And Janey? God, she must be pretty devious to have seduced him like that, especially as she wouldn't go to bed with him." Jill shuddered, it was all horrible. " I still can't believe what you've done."

"Janey is the most single-minded person I've ever known. She was absolutely determined to get to the States and I was able to help her."

"That's a poor excuse and you know it," Jacqui pointed out. "There are plenty of decent ways to earn money."

The silence sat heavily between them - the tension as powerful as a physical barrier.

They'd sat in this corner so often, laughing and gossiping, bolstering each others' egos and supporting one another through every crisis under the sun. Would this be the end of a friendship that was one of the most important things in her life? Without Jill and Jacqui she wouldn't be able to go on.

"Gaby, don't cry," Jill rooted in her pocket for a tissue. "We've been very hard on you, I'm sorry. I know it wasn't a lark and how you must have been hurting. It's not even the immorality of it, and it *was* a dreadful thing to do, but it was dangerous too. Gaby, I'm terrified now, he might do anything."

Jacqui reached across and took hold of Gaby's hand. "I'm scared too, Gaby, and I can't help saying it again, I think you should get in touch with the police."

"Trust me, they were idle threats," Gaby said, blowing her nose. "I thought you were going to leave me high and dry, that upset me far more than anything that stupid Myles had to say."

"That's the most ridiculous thing you've said today - and boy, what you've said today takes some beating."

A watery smile lit Gaby's face, her nerves were so raw that nothing made too much sense. At

Anne Schulman

least she hadn't lost the loyalty of her two friends.

The triumph of revenge still hadn't registered. When she returned to the cottage after what had seemed to be endless hours she took a long hot bath. Her mind wouldn't focus so she lay in the water allowing an endless stream of jumbled thoughts to run through her mind. Later, wrapped in her bathrobe, she made a cup of tea and went outside to the little rustic table and wrote to Janey. She sealed the letter. It was then that relief came, it engulfed her like a flood. No more Janey, no more phone calls or guarded talks. No clandestine lunches, hidden away in poky little cafes in case Myles should discover them. It was all over. Myles no longer mattered to her. She could forget him at last.

She thumped the stamp on to the envelope with the side of her clenched fist. She pulled on a pair of culottes and a cotton sweater and ran to the post box. "Good-bye, Myles," she said, thumbing her nose at the green box in the wall, "and good riddance."

CHAPTER SIXTY

Stephen Drake kissed Gaby chastely on the cheek and with a long wistful look left her to follow the porter into the airport terminal.

She had half an hour to kill before her flight was called, plenty of time to browse in the splendid new bookshop and to buy some of the Irish smoked salmon that Claude d'Albion adored. She thought of the dapper little man with affection. He'd never let her down no matter how late she made her booking.

Lost in one of her new books, Gaby was astonished to hear the landing announcement.

Searching amongst the tanned faces at the barrier she saw Joseph. She waved and walked towards him smiling widely.

"Welcome, M'mselle Gaby, you had a good flight, yes?"

"Hello, Joseph. The flight was excellent, thank you. How's everyone at the château?"

Joseph negotiated the busy roads and told Gaby all the news. He liked this Irish M'mselle, always so polite, so friendly - her father too. She had only been a schoolgirl when they'd first met and here she was, a beautiful young lady. She and her friends had had such fun last year, they'd given a sparkle to the atmosphere at the château. M Claude had a soft spot for her too. Only this morning he had told Marc to be sure to include her favourite gâteau on the dinner menu. He peeped at her in his mirror and thought she looked rather sad, there was a slight down-tilt to her mouth.

"Here we are," he smiled as the black gates parted with a quiet swish.

"Oh Joseph, just smell that perfume, look at the lemon tree, it's grown at least a foot since last year." Joseph was just as proud of the magnificent grounds as Claude.

"I have my own garden now," Gaby said, "I'll be able to take some cuttings from here, when Monsieur Claude isn't looking."

They both laughed. All the château's regular guests knew the rule, taking cuttings was strictly forbidden without M Claude's permission. "Don't let him catch you, M'mselle, I would hate to lose you as a guest," he smiled. Gaby believed his warning, it had happened before.

"*Gabrielle, tu es bienvenue ici,*" Claude d'Albion said, his normally solemn face smiling affectionately.

"Claude! Oh, it's so good to be back." Gaby sprang from the car and threw her arms around him. It was known to be a sign of his esteem when he left the marble entrance hall and came to greet someone at the hotel limousine.

"Let me see you, Gabrielle," he said, extricating himself from her exuberant embrace. "You are well?" A slight frown creased his brow. Although she was as beautiful as ever, she had lost weight and he noticed purple circles under her eyes.

"Absolutely fine," she assured him, then clapping her hand to her mouth, she groaned. "Oh my goodness, I forgot to bring you smoked salmon."

His expression didn't alter. "Please, it is of no matter," he assured the laughing girl. "Gabrielle, you are teasing me, I know it from your eyes."

"Yes I am - as if I'd forget!"

"*I* forget, you are trouble with your jokes. Please Gabrielle, no mischief now."

"I promise, I'll behave like a proper young lady, you won't know I'm here."

Why did the sun shine brighter whenever Gabrielle O'Neill came to Beaulieu?

"Hi, Claudine!"

"M'mselle Gaby, we are pleased to have you back with us." Claudine smiled, opening the lid of Gaby's suitcase. Lifting out the pretty dresses she smoothed the creases and placed them on the padded hangers. "Such lovely colours, perfect for the sunshine, *non?*"

"You must remember them from last year," Gaby said.

Claudine began to hang the clothes in the tall wardrobe while Gaby stared through the window at the people lounging under the shady trees. "No one I recognise," she said, impatient to join them. "We'd better hide that wire hanger, Claudine, or M Claude will have a seizure." Gaby clutched one hand to her heart and the other to her brow. She collapsed dramatically on the bed. "Wire hangers, wire - in my château, *mon dieu!* Please leave the Château d'Albion immediately, Gabrielle."

Claudine laughed, the young Irish lady was a good mimic.

Gaby walked through the foyer towards the garden, swinging her beach bag. "You have protective cream for your skin, Gabrielle?"

Claude, sitting at the reception desk, enquired.

She resisted the urge to giggle. "Yes thank you," she said decorously.

Gaby emptied her bag onto the middle of the wide sun mattress and rooted until she found her sunglasses, her suncream and a bag of toffees. Scooping everything else back into the bag she slipped off her jacket and slathered herself with cream. She thought for a moment of Janey, reunited with Hugh. Where was Myles? Licking his wounds in Wicklow no doubt. Those stupid threats he'd made, like something out of a melodrama. Despite the heat of the sun she shivered as if someone had walked over her grave. Forget them, she told herself sternly.

With her sunglasses perched on her head, she lay back on the striped bed and sighed with bliss. Roll on new life, I'm ready.

Edward

CHAPTER SIXTY-ONE

Edward hated to admit it after just one week but their marriage was not working well. Was it emotion or sympathy for his financial loss that had weakened Nicole's resolve and prompted her to marry him? If David Lock had any opinion about Edward's unwise investment he had kept it to himself.

The showgirls, with their great plumed headdresses, formed a feathered archway under which he and Nicole made their way from the wedding chapel to the stretch-limo. David Lock hosted their reception and it lasted practically all day to allow his friends on the staff to wish him good luck as they changed shifts. Nicole kept herself slightly aloof, even from the other girls in the show, but Edward was friendly with every one of the hotel staff, from the busboys to the boss.

"I'm afraid a honeymoon will be out of the question," he confessed reluctantly.

Nicole's mouth formed a pretty pout. "Couldn't we use credit cards? Everyone else does."

Edward had roughly calculated the cost of a week in New York. Hotels and air fares were expensive and the thought of Nicole's shopping assault on the stores made his blood run cold. No, it would have to wait until he had begun to recoup at least a fraction of his loss. She avoided him for a couple of days after that. On the day of the wedding when his watch showed five minutes after the appointed hour and she hadn't yet arrived, he was sure he'd blown it.

Nicole's petulant bridal face was noticed by the girls. Few of them would have turned down the opportunity to be standing in her Maud Frizon shoes that day.

"A toast to the happy couple," David Lock proposed, raising his glass. Frowning, he wondered, "What's her beef?" He'd never liked the girl but she was a talented dancer and that was all he cared about. If there was some way he could prevent members of staff marrying each other he would have done so. It so very rarely worked. Edward didn't look like a happy bridegroom either. Now that he came to think of it, Edward had changed since that day the young Irishman had sat in his apartment and told him about the scam he had fallen for. David had heard Edward out, nodding sympathetically where necessary. Although he was slightly hurt, he didn't ask why Edward hadn't told him about it first. But it was done now. Maybe his wedding gift to them would cheer them up.

Within seconds Nicole's eyes were alight with excitement, ten days in New York all paid for and a handsome cheque to boot.

"Oh David, how fabulous," she gushed, hugging him warmly.

"This is more than generous," Edward said gratefully, pumping David's hand. "It will certainly start our marriage off in style."

The limousine was decked out in style too. Strings of silver balloons trailed in its wake as, showered with confetti, paper rose petals and good wishes, they left the hotel to spend the night at Edward's apartment before leaving for New York next morning.

Nicole's happy mood was infectious and he didn't even mind when she wouldn't allow him to kiss her and pushed him away, frowning in the direction of the driver.

Although they were no strangers to lovemaking Edward had imagined their wedding night would be something special - magical even - but when he caressed her beautiful body and kissed her soft lips he sensed a feeling of distance and impatience in Nicole. She didn't respond. He grabbed her hands and forced her legs apart and plunged inside her with fast rhythmic strokes of anger and disappointment. She made no protest, didn't cry out, she just turned her back to him. In the dim light of the room he watched her - smiling in her sleep. She was probably dreaming about the trip, he thought bitterly. What sort of spell had Nicole cast over him? Was it her aloofness that attracted him so much? He'd had so many beautiful girls to choose from but she was the one who'd fascinated him from the moment they'd met.

The flight had been uneventful but he found it difficult to concentrate on the film. Nicole had woken that morning dewy-eyed and excited. She rushed around doing last minute packing, but didn't seem to notice his air of preoccupation.

"One more hour and we'll be in New York, I can't wait!"

"Me neither," Edward had shrugged off his grudging mood, last night was better forgotten.

Nicole's eyes glowed with such intensity that he laughed and squeezed her arm affectionately.

Anne Schulman

She gave him a long lingering kiss. Maybe it wasn't going to be so bad after all.

The exit doors of the air terminal parted and the freezing air cut across their faces with the sharpness of a razor. Edward took a long deep breath which stung his nostrils like acid.

"Quick, there's a cab," Nicole dashed to the waiting car. "Edward, come on, it's freezing!"

"Wonderful, I love freezing," he gasped, fighting against the icy breeze.

She tucked her arm through his as they drove towards the city. "I never get used to those skyscrapers," she remarked. "I always feel they'll topple over."

"They're amazing aren't they? - defying gravity," he laughed.

When they entered the plush lobby of the Plaza Hotel the sound that greeted them was audible - the sound of silence.

"Listen," Edward said. He stopped suddenly.

"Listen to what? I can't hear anything."

"Exactly. No noise, no music, no slots, no laughter, just muffled calm."

Within an hour they'd booked seats for the ballet, two Broadway shows and, though Nicole was less than enthusiastic, an off Broadway, Neil Simon comedy.

Nicole whirled and twirled around the room, pirouetting with such abandon that Edward ducked out of the way of her long swinging legs.

"This is going to be incredible," she said, squirming and protesting as he pulled her down on to the enormous bed. "Let's save that till later, New York is waiting."

Edward frowned at himself in the mirror and

wondered how he was going to spend his day. Snow was forecast and he couldn't wait to feel the white flakes falling on his face, catching them - tasteless and cold - on the end of his tongue just as he had when he was a child.

He had walked more in the last week than he had for years. Each morning at nine o'clock Nicole was ready for action, but the action was shopping. Edward did most of the sight-seeing on his own. Every afternoon she came back to the hotel laden with packages. Shoes were her particular weakness and she'd strewn boxes of them all over the bed. Edward had laughed and told her she was trying to outdo Imelda Marcos. Then came the clothes; dresses, blouses and skirts, sweaters. She made a beeline for a shop which specialised in dancers' outfits - leotards, lycra body suits, leg warmers, ballet shoes - and she bought them, in all colours and shapes. David Lock's cheque didn't begin to cover all this reckless spending and she'd spent her own savings on the first day. Edward warned her that she had to stop. That night she hardly spoke to him and her rigid spine next to him in the king-sized bed told its own tale.

Contrite, the following day she arranged to meet him for lunch at Windows On The World on the 107th. floor of the World Trade Centre. From their window table they gasped at the magnificent view of Manhattan below them. Teeming traffic moved in neat grids like children's toys, stopping now and then to permit little colonies of pedestrian ants to cross their path. Nicole produced a gift for him. Perhaps it was an apology. His face paled as he unwrapped it. A Missoni sweater which, without seeing the price tag, he knew cost the earth.

"Don't you love it?" she asked, her eyes wide in expectation of his gratitude.

"It's beautiful, Nicole," he said, fingering the knitted garment with its soft understated colours. "There's no way that we can afford it. I'm sorry, but it must go back." His voice was firm, harsh with frustration. "Don't you understand, this shopping-fest must end? We'll finish up in such debt it'll take us years to clear it."

She flounced out of the restaurant without having eaten, leaving the sweater on the table. Edward cancelled the order, he'd lost his appetite. The shop on Madison Avenue was packed with wonderful knitwear and he returned the sweater without difficulty. As he walked disconsolately past the designer shops he wished he could give Nicole carte blanche and indulge her every whim. With her lovely face and perfect leggy figure it would have been difficult to find anything that didn't suit her, he thought sadly. Later that day they had their first really bad fight. She slammed into their room flaunting a dozen large carrier bags, bearing the names of some of the world's top designers.

"There." She slammed the bags on the bed. "Now you've really got something to belly-ache about." She faced him, her violet eyes almost black with rage.

"You can take them back first thing in the morning," he said quietly. "Even a child wouldn't behave like this. What's the matter with you, Nicole, don't you understand simple finance?"

She ranted and screamed for an hour until

Edward calmed her down with the promise that she could keep the item she most favoured. "But that's it, Nicole, the end, no more."

They patched up their troubles and made plans to spend the following day in Greenwich Village but within a hour she was off again to the bijou shops, leaving Edward to mooch on his own.

✿ ✿ ✿

"What are you going to do while I'm gone?" Nicole asked, tucking her luxuriant blonde hair under a bright red knitted hat.

"I think I'll go to the Frick Museum," he replied, "I'm hoping it'll snow."

"You're crazy, no one over the age of ten looks forward to snow," she laughed, "have a good day whatever you decide. See you back here about six o'clock."

"And you," he said, kissing her tenderly. "Say hello to your girlfriends from me."

Edward was pleased that she had arranged to meet her friends from her club days in New York. He offered to go with her but she refused, saying it would look odd taking her husband along on an all-girls-together day. He didn't really mind, quite the opposite, she had made so few friends in Las Vegas it would be good for her to indulge in some girl-talk.

There was something familiar about the back of the tall figure closely examining the painting. Edward took a few sideways steps and looked at the man.

"My God! Henri!" Edward's voice echoed

loudly in the quiet room.

Wheeling round at the sound of his name, Henri Ducroix's face wore a look of total astonishment. "Edouard, my friend, what are you doing here? It is so good to see you again. I thought you were in Las Vegas, do you live in New York now?" asked Henri.

"No, I'm here on honeymoon. I still work in Las Vegas. I meant to write, but time flies by and, well, I'm sure you understand. And you, Henri Ducroix? What are *you* doing here?"

"No name, please," Henri said, putting his finger to his lips. "Let us go and have a cup of coffee and a drink, then we can talk."

"Oh this terrible cold, it seeps into the bones and numbs the brain. *Salut!*" Henri swallowed the warming brandy in a gulp. "That's better," he smiled, wrapping his big hands round the hot coffee cup. "Now we can relax. It makes me nervous to hear my name mentioned in a gallery or museum."

"What brings you to New York? How long will you be here? Can we spend some time together?"

"One question at a time! I am here to copy one of my forgeries. Crazy, no?" he said in a low voice. He laughed at Edward's puzzled face. "I will explain in a moment - as for time, I leave tonight for Paris but the day until four o'clock is my own."

"At least we can have a few hours together."

"That will be good. I have missed our journeys together and I am pleased to see that maybe I have given you some love of art, yes?"

"Yes, I suppose you have. So this crazy job of yours, tell me about it."

"No names, you understand?"

Edward nodded. Henri had always been frank with him, dangerously so, Edward judged. But he'd never told Edward the names of any of his buyers or clients.

"The picture in question has been authenticated by one of New York's art 'experts' as genuine and the owner, who wishes to sell it, desires a copy. There is but one twist in the tale, the authenticated original is a fake - my own forgery!" A wicked grin spread across Henri's canny face.

"Are you sure?" Edward asked unnecessarily. Henri would be positive.

"Of course, have I taught you nothing?" he sighed.

"Silly question, I'm sorry."

"No, I am being too clever, I have total proof in one second. Something nobody knows. Can I trust you?"

"You *know* you can," Edward assured him with a hurt look.

"Every canvas that I paint bears a mark known only to me. It is invisible to the naked eye and I would challenge anyone to find it. Not with a powerful magnifying glass or with x-rays or by any other known method."

"And you're not going to tell me what it is?"

"I'm sorry, but you understand?"

Edward understood perfectly. "So the owner is selling his painting in good faith?"

"*Absolutement,* and it is not for me to tell him otherwise."

"So the copy you make, is it identical to the original? I often meant to ask you that."

"There are small changes, slight differences when I paint a copy. A forgery is as near perfect as possible."

"It still fascinates me after all these years," Edward admitted.

"Me too!" Henri laughed. "Now tell me about your marriage, where is your bride? Will I meet her?"

"Not today unfortunately. She's meeting some of her friends, girls she worked with in New York before going to Las Vegas. Her name is Nicole, French-born, and very beautiful. She's a dancer in the hotel where I work but she wanted to be a ballerina. Her height - she's six feet tall - made that impossible."

"And you, you are successful in Las Vegas? Happy there? Wait, before you tell me we will go to the best little French restaurant in New York, it's getting too noisy here."

"You should try Vegas. You'd go crazy with the noise, it never stops – twenty-four hours a day," Edward said, striding along beside the big man with his flapping cape.

Henri poured the last of the wine equally between their two glasses. "It is bad for you, Edouard, to lose all your money like that, I am very sorry. All those years and - *pouf!*"

Edward hesitated. He wondered if it would be totally disloyal of him to tell Henri the rest of the story; his problems after one week of marriage, about Nicole's mad spending spree and her obvious dissatisfaction. He needed to talk to someone and who better than Henri?

"What do I say?" Henri asked, his eyes searching Edward's unhappy face. "One thing I do not understand, you lost your money before you were married, so it has not been a shock for her, no?"

"Right, and that's what makes it so difficult to take. I'm sure she regrets having married me."

"In that case, she's a fool. Give her a little while, but be the master." Henri glanced at the ormolu clock above Edward's head. "Sadly, I must leave now. I wish we could have had more time. From now on we keep in touch, yes?"

"I promise. I'll write, you can draw!"

Edward watched Henri disappear into the inevitable melee of traffic. Seeing Henri had taken him back to the days they spent together visiting art galleries, to long lazy lunches, to the old camaraderie. A sudden longing for France threatened to overwhelm him. He could almost smell the diesel and the fresh paint of the boats. It was cold standing there daydreaming in the middle of the busy street and he started to walk back towards the hotel.

He stopped at Tiffany's. Their window displays were ingenious. A miniature model of a New York brownstone, a row-house faced with reddish-brown stone, was featured in each of the windows. It took a minute before Edward realised that, sitting in a miniature trashcan in a tiny alley, was a magnificent pear-shaped diamond. He retraced his steps to the first of the displays and searched until he found a huge cabochon ruby partly concealed in bits of torn newspapers. At the next house, hidden amongst the weeds on its steps, an emerald nestled. A tiny cat clawed amongst some diminutive trash cans revealing a glistening stream of glittering stones.

Anne Schulman

They were almost lost amongst papers, fish bones and empty cans. Edward was so engrossed in his game of spot-the-gems that he failed to notice the first flurry of flakes until a cold drip of melted snow ran down his cheek. Smiling broadly, he turned up the collar of his coat and continued on his way. Within minutes he was back at the hotel and by then snow was falling fast. For a moment he stood outside allowing the lacy white discs to fall on his open palm and then melt into an almost invisible drop of water. He laughed uproariously as a scurrying passer-by dropped a nickel into his outstretched hand. Maybe it was time to go inside.

The hotel was usually quiet at this time of the day but as he looked around him he saw people heading towards the Oak Bar, brushing the snow from their shoulders. Nicole wouldn't be back for a couple of hours. The lively bar would be better than sitting alone in the bedroom watching television.

Edward chose a table at the window facing Central Park and watched the hurrying crowds huddled in scarves and heavy coats battling against the driving snow. The open horse-drawn carriages, so much a feature of the corner site, had disappeared early. There would be very few people brave enough to face a slow drive through the park in this weather, he thought. He looked back at the bar which was filling up with commuters and hotel guests. At the table beside him a powerfully built man with thinning grey hair, light-framed glasses and a benign rounded face glanced at his watch. He was probably worried about his wife. Edward was beginning to wonder if Nicole would be delayed also.

"Makes you yearn for the sun, this weather," the man remarked, spearing an olive with a cocktail stick and pushing aside the empty bowl.

"It probably sounds ridiculous, but I've been yearning to see the snow," Edward said sheepishly.

"Obviously you live in a hot climate."

Before Edward had a chance to reply a tall, fair-haired man rushed through the door removing his raincoat as he walked. "Sorry, Bob. It's from hell out there. Every cab in the city has vanished."

"No sweat. I had trouble getting here myself. I ordered you a Scotch, reckoned you could use it in this weather."

Shaking off his coat, he folded it loosely and threw it over the back of a chair, brushing his long damp hair away from his thin face. The young man withdrew a large sheet of rolled paper from a cardboard cylinder. Propping the cylinder against his chair he sat down and unfurled the sheet, anchoring one end of it with an ashtray. He held the other end in his hand. "Coming up to the home straight at last," he smiled at the man he'd called Bob who bent forward to examine the drawings.

"Looks good, how about that problem with the aft deck, have you been able to sort it out?"

"Yes. I'm ashamed to say that the solution was staring me in the face and I couldn't see it. Here, let me show you." Using his forearm to prevent the blueprint from curling, he pointed awkwardly to the deck in question.

Edward had heard the word *deck* and his

interest was piqued. The plan was far too large for the small table. Edward watched the man struggle to spread it fully. He put his glass on the window ledge and pushed his own table nearer to the two men.

"Use the bowl and ashtray as well," Edward offered.

"Thanks, that's better," the young man smiled gratefully. He put his glass down by his feet. The two of them continued to pore over the diagrams. The man, whom Edward had now realised must be a naval architect, pointed out the changes that he'd made. Edward found it impossible not to sneak a glance at the plans. His eyes were drawn to the outline and then to what appeared to be a large number of staterooms and cabins. When they finished their discussion, Bob asked Edward if he'd like a drink. Edward said, "No thanks, I'll nurse this for a while." The wine at lunch had made him a bit sleepy, he ought to take it easy.

The architect reached behind him for the cylinder and removed a second, slightly smaller diagram. As he opened it Edward automatically reached for the corners and tucked them under the bowl and ashtray.

"This is a nuisance for you," the architect said apologetically.

"Not at all. To be honest boats fascinate me. I have to admit I've been trying to look at your blueprint without wanting to be nosy, it looks fabulous."

"Thank you," the man smiled, "please be my guest - I don't imagine Bob would mind."

"Bob would mind what?" Bob said, a genial

smile lighting his face as he placed the drinks carefully on the edge of the table.

"I've been sneaking a look at your plans. I adore boats, ships, yachts - you name it. Living and working in Vegas, I don't see too many of them floating up and down the Strip."

They laughed and Bob moved up slightly to allow Edward a better view.

"This is the interior plan," Bob said proudly.

"It looks enormous," Edward said.

"I suppose you could say a hundred and fifty feet is pretty big."

Edward whistled softly. "That's an understatement. What are you going to name it?" he asked, looking from one man to the other.

"Good question. We've all been tossing names backwards and forwards for months. My wife suggested *Big Bucks* - as you gather from that, she can't see the value of it! I thought perhaps *Moon Swell,* don't ask me why. Justin here, when pushed, came up with *White Arrow.* Care to throw in your ten cents worth? We're open to suggestions."

Edward looked at the drawing. Such luxury, what sleek lines, a dream of a yacht. "How about the *Bon-Vivant?*"

"I like it," Justin said.

"I love it." Bob's eyes beamed approval behind his glasses. "Terrific, don't you think, Justin?"

"It certainly has an sybaritic ring to it. Yes, I really do like it."

"Now you *must* have a drink," Bob insisted, calling a waiter. "Let's christen her here and now."

"To the *Bon-Vivant,*" Bob proposed, as he

handed Edward a glass.

"To safe seas and smooth sailing," Edward added.

"Amen," Justin echoed. "That's all we can do today. I'll leave the interior designs with you and here's the list of fabrics and sample colours. If you could make a decision tomorrow, we can order them right away. Everything else is fine, I should have the rest of the materials by next Monday at the latest."

"I'll make the decision tonight," Bob promised, glancing through the window. "Still swirling around out there. I think I'll wait here a while."

Justin shook hands with them both. "I'll expect your call," he said to Bob. "Nice to have met you, thanks for the name. The more I think about it the better I like it," he smiled at Edward.

"Any time!" Edward laughed. "By the way, congratulations. I'm sure it'll be superb."

"He's a brilliant yacht designer, streets ahead of anyone else, I think," Bob said, watching Justin's lanky frame as he left the bar.

"I gather it's almost finished."

"Almost. Another week and she'll be ready for the interior designers and then, the maiden voyage." Bob's chest swelled up proudly over his rotund stomach.

"Where will that be?" Edward could just see Bob in his yachting gear, standing proprietorially in the wheel house.

"Across the Atlantic."

"That's some maiden voyage!" Edward was impressed. "You must be very excited."

"I would be, but I won't be aboard," Bob said wistfully. "My wife is a lousy sailor so we've reached a compromise, the crew will take the yacht to France and we'll join it there in calmer waters. This," he said, prodding the page with a stubby finger, "is the fulfilment of my ambitions, my dreams - an ocean-going yacht."

"I don't blame you. I lived in the south of France for some years. Nowhere better than Monte Carlo or Cannes for your wife if she's unhappy at sea."

"Did you have a boat there?"

"I wish I had. No, I couldn't afford one." Edward told the story of his hasty flight to France.

"Irish blarney?" Bob smiled cynically.

"No way. It's all true," Edward frowned. "If it wasn't, I'd be practising law in Ireland today."

"Do you have any regrets - leaving France, I mean?"

"Sometimes, yes. Today, very much so. I ran into an old friend at the Frick Museum. Talking to him brought it all back, the port, the bistros, our outings ..." Edward stopped as he saw Nicole, laden with parcels, at the entrance to the bar. She waved to him and made her way across to the table.

"Were you worried about me? The subways are crowded and there isn't a yellow cab to be found in New York," she said, her face flushed.

Edward introduced her to Bob. "Good shopping, I see?" Bob smiled, "unlike the cabs, there's always a store when you need one!"

Nicole avoided Edward's glaring eyes. "If you'll excuse me I'm going to take a hot shower. No, don't get up, Edward, stay and finish your drink." She smiled and left the bar, her perfume lingered.

"Did I detect a slight accent?" Bob asked.

"Nicole was born and brought up in France then the family moved to the States."

"How does she like Vegas?"

"She doesn't. I think she'd be happy to go back to France, even though she was so young when she left."

"Do you have plans to return?"

"Not at the moment. Things are tight financially, I had a bit of bad luck recently."

Bob's eyebrows rose. The Plaz. was not exactly the cheapest hotel in New York and, judging by the designer names on the bags Edward's wife had been carrying, that was an expensive excursion. He thought Edward hadn't looked too happy when he saw his wife. Maybe she'd gone a bit crazy in the stores.

"What's your job in Vegas?"

Edward told Bob about a typical week in his life as a manager.

"After that even I'm exhausted, here let me buy you a drink." Bob stood up and made his way to the crowded bar.

Edward looked through the window. Nighttime in New York held a special fascination for him. The sable sky was illuminated by the light of high-rise buildings. Countless thousands of tiny golden lights in the square windows paid homage to the dusk. A city vibrant and alive. Through the flurry of snowflakes he could see the ever-moving traffic. Taxis were stampeded by jostling groups as they elbowed the competition aside. Cars and buses, limousines with their mysterious darkened windows, all moved more slowly than usual on the slushy roads. Even the snow hadn't deterred the new breed of roller-skaters, whooshing and splashing jets of slushy water on pedestrians too cold to argue.

"So, you're impressed with the yacht?" Bob asked.

"And how. Who wouldn't be?"

"How much time have you spent around boats?" Bob twirled the ice in his glass.

"Not as much recently as I would have liked. I've always been around boats and the sea since I was a small boy. The fishermen would let me help them with the nets, repairs and all that. I did odd jobs and they paid me by taking me to sea with them. I became part of the scenery. When I wasn't working at the casino bar in France, I used to earn money that way. The yachts in the port at Cannes were fabulous but not remotely like yours. I once saw a magnificent yacht which belonged, I think, to an Arab prince. It was so big it had to be berthed at sea. We used to watch it from the port, swaying gently at anchor. There were launches ferrying people backwards and forwards all day. You'll have to do the same, I imagine," Edward said thoughtfully.

"I believe so, according to the captain. He's experienced in those sort of details. I just want to get my feet on the deck and let someone else do the worrying."

"You obviously have a crew?"

"Sure, ready to go. But I'll tell you what I don't have, I don't have a manager or a caretaker, if that's the word. Someone responsible and trustworthy. Someone to make the crossing in my absence."

Edward was confused, surely the crew would

fulfil that role? After all, Bob trusted the captain with his life, why not his boat?

"You look surprised. I'd like to have someone on board while I'm not there, aside from the crew."

"There must be a thousand people who'd love that job. A security firm could supply someone, an ex-cop perhaps? You should have no problem in finding any number of men - or women," Edward suggested.

"That's obvious," Bob's tone was slightly condescending. "The person I need has to be able to stand in for me without antagonising the crew."

"I understand what you're saying," said Edward, "what I don't understand - and it's not my affair - is why?"

"I have my reasons." All his life Bob had been guided by his intuition and his gut feeling told him that Edward could be the right man.

"Would it appeal to you? I gather you'd like to go back to France. You love the sea and, if you could supply me with a sound character reference, I think you could be the person I'm looking for."

"Me?" Edward asked. "Why me?"

"Why not?" Bob replied, "I think you'd love the experience and you seem to have the necessary qualifications. Interested?"

"I could think of nothing I'd enjoy more, but I do have an excellent job already."

"Yes, I appreciate that but what I'm offering would take a month at most. You could combine it with a vacation. You could make use of the yacht until we arrive. Of course I'd pay generously for your time. The trip will also involve one week in France without the crew, I've promised them a vacation before we set off round the Mediterranean. The captain has found a temporary replacement for the week, a friend of his whom he can trust with *his ship!* We'll have to hire a couple of experienced and reliable locals too. You know the area and I gather you speak the language?"

Edward's mind was working furiously. Paradise, handed to him on a plate. He would have to discuss it with Nicole, but what about David Lock? He'd need his permission to take time off and he'd need a reference. But an offer like this was a once-in-a-life-time opportunity.

"A reference would be no problem but I must get the OK from my employer first. I can call him tonight and I'll let you have my answer later. It sounds wonderful."

"Sooner the better. Let me give you my card, you can call me any time up to midnight. If it pans out, you've got yourself, and your wife of course, a first class ticket across the Atlantic. If it doesn't, well, I've enjoyed meeting you."

"Me too and either way, good luck with the *Bon-Vivant.*"

CHAPTER SIXTY-TWO

Nicole finished brushing her damp curls and then lay on the bed wrapped in a fluffy blue towelling robe. It flattered her colouring, made her look vulnerable. Apart from the awful weather she had enjoyed her day. It had been fun to see the three girls again but she hated the sleazy little bar they chose for lunch. After a few drinks it began to look better. Nothing much had changed for any of them since she had left New York. Darlene had been offered a small solo part in a musical but that meant going to Chicago and she was still undecided. The girls wanted to hear all about Las Vegas and her new husband. Nicole supplied some of the details. Her finances were none of their concern. They had fingered her cashmere cardigan reverently, their envious glances made it all seem worth while.

Edward could no longer be angry, she'd solved her money problem. One quick phone call to her bank was all it took. She arranged extended credit and in under an hour she had collected all those returned garments and added some extra items that she'd missed on her first trip. She'd worked hard in that awful chorus line and now she deserved some fun. It wouldn't cost Edward a cent so he could no longer gripe and rage. She had blanched a little as she added up her bills. Fifteen thousand dollars in one afternoon was a bit much, but so what, the clothes were stunning. She stuffed the receipts quickly into the pocket of her robe as Edward entered the room.

"He seemed a nice man. Did you enjoy yourself today?" she asked brightly.

Edward's gaze softened as he looked at his wife lying seductively in the centre of the big bed. "More than you could imagine. This morning at the Frick Museum I walked into Henri Ducroix - you remember? I told you about him, my friend from Cannes, an artist." He'd never told her Henri's real profession. "We had a long lunch together, it was wonderful to see him again. I hadn't realised how much I have missed his company."

"That's wonderful, I'm pleased for you. Will I meet him?"

"No, he left New York this evening. But that's not all. The man I was talking to in the bar downstairs, Bob..." He removed the card from his pocket and looked for Bob's last name. "Bob Howell."

Nicole nodded her head.

"He's offered me a job for a month," Edward said. *"Us* a job for a month, caretaking his yacht on its first voyage across the Atlantic."

"You're not serious." Nicole's face had turned pale. "Are you nuts? People die out there on that ocean."

"Don't be silly, this is a huge yacht almost as big as a liner. It looks fabulous from the drawings."

"I don't care if it's the size of the QE2. You're kidding, aren't you?"

"No I'm not. This is the chance of a lifetime. You'd adore it, Nicole. Think about it - a crew to look after your every need, untold luxury and then a few weeks in Cannes or Monte Carlo living on the finest yacht in the harbour. Not even in the harbour, it's too big, it would have to anchor at sea." Edward moved to the table at the side of the bed and lifted the phone.

"Who are you calling?" she asked, her eyes full of alarm.

"David Lock," he answered. "If he's agreeable I'm going to go. It's up to you whether you join me or not." "Be the master," Henri had said.

Edward replaced the receiver and gave a couple of whoops of delight. David had been surprisingly understanding. When he knew that Edward would be back by the July fourth weekend, he had given him his blessing. "You could do with a bit of luck. I'll expect his call - what name did you say?"

"Do you want to eat out tonight?" Edward asked. "The snow seems to have stopped. We can eat here in the hotel or call room service."

Nicole shrugged, "I don't care, you choose. My opinions don't seem to count."

She slid off the bed and padded her way towards the bathroom, crumpled receipts falling from her pocket on to the carpet.

"You dropped something," Edward said, bending to retrieve the crackling wad of papers.

"Damn, I forgot about those." Darting back she tried to snatch them from his hand. The rustling sound of the credit card slips was unmistakable. "What the hell are these?" his voice lashed her. "After all your promises. You're sick, Nicole, you need help. This is insane."

"For your information, these are *my* receipts, *my* responsibility." She faced him, her violet eyes insolent with satisfaction. "My spending is no longer your problem."

"How the hell can it *not* be my problem, what did you do, rob a bank?"

"No, I called one. They were happy to extend my credit."

"You idiot," he yelled, "of course they were. Just how do you propose to repay these amounts? Get it through your thick skull, Nicole, you - me - us, it makes no difference."

Nicole had never thought Edward was capable of such rage. Tears spilled down on to her robe, why could he not understand her simple needs?

The strength ebbed from his body, his elation of a few minutes ago drained to frustration. She's spent almost fifteen thousand dollars, he reckoned, not counting the other things she'd bought - shoes, bags, lingerie, and the stage wear. He sat, head bowed, helpless. Her sobbing filled the quiet of the room. Rousing himself, he asked, "Why are you the one crying?"

"I thought you'd want to be proud of your wife," she wept with gulping breaths.

"I am proud of my wife. But we can't afford Chanel and Yves St Laurent or any other fancy designer-labels." He was sick of repeating the same thing.

"I could wear them in France," she ventured.

"Give it a rest, Nicole." If it wasn't so cold out there he would have walked the streets and avenues until he calmed down.

"Let's order dinner," she wheedled.

"You order, I'm not hungry."

Bob Howell's voice was thick with sleep when he answered the phone.

"Sorry," Edward apologised, "have I woken you?"

"Fell asleep in front of the television."

"The right night for it. I have news for you, I accept your offer."

"Hey, that's great, that's worth waking for," Bob's laugh boomed down the line.

"David Lock will be happy to answer any questions, you'll need his number."

"OK right ... got it. Talk to you to-morrow." Bob Howell replaced his receiver abruptly.

Next morning it was Edward's turn to be woken by the ringing telephone. It had taken a long time to fall asleep. It had dawned on him that there was no future for them together, there was no common meeting ground.

"Hello?" Edward said in a furry voice.

"Can we meet for a drink about four?" Bob Howell asked abruptly

"Fine," Edward responded shortly. "Where?"

"How about back in the Oak Bar? Suit you?"

"Perfectly, see you then."

Nicole stirred in her sleep and threw a long slim arm across his chest. He turned towards her and looked at her innocent face half-smiling in repose. What was he going to do? How could he leave her, this half-woman half-child. Stroking her bare arm, he could feel his resolve weakening. He moved closer to her. She wrapped her long legs around him and he could feel her sweet breath on his mouth. He would try talking to her once more.

❀ ❀ ❀

"I'm afraid my wife has a problem," Edward explained, apologetically.

The salesgirl looked at him sympathetically. It

wasn't the first time she'd heard that story.

"We can do it this time, but I'm afraid if she makes any further purchases, the goods can not be exchanged," she said, quoting the company's rule.

"Then don't sell them to her, that is, if you want paying," he snapped. He issued the same instructions in two other boutiques, this time with assurance and no apology.

Bob was already seated when Edward arrived at four o'clock on the dot.

"What will you drink?" he asked Edward, snapping his fingers to attract the waiter's attention.

"Scotch on the rocks," Edward ordered.

"You certainly come highly recommended," Bob Howell smiled, his eyes twinkling behind his lenses.

"Thank you. I presume you spoke to David?"

"I did. As long as he has you back by the beginning of July, he's happy."

"It's a busy time in the hotel," Edward admitted.

"OK, here's the deal." Bob gave him a rough outline of what was required from him. If all went according to plan, Edward should be ready to leave towards the end of May and be back in the States around the end of June at the latest, even allowing for snags. They would meet two days before sailing and then Bob would take him round the yacht personally, give him full instructions and introduce him to the crew. Bob would contact him two weeks before the *Bon-Vivant* was ready to sail.

"How does that sound?"

"I can't wait," Edward confessed truthfully.

CHAPTER SIXTY-THREE

He woke to the gentle, rocking motion of the *Bon-Vivant*. Edward stretched and yawned and pressed the bell for the steward. Breakfast would take exactly ten minutes, it always did. Raising himself on his elbow he looked through the large windows - too big to be considered portholes. The sun was shining brightly and, judging by the even swell of the waves, it was going to be another fine day. Falling back on his pillows he glanced at Nicole's sleeping form beside him. Despite her misgivings, at the last moment she had decided to make the voyage. Each night she dosed herself with two sleeping tablets declaring that if she were going to die at least she would be unconscious at the time. Edward didn't argue nor did he point out that ships could sink in daylight too, why make her more nervous?

The sea had been kind. With the smooth motion of the *Bon-Vivant* it was difficult at times to realise that they were in the middle of a vast ocean. Only one and a half more days before they anchored. Three more weeks at least before they need say goodbye to the floating palace.

It was just over a week since Edward had boarded the yacht for the first time. The blueprints at which he had so furtively peeped bore little resemblance to the finished craft. It lay long, white and sleek in the water justifying the naval architect's suggested name, *White Arrow*.

How apt that would have been. The one hundred and fifty foot yacht was more elegant than anything Edward had ever seen. Each room on the upper deck was painted white. A semi-circular step surrounded by a modernistic wrought iron balustrade separated the dining section from the living area. Suede couches, chairs, curtains and carpets were furnished with snowy textured fabrics. The dining-table and its matching padded chairs were upholstered in white hide and so too were the expanding armchairs with their companion footstools. Occasional tables with bowls of white silk roses followed the theme. The only concessions to colour were the narrow bands of pastel shades on the scatter cushions and two vividly bright paintings, one either end of the salon. A collection of Egyptian bronzes in a glass-shelved niche broke the monotony of the white walls. The main stateroom had received the same bleached treatment, but here the canopied four-poster bed with its luxuriously quilted cover and cushions was relieved by a dramatic flame-coloured motif in the Greek Key pattern.

Together they had explored every inch of the ship. Bob pointed out the details both technical and decorative. No expense had been spared, every material had been chosen for its fire-resistant properties and the most up-to-date methods of fire fighting and prevention had been installed. The galley and pantries gleamed with chrome and brushed steel. They were equipped with every labour-saving gadget possible.

Each door that had been opened revealed more and more wonders. Justin's eye for detail was extraordinary. The yacht was a push-button wonderland. Music played at the press of a switch, curtains swished open or closed, doors slid silently and, most impressive of all, a square of carpet in the main salon rotated, revealing a polished wooden section of floor for dancing. Edward's lower jaw felt quite uncomfortable after the first half hour of the tour, he doubted that he had closed his mouth once during all that time.

"You haven't said a lot, what do you think?" Bob asked, a little disappointed by Edward's silence.

"It's amazing, I can't take it all in. This must be the finest yacht afloat."

Bob grinned and threw a friendly arm round Edward's shoulder as they walked under the blue and white awning of the sundeck.

"It was a toss-up between blue and yellow," he remarked, "but the blue won out, a tribute to the sky and the sea. Now, destination. My wife suggested we flip a coin, heads or tails, Cannes or Monte Carlo. Cannes it is."

Edward was delighted, the perfect opportunity to spend lots of time with Henri.

A light tap at the door brought Edward's deliberations to a halt. Reaching sideways he pressed a button on the panel near him and a small table swung silently from under the top of the bedside locker. The steward smiled and set the tray on the waiting table. He handed Edward a print-out of the daily news picked up on the ship's satellite. The aroma of warm croissants and coffee assailed his nostrils as he hoisted himself up on his pillows. Contentment washed over him as he sat eating his breakfast. There was no noise, no loud music, none of the sounds which had irritated his ears in Las Vegas, just the gentle slapping of the waves against the ship and the soothing throb of the engines.

In her sleep Nicole flounced over on her side and grunted. It would be ages before she would be fully awake, nearly lunch-time probably. Each morning he worked out in the exercise room for an hour, it was still too cold to use the swimming-pool. He had examined everything from the engine room to the wine cellar - which was cooled to exactly the right temperature. He had watched the steward gently removing the bottles of wine from their boxes and stacking them on the racks. The yacht had a cellar of which anyone could be proud. He shuddered to think of what it must have cost to stock this room. None of the desirable vintages here had been laid down over the years or bought when the price was right. As he had glanced through the computer print-out cataloguing the stocks, he thought of the leather-bound book that he had frequently consulted at the Château d'Albion, every bottle meticulously logged in and out in Claude d'Albion's neat writing.

As the breeze picked up slightly Edward returned to the main salon and picked up his book. Lying on the sofa he became engrossed in the story.

"Here you are!" Nicole's voice startled him. "I thought you'd still be on your tour of inspection."

She had taken little interest in anything other than the main rooms. She preferred to stay on the one deck with the exception of an odd breath or two of fresh cool air. He had tried to teach her to play chess but it had been a thankless task, ending in frustration for them both. Reading held no magic for her and she missed the television. On a screen, concealed when not in use, they had watched one of the latest film releases each night after dinner. The trip bored Nicole to distraction and she couldn't wait for the anchor to drop so she could plant her feet on land again. At least she couldn't shop here at sea, Edward thought thankfully. He resented the bank statements which arrived with depressing regularity each month after their New York excursion. Pushing away the reality of their problem he put up his hand and dragged her down beside him.

"Only one more day," he smiled.

"Wonderful," she sighed, kicking off her shoes and snuggling up to him. "What are you reading?"

He showed her the cover of the book and she pulled a face. "You and boats, you should definitely have been a sailor."

"Maybe one day I shall. But it's an interesting book, the story of a man who started out as a stowaway and ended up as a commodore," he defended his choice.

"How long until lunch?"

"About quarter of an hour."

She prowled the room, sitting first in one chair then another. Edward closed his book and stared through the window at the endless stretch of grey-green water, Nicole's restlessness was infectious. He walked the length of the cabin and looked at the attractive seascape hanging on the wall, the blues, greens and yellows of the sky soft against the white wall. It served its purpose well. The glass-framed picture with its bright hues gave no clue as to its extraordinary value. The painting itself was worth little but, in the hollowed out wall behind it, embedded in a hermetically sealed frame on the reverse side, was the Van Gogh.

Of all the surprises the yacht held in store, none equalled the shock of discovering the presence of such a valuable object on board. Bob locked the cabin door, then pressed a button to close the curtains, blocking out the light. Edward watched fascinated as the big man removed a bronze cat from the niche and placed it deliberately on the open end of the balustrade pushing it down firmly. Edward heard a click. Grasping the bronze Bob turned its head, two full turns to the left then one to the right. A whirring sound could be heard as the mechanism behind the frame was activated.

"Watch," Bob commanded, his eyes narrow and flinty.

Slowly the painting edged forward until it was clear of the wall. Edward noticed that it was held on either side by an expanding bracket. The picture revolved from top to bottom revealing the precious canvas. When the movement was complete the bracket hummed into life again this time sucking the seascape back into the hollow. The frame was in perfect position.

"A Van Gogh," Bob announced.

Edward saw a look of smug sensuality cross Bob's face, the sort of glint that he had seen in men's eyes when escorting a beautiful woman. He looked again at the painting, a sheaf of lilies in a tall vase, their silken trumpets open and dewy. It was an unusual subject for Van Gogh.

"*This* is the reason I needed someone trustworthy," Bob said simply.

Not surprising, Edward thought. There were a dozen questions he longed to ask.

"No one knows it's on board - not even Justin. I made the final arrangements myself," he volunteered, his eyes glued to the flowers in the frame. "As you can see, there's no chance that the painting could be found by accident."

Asking the most irrelevant of the questions queuing in his mind, Edward queried what would happen if the cat's head was attached to the opposite side of the balustrade?

"Nothing. It wouldn't work," Bob answered brushing the question aside. "It's important that in an emergency you should be able to do this quickly. Now you try it."

Edward took the heavy ornament from Bob's hands and placed it on the metal bar.

He had difficulty at first locking it in to position. After several attempts he succeeded and the valuable work of art revolved as before.

"The frame is watertight which of course also protects it from the salt air."

"Why keep such a valuable picture on board a yacht, especially if it's hidden?" There, he'd asked the real question.

"That's my business, I think."

"I didn't mean to be nosy," Edward said, but he had. For a man who was so out-going about his possessions, Bob was totally close-mouthed when it came to disclosing either what he did for a living or how he'd amassed such a vast fortune.

The eyes behind the pale tinted lenses changed colour like a chameleon and the round, jolly face hid a ruthless mind, Edward suspected.

"That's all right. I suppose it's a reasonable question." But he made no attempt to answer it. "Now that you know how it operates, there is no need for you to expose it again unless an emergency arises. Should that occur, then slide it down, like this." With his thumbs he pressed the frame lightly towards the wall and then slid it downwards. Smoothly the base detached itself from the frame. Continuing to hold it firmly, he eased it down until it freed itself. "It's still completely sealed as you can see. Now I'll put it back and you do it."

This time Edward had no problem but he felt patronised, like an inept schoolboy. He realised that he had begun to dislike Bob. After tomorrow he wouldn't have to see him again, except for the day he handed back the superb burden of responsibility. The man's condescension was a small price to pay. He could live with that.

"Let me put it all together again," Bob's voice became more friendly, "then I'll show you where you must take it in case of fire or shipwreck."

Bob made sure that none of the crew was on the boat deck before he removed the cushioned seat from the motor launch and searching with his hand pressed a hidden button. With a similar droning noise to that in the cabin, Bob had detached the apparently fixed top of the seat, revealing a metal-lined locker just large enough to hold the painting. "Waterproof and fireproof," Bob explained.

Wheeling around he gave Edward an icy

glance. "I must warn you, Edward, that should you at any time discuss the existence of this painting, then you can expect the direst of consequences, *my arm* reaches far - to all parts of the globe. This applies to your wife too."

Edward understood the deadly implication of his warning and he shivered in the cool air.

After lunch the increased rocking motion of the boat sent Nicole scurrying back to their stateroom. Rain was lashing against the windows of the salon and the waves were higher than they had been during the voyage.

"Shouldn't be too bad," the captain said, popping his head round the door. "An hour or so and we'll be clear of this squally weather."

"I don't mind a bit of rocking and rolling, my wife isn't too happy though," he smiled ruefully. He liked the captain, a quiet man who spoke only when necessary. If he had any interesting tales to tell Edward had not been privy to them, they exchanged pleasantries each day and he kept Edward up to date with their progress but it went no further than that.

The book dropped on to his chest and, lulled by the rocking of the boat, he dozed lightly. He dreamt of pictures hanging in the engine room, paper boats floating through the salon. Yards and yards of white carpet floated on the sea. From the waves Henri Ducroix appeared holding aloft a canvas and Edward extended an arm the length of three decks and helped him aboard. Tugging him by the sleeve, Edward dragged him to the engine room where the Van Gogh hung swaddled in yellow cladding. "I can make a copy for the stateroom," Henri said. His voice sounded just like Nicole's. With every dip of the ship the carpet expanded then separated into narrow streams of ribbon. As Edward floated lazily on the sea of white, the ribbons began to wrap themselves around him, choking him, pulling him down into a white vortex, he was drowning.

He awoke with a start, sweat running down his face. The sweater he had thrown over himself had worked its way up until it covered his mouth. The dream was vivid in his mind as he stood up shaking his wrist, numb at first then stinging with pins and needles. The rain had stopped and the boat had stabilised. He looked at the picture which was still in place. Henri would laugh if he told him of his day-mare. Should he show Henri the Van Gogh, he wondered? He would appreciate it more than anyone. Edward could almost see Henri standing there silently in front of the painting, measuring it all in his mind's eye. Maybe he'd know something about the buyer, the owner of all this. Little of importance took place in the art world without Henri being aware of it. He would definitely tell Henri.

As he stood unseeing in front of the canvas an incredible idea flashed into his head, what if Henri *did* make a copy? What if they substituted a forgery for the real thing and sold the original? Would Bob Howell even realise his multi-million dollar Van Gogh was a fake? How do you dispose of a painting of that calibre? It would be impossible. Still, it was fun just thinking about it.

CHAPTER SIXTY-FOUR

The dream refused to go away. It snaked around in his brain. Nicole felt queasy and decided to stay in their cabin.

"You don't mind, do you?" she asked, her face pallid.

"No. But you'll be fine, the captain says it should be clear sailing all the way now. By tomorrow afternoon we'll be anchored and your worries will be over. I'll come back after dinner to see if you fancy a movie."

She nodded and burrowed deeply into her pillow as if stabilising herself.

Each morning the chef presented them with a menu to choose from. Edward thought Bob had picked a winner in this man. He and Nicole looked forward to every meal. The chef's cooking was superb and whenever they complimented him he brushed their praise aside nonchalantly. "On the sea, food is more important than on the land," he replied, not letting his pleasure show.

Edward selected the wine himself each day. He opened it, letting it breathe or chilled it in one of the ornate ice-buckets.

Tonight's meal, medallions of beef with a sauce of natural juices would demand a bottle of red, a Bordeaux perhaps.

He made his way to the cellar, a fair-sized room beside the pantry. Shivering slightly in the chilled atmosphere he consulted the continuous sheet of computer paper and leafed through its contents. He stooped to catch it as it slipped through his fingers threatening to unwind its full length on to the floor. *Chateau Petrus 1975* the name caught his eye. *Superb vintage, plummy and full-bodied,* the wine-merchant had commented in the next column. It received the maximum award possible, the perfect ten.

Reverently pulling a bottle from its rack, Edward looked at it longingly. It was his last night of sailing and, so far, they had used only the most modest of wines.

Edward sat at the table in isolated splendour and sipped the precious liquid, savouring every drop. The tender beef with its reduced sauce was perfectly cooked, how well the food and wine complemented each other. He wondered if Bob Howell had organised the stocks himself or had some impersonal wine merchant filled his order, like buying books-by-the-yard?

Henri was very much on Edward's mind. He must contact him on ship's telephone as soon as they docked. Since their meeting in New York they had kept their promise and written to one another. Henri had sent his humorous replies in the form of strip cartoons.

Edward filled his glass again. His fantasising knew no bounds. Armed with a perfect forgery of the Van Gogh he sallied forth mentally into the world of art buyers, selling to the highest bidder for untold millions. Dollars, yen, pounds - he didn't care. With his ill-gotten gains, he and Nicole would disappear from view, out of reach of the long arm of Bob Howell and the law, then reappear in unrecognisable form. Nicole could shop to her heart's content and he would be able to afford his dream of buying a boat. He could mess about on the water to *his* heart's content.

But the fantasy came to an abrupt stop as he remembered the real facts. Nicole's shopping! New York loomed large, they were still paying dearly for that crazed spree. How was he to make sure it didn't happen again? In the weeks before this trip he had brought up the subject several times. He'd begged, pleaded, insisted that she should be sensible. She had been hurt and then placatory. Before they came on board he had warned her that if it happened again, he'd cut up her credit cards.

Nicole had fallen asleep so Edward quietly left the cabin and returned to the salon. He was not in the mood to watch a film and for the first time since he had boarded the yacht he wished he was on land. The fantasy world he'd created came back to him as he paced the room. For one crazy moment he wondered about the painting on the opposite wall, a pleasant landscape identically framed. Could there be another art treasure concealed behind its innocent facade? Ridiculous nonsense, he told himself. If there were, surely Bob would have been anxious to protect it too? He tapped the wall surrounding the frame and listened to the noise it made. Then he carried out the same exercise around the Van Gogh, the sound was identical. Full of Dutch courage, he took the bronze from the shelf and tried clicking it on to the side of the balustrade, but it just toppled ineffectively into his hands. The wine must have addled my brain, why would Bob protect one painting and not another he reasoned, replacing the bronze on its shelf.

"Earth to Edward, come in Edward." Nicole's voice broke through his thoughts.

"Sorry darling, I was miles away," he apologised, smiling at his beautiful wife who was immaculate in white trousers and a violet shirt the colour of her eyes. A wave of sympathy for her overtook him. She had really suffered these past days, her fear of the sea agonising to watch. But now that they were in calm waters, with land so near she had come alive, her eyes dancing with vitality.

"You're ready, I see," he smiled fondly.

"You bet - the second that anchor is in place."

"We'll cross in the launch, you'll find that very smooth. You know I'm meeting Henri?"

"What do you mean, cross in the launch?" she frowned.

"It takes less than a couple of minutes, we're too large a vessel to berth at the dock."

"Why didn't you tell me that before, are you sure it won't be rough?"

"I promise it won't."

"OK then, I really need to get my hair done, it's felt sticky all week. It'll be nice for you to spend some time with Henri."

"Do you know where to find a hairdressers?"

"There are bound to be several on the main street," she said confidently.

"Let's arrange to meet on the Carlton Hotel terrace for a drink, say about five o'clock?"

"That sounds lovely, after all your publicity I'm looking forward to it."

"It's a quiet time but we'll go one evening too. Nicole, don't forget your promise. Stay out of the shops."

She kissed him, careful not to smudge her lipstick. "I won't forget."

Edward wished he could believe her.

CHAPTER SIXTY-FIVE

Henri Ducroix watched as the motor launch approached. The girl beside Edward hopped out of the swaying boat the moment it tied up. Edward paused on the quayside and breathed in deeply, a wide smile on his lips. There it was, that tantalising smell of garlic, seafood and the tang of the harbour. It was wonderful to be back.

Henri moved towards the couple. He was wearing a heavy suit, making no concession to the warm weather. The two men hugged each other fondly while Nicole stood waiting to be introduced to Edward's flamboyant friend.

"Enchanté," Henri bowed gallantly over her hand.

"It is good to meet you, at last," she responded in their own language. "I'll leave you to your reunion and will see you at - five o'clock?"

"Five, yes, at the Carlton."

"Shall we go to Michel's Bar and catch up on the news?" Henri beamed, he'd missed Edward's company.

"No, I want to show you the yacht. You've never seen a boat like it. We can spend a couple of hours aboard then come back here at four o'clock. The chef and his chief steward have gone to the market to stock up with provisions for us, and they'll need the launch."

"You're the captain," Henri said amiably, "my time is yours."

Expertly Edward picked his way between the

moored boats then opened the throttle and headed out towards the yacht.

"You spoke earlier of something that might interest me, what was it?"

Edward tapped the side of his nose with a finger and smiled mysteriously. "You must wait a little longer," he said, grinning.

Edward enjoyed watching Henri's amazed reactions as he gave him the grand tour of the yacht.

"Something else, isn't it?" he asked, handing Henri a drink.

Henri agreed. "It's magnificent, so different. And that wine cellar!"

"What do you think of the paintings?" Edward asked innocently, waving a careless hand towards the canvases.

Henri rose from the armchair and pursed his mouth. He nodded, then shook his head. "Nothing special at first glance." By the tone of Edward's voice he knew that there was something hidden behind the casual question.

He looked for a moment at one then walked to the other. Curling his lip, he returned to the chair. "Pleasant - harmless. Like I said, nothing special."

Edward took a sip of his drink and frowned.

"Edouard, there is something more here than meets the eye."

Jumping lightly to his feet Edward walked to the alcove, and grasping a bronze cat he expertly balanced it on the finial of the balustrade. "Two to the left, one to the right," he said aloud. They could hear the hum of the mechanism and he told Henri to watch carefully. Henri gazed at the seascape. As the painting revolved and the concealed canvas appeared Henri needed no invitation to view it. For a big man he was remarkably fast on his feet. "Is this... ?" He looked again closely. "It is! It's a Van Gogh, I'm sure of it. Certain." He stepped to one side and peered at it, then moved and examined it from a different angle.

"Oh yes, this is genuine," he assessed.

Edward didn't speak, when he was ready Henri would discuss it. Suddenly he felt as if he couldn't stand and he collapsed abruptly on to the nearest chair.

"Do you want to tell me all about it? The history of the Van Gogh?" Henri asked calmly.

"I was hoping that you'd tell me." Edward's voice shook slightly. "The whole thing is a mystery. Wait, let me lock the door, we don't want anyone barging in." He sat on one of the footstools. "I'd better start at the beginning. As you know already I was hired to act as - custodian. Bob Howell showed me the Van Gogh when I first came aboard, how to remove it from the frame and where to stow it in an emergency. He's the owner of the yacht and although he trusted me with its safe-keeping, I know very little about him. He paid me handsomely - in cash. We're to stay aboard until he and his wife arrive. By the way, he threatened me in no uncertain terms - and Nicole too - if news of the picture's existence leaks out, we are as good as..." Edward drew his hand across his throat. "I believe him, Henri, I think he meant every word."

Henri nodded reassuringly. "Don't worry, I

won't betray your confidence."

"I trust you absolutely. I think I should put the Van Gogh back, it's making me nervous."

Edward refilled their glasses and they sat opposite each other, silently sipping.

"What I suspect is that the painting may have been stolen," Edward voiced his thoughts. "Or it could have been bought with dirty money. Something isn't right, I just know it," Edward said.

"Anything is possible. If the picture has been stolen it will be listed and I can find that out when I return home. Stolen money, dirty money - I suppose considering these elaborate precautions… " Henri inclined his head sideways towards the picture. "But tell me, why are *you* worried? It's just a job, no?"

"Yes and no. The other afternoon I fell asleep and dreamt that you made a copy of the Van Gogh and I sold it as genuine." If he had expected Henri to be shocked, he was disappointed. "Crazy, I know, but the dream wouldn't fade. I began to think what if it was for real, what if you did copy it? I could substitute the forgery for the real painting, how would Bob Howell ever know? Are you horrified?"

"Forging pictures is my life, you're more appalled than I am."

"Things are pretty rotten for me at the moment. I can't keep Nicole happy in Vegas. If we stay there it's just a matter of time before we split up. We're living in constant mind-destroying light and noise and, after all those years of work, I'm back to square one, worse than square one - broke and deeply in debt as you know. I love

Nicole and don't want to lose her, but she's unhappy, suffocating."

"What does she think about your idea?"

"She knows nothing about it. Nothing. Nor about the painting either, it's safer that way. As I said, I don't doubt for a second that Bob Howell would carry out his threat so it's better that she remains in the dark. By the way, she thinks you're an artist, I've told her nothing more."

"I have always trusted you, my friend. Now, let us think. Naturally I can make a perfect forgery."

Despite himself, Edward smiled, this was the Henri he knew and loved.

"The problem will be making the exchange," Henri said. "That frame is very well sealed, it would be difficult to remove the canvas and then replace it with another. *We* could not do it ourselves and letting anyone else know about it would put you in danger."

"I knew it was a crazy idea, a pipe dream."

Henri leaned forward, his hands cupping his chin. "Let me think about it tonight. Tomorrow we'll talk again."

Edward knew better than to pursue it further, Henri had his own methods of working things out, of finding solutions.

"We had better make tracks, the chef will be waiting for the launch. I almost forgot, did you find someone for me? The crew go on vacation the day after tomorrow."

"I forgot too. Yes, I think so, two people. I can vouch for their honesty - my landlady's daughter and her husband. He has been around boats all his life and I think you'll like him, she will be an asset too. I'll arrange for you to meet them tomorrow morning."

"Thank you, Henri. What would I do without you?"

Henri patted his hand but didn't reply.

"It's good that the crew will be away, if we decide to go ahead with your scheme that will make it easier to remove the picture to my studio."

Edward hadn't considered taking the Van Gogh from the yacht.

"It would not be possible to paint on a moving boat, Edouard," Henri reminded him.

"No, I suppose not. To be honest it was such a mad idea I hadn't given it any real thought at all."

"Come, forget it for now. Where would you like to eat tonight? You must have thought about that."

Every head turned as Nicole walked up the steps of the terrace and stopped momentarily. In a resort where glamorous women were always in evidence it was a great compliment to her. Her shiny blonde hair bounced as she walked and Edward noticed that her blouse had been replaced by a top which left her midriff bare and covered little of her magnificent figure. In one hand she carried a slim shiny carrier bag bearing the name of an exclusive shop on the Rue d'Antibes. She looked so lovely, so vibrant that he could not bring himself to censure her. One top, he supposed, wasn't the end of the world.

"Do I look better now?" she asked, bending to kiss Edward. He was sure he was the envy of every man in the place.

"You look better than better," he smiled indulgently.

"Cannes is so exciting, such beautiful people, so smart," she enthused.

"Perhaps so," Henri replied. "You should have been here last week - the film festival. The women all trying to outdo each other, the less they wore the more cover they got!" He laughed uproariously at his own pun.

"How exciting, I'd forgotten the festival. Edward has told me all about it, the stars, the directors and the wheeling and dealing. It sounds fun."

"Depends," Henri said dourly. "I do not like the crowds, the resort changes into one big carnival of flesh."

Edward nodded in agreement.

"Are we going to the casino tonight?" Nicole asked.

"I don't think so. We can go later in the week, we'll dress up and make a night of it. Henri has invited us to be his guest tonight and the choice of venue is mine. You'll enjoy it I promise."

"Let me telephone for a table," Henri suggested. "It is not like it was in your day, Edouard, now everything needs to be arranged in advance."

"Did you enjoy visiting with Henri?" she asked, nervously pulling at the skimpy top. "This was very good value and I paid for it - in cash," she said, nervously meeting Edward's eyes.

"It would need to be good value, there's very little of it." His bantering tone won him a dazzling smile.

Henri flapped his way back to the table, his loose black jacket bulged with its usual complement of sketch pads, crayons and charcoal sticks. "We will have to eat early I'm afraid, seven o'clock?"

"Perfect, we can walk slowly along the Croisette, it will give Nicole a chance to see the hotels and soak up the atmosphere."

Henri shook the *patron's* hand and then introduced Nicole and Edward.

"Bonsoir," Edward smiled, "you don't remember me, do you?"

The man looked puzzled then pretended recognition. Edward didn't mind, he'd probably changed considerably. They sat at a table close to the railings which divided the restaurant from the road, here they could watch the strolling world pass by.

The waiter brought a big basket of crusty bread and opened the wine.

"This is wonderful," Edward sighed. "I've often dreamed of sitting here on a warm night like this."

"Messieurs, 'dame." The *patron* himself carried the enormous wooden platter covered with fish netting. As it was lowered on to the table all three of them sniffed appreciatively. The board was garnished with large chunks of lemon and held every type of seafood imaginable, langoustines, lobster, prawns and crabs and several smaller crustaceans. The waiter followed with a jug of hot butter sauce and a bowl of creamy garlic mayonnaise.

"Bon appétit," they chorused and left the trio to enjoy their meal.

With buttery juices, messy fingers and satisfied smiles they tackled the wayward shellfish - too engrossed to talk.

"That was better than I remembered." Edward sat back in his chair like a satisfied cat. "The journey was worth it for tonight alone, good food, good company."

"For me too," Nicole agreed, still delicately picking at the shells.

"Here's to many good nights," Henri raised his glass in a toast.

The table was cleared and a pot of hot strong coffee accompanied the glasses of liqueur. "With the compliments of the *patron,*" the waiter said.

"I'll fall asleep right here if I drink any more," Nicole laughed, pushing her glass towards them. It pleased Edward to see her so happy, so full of gaiety. Like a wilted flower placed in water, she had sprung to life and was beginning to blossom in vibrant colour. There was even a faint golden tinge to her skin, a few days in the sun and she would lose her pallor.

"What are we going to do tomorrow?" she asked, patting her stomach. "Not eat, I hope!"

"In the morning I must come ashore and meet a couple Henri thinks would make good replacements on the yacht, don't forget the crew go on vacation the following day."

"I had forgotten," she admitted. "Would you mind if I went to the *plage,* the one at the Carlton?"

Edward was surprised, Nicole rarely sat in the sun.

"Not at all. You can come with me on the launch early in the morning and perhaps we'll arrange to meet for lunch, does that suit you too, Henri?"

"I am at your disposal."

Edward joined Henri and the young couple who were waiting eagerly in the café to meet him. Although he had finished breakfast not an hour before, Edward could not resist a cup of Michel's hot frothy chocolate. He liked Henri's friends on sight and within half an hour had offered them the job. Edward outlined their duties. He was pleased when Luci offered to do any cooking that was necessary as well.

"Accept!" Henri instructed, smiling at the sweet-faced girl. "You will never taste better."

Luci and her husband Adrien each shook hands politely before taking their leave of the two men.

"Thanks, Henri, I think they'll be ideal."

"You will not be disappointed. I have some information for you - the painting *is* on the missing list. The last known record of *Les Lis Blancs* - The White Lilies - is when it was sold at auction in New York to an anonymous buyer ten years ago. The price then was two million dollars. It is rumoured that it changed hands less than two years ago for *twelve* million American dollars." Henri paused.

Edward's face lengthened by several inches when he heard the astonishing figure.

"Twelve million?" He was stunned. "I thought perhaps four or five."

"There are many fluctuations in the price of art. Two people anxious to purchase the same item and..." Henri raised an arm, indicating the cloudless blue sky outside.

"A sum of money like that is staggering. It's unfair, isn't it? Just think how many of these talented artists almost starved to death, often giving away their masterpieces for the price of a loaf of bread or a bottle of wine," Edward struggled with his own conflicting thoughts and feelings.

"Life is unfair." Henri shrugged, he had come to terms with that long ago. "Before I give you the benefit of my advice, I want you to know that I have requested any available information about Howell. Maybe we'll be lucky - maybe not. We must wait and see."

Edward was fascinated that Henri's network stretched so far and so wide. "Can you really check on him?"

"I have taught you little," Henri sighed. "When it comes to works of art, the world becomes a village."

"I'm probably being stupid, but if there's no record of Bob having bought the painting, how will your contacts be able to get information?"

"Not stupid, inexperienced. Think, if a man is prepared to spend that kind of money for a painting which must remain hidden, then it is certain that he would purchase other things too; sculptures perhaps, works by lesser artists than Van Gogh, porcelain or something else that would have established him as a collector."

"That sounds logical," Edward acknowledged.

"*Alors*, we have: one genuine Van Gogh, one brilliant forger, one sealed frame, we also have one dangerous man."

Henri loved to present his arguments in a stabbing, accentuated manner. Edward bit his lip, he could clearly recall Bob's steely eyes as he delivered his threat.

"Now," Henri continued, assured of Edward's rapt attention, "we need - one copy, one buyer and one week." The forgery could be completed in four days but that would have spoiled the impact of his speech. Henri never tired of word games. His frivolous delivery became serious.

"Exchanging the canvases will not work, therefore you must be prepared to sell the copy, it is the only way. Wait! Do not interrupt. I cannot get involved personally, you understand, however it is not difficult to spread the word in certain circles that such a renowned canvas is for sale. When, or if, the time comes, you will show the buyer the real Van Gogh and, believe me, there is always a queue of buyers. He will examine the picture and if he is satisfied you will demand the money in cash. Then you will meet him again, this time away from the yacht and hand over *my* canvas. That appears to be the best way, the only way, if you do not want to risk discovery."

"It sounds so simple," Edward groaned. "But there are so many *ifs* and *buts* in my mind."

"Tell me," Henri said. "That way we'll face the problems together."

"The painting would have to be shown to the buyer on board the yacht, that will tell him its whereabouts. What if the buyer should report it to the police?"

"The buyer will be known to my contacts, so set your mind at rest. What next?"

"How much could I ask for it? Would anyone have that much money available? Just think about the difficulty of carrying that amount of cash. It's all quite frightening, Henri." Edward was beginning to find the whole prospect terrifying.

"It will not be easy. But it is up to you to

decide whether the risks are worth it. Naturally I will help you but you must think about it all very carefully. Also, should you decide to go ahead, for your own safety and Nicole's it would be imperative that you disappear for a time. For instance," Henri added as an afterthought, "would you be prepared to give up your job in Las Vegas? You could not go back there, it would be too easy to find you."

"Absolutely. With that kind of money I wouldn't need to work there, or anywhere else for that matter. It's just that there seem to be so many obstacles in the way, and I don't mean little things. I'm thinking of Bob Howell's threat, letting the existence of the painting be known, proving ownership - that's another thing I hadn't thought of. What if the buyer contacted him? If only there was a guarantee that it would go even fairly smoothly."

"Would you expect to receive nine or ten million dollars without *some* worry?"

"Is that how much I should ask for it?" They were discussing the money as if the operation were a faît accompli.

"That would be the sensible amount. You may be sure that, whoever the purchasers, they will haggle. The other important point, Edouard - you need to have a reason for selling it, a good reason. That will take some thought."

The difficulties were piling up like toy blocks, one balancing precariously on top of another. Surely it would be just a matter of time before they would come crashing down around him. Henri took a sketch pad from his pocket and began to draw, his way of giving Edward the opportunity to sit quietly and think it all through.

CHAPTER SIXTY-SIX

Edward had never considered himself a prude. Walking down the steps to the beach he saw Nicole, the top of her bikini discarded, surrounded by a group of practically naked young people. Unaccountably he felt angry, embarrassed.

"Hi, Edward," she called, waving to attract her husband's attention.

He tried to smile but failed dismally.

"Nicole," he said coldly.

"Let me introduce you." Gaily she reeled off the names of the crowd, laughing as she got muddled.

"We're meeting Henri in a few minutes, I think you should get dressed. I'll wait for you at the bar, over there." Nodding curtly to her companions, he walked across the sand to the shaded bar and ordered a drink.

"Here I am." Nicole, the top of her bikini now in place under the diaphanous coloured beach robe, tucked her arm in his. "I can't remember when I've enjoyed myself so much. They're a great crowd, aren't they?"

"They don't go to great lengths to hide their charms, do they?" he asked sarcastically.

"Oh Edward, don't be such an old woman, everyone goes topless here."

Edward released his arm from her grasp as they climbed the steps to meet Henri.

"I thought we were going to eat at the beach,"

she frowned, disappointed.

"Well, we're not," he snapped.

Nicole eyed him warily. What was his problem? "What's bugging you?" she asked, her voice sharp.

Suddenly he felt foolish. What she'd said was true. On every beach, women were swimming, walking or sunbathing, topless.

The difference was that none of them was *his* wife, he argued silently.

"Nothing's bugging me, maybe I'm just overdressed in this heat." He hadn't intended the jibe.

Immediately after lunch Edward returned to the *Bon Vivant* leaving Nicole to her sun-worshipping. Locking the salon door and closing the curtains he operated the mechanism. For a long time he sat looking at the canvas as if willing it to give him some sign or answer. He supposed he should take a sheet of paper and make two columns, for and against the theft. He shuddered, but there was no other word for it. He drew a dividing line on a sheet of the *Bon Vivant's* stationery and began the exercise with the word - dangerous. Then followed - immoral, risky, unlikely, floundering, inexperienced. The list on the left hand side of the page grew alarmingly. The right hand column bore one solitary entry - ten million dollars. The figure stood out starkly, he could imagine the flashing lights of Las Vegas highlighting it, bells ringing, the buzz of excitement, the rush of people to witness his triumph. "Was *that* a jackpot or what?" he could hear them say. He carefully shredded the paper into tiny pieces. He was no nearer a decision. He wished Henri would advise him, say "yes do it," or, "no, don't touch it."

Restlessly he paced the deck. He leant on the rail and watched other boats whizzing across the path of the *Bon Vivant,* their carefree, laughing occupants waved to him. On the long stretch of beach, delineated by their differing-coloured umbrellas, he could see figures moving about, heads bobbing in the water like tiny coloured bubbles. Where was Nicole amongst that lot? Topless again no doubt, he thought savagely. The only saving grace was that at least it kept her away from the shops. He'd probably exchanged one problem for another or was she right, was he being stuffy? Now that he'd complicated his life beyond reason, he was probably the only person in this holiday resort having a miserable time. He stripped off his shirt and lay on one of the long blue-striped beds and tried to make sense of the situation.

"Wake up, sleepy head!" Nicole's voice lilted.

He looked at his watch, he had slept for hours.

"You're quite red," she observed, "we should find you some cream, it will soothe that skin."

He didn't recognise the smart cover-up she wore, certainly it wasn't the one he'd seen at lunch-time. He eyed the straw bag slung over her shoulder.

"What are you doing?" she protested, hanging on tightly as he grabbed at the strap.

Edward wrenched it free, tipping its contents on to the sunbed beside him. "Oh my God," he groaned, as he looked at the scattered heap of items piled on the blue stripes. Several bikinis and matching beach wraps fell from the smart bag that had been hidden in the large straw hold-all.

"I had to buy *some* new beach wear, mine is worn out and passé," she replied indignantly. She didn't mention the two pairs of finely-strapped sandals, one pair gold, the other silver.

A blinding rage seized him. "Right, that's it!" he stormed. Edward scooped up her purse, rifled through it until he found her credit cards and cheque-book. With the strength that only fury and passionate anger could bring, he folded the credit cards in half, bending them backwards and forwards until they snapped. He grabbed her cheque-book just before she did, and ripped it into shreds. He walked deliberately to the rail and flung the pieces overboard. They drifted away like pieces of flotsam. Turning, he pointed to the beach wear. "Return these first thing tomorrow," he ordered. "Now, get out of my sight."

Tears of indignation filled her eyes as she gathered up the glamorous swimwear. He had no right to do that, they were her cards, her cheques. Edward's actions had astonished her, his anger was mesmerising. In total silence Nicole left the sun deck and slammed into the stateroom, locking the door behind her. She would teach him a lesson, just wait until he came knocking on the door.

Edward was still shaking with rage when he banged on the cabin door. "Open it immediately," he ordered. Nicole hesitated, his fury was frightening. In this mood he might break it down anyway. She unlocked the door.

Ignoring her totally, he used the bathroom to shower and change.

"Where are you going?" she demanded. Edward's truculent silence unnerved her. He left the cabin without speaking and a minute later she heard the roar of the launch as it left the ship. This was the last straw, a prisoner and penniless too - when they returned to the States she would leave him.

Tactfully Henri remained silent as he recognised Edward's anger.

"I need a drink, come on," Edward said. His eyes were black as thunder.

They didn't speak a word until they reached a small bar just off the Croisette. "Double Scotch for me, what will you have?" Edward asked tersely.

Swallowing his drink in one mouthful, he ordered another. "I've made my decision. If it's OK with you, I'll go ahead with the idea. At least, if nothing else, I have the perfect excuse now for wanting to sell the painting - a wife who can't stop spending money and whom I intend to divorce."

"What happened? Everything was all right at lunch-time."

"I'd bet that Nicole could work her way through even that amount of money and then some. It's sad to accept that our marriage was probably doomed from the start, perhaps I was too blind to see it," he said.

"You know best how you feel. I am sorry, sorry for you both. I hoped after we spoke in New York that you would have sorted out your problems, but as you say..." Henri shrugged.

There was nothing more he could say, it was obviously pointless.

"Where do we go from here?" Edward asked, considerably calmer.

"Tomorrow you are picking up Luci and Adrien? I will go with you to the yacht, we'll remove the painting and then take it to my studio. It's best that I collect it, people here are used to seeing me carrying canvases so they won't think it strange. We must not take any unnecessary chances. I'll bring a painting with me to the yacht and substitute it for the Van Gogh. You can hide my painting for a few days?"

Henri was a familiar figure in Cannes. He often toted canvases covered by fine unbleached sacking bags, he had established a reputation as an artist, modest but eccentric. The role amused him and it had paid dividends. No one bothered him and he was able to carry out his real work undetected and unheeded by the locals.

"What am I going to do about Nicole? We certainly don't want her around tomorrow."

"I'm sure that she will want to return to the beach, but we can take things as they come. I suggest we have dinner and a good bottle of wine, things always look better on a full stomach," Henri advised.

Edward readily agreed. It was getting late and he realised how selfish he had been.

As Henri had predicted, Nicole intended to spend the day at the beach. She told the captain that she wished to be informed when the launch was ready to leave and sat on the sundeck, sulking.

Edward had used one of the guest cabins the

previous night. When he returned to the stateroom, he found the door unlocked. He ignored his wife. He was angry that he had been forced to order breakfast in another cabin. The steward had served him without comment, no doubt by now all the crew would know of their separate sleeping arrangements.

"I'll be at the beach all day and I need money. That is unless you intend starving me too," Nicole said coldly.

Edward took some cash from his wallet and threw it on the bed. "The launch will return for you at six o'clock, please don't keep Adrien waiting." His voice was icy.

As far as he could remember, she hadn't even bothered to ask if the young couple he'd been meeting were a suitable replacement for the crew.

Luci and Adrien waved as the launch approached. Their faces were bright and alive with excitement. Edward watched them standing close together, each with an arm around the other's waist. A feeling of bitterness suddenly engulfed him, he felt old beyond his years, disillusioned. It had taken less than six months for his own happiness to dissolve into this crumbling mess.

"Bonjour M Edouard!" they chorused. His cynical mood vanished as abruptly as it had appeared. The couple exuded an air of gaiety, a joyous anticipation. Edward welcomed them aboard. Adrien shyly offered to take Edward's place at the wheel. "Why not?" he replied. It would be a good opportunity to make sure the young man could handle the launch.

"Have you seen Henri this morning?" he asked.

"Yes, he said he would be a few minutes late. He went to collect some art supplies," Luci said, shading her eyes with her hand. "Look, there he is."

Edward smiled as his friend, huffing and puffing, climbed aboard the launch. "I've kept you waiting, my apologies." He propped the large flat parcel carefully against his legs and wiped his perspiring face with a handkerchief.

Adrien handled the launch skilfully, which reassured Edward. The captain's replacement had come aboard the previous night. At their brief meeting earlier, Edward had judged him to be a private man, able, uncommunicative, and a little surly. "He has been thoroughly briefed," the permanent captain assured Edward.

Henri smiled broadly at Edward as the two of them witnessed the young couple's delight. Edward gave them a quick tour of the yacht, and was pleased by their undisguised enthusiasm. When he had delivered them into the captain's competent hands, he and Henri shut themselves in the salon to discuss their plans.

"Any information yet about Bob Howell?" Edward asked.

"No, but it's early days. Patience, my friend," Henri cautioned. "I have however intimated to a contact that there could be an important canvas on the market within a week or so. I suggest that we now remove the picture so I can get back to my studio and start work."

After taking the usual precautions, they carefully removed the picture from the frame. Henri slid the bottom of the frame from the sealed canvas and slotted it back into place on the seascape. When they turned the head of the bronze they breathed a sigh of relief. The painting again rested innocently on the wall.

Edward laughed as he studied the picture Henri had taken from the bag. On a canvas almost blackened by age he could just about make out the face of a bewigged man, his eyes looking inwards towards his long skinny nose. "Where did you find this?" he asked. "If you tell me that this is a good painting I'll eat my hat."

"Start chewing!" Henri grinned. "I'm teasing you, but it is very old. The canvas and the stretchers are of value and the frame too. Remind me to show it to you when you come to the studio, it is magnificent."

"In that case I'll put him away carefully," Edward said, laughing again at the unfortunate portrait.

"See you tonight?" Henri asked, as he prepared to leave.

CHAPTER SIXTY-SEVEN

The next four days had passed more slowly than a week. He and Nicole hardly spoke to each other. Early each morning from his cabin he could hear the engines of the motor launch as Adrien left to take her across the short stretch of water. Edward spent his days visiting old haunts and, except for a couple of café owners, found few people that he remembered. He'd imagined a nostalgic reunion at the casino, but he found to his disappointment that it was closed.

"The casino at the Carlton is fashionable now," Henri said, standing back from the canvas.

Edward lounged on the settee, his face glum. "Everything seems to have changed," he grumbled.

"You've been away a long time."

"I suppose so. How are you getting on?" Henri had forbidden him to look at the picture until it was finished. He could see only the backs of the canvases side by side on their easels.

"One more day - maybe even this afternoon," Henri said in an appeasing tone. He felt sorry for Edward who was mooching around when he should have been lying on the beach with his beautiful wife. But Nicole obviously had other ideas. Henri had gone to collect a tube of paint from his suppliers a couple of days ago and he'd stopped to have an espresso coffee in the open air café before going back to the studio. He was idly watching the passing scene when his eyes had been drawn to the unmistakable figure of Nicole. She was going into the hotel opposite and she was not alone. Henri's heart beat uncomfortably as he called to the waiter who leaned against the door. "That hotel - there," he asked, pointing to the building across the road, "does it have a good restaurant?"

"No *Monsieur,* they have no restaurant. Rooms only, I understand. "

Henri lingered over his coffee but the couple failed to reappear. Then he ordered beer and a sandwich. He watched and waited, half hidden by the glass screen. He was there for over two hours and was losing valuable time. He was about to rise from his chair when he saw them - there they were, kissing each other passionately as they separated. Nicole's swinging stride took her towards the sea, the man walked in the opposite direction. Henri shook his head sorrowfully, he would never hurt Edouard by telling him what he'd seen. The sooner he was free of her the better.

Edward lifted the mattress from the bed in the unused cabin and placed Henri's carefully packed Van Gogh on the base. He replaced the mattress and remade the bed then he smoothed the quilted cover, making sure everything was in place. Although the cabin was not in use, he locked the door and removed the key. He'd been speechless when he'd finally been allowed to see the canvas. When the two pictures were side by side he was unable to detect even the slightest difference, Henri's was a photographic likeness of the original.

"It's perfect, it's quite uncanny," Edward said.

"Yes, I'm pleased," Henri replied, "it is an excellent forgery."

Luci came out on the deck. "M Henri is telephoning you," she said, as she placed a cup of coffee on the little table beside him.

"Edouard? I must talk to you regarding the eh … matter that interests us both."

Edward felt a curl of excitement rise to his throat. "I can be with you in half an hour."

"We'll meet at Michel's?"

"The buyer wants to remain anonymous - which is not surprising. He will send his agent to view the picture, someone who is an expert on Van Gogh. Naturally it is all totally confidential so have no worry. You must begin by asking twelve million dollars then be prepared to accept nine or ten. They will no doubt offer you as little as six million to start with, but that is to be expected."

Edward laughed hysterically, *"As little as six million."*

Henri frowned. "I wish I could be there with you, especially if that is how you are going to behave."

"It's such a crazy amount of money I couldn't help it," Edward apologised.

"My other news - or lack of it, is about your employer. All enquiries seemed to lead nowhere, a wall of silence surrounds him. There is little doubt about his wealth but exactly how he acquired it no one is prepared to say. A hint was dropped that drugs may be involved, but I suspect that was just a guess. At this stage it is more important that you should complete the transaction."

Edward waited as calmly as his fast-beating

heart would allow. The smart motor launch drew level with the yacht and he caught his first glimpse of the dealer. An attractive woman climbed aboard gracefully. She was wearing white trousers and a black shirt with a white cravat. It was a shock to discover that the agent was female, not that it mattered. Luci and Adrien had left in the launch to buy provisions so Edward and his guest would not be disturbed. He led the way to the salon and the woman followed, expressing admiration at her surroundings.

As they entered the room she stopped abruptly, the Van Gogh was in full view.

"Ah!" she said. She made no attempt to move nearer.

"Would you like some coffee … ?"

"Call me Nicole," the woman smiled.

"That's not your real name?"

"No."

"Good, in that case let's find a different name." His voice was harsh.

"OK, try Jeanne."

"Jeanne. Nicole is my wife's name and frankly it sticks in my throat."

"Jeanne" walked towards the painting and stared at it closely. "I understand it will not be possible to remove it from its seal?"

"Only when it's sold. We have to be careful - the sea air, damp?"

"Of course," she smiled rather coldly.

"Would it be possible to take it from the wall? I would like to examine it by the porthole, Mr Howell."

"I'm … sure that will be all right." Just in time

Edward stopped himself from denying he was Bob Howell. That would have been a serious mistake.

"Would you mind turning away while I unlock it please?"

"Not at all, I'll sit over there."

She turned a chair to face the landscape on the other wall and sat, one leg neatly crossed over the other. Edward reached towards the picture and slid it from its frame. As he walked towards her he admired her long auburn hair shining in the sunlight.

"Here you are," he said handing it to her carefully. "It's heavy."

She walked to the window and stared at the flowers, then she turned the picture round and studied the reverse side. "When did you buy it?"

"A couple of years ago," he said.

"Who did you buy it from?"

"Oh come now," Edward smiled, "you don't expect me to answer that." Henri had schooled him well.

"No, but there's no harm in trying!" This time her laughter was sincere.

"Why do you want to sell it? It's not been in your possession long."

"Do you really want to know?" he asked.

She nodded her head and went on examining the canvas.

"Put it down on the floor and have some coffee," Edward urged, "unless you're in a hurry."

"I've plenty of time, after all you don't discover a beautiful painting like this every day."

Edward turned the lid on the vacuum flask and poured steaming liquid into the cups. "Are you interested in buying the picture?" he asked bluntly.

"Perhaps," she parried.

"If you do decide to buy it, then I'll tell you why I'm selling." Edward sat back in the chair in a casual manner, his actions belying the turmoil that raged inside him.

"Where do you come from?" he asked, he couldn't place her accent.

"Somewhere and nowhere," she replied.

"I've been there too!"

"What's your asking price for the picture?"

"You already know that, I'm sure, but it's twelve million American dollars or the equivalent - in cash of course."

"I'm instructed to offer you five million."

"That's an insult not an offer."

"Take it or leave it," she shrugged.

"I'll leave it, thank you. There are several other people interested so we've nothing to talk about."

"Who else is interested?" she demanded.

"Please, Jeanne! ... Let's enjoy our coffee, forget the picture."

"All right, I'll go to seven million."

"I'll tell you what, eleven million and it's sold, if not I prefer to wait."

"Eight, and that's my final offer."

"Sorry, no. You know its value. No harm done, and I realise that you're acting for someone else. If the others don't come up with a better offer, I'll contact you again. But you might have a long wait."

Her amber eyes stared at him steadily. He forced himself to return her gaze, unflinchingly.

Could she see the pulse beating double-time in his throat or did his shirt hide it? She was attractive in a hard sort of way, wide-nosed with undefined cheek bones. Edward recognised a stubborn chin when he saw one and her mouth, although generous, was set in a grim line. It helped to be sitting in the shadow as he was.

"It's academic now, but what do you really hope to get for the painting?"

"Eleven million dollars."

"Don't budge until the end," Henri had warned.

"No you don't," she accused. "I bet you'd grab nine million happily."

How right you are, Edward agreed silently. "You're wrong, but as you're no longer interested I'll tell you that ten million would make me think twice," Edward smiled.

"Nine."

"Ten, not a penny less."

"You're a tough man. All right, you've got yourself a buyer, ten million dollars less a hundred thousand for me."

He didn't let out a scream of delight, didn't jump up and hug her, he just sat frowning, considering her proposal. "I suppose so," he said with great reluctance. "Cash, of course?"

"Cash," she agreed. "I was going to suggest that we deposit it in an account in Switzerland, but if you insist on cash, my client will arrange it."

"A Swiss bank? Mmm, that's an idea, but I don't hand over the painting until the money's in place."

"That's understood. It'll be placed on deposit

in a bank of your choice and when you're satisfied, we can make the exchange then."

"That sounds all right. If you don't mind waiting a moment, I'll make a telephone call to my legal adviser."

"By all means. Do you have any authentication?"

"Hardly, believe it or not they didn't give me a receipt, nor did they charge me tax!"

His tone was light, teasing but again his heart was thudding. He prayed she wouldn't notice how unsteady he was on his legs.

"That will be acceptable," he said, returning to the salon. Henri had been delighted by Edward's handling of the deal and approved the idea of the bank. "Far more practical, safer that way - and a lot lighter," he laughed. They arranged to meet later when the launch returned, and Edward rang off.

"I'd like to know your reason for selling now that we have a deal."

"My wife is entitled to half of everything in a divorce situation. We're going to split up. That will mean giving her half the yacht, half the houses, half the art collection, need I say more?"

She shook her head.

"The one thing she's not entitled to is the Van Gogh."

"How come?"

"Because she doesn't know it exists."

Jeanne's eyebrows rose.

"Some women like to gossip, and to boast about the things they own and my wife is one of them. You're a woman of the world, I don't need to spell out what would happen if information like this became public knowledge. I thought it wiser to tell her nothing, she's not interested in art, doesn't appreciate it. Now that our marriage is over - kaput - I'm damned if I'm going to let her get her hands on one penny of this money. I'm going to sell the painting now, as a precaution. After all, if the houses go and the yacht too, I can hardly travel around with the Van Gogh stuffed in a suitcase, can I?"

"No you can't, but surely the property can be divided up."

"Who knows what can happen? I wouldn't be the first to get taken to the cleaners by a smart lawyer. This way I'm taking no chances."

For a few minutes they sat silently. "What do I get for my hundred grand?" Edward asked.

"I don't understand," she said, her eyes wary.

"Information, I mean."

"What kind of information?"

"Who's your buyer?"

She laughed heartily. "Nice try, you're as cheeky as I am. You had me worried for a moment. The only thing I'll tell you is it's not me."

"That's what I call rotten value for money."

"That's the name of the game."

"Seriously, how come you're involved in this ... kind of work? Aren't you considered to be the expert on Van Gogh?"

"I am. But if you can tell me where I can make the sort of money I just did now by working in the basement of a museum or in an art gallery, then I bow to *your* expertise."

"Touché," Edward laughed. "There's one question that I'd like to ask, how do you know the painting is genuine?"

"Simple, fifteen years hard study. Van Gogh for breakfast, lunch and dinner, also I have seen this painting before. To be honest I missed it last time it was on the market. That's when it was sold to you so you see I already know all about the purchase. Now you can discuss it freely."

"If you do know all about it, then we've nothing *to* discuss."

"You're a smart man, aren't you?"

"Let's put it this way, I'm not a fool." Not half, that's why I fell for the con in Vegas, he reflected silently.

"I'd like to leave Cannes as soon as possible," Jeanne said, "so let's shake hands on the deal. Would you care to tell me which bank you'd like to use?"

Edward named the bank Henri had suggested.

"Very well, as soon as the money is there I'll phone you. We'll meet at Nice airport and you'll bring the painting with you. You must take it from its frame and put it in a cylinder - you can buy one in any art shop. I'll examine the painting and then we'll telephone the bank to release the funds. Does that suit you?"

"Where will you examine the painting? Surely not on the concourse?"

"I'll take it to the ladies cloakroom. If you want you can send someone with me but, remember, it's in my interest too that everything is above-board. Then you order the transfer of one hundred thousand dollars to me. At that stage you can leave me to make my own arrangements. By then your money will be untouchable."

Anne Schulman

"That sounds all right, when can I expect to hear from you?"

"Tomorrow morning after eleven o'clock. You should be prepared and ready. Good-bye, Mr Howell, it's been nice doing business with you and I hope your divorce doesn't cause too many problems."

CHAPTER SIXTY-EIGHT

Edward could barely contain his excitement as he packed the last of his clothes into the hold-all and made sure that the tube holding the picture was well hidden. He looked around the stateroom. He'd left Nicole's passport on the dresser with a hundred dollars in cash and her air ticket. Now that the time had finally come for them to part he felt a pang of sadness despite the mayhem of the previous night's party.

"It's better that you leave right away, as soon as the money's in the bank," Henri advised. "This is a dangerous game you play, Edouard. Contact me when you can, but give no name, no address. Sooner or later my friend, we will meet again, good luck and be happy. Do not let that money spoil your life."

With a heavy heart he had said goodbye to Henri who utterly refused to accept any payment for his contribution. Edward didn't press the matter further but, whether Henri liked it or not, he would send him a draft for a million dollars when the money was paid into the bank. Henri would have to accept it, especially if Edward couldn't be found.

Why was he feeling so low, Edward wondered? The lights of the Croisette twinkled as brightly as the starlit sky, he could hear the rhythm of music floating across the calm sea. As he came nearer to the yacht the music was quite deafening. All around the *Bon Vivant* small craft bobbed on the water, rowing boats, motor launches and even rafts. Edward made his way across the crowded deck. Adrien's worried face greeted him. "Thank goodness you're back, Monsieur, I think things are out of control."

A splash was heard, then screams of laughter. Adrien caught Edward's arm as he tripped over a half-empty bottle which rolled along the deck. The swimming-pool was packed with naked bathers. He rushed to the salon where the remains of a buffet spilled from the table. Plates were scattered everywhere and disgusting morsels of food smeared the carpet and white couches. A drunken youth had taken the smallest of the bronzes from the display shelf and was lobbing it at a row of empty champagne bottles. Hit or miss, everyone cheered as he tossed the precious ornament at the targets. A sweet sickly smell hung in the air and in the centre of the room the small wooden floor was tightly packed with weaving couples, the motion of their bodies bearing no relation to the music. Everywhere he looked there were people drinking wine straight from the bottles. Grabbing one of the bottles, he looked at the label, Mouton Rothschild, one of the more precious vintages from the wine cellar. Nicole ran along the deck laughing, and drew to a halt in front of her furious husband. "Look everyone," she shrieked, "Mr Credit Card is home, three cheers for Edward, hip ... hip ... rip! Hip ... hip ... rip!"

Edward slapped her across the mouth with the flat of his palm. Everyone screamed with laughter. "Rip ... slap, rip ... slap," someone chanted.

"You bastard," Nicole screeched, flailing her arms in Edward's direction.

"Get off the ship now," he yelled at her drunken companions, startling them into silence. "If any of you are still here in two minutes I'll throw you overboard myself."

Luci ran along the deck calling to him, "Quickly, Monsieur Edouard, the stateroom."

He and Adrien ran to the cabin. A billow of smoke curled from under the door. As they burst it open they could see the figure of a man lying on the smouldering bed. They threw open the window and dragged the drunken man towards the fresh air.

"How did all this happen?" Edward asked the stricken Adrien.

"Madame told us to prepare for some guests. Twenty she said, but they just kept arriving. Some of them even swam across."

"I'll soon get rid of them. Don't worry, Adrien, it's not your fault."

As they passed the galley they heard a heart-stopping crash.

"Now what?" Edward groaned, as Adrien pushed open the door. There was no one there. They could hear moaning and a stream of red liquid oozed from under the cellar door. With the agility of a cat, Edward jumped aside as the rack crashed forward when Adrien turned the handle. Dozens of bottles of wine had fallen, smashed to smithereens and wine flowed through shards of glass. A young girl lay beneath the fallen racks, grinning foolishly, a bottle of champagne clutched tightly to her chest.

"Throw her overboard," Edward ordered.

Adrien stared at him, shocked.

"But Monsieur, she is drunk or even unconscious perhaps, she would drown."

"Then find her friends, but get rid of her." The last thing he needed was a police inquiry on the yacht.

Edward picked up an unbroken bottle and searched through a drawer until he found a corkscrew. He took two glasses from the tray on the table and poured a drink for Adrien and himself.

"Sit down, you need a drink. I certainly do."

Luci was scurrying around the salon collecting glasses and bottles in a big bin. Word had spread quickly that Monsieur had phoned for the police. Like rats leaving a sinking ship they scurried to their boats and disappeared into the night. Nicole went with them.

The captain had slept through the whole episode, his "tonic bottle" empty beside him on the night table. "Leave him, there's nothing he can do now," Edward said in disgust. "The crew will be back tomorrow, they'll clean the carpets and the furniture."

The three of them set about tidying as best they could. "Please let things go right tomorrow," Edward prayed, as he finally climbed into bed. The wine had done nothing to relax his taut nerves and he lay in the cabin waiting for daybreak.

At eleven o'clock Jeanne phoned. "Everything is ready. I'll meet you as arranged, two-thirty sharp." Her voice was thick, almost unrecognisable.

The airport was buzzing with holidaymakers,

tanned faces contrasted with those of new arrivals. Jeanne was waiting for him. He took the cylinder out of his bag and handed it to her. "I won't be a moment," she assured him, as she disappeared into the ladies cloakroom. He walked up and down, his heart slamming against his ribs.

"We'll phone the bank now," she said. Her hands were empty.

Edward looked at her, frowning. "Where is it?" he asked.

"Don't worry, it's in safe hands."

The bank handled the transaction with smooth efficiency. He wrote down the number of his temporary account and repeated it twice to make sure it was correct. He told them to transfer one hundred thousand dollars and he signalled to Jeanne. Edward stood out of earshot as she gave them the name of her bank.

"It's all arranged," she said, holding out her hand.

"Thank you," Edward smiled nervously.

"Goodbye," she smiled in return, moving away. "By the way, my congratulations. Between ourselves - it's an excellent forgery."

CHAPTER SIXTY-NINE

Bob Howell crashed the receiver back into place, the man had just disappeared into thin air. Even his world-wide network had failed to find him.

The young couple Edward had hired were unable to tell him anything about Edward's whereabouts, and he believed them. The temporary captain, when they finally caught up with him, was equally unhelpful.

The yacht had escaped virtually unscathed from the orgy apart from the decimation of his wine cellar. If the young couple were telling the truth it was Edward's wife who had been responsible for the party. For a time Bob even felt a certain sympathy for Edward, obviously his wife was totally out of control. She hadn't been difficult to find. She was in a nightclub in Paris and after some not so gentle persuasion, the heavies he'd sent had been satisfied that she neither knew nor cared where her husband was. Pity about the face, but it would heal.

A telephone call from Bob Howell's scout in New York finally disclosed the true reason for Edward's disappearance. The hunt for him began.

Bob experienced a rush of pumping adrenaline that only the promise of an important find could bring. The painting was here in Nice, not an hour away. "Of course I'm interested, set up the appointment," he urged.

Another Van Gogh, quite a coincidence - lilies.

Perhaps they were a pair, but he doubted that somehow.

Bob Howell walked into the gallery and strolled about casually examining the exhibition of primitive art. The flamboyant gallery owner watched him on a screen in the director's office and was satisfied. The man fitted the description his agent had given him. He greeted Bob Howell effusively. They discussed the exhibition, played for time, sized each other up.

"Not quite what I had in mind," Bob Howell ventured.

"What type of painting were you looking for?" the man asked.

"Oh, something more ... flowery?" he suggested.

"I see, any flowers in particular?"

"Lilies."

"Follow me," said the pink-suited man with the red spotted cravat.

He locked the door. Behind him Bob could hear the rattle of keys, racks sliding, something buzzing. He forced himself not to turn his head.

"Voilà." said the art dealer triumphantly.

Bob swung around and saw the painting on the display easel. *His* painting.

"It can't be," he said angrily, "this is a forgery. I already own this painting."

"I'm afraid not," the dealer said calmly. "This has been verified by the foremost expert on Van Gogh's works."

"Then you have been misled ... or," he stopped. It wasn't possible. His picture was safe, sealed in its frame in the salon, untouched.

He left the gallery, agitated and confused. He

had to agree that one of the canvases must be a fake, but which one?

The intervening week stretched endlessly. His anger and frustration grew with every passing hour. A terse phone call sent him scurrying back to Nice.

"I have the forgery," said the grey-faced man, dressed in mourning-black.

Relief flooded through Bob Howell.

"I'm sorry, really sorry," Bob managed to say. "What happens now?"

"The word is out. My *expert* is conveniently incommunicado, but don't worry - we'll find her." The gallery owner's voice was malevolent. "I appreciate your concern. However, I feel it my duty to point out that the fake is a recent one, not more than three months old. If, as you say, the painting has been in your possession for some time, how do you explain that?"

A deep purple flush spread upwards from Bob's neck.

Bob lay comfortably on the deck in the morning sunshine. A small item in a local newspaper meant nothing to him. It reported the mysterious death of a young woman found on a lonely stretch of road in her burnt-out car.

CHAPTER SEVENTY

Edward stared at the stranger in the mirror. He was a fine-looking man with a tanned face, prematurely grey hair, a straight narrow nose, flat ears and piercingly blue eyes.

The stranger grinned at him cheekily. "Good morning, stranger," Edward bowed.

When he first looked in the mirror he had refused to believe it was possible. The hair had been a shock, brown to grey in one easy application. The contact lenses had been startling too, so blue - his brown eyes were a thing of the past. He smiled as he remembered the day the surgeon had shown him his new, streamlined nose; shorter, straight as an arrow, the tiny bump gone. The flat ears had not been so much a matter of vanity as of necessity. He remembered the taunts of his school-friends, "Ask jug-ears. Come on, loopy-lugs." His ears looked good now.

The time had come. This was the moment of truth. He snapped the locks on his briefcase and left his tiny flat in the Swiss village for the last time. The Ferrari suited his new image. Edward threw his case, then his briefcase, on to the passenger seat and turned the key in the ignition. He began the journey that would take him, Eduardo Conti, to France.

He was pleased now that he'd had driving lessons, voice classes too. The change of accent had been Henri's idea. Their guarded phone calls had been the only contact with his past life during his year of isolation. Henri told him about the discovery of the forgery, the "coincidental" death of the girl he had known as Jeanne, and the questioning of Luci and Adrien by Bob Howell. Edward's change of face had been the biggest challenge of all but that surgery was his passport to life.

The powerful engine growled beneath him as it ate up the kilometres. Claude d'Albion would approve of the elegant car, but would he approve of his guest? The expensive clothes, the lightly accented voice? In a very few minutes he'd find out.

The big black gates parted and he drove slowly along the drive. He wanted to enjoy the smell of the flowers and he didn't want to anger Claude d'Albion. Fast driving sent the gravel flying.

As he rounded the curve he could see the dapper proprietor standing on the marble steps.

"Make or break," Edward muttered to himself, his pulse quickened as he opened the door of the car.

"Signor Conti, welcome to the Château d'Albion. I hope you will enjoy your stay with us."

"This is delightful!" Edward spread his arm in a wide sweeping gesture. "I cannot fail to enjoy such a place - a heavenly oasis."

Claude smiled at the man. So poetic, the Italians. He was a handsome man too, casually but beautifully dressed, he approved. The shirt was silk, the trousers uncreased even after his drive. Edward stopped himself in time from

Intrigue

dragging his suitcase from the car. He picked up his jacket and document case and gave his keys to the young porter. No need to warn him about the power of the Ferrari, Claude wouldn't let him touch it unless he could handle it competently.

"Your luggage will be in your room in a moment. Please join me in a glass of champagne, it will rid you of the dust of travel."

Edward sat on the bed, a satisfied smile on his face. He had passed the test so far. He was unrecognised, respected and an honoured guest at the Château d'Albion.

Rachel

CHAPTER SEVENTY-ONE

It wasn't like Harriet Whitney to be so insensitive. Rachel had purposely turned her head away from that side of the street. She didn't want to see Caprice - the whole experience was still too raw.

"Rachel, look." Harriet tugged at her sleeve.

With reluctance Rachel turned to look through the cab window at the boutique. It was shuttered and the interior blinds were in place. Harriet's poor eyesight had prevented her from seeing the notice taped to the window but even for Rachel the message it bore was too small to read from that distance.

"I wonder why it's closed?" Rachel asked herself.

The taxi drew up in front of the medical centre and Rachel helped Harriet out of the vehicle and paid the driver. Drawing a deep breath, Harriet strode purposefully into the reception area. She wished she hadn't agreed to this examination. Wasn't one ophthalmologist just like another? Her sight had deteriorated, *she* had accepted that long ago - why couldn't Rachel?

Rachel smiled her encouragement but Harriet scowled as they sat in the waiting-room which was decorated in soothing shades of pink and beige. A white-coated nurse approached Harriet who rejected her helping hand. She followed the nurse into the doctor's office, her tiny figure proud and erect.

Rachel's thoughts wandered back to Caprice. What had happened to Meg Adams? Tuesday was usually one of their busiest days. It was unlike Meg to be away, especially as she had no help in the shop. She was never ill, perhaps she'd had an accident? She might ask the cab-driver to stop on the way home so that she could read the notice. Rachel leafed through the magazines but they didn't hold her attention. She walked to the window and absent-mindedly watched the passing traffic.

"Rachel?"

She turned quickly. Harriet Whitney was smiling broadly at her.

"What did the doctor say?"

"Sit down for a moment and I'll tell you what she said."

Harriet groped for a chair, her eyes slightly blinded by the drops which the doctor had used.

"Apparently I have a cataract in my right eye which can be removed and a lens implanted. The left eye is also affected but that can be cured in a couple of years' time when the cataract is fully developed."

Rachel was overjoyed to hear the news. "See, I told you it was worth a visit." She couldn't resist the temptation to gloat.

"Come on, let's treat ourselves to a good lunch," Harriet said. She hadn't had lunch at a restaurant for eight or nine years, she felt they deserved a celebration.

Rachel left the cab to stare at the notice in the window.

Closed due to unforeseen circumstances
Reopening shortly

"What did the notice say?" Harriet asked.

"Very little, just that it was closed due to 'unforeseen circumstances', it would reopen soon. There was a phone number to contact."

"That's very odd. Let's phone the number when we get home."

"No. I don't want to," Rachel replied sharply.

"You're probably right. That was tactless of me."

Rachel assured her that it didn't matter. Harriet meant well.

The days passed slowly in the Whitney household. Rachel held Harriet's tiny trembling hand until they came to take her to the operating theatre. The surgeon was pleased to tell the waiting family that the operation had gone smoothly, in two days Harriet would be back home. Harriet was pampered by Rachel, by Enid Saunders and her husband, and visited by her family. She revelled in all the attention. They filled the house with fragrant bouquets and magnificent baskets of exotic fruits.

Rachel was determined not to allow the euphoria to be spoilt by her own problems. With a mug of coffee in front of her she scoured the classifieds each morning circling every advertisement which might be suitable. Although Rachel said that she would take any job that she could get, Harriet begged her to wait until the right one came along. "There'll be something that's right for you, Rachel. You don't need to worry about rent or food. Be patient. Besides, I need you here with me at the moment."

Rachel knew that Harriet loved her. She also knew she could manage perfectly well without

Anne Schulman

her. She promised to wait for two weeks, no longer, then she'd accept the first offer that came along.

Rachel left Harriet dozing, and spread some fabric on the table in the kitchen and pinned a pattern to it. She'd seen a photograph in a French magazine of a woman who looked like Harriet Whitney and Rachel had sketched the elegant dress that the chic woman had been wearing. The day she left Caprice she'd torn out the page - to hell with Meg Adams. Rachel would keep the photograph to show Harriet when the time was right. She used one of Harriet's dresses for the measurements of the pattern. Rachel was pleased with the material she'd bought. Enid Saunders abandoned her chores to watch Rachel skilfully cutting the fabric, a delicate wool crepe in soft sky-blue.

"God you're brave! I'd be terrified to slice into it like that," she observed, hardly daring to breathe.

"It's practice. I was scared stupid the first time I had to cut material," Rachel told her. "My hands wobbled so much that the seams were as wavy as the sea!"

Rachel threaded a bright tacking cotton into a large needle and she sat down to begin piecing the parts of the dress together.

She was lost in her work when the sound of the telephone disturbed her.

"Rachel!" Enid Saunders called, "it's for you."

Who could be calling *her?*

"… and so, if it is convenient, we would like you to call at our offices," the voice concluded.

Rachel made a note of the address. Tomorrow

at ten-thirty would be fine. Thoughtfully, she replaced the receiver and tried to make some sense of the call.

"He said they wanted to talk about Caprice."

Harriet gave her full attention to the details of the call. The man from the firm of accountants responsible for the boutique, had been mysterious. "He just said it would be in my interest to visit them. He was a tough nut. He wouldn't answer my questions; why was Caprice closed? What happened to Meg? He promised to explain it all when we meet. I admit that the call left me intrigued and frustrated."

"They've discovered you were cheated," Harriet declared.

"Could be. They might want to check out Meg Adams. Whatever. He wasn't going to discuss it on the phone. I tried, believe me!"

"At least you only have to wait until tomorrow for an answer."

The reception area was insulated by a deep-pile carpet which cushioned every footfall. A selection of minimalist art hung on the white walls and large green plants flourished in huge tubs at regular intervals in the pale space.

"Please go right in, you're expected." The glossy receptionist indicated a door facing her uncluttered desk.

"Thank you for coming." The man in the three-piece suit pulled back a chair for her at the glass topped table.

Two other men rose politely as the spokesman of the group introduced them.

"Avery Salk and his assistant, Teddy Lawrence - our lawyers. I'm Gideon Seaforth."

Rachel smiled at the men. They tried not to stare at her lovely face.

"You're aware that Caprice is temporarily closed. Before I answer your questions we have some questions for you," Gideon said, his face grave. "Apart from your salary, did you receive any commissions on sales?"

Rachel shook her head. "None," she answered briefly.

"Why were you dismissed?"

That unfair dismissal still hurt. But she explained the circumstances in a clear, cool voice. "Mrs Adams was very angry with me," she said, "and I was asked to leave that week and was paid a month's salary in lieu of notice."

"I see." Gideon Seaforth took off his glasses and rubbed the bridge of his nose.

Avery Salk continued the questioning. "How did Mrs Adams deal with the cash sales?"

Rachel had no idea. She'd known nothing about Meg Adams' accounting system. They continued asking questions but Rachel had no answers. She began to feel uncomfortable and irritable. Why was she here? Was it a witch hunt?

"Can you tell me what happened, *please?*" Rachel was beginning to lose her temper.

"Just a couple more questions," Avery Salk smiled.

How could she beat the system? Rachel wondered. These men were masters of evasion.

"Let's break now," said Gideon Seaforth. He sensed that their unrelenting enquiries had yielded all the information possible.

"You do have time for lunch?"

Rachel took it as an order rather than an invitation.

Intrigue

They stretched their legs and waited until the receptionist had unloaded her tray of sandwiches and coffee pots. Conversation became general and "the suits" became positively human. Avery Salk showed Rachel photographs of his family. His hobby was photography, he said, proudly explaining who was who. Gideon Seaforth recommended a novel he was reading and Teddy Lawrence said little, but his smiling eyes met Rachel's with shy admiration.

As the informal lunch ended, Gideon Seaforth raised an eyebrow and put forward his proposal. "Would you be prepared to accept the management of Caprice, Rachel?"

She choked on the last crumbs of her sandwich and Teddy Lawrence jumped to his feet and tapped her firmly on her back. Her eyes watered and she took great gulps of air. But she nodded her astonished agreement.

"Take your time," Avery Salk counselled.

As soon as her voice returned to normal, she said yes. "But *please,* tell me what's happened, why did the boutique close?" she begged, unable to contain her curiosity any longer.

Gideon's face softened. He smiled fully for the first time. She was so appealing - those huge dark eyes. "Mrs Adams appears to have had several ... shall we say, irregularities in her bookkeeping."

"My commission I suppose?" Rachel interrupted bitterly.

"Yes, that and other things. That's only the tip of the iceberg."

"So that's why you were asking all those questions." Rachel felt she should have realised the reason for the third degree.

"Yes, but you obviously don't know just what she did. The extent of her deception." Gideon marvelled at how wide those beautiful eyes could grow as he told her the details of Meg Adams' activities. "Now, let's discuss your contract."

Rachel listened avidly to the various details. It all appeared to be straightforward, at least as far as she could tell. She was totally inexperienced in these matters. Rachel made her dazed way to the waiting taxi. Her mind was in turmoil. These days, she grinned ruefully, she stumbled from one crisis to another - but this one was heaven-sent.

They sat on the patio finishing dinner. Rachel ignored her meal as she attempted to recount every word of the meeting to Harriet.

"It seems that Meg Adams was taking my commission as well as her own, not that *that* comes as any surprise. She fiddled the cash sales too - the money went straight into her pocket. To cover herself she reduced them in her books at sales time, *sold* for a third of their ticketed price."

"Wait a minute, let me see if I understand. She sold the garments at their full price then pretended that they'd been in the sales? She pocketed the difference?"

"Exactly. And worse still she lent gowns to customers for a dance or dinner and charged them a hefty fee. They wore a frock just once, paying a tenth of the price it would have cost them to own an up-to-the-minute ball gown or cocktail dress of such quality."

"My lord! What a opportunist she was, so enterprising. What are they going to do about it?"

"They're prosecuting her. They were very definite about that."

"Quite right too. Will you have to go to court?"

"I don't think so, they seem to have all the information they need."

"So, tell me about your contract."

"I'm to manage the boutique," Rachel said proudly, her eyes sparkling. "The buying will continue as before and I have to hire an assistant."

Harriet was pleased. Justice had been done. She'd spent long hours trying to find a way to right matters but had drawn a blank.

"I begin on Monday, and report to Gideon Seaforth twice a week. The fine print seems to be OK.," Rachel said hesitantly, "but I'm not very good at those things."

"Do you have a copy of the contract?"

"It'll arrive tomorrow. I have to read it through and, if I'm satisfied, sign it. "

"We'll take a look at it together and if there are any problems or unusual conditions we can call my lawyer. This is a well-deserved opportunity for you and I know you will be 'A OK' as they say."

They laughed at the incongruity of the expression coming from Harriet's lips. She was coming out of that tunnel in a big way.

Rachel couldn't wait to finish Harriet's dress.The next step on the "nag list", as Harriet called Rachel's requests, would be to drag the liberated lady to the beauty parlour and get rid of that unflattering bun.

Sitting in the fading light Rachel glowed with happiness as they discussed her plans for the running of Caprice. "Of course I'll be limited in what I can do but I have some really exciting ideas." As Rachel enthused Harriet stifled a yawn, Rachel needed to talk and there was no way Harriet would puncture the girl's excitement.

The written contract was simple. The salary and commission she would receive were more than generous, so too was the allowance for clothes from the boutique. The clause that stated that any form of theft or fraud would be liable to instant prosecution irritated Harriet. "You can't blame them, I suppose," she said edgily. "Other than that, it looks fine to me. I suggest you go ahead and sign it."

With a flourish Rachel added her signature to that of Gideon Seaforth. "There, signed and sealed. I'll post it right away."

"There's been a call for you, Rachel, from Daniel Hunt. He'll phone back in an hour."

Rachel flushed and Harriet gave her a knowing look.

"What?" Rachel asked.

"What, what?" Harriet replied innocently.

"Why the funny look?"

"I don't know what you mean." A grin broke out on Harriet's face.

"You're wicked and you know it."

"What have I done?" Harriet fenced.

"It's like you know something that I don't."

"I can't help my face, Rachel."

"I give up, I can never win with you."

"You haven't done badly in the past."

"Wait till you see what else I've in store for you," Rachel threatened.

"Bungey-jumping?" Harriet suggested.

"How do you know about that?" Rachel looked at her friend in amazement.

"I don't live in the stone age Missy, and I do read the papers." She tried not to look as pleased as punch; reading had become a renewed pleasure for her and television fascinated her. "You've created a monster."

"A loveable monster," Rachel smiled fondly.

CHAPTER SEVENTY-TWO

Harriet was flabbergasted when Rachel produced the dress. "It's beautiful. How did you know my size?" It was such a long time since she had bought herself any clothes.

"I borrowed one of your dresses and cut the pattern from that."

"It's so elegant." Harriet marvelled.

"There is a *but*."

"There always is."

"A little self-improvement."

"What now?" Harriet sighed resignedly.

"You have to get your hair styled."

"Forget it. I like my hair the way it is."

"It's too severe. You have a lovely face but your hair makes you look old."

Rachel stopped, she hadn't meant to be hurtful. She put her hand over her mouth. Why had she said that?

"I *am* old," Harriet observed tartly.

Grateful that the feisty little lady had taken no offence, Rachel argued the point.

She showed Harriet the likeness of herself that she'd torn from the magazine.

"My goodness, we do look alike, don't we?" She stared at the woman who appeared to look back in her own image. *Her* hair was short and softly waved. It was very attractive, she grudgingly conceded.

"*Please*, Harriet?" Rachel waited.

"I'll be pleased when you go back to work and

get out of my hair," Harriet laughed.

"Tomorrow afternoon?" Rachel enquired straight-faced.

"You're a pest." Harriet swatted her with the television guide.

"I aim to please." Rachel ducked the swinging paper.

"Daniel! How are you?"

"Mending fast. Another week and I'll be released from medical constraint and become "real-people" again."

Rachel laughed, he was so impatient. He had crossed her mind a thousand times but the traumas of the past weeks had taken precedence.

"I have so much to tell you," she bubbled.

"Good, I hope?"

"Wonderful news, on all fronts."

"How about saving it for another week?"

Rachel said nothing but was disappointed. Now I'm being impatient, she thought.

"Will you help me celebrate my return from the world-of-white?"

"I'd love to." Rachel smiled at his description of the medical profession. "You should be grateful to the nurses."

"You're right. I am really but I hate being followed by a starched apron carrying a hypodermic."

The nurses who had looked after him at the hospital had taken his humorous protests in good part and she knew that he really did appreciate them but didn't take kindly to restrictions.

"Let's say a week from tonight. We'll have dinner - I'll call for you at seven o'clock if that's all right."

"Fine, I'll be ready."

"You can tell me your news then and we'll have a double celebration."

"You look pleased with yourself." Harriet had been eavesdropping unashamedly.

"We're going out for dinner next week."

"You're fond of him, aren't you?"

"Very, he's such a nice man."

"There's a very big difference in your ages." Harriet said sceptically.

"We're just going to have dinner."

"You know best." Harriet didn't want to upset Rachel but she did have misgivings.

The transformation was magical. Harriet looked ten years younger as the full, short, soft waves bounced about her face. She turned her head this way and that and Rachel insisted that they must go out to eat that night. "Such beauty shouldn't be wasted."

"Flatterer!" Harriet was thrilled with the new hairstyle and the pretty polished shell-pink nails. Rachel had cunningly booked the manicurist without telling her, no wonder she'd rushed out of the salon without a word.

The waiter seated the two ladies and produced the menus. The restaurant overlooked the Potomac River which reflected the Kennedy Centre in its still dark waters. They both chose scallops and side salads. Harriet ordered a bottle of light white wine. Rachel stared at her – grinning.

"You're unnerving me, Rachel."

"I can't believe how wonderful you look," she answered.

The Saunders had been equally unstinting in

their admiration. "Oh Mrs Whitney, you look like a debutante," Enid Saunders had said.

"Get away with you." Harriet dismissed the compliment out of hand but she was delighted all the same.

"What are you planning now?" Rachel asked. There was a mischievous glint in Harriet's eyes.

"Nothing. I'm just thinking how surprised my family will be when I swan in at the weekend with my debutante look."

"I'd give anything to see their faces," Rachel laughed.

"Come with me. Yes, you must."

"No, I couldn't impose." Rachel was embarrassed.

"Nonsense, it wouldn't be an imposition, you'd be most welcome. Why didn't I think of it before? Of course you must come with me, after all, you're as dear to me as my family."

The waiter brought their meal. The scallops, a first for Rachel, were delicious. All around them people were chatting and laughing, some in pairs others in large groups. Unable to finish the over-generous dish of delicate seafood, Rachel leant back against the softly-cushioned seat. Never could she remember being so content, so cosseted. Had it really been just a matter of weeks since she felt that the bottom had dropped out of her world, again? She was a lucky girl.

Harriet's elder daughter phoned Rachel to congratulate her. "We're delighted for you, your dismissal was outrageous," she said crisply.

"Thank you," Rachel was flattered, "I must admit I'm relieved to be going back."

"We hope you'll come with Mother on

Saturday, you'll be very welcome. We're planning a barbecue - very casual."

"Thank you," Rachel repeated, "I'd love that."

As she replaced the phone the thought struck her - she had never been to a barbecue, something to look forward to.

The day was perfect. Rachel looked striking in a crisp white blouse, black straight-legged trousers and flat black pumps. They drove through the Virginia countryside and Harriet pointed out the houses which were owned by people Rachel might have come across at Caprice.

"Look at that one," Rachel said as she briefly glimpsed a beautiful white mansion set in its own grounds. Their view was blocked by big gates as they swung shut behind a limousine which entered the path between rolling lawns.

"Do you know whose house that is?" Harriet queried.

"No, should I?"

"That's your friend Daniel Hunt's home." Harriet paused for maximum effect.

"It's beautiful and so big." Rachel somehow had only pictured him in his Georgetown house, one similar to Harriet's.

In a couple of twists and turns they turned off the road and followed a path which revealed a sprawling house nestled into the hillside. As they reached the door Debrah Whitney-Lloyd came forward to meet them. She seemed less forbidding than she had that day at Caprice. Rachel was sure her first instinct had been correct, the woman was far more at home in trousers than in a ball gown.

"Mother! What have you done to yourself?" Debrah stared open-mouthed. "You look fantastic!"

Harriet was thoroughly enjoying her daughter's confusion. She'd got used to her new image and loved the impact it made on everyone who saw her.

They followed Debrah through a sunny hall which opened directly on to a patio and enormous gardens at the rear of the house. Four heads bobbed and splashed in a rectangular swimming-pool. Netting around the clay tennis protected the less energetic sun-bathers on the patio. A tall man brandishing barbecue tongs approached them. "Is that really you, Harriet?" He stared at his mother-in-law in astonishment.

"Hello Frederick. Yes, it's me!"

"I married the wrong Whitney." He bent forward kissing her pink-tinged cheek.

A young girl left the pool and slip-slapped her wet feet across the red tiles of the patio to see what was happening.

"Say hello to Rachel and your grandmother," Debrah said.

"Where is she?" The dripping youngster, blond hair slicked to her tanned face, looked around. Each member of the family in turn praised and delighted in the rejuvenated matriarch. Harriet had more fun than she'd had for years. Emily, Harriet's younger daughter, congratulated Rachel on her tenacity. "You're a miracle worker," she said, smiling fondly at her mother. The sisters were well aware of Rachel's influence and they were grateful. At one time Rachel had worried that Harriet's affection for her might cause jealousy but she quickly realised from brief telephone conversations with them both that nothing could be further from the truth.

Within minutes, Rachel's shyness had disappeared and she began to relax in the informal atmosphere.

"Men's work today, we're guests," Debrah announced and led them to a drinks trolley at the patio.

The four women sat on brightly-coloured chairs sipping their iced drinks.

"We're really pleased that you've been made manageress of Caprice," Emily said warmly. "I'm sure you must have hated that woman Meg Adams. Personally, I couldn't stand her hard-selling ways."

"Forgive me," Rachel puzzled, "did I ever see you in the boutique?"

"No you didn't, I stopped going there ages ago. I had a sickener one day when she tried to cram me into a dress for a teenager - young and beautiful though I am, that was it for me." They all laughed as she patted her hair and pouted her lips, one tanned leg displayed in a sexy pose. "I'll be back now, never fear, and I'll drag my friends with me by the roots of their dyed hair."

"There's one thing I must say in her favour," Rachel admitted, "I met all of you through her and that can't be all bad."

The look of understanding that passed between mother and daughters spoke volumes. "You really are a charitable girl," Debrah said awkwardly.

"Come on, folks, five minutes to chow time," Frederick called.

"Help me grab a salad from the kitchen," Debrah said, energetically springing from her chair.

The kitchen was a mass of plants and colour. Herbs in bundles hung on hooks from a brass rail. Prints of clowns added their own character to the walls and rows of graduated copper pots gleamed in the sunlight and gave the room a mellow look.

"What a wonderful kitchen," Rachel admired, "it's so ..."

"Messy?" Debrah laughed.

"No, so ... alive." Rachel struggled to describe the homely atmosphere.

They each carried large bowls of salads to the table at the shaded end of the patio. Debrah tossed a bundle of herbs on to the coals and Rachel sniffed appreciatively as the two men brought huge platters of char-grilled ribs, chicken and burgers for their inspection. The four teenagers, lured by the smell of food, dashed to the table. They were collapsing from hunger they said. Politely they shook Rachel's hand and kissed their grandmother. "You look hip, Gran," said her lanky eighteen-year-old grandson.

"You're a man of discernment," Harriet replied straight-faced.

"For once the dweeb tells the truth," his lovely coltish sister agreed.

They bickered in a good-natured way helping themselves to hot biscuits which had appeared like magic from the kitchen along with an enormous dish of sweet potatoes and foil-wrapped baked ones. The food was wonderful, barbecues *were* all they were cracked up to be,

Rachel thought happily, chewing one of the wonderful charred ribs. Everyone went to great pains to make her feel part of the family and Harriet's nonchalant grandson instantly fell in love with her. The youngsters cleared the debris and returned with platters of apple crumble and a light lemon chiffon pie. Emily's husband, a kindly, jolly man volunteered to act as coffee-chef and the afternoon drifted by in a desultory haze of easy conversation.

"It's been a wonderful day," Rachel thanked Debrah and Frederick Lloyd.

"You're welcome any time," Frederick said.

"We're delighted to meet you properly at last." Debrah noticed her husband's glance linger on the girl with the lovely face and didn't blame him.

As they drove home in the Lloyd's limo, Harriet fell into a gentle doze and Rachel counted her blessings, the delight of the day and the exciting prospect of returning to Caprice. Then there was the thought of seeing Daniel again. It was all too much.

CHAPTER SEVENTY-THREE

Rachel took the key from its special delivery envelope and paused, savouring the moment. This was it, the beginning of her new career. The boutique was exactly as she had left it, newspapers and magazines neatly stacked, rows of clothes on padded hangers. "Mine, all mine," she sang as she whirled around. Her eyes lit on the chaise-longue and an involuntary shiver ran down her spine. Roberto, what had happened to him? She never wanted to see him again, he was an episode in her life that she needed to forget. She scooped up the out-of-date newspapers and dumped them in the waste basket reminding herself to collect new magazines on the way home. Pulling up the blinds she removed the notice from the window and deliberately ripped it to shreds - Caprice was no longer closed.

The hours sped by as she chose garments for the windows, dusted glass-topped display tables and reorganised shelves to suit her own taste. She phoned for a sandwich and settled herself at the desk which had been Meg Adams'. She opened the mail. For the first time she felt a bit daunted: notices of incoming autumn stock, bills which needed paying, queries from out-of-town customers. The telephone rang at the same time as the door buzzer sounded. Rachel prayed she could cope. By the end of the day she had calmed down and had sorted the mail into separate piles. A beautiful posy of flowers arrived from Harriet Whitney, and a colourful plant from Debrah and Emily. She phoned to thank them and they promised to pay her a visit later in the week. The second delivery of mail brought a horseshoe hanging from a card which bore the Saunders' good wishes and Rachel called them too. Finally, she drafted an advertisement for an assistant and sent it to *The Washington Post.*

They were at the front door waiting for her when she arrived home, tired but content. Things were under control.

"I'll just get changed and then I'll tell you all about it," Rachel promised.

Dressed in her jeans and a cotton sweater, Rachel relaxed.

"We're so proud of you, honey," Enid Saunders beamed. Her husband nodded his agreement as he handed her a glass of iced Coke.

"It was scary this morning," Rachel said honestly, "the paper work mostly. I'm still at sea with some things but Gideon Seaforth will sort them out until I'm used to handling everything."

This was always the best part of the day, dinner with Harriet. At Harriet's insistence they decided not to mention Caprice until after the meal.

"You have to unwind and eat now, we'll discuss everything later," she advised wisely. She noticed how hyped-up Rachel was.

"I was wondering today, has that young man you were seeing come back to Washington yet? You never mention him."

"I haven't heard from him." Rachel's cheeks flamed at the mention of Roberto. She remembered the convenient lie she'd told Harriet.

She'd said he was working out of state. This was the second time today she wished she'd never met him.

Mistaking her blush for embarrassment, Harriet changed the subject to Rachel's dinner date with Daniel Hunt.

"What are you going to wear?" she demanded.

"I don't know. Smart dinners haven't really been my thing up till now."

"Why don't you use your allowance and choose something from Caprice? Tell you what, why don't I come to the shop tomorrow and your *hip* friend will help you choose something."

"That's a great idea, I'd love that. While you're there we'll have a look at something for you."

"Me and my bright ideas! Perhaps you'd like me to stop off on the way and have a face-lift?"

"Now that you come to mention it..."

"Enough of that, my girl. Now, tell me all the problems you had today."

Somehow in the relaxed atmosphere most of her earlier misgivings seemed to fade and, apart from a couple of minor niggles, Rachel recovered her confidence. She realised how wise Harriet had been to forbid all shop talk for the couple of hours.

They chose a magenta-coloured silk jersey dress which fell into soft foids accentuating the slim curves of Rachel's body. It would be a difficult dress for most women to wear but Rachel's slim figure showed it off to perfection. Rachel sat elegantly on the arm of a chair. Harriet marvelled at the girl's lack of conceit. She hesitated to suggest that Rachel should invite Daniel in for a drink, but the matter was taken out of her hands when Gates rang the bell.

"Mr Hunt is still a little restricted in his movements," he explained.

"Have a fun evening," Harriet smiled. "See you tomorrow afternoon at Caprice around three o'clock."

The hotel restaurant was one of the best in Washington and the maître d' welcomed Daniel with open arms. It was good to see him up and about again after his unfortunate ordeal. Guilt washed over Rachel like a bucket of cold water but, with all the attention and ceremony, it soon receded.

"Will you have a drink first?" Daniel took command.

"I'd love a glass of wine." Rachel had discovered that a glass of wine could calm the butterflies which fluttered in her tummy. Tonight they were actively flying around inside her.

"How about champagne?" Daniel suggested.

As she sipped the pink liquid with its effervescent bubbles a feeling of well-being spread through her. The flying beauties had been anaesthetised.

"You look much better," Rachel said, she could see Daniel now in the light of the elegant room.

"I feel it too. Honourable discharge today!" He saluted in mock gratitude. "You said you had good news. It seems like a lifetime since we saw each other."

He had deliberately prevented himself from contacting her sooner. It was crazy to be interested in such a young girl but reason lost out. He was haunted by her gentle simplicity and sheer beauty.

"So much has happened I don't know where to begin."

"At the risk of using a cliché, how about at the beginning!"

"You remember I told you about the paper I found on the office floor?"

Daniel nodded, not interrupting her flow.

"I finally plucked up courage to tackle Meg Adams about it - I got fired for my trouble. It was awful. She was so unjust. So adamant."

Again Daniel nodded. She glowed as she told him about the successful operation on Harriet's eye and she made him laugh uproariously at the story of Harriet's visit to the beauty salon and everyone's delighted astonishment. "She looks amazing," Rachel was proud of her part in the make-over.

"It gets better, even more good news," she told him, stopping to take a sip of her champagne before giving him the full story of her visit to the accountants. Saving the best till last, she repeated verbatim their offer to reinstate her, this time as manageress of Caprice.

"I'm really pleased for you. Sometimes it takes courage to stand up and be counted. How do you think you'll cope with your new responsibility?" he asked.

"OK I reckon, especially if I get a good assistant. Naturally there are some difficult areas - bookkeeping, accounts and a few odd bits and pieces but Gideon Seaforth has assured me that he's at the end of the phone and that I can call him if there are any problems."

"You'll handle it beautifully I'm sure," he said, seeing the frown on her smooth brow.

"I hope so," she laughed, "otherwise I'll get fired from the same place twice, quite a feat."

A senator and his wife stopped at their table. Daniel introduced Rachel who was sure she detected a supercilious look in the woman's eye. The senator's admiring stare was something she was beginning to get used to. Their meal arrived, the lobster recommended by the attentive maître d' was all he had promised. Daniel seemed to know at least half of the diners in the elegant room and they all stopped by to wish him well and rejoice in his recovery, barely concealing their curiosity about his gorgeous companion. That night Rachel became aware of her beauty, self-conscious because of their flattery.

"I haven't stopped chattering," Rachel apologised. "You're too good a listener." Daniel called the wine-waiter to order another bottle of champagne but Rachel begged off, "I have to work tomorrow!"

"I suppose I shouldn't indulge either," he laughed ruefully. He contented himself by telling her of a trip he'd made to the champagne district as a guest at one of the magnificent châteaux. "To be honest I went to so many wonderful tastings that half of the details escaped in a haze of bubbles!"

"I'd adore to go to France - and to Italy and to England and to everywhere." She laughed at herself. "I've had too much champagne."

"It's good for you."

Rachel was sorry when the evening came to an end. They were the last two people to leave the dining-room but only after they noticed the waiters, shuffling from foot to foot, making valiant attempts to hide the fact that they would like to leave even if Rachel and Daniel were prepared to stay.

"How about doing this again the same night next week?"

"I'd love to but it's Harriet's birthday and I wouldn't miss that for the world."

He admired her loyalty. Affection for Harriet shone on her unclouded face making her even more attractive, if that were possible. He loved everything about this girl not least, he groaned inwardly, the girl herself.

"Let me take you both to dinner. I'd really like to meet her."

Before she could reply Daniel signed the check and they were helped from their chairs by a relieved pair of sleepy waiters. The maître d' rushed to their side from the kitchen to bid them goodnight.

The limousine purred quietly along the empty streets. "Thank you for making it such a lovely jail-break," Daniel said as they drew up in front of the townhouse. Leaning sideways, he kissed her lightly on her cheek and excused himself for not leaving the car. Rachel could see black circles under Daniel's eyes, they were visible even in the dim interior. Obviously he must still be in considerable pain.

"How selfish of me, we should have left earlier."

"Nonsense, I've enjoyed every second of the evening. Tomorrow I'll call Harriet and persuade her to join us next week."

CHAPTER SEVENTY-FOUR

Rachel pulled a face as the phone rang for the umpteenth time that morning. She made an appointment for Friday afternoon and tried once again to finish pressing the dress which was to be collected later that day. She was happy that there had been such a good response to her advertisement, ten appointments so far. Looking at her watch, she discovered it wasn't yet twelve o'clock. Neatly stacked in the corner were the boxes that had been delivered earlier that morning. The first delivery of the autumn stock, but they'd have to wait until the shop was closed and the phone had stopped ringing. She must call the house and tell them she'd be late for dinner. As she reached for the phone, it rang again.

"Yes, you have the right number," she assured the nervous voice on the end of the line. "Ten minutes? I suppose so. Where are you calling from?"

The girl was anxious to get there as soon as possible. Rachel was reminded of her own enthusiasm when she had first applied to Caprice. It was going to be impossible to settle down to any routine work today. "All right, ten minutes." As she gave the address of the shop to the girl the door-buzzer sounded.

Rachel covered the distance from the office to the door, checking on the way that everything was in order. Pasting a smile on her face she pulled open the door. She tried desperately not to stare at the apparition standing in front of her. *Ugly* was not a word Rachel cared to use, fascinating, astonishing or startling possibly. "Come in," she stammered, her eyes spellbound by the earrings which dangled and danced ten inches below the woman's jet black hair.

"Good morning. Rachel?"

Rachel nodded mutely, mesmerised by the bracelet on the outstretched hand, reaching almost from wrist to elbow. On her other arm was its match. Tearing her gaze away from the golden manacles Rachel smiled.

"I am Sylvie Vadim, the buyer for Caprice."

"Oh!" Rachel stammered, unable to find anything better to say.

"Did Gideon Seaforth tell you I was to visit you? I thought we should meet and have a talk," Sylvie suggested, smiling with large crimson lips.

Pull yourself together, Rachel warned herself. "No, I haven't spoken to Gideon, but the phone's been busy this morning. It's nice to meet you," she said with what she hoped was a welcoming smile. Rachel took inventory of the Frenchwoman's startling appearance. She was almost as tall as Rachel and stick-thin. Her height was accentuated by six-inch stiletto heels. Her tights, Rachel observed professionally, were no more than a whisper. A skirt barely showed beneath her jacket, the suit shrieked haute couture. Her collarless neckline sat faultlessly and was entirely filled by gold chains. Swinging earrings missed her shoulders by less than a centimetre. They'd started their journey somewhere under the jet black cap of hair plastered flat to her head, its fringe symmetrical with her black eyebrows. Her skin was snow-white. Her nose with its flaring nostrils covered at least three quarters of the length of her face, it was her most commanding feature. It was impossible to take in her presence all in one go.

Rachel blushed to the roots of her own hair as Sylvie read her thoughts.

"*Jolie-laide,* that's the expression the French use."

"Excuse me?" Rachel played for time as she tried to recover from the embarrassment of being caught staring. Poor though her French was, she had fully understood the phrase. She had come across it in an article in one of the fashion magazines.

"Pretty-ugly, I think you say," Sylvie's tone was without rancour.

"Oh no! I was thinking how unusual it was that you have such blue eyes with your dark colouring." Rachel protested in a desperate attempt to rescue the situation.

"I'm used to people staring at me. I *like* to exaggerate my features, my faults - and flaunt them."

"Would you like some coffee?" Rachel offered, searching for a way out.

"It is a long time since I have been here," Sylvie said amicably, looking around the boutique. Rachel busied herself pouring the coffee and joined Sylvie on the chaise-longue.

"Did you know Mrs Adams - my predecessor?"

"No, we never met. I understand she will not be returning?"

"No, she's gone." Rachel did not feel that it

was her place to discuss the reason for Meg Adams' dismissal. Following Sylvie's gaze to the pile of boxes lining the corner, Rachel said, "I always look forward to opening the boxes, you have such flair and good taste. Today's been hectic. I'm advertising for an assistant so the unpacking will have to wait until tonight when the shop is closed, then I can give it all my attention."

"You certainly need help," Sylvie said as Rachel returned from yet another call. Before she could reply the door buzzer sounded. A plump girl with greasy hair was standing in front of the glass door. Her T-shirt was grubby and her torn jeans were dotted with telephone numbers. Tactfully Rachel took her name and address and firmly edged her towards the door. The first interview lasted less than three minutes.

"Not quite right for the boutique!" Sylvie laughed, her white teeth in startling contrast to her crimson lips and suit. She could read the disappointment on Rachel's face, what a shame that this had to happen at the beginning.

"You can say that again," Rachel agreed. "Imagine applying for a job looking like that, no wonder she was covered in telephone numbers."

"I wondered if we could have dinner tonight?" Sylvie said frowning, "but I see you have so much work."

"I would love to have dinner with you, there's so much I want to know. But as you so rightly say, I do have to work tonight."

"Maybe I could help, I have a free day. I can undress the boxes and hang the clothes ready for you to label. That is, if you do not feel I am interfering."

"Not at all, I'd be grateful," Rachel said, rising to answer the telephone yet again.

Sylvie tidied the cups on to the small tray and, taking a nail file from her bag, began to slit the wide tape on the cardboard cartons. She clucked with annoyance as she discovered that the manufacturers had forgotten to include hangers. Pulling the box aside she opened a second one. *"Ah, voilà!,"* she said aloud. They would have had a sharp phone call from her if the hangers hadn't been included. She hung each garment on the rail, satisfied anew with the choice she'd made so many months before. Rachel joined her. Together they examined and admired the fine wool dresses, which heralded the autumn season, and appreciated the elegance of the evening wear which would grace dinners and the more formal occasions of Washington's winter.

"They're wonderful," Rachel approved, "so wearable."

"I am glad you like them, it is easier to sell something that you would like to wear yourself. That is how I try to buy. The separates and the cocktail wear should be here soon, in a few days or so perhaps."

She mustn't forget to phone Enid Saunders. On second thoughts, at this rate she'd be finished well before closing time. Maybe she could invite Sylvie back to the house for dinner, she was sure Harriet wouldn't mind - she'd probably enjoy meeting Sylvie and listening to the shop-talk.

"Why not take the phone off its cot?" Sylvie suggested as once again the ringing interrupted them.

"It could be a customer," Rachel replied,

captivated by Sylvie's expressions. It had taken her a couple of seconds to realise she probably meant *cradle*.

Conscientious too, Sylvie thought as Rachel crushed the carton into a flat sheet - she was very impressed with Gideon Seaforth's young manageress. The girl was gorgeous with those huge almond eyes and glossy hair, but, more importantly, Sylvie was struck by her manner and obvious dedication to work. The salon was immaculate and the window display showed great flair. The suit Rachel wore was beautifully made and Sylvie, who was always interested in labels, was astonished to learn that Rachel had made it herself. "You *are* talented." She praised the choice of fabric and the workmanship.

"I love making things when I have time," Rachel admitted, flattered by Sylvie's appreciation.

Rachel carried the flat sheets of cardboard to the trash can at the back of the shop and phoned the house. Harriet answered the phone and in a quiet voice, Rachel filled her in on the situation and made her suggestion.

"Of course!" Harriet replied without hesitation, "it would be a pleasure. By the way, Daniel Hunt called to invite me to dinner next week. Your doing, I imagine." She sounded pleased.

"Absolutely not my idea. He wanted to meet you and when he discovered it was your birthday he insisted that we celebrate it by going out to dinner."

"It's kind of you both," Harriet chuckled, "I'm looking forward to it."

"Me too," Rachel said, "see you later."

Sylvie was delighted to accept the invitation. "It will be good not to spend the evening in a restaurant," she observed.

Rachel dashed up to her room to have a quick shower and change before Sylvie arrived. She'd been an enormous help, even answering the phone while Rachel attached price tags and checked invoices. By four o'clock everything was on the rails and Rachel was totally captivated by Sylvie's charm and her delightfully accented voice.

"She's unusual," Rachel warned Harriet, "striking I suppose you'd say, so don't get a surprise."

Harriet looked puzzled. "What are you trying to say?"

"Just that when I first saw her I thought she was... well, different." Rachel felt disloyal.

"And?" Harriet, shrewd as always, got to the point.

"After a few minutes you get used to her appearance, she has great charisma."

Sylvie carried a little box, beautifully wrapped with a complicated bow. Harriet's smiling expression didn't change when Rachel introduced her to Sylvie. Sylvie wore a black dress and shoes - suede stilettos this time, the heels even higher if possible. To relieve the severity of the dress she wore pearls, row after row which grew larger and larger; by the time they reached her waist they were the size of pigeons' eggs. The jet and pearl earrings, Rachel decided, would have been outrageous on anyone else, but they suited Sylvie. The bracelet and rings too were an interesting combination of jet and pearls and the vermilion lipstick on Sylvie's full mouth added the only touch of colour to the whole ensemble.

"How *chic* you look, Madame Whitney, and how kind you are to invite me to your home." Sylvie kissed Harriet on both cheeks and handed her the beautifully packaged square.

"I'd like to return the compliment," Harriet said suavely, "may I open my gift?"

"Mais oui, please," Sylvie smiled.

"How gorgeous! Look Rachel," Harriet exclaimed.

Rachel leaned forward, in the box was a rose made of sheer fabric, light blue in the centre deepening to royal blue round the edges. Harriet placed her thumb and forefinger into the box and eased out its contents. As she did the rose unravelled and a wisp of pale blue silk chiffon appeared in her hand. Harriet looked guiltily towards Sylvie, "I'm afraid I've damaged it," she said apologetically.

"No, no, it is right," Sylvie assured her, "continue."

Just like a stage magician, she pulled a seemingly endless stream of shaded gossamer-thin silk from its nesting place. "It's beautiful Sylvie, thank you," Harriet exclaimed, holding up the exquisite scarf between her tiny hands.

"And perfect with your dress," Sylvie exclaimed, gently taking it from her. With the touch of an expert, she draped it elegantly round Harriet's neck allowing it to fall softly on one shoulder.

Enid Saunders, who was carrying a tray of appetisers into the room, admired Harriet's beautiful gift. Sylvie put the finishing touches to the gauzy silk, and Rachel bit her lip as she met Enid's rolling eyes. "Dinner in ten minutes, Mrs Whitney," she announced. To Rachel's relief she left the room.

"You are in the wrong length of the business, Rachel," Sylvie said, when Harriet proudly told her that her dress had been made by Rachel.

They found her mistake most attractive.

"Wrong *end* of the business," Rachel smiled. Earlier, Sylvie had begged Rachel to correct her speech errors. "It will help me to learn properly."

"I was admiring your tights," Rachel said as Sylvie rose to follow them to the table.

"Merci. If you would like some I will send them to you from Paris when I return."

"I'd love them, but I was thinking how well they'd sell in the boutique."

"Why not? I will arrange a shipment, tell me what colours will be best and I will have them sent."

Harriet and Rachel were entranced as Sylvie told them about her life in Paris. Enid Saunders lingered as long as she could between courses, eager to hear the strange but pleasing voice.

Sylvie had worked in a shop, "Not unlike Caprice. I heard of a vacancy at one of the top couture houses and presented myself without an appointment, and won the position. It was not as I expected. I was an assistant to an assistant," she explained her face breaking into an alarmingly-wide grin. "Three years passed before I was permitted to serve a customer and then only in the boutique, not the main salon. I learnt how to make a plain dress more *exotique* by the addition of jewellery or a scarf; how to put it all together, as you Americans say. Rarely was I permitted even a glance into the beautiful grey salon where fashionable women from all over the world paid homage, and usually their husbands' hard-earned money, in return for the magnificently sculptured clothes. Finally, I became a *vendeuse* and had my own *clientèle*. One of my favourite customers, an attractive Italian lady living in Paris, invited me to her home one weekend. She and her husband were *charmant* and, during the course of my stay, she put a proposition to me that I could not refuse. She intended opening her own shop with her husband's blessing and support and needed someone to run it and help her with the buying. Such an opportunity! I accepted immediately. It proved to be a big success. We worked well together; naturally, at first we made our mistakes but nothing - how do you say - disastrous. A few years later we opened another shop, this time in Rome. Buying became my full-time occupation. During this time I married. It was, alas, short-lived. I threw myself into work to forget my problems."

Harriet and Rachel sat quietly, both noticed the troubled look that crossed Sylvie's extraordinary face. Harriet's eyes were glued to Sylvie's hands which weaved hypnotically as she spoke. Composing herself, Sylvie continued. "It was then that I was asked to take on the buying for Caprice."

Harriet jumped in with the question that hovered on Rachel's lips. "Who are the owners of Caprice?" she asked, her bright eyes burning with curiosity.

"I deal with Gideon Seaforth," Sylvie replied quickly.

Evasively? Harriet wondered.

"So, that is where you find me. Now you know it all." She picked up the delicate glass and took a sip of wine.

"It sounds such an exciting life, travelling like that, visiting all the famous couture houses, seeing the best clothes in the world and having the power to choose or reject what you want." Rachel's imagination ran riot.

"It is, but it can be very lonely at times too, strange cities, hotel rooms, your own company. One day, *cherie*, you will accompany me and then you will see for yourself."

They had their coffee on the patio - the scents of the late summer garden were not as pungent as in earlier months. Harriet shivered slightly in the night air. "Bed time for me, I'll leave you two to talk."

"She is a delightful lady," Sylvie remarked. Rachel could only guess at the emotions which hearing about France had stirred in Harriet. Was she remembering her lost love?

Rachel told Sylvie how she had come to live with Harriet and how close they had become. "She's my family now, *closer* than my family." The bitterness in Rachel's voice didn't escape Sylvie's notice.

"We haven't discussed the boutique yet," Sylvie gently reminded her. "I wondered if there were any ideas you would like to add, any changes you would like to make, any suggestives? Space permitting, of course," she laughed.

"It's a bit crowded at the moment," Rachel admitted, letting the mistake pass. She had wondered if more hanging space and shelving could be added, to extend their stock but she'd abandoned the idea - "none of her business," Meg Adams' ever-threatening cry.

"It would be useful to have more space," she agreed, "to be honest I haven't had time to give it much thought up to now. There are marvellous jewellery craftsmen here in the States, excellent designers whose labels we don't carry. At one time I thought it would be terrific to do custom-made clothes but, after the last day or so, I can see it could be a real headache, we're busy enough with alterations."

"Rachel, I have a few days free before I go to New York, would it be of value to you if I spent them with you at Caprice? Please, if you do not like the idea I will not be defended."

Rachel laughed and gently corrected her error. "I'd be delighted to have you there. I was wondering how I'd manage for the next couple of days - with all the interviews," she grimaced. "Maybe you could help me decide?"

"Whatever you desire, but you are very capable Rachel, don't be nervous. When the right person comes along you will know."

As if word had spread by osmosis, customers flocked in to view the newly-arrived autumn collection. The constant ringing of the telephone, the customers and the interviews whisked away the hours until closing time. Harriet had phoned the shop telling Rachel that she thought it would be a good idea if she took Sylvie to dinner. "On me," she insisted. "I'm sure the two of you will have fun."

Rachel was pleased. "It's very kind of you and

it *would* be a nice way to say thank you, she's marvellous," she whispered loudly into the receiver.

"Have you had any luck with an assistant yet?" Harriet enquired before ringing off.

"Not yet," Rachel said ruefully.

She too had been feeling a little bit sorry for Sylvie, going back to an empty hotel room, but she was torn between a desire to have dinner with Sylvie and not wanting to leave Harriet alone. With her improved eyesight Harriet had become an avid television viewer and one of the first things she had done about her new addiction was to have cable television installed. Not until now had it struck Rachel that the reason for her being in Harriet's home was obsolete; her reading skills were no longer necessary. She'd come to regard it as her home too, Harriet and the Saunders as her family. She presumed Harriet must feel the same way, since there hadn't been the slightest mention of her leaving.

Sylvie stood in the centre of the floor and with alert eyes scanned the walls with their open hanging spaces. "Ah! I have the answer, Rachel."

Rachel frowned. "The answer to what?"

"If we move the entrance to the office and your workroom to the right, you can have almost the whole length of the wall either for hanging or whatever it is that you prefer."

Rachel's eyes followed the sweep of Sylvie's elegantly expressive hand.

"Do you think that Gideon will allow that?"

"Why not? More space, more profit," Sylvie said, shrugging her shoulders. "Why not ask him when you speak to him? Now is the time - a new brush sweeps clean," she misquoted charmingly.

As they left the restaurant, soothed and calmed by a bottle of light, sparkling Californian Chardonnay - which Sylvie swore was every bit as good as her native French wine - and a leisurely meal, Rachel signalled a cab. She dropped Sylvie at her hotel and continued on the short homeward journey. How confident she felt, how clever Sylvie was, she chuckled. Her thoughts strayed to Meg Adams, so embittered towards a buyer she had never met.

Harriet Whitney's laughter stopped her as she passed the living-room door. Rachel smiled fondly as she peeped inside and saw Harriet's diminutive figure curled up in a chair. She was watching the latest episode of Benny Hill's comedy show. It was way past her normal bedtime.

"You're early," Harriet accused, hastily pressing the button on the remote control.

"Don't switch it off because of me," Rachel said.

"I wasn't really watching it, I was waiting for you."

Rachel hid her smile, Harriet hated to be caught out. "We had a lovely meal, Sylvie's very good company and so helpful."

"She's something to look at it, isn't she? But charming," Harriet hastily added. "I haven't had a chance to talk to you since last night. You were right, she's fascinating, so ... challenging, in her appearance. I'm glad that she's there with you, it must be a bit daunting for the first little while."

"You should see what she came up with today. She suggested that we move a door, that would give me practically a whole wall at the end of the shop. It was so obvious when Sylvie pointed it out. Everything is falling into place now and, if I can find someone to help me, I'll be able to manage."

"No luck today with the interviews then?"

"No. I was beginning to despair, but as Sylvie said, the right one will turn up."

"She makes a whole lot of sense. Of course she will," Harriet soothed. Rachel was certainly taken with the agreeable Frenchwoman - quoting her with every breath.

"Enough shop talk," Rachel insisted. "Are you looking forward to meeting Daniel Hunt?"

"Absolutely," Harriet's eyes sparkled. "He said we're going to eat somewhere that's fun, so I should wear my jeans."

Rachel shook her head and smiled, what on earth was he up to? He seemed to have won Harriet over before they'd even met, what a resourceful man. "I'm off to bed," Rachel yawned, and bent to kiss Harriet goodnight.

"I'll follow you up in a moment."

As she made her way up the stairs, Rachel could hear the sound of laughter again. If I do nothing else in this life, she thought, I can at least be content that I've improved the quality of Harriet's.

CHAPTER SEVENTY-FIVE

The windows were dressed and Caprice was ready for the day's business. From sheer habit, Rachel glanced along the street. She missed seeing Daniel and exchanging waves through the glass barrier. A little frisson of pleasure made her heart flutter. She'd noticed the deference shown to him both in hospital and at the hotel. It was natural, too. It wasn't just because he was a generous tipper. In the restaurant she had been guilty of basking in the reflected glory of his charisma as the members of the administration and diplomats had paid their respects. She longed to know more about his family and was consumed with curiosity about his wife. There was Wednesday to look forward to, their outing with Harriet.

"I think you should pick your clothes now before they are all sold," Sylvie said, her head on one side.

The thought of choosing a "wardrobe" had never occurred to Rachel. True, Seaforth and Associates had made her a generous allowance, but everything was moving so fast she'd forgotten that as a representative of Caprice, she should look the part. "I bet you've something in mind."

"You are getting to know me," Sylvie smiled. "But yes, I have."

Purposefully she strode to the open cupboard, removed the protective sheet and pulled out several woollen dresses. From the temporary rail which held the sales items, Sylvie chose an exquisite white and silver evening dress. "Try them on now, while it is quiet," she instructed.

As they came to the last dress, Sylvie groaned.

"What's wrong, don't they suit me?" Rachel asked. Personally she had been entranced by some of the garments.

"That's the trouble, they all suit you. I have good taste for you, no?"

Rachel was pleased by Sylvie's dilemma. "I can't afford them all, that's for sure. I certainly don't need the evening dress."

"But you must have it. It was *made* for you and when will you ever find anything so beautiful again and such good value?"

It wasn't a snip, but it was vastly reduced in the sale and, with her hefty discount, she could afford it.

"Try them again," Sylvie insisted, "then I decide."

With great difficulty they made their decision. Sylvie twisted Rachel's hair into a sophisticated topknot. "It is wonderful, that gown. Right for all times of the year." Rachel stared at her reflection in the long mirror. The dress swirled and fell in graceful folds with every move of her body. Sylvie was right, it could have been made for her and if Daniel invited her to a formal function, she'd be properly dressed. Sylvie made Rachel promise that she would invest in some shoes and good bags. "Two colours are all you need. And white satin for the evening dress," she insisted, wagging her finger.

The last interview of the day brought the only promising applicant for the job. She was a pleasant girl full of wide-eyed admiration for the beautiful clothes. She didn't have much experience but Rachel remembered her own early enthusiasm and the girl was able to sew, so she decided to take her on a month's trial.

"Good decision," Sylvie applauded. "She displayed all the right reasons for wanting to work here and besides, she admired my suit!" She grinned her wide scarlet-gash of a smile.

"I'll miss you when you leave today," Rachel assured her sadly.

"You will not have time to miss me," Sylvie responded. She had thoroughly enjoyed her brief busman's holiday; being on the shop floor again. Rachel was a delightful *jeune fille,* in her opinion an excellent choice as manageress for Caprice. How unaware she was of her extraordinary beauty and of her ability. A couple of weeks and she would forget any nervousness. It will be a *plaisir* to buy clothes with Rachel in mind.

"How are you going to spend your time this weekend?" Harriet asked, as they sat watching a wildlife programme.

"Reading and sleeping," Rachel decided aloud.

"How would you like to show an old lady round the art gallery?"

"I'd like to, but I don't know any old ladies," Rachel retorted.

"My, my. Isn't Sylvie's Gallic charm catching!"

"You're *not* an old lady," Rachel stressed, "you talk as if you're a hundred years old. Just look at you, you look terrific. You're slim, pretty and smart, well, *almost.*"

"Here we go again," Harriet groaned, recognising that special tone in Rachel's voice.

"Nagging time is back!"

"OK. Your clothes could do with updating a bit, otherwise, you're together."

"Sharp, Missy, aren't you?"

"We're always honest with each other, aren't we?"

"Some of us are more honest than others," Harriet snorted.

"Let's make a deal. I'll go with you to the gallery tomorrow if you'll come into the shop on Monday."

"Deal," Harriet agreed. She didn't mean to tell Rachel but, in honour of the outing on Wednesday, she'd intended purchasing a new outfit anyway. This way Rachel felt that she had won a victory. For the most part Harriet enjoyed the raillery between them. But not for the world would she admit that Rachel was usually right.

"How come you're not visiting the family this weekend?"

"They're staying with friends at Charlottesville."

Harriet was enthralled by her visit to the gallery - so many new artists whose names were totally unknown to her. She studied the pictures and her knowledge was impressive. Roberto Maroni's image flashed through Rachel's mind. It was the first time she had thought about him for a long while. What a no-good he was. She was blessed that she had so much to occupy her, that her work left her little time to think about him. *Never* would she forgive his dreadful attack on Daniel.

"Let's have coffee. I think I've taken in all I can," Harriet suggested, breaking in on Rachel's black mood.

It was warm enough to sit outside and they basked in the late afternoon sunshine watching the families; mothers or fathers explaining the exhibits to their interested or, in some cases, bored children. Harriet still wore her light-to-dark sunglasses outdoors but her improved sight had opened up vistas which she had thought buried forever.

"I'm considering calling in a decorator to give the house a bit of a face-lift," Harriet said. "It's all a bit miserable now that I can see it clearly again."

"It's a lovely house, but I suppose you know best," said Rachel.

"Seeing the colours here this afternoon set me wondering. I think a change of wallpaper and drapes is in order. I'd enjoy working with someone, although I have some ideas of my own."

"Go for it, Harriet," Rachel laughed.

Daniel Hunt refused to tell them where they were going.

"It's different, that's all I will tell you." He was casually dressed in an open-necked shirt with a lightweight checked jacket and navy trousers. The stick was gone. Although his gait was slow he walked straight and tall as he escorted them to the waiting limousine. The restaurant he had chosen was in Chinatown. "Much smaller than some other cities," he admitted, as he helped them from the car.

"It's Mongolian!" Rachel commented, seeing the sign over the door.

They were shown straight to their table and Daniel ordered drinks.

"There are no menus, you help yourself from there," he said, pointing to the centre of the room.

"How are things going at Caprice, Rachel? I feel I've lost touch in the last week."

Harriet was sure there was a wistfulness in his tone.

"I miss seeing you in the mornings," Rachel smiled shyly. "Everything's working out well. I have an assistant now and she's very enthusiastic and keen to learn. The buyer, a charming French lady, appeared out of the blue like an angel of mercy and thanks to her I settled in smoothly. The accountant is very supportive and if I do have problems he's there at the end of the phone. Yesterday I heard that Meg Adams has been charged with fraud, she was my predecessor," she reminded Daniel. "It's a shame, she's lost her job and that seems to be punishment enough."

"And cost you yours if you remember. She committed a crime and should be punished." Daniel's tone was harsh.

Unlike Daniel to be so tough, he was usually very understanding. Rachel peeped at him from under her long lashes.

"At the risk of using a cliché, there's no sentiment in business, Rachel. That's something you have to get used to. She stole from her employers and, in my opinion, deserved no better than she got."

He's right of course, I don't suppose Daniel built a billion dollar empire by turning a blind eye. And true, Meg had been the cause of her own misery.

"Would you like to serve yourselves?" the waiter asked, removing their empty glasses. "The chefs will help you if you need it."

They made their way to the enormous gleaming hot-plate which filled the centre of the room. Between the cooking area and a circular counter - which was set out with an amazing variety of food - four chefs waited to cook their meal.

"Where do we start?" Harriet asked, tickled pink with the array.

"Start with the meats," Daniel advised. "There's chicken, beef and lamb. They freeze the raw meat, that's how they're able to shave it so thinly." He handed them both a large heavy bowl into which they placed the ingredients for their meal.

"Vegetables next," he said, spearing some bean sprouts and finely-shredded onions, ribbons of carrot and bamboo shoots from amongst the big display. He added pineapple for sweetness. One of the chefs explained the contents of the sauce boats which contained a bewildering selection of seasonings and oils. These were ladled over their heaped dishes before the food was tipped onto the sparkling hot-plates for cooking.

"I feel greedy," Harriet protested as the chef added more ingredients to her dish.

"It diminishes in cooking, Ma'am", he assured her cheerfully, adding a tiny spoon of chilli oil.

A wonderful aroma of garlic and oils assailed their nostrils as they watched the chefs expertly tossing the piles of food over and over to prevent it burning. It took just a couple of minutes before they returned the cooked food into clean bowls with their flat metal spatulas. "Please come back as often as you like," the chefs chorused as they handed them their dishes. On the table waiting were hot buns encrusted with sesame seeds.

"It's delicious," Rachel said between mouthfuls. "Every bite has a different flavour."

"Lovely, I agree." Harriet chewed contentedly. "You said it was a fun place and it is." Behind them a large party were celebrating a birthday with a dessert lit by sparklers. Everyone joined in singing *Happy Birthday* to the embarrassed girl whose birthday it was. Harriet led the delighted applause.

"Who's going to make a second visit?" Daniel challenged.

"Twist my arm," Harriet grinned.

"Me too." Rachel was not going to be outdone by the two of them.

Daniel set out to be a charming and attentive host. Harriet's attitude towards him so far had been cordial, but a sixth sense warned him that she would need to be strongly convinced that he was the right companion for Rachel.

Daniel had visited Mongolia, "A long time ago. I was cold from the minute I got there until the moment I left," he laughed, shivering at the memory. He painted a vivid picture of the factories he had visited where the workers had never before seen a westerner. "They giggled like children at my layers of clothes, I must have looked like an Eskimo! The food was dreadful and the liquor was rough in those days but, from a business point of view, it was a most successful trip. My sons go to far distant places now, and I grab all the good trips like London, Rome or Paris!"

"I'd adore to go to Paris," Rachel said longingly, "Sylvie Vadim really whetted my appetite."

Daniel checked his instinctive response, nothing would give him greater pleasure than to take her to Paris, but he must tread warily. His gaze rested on Harriet's shrewd face. What was the matter with him, a grown man afraid of a tiny scrap of a woman he hardly knew. Why was her opinion so important to him, he wondered? A man who dined with presidents intimidated by a canny little lady.

Rachel excused herself to go to the powder-room.

"You're in love with Rachel, aren't you?" Harriet asked bluntly.

Daniel choked on his beer. He prided himself that nothing in this world surprised him but in one swift blow she had succeeded. "You are direct," he coughed, "yes, I do love her. She's an exceptional person. Honest, sincere, kind, interesting, clever and just about everything else that's good."

Harriet digested his remarks. "What are you going to do about it?"

Daniel shook his head from side to side, smiling at her. "First of all I'm not sure how Rachel feels about me. Then there's the age difference which obviously is not ideal in other people's eyes. Personally, I don't think it matters a damn."

"You're probably right." Harriet was impressed by Daniel, there was something about his manner that reminded her of the man she had loved.

Daniel stared at her in amazement. Now that

Anne Schulman

he analysed his feelings he realised that it was Harriet's objections that he most feared and here she was, an unexpected ally. His sons would be happy for them and Nicholas's wife, Jennifer, would be too. Jonah's wife, Caroline, would be the fly in the ointment, he knew that. He grinned to himself as he pictured her outrage. Rachel's beauty would put Caroline's snooty nose out of joint.

"Share it?" Harriet's voice cut across his thoughts.

"I was thinking about my daughter-in-law. She will, as they say, go ape."

"Is she protective of you?"

"Not really! I'll tell you about her sometime," he said as Rachel returned to the table.

"What have I missed?" She looked at them both questioningly.

"Nothing. I've been my usual forthright self," Harriet said equably, "asking questions."

"Shall we have coffee now?" Daniel could see this was getting complicated.

"Let's have it at home," Harriet suggested.

"Fine by me," he said, calling for the check.

* * *

Rachel put her fingers to lips still tingling from Daniel's gentle kisses. He had caught her unawares.

"I haven't offended you, have I?" he asked.

"Do I look offended?" she replied softly. Why did Roberto's face suddenly loom large in her mind? Would he always cast a shadow between them?

598

"Rachel, I'd like to take you to a luncheon on Saturday - if you're free."

"What kind of luncheon? I mean ..."

"Don't worry, it's just a few senators and congressmen - and their wives, of course. You'll enjoy it, it'll be very informal," Daniel reassured her.

"Then yes, thank you."

"Much as I'd adore to stay here with you I'm afraid I'll have to make a move; the effects of my injection are wearing off," Daniel said regretfully. His face was pale and his pain was obvious.

"It was so good to see that you weren't using your stick that I forgot about the pain you must be suffering."

"No, I'm fine, but I do need my medication."

Rachel stood at the top of the little flight of steps and waved as the limousine drew away. Her dependence on Daniel, her fondness for him was growing by leaps and bounds. His companionship was like a ribbon which bound them more closely week by week. She was nervous about meeting his famous friends but she couldn't wait for Saturday.

Rachel arrived at Caprice at the same time as Amy.

"Hi, Rachel, you're early," Amy called as she watched Rachel approach. She positively glows, Amy thought, those long legs, that slim figure and that wonderful streaming hair which falls back into shining place no matter what she does. If only I could look like her, she wished.

"Hi, yourself," Rachel smiled, unlocking the door.

Together they opened back the protective

curtaining which shielded the clothes from dust and chose the garments for the windows.

Amy had adapted quickly to the routine. Her relaxed style and easy smile hid a capacity for hard work and efficiency. She had shown the tact and skill necessary when dealing with customers, always of the utmost importance at Caprice. This week had been a tough test, Rachel reflected, and she had come through it well. Deliveries had arrived almost daily, and so too had the customers anxious to get the job of selecting their winter wardrobes out of the way.

"Word spreads quickly on Capitol Hill," an attractive client confided in Rachel, "and the word is that Caprice and its new manageress empathise with the problem of dressing well on a restricted budget. After all, a fashionable jacket and a couple of blouses and skirts can take a girl a long way."

So that explained the influx of professionals from the Hill. From day one as manager Rachel decided that no client would be harried or pushed into buying anything she was unhappy or unsure about. "You catch more bees with honey than with vinegar," her mother used to say. Rachel's eyes clouded with momentary sadness - where is my mother now? She would be so proud of me, if only I could talk to her. It isn't natural, a mother and daughter as close as we were, separated by a beer-swigging lecher. That was a fair description of the revolting man who had parted them. Shaking her head she pulled herself out of her self-pitying mood and turned her attention back to Amy.

"If I slip out for a couple of hours this

afternoon, can you manage alone?"

"Sure, no problem." Amy was delighted to have the responsibility. Her first week at Caprice had been a challenge. She liked Rachel's gentle ways. Rachel guided but didn't push her.

"I felt I had nothing to lose when I applied for the position. I knew I didn't have a lot of experience. I was overjoyed when you said you'd take me on a month's trial," she admitted to Rachel one day. "My boyfriend is studying at Georgetown University and with my support he has been able to start his law course with a relatively easy mind. It would be the icing on the cake for us if you keep me on."

For the first time in years her waist-length hair was cropped to her shoulders. Rachel watched as her long hanks of hair fell to the floor.

"Split ends," Alphonse tutted, "no lift, it needs lift."

While Alphonse - his real name was Al, he confided - cut and snipped a manicurist polished Rachel's oval nails and applied a discreet shade of pink nail varnish. "You have beautiful hands," she said, massaging cream into Rachel's long fingers. At last the cutting ended and, taking a drier, Alphonse began to lift and sculpt his artful cut, insisting that Rachel must relax and close her eyes. The soothing movement of the massage lulled her anxiety, there was no going back now. She had kept her promise to Sylvie and bought shoes and bags to complete her new outfits. She walked up and down the carpet of the shoe shop in the soft calf-leather sling-backs which were feather-light on her feet. Rachel introduced herself as the manageress of Caprice to the friendly woman who served her. The saleswoman pricked up her ears at the mention of the elegant boutique. Meg Adams had approached her in the past and offered to send clients to the shoe shop in return for a percentage of sales. She'd been disgusted by Meg's greed and had turned the offer down flat. She had been cold but polite whenever Meg Adams came in to buy shoes. Rachel didn't strike her as being the same type, quite the opposite in fact. "You're welcome to a trade discount," she offered.

"That's an unexpected bonus, it certainly takes some of the sting out of the check!" Rachel browsed around while her parcels were being wrapped. She examined the bags and their matching shoes. "They're beautifully made," she said appreciatively. "I have a suggestion. Why don't you come and see me at Caprice and take a look at the clothes. If we can co-ordinate colours, I'll put the shoes and maybe the bags on display. Good for us both."

"I'd be delighted but I must ask, what would you expect in return?"

Rachel looked at her sharply. "Why should you think that I want something in return?" she queried.

"Mrs Adams," the woman explained apologetically. "She demanded a cut on anything sold to one of her customers, a big cut. I'm sorry, but I have to be sure."

"All I want is to give my clients the best service possible. I think you'll find that I run things very differently."

How many other scams did Meg Adams have

going for her? Rachel wondered as she made her way down the street to the beauty parlour. It was pointless mentioning any of this to Gideon Seaforth - water under the bridge, she decided.

"You can look now," the stylist's voice interrupted her daydreaming. Her hair tumbled round her face and fell to her shoulders in soft bouncing blue-black waves. Riveted she gazed at her own image. Her eyes and high cheekbones were accentuated by the spilling softness. Her slender neck formed a perfect column around which the leonine mane ended in glorious profusion. A feeling of déjà-vu overcame her - Harriet's visit here, not a month before.

"Are you ecstatic?" Alphonse demanded dramatically, holding a hand mirror to allow Rachel a back view of her head.

"Thrilled, where did all that hair come from?"

"Layering makes it look thicker and, as you can see, it's still long enough to wear it up," he said, pulling a wave into perfect position. "I bet you didn't know you had a natural curl in your hair."

Amy's reaction made Rachel feel even more delighted. "You look incredible!" she gasped. "I always envied your hair but now I'm green with jealousy."

Their looks were strikingly different - Amy's skin, peaches and cream, contrasted with Rachel's olive colouring, her hair was as fair as Rachel's was dark. Even the shape of their faces differed, Amy's was heart-shaped, Rachel's a perfect oval. Rachel was the taller of the two but Amy's slim figure was in perfect proportion to her height. "You have beautiful hair," Rachel objected, "you can have no complaints in any department. Your eyes are a wonderful shade of blue and I've always longed for blue eyes. Women are never happy, are they?"

A call from Gideon Seaforth ended their session of self-criticism.

"How's it going?" Gideon asked in a friendly voice.

"Everything's under control - Amy's working out well. If it's OK with you, I've arranged to take some items from Le Sac, the shoe and bag boutique, and display them at Caprice. They're superb," she finished tentatively.

"Good idea. By the way, the contractors are ready to start work on Monday, if that suits you?"

"Absolutely," Rachel assured him. As Sylvie had predicted, Gideon had no objections to enlarging the display space, and had offered to find someone to carry out the work. "Have a good weekend," he said before replacing the receiver.

Rachel put the finishing touches to her make-up. The new hairstyle and the soft coral dress hanging on the open closet door made her feel more confident. There was still an hour to kill before Daniel was due to call. Restless, she knocked on Harriet's door.

"Come in," Harriet called from her bed. "You're ready early and you look fabulous."

"I don't want to keep Daniel waiting," said Rachel. She felt herself blushing at the forthright compliment. "To tell you the truth I feel a bit nervous, I won't know anyone there today except Daniel."

"Oh pul-eeze!" Harriet laughed playfully,

practising her latest television-inspired expression. "You won't *need* to know anyone, they'll get to know you fast enough." If anyone had told her that Rachel's beauty could be improved upon she would have bet her last dollar they were wrong - yet the nervous girl sitting cross-legged on her bed was utterly stunning.

"Trust me, for once *I'm* right. You'll see."

Daniel gasped when he saw Rachel standing in the doorway.

"You look incredible," the truth tripped from his lips. "Is that a new hairstyle? Stupid question! Incredible," he repeated, transfixed. "I bet that dress came from Caprice."

"Right first time - at Sylvie's insistence," Rachel said, giving credit to her friend. The softly draped neckline was fastened on the shoulder by a single triangular button. The bodice moulded itself to her high breasts and tapered to a point at her tiny waist. As she walked the skirt echoed her every move, rippling and swaying in time with her step. Coral was an inspired choice for her colouring. Daniel followed her to the car, the subtle aroma of her perfume lingered on the air.

"You'll seduce all the men, and the women will be thoroughly jealous of my beautiful Rachel."

"Thank you, kind sir," she smiled, attempting a limited bow. *"My beautiful Rachel."* That was music to her ears.

"Just a word of warning," he said in a quiet serious voice. "If anyone asks you more than a couple of questions, beware. People love to snoop. They won't pass up a chance to find out all about a beautiful woman. They're always interested in adding up two and two and making ten where Daniel Hunt is concerned."

Rachel considered the implication of his statement as she relaxed against the cushioned seat. How had he escaped so far? she wondered. Apart from his legendary wealth, his good looks and easy charm must make him a desirable target for any unattached woman. He must have escaped in the heel of the hunt, she giggled at her unintentional pun. She knew so little about this distinguished man sitting at her side.

The hostess welcomed her warmly and with ill-concealed interest. "Where did you find this gorgeous creature?" she quizzed, kissing Daniel on the check.

"At the end of the rainbow." God, he groaned inwardly, I don't believe I said that. What on earth prompted me to answer her like that? He was spellbound by Rachel, that's why. He must pull himself together and behave more cautiously in front of these people with their unquenchable curiosity. Within seconds Rachel had been whisked away by the hostess to be introduced to everyone. Daniel could hear the ripple which ran round the room. Who was she? Had she come with Daniel Hunt? Daniel's attention was demanded by two congressmen anxious for his advice and, reluctantly, he allowed himself to be dragged into a quiet study where their conversation could not be overheard.

"This matter is far too complex for discussion at a party," he advised, "come and see me next week then we can talk at leisure." Tactfully he made his escape anxious to find Rachel. Cricket

Mancelli, the queen of the gossip columnists, was working her way round the room gleaning information at every deliberate stop. The sole topic on everyone's lips was Daniel Hunt's stunning companion so she headed in Rachel's direction. Daniel reached Rachel's side at precisely the same moment as Cricket.

"Daniel, nice to see you about again. Who's this lovely that's causing all the buzz?"

"An old friend of mine," Daniel fenced nonchalantly.

"She's too young to be anyone's *old* friend," Cricket glared at him.

"There you go! Please excuse us, I'm sure you have someone else you want to talk about."

"Not at all, you know how much I enjoy your company, Daniel," she simpered, clutching his sleeve in a vice-like grip.

Cricket Mancelli had been a constant thorn in his side since she'd first discovered the extent of his vast empire and his single status. When they had first met, she had made it bluntly clear that a quiet affair would buy her silence in the thirty-five daily syndicated columns where she spread her poison. His curt dismissal of her advances infuriated her. She targeted Daniel and his family with all the dedication of a heat-seeking missile. Every week some little tit-bit of rumour or innuendo came tumbling from her venomous word processor.

"Please let go of my sleeve, Ms Mancelli, you surely don't want to be charged with assault - do you?" Daniel took Rachel's arm and steered her away from the tangle-haired reporter with the bulging eyes and slack mouth. But not before a flash bulb popped in their faces. Temporarily blinded by the bright light they were halted in their flight for a moment.

When her vision cleared, Rachel saw Gates' burly figure collide with the photographer. The camera fell to the floor and deftly Gates bent to retrieve it and returned it to its owner, apologising for his clumsiness.

"Shouldn't we say good-bye or thank ... " Rachel's voice trailed off as she saw the grim set of Daniel's face.

"Let's just get out of here," he said tersely.

"Sorry you missed out on lunch," he said, "but I know a lovely little restaurant where we can have some privacy."

Daniel was so angry when they had left the party Rachel was sure that he was going to take her straight home.

"Go and have some lunch, Gates, you can pick us up at five, and Gates - thank you."

"My pleasure, Mr Hunt," his driver grinned as he handed Daniel a black cylindrical canister.

Rachel looked around the pretty room. It was exactly as she had pictured a country inn; broad wooden beams, shining brasses and a low burning log fire - even this early in the year. Flower-patterned chintz drapes matched the sofas and the deep buttoned cushions on the slatted wooden chairs. Vases filled with early autumn blooms lent splashes of colour to the intimate restaurant. Well spaced tables gave diners perfect privacy. The host greeted Daniel with affection. "We're delighted to see you again, Mr Hunt, it's been a long time."

"Thank you, good to be here. You have a

table for us?"

"No problem, would you like to sit by the window or in the corner?"

"The corner, I think. How's that with you, Rachel?"

"The corner, it looks cosy."

"I must apologise for my odd behaviour," Daniel said spreading a crispy roll with butter. "Mippy, our hostess, should have known better than to invite Cricket Mancelli to a private lunch and, as for the photographer, that was unpardonable."

"I don't really understand," Rachel admitted.

"No. I'm sorry, of course why should you? Mippy and I have known each other for a long time. Her husband asked for a divorce - out of nowhere - and she was devastated. When she was younger she gave up a promising career as a concert pianist - she was immensely talented - and threw herself into building his career in politics. They couldn't have children and he wouldn't agree to adopt. She accepted that and devoted one hundred per cent of her time to entertaining for him, attending charity functions, attracting the right people and doing the right thing. But he'd been seeing someone else for years and one day, without warning, he just upped and left. I was disgusted with him and I was fond of her. I became the proverbial shoulder for her to cry on. We spent a fair amount of time together until she got used to her situation, strictly platonic, I must add. She finally came to accept the split but naturally it took time. Unfortunately, she began to rely on me and I found myself in an uncomfortable position. 'We'll

Anne Schulman

go here and we'll go there and I've got tickets for this concert and that play.' You know, fait accompli. I began to opt out, I refused her invitations and, I must confess, she didn't take kindly to that. I'd taken the place of her husband. Cricket Mancelli had a field day. She constantly linked our names in her columns. Mippy knows full well that I don't like publicity - more than that, I loathe it. We meet once in a while and when she invited me to her lunch today I accepted but I told her that I'd bring a friend with me. Obviously that's not what she had in mind and she tipped off that awful woman."

"Hell hath no fury … " Rachel didn't blame him.

"We won't escape unscathed from that gossip queen's column on Monday I'm afraid, but don't let her upset you. At least there'll be no photographs."

"How do you know? The photographer certainly got one picture."

Smiling, Daniel slipped his hand into his pocket and produced the film which Gates had cunningly taken from the fallen camera.

"Crafty man," Rachel laughed delightedly. Harriet would enjoy hearing all about this. "How did Gates know to come in just at the right time?"

Again Daniel's hand reached for his pocket. Rachel examined the neat black box no larger than a cigarette packet and much slimmer. "This is the latest technology in personal alarm protection. I have to confess I'm a technoholic where it comes to alarm systems and communications," he admitted sheepishly. "Gates carries a device like this. A necessary evil in this day and age, the penalty of being rich I'm afraid."

Their conversation was interrupted by the arrival of their first course, smooth duck liver pâté on a bed of tiny oak lettuce garnished with orange slices. "It's good isn't it?" Daniel smiled.

"Wonderful," Rachel agreed, "the oranges cut through the richness. Who's that man, over there at the table in the window? His face is familiar," she puzzled.

Daniel turned in his chair to look. "It's Ted Kennedy, with some of his family."

"No wonder I recognised him!" she said taking another peek.

"Sooner or later most of the politicians come here, especially at the weekends if they're in Washington. The food is first rate. Home away from home."

"If you think I'm out of order, Daniel, just say so, but you never talk about your wife."

"I don't, do I? You have a right to ask." Daniel's face was pained. Hesitantly at first he described the day his pretty, vain young wife walked out on him and their boys. "She had everything going for her, a loving husband, gorgeous twin sons, a fine apartment, no shortage of money. Obviously it wasn't enough - one day I came home and found she'd gone. My world fell apart. For weeks I tortured myself. What had I done wrong? I blamed myself. After a while I could see that that was pointless. I decided to leave New York and start a new life in Washington. At college I'd worked hard. I didn't have much time for personal relationships. So, when my wife left me it wasn't difficult to begin again. Nobody knew me. My parents were dead and my sister was working somewhere in the wilds of Africa. I hired the services of a private investigator and eventually he found my ex-wife. For years I kept him on a retainer - still do, for business reasons now - and he reported to me twice a year. Things went from bad to worse for her but I never lifted a finger to help. Not even when she made a real mess of her life. And I didn't forgive her either. She died five years ago. She had no money. She was alone. I told the twins that their mother died when they were babies and they accepted it, without question. I feel bad about lying to the boys, but that's my sin - I have to live with it. I had my reasons. I loved my boys and I didn't want them to be hurt or feel rejected. I never want them to know the truth, Rachel."

Rachel wouldn't tell his secret but she did feel that his sons should have had the opportunity to know the truth. Now it was too late.

Daniel leaned back in his chair. The haunted look had left his eyes. "It's wonderful to be able to talk about her and the way she left me after all those years of denying her existence even to myself."

For the first time Rachel saw the intransigence of the man she had begun to love and felt a shiver run down her spine. She knew now that Daniel would never tolerate any form of deception.

"What about you, do you have any hidden young men in your life?" He asked the question lightly but his eyes narrowed as he waited for her reply.

Rachel started. Could he read her thoughts?

"No, no one. I did go out with someone for a few weeks but he left to get a job in another state."

"Which state?"

"I don't know where he went," Rachel answered truthfully. "I never heard from him again."

"Did you love him?" Stop acting like a jealous fool, Daniel chided himself.

"I was attracted to him but he really wasn't for me. I wasn't sorry when he left Washington."

Daniel felt extraordinarily relieved by her reply, he couldn't bear to share her with anyone. "Jonah and I are going to Mexico early on Monday. There's an excellent chance that we will be able to buy a manufacturing plant there, it would be ideal for us."

He told her about their plans. What an intelligent listener she is, he thought, as he answered Rachel's pertinent questions. Those eyes, how could any man resist them?

"Will you come to dinner at the house next Saturday? It's just the family, the Ambassador from Brazil and his wife, and another couple, old business friends from Boston. Please say yes!"

Rachel smiled at him. "I'd love to, Daniel."

"I'll send Gates for you at seven-thirty, we dress formally."

At least that wouldn't be a problem, it would give her the chance to wear the white evening dress that Sylvie had insisted she buy.

"My elder daughter-in-law acts as hostess for me," Daniel explained, "that's something she does well. You may find her a little - outspoken. She can be a bit off-putting at times but don't let her get to you."

"I won't," Rachel reassured him.

"We seem to specialise in overstaying our welcome in restaurants," Daniel laughed as he watched the first of the evening's diners arriving.

Rachel noticed how he arched his back as they left the table. "Are you uncomfortable, Daniel?" she asked.

"A bit, yes. My tablets are due in an hour, that will oil the joints," he said but she could see how drawn his face was.

"You'll be more comfortable in the car," she soothed.

Gates drove them as they sat in companionable silence, smiling at each other now and then. "Forgive me if I don't see you to the door. I'll look forward to Saturday."

"Me too," Rachel smiled and leaned sideways to kiss his cheek. "Thank you, it's been a lovely day."

Daniel put his hand to her head and stroked the silky waves. "We'll share many more happy days," he promised, "without Cricket Mancelli."

CHAPTER SEVENTY-SIX

Twenty-three … twenty-four … twenty-five. Caroline Hunt counted as she dragged the brush viciously through her short brown hair. How could he? she raged silently, the girl was younger than his own sons. That bang on his head must have caused brain damage. Until now she'd always respected Daniel but this situation was utterly ridiculous. Where was Jonah? Trust him to be late tonight. Bad enough that they were facing the humiliation of being paraded in front of a money-hungry little bimbo, Jonah shouldn't make them late. That was just not her style.

"Jonah, is that you?"

"Yes, Caroline, it's me." Who did she think it was? he wondered. He always felt irritated when he entered the immaculate bedroom. Caroline's compulsive neatness agitated him these days, he had a sudden urge to wreck the ordered room, to sweep everything from her perfectly arranged dressing-table on to the floor. How would she react if he ripped the brown silk jersey dress, sitting perfectly pressed on its hanger, or broke one of the stilettos from her brown satin shoes?

"What time are we expected?" he asked.

"Seven thirty, and it's quarter to now. You're cutting it fine," she snapped, blotting her lipstick on a tissue.

Jonah ignored her accusing tone and switched on the bathroom shower, drowning out her voice. She had been simmering like a slow-boiling pot from the moment she heard the news that the young girl who rescued Daniel after the mugging was the guest of honour tonight. That might *just* have been acceptable in her eyes, but the fact that they had been out together several times was not. Thank heaven I was away for most of the week, Jonah thought, she'd have driven me crazy dissecting Dad's motives, questioning his interest in her. The sharp needle spray eased the tension in his neck muscles. Tonight would be a testing time for them all. He altered the dial on the shower so that soft jets of water cascaded over his head and body, soothing his troubled thoughts.

Never had he seen his father so happy, so full of life. He and Nicholas trusted Daniel's judgement in all things. Nicholas had met the girl briefly at the hospital and confessed to being impressed. "Unreasonably beautiful and, from what I could tell in such a short time, a very nice person." During their Mexican trip, Daniel revealed a side to his nature that Jonah felt ashamed he'd never even suspected. He had always seen his father as successful and respected, constantly in demand. The loneliness which Daniel confessed dismayed him.

"I've met a lot of women over the years and I'd like to have remarried but somehow the right one never came along. Then I met Rachel and the better I got to know her, the more I knew that she was the person who was missing from my life. You'll like her, Jonah, I know you will."

For Daniel's sake he would welcome her to the family whether he liked her or not. "Are you going to marry her?" he asked.

His sons' approval was very important to

Daniel. "I'd like to but she's very young. Believe me I've thought about that non-stop but what are the guarantees for any couple today, irrespective of age?"

"Too right," Jonah said bitterly.

"Do I detect trouble on the home front?" Daniel asked.

Jonah longed to unburden himself but wasn't sure that this was the time.

"Jonah, if you have a problem, tell me," Daniel pleaded.

"If you consider a wife I can't stand, a son who's spoilt and arrogant and a woman whom I adore but can't marry, then yes, I suppose you could say I have a problem."

Daniel wished that he could have been more surprised, but he wasn't. He'd harboured feelings of guilt about Jonah's marriage for more years than he cared to remember. It was he who had urged Jonah to consider Caroline as a suitable partner, pointing out her impeccable pedigree. Caroline came from the right sort of family, she'd been to all the right schools, had a degree from Vassar and was debutante of the year. Her parents encouraged the match. Jonah was handsome and well-educated - he was set to have a brilliant future. His father's increasing wealth was a well known secret and that hadn't harmed Jonah's chances. Several months later their marriage had been reported as "the wedding of the year" in all the journals and newspapers.

"Caroline had her first headache on the second night of our honeymoon." Now that Jonah had started to tell Daniel the truth, he might as well get it all off his chest. "Sex was always, quote, a favour she bestowed, something that had to be suffered. Having a child was a duty she performed. I think that even she was taken by surprise at how attached she became to Zack. After a time I realised that she was the most mean-spirited person I had ever known. I never knew that anyone could be that self-seeking."

"That does surprise me," said Daniel.

"Oh yes, she hides it well but trust me, she's an expert. Caroline has never done a thing in her life that wouldn't benefit her. She picks other people's brains shamelessly, then claims their ideas as her own. Sharing is something she doesn't understand. People are either useful or expendable. Unfortunately she's brought Zack up to think the same way - he's horribly arrogant for a boy of his age. I suppose I have to share some of the blame, I should have put my foot down years ago. But Caroline has made my own son a stranger to me."

"Don't worry, when he goes to boarding school he'll level out." Daniel had already begun to notice a new maturity in his grandson. When Zack got away from Caroline's compulsive control he was sure the youngster would straighten out. How lucky he had been with his twins.

"Jonah, are you out of the shower?" Caroline's voice was impatient. The water had run cold and he shivered as he wrapped himself in a towelling robe and began to shave.

❈ ❈ ❈

"Nicholas, are you out of the shower?" Jennifer Hunt called, as she struggled to tame her stubborn, curling hair. She was looking forward to meeting Daniel's rescuer even though Nicholas had described her as a stunner. "As long as she's a nice person she's OK with me," Jennifer had said when Nicholas told her about Daniel's guest. Jennifer had been brought up by a loving mother, and she regarded Daniel as the father she'd never had. She adored him. Daniel's affection for Jennifer was a constant source of jealousy to Caroline and she countered it by undermining her sister-in-law at every opportunity, subtly at times, cruelly at others. Jennifer's gentle nature prevented her from retaliating, but Nicholas parried with Caroline - he ridiculed her bitchy pretentiousness with humorous insults and rarely let her away with anything.

"Oh Nicholas, just look at this hair," Jenny growled at herself in the mirror. "It looks like a scouring pad."

"It's beautiful," he said, and meant it. Jenny always looked beautiful to him and she worried far too much. Any meeting with Caroline set the wheels of her self-doubt in motion.

"Come on, smile, you're on Caroline camera!"

Jenny laughed, he could always make her feel better. Carefully she pulled on the long black dress, avoiding her lacquered hair. "Oh no! The zip's broken."

Between them they pulled and tugged at it until she was able to step out of the dress. It was her favourite - mostly because it didn't show the few extra pounds she had gained. "I've got to mend it," she said, panicking. "We're going to be late."

"We won't be thrown out, take your time. They won't start dinner without us." Calmed by his patience, Jenny began to sew the zip back into place, her fingers moved deftly along the delicate fabric.

"Right, I'm ready," she finally announced as she picked up her purse and hurried to the waiting limousine.

CHAPTER SEVENTY-SEVEN

The limousine swept along the drive. Rachel craned her neck to see the mansion that had been faintly visible the day they'd visited Harriet's family. It was still difficult to see much more than an outline peppered by blocks of light which shone from the windows of the huge single-storey residence.

Daniel was waiting for her as the car stopped. How distinguished he looked in his tuxedo, his face tanned from the Mexican sun.

"I've missed you," he said, kissing her gently so as not to spoil her make-up.

"It seems like you've been away for a year." He had phoned her twice during the week, and that had delighted her.

Jonah Hunt's gaze widened when he saw the exquisite woman enter the room with his father. Her white dress, its sleeves delicately laced with silver, flowed gracefully on her slim body as she moved. He'd never seen more wonderful hair. Her flawless olive skin was a perfect foil for her coal-black eyes. Her generous mouth was parted in a smile. He struggled to remember where he had seen her before.

"How nice to see you, my dear." Caroline Hunt walked forward to greet Rachel, hand outstretched.

Daniel made the introductions as Caroline sized Rachel up. She'd seen this girl somewhere before, certainly she was attractive, she grudgingly acknowledged. "Haven't we met … ?" Her question was interrupted by the arrival of Jenny and Nicholas Hunt.

"Sorry we're late," Jenny apologised, kissing Daniel.

"Don't worry, you're fine. Come and meet Rachel."

Jenny followed him hurriedly across the room, knocking over a small table. A dish of nuts scattered in all directions and Jenny clapped her hand over her mouth in horror. "Oh no, look what I've done," she said, bending to gather up the mess.

"Jenny, sweetheart, leave it," Daniel pleaded.

As she got to her feet she caught the hem of her dress in her shoe and bumped against Jonah, tipping some of his drink on to his tuxedo. "Oh, I'm a walking disaster, I'm really sorry." She was red-faced with embarrassment as she rubbed the offending stain with a tissue spreading little nubs of white paper on the black surface.

"It needs seasoning, alcohol will preserve it," he laughed, trying to put her at ease. Jonah was very fond of Jenny. He knew that she was clumsy when she was nervous. In her own home she was a master of efficiency and good humour, entertaining everyone with the earth-mother touch. He loved the easy-come easy-go atmosphere, drinks in the garden while the two brothers barbecued for friends, spiced punch in winter sitting round the table in the large cosy kitchen. Jenny always chattered happily when she cooked lunch, it invariably stretched to include anyone who dropped in. Caroline rarely came with him, possibly that was why it was all so relaxed. Inevitably Jenny became all thumbs in her presence and it suited them all when Caroline was conveniently "otherwise engaged".

Rachel's face remained impassive as Daniel introduced her to his son and daughter-in-law. Caroline, she remembered, had come into Caprice when she had first worked there. She'd criticised the stock, and pulled and pushed disdainfully at the garments on their hangers. Jonah's hand trembled as he clasped Rachel's, his face was troubled. What was bothering *him*, Rachel wondered? Then she remembered - the lovely excited girl, the man in the waiting limousine, carrying the parcels, their loving glances. "How do you do, Jonah," she said, meeting his gaze. "It's really nice to meet you." He relaxed. Her unwavering eyes and the firm pressure of her hand told him that his secret was safe with her. Jonah smiled his unspoken thanks. His father was right. Rachel was something else. Strange that during their lengthy conversation in Mexico Dad had never actually mentioned where she worked, thank goodness for her tact.

Nicholas greeted her like an old friend.

"Still ugly, I see," he said, affectionately kissing Rachel on the cheek. Jenny dimpled with pleasure when she finally reached Rachel's side. "Oh Rachel, it's lovely to see you again, I didn't realise it was you. Do you remember, you sold me this dress?"

"We were both so scared of Meg Adams, we communicated by signals," Rachel laughed.

"Do you still work there?" Jenny mouthed silently.

They both giggled as Rachel put her finger to

her lips and nodded exaggeratedly. She liked Jenny, obviously she had a good sense of humour.

"I admire your courage," Jenny whispered, looking over her shoulder as if she expected Meg Adams to appear behind them.

"What are you two doing?" Caroline demanded, watching their antics.

"Private joke," Jenny giggled.

"I must give you the name of my hairstylist, Jenny. Are you having a problem with your own?" Caroline enquired solicitously.

Rachel watched the merriment die in Jenny's eyes.

Caroline complimented Rachel on her dress. "It's beautiful dear, did you make it yourself?"

"Thank you, Caroline. No, I didn't make it. Don't you remember, you tried it on - at Caprice? Unfortunately it was too tight for you." Rachel's reply was more in defence of Jenny than of herself. Jenny tried to hide her laughter but a grateful giggle escaped. That put Caroline in her place beautifully, she thought.

Caroline flushed with anger at Rachel's stinging reply. This one may not be quite the push-over that her sister-in-law was. If Daniel committed the grave error of marrying this girl she would be Caroline's mother-in-law. Great, just great.

"Oh! Now I remember, you were the little assistant who served me," she responded patronisingly. "I do hope your stocks have improved."

"Caroline!" Daniel's voice cracked like a whip in her ear.

"Mr Hunt, the Ambassador has arrived." A

woman dressed in black appeared at his shoulder.

Caroline breathed a sigh of relief. She hadn't known that Daniel was standing behind her. Daniel was rarely angry but she feared him more than anyone else when he was, he could be quite ruthless at times. Reluctantly she left Jenny and Rachel and followed Daniel to greet the couple.

Rachel looked admiringly round the big square room with its pale ash panelling, cheerful fire and soft, diffused wall lighting. Comfortable looking lemon-coloured sofas with huge downy cushions, placed either side of the great stone fireplace, brought a warmth to the severity of the walls. An enormous coffee table linked the space between the two couches. There were plates of appetisers and napkins on its glass surface. A huge marble bowl piled high with multicoloured stones twinkled in the night light. Two small sculptures of twin boys brought a smile to her lips. The sweep of curtains hid the garden from view, she imagined it must be enormous judging by the telescope standing in front of the drapes. Cosy armchairs dotted in pairs filled part of the room, occasional tables at their arms. What a good feeling this study had, homely and welcoming. She could picture Daniel sitting here on a winter's night reading or watching television.

"What a lovely room," she said to Jenny who was thinking how lovely Rachel was.

"It's my favourite room in autumn and winter. I love a real fire, don't you? Have you seen the rest of the house? Most people call it a mansion but Daniel hates that, he prefers to call it a home."

That would be typical of Daniel's low-key approach, Rachel thought recalling his telephone call from Mexico when Cricket Mancelli's sniping comments had appeared in the Monday editions. That had annoyed him intensely. *"Rachel goes on a Dan hunt,"* Cricket had written. Daniel was furious when he read the vitriolic column. "I wonder if Cricket's own private life would stand up to that kind of scrutiny?" he had remarked acidly.

"Maybe not," Rachel replied, "but she's the type who'd probably welcome the publicity. Don't let her bug you - she's not worth it."

"You're right," he said, relieved that the article hadn't upset her. "One day I'll get even with her, it's just a question of how and when."

"May I refresh your drink, Rachel?" Jonah's voice broke into her thoughts.

"No, it's fine. I've been admiring the room, so many interesting pictures and knickknacks. I love the sculptures of the twins."

"Dad's an incurable collector. He looks for new artists, crafts people too. He buys what he likes. He's not really interested in what's fashionable. He couldn't care less if they're famous or not. He doesn't care if they've never exhibited at one of the galleries, he's only influenced by what he sees. Mind you, he's had a hand more than once in helping young artists he considers to be good. See that one there?" Jonah pointed to a portrait hanging over the fireplace. "It's Dad, obviously. That was painted by a young handicapped girl who was earning a few dollars by doing watercolour portraits of children in the local park. He was fascinated by her work and had her paint a head of my son, Zack. It was so good that he encouraged her to work in oils. He arranged a studio and equipped it for her. Dad, being Dad, made sure that it had wheelchair access. When she was settled in, he mounted a one-man publicity campaign amongst his friends and business acquaintances. Now she's so busy you can't get an appointment for a sitting in under three months. That portrait was her gift to Dad for all his help."

The likeness was unmistakable, the face rugged, dominated by his powerful personality.

"Rachel, thank you for your understanding." Jonah's blue eyes, so unlike Daniel's, were sad. "I hope it doesn't embarrass you... Jemma, the girl you met, is more than just a friend..."

"What are you two talking about?" Caroline's voice was harsh and grating. Jonah, cut off in mid-sentence, was lost for words.

"Jonah was telling me about the artist who painted Daniel's portrait," Rachel leapt to his rescue.

"Oh that," Caroline dismissed disparagingly. "Another one of Daniel's good causes."

"That's a mean thing to say," Jonah snapped. "I didn't hear you complaining when your gardening club ladies admired Zack's portrait the other day."

She threw him a look that would have shrunk lesser mortals.

"We're just waiting for Bart and his boring wife, then we can go in to dinner." Jonah shook his head, disgust showed on his handsome face.

Anne Schulman

Everything she said these days was barbed. Just one more year, one year then he would be free. Zack would go to boarding school then Harvard, just as he and Nicholas had done. Then he would be free of Caroline and his miserable marriage. Warmth flooded through his veins as he conjured up a picture of Jemma; her halo of fair hair, eyes as blue as his own. How she loved life - almost as much as she loved him. She never pressurised him. She accepted their difficult situation with loving grace.

"Happiness is for the moments that are, not for the ones that might be." Every stolen hour with her was a joy. Just one more year.

Bart Graham's "boring" wife turned out to be a shy pleasant woman. She was overawed by the Hunt family in general and Caroline in particular. Rachel recognised the symptoms and went out of her way to be pleasant. She drew her into the conversation. Seated with the Ambassador on her left and Nicholas on her right she smiled at Daniel, who was talking to the Ambassador's wife about his travels in Brazil.

The blue, gold and white of the high-ceilinged dining-room was impressive and formed a perfect background for the candle-lit table which was covered with a delicate snow-white embroidered cloth. A magnificent épergne, cascading with gold and white flowers interwoven with fruit was flanked by sweet burning candles. It presented an imposing centrepiece. The sight of the exquisite crystal and the delicate Royal Doulton china filled Rachel with admiration. She fingered the gleaming Cristofle silverware timidly, never could she have imagined a more beautiful setting.

"The table has been shortened to half its length - at full tilt, it holds thirty," Nicholas explained.

"Imagine cooking for thirty people," Rachel groaned, realising just how undomesticated she had become. These days she did little more than boil an egg and make some toast. Living at Harriet's had spoilt her.

"We usually dine à deux if Jonah is at home. Zack often prefers to eat with his friends at night," Caroline interrupted.

"I wonder why?" Nicholas jibed in a low voice.

"I favour French cuisine myself," Caroline pontificated. "How about you, Rachel, what kind of food do you like?"

"Oh, anything really, I'm easy."

"So I imagine," Caroline said, quietly but acidly.

Rachel seethed at the woman's overt rudeness and her eyes sought Daniel's. Apparently he hadn't heard his daughter-in-law's remark. Bart's wife blushed with embarrassment and Nicholas glared at Caroline. What a bitch she was, was it possible that anyone could be *all* bad? He smiled at her cherubically and quietly said, "How attractive you look tonight, Caroline, all in brown - like a symphony in shit."

Jenny, who was taken by surprise by the quiet vehemence of Nicholas's insult, spluttered with laughter. Blinded by tears she replaced her glass on the table where it tipped the edge of a fork. She watched helplessly as a dark red stain spread remorselessly across the beautiful white cloth.

"Dab white wine on it," Daniel advised calmly. "Don't be upset, Jenny, it'll wash out."

"I'm such a klutz," she moaned, "why does everything happen to me?"

"Because you are, as you say, a *klutz* - whatever that means," Caroline muttered. Jenny's discomfort had been the only saving grace of the whole rotten evening.

"Have you visited our beautiful country?" the Ambassador asked tactfully, turning his attention to Rachel.

"No, I haven't been anywhere outside the United States. There are so many places I'd love to visit. Maybe one day I will."

"Oh, she'll find a way no doubt." Caroline's sarcastic voice rang the length of the table. Daniel avoided Rachel's beseeching eyes but his face was suffused with colour. Caroline tapped her glass imperiously. Gates, white-coated and acting as wine waiter for the meal, refilled it.

"Don't you think you've had enough?" Jonah whispered in Caroline's ear.

"Let me be the judge of that," she flared, not bothering to lower her voice. "Tell me, Rachel, how is your little boutique?" Her voice was slightly slurred.

"Fine," Rachel replied tersely.

"Don't you get tired of seeing the same old clothes day in day out?" Caroline yawned.

"Not at all, there's so much to do, so many people to look after. Half the time women need something 'yesterday' and we have to find them an outfit quickly. It's pressured at times but very rewarding."

"It sounds terrific," Jenny said. "I'd love to meet all those people, to be caught up in the rush to organise an outfit for someone." Nicholas looked at his wife in amazement. She'd never expressed any desire to work outside their home. It must be lonely for her all on her own, especially when he was away. A frown creased his chubby face, they must talk about this later.

"Pity I didn't know that sooner, I've just taken on a new assistant."

"It was just a thought," Jenny answered, but her face was unusually serious.

Daniel excused himself to take a telephone call and the conversation around the table became more general. Jonah sat quietly, barely listening to the chatter. Caroline's behaviour tonight had been unpardonable. What must their guests think of her? He knew she was a bitch but snobbery and a notion of good breeding normally kept her rudeness confined to the occasional remark. Poor Rachel, a real baptism of fire for her. He looked at her lovely face, serene and glowing in the light of the candles. His father was a lucky man.

Vaguely he heard Caroline speaking in French to the Ambassador's wife. It was the first positive sign of her role as hostess he had noticed all evening.

Daniel returned, smiling and looking pleased with himself. He signalled to Jonah. He left his seat and they spoke together for a minute. Daniel rejoined his guests as Jonah left the room.

"Do you speak French, Rachel? That's so important these days, especially in Washington." Caroline smiled ingratiatingly at the Ambassador.

"Very little, I'm afraid," Rachel said.

"Were you not taught in school? What subject did you take instead?"

"Good manners, Caroline. Obviously something missing from your curriculum."

"Touché." Nicholas applauded softly, nudging Rachel's elbow.

Rachel found no comfort in his support. She was trying to hold back her tears. Daniel *must* have heard his daughter-in-law's patronising remarks, how could he allow her to get away with it? She wanted to run from the room, go home to where she was safe. Sheer willpower kept her in her seat. For the first time since she had known Daniel he had utterly deserted her. It was no wonder that Jonah had shown such affection for the girl who had come to the shop, how different she was to the hard, brittle woman who was his wife.

"Come on everyone, let's have coffee in the study," Caroline marshalled them, swaying slightly as she stood. "Where did I put my purse?"

"You probably left it with your broomstick," Nicholas whispered in her ear.

"How dare you!"

"Believe me, I dare," he said, and in a voice inaudible to the others he added, "I hope that you're smashed, Caroline, because there's no other explanation for your disgusting behaviour. If you were my wife I'd take you home, lock you up and throw away the key."

Daniel caught up with Jonah as he re-entered the dining-room. "A quick word," he said to his son.

"Dad, if you're going to say that Caroline should've been drowned at birth - I agree. I telephoned Avery Salk as you suggested and told him to start the ball rolling on the divorce papers."

"That's good. Tonight said it all, you have my total sympathy. Now, I need your blessing. I'm going to propose to Rachel - so wish me luck."

"Oh Dad, I really do. She's delightful and I'm sure you'll be happy together."

"I'm sure we will too, that's if she's still speaking to me!"

Daniel grinned cheekily at Rachel who gave him a frosty glare. "Can I have a word with you?"

"You certainly can, after I'm finished saying what I have to say."

They left the study and Daniel led the way through the circular hall to his office.

"How could you allow her to treat me like that?" Rachel rounded on him, her eyes blazing. Daniel closed the door behind them. "You must have heard what she said. Everyone else did." Her voice was deep with hurt but her eyes were fiery.

"Make no mistake, I heard every word."

"Then why didn't you do something?" The tears that she had held in check up till then spilled down her cheeks, splashing on to the white dress in little oblong drops.

During the week Daniel had been in Mexico she had thought about him every moment. She'd finally come to accept that she was in love with him, wholly and completely. She'd thought that he was very fond of her, loved her perhaps, but after tonight she wasn't sure of anything.

"I did do something, darling," he smiled.

"*What* did you do? Nothing that I could see or hear," Rachel retaliated sarcastically.

"I encouraged Jonah to telephone our lawyer and he instructed Avery Salk to go ahead and start divorce proceedings."

Rachel's look of astonishment almost made him laugh.

"I thought perhaps you might be a match for Caroline. You and Jenny certainly seemed to hit it off."

"We did. As you'll have realised we met before."

"I think the two of you stitched Caroline up!"

"Daniel, that's not funny."

"No, it's not, is it? When we were in Mexico I tried to persuade Jonah to wait until the boy had gone away to school before divorcing Caroline. But after tonight's performance I felt that was crazy. Jonah said that I could tell you. He's angry that your introduction to our family was spoilt. Now, let's forget all about Caroline, after tonight, she's history."

"Like Lucrezia Borgia?"

Daniel cleared his throat. "This isn't how I planned things but, Rachel, if you're not doing anything on New Year's Eve, please, will you marry me?"

His proposal caught her totally by surprise and she stared at him.

"Please Rachel, say something."

"I ... I ... I don't know."

"I love you, Rachel. I think I loved you from the first time I saw you struggling with a mannequin in the window at Caprice. All the time we've spent together has convinced me that we could be happy. Dare I hope that you love me a little in return?" His teasing mood had vanished, his eyes were dark with pleading.

"I think that might be arranged." Two could

play at his game.

"Then it's yes?"

"Then it's yes!"

A look of joy swept his solemn face and he enfolded her in his arms. Tenderly he kissed her first on her eyes then on her cheeks and finally on her trembling mouth, her tears were salty on their lips. "Rachel, what's wrong? Why are you crying?" He pulled a handkerchief from his breast pocket and gently wiped her cheeks as she laughed and cried together.

"Because I'm happy, silly. I do love you, Daniel. I've always liked you but when you were away I felt so empty somehow, like half of me was missing. Then I knew I was in love with you." As he took her in his arms again they heard a tap on the door.

"Come in."

"Mr Hunt, I am sorry to disturb you, but there's a lady here to see you."

"Thank you. Don't go, I was just about to ring for you. Rachel, this is Katie who mothers and smothers me. I want you to be the first to know, Katie, this young lady has just consented to be my wife."

Katie smiled broadly. "Congratulations. That's marvellous news. I hope you'll both be very happy." Then her smile vanished as quickly as it had appeared. "I suppose you won't need smothering any more now?" she asked tentatively.

"Of course he will," Rachel answered for Daniel, touched by the look of dejection on Katie's face. "Me too, if that's all right with you."

Katie's face was even brighter than before.

This girl is nice, really nice, she thought.

"Katie, could you and Gates rustle up some champagne? On your way out would you ask the lady to come in. Now, where were we?" he laughed. Kissing Rachel briefly Daniel walked to the door and invited the caller to come in.

"Sylvie!" Rachel yelped, unable to believe her eyes.

"Rachel, *ma cherie*." Sylvie grinned. "Surprise, no?"

"Surprise, yes! What are you doing here?"

Rachel watched Daniel's face. She had seen that same look of amazement before. It happened to most people when they laid eyes on Sylvie for the first time. Tonight she was gowned - the only word for it, Rachel grinned inwardly - in scarlet. The inevitable earrings, diamanté and glittering, ended at the top of her stunning strapless dress. Its boned top swirled in silken circles to her nipped-in-waist and the miniskirt in front graduated in length until it reached the ground in a full train at the back. Her lipstick and nail varnish matched to perfection. She wore a ring on each finger, the glitter was quite blinding. Her hair was shorter than Rachel remembered and gelled flat to her head with just one curl coaxed into place on her forehead. Still, that didn't answer the question. What was Sylvie doing here? It was obvious by his stare that she and Daniel had not met before.

"Welcome, I'm Daniel Hunt," he recovered his voice. "You must be tired after your trip, come and have a drink."

"Will someone tell me what's going on?" Rachel pleaded.

"Shall we tell her?" He cupped his hand round his chin and frowned.

"Someone better. I can't take much more tonight."

"Sylvie has brought you a gift, a gift of thanks and love from me."

"Excuse me a moment, I will get it from my wrap." Sylvie returned to the room carrying a long envelope which she handed to Daniel. "Perhaps I will go and have the drink now," she suggested.

"I'll call Katie, she'll look after you. You must be starving after your long journey."

"With my undying love and gratitude," Daniel said, handing the envelope to Rachel.

"What is it?"

"Open it and see."

"It's in French, the only word I recognise is Caprice."

He took the documents from her and spread them on the desk. "Can you see that?" he asked pointing to her name. "These are the deeds of ownership to Caprice. You're now the sole owner."

Rachel couldn't quite take it in. "But where did this come from?"

"From Paris. Let me explain. Originally the property was ours. It was leased from us by the same people in Paris for whom Sylvie works - that's how she happens to buy for Caprice. After the mugging I wanted to find some way to repay you for all your kindness and help but I couldn't think how. When you came to the hospital and spoke so enthusiastically about the boutique, I had the answer. Oddly enough, the agreement was negotiated the day you were fired but it hadn't been finalised - otherwise I wouldn't have put you through all that upset. Sylvie supervised the legalities in France and Gideon Seaforth acted for us here in Washington. All that remains now is for you to sign both copies. I'll finance the buying now and the profits will be all yours."

"I don't know what to say. How do I thank you? The whole thing's too much to grasp. Everything's spinning so fast, there are so many questions I want to ask. I'm dizzy, happy and puzzled, going round the twist with it all." She shook her head and then laughed. "'All in good time, Rachel,' your face says. See, I'm beginning to read your expressions, Daniel."

"Absolutely right. All in good time, Rachel. Come on, let's go and break the wonderful news."

"Could I use a mirror first? At this stage my make-up must be all over the place."

"There's a powder-room just across the hall, come on, I'll show you." He kissed her again and reluctantly released her.

"Daniel," called Rachel as she left the room.

"Yes darling?"

"What do you think of Sylvie?" She smiled mischievously.

He rolled his eyes. *"Fantastique."*

Everyone crowded round the smiling pair, congratulating them and wishing them well. Caroline slipped from the room unnoticed. Jenny hugged Rachel. "It will be fabulous to have such a beautiful mother-in-law," she said generously.

"I'd rather be your friend." Rachel returned her hug warmly.

"Cherie, I am so happy for you, he is *charmant,"* Sylvie said, and then lowering her voice she whispered, "see how beautiful you are in the dress, now admit, Sylvie was right."

"You're always right. You know exactly what suits me and what I should wear."

"But alas, now you will no longer need me, now you will do your own buying. *Naturellement,* I will assist you at first if you like."

"Of course I need you. You must continue to do the buying, Sylvie. You will, won't you?"

"I would be happy to, but now you must come with me and you will learn too."

"Can you imagine, the two of us in Paris? I'm totally dazed tonight. I'm excited and mixed-up. Daniel's wonderful, isn't he?"

"Trés distingué, he will make the best husband you could desire," Sylvie said emphatically.

Daniel was at her side. "Happy?" he asked, putting his arm around her. "Would you like to phone Harriet and give her the good news? You can use the phone in my office, I'll have a word with her too."

"In all the excitement I forgot about Harriet," Rachel said, stricken with remorse.

Harriet sounded delighted but unsurprised. "About time too," she chirped when Daniel took the phone. "Yes Ma'am," he laughed. "You must come for dinner next week, we'll arrange it tomorrow. Nothing is making much sense at the moment."

He put down the phone and opened a drawer in his desk and produced a telephone directory. "There's something I promised myself I'd do - no time like the present," he said.

Rachel was getting used to his ways, he enjoyed being mysterious. She sat at the edge of his desk while he tapped out a number.

"Bonnie? This is Daniel Hunt. No, it's not a hoax. How'd you like an exclusive?" He winked at Rachel. "I'm about to be married. Yes, it *is* the girl in Cricket's column and Bonnie, I hunted her, she didn't hunt me. No, of course, Cricket doesn't know. Right ... correct ... yes, that's it - you've got it. And Bonnie, you owe me one!"

"So that's how you get even!" Rachel laughed.

It was after midnight and time to leave. Rachel was tired, excited, enervated.

"Do you mind if Gates drives you?" asked Daniel. "In all the fuss I forgot my pills and I'm paying for it now. Unless, that is, you'd like to stay the night, there's plenty of room in my bed." He grinned lasciviously.

"Not tonight, Napoleon. Besides, Harriet will be waiting for me, she'll want a full detailed description of the evening!"

"No harm in asking. I suggest that tomorrow we spend a quiet day here, we've a lot to talk about."

"I couldn't think of anything nicer," she said, kissing him goodnight. "And Daniel, I love you."

CHAPTER SEVENTY-EIGHT

Rachel lay on her back, warm sun soaked into her oiled skin. At the first stroke of midnight on New Year's Eve the minister began their marriage service. At Rachel's request the wedding was restricted to family and close friends. Daniel wanted to show her off to the world but there would be time enough for that later.

Harriet and Debrah Whitney-Lloyd offered to organise the wedding at Daniel's home, and both Rachel and Daniel accepted gladly. Daniel had grown fond of Harriet. The pair of them argued and bickered happily together, each scoring points from the other. Harriet had quickly dabbed her eyes as Rachel, beautiful in a cream dress which Sylvie brought from Paris, made her vows.

The news of their engagement was a scoop for Bonnie. Rachel prayed that her mother would see the item in one of Bonnie Drake's many syndicated columns and contact her but it was a forlorn hope. Daniel set his own investigator to find Rachel's mother. He didn't tell Rachel about that. But the investigator drew a blank in all fifty states. Rachel enjoyed every minute of their wedding when she could forget about her mother. She was overjoyed when Sandi called to accept the invitation to be her bridesmaid. Harriet insisted that the girl must stay with them and she regressed to her own girlhood as the three of them laughed and giggled, experimented with make-up and generally behaved like happy fools. Sandi was awed by Rachel's success at Caprice and Rachel made her a gift of several outfits which Sandi tried on again and again in the privacy of her bedroom. After Sandi went to bed, Harriet and Rachel sat on Rachel's bed too excited to sleep.

"I haven't given you your wedding gift yet," Harriet said, her little face serious. "I want you to have the Canaletto. I know that you love it and will treasure it."

"Your beautiful picture, Harriet I couldn't, all your memories … "

"I don't need a painting to remind me of my love, it's all here inside," she said pointing to her heart. "I give it to you with all my love, Rachel."

Rachel put her arms around Harriet and they clung together.

"I don't know about you," Harriet snuffled, "but I've got to look good tomorrow so no crying. Incidentally, it's all right for you to tell Daniel the truth about the painting, but please, no one else."

Wiping her eyes, Rachel promised.

They had all noticed a vast change in Jonah since he and Caroline had officially separated. They made changes to Daniel's Georgetown house with Jemma's help.

Daniel sent Jemma her own invitation to the wedding and she and Jonah stood closely together, secure in the knowledge that they too would be married in a short time. Nicholas and Jenny took to Jemma immediately, as did Daniel and Rachel. "No one should be as unhappy as he was," Daniel rationalised. "He was becoming a shadow of himself."

Sylvie returned for the wedding as promised. She stayed on to look after Caprice with Amy while Rachel and Daniel were on honeymoon. She charmed them all and Rachel was content that Jenny and Jemma would do their best to entertain Sylvie on some of her off-duty time.

Enid Saunders and her husband were as proud of Rachel as if she was their own daughter. "How we'll miss her," Enid said sadly to Harriet as they drove through the quiet streets. But Harriet, exhausted from all the excitement, fell asleep rocked by the gentle motion of the moving limousine.

"It all seems like a dream now," Rachel said, wiggling her toes in the warm sand. "It was a perfect wedding, wasn't it?"

Daniel smiled at his young bride. She was so beautiful, suntanned and slim in her scanty blue bikini. Rachel had passed up the chance to spend time in Europe. She insisted on Barbados for their honeymoon instead.

"I thought you'd have preferred to see London and Paris and maybe Rome, you longed so much to go to Paris," he said, surprised that she chose the tranquillity of this island instead of the bustle of famous European capitals.

"We can go there in the spring perhaps, but think how good the warm climate will be for your back."

The cold weather had already affected Daniel. Although he tried to hide his discomfort whenever he could, Rachel began to avoid situations which would add to his pain.

She clutched his hand tightly as the ten seater

jet screamed along the runway and lifted into the air. Daniel had forgotten that this was the first time Rachel had been in a plane and he tried to soothe her fears by explaining the reason for each changing noise. The flight was calm and that helped Rachel to forget her alarm.

She explored the sleek silver-bodied jet with interest. Lush, royal blue carpet covered the floor and lower section of the cabin walls. Neat shelving, a refrigerator, fold-away tables and hanging wardrobes were cunningly concealed behind white-panelled doors in the upper section of the bulkhead. Over the entrance to the pilot's cabin a cinema screen was neatly rolled, ready for use at the touch of a button. On either side of the aisle were large, roomy armchairs, upholstered in light blue tweed, which swivelled, allowing four people to face each other in intimate comfort. Two armless white leather chairs and two royal blue leather desk-tops supplied a stable office for working trips.

"Take a look at the rear cabin," Daniel said, putting out a hand to steady her as the plane banked suddenly. "It's OK, we're just changing course."

A larger than average single bed and a night table were bolted into place, an intercom and telephone were the only movable objects. The tiny bathroom adjoining the bedroom was equipped with everything necessary for a traveller. Rachel checked her hair in the theatrically lit mirror over the hand-basin and then returned to the main cabin.

"It must be wonderful for you to own your own plane. Such comfort. No waiting at airports, no standing in line waiting for baggage..."

"Rachel, it's not my plane, it's our plane, or yours for that matter," Daniel reminded her.

"I suppose it is," she giggled, "It seems ridiculous. I've never even owned a bicycle let alone a plane."

They walked along the white beaches hand in hand; a little further each day. Time hung motionless. They talked for hours or just lay in the sunshine, content to listen to the lapping waves breaking lazily at the edge of the glittering sand. Even the coconut palms swayed slowly, fanning themselves with their leaves. Rachel swam in the clear blue sea. Daniel hired one of the glass-bottomed boats so that they could marvel at the exotic tropical fish swimming below them in shoals of iridescent colour. At night they ate under the stars and then made love until they fell asleep in each other's arms. Daniel was a skilful lover and all thought of the night of nervous passion spent with Roberto was banished from Rachel's mind.

Daniel insisted that they should spend at least a few days in New York before going back to Washington. "I want to show you the city, to watch your face as your head reaches backwards and your eyes follow the skyscrapers on their path to the skies. For fifty cents we can take the ferry to Staten Island, that's the economy section of our honeymoon. Climb the steps to the observatory in the Statue of Liberty, or at least *you* can. Then there's the opera and the ballet, a chance for you to show off your lovely gowns. If you like, we can visit the museums and galleries. *My* number one priority is to take you to Tiffanys and buy you a wedding gift. After that, you can browse around the stores - you'll love Bergdorf

Goodman. We can go to Saks, or anywhere the fancy takes you. It'll be a thrill for me seeing it all again through your eyes."

"Sounds as if we'll need a month to do all that! I'll be sad to leave this island paradise, won't you?" Rachel sighed, turning over to toast her back.

When the time came to board the jet she'd lost any vestige of nervousness. The pilot called to advise them that it would be necessary to leave earlier than planned. "There's a blizzard forecast for New York. We could just about avoid it if we leave in the next two hours," he said. But even Daniel couldn't control the weather. Less than an hour after the start of their journey, radio contact informed them that the airport at New York was closed, the expected snowstorm had arrived sooner than anticipated.

"What are the options?" Daniel asked the frowning pilot.

"In that area - Boston's open, Washington?"

"Would you like to go to Boston?" he asked Rachel, "It's a lovely city. Maybe we could fly on to New York in a couple of days if the weather improves."

"Do you know what I'd really like to do? I'd like to go home." Boston, she thought, would be just as cold as New York.

"You heard what the lady said," Daniel said resignedly, "home it is."

✻ ✻ ✻

The snow was still falling heavily as they sat contentedly by the blazing fire. It was hard to imagine that in a few days it would be April - spring. Daniel, engrossed in his papers, signed and marked them as he read. Rachel sat on the thick carpet by his feet, sewing. The rustle of the fabric as she turned it over broke his concentration. He glanced at her shining head bent over her work. How much I've missed all these years, he thought. Her beauty and gentleness delighted him each time he saw her. He listened like a child for the sound of the car bringing her home each evening. She wanted to learn to drive herself but her pleas fell on deaf ears. Daniel was adamant - she must have a driver. "Learn by all means, but you'll have to have a bodyguard and you might as well do what we all do, grin and bear it. None of us likes the idea, Rachel, but in today's world we accept it." It worried him that she seemed to have no concept of the family's enormous wealth. When Avery Salk strongly suggested to Daniel that Rachel must sign a pre-nuptial agreement, it had taken him a couple of days to bring himself to broach the matter.

"Don't worry," she said cheerfully signing the paper without bothering to read it. "If I misbehave you can cut me off without the proverbial penny."

Even though he had his own office here at home he missed the bustling Georgetown Streets, his early morning stroll before the day's work began. His doctors had told him in no uncertain terms that another fall could damage him permanently, paralyse him even. He had a lot to live for so, grumbling, he followed their advice, for the winter months at least.

"I'm tired," Daniel yawned, "I think I'll turn in."

Rachel put up her face to be kissed. "I'll finish this, just a few more stitches and it's done."

"Goodnight darling. Don't stay up too late."

Rachel watched as he crossed the room. His movements were slightly stiff and slow. The cold weather had taken its toll on Daniel. She thought of Barbados. That had worked magic. He'd been able to cut his medication by half there. When her busy season was over she would suggest that they take a break somewhere dry and hot. She packed away her sewing kit and sat quietly against the sofa, which was still warm from Daniel's legs and rested her eyes.

The last three months had been blissful. Daniel anticipated her every need. He was loving and gentle, intelligent and fun. Katie ran the house as she'd always done, leaving Rachel free to expend her energy at Caprice. Jenny and Nicholas had taken to popping over a couple of nights a week. Jonah too made the trip from Georgetown often bringing Jemma with him. Katie always managed to rustle up a meal even at short notice. Rachel and Daniel rarely missed one of Jenny's Sunday lunches. One night a week Harriet either came to dinner with them or they visited her. Rachel phoned her every day. Her newly restored sight encouraged Harriet to join several groups and she'd even bought a car which Saunders drove, very slowly and carefully. Debrah telephoned Rachel if she was going to be in town and they'd lunch together. Rachel realised she'd been wrong about Debrah. She was brusque but kind and Rachel looked forward to their outings.

Jenny often called into the shop around lunch-time on the off-chance that Rachel would have a free hour. She thoroughly enjoyed standing in for Amy, the day Amy had finally been persuaded to visit her dentist with an excruciating toothache. Jenny plunged in to help Rachel to serve an onslaught of customers who invaded the boutique. When Amy returned, smiling and free of pain, Jenny dragged Rachel out to lunch. They had to celebrate the launch of her half-day old career. Rachel frowned - what a good saleswoman Jenny could be. She was obviously bored at home during the weekdays and would like to work. Perhaps when Amy took her spring break she'd ask Jenny to help. If that worked out, Jenny could fill in for herself too. And Daniel and she could go sun seeking. As Rachel made her way along the corridor to her room she felt satisfied that she'd solved two problems in one go. She would have someone to depend on, Jenny would be over the moon to spend her days in Caprice.

Although both Daniel and Rachel hated the idea, they agreed that it would be better to have separate bedrooms. When Daniel's pain was bad at night he had to walk up and down to stretch his back. Rachel, the lightest of sleepers, would be woken up. So with great reluctance he called in decorators and together they redesigned a beautifully proportioned room for her.

"We'll take it in turns to visit each other at night," Daniel said. "Just like those old movies when people tiptoed along the corridors sneaking into someone else's room."

"What are they?" Rachel asked, pointing to the four black tiny discs which had been installed at each corner of the ceiling.

"Security devices," Daniel explained. "Nothing for you to worry about. Besides, your beautiful Canaletto deserves protection."

Rachel loved the sprawling mansion with its high ceilings and beautiful semi-circular bays. Daniel installed the most sophisticated security system available. Every inch of the house was protected, even the conservatory he'd added to indulge his passion for orchid growing was inconspicuously wired.

The rolling grounds surrounding the house were magnificently landscaped. Daniel was proud of his gardens. He spent hours poring over catalogues. He was always searching for unusual and rare plants.

Rachel started slightly as the telephone sounded beside her bed. "Hello?"

"Hi girl! Do you remember me, your Roberto?"

The blood drained from Rachel's face as she held the receiver in her motionless hand.

"You there, girl?"

"What do you want? How did you get my number? It's unlisted."

"Hey sweet girl, that doesn't matter. You haven't forgotten your Roberto, now that you've married Mr Mega-Bucks?"

"You're *not* my Roberto."

"I want to see you again, sweet lady."

"Certainly not," she snapped, her heart thudding uncomfortably, her mouth dry. "I want nothing more to do with you. I'll never forgive you for what you did. You just vanished and left me to deal with the police. Don't *ever* call me again, do you understand?"

"OK. Maybe I'll call Mr Big instead. I'm sure he'd be very interested in hearing what I have to say. Maybe he should know you were there. Your part, girl, in his 'downfall'?"

"You leave my husband alone, leave me alone *and stop calling me girl.*" Rachel's voice rose.

"Touchy, sweet ... Meet me, girl, or I call him - and when he hears what I have to say that could be the end of the lovely Mrs Daniel Hunt. Wednesday, at my place, and don't try anything funny. See you, girl."

The phone went dead. She felt sick, as if her worst nightmare had come back to haunt her. With shaking hands she wrote down the address he had given her and climbed miserably into bed praying that Daniel wouldn't come to her room tonight. What did Roberto want? She didn't have the slightest doubt that he'd carry out his threat to contact Daniel. After that cold-blooded mugging, she was sure he'd stop at nothing. She must stop him. All night long she tossed and turned half-awake, half-asleep somewhere between dreams and nightmares.

Nine o'clock, heavy with sleeplessness, Rachel's eyes were burning and her head ached. The open drapes reflected the piercing white light that only snow could bring. She dragged herself from the bed and walked to the window. There'd been another blizzard during the night. It would be late before she could get to Caprice. Amy's cheery voice answered the phone after a couple of seconds. "I'll be late, Amy," Rachel said, her voice thick with tiredness. "The snow's bad here so it'll take some time to get to town."

"Everything's dead here too, there isn't a sinner

about. Why not stay home? I bet there won't be a single customer today."

Amy's suggestion was very tempting. Apart from her honeymoon Rachel hadn't missed a single day at the boutique.

"I'm sure you're right. I think I'll do just that. If it snows again, Amy, lock up and go home, OK?"

"Will do. Enjoy your day and make a snowman for me," Amy said brightly.

"You're quiet today, Daniel," Rachel said, as they sat having lunch in the study.

"Problems to sort out in Mexico," he said brusquely.

His preoccupation with his papers and phone calls disappointed her. She needed comfort. As soon as lunch was finished, Daniel picked up the unfinished stack of papers and went back to his office. She wrapped up warmly and slipped and slithered round the paths. Then she gave up and returned to the house and gazed moodily through the long windows at her own odd shaped footprints. For once the cheery logs burning in the grate failed to warm her.

"You don't sound your usual bright self, are you OK?" Harriet questioned.

"I'm fine, just a little chilly, the garden looked tempting so I went for a walk."

They chatted for a few minutes then Rachel excused herself. "Daniel's calling me."

She put down the phone and picked up a magazine, browsed through a few pages, and flung it on the table. The muffled sound of a car took her back to the window. She watched a man, huddled against the biting wind, leave his car and struggle towards the front door. She'd seen him once or twice before, he did investigative work for them, Daniel said. Jenny telephoned to cancel their dinner date and Rachel had to admit she was relieved. The strain was getting to her.

The noise of dripping water woke her next day. She must have left a tap running. She jumped out of bed and went into her bathroom but everything was in order. She ran the water for her bath and looked out of the window. So that's what it was, the thaw had set in, the snow was melting fast, dripping streams of water from the roof and trees. Daniel was reading *The Washington Post*.

"Morning," he said, glancing up at her. "You going to work today?"

"I can't play hooky again." She crossed to the table and bent to kiss him.

"Anything planned for tonight?" asked Daniel.

"No, Harriet prefers not to go out in this weather. I don't think she trusts Saunders' driving on these slippery roads."

The day dragged. Rachel sent Amy home after lunch, and locked up at three-thirty. There hadn't been a customer all day. If only it was this time tomorrow. Her meeting with Roberto would be over and she would be free of him. Life had been so good before he called, so smooth. It will be again, she promised herself - come on, be positive.

"I'm going to Quartz for lunch today," she told Sven, her driver, "so I won't need you. Pick me up at five o'clock would you?"

The chic little restaurant was only two minutes walk from the shop. Rachel sat at a table near the window. She wanted to be sure that Sven was nowhere in sight. Five minutes later, she made her apologies to the owner, and slipped out of the restaurant and hailed a cab. She gave the driver the address near 14th Street and New York Avenue that Roberto had given her. The building was shabby. Its hallways smelt of stale cooking. It seemed a lifetime ago that she'd walked along this very street when she'd been looking for an apartment. The area had scared her then and it was frightening her now. Despite the cold, several groups of tough-looking young boys and even tougher-looking men lounged in doorways, their eyes menacing as they stared at her. With every fibre of her being she longed for the security and comfort of the serene house in the Virginia hills, for Daniel's soothing voice and loving ways. Suddenly her throat was dry. Fury began to eat at her, she would *not* allow Roberto to jeopardise her happiness.

With a determined step she entered the building and began to climb the stairs. A clatter of feet and a man's screaming voice halted her in her tracks. Two uniformed men appeared above her on the stairs. Handcuffed, his hands behind his back, Roberto half walked, half fell down the stairway. One man in front of him, the other behind. "I've been set up, it's not mine," he screamed, "it's a frame." The taller of the two cops told him to shut up. Rachel stayed where she was, she couldn't move, she was shaking so much. As they reached her the policeman told her to move out of the way.

"You!" Roberto yelled as he saw Rachel cowering against the wall, her face chalk white.

"It was you. I should have known. You scummy bitch, you planted it." He suddenly lunged at her. She screamed in terror as both men grabbed him and threw him against the opposite wall. "I'll kill you for this, you've messed with the wrong guy. You wait, I'll get even with you if it's the last thing I do - *girl.*"

"Shut up, you punk!" the officer shouted.

They opened the door and pushed Roberto outside. As it slammed behind them, Rachel, still dazed and shaking, saw a bag of what looked like flour catch in the door. The door crashed open again and Rachel could hear a chorus of grunts, squeals and "oink, oink" as the police officers appeared. The trapped bag disappeared. She had no idea how long she'd been standing in the freezing hallway. She must get out of here, get back to the shop. Her feet barely carried her weight as she left the apartment building and breathed the cold air of the street. She put her head down and ignored cat-calls, whistles and suggestive comments. Somehow she made it to the end of the street.

"Oh please, let there be a cab," she begged as she stood on the corner in a bitter wind. Blindly she began to walk, she had no idea where she was headed. She waved her arms to flag a passing cab but it didn't stop. She pushed up the sleeve of her coat. Her watch showed three-thirty. She had to get back to Caprice. A car stopped and the driver leaned across offering her a lift. She ignored him and walked faster as he drove alongside her. Suddenly she saw a cab on the opposite side of the road and darted across the street, flailing her arms to attract the driver's attention. Rachel fell onto the back seat and gasped for breath.

"Rough neighbourhood for a pretty lady like you," he remarked amiably, noticing her expensive coat. Rachel just nodded her head. The cab-driver eyed her through his rear-view mirror and asked, "You all right, honey? You look like you've seen a ghost."

"I have," she replied. The anger in her voice persuaded him to leave her alone and concentrate on his driving.

CHAPTER SEVENTY-NINE

D aniel prowled the room like a caged leopard. How long would it take for this snow to melt? He was losing all patience with this enforced idleness. Thank goodness he'd had the foresight to build a connecting passage from the house to the conservatory, otherwise he would've had to give up the pleasure of pottering with his orchids too. The shadow of Rachel's car passing the window put an end to his restlessness and he listened for her familiar footsteps as they entered the house.

"Hi darling. Sorry I'm late tonight, the traffic was snarled up for miles." Without removing her coat she sank into the cushioned sofa, sitting as near as she could to the fire.

"At least you saw traffic. The only things that moved here today were the branches on the trees," he said grouchily.

Normally Rachel would have sympathised. She would have coaxed him back into his usual good humour. Instead she asked him if he would get her a scotch. He couldn't ever remember her doing that before. "You look pale, you're shivering." He poured her a large measure of the golden liquid and a smaller one for himself. She swallowed a mouthful and it made her cough. Daniel sat beside her and put his hand on her forehead.

"You're burning up," he said, moving his fingers to her cheeks. "You must go to bed, you have a fever."

Rachel nodded dumbly and dragged herself to her feet.

For three days she drifted between consciousness and delirium. Snow fell on her head from plastic bags and, all round her bed, teams of policemen swept it away. She tried to sit up but they pushed her back against the pillows, threatening to kill her. Roberto shouted at her to get up and go to work - if she didn't, he'd come and get her. He was trying to kiss her but she beat him off with her fists. "I hate you," she screamed, but that hurt her throat. Someone was sprinkling ice on her head and it was so cold it burnt. With a cry of joy she put her arms out to her mother but, as she tried to touch her, she floated further and further away, disappearing into the walls like a ghost. Her eyelashes hurt and someone had broken her arms and legs. "Daniel, make them stop," she sobbed, but tears hurt too.

When she awoke from her nightmare Daniel was sitting by her side, his face was gaunt. There were dark shadows and smudges under his eyes. Rachel smiled at him weakly, glad to be free of the terrible dreams. "I must have fallen asleep. Have you had dinner?"

"Three times! You've been very sick, a bad dose of pleurisy."

She hoisted herself up on her elbow but fell back again as her head swam. "How long have I been here?"

"Three days. Don't try to move, you must stay in bed. Now, I'm going to get you some bouillon, you must build up your strength."

She tried to shake her head, to say no, just the mention of food made her want to throw up.

The doctor made her stay in bed for another week. "What about Caprice? How will Amy manage on her own?" she asked. She was almost crying.

"It's all under control," Daniel assured her. "Jenny's filling in for you, so relax and concentrate all your energy on getting well."

Each day he sat by her side and at mealtimes he read to her, snippets from the newspapers, while she forced herself to eat some light food. Sometimes she lay with her eyes closed and just listened as Daniel read. Cricket Mancelli had found new victims to torture. The temperature had risen fifteen degrees - spring was in sight at last. Someone called Roberto Maroni had been arrested in possession of cocaine. Rachel didn't open her eyes, she couldn't. Sheer willpower kept her silent as Daniel, who thought it was funny, read the whole item aloud.

"Last Wednesday, two police officers, acting on a tip-off, arrested Roberto Maroni for possession of cocaine. Protesting his innocence, Maroni, in a blind fury, almost kicked a hole in the door of the police car. Asked if Maroni would be charged with malicious damage to police property the officer in charge said, 'No comment'."

Her own weak laugh sounded false in her ears. She shivered as she remembered Roberto, cuffed and yelling in that cold hallway. Daniel was suggesting that she might like to play a game of Scrabble in a day or two when she felt better. She nodded. She didn't trust herself to speak.

As they walked in the garden, Daniel pointed

out the rare shrubs. The rich soil in the borders
was dotted with tiny plants pushing their way
into the spring air. "They look as if they're testing
the weather," Rachel smiled. Even though she
wasn't back to normal she knew she was a little
stronger. Harriet had visited her several times and
was concerned by her lethargy. Jenny came to
see her most evenings on her way home. "I
adore working at the boutique," she enthused,
"the day flies by. You chose well when you
picked Amy, she's so conscientious and the
customers adore her."

Rachel smiled fondly at her daughter-in-law.
"Something good always comes out of something
bad." She squeezed Jenny's hand. "I'm so grateful
to you both."

Sylvie telephoned from Paris, she was starting
her winter buying in a few weeks and wanted
Rachel to join her. Daniel saw the lively flush of
interest that illuminated Rachel's expressive face.

"What brought that glint to your eyes?" he
asked as the call ended.

"Sylvie wants me to join her on her next
buying trip in Paris. She'll be starting in a few
weeks."

"Why did you say no? You've always wanted
to go to Paris."

"I don't know really, I always imagined we
would go there together, I suppose."

"Some day. Don't refuse it out of hand - think
about it. In a few weeks time you'll be much
stronger and it would be good for you. Sleep on
it, you can decide tomorrow."

The more Rachel thought about it the more
enthusiastic she became. She had always yearned
for the day when she would walk through the

doors of the famous fashion houses. To see for herself the wonderful clothes in the city of their creation. With Sylvie to guide her, that would be the fulfilment of a dream.

"Are you sure you don't mind?" she asked, for the fourth time.

"If you ask me that again, I'll be glad to be rid of you! Call Sylvie and make your arrangements. You can fly Concorde directly to Paris, that way it'll be less tiring for you. Find out the dates and I'll make the booking."

"Won't you change your mind and come with me?" she pleaded.

"I could imagine nothing worse than having to sit on a tiny gold chair, watching models parade up and down all day."

Daniel had been unusually irritable the last few weeks. Things that normally would have amused him had met with stony silences. Rachel went out of her way not to ask him if he was in pain, that annoyed him too.

"You and Sylvie do all your running around in Paris and when you're finished you can fly to Nice. Just outside Beaulieu on the Côte d'Azur there's a beautiful hotel - the Château d'Albion. I'll join you there and we can have a vacation."

"Oh Daniel, that's perfect. It was the thought of being away from you that I hated so much, now we can be together, at least part of the time."

❊ ❊ ❊

Sylvie impatiently waited for Rachel's flight to arrive. She'd made plans for the first few days of Rachel's visit. It would be an opportunity for

Rachel to see something of Paris and become used to French ways before they had to start work in earnest. It was too late in the season but Rachel hadn't been able to make the trip earlier and Sylvie, disappointed, had done the bulk of her buying alone. The elegant figure of a young woman with raven hair followed a porter wheeling a loaded trolley. How marvellous Rachel looked in the pale grey suit that Sylvie recognised instantly. Rachel's beautiful face broke into a wide smile when she saw Sylvie waving wildly. They hugged each other with delight as Sylvie welcomed her with a posy of yellow and white freesias.

"So you will not be sick-from-home," she said.

It was so good to be with Sylvie again, how she loved those mixed-up expressions of hers. They stored the baggage in Sylvie's little Renault and headed for the city. Rachel clung on to her seat for dear life as Sylvie zipped in and out of the traffic with gay abandon, honking her horn and swapping insults with other drivers. Rachel closed her eyes more than once, sure that any second now they'd crash into another car being driven with equal recklessness. To her great relief they reached the deluxe hotel on the Avenue Georges without mishap.

"… and it reminded me of a chariot race - with Sylvie in the role of Ben Hur. It was terrifying!"

"Traffic still as bad, eh?" Daniel laughed, his voice distant and crackling. "Don't fret, I've arranged a car and driver for you. He'll contact you shortly."

Rachel glanced at the unopened envelope lying on the bed. She propped the receiver under her chin, picked up the envelope and slit it open. "There's a note here from the rental agency, the driver's at the hotel now."

"Sorry, I can't hear you, this line is terrible. Talk to you tomor..." The rest of his words were lost as the connection was broken. The hotel operator offered to reconnect the call but Rachel declined, there was nothing more to tell him.

She quickly unpacked, ordered coffee and asked for the valeting service. Then she explored the rest of the suite. Flowers, fruit and a bottle of champagne, in an ice-cooler, gave the living-room a welcoming air. She switched on the television and listened for a moment to the rapid-fire speech of the presenter. "Too *formidable* for me," she said aloud, pressing the off-switch. The coffee was strong and pungent and, as she sat in a comfortable chair, leafing through the glossy visitor's guide, her energy slowly returned. There was plenty of time for a leisurely bath before Sylvie was due. In fact, why didn't she send the car for her? It would save Sylvie the problem of parking - to say nothing of her own frazzled nerves.

"You are frightened by my driving, no?" Sylvie laughed. "I am happy. It will, as you say, save me the hustle of parking."

"Hassle of parking," Rachel corrected, "hustle means rushing or hurrying."

"So I *was* right! You don't like my driving." Sylvie laughed again.

Rachel lay sleepily on the bed and waited for Daniel's call. Each night she eagerly told him about her day and he reported the happenings back home. "Everything's running smoothly at

Caprice, you just forget about it. By the way, Meg Adams's case came up today, she got two years."

"Oh that's terrible, poor Meg..."

"It *was* fraud," Daniel intercepted coldly, "she deserves her punishment. In this life Rachel, there's no room for deception."

"Daniel, who was responsible for taking her to court? I know Gideon Seaforth brought the charges but on whose behalf?"

"Mine. The sale of Caprice had already been agreed, remember?"

Miserably, Rachel listened as he told her about the trial. With nothing to lose Meg had made public her husband's dependency on her. "He disappeared the day she was charged. She was of no further use to him. She'd spent little or none of the stolen money on herself. Maybe she hoped that might help her case."

They talked for another ten minutes. In a way Rachel felt responsible for Meg's imprisonment and she felt wretched. Daniel confirmed the time of her flight to Nice on Monday - a car would be there to meet her when she arrived. He would follow next day.

They said goodnight and for a long time after she replaced the receiver she just lay there, mulling over Daniel's news. She forced her thoughts in a different direction. Sylvie had been an incredible guide and mentor. It wasn't just the elegant shops on the Faubourg St Honoré or the Avenue Montaigne - though she'd spent a small fortune in those places - that would stay in her mind. It was the shop that sold nothing but oils, the button shop stocked from ceiling to floor with every imaginable shape and colour of fastening, the antiquarian book store, musty and dusty - they were the ones that had enchanted her. Sylvie chose out-of-the-way restaurants where the food surpassed the cost and Rachel insisted that they dine at Le Grand Vevour and at the astronomically priced Maxims. They drank red wine, full-bodied, mellow and heady, and white wines, light, sparkling and fruity. There were invitations to private showings at fashionable art galleries or hastily converted studios.

Rachel, who was walked off her feet, begged to sit down at one of the bistros which seemed to spring up wherever there was a space on the pavements. When time was running short they viewed the magnificent gardens, churches and historic buildings from the open windows of their car. At Le Sentier, the wholesale garment district, they examined the stocks, picking and choosing from the latest collections. Rachel respected Sylvie's skill. Sylvie could spot a flaw, reject an unsuitable fabric, drive a hard bargain, demand concessions - always with a smile and her own idiosyncratic charm. And then there were the markets, fruit and vegetables, their sweet scents mingling with the flowers - a kaleidoscope of colours.

It was almost over now. Tomorrow morning they were going to Fauchon's, the best food shop in the world. As Sylvie had invited some friends for lunch on Sunday she'd finally agreed that Rachel could spend her money in that famous shop and make her contribution to the lunch. Rachel had already decided what she would like to buy, pâté de foie gras, truffles, chocolates and some of the exquisitely displayed fruit and vegetables that she'd seen through the window as they passed.

Saturday was probably not the best day to visit Versailles. It was full of tourists at this time of the year, but somehow they'd never found time to go there during the busy weeks. And, to Rachel's delight, Sylvie managed to get two much-prized tickets for the opera.

Maybe she should phone Harriet now, the next couple of days would be choc-a-bloc.

"Rachel! What a lovely surprise. Are you enjoying Paris?"

"It's unbelievable, better than I could have imagined. Sylvie sends her love to you, she's a fantastic guide."

"When do you leave for the south?"

"Monday afternoon, the weeks have raced by."

"By the way, do you remember that young man you went out with? Wasn't his name Roberto Maroni?"

For a second Rachel's heart seemed to stop beating.

"Yes, it was," she said.

"I was just reading the paper as you phoned. He must have returned to Washington because he was arrested on some drugs charge or other, possession I think. Well anyway, when he was being transferred for trial, the police truck they were travelling in crashed into a bus and Maroni and some other man escaped. Thank heaven you stopped seeing him, can you imagine being involved in all that?"

Rachel could find no quick way to say goodbye to Harriet. What other bad news could the night bring her? She answered Harriet's questions mechanically and put the phone down as soon as she could. "Bye Harriet, I'll call you in a few days."

She felt sick. Would Roberto be recaptured or would she have to live in fear of him for ever? Sven couldn't guard her twenty-four hours a day and she certainly couldn't tell Daniel anything about this. He would never forgive her if he found out that she knew who his mugger was. If only she'd owned up there and then, but she'd been too scared and shocked. Roberto was right, that would be the end of Mrs Daniel Hunt and her marriage. What could she do? Nothing here in Paris. Could she tell Sylvie, could she trust her? If only she'd told Daniel the truth from the beginning.

"Pull yourself together," she instructed herself in a sharp voice. But, no matter how much she tried to reassure herself that Roberto would be locked up again before she got home, it was almost daybreak before she fell into a deep sleep.

CHAPTER EIGHTY

The heat hit her with force as she walked down the steps of the plane at Nice Airport. The Château d'Albion's driver was waiting to whisk her into the cool of the limousine. The drive along the coast road captivated her. Houses clung to the hillsides above the attractive villages. All around them were the vibrant colours so special to this part of the coast. The limousine turned off the main road and stopped at a pair of tall black gates which slowly parted, revealing a breathtaking profusion of flowers and shrubs. Ahead Rachel could just see the azure sea, more vivid, if possible, than the cloudless sky. The car swung gently round a curve and there, in its pristine glory, stood the Château d'Albion. As they pulled to a dignified halt a man, not tall but immaculately dressed, came down the pink marble steps and opened the door of the car.

"Welcome to the Château d'Albion," he said, taking her hand to help her from the vehicle. "I am Claude d'Albion".

"Thank you," Rachel smiled, "I've heard so much about the château. What wonderful gardens you have, I'm looking forward so much to seeing the rest of them."

"It is the best time of the year here at the château, a summer celebration."

As he spoke he studied the soignée young woman. She had a sweet, wistful madonna-like face. She was expensively and beautifully dressed in a cream silk pants-suit with navy blue accessories. She was courteous and appreciative of his gardens - he approved of that. Yes, she was just the type of guest he liked to have at the château.

"Mme Hunt, your husband telephoned this morning. He regrets but there has been a change of plans, he has had to go to Mexico and will arrive here on Saturday. He will telephone as soon as he can. But don't worry, you will be in good hands here. I will take you to your room and Claudine will help you to unpack."

The porter placed the luggage on a rack at the end of the bed and drew back the wooden shutters. Rachel went to the window and looked out at the magnificent vista below her. People relaxed in the gardens, uniformed waiters served cool drinks, sunlight shone on the glittering sea. Heaven. There were four days before Daniel was due to arrive, four days to laze in the sun, swim and read. This would be the perfect ending to her vacation; if she could just forget Roberto.

Claude

CHAPTER EIGHTY-ONE

The ticking of the tiny jewelled clock was a comforting sound. Claude was not consciously aware of it, he just knew it was there in the silence of the little room. The rickety chair creaked as he leant against it, easing his neck with linked hands. His eyes travelled from the crate which served as a filing cabinet to the unpainted walls and then upwards to the single light bulb hanging by its cord. The scarred trestle-table which held his precious leather-bound black books was hidden by sheets of clean white paper. Clean white cotton sheets protected his clothes which hung on an open rail. Only the precious clock and the divan bed, with its luxuriously thick mattress and spotless cover, were to his taste. He was very proud of this room, the first semi-habitable room in the château.

He mustn't allow his daydreams to interfere with his work, although he could hardly think of the scene with Thierry Thibault and his father, Pierre, as a dream - a nightmare perhaps.

Pierre's angry demand for an explanation caught Claude unprepared. Why were the lawyers writing to *him* and not to Pierre? Claude would have preferred the dignity of a private discussion not a screaming match in the hotel foyer. Thierry had snatched the letter confirming Claude's successful bid for the château from his hand and read it out loud. His face was ugly with anger.

"Let's talk privately," Claude suggested, "there are guests in the hotel."

"What does this mean?" Thierry shouted.

"Its meaning is obvious," Claude snapped, "but my business is with your father not with you."

"Maybe Claude's right, we should discuss this quietly," Pierre said in a choked voice.

"Why should we save this little parasite the embarrassment? Let the world know how he repays your years of kindness - by stabbing you in the back." Thierry's face contorted with rage. He wasn't ready to give up his life in Zurich. The hotel management training had given him amongst other things, the chance to meet rich, spoilt daughters of men and women who expected the best of everything. He was too young to give up this opportunity. He didn't want to run a hotel in a side street - a place where he'd be lucky to see daylight once a week - this was not for him. Plenty of his fellow trainees had been transferred to other international hotels in the group, some to New York, others to Paris. Only last week two of them had left for Rome. His father would expect him to come back and take over Claude's job. Managing the château mightn't have been too bad, but a glorified *pension* hidden away from the activity and glamour of Cannes was too dreadful to consider. His personal preference would be to manage a prestigious hotel in Paris or London for a start. The world could be his oyster but with one fell swoop, Claude had stamped on his hopes and reduced him to a squashed shrimp.

"How dare you accuse me of stabbing *you* in the back. That's ridiculous!" Claude retorted, his voice rising with fury. "I changed the image of the *pension*. I was the one who doubled its size, who hired the staff, supervised the management. And who looked after the welfare of the guests? Made sure that each one was treated with care? Who increased the profits so that you could go to Switzerland and swan around Zurich in your sports car? *I did*. And my reward? The promise of a partnership that was a hoax, a delaying tactic for poor stupid Claude, until such time as you decided that you would honour us with your presence - if ever. Oh yes, Pierre, don't look so surprised. I knew about your plans, I heard it all when you foolishly left your door open - the day you spelt it out for your son."

Pierre just stood there. He was helpless now. He could find nothing to say in his defence.

"You should have spoken to me," he finally managed weakly.

"And how do you hope to find the kind of money it would take to restore this château?" Thierry asked, his tone patronising.

"That's none of your concern," Claude retorted.

"It will be when the château comes up for sale again," Thierry sneered.

"This is getting us nowhere. We should sit down and see if we can come to some arrangement - one that would be fair to us all," Pierre pleaded. Thierry was too inexperienced to realise how much they depended on Claude. What a good son he was, jumping to his father's defence like that. Father and son together, the day couldn't come quickly enough for him.

"There is *nothing* you can say that would

interest me, no words that would persuade me to trust you again. I'm sorry for you, Pierre, this son of yours will bring you nothing but heartache."

"Why you little..."

Pierre grabbed Thierry's hand. "That kind of behaviour will get you nowhere," he warned.

"So, it begins already," Claude remarked acidly. "I am, however, prepared to stay here for a month if you wish. That will give you time to find new staff."

"What do you mean - staff?" Thierry seized on Claude's words.

"Staff, people who will run the hotel. A chef, a porter, cleaning staff, a manager."

"They're all leaving?" Pierre's voice was incredulous.

"That's their decision, but I'm sure they'll give you time to replace them."

This time Thierry's punch found Claude's face before Pierre could stop him. Claude was knocked backwards. He fell awkwardly into a chair behind him.

"Idiot, imbécile, you could've killed him - that marble floor!" Pierre roared at his son.

Joseph came running from his post at the front door. "Are you all right, M Claude?" he asked.

"Traitor, ingrate," Thierry shouted at the confused man. "Get out, all of you, get out now."

"Gladly," Joseph replied. "I'll tell the others."

"Joseph, wait," Pierre begged. "Thierry is upset for my sake. He didn't mean it."

"I'm sorry M. Thibault, but I could never work with a man like that, none of us could."

One after the other they said goodbye to Pierre Thibault, but ignored his glowering son.

They waited outside the hotel for Claude in a straggling group. Joseph offered to stay with him as he packed. He was afraid that Claude might be assaulted again.

"Thank you, Joseph, it isn't necessary. I'll be with you shortly."

Relief mixed with sadness as he left the hotel, his jaw tingling painfully from Thierry's powerful blow.

"I've sent Joseph for a taxi," Marc said, taking command. "You'll stay at my parents' home for a day or two until you decide what to do. We've arranged to meet there later."

Claude nodded gratefully as they took his case and the extra clothes he carried over his arm. Pride wouldn't allow him to ask for a box to put them in. Lisette Garnier's clock was carefully wrapped amongst his sweaters in the suitcase with his precious leather-bound books.

It took them a week to make their plans. A couple of times Claude found himself close to tears, he was so touched by their stubborn kindness. Marc's mother fussed over him. Each day when they all met at the house, she fed them on gigantic casseroles fragrant with herbs.

"It's no wonder you're such a good cook, Marc," Joseph said in a loud voice so that Marc's mother couldn't fail to hear.

"*Merci,* Joseph," she responded smiling. He was a silver-tongued flatterer, that one.

It took all Claude's persuasive powers to convince Marc that he should study under Georges Liseaux. The man was regarded as one of the best *pâtissiers* and chefs in France. "There's nothing you can do at the château and you may never get a chance like this again," Claude reasoned. "It's only because of your own reputation that you've been offered the place. *Le maître* accepts only a few people at a time and there's a long waiting list."

Marc agreed reluctantly. "But how will you manage?" he asked plaintively.

"We'll live on *les sandwiches* and dream of your fine cooking," Claude teased.

❊ ❊ ❊

He stood like a mother hen with her chicks and watched their every reaction. His own possessive excitement rose as they walked from room to room.

"Magnifique!" Joseph declared, shaking his head in wonderment as he examined the thick walls of the enormous rooms.

"My kitchen will be wonderful, a little dark perhaps, but we can light it well," Marc said, pacing it out.

Claude smiled, his plans included knocking out large sections of the walls in order to flood the château with sunlight. But let that come as a surprise.

Each one of them had points to make and Claude listened to their opinions. Claudine's father, Jules, was more than pleased to work for Claude. "It will be an honour," he said sincerely, "to have an employer who appreciates beautiful gardens."

"It's not necessary to take out every tree, M Claude," Jules said after he'd looked briefly at the neglected grounds. "A lot of this will thrive with a little care."

Claude gave him the task of designing the grounds. He would hire other gardeners. It was Jules who had solved their biggest problem; where to live during the re-building.

"Two caravans, in the shadow of the château," he suggested.

"Of course! " Joseph said enthusiastically. "That way we can be here all the time, we won't have to travel backwards and forwards."

With the exception of two girls who lived with their families in Cannes, the rest of the Hotel Thibault's staff volunteered to work at the château. None of them would allow Claude to pay them while they worked elsewhere in the interim. Jules promised to clear a suitable area for the caravans and Claude left him to start work as soon as possible.

They all escorted Marc to the station, and promised to keep him up to date with progress at the château.

"You'll need help in the kitchen when you come back, where better to find it than at M Liseaux's?" Claude said as Marc boarded the train.

"Bonne chance," they shouted, waving wildly at Marc's rapidly diminishing figure.

It was difficult to find the right architect and the best builders. Not everyone agreed with Claude's ideas, but in the end he felt he'd chosen well. As he sat in the quiet room, with nothing to disturb him but the ticking of the clock, he glanced towards the neatly folded documents in their cardboard nesting place. His dreams on paper.

CHAPTER EIGHTY-TWO

They crowded around the doorway as Marc inspected his domain. They smiled as they watched him open the doors of the gleaming refrigerators, run his hand over the bars of the charcoal grill and caress the cold shining surface of the counters. His eyes approved the rows of burnished copper pans and the lethal steel-bladed chopping knives in their protective wooden blocks. Silently he moved to the huge ovens. There was nothing more he could have wished for. It was all here; the butcher's table, the marble top for pâtisserie, a fully automated icecream churn and every labour-saving machine imaginable. The big table in the half moon of the jutting turret pleased him most. A place setting of the château's china, silverware and glass was laid out on its virginal wooden surface. The kitchen table was the heart of a home Marc always maintained. He examined each piece of elegant china and his smile broadened. The glasses, fine crystal, might be a little too delicate, but M Claude wouldn't have it any other way.

Marc turned to face his waiting friends and shook his head. *"Fantastique*. It really does the business," he said, proud of the expression he'd picked up from a young English chef. Claude released his breath, his face quite pink with delight.

"Are you surprised by the light?"

"You kept that secret from me very well," Marc

replied, looking again at the big expanse of window that had been cut into the thick stone walls.

Joseph brought two cups and saucers and a jug of coffee to the table.

"I imagine you've plenty to talk about," he said. "Call me if you need me."

"You've done wonders," Marc reflected, as he looked around the big kitchen again. The fans whirred overhead, cooling the air.

Claude was pleased by Marc's praise, but he shrugged. "It's beginning to come together. When does your assistant chef arrive?" he asked. "You really think highly of him?"

"He'll be here next week and I'm sure he'll make a fine chef. He has a great talent, wait till you taste his pastry and *le chocolat*, I think he was born to create wicked desserts. Even le maître learnt from him. You'll be pleased, M. Claude."

"Marc, when we're alone please call me Claude, Monsieur is too formal."

"Eh … Claude." The name seemed strange without its prefix. "How long before we're ready for our first guests? Are you planning to have a special opening? Will we advertise in the holiday brochures?"

"I was waiting until you came to discuss these matters. I've given it a lot of thought and advertising doesn't appeal to me, I think it best to attract our guests by recommendation."

Marc thought about what Claude had said. "But where do we start? How will people know we're here?"

"That's simple. Before the official opening

we'll invite travel writers from the most prestigious journals to spend a weekend here at the château as our guests. Each of them can bring a partner. It won't make much difference to the cost, all the rooms are doubles anyway." Claude reeled off an impressive list of names. "I doubt if anyone will refuse an offer like that."

"That could be expensive," Marc frowned, but he agreed it would be excellent publicity.

During the long empty evenings the previous year, Claude had formed many of his ideas in the letters he'd written to Marc, using him as a sounding-board. Marc was well aware of Claude's ambition - to turn the Château d'Albion into a world-class resort hotel. He had been horrified when he'd learnt about the prices Claude intended to charge and was honest in his criticism. Claude had written and spelled out the costs involved in running the venture. Eventually Marc conceded that Claude was right and he was flattered to have been consulted.

"There's something else," Claude said, as he doodled on the surface of his coffee with a spoon. "As you know, I left the Hotel Thibault because Pierre refused to give me a partnership which I felt I deserved. We've worked well together, you and I, and I think a lot of you. I want you to be happy at the château, so I'm going to give you a ten per cent share of the overall profits - not just the food."

Marc's eyebrows shot up, his eyes round with amazement.

"You're loyal and hardworking. I really appreciate that. So that will be the arrangement for five years, after that we'll talk again. You can't expect very much for a couple of years, naturally. But after that..."

"M Claude ... I mean, Claude, this comes as a total shock. You've already offered me a very generous wage, I never expected such..."

Claude had expected Marc to be astonished. He'd been thinking about this for some time. He was not going to make the same mistake Pierre Thibault had made. Marc's bonus could avoid discontentment later, besides, he valued Marc's opinions and trusted his integrity.

"We must always discuss our ideas with the rest of the staff. It's important for everyone to be consulted."

Marc nodded slowly. He was still coming to terms with his unexpected windfall. He pulled himself together and turned his full attention to what Claude was saying. They decided on a date for the opening weekend, two months away. "If everything is ready in a month then that would give us plenty of extra time for any hiccups."

Marc insisted on cooking dinner for everyone that night. He checked the supplies and wrote a list of items they needed, then called Joseph.

"Would you mind going to the market for me?" he asked. "Tomorrow I'll stock the kitchen."

Claude was glad to have Marc's support. Some of his ideas amazed Marc. "There's so much to think of," Marc admitted. "You're right, we do need a little van for the market. We can't have the hotel limousine smelling of garlic!"

"Or fish!" Claude laughed.

"I can see it now, Louis Vuitton suitcases covered in fish scales. Suit carriers decorated with onion skins."

"Think of it, fur coats reeking of melons."
Claude was enjoying the silly conversation, he
needed a little light relief.

They squashed around the table, all thirteen of
them. Claudine ran to her room, and returned
with a rag doll which she put on the chair beside
her. "Thirteen's an unlucky number," she said.
Marc's parents beamed at their son's friends.
They looked forward to tasting the results of the
year spent with M Liseaux. Jules, who had
brought his wife and Claudine's young brother,
was responsible for the perfectly grown blooms
on the table. Joseph was wine waiter and
Claudine, who had lost some of her shyness,
volunteered to serve the meal with Marie. The
others added gaiety to the gathering with their
chatter and Claude, in his place of honour at the
head of the table, beamed proudly at his adopted
family. A momentary pang of sadness gripped
him. How happy he would have been to see his
mother and Lisette Garnier at this table. Silently,
he drank a toast to them.

"The meal was perfection!" Claude said, when
forced to make a speech. He was unused to the
sound of his own voice in company and he
fumbled for words. "The company was perfect
too. Thank you *all* for your support. I know we'll
be happy and successful together." He smiled
shyly and sat down again. His "family" cheered
loudly.

CHAPTER EIGHTY-THREE

Pierre Thibault wiped the splashes from the edge of the bowl and placed it on the hot-plate. Where was that girl? He eyed his splattered apron and resigned himself to waiting here in the kitchen. It was a pity that Thierry hadn't been able to help today.

"I have an urgent appointment which I can't break," he said. Pierre didn't like to question him. The other young waitress that Thierry had hired telephoned earlier to say she was sick, although the giggling Pierre could hear made him doubt it. He must talk to his son tonight about replacing her.

He wiped his brow on the stained cloth that hung from his waist, and went to the dining-room to see what had delayed Michele. His head pounded with anger when he saw her, lolling against the wall as she chatted to a handsome fair-haired man, ignoring the calls of other diners. As Pierre watched a couple stood up, the man threw some money on the table and they stormed out of the dining-room. Furious, Pierre called to her from the door. She pulled a face, apologised to the man and sauntered slowly towards Pierre.

"What is it, Monsieur?" she asked insolently.

"There's more than one table to be served, Michele. Food is piling up on the hot plate and one couple have just left."

"So?" she shrugged. "They're impatient, that's all."

"They're customers and deserve courtesy and attention." That had been Claude's constant slogan, Pierre recalled bitterly. This could never have happened while Claude was in charge.

"I'm only one person and I'm doing my best," she whined.

"Then your best isn't good enough. You've been talking to that man for at least five minutes. Come on, Michele, get those plates to the table before anyone else leaves."

Petulantly she walked in and out of the kitchen carrying one plate at a time. In sheer frustration Pierre tore off his apron and donned his last clean one. He scooped up the rest of the covers and rushed to the dining-room to appease the few hungry diners, apologising for his lack of staff. How the two of them would have managed if they had been busy he shuddered to think.

"You'll have to speed up in future, Michele," Pierre warned her.

"Maybe if that precious son of yours didn't disappear with Claudette every other day, we'd have some service around here," she sniped viciously. "Or haven't you noticed?"

Pierre looked at her, his eyes narrowed. Was she telling the truth? Thierry wouldn't leave him here to manage with only an inexperienced waitress. Would he?

"How dare you say that," he thundered.

"It's true. I heard them whispering in the foyer last night, they were making arrangements to meet."

Pierre had heard Claudette giggling this morning. He didn't expect Thierry back till seven o'clock and wondered what appointment could take a whole day?

"Get on with your clearing," he snapped.

"Clear it yourself," she retorted. She unpinned her apron, threw it at the dishes piled on the table and flounced out of the hotel slamming the door behind her.

"That's all I needed," Pierre groaned, sinking on to a chair. He was no longer able to stand in the kitchen all day, it exhausted him. It looked so grubby now. He'd had no time to put the plates into the big dishwasher. His indigestion bit savagely at his throat and chest. Rooting through the drawer he found his tablets and popped two of them into his mouth at once.

He sank down gratefully on to the hard chair and sipped a glass of cold milk. How much longer can we go on like this? he wondered. It had taken all his energy to persuade Thierry to give up his course for a term until things straightened out. The promise of a new car had finally won Thierry over. But things had not improved, if anything, they had got worse, Pierre knew that. Bookings had fallen off considerably. Many guests had left without confirming their annual reservation. He couldn't forgive Claude for provoking Thierry but his son should not have punched him. How his feet ached. Claude should have stayed until they found someone else. Had Claude enticed away his staff? The two girls who stayed on lasted only a week, then they left too. His head throbbed. Could he have a little sleep for a few minutes before he started the evening meal?

"Papa, wake up, it's almost seven o'clock."

Pierre swatted the voice with his hand and laid

his head down again.

"Papa, Papa." The voice annoyed him. Someone was shaking him, he wanted to go back to sleep.

The clink of a glass on the table startled him. Thierry's face was peering anxiously into his.

"What time is it?" Pierre asked.

"Seven o'clock. How long have you been sleeping there?"

"Nearly three hours," Pierre said, scrambling to his feet. "I slept for almost three hours! Quick Thierry, help me prepare the vegetables. We're going to be late with dinner."

"But Papa, I'm going out tonight, have you forgotten?"

"You can't leave me on my own. Michele has left, and Claudette is sick, or so she says."

"We've only ten covers, surely you can manage that?"

"Thierry, I need you here. I wouldn't be so tired if you hadn't spent the day with Claudette." He hadn't meant to say it, but exhaustion had made him angry.

"Who told you that?" asked Thierry warily.

"Michele. She overheard you talking last night. Now please, Thierry, start on those vegetables."

"But Papa!"

"Now!" Pierre thundered. Maybe Claude was right after all, Thierry was not reliable. "Stop slamming and crashing, Thierry, it won't do you any good. We'll look for someone else to serve and help me in the kitchen tomorrow, but you must stay here tonight."

He could never remember speaking so firmly to his son, but he was desperate. His indigestion was getting worse, burning in his chest.

"I'll help you for a short time," Thierry said, "but then I'm going out."

Pierre could no longer hear him. He clutched his chest, his eyes rolled upwards. He was dead before he hit the floor.

Thierry screamed for help but it was too late.

Thierry Thibault stared at the solitary bunch of flowers on the grave. "Claude d'Albion is to blame. He killed my father as surely as if he'd shot him or stabbed him to death. Some day, I'll make him pay for that. He will pay with his life Papa, I promise you."

He left the graveside and walked slowly to the chapel. He stood alone in the silence and repeated his promise. At precisely the same moment near Beaulieu, Claude d'Albion too stood alone - on the marble steps of the château awaiting the arrival of his first guests.

CHAPTER EIGHTY-FOUR

J oseph listened to the reactions of his travel-weary passengers as he carefully turned the limousine into the drive. He heard their cynical remarks. They'd seen it all - been there, done that.

The gardens brought grudging sounds of approval. As he rounded the bend leading to the château, he heard surprised grunts.

"Impressive old pile," the representative of a prestigious British journal commented.

"Great building," the American columnist remarked to his companion, but her eyes were glued to her hand mirror as she examined her face.

"Uh huh," she responded without looking up.

M Claude wouldn't take kindly to that, Joseph thought, as he brought the car to a gentle halt.

Claude straightened his tie nervously and came down the two steps to meet his guests. Joseph opened the limousine door.

"Looks fantastic," the journalist gushed. "I could just do with a hot shower then some good French food and wine."

"Welcome to the Château d'Albion, I'm sure we can satisfy all your needs," Claude said proudly, leading the way into the château. People were always amazed by its airiness, they expected it to be dark and dismal.

"Philistine," one architect had accused. He was outraged that Claude was determined to break open the beautiful old walls.

"Hey, just look at this," the American exclaimed when he saw the entrance hall of the château. The pink marble floor of the foyer was spread with soft rugs of apple-green and white. From one corner of the reception desk - an ornate boule table - flowers cascaded. As Claude led the couple into the living-room, the journalist's partner forgot her boredom. "It's out of sight," she exclaimed.

The pinks and greens of the room blended harmoniously, highlighted by touches of white. Informal groupings of downy settees and chairs divided the room. Artfully placed flowers drew their eyes away from the bare walls. There were still very few paintings or ornaments. Claude's delicate jewelled clock ticked merrily on the white stone mantelpiece. Sweet-scented logs crackled in the grate.

"A glass of champagne?" Claude offered.

"Faahb-ulous," the young woman replied, as she helped herself to a tempting snack from the big silver tray. Popping one after the other into her mouth, she said, "Hey, these canapés are really great, try one Cy."

Marc and his assistant, Didier, planned the weekend menus with the precision of a military campaign. The two men left nothing to chance. With the aid of two young trainees, they tested each of the dishes on the staff. "It's a trial run," Marc said. But he refused to give them any hint about the culinary delights to come. Claude was also left in the dark. They learnt to guess what food was being prepared by the music which floated from the kitchen. A Strauss waltz heralded feathery soufflés, Swan Lake meant airy, melting meringues, Handel's Water Music, they guessed, would result in a delectable fish course. Claude frowned as the sombre tones of Wagner thundered from the speakers. Not the time, he decided prudently, to approach the artists at work. He'd find out later what disaster had taken place.

Claude had his own master plan. He would have lunch or dinner with a different journalist each day. That way he'd be able to answer any questions they might have, also he could judge their reactions. The Italian delegate had expressed a desire to eat alone. Claude's biggest regret was that it was winter, they wouldn't be able to enjoy the lovely gardens.

The delicate tones of Chopin were reassuring. All was peace in the air-cooled kitchen.

"The canapés were a great success," Claude announced, *"Faahb-ulous,* according to the American m'mselle!"

"That's *fan-taas-tique,"* Marc's laughter bordered on hysteria. "Your American accent is improving."

"We're about to light the candles in the dining-room. I thought you might like to see it before dinner."

Warning the two trainees not to take their eyes off the bubbling pots, the two chefs, in their starched white uniforms, joined Claude. Some of the tables were round, others square. That lent an air of individuality to the room as did the alternating colours of the cloths. Flickering candlelight bathed the room in a soft glow enhancing sparkling crystal and gleaming silverware.

"It looks wonderful, M Claude," said Jeanne who had taken time from her housekeeping duties to see the finished product. She too called him Monsieur if they were not alone. During their setting-up period, Jeanne had proved herself to have organisational skills which Claude had never suspected. She installed a system of keeping linens in check. She made sure that all the uniforms fitted. She arranged for a local firm to collect and deliver the laundry, insisting that everything must be perfect for M Claude. Jeanne trained the young women who'd be responsible for keeping the château squeaky clean. "No dust will be allowed in M Claude's château," she warned them.

There hadn't been a single hitch, even by Claude's critical standards. The waiters moved about the room with quiet efficiency, they were friendly but not intrusive. Each course brought raves from the Americans, four of whom had joined forces. Snippy, the American m'mselle, led the praise and Claude, whose ear was becoming attuned to her strange turn of phrase, smiled benignly at her. The two journalists were generous to ecstatic, but Claude refused to get excited. He'd rather wait for their reviews.

They gathered together in the cheerful salon to drink coffee from delicate demi-tasses. Claude moved around offering a tray of perfectly arranged petit-fours. He was anxious to hear their comments.

"He'll never keep this up," a cynical voice remarked as they sipped their liqueurs. "That was a superb meal."

He must remember all their comments and

report them to Marc.

As Claude left the room, Joseph ran towards him, a look of alarm on his face.

"It's Thierry Thibault, he's outside, he's shouting and he's drunk."

Claude stopped dead in his tracks, this could be disastrous. Thierry must have escaped from his father and wanted to pick another row.

"Quick, get Marc and a couple of the others, we can't allow him into the château."

"What do you want?" Claude asked, his voice icy.

"I want you - you murderer," Thierry shouted, slurring his words.

"You're drunk. Please stop talking nonsense and get off my property." Claude's legs trembled with fear and suppressed anger. He must not allow this man to be heard inside the building.

"Do you know where I was today?" Thierry said belligerently. "I was at my father's funeral."

Claude gasped. "Pierre? Dead?" he replied. "When? I can't believe it - Pierre?"

He could hear the sound of running feet and turned. "Pierre has died," Claude repeated. Of the four men who ran from the château, Marc and Joseph were the only two who knew who Pierre was.

"Do you want me to phone the police?" Didier asked, he was clutching an evil-looking meat cleaver in his upraised hand.

"No, wait," Claude said.

"Yes, wait. You might like to hear how my father was murdered by this man - your boss?"

"Don't talk rubbish," Marc said sharply, "Monsieur Claude was nowhere near your father.

But I'm very sorry to hear your terrible news, Thierry. I'm sure we all are."

"It's too late to be sorry now, isn't it? What do you say, Claude, are you sorry too? Sorry that you murdered my father, sorry you left him on his own without a word of warning, sorry he dropped dead from exhaustion. Tell me how sorry you are Claude, I can't hear you." Weaving unsteadily, a hand cupped to his ear, he moved towards Claude.

Didier stepped between them. Even in his drunken state, Thierry could see the glint of the moon on the metal blade. Claude stood silently, stunned by the news of Pierre's death.

"You'd better leave," Joseph suggested quietly. "You're upset, don't make matters worse."

"Upset? *Upset?*" Thierry screeched. "Is that how you put it? This man ..." he pointed a shaking finger at Claude, "he killed my father. Not with a knife or a gun, oh no, it was far more subtle than that. He ruined him, destroyed him, left him alone to cope."

"Where were you while all this 'alone' was happening?" Marc demanded angrily, "out chasing girls in your sports car? And, don't you forget it, Monsieur Claude *offered* to stay - your answer was a punch in the face."

"Ignore him," Claude said. "We're not going to go over all that again. Leave now, Thierry, and whatever you may think, I do regret that your father has died."

"You *will* regret it, more than you know. Some day when you least expect it, you'll pay, *Monsieur Claude.*"

"See him to his car," Claude ordered firmly.

"Don't attempt to come here again, Thierry."

"Joseph, from now on we'll keep the gates closed at all times. I'll arrange to have locks fitted on Monday. We'll have a viewing screen installed, then the gates can be opened from inside the château too."

The sound of the car's engine screeched through the quiet garden as Thierry drove away. They winced as they heard the scraping of metal against metal.

"You'd better check that he didn't paste himself to the gates," Claude instructed.

"I'll go with you, just in case," Didier offered, swinging the cleaver through the air. "If he's still there, he won't argue with this."

Stooping to pick up a leaf from the step, Claude returned to his guests. He was still shaking.

"Do you think it was my fault?" Claude asked. He gulped the cognac Marc had poured for him.

"You *know* it isn't, I'm surprised you even ask. It's over a year now since we left the hotel and if they couldn't work things out in that time, too bad. Don't forget the reason you left. They thought nothing of using you," Marc reminded him, indignantly.

Claude nodded, "I suppose you're right. But it's a shock. Poor Pierre. His biggest sin was loving that useless son of his too much and where did it get him? I must admit, Marc, I'd like to know what really happened."

"I'll try and find out. I'm curious too."

Claude left the main château, unhappy and deflated. The row with Thierry had robbed him of the triumph of his success. The two-storey

circular turret had proved to be the perfect home
for him. It was joined to the main building by a
short corridor and it provided him with both
privacy and proximity. The upper floor had
yielded enough space for a large bedroom and
bathroom. There was ample room on the ground
floor for relaxing and dining. Claude hoped
before long to knock out the windows and
replace them with a door leading to a large
terrace. He'd bought the marble but the work
would have to wait. A call from his bank
manager had warned him that his funds were
getting low. "Take care, Claude," he cautioned.
"You must slow down now, recoup some of your
expenses." He was acting as a friend as well as
an adviser. He'd felt it his duty to curb Claude's
dreams. There wasn't a doubt in his mind that the
château would become everything Claude hoped
it would. But slowly. Carefully and slowly.

Claude had taken heed of the warning. Quality
not quantity had become his maxim but he ached
to do everything - now.

He waved from the steps as the last of the
guests climbed into the limousine. Joseph
grinned at him cheekily as he walked to the
driver's door. Tonight they would celebrate. If the
hard-bitten critics had been telling the truth then
the Château d'Albion would be well and
magnificently launched.

CHAPTER EIGHTY-FIVE

It was a long wait. Weeks of nail-biting anticipation interspersed with despondency. Had his policy of low-key exclusivity been foolhardy? Claude began to doubt his own wisdom.

"M Claude, there's a telephone call for you from the United States," the attractive receptionist said. Covering the receiver with her hand, she whispered. "M'mselle Snippy!"

"Bonjour M'mselle Snippy."

"Bonjour. Hey, drop the m'mselle bit. How are you Claude?" She didn't wait for his reply. "I've been raving about your château back here in the States and a friend of mine is keen to take over the whole shmeer for a long weekend in June. Can do?"

Did she mean that her friend would like to book all the rooms in the château? wondered Claude. I must learn these expressions.

"I'm sure that the shmeer will be available in June, just let me consult the diary."

Marie-Claire grinned at him as she opened the big black book.

"That would be satis ... Can do, Snippy." He was learning already.

"Faahb-ulous," she enthused, "here's the deal. They want to fly their closest friends to France to celebrate their fifth wedding anniversary. You can get back to me and tell me how many people you can accommodate and I'll take it from there, OK?"

"I can tell you now. We have eighteen rooms at the moment - so we can take thirty-six people if they are sharing."

"Pencil in thirty-five, I'm not sharing with anyone."

"You are coming too? I am very pleased to hear that."

"You bet I am, I'm not passing up the chance to gorge on all that wonderful food! And Claude, my friend is loaded, don't be afraid to order the best. I'll confirm in a couple of days. Would you like a deposit?"

"I think that would be desirable," Claude agreed.

"Leave it with me. And Claude, you owe me one."

With a click the line went dead. Claude scratched his head, what did he owe her?

They scanned the magazines and journals eagerly for articles about the château. The reviews were better than they dared hope for. A couple of the journalists wondered sceptically if the standards set during their stay could be maintained. Cyrus Hertz, Snippy's companion, sent a copy of his exclusive travel publication and was unstinting in his praise. Even the British journalist recommended the château unreservedly. One of the French contingent waxed lyrical about the food and wines. He was in fact the magazine's restaurant critic. He'd been standing in for the travel journalist who was touring the Far East. Marc and Didier positively swelled with pride. As yet, the lone Italian had failed to report.

The full complement of staff numbered twenty-three. Fifteen of them lived in the staff wing, the rest were daily or part-time workers. Claude had been very careful to ask residential staff how they would like the stables converted. They'd opted to have one large communal room. Claude carried out their wishes to the letter. He added a wing to the stables which now housed bedrooms and bathrooms and fenced off a section of garden for their private use. Jules planted the enclosed garden and already tiny snippets of green were visible.

The bookings began to trickle in and the pages of the diary lost their pristine stiffness. They were regretful but proud to refuse a booking for the June weekend. "We're fully booked, I'm afraid," Marie-Claire fought to keep the victorious note out of her voice. "Yes, that's available, first weekend in July. Thank you."

Arrangements for the fifth anniversary weekend were under control. Nothing but the best, Snippy advised in her long detailed call. The cheque for the deposit put a smile on the bank manager's face. "Now that's more like it," he said.

Snippy would arrive two days before the rest of the party, to talk over last minute details. Jeanne checked that her room was filled with flowers. She'd put the ice cooler with its bottle of Roederer Cristal champagne in the room just before Snippy arrived. Marc suggested that she and Claude should have dinner in his apartment as the dining-room was quiet that night.

"It's a *swell* idea," Claude said, practising his American vocabulary.

The dinner was an unqualified success. Claude consulted his book. Snippy loved veal.

"Veal it is," Marc agreed.

"This veal is sublime," Snippy raved, helping herself to a second portion. Didier had, in her honour, produced a tarte au citron, frothy and sharp. She had refused to eat the tiny jug, fashioned from chocolate, which held the crème fraîche. "It's out of sight," Snippy said holding it up gently. Seeing Claude's puzzled look she explained.

There were several things that Claude didn't understand.

"May I ask, why did *you* make all the arrangements for the weekend?"

"That's what I do. My firm, No Worry Inc., organises social events - from christenings to funerals and everything in between. Mike Noble, as you know, wants this weekend to be a complete surprise for his wife so he hired us to come up with something different. The château was something else, so I thought, why not? How different can you get! End of story."

"I'm pleased you thought that way," Claude said. "I wanted to ask you something else. You said on the telephone that I owed you one - can you tell me please, what is it that I owe you?"

Snippy smiled, breaking off a little piece of the chocolate jug. It was no use trying, she couldn't resist it. "It means I've done you a favour so you owe me one in return. But hey, after tonight and that wonderful meal you're all paid up. I hope the Nobles will be the first of many clients I send you."

"In that case, I will owe you more than one!"

Anne Schulman

"Sure will, and I'll collect too."

"You must consider yourself my guest at the château whenever you care to visit."

Claude hadn't liked the American girl when he first met her. She'd seemed brittle and shallow but as the opening weekend had progressed she'd endeared herself to all the staff. In her open way she had confided in Claudine that if Cyrus Hertz hadn't come up with a proposal by the end of her stay, she was going to dump him. Claude didn't dare to mention his name.

"Did you see Cy's review?" she asked as if reading his mind.

"It was very flattering."

"He was crazy about the whole shebang," she said bluntly, eyeing the other chocolate container. "May I?" Claude passed it to her with a smile. How did she manage to stay so slim?

"Will M Hertz come to France again soon?" He was curious to know if she'd carried out her threat.

"No idea. I don't return his calls anymore," she explained simply. "The bum kept me on a string long enough. He's history now."

Claude presumed the affair was at an end.

It was well past midnight when Snippy yawned and said, "I'm bushed."

Claude had learnt a lot from the forthright girl. "Never fail to write everything down, that's my motto. Every detail about everyone. For instance - take me - *Snippy is a greedy pig, she loves veal, adores chocolate. She talks non-stop and is a pain in the butt,*" she smiled, tapping herself on her rump. "See what I mean?"

Claude laughed. "I do see. I've kept a record

of guests' likes and dislikes. Those black books, over there," he pointed to the neat row of official-looking ledgers, "they contain just such details."

"I don't suppose they hold the secret of Marc's veal?"

"No, but I am sure he would give you the recipe." Claude frowned. He was not at all sure that he would.

Claude knew that Snippy had done her job well when a fleet of limousines arrived in a steady stream. He must make a note of the firm who supplied them. Within minutes the sound of laughter rang around the château. Terri Noble confided in Jeanne, who was unpacking for her, that she'd been delighted to discover so many of her friends had come to wish them bon voyage.

"When Mike and I boarded the plane, I couldn't believe it, there they all were, twenty-eight of them, and us. The party started right there and then, but no one would tell me where we were going, not even the stewardesses. It was only when the landing announcement was made that I discovered we were in France!" Jeanne's eyes were positively misty, she thought it was incredibly romantic.

The Americans were determined to make the most of this luxurious break. Dinner that night was served on the terrace for the first time. The weather was balmy and the sky starlit. The Nobles and their friends forgot their jet-lag and enjoyed themselves energetically. Marc excelled himself. Compliments flew. Waiters were despatched to the kitchens with demands for various recipes. The mellow wine began to take its toll. They tried hard to keep the party going but, one after another, the weary travellers succumbed to the temptation of a night's sleep.

Everyone was gathered in the foyer early next morning. Picnic hampers were stacked in the back of the limousines, the wines in ice-cooled boxes. Snippy had planned a day of sightseeing while the château prepared for the party.

As dusk fell, strings of coloured lights leading from the château to the garden terrace - which was cantilevered from the cliff overlooking the sea - cast a magical glow on the gardens. Spotlights nestled by the base of the trees. Candles, shielded from any vestige of breeze by glass lanterns, supplemented the moonlight.

Claude purred with satisfaction. He had dreamt of this moment. The guests were beautifully dressed, men in white dinner jackets, ladies in flowing dresses whose colours blended subtly like a bouquet of exotic blooms. A green and white striped awning, with its supporting pillars hidden by fragrant night-scented flowers, set the stage for the outdoor dining-room with its pink-covered tables and green and white chairs. The huge charcoal grills were hot, ready for the delicate skewers of seafood, which would be cooked at the last minute. A buzz of appreciation spread throughout the moonlit terrace.

"Dinner is served," Claude announced. They needed no urging. The succulent seafood with its delicate sauce brought groans of delight. "We've got to try this on the barbecue back home," said a muffled voice.

"Bouef en croûte." The waiters assigned to each table presented a dish of golden pastry before removing it to the burners to be carved. The tender beef with its garnish of truffles and pâté brought a fresh onslaught of praise. "I think I've died and gone to heaven," one man sighed. Sounds around him of, "Um and ah," were heard as petits pois and crisp puffs of potato were added to the plates. A round of spontaneous applause greeted Marc and Didier as the celebration cake came into view, a towering pyramid of choux buns glistening with spun sugar. The smell of freshly brewed coffee wafted on the air. The cream for the coffee was contained in tiny chocolate jugs - Didier's trademark. The guests clamoured to know how Didier made the jugs. Snippy begged him to give a demonstration the following day. Looking first at Marc who nodded his assent, then at Claude, Didier shyly agreed.

"Tomorrow afternoon at three o'clock?" Grateful applause followed that announcement.

The chefs left the terrace and the happy party resumed their conversation. All the lights, except those on the path, were extinguished. The sound of a rumba could be heard from somewhere in the hidden darkness. Suddenly the path was floodlit from the ground. Tall, exotic girls in single file swayed to the incessant beat of the music as they came down the path towards the terrace, their sequinned turbans and frilled trains glittering in the coloured lights. A rhythmic throb echoed over the quiet sea. The girls held out their hands to any of the men who would join them on the floor cleared for dancing. Soon everyone joined in and danced to the Latin-American rhythm. Shaking jewelled maracas the girls shimmied back towards the château. The applause of the guests lasted until they were out of sight. After an hour the band took a break and was instantly replaced by a lively trio. The two bands alternated every hour until, at four o'clock, the party gave up the ghost and retired for what was left of the night.

With less exuberance than the previous morning the guests wandered down to the dining-room terrace to enjoy a late breakfast of coffee or hot chocolate with fresh croissants. Wisely, Snippy had made no plans for the day. She'd known that the party would go on into the early hours. The sunbeds, in pairs under the trees, were spaced for privacy and tranquillity. But gradually they were moved into a huge circle and, from the château, roars of laughter could be heard. The terrace bore no signs of the night's entertainment and the big grills again glowed in readiness for lunch. Claude laughed as he watched the guests straggle towards the open air restaurant. They'd been lured by the aroma of herbs and garlic streaming towards them in an invisible ribbon. Pledged to gastronomic celibacy, one by one their resolve weakened as they sheepishly followed each other to the source of temptation.

"Just fruit and a salad for me," one skeletally-thin girl vowed.

"You could do with some meat on those bones," her husband remarked. "You can go back to your air and lettuce leaf diet when you're home."

Didier postponed his demonstration until four o'clock, at Snippy's suggestion. "You won't hear a sound from them till then - except snoring," she grinned.

When they arrived en masse in the air-cooled kitchen, Didier was overwhelmed. Waiters rushed around crowding more chairs into the available space. The guests watched, fascinated, as the chocolate was tempered and then cooled to the right temperature. As he covered the moulds, Didier explained in halting English the importance of using the right materials, the best chocolate and the need for patience before removing the little jugs.

"I think I'll send for some of yours, Didier," Terri Noble groaned.

"It needs practice," Didier responded, deftly removing a perfect jug from the mould and handing it to her. "Now I'll show you how to make the little swirls you all admired."

He used a piping bag to trace a decorative fine stream of chocolate over the waxed paper. Circles, stars, initials, squares appeared in perfect formation.

"What about those long curls? They're wonderful. Can you show us how they're done?" someone asked.

"Of course," said Didier, warmed by their admiration. He took a marble slab from the rack. They crowded about him as he scraped and moved the chocolate around and then returned it to the double saucepan. Finally satisfied he poured it on to the clean slab. Nobody spoke. He dragged a sharp spatula at an angle along the block of chocolate until it formed long rolled curls which he expertly flicked to one side. In seconds he had cleared the hardening chocolate and invited everyone to help themselves. In even fewer seconds the slab was bare. He blushed as the crowd gave him a round of applause.

Snippy organised a visit to the casino in Antibes.

"How about a buffet?" Marc suggested.

"That's a great idea, they can eat either before or after the casino," Snippy agreed.

To the château staff's amusement, they did both.

In spite of all the nerve-racking hard work and anxiety, they were sad to see the light-hearted group leave. The guests promised they'd be back again and would recommend the château to their friends. Clutching brochures and tariffs, a few faces paled when they saw the prices. Terri and Mike Noble thanked everyone profusely, and handed out huge tips.

"Book us in for our tenth," Mike Noble said, "you know the date."

Snippy was travelling back to the States with them. Claude knew he'd miss her funny speech and friendly manner. She hugged him warmly which made him feel a little embarrassed.

"You will be my welcome guest whenever you choose to return," Claude insisted.

"The weekend was faahb-ulous and no, you don't owe me one!" she whispered. "But Claude, honey, get that swimming-pool built, pronto." She climbed into the last of the cars and was gone.

"It's so quiet," Claudine said, as they sat round the big table in the staff room.

"I never thought I'd miss M'mselle Snippy," Claude admitted.

Intrigue

There were no guests in the hotel that night. Claude suggested that Marc and Didier need not cook, there was more than enough food left over from the buffet. Relaxed, they sat around the table and discussed the weekend, the guests and their comments.

"We must talk about our problems," Claude said, "who'd like to start?"

"I will," Jeanne said. "It's the hot water, Monsieur."

"Yes, I noticed that too. I've already telephoned to the builders, we must add more tanks. When everyone bathed and showered at one time, the water almost ran out completely. And remember, not every room was in use."

"Anything else?"

Again Jeanne spoke. "I think we need to buy more towels. If we change them twice a day as we planned and the château is fully booked, we'll be short at the weekends."

"Make a list of what we need then," Claude nodded. "We must have plenty of spares."

"Should we order more bathrobes?" Claudine asked softly.

As one, their heads turned. She was still very shy and gentle. They weren't used to hearing her voice an opinion. "The American ladies love the gowns instead of towels."

"You're right Claudine, I'll look into that."

"What about broken glasses?" a red-haired waiter queried. "People wander around the garden terrace barefooted and it's not always possible to sweep up the broken pieces."

"That's true," Claude agreed. "You're not suggesting we use thick glasses, are you?"

The waiter had been thinking exactly along those lines but Claude's look of horror made him back down. "I don't really know, but I feel it's dangerous as it is."

"Anything else apart from the problem with the glasses?" Claude queried.

"Nothing." Marc said, yawning.

"Marc, I'd like to talk for a minute," Claude said. Leaving the others they walked outside and sat in the garden. "Before M'mselle Snippy left, she said I should build a swimming-pool. If we do, we'll make no profit for a year at least. What do you think?"

"She's right, Claude. I didn't like to suggest it. I know finances are tight. But it's difficult to get to the beach. I know those steps are only temporary but most people would prefer a pool to the beach anyway, especially if they have children. I'd build it straight away. It should be ready well before next season."

"You realise that you'll have no bonus if we do this?"

"With God's blessing, we'll be here for many years. What does one year matter, or even two or three?"

"I'm a lucky man to have you as a friend, Marc," Claude said in a rare show of affection.

CHAPTER EIGHTY-SIX

Claude closed the pages of his big black book. What tales they told, his books. It was a diary of his guests. Every guest that had stayed at the château was faithfully recorded between their black covers. Their foibles were noted, what room they liked, their taste in food, which wines they favoured and just about everything else he could think of that would make future visits ideal. He was well aware that he was considered eccentric, obsessive perhaps, but anything short of perfection hurt him and wounded his heart. There were four books now all written with black ink in his neat handwriting. Hidden amongst their pages, three or four red entries. Indulging himself he took out the other three books and brought them to his desk, piling them neatly in a stack.

The opening weekend. All so long ago, Claude sighed. There were the menus, journalists' comments, suggestions - mostly Snippy's, and a record of the château's problems. The Italian journalist - the first of Claude's red entries - had never published his article. Any name entered in red ink meant a guest would no longer be welcome at the château should they ever try to return. He shivered involuntarily as Thierry Thibault's name came to mind, that drunken haranguing in the garden. Many years later they had come face to face in Cannes. Bloated and weaving slightly he had approached Claude.

"Ah! Monsieur Claude. Have you destroyed

anyone else lately, Claude?"

Claude had backed away. He hated confrontation. "Don't forget my promise, I haven't," Thierry warned, as he staggered away. It had taken Claude days to recover from that meeting.

Every detail of the Nobles' anniversary party weekend was noted. That had taken up several pages. And what a shock it was when, four months later, Snippy had told him that the couple had split up.

The O'Neills. They were amongst the few guests to be awarded his three-star rating. Gabrielle had won his heart with her warm affectionate ways. She'd been the first person to use the swimming-pool, he remembered as he read his comments. There had been no surprises on the dessert menus whenever Gabrielle was due to visit the château. Marc and Didier actually allowed her to help them in the kitchen when the weather was bad, and that was recorded too.

Claude smiled gratefully as he flicked the pages. Snippy had been as good as her word. She'd sent him "packages" of eligible and smart clients, mostly in the quiet months.

Hers had been the first wedding held at the château. He could still remember the day she called to give him the news.

"Hi Claude. I have a surprise for you, I'm getting married." Snippy never wasted any time getting to the point.

"That's wonderful news! I am so pleased for you." Claude's congratulations were sincere.

"How about coming to the States in May for the wedding?"

"I wish I could, but May is a busy month here," Claude said regretfully. He'd love to go to America.

"Darn it. I have so little family and I would've loved it if you could have given me away."

Claude wondered for a moment why she should want to be given away and then he understood. She sounded so disappointed, but it would be impossible for him to leave the château.

"Snippy, I have an idea for you. Why not have your wedding here? Then I could do as you ask - give you away. It would give us all great pleasure."

"I couldn't … I … thank you Claude, you can't be serious."

"I do mean it, will you think about it?"

"Thanks Claude, but you've done enough. I couldn't accept that."

"Snippy, talk to …"

"Cy, Cyrus J Hertz," she supplied.

"You finally answered his calls?" Claude laughed.

"Big deal, so?" she said defensively.

"Talk to him, Snippy."

"OK. Call you tomorrow."

Claudine had been delighted to hear the news. "She's not as strong as she pretends. Wouldn't it be wonderful? M'mselle Snippy, married here."

When Snippy didn't call the next day, Claude made one of his rare transatlantic calls. "Snippy, this is Claude. What have you decided? Everyone is anxious to know."

"It's too much, Claude. I spoke to Cyrus … "

"And what did he say?" Claude asked impatiently.

"He thought it was an incredible idea."

"So why did you not telephone? Don't you like the idea?"

"I love it, it's a beautiful thought, but hey, it's over the top."

He wasn't prepared to waste money arguing long distance. "Let me have the date and tell me how many people will come with you. This time *we'll* do the arranging."

It had been a perfect day. They were married in the garden. Marc and Didier excelled themselves. Claude invited the other guests to join in the celebrations. Gabrielle O'Neill, then a pretty teenager, had strewn rose petals in front of the bride. Snippy clung nervously to Claude's arm as they walked along the red carpet to the flowered altar. She looked beautiful but pale in a blush-pink dress. Immaculately attired in a dark formal suit, Claude took his duties seriously. He handed the bride to her beaming bridegroom and stepped back. He listened intently to the service. The wedding reception had been held on the lawn. Snippy always loved to eat outside.

The happy pair had spent ten days at the château. From his usual vantage point at the top of the steps, Claude watched Joseph drive them away. She and Gabrielle always took a little of his sunshine with them when they left.

He stopped as he saw another red entry, one which had caused a lot of heartache at the time. A guest, a chic Parisienne, reported a blouse missing. Puzzled, Claude had gone with her to her room. Together they searched through her wardrobe, under the beds, in her suitcases but there was no sign of the missing garment. He asked if it could have been sent in error to the cleaners, but neither Claudine nor Jeanne had sent anything belonging to Madame for laundering. It was a mystery. The following day, Joseph told him that M Holt in room four had reported that his pen, always kept on the table beside his bed, had also gone. Before Claude could talk to the man, the phone on the reception desk rang.

"Monsieur Claude? This is Marcie Oppenheim, could you check if I left a pair of red shoes outside my door to be cleaned. They seem to have vanished."

Claude picked up the sheet of paper that stated which shoes belonged to what room. He saw no record of Mme Oppenheim's shoes.

"No, there were only three pairs altogether last night," insisted Paul, the young porter. "I returned them myself early this morning."

A knot formed in Claude's stomach. He knew his staff were completely innocent, but who was responsible? Each room had been thoroughly checked. A pen might have fallen into the wastepaper basket but a search of the big refuse sacks failed to produce a result. The shoes were not to be found, nor was the blouse. Claude called a meeting of all his staff and told them what had happened. "Frankly I don't know what to do. We've never had a problem like this before."

"It's bad for us," said one of the cleaning girls.

"It's bad for all of us," Claude corrected her. "I must emphasise that in no way do I suspect anyone here any more than I suspect myself."

"Why not call in the police?" Joseph suggested.

"No, I don't want to do that, think of the château's reputation. We must wait for a day or two."

"Could a stranger have entered the château without us seeing them?" Claudine asked.

"I doubt it," Claude replied. "The gates are always locked. Even if an intruder sneaked in, there's always someone around. A stranger would be noticed immediately."

"Maybe we should do as you suggest, M Claude," Marc said. "Wait a day or so. Everyone should be vigilant, that way we might discover something - anything - that would solve this mystery."

A further complaint was launched. This time it was a bottle of perfume. An air of despondency spread through the château. The staff snapped at one another and at Claude. Even Joseph's sunny smile disappeared. But there was still no solution. Claude couldn't understand it. No jewellery was missing, or anything of great value.

"We must compensate everyone fully, it's all we can do. But what about the château's reputation?" Claude fretted.

"You're right. I don't know what to suggest. It's affecting everyone - badly," Marc replied dejectedly.

Joseph had come into the kitchen looking glum. "Monsieur, Ambassadeur Renault wants to speak to you."

The three men looked at one another and Claude's heart went right down to the tips of his gleaming shoes. "There's no escaping it, if someone else has been robbed we don't have a choice. The police must be called in, things have

Intrigue

gone too far." Claude's face was wreathed in misery.

The other two agreed. "It's a sad day for the Château d'Albion. But you mustn't allow this to get you down," Marc urged.

Claude entered his office and shook hands politely with the distinguished diplomat.

"Please," he said, as he pulled out a chair. At a quick glance Claude could detect more trouble, serious this time perhaps.

"I wish to speak to you on a delicate matter, Monsieur Claude." So his guess had been correct. He would hear the Ambassador out then explain that he intended calling in the police.

"My wife," the ambassador began, "she hasn't been well recently. The thing is, she has developed an unfortunate illness."

Claude had not been aware that Madame had been ill but he offered his sympathy anyway.

"No, it's not that kind of illness. Quite frankly, she has begun to take things from people, things that belong to them. This is so embarrassing. I heard that several items were stolen so I searched my wife's wardrobes and suitcases. I'm afraid it is my wife who's to blame, Monsieur."

Claude's emotions ran riot. Relief, anger, thankfulness, pity.

"I can only offer you my deepest apologies and those of my wife. This isn't the first time it's happened and I suppose it won't be the last. Could I ask you … what do you intend to do?"

"I don't know," Claude answered truthfully. He was still shocked by the grey-faced man's revelation.

"I know. It comes as a shock. Whatever you

decide, will you let me know?"

"Of course. But how did she manage to get into the rooms?"

"At first she wouldn't tell me but apparently you keep a spare key in the cupboard, hidden behind the linens. Is that correct?"

"No. The spare key is kept here in my office for emergencies." Claude opened a drawer and searched for the key. "It's not here," he said, "it's always at the front of the drawer. See for yourself, there are no keys."

The ambassador sat helplessly in his chair. "Then she hid it in the linen cupboard," he said wearily. "It's so difficult, I don't know what to do. It will ruin us both, this sickness."

Like a trigger, the word *ruin* acted on Claude's brain. "You have ruined us..." Thierry Thibault's accusation echoed loudly. *Ruin.* Never again would anyone accuse Claude of that. He would not be the cause of the ambassador's destruction.

"I have decided, M Ambassadeur. There will be no need for you to worry, about me, that is. It's best that you leave the château as soon as possible. But I'd like to tell my staff the truth. All this has caused them considerable distress."

"You've been very kind and I thank you for it. Of course you should tell your staff. If you'll allow me, I will tell them myself."

The staff grouped quietly in the office, wondering what M Claude had to tell them. Claude admired the ambassador's courage as he explained the circumstances. He was a gentleman and a diplomat, normally Claude would have awarded him three stars.

Claude had taken his usual place of salute at

the top of the steps. He could be a gentleman too. He had looked into Madame's eyes. They were clear and untroubled like the eyes of an innocent child.

The second book on the pile brought a smile to his face as he read the first entry. That had been another shock, but a pleasant one. Claude had suspected nothing out of the ordinary in the staff's relationships with each other. He was astonished when Marc took him aside one day and told him that he and Claudine were engaged.

"You're a close one," Claude accused.

"I knew you'd say that," Marc laughed. "We only decided last night, it is very sudden. You're the first to know." They'd shared most things and Marc knew this would be a surprise to Claude. It had surprised Marc too.

"When is the wedding? I presume you will tell me that?"

"Come on, Claude, after all we only made up our minds last night."

"Well, when is it to be?" He supposed Marc was right, and he *was* the first to know.

"When else?" Marc grinned.

"February?"

"Of course."

The château closed for the month of February every year. That was the time when Claude arranged for any necessary repairs or refurbishing. He stayed at the château on his own, sustained by a freezer crammed with food prepared by Marc and Didier. It was a time to catch up on his reading, to walk undisturbed through the rooms, noting in a small book improvements that could be made. As the years passed his notes had grown shorter.

None of the staff left the château till after the wedding. Didier offered to do the catering for the reception, he refused Marc's help. Jules and his wife and Claudine's younger brother all stayed at the château the night before the wedding. Marc's father was too ill to attend. Joseph collected Marc's mother early that morning so that she could take part in the excitement building up to the great moment. The château had never looked so beautiful. Jules begged, borrowed and stole every scrap of greenhouse space for miles around in order to force unseasonable blooms for his daughter's marriage. Claudine chose a lemon and white theme. Jeanne bought metres of material in both colours and spent happy evenings whirring away at her machine making two-coloured tablecloths and napkins. Claude snapped his mouth shut tightly when he noticed an odd crooked seam.

He toasted the happy couple with great ceremony. Speechmaking had become a little easier for him by then.

Claudine was a radiant bride, her dress was every girl's dream. Marc, handsome in his black suit, had to exercise every ounce of his willpower to stay at the table. Someone had posted a large notice on the door of the kitchen:

No Admittance to the Bride or Groom.

Claude had straightened it and added another piece of sticky tape.

Didier coped beautifully with his self-appointed labour of love. The wedding cake had been a mystery at first. It was a small but perfect replica of the Hawaiian Islands. Claudine was puzzled by this until everyone began chanting, swaying their hips and making snaking gestures with their arms. Then she realised what it all meant. She flung her arms around Marc. "I can't believe it! What a wonderful place for a honeymoon."

Didier and one of the trainee chefs carried in his speciality, a pyramid, made of Claudine's favourite - meringue. It was two metres high, scattered with silver almonds and good luck charms.

"Tradition says you have to eat it all yourself," Didier teased, kissing the bride on her cheek.

They all stood on the steps to wave the couple goodbye. What a surprise they'd have the following day when Snippy and Cy met them at the airport in New York. Marc and Claudine had no idea Snippy knew about the wedding. Marc had left the bookings for the islands to Claude and he in turn had contacted Snippy.

"No problem, that's just my thing," she offered immediately. "I'll see they get royal treatment. Call you."

The following day she phoned to confirm the arrangements. "They'll be upgraded wherever they stay, except at my house! We want to show them around New York for a couple of days. If they notice the discrepancies of the dates for the islands, tell them you'll fix it. *Ciao,* Claude."

But Marc hadn't noticed and Claudine hadn't seen the tickets at all.

The following morning the builders arrived. They began the extension - a bedroom, bathroom and living room for the couple. Marc mentioned in passing that their rooms would be a little cramped but Claude brushed that aside. He suggested they should see what could be done when the newlyweds returned from honeymoon.

❋ ❋ ❋

There were two red-ink names in the book, one a pop star who had torn his room apart, half-crazed on drugs. Furious, Claude had faced him.

"Name your price, old son, any amount of dosh you want. Just don't call the gendarmes," he pleaded.

"Do what he says, make him pay for this," Marc advised. "You'll never see him again."

Claude wrote a figure on a sheet of paper. It was enough to redecorate three rooms.

The scrawny young pop star had smiled and written the cheque. Claude slipped it into his drawer and tried to warn him of the damage he was doing to himself, never mind the château. He laughed uproariously. "Ta for the warning, but it's OK, I can kick the habit anytime. Cheers."

Joseph escorted the brash performer to his limousine. It was the first time Claude simply could not bring himself to stand on the pink marble steps. He'd better add the cheque to the lodgements. He took it from the drawer. His eyes opened wide when he read the pop star's error, he'd added one zero too many. Looking again, Claude realised there was no mistake - the sum was written in words too. Claude bought his first good painting with that money. After, and only after, he'd given Marc a percentage.

The second and more serious offender inked out of the château's future existence was one of the most charming ladies that Claude had ever met. She'd been titled too. She had entertained the cream of society at the château. Her final bill had been enormous. She always ordered the most expensive wines and champagnes. Everyone adored her, she was definitely three-star quality. A week later the myth exploded when the police arrived at the château in force, armed with picks and shovels.

"The English Milady is no more titled than I am," the chief of police told Claude. "Betsy Briggs is her name, she's the leader of a pack of jewel thieves."

He gave Claude time for the news to sink in.

"Did she eat here at the château often?" another policeman asked.

"Yes, I suppose she did. Why?"

"Did she have guests here to dinner?"

"Yes, often."

"That's what we thought."

"Can't you tell me more about this?" Claude was uneasy. The château had never been involved in a scandal and he didn't want it to happen now. He pressed the intercom on his desk and asked Marc to come to the office. By the time Marc arrived, Claude was paper white.

"I suppose it'll do no harm to tell you this. We have to dig up your garden anyway."

Claude was appalled. "Why?" he demanded.

"Because we think that they may have hidden their stolen jewels there."

"What's going on?" asked Marc.

Claude explained. It wasn't funny, but Claude's lips quirked slightly as he watched his friend. Open and shut, open and then open wider went his lips. Marc was like a fish out of water.

"While the lady was dining here, one of her accomplices would rob a residence. She was pretty smart. She knew the best targets - wealthy people in rented villas, or people with only a small staff. There were lots of gala nights, and many private parties. And women love to flaunt their jewels. Her accomplices were a man and a woman. The man was unbelievably handsome and the girl was beautiful. They'd turn up at a selected villa, lost and needing help. While the girl kept a manservant enthralled her partner would enter the house and ransack it, and vice versa. We suspect that all this happened while the owners of the villa were here in your château as her guests."

"I'm amazed," Claude said, "she was so charming."

"So I'm told. But that brings me to my next point. None of their cache has been found and we think that they may have hidden it here in the grounds of the château."

"That's just not possible," Claude interjected. "We'd know if anything had been disturbed."

"Do you check every day, do you look under trees? Why should you?"

Claude knew that was true. They wouldn't. "Marc, call Jules. He's our head groundsman, he'd know if anything has been disturbed."

Jules had noticed nothing unusual, but he recognised one of the policeman, leaning against his shovel, as a neighbour. He left the château and had a word with the man. By the time they had all reached the garden Jules, with the aid of his friend, persuaded them to let him do any digging that had to be done. He could tell immediately if anything had been touched. For two days Jules obligingly dug any suspect patches.

"Surely they'd have taken their haul with them?" Claude reasoned.

When they were finally satisfied that there was nothing to be found in the gardens the police left with a minimum amount of damage to Jules' prized beds.

Claude took his red pen and, with customary neatness, added the lovely English "Lady" to the banned list.

The last of the books held no bad memories. Quite the opposite. It recorded the addition of six luxurious suites, an extension of the dining-room terrace and a recreation room with a small galley kitchen for the staff.

Claude had been bitten by the collecting bug. He was never one to do things by halves and he'd become an addict after he'd bought his first painting. He combed the galleries and antique shops. Whenever he found something he liked his friend Henri Ducroix, the artist, would advise him whether it was good value or not. He was a strange man, Henri. Once when Claude discovered a really good painting, Henri had been almost angry. "Don't buy it," he said, but he wouldn't give Claude a reason. Still, Claude trusted Henri and respected his opinion.

Claude subscribed to several antique collectors' journals. He read them from cover to cover. A little jewelled clock finally tempted him to make his first journey abroad. Sotheby's in London were the auctioneers. It was his first auction. The faintly musty smell of old furniture, tapestries and carpets excited him. He loved the viewing rooms, full of items each with a history. He hardly dared blink in case he'd end up buying something he didn't want. He listened to the bidding in the auction room. Then suddenly there it was, a porter was showing the clock, the next lot for sale. Claude wiped the sweat from his brow and timidly he held up his hand. The auctioneer nodded in his direction. Bids were raised in fifty pound jumps. His opponent was taking a long time between each one, Claude was already at his self-imposed limit. One more, he decided, just one more bid. "It's with you, sir," the auctioneer prompted. Claude appeared confused.

"Sold." The gavel echoed loudly on its base. "The gentleman in the second row," the auctioneer instructed his clerk, and pointed at Claude.

The week passed in a flash. He phoned two couples, regular guests at the château, and they took him under their wing. On his last night in London he invited them to dinner at Gavroche. He'd heard so much about the restaurant and he wasn't disappointed. The two couples had been most compatible and they'd arranged to meet each other three weeks later.

Everyone gathered round the big table as he told them of the sights he had seen and the places he had visited. For a moment he could picture himself back in the Hotel Thibault after his trip to Paris, but that was something he wanted to forget.

Claude looked at the elegant bookcases and sighed with satisfaction. His stack of catalogues was piling up nicely. He'd learnt a lot by studying them. He thought about the times he'd placed his bid by telephone, waiting anxiously to hear if it had met with success or if he had been outbid. Always in the quiet of his room his precious little clock ticked, Lisette Garnier was never far from his mind.

He stopped at the page which recorded the first of the dinners on his own private terrace. John O'Neill and Gabrielle, a friend of Snippy's from Chicago, Sir Rudolph and Lady Keyes and himself. It had been an interesting experiment and a delightful evening. Gabrielle, tanned and with a new-found sophistication had added an air of youthful gaiety. John O'Neill was one of his most favoured guests. They always had a drink together and talked for hours. John always brought Claude a gift of wonderful Irish smoked salmon. That had become one of the few things he refused to share.

An entry bordered with black ink reminded him that Marc's father had died. It had been a merciful release after years of ill-health.

Marc's mother had joined them later on. That was in the diary too. Claude had reservations - would it work - a mother taking instruction from a son? But it had been spectacularly successful. Marc's mother had great respect for her son's talent and Marc always listened with interest to his mother's suggestions. After all, as Marc said, "My mother taught me to cook."

Claude closed the book. He was proud of his achievements. He never forgot how much his loyal friends had done for him. Most of them had stayed with him. Those who worked and lived at the château were assured of a comfortable home and considerate treatment. Joseph would be married next February, his bride-to-be would join the staff permanently. She had worked at the château from time to time as a trilingual secretary. The addition of a high-tech office with fax machines, computers and clacking printers had almost broken Claude's heart. His dream of the château as a haven of peace - crudely destroyed by modern machines. It was rumoured amongst the château's guests that M Claude winced every time he passed the door of this technological carbuncle.

Once, Joseph had ferried a guest backwards and forwards to the nearest secretarial bureau three times in one week. Claude rapidly cast aside his selfish principles and hired one of the bureau's super-efficient secretaries on a retainer. Joseph collected her whenever her services were required. From there the friendship between them developed and turned to love.

Claude smiled as he thought of the coming week. Gabrielle O'Neill would arrive tomorrow. He could almost hear her teasing laughter. He would give one of his dinners on Friday, she always enjoyed that. Last month when he had placed his order for more velvet-padded hangers for the château, he had specified that a dozen of them were to be initialled with the letter "G". Gabrielle would be pleased. She shouldn't use those dreadful wire things on her beautiful clothes. Maybe he was being fussy, presumptuous, but the hangers were just a little gift to her. He would put her in room three overlooking the gardens and the sea - her favourite room - all peach and cream. Each of the bedrooms had been individually colour-matched. The green, white and pink of the salon, dining-room and gardens stopped at the ground floor. His own apartment was a combination of pink and gold. His marble terrace matched the others. There were still places on his walls which begged to be filled and one day they would be. He'd taken his time buying furniture, one piece at a time. He was proud of each and every item.

Claude replaced the books and dusted his desk. He checked that everything was in order then made his way upstairs to his bedroom. He took off his jacket and brushed it carefully. He made sure it hung perfectly on its hanger then placed it inside his wardrobe. He polished his shoes then buffed them with a tiny velvet cushion, a hundred times for each shoe. Satisfied, he inserted the shoe-trees and lined them up beside the others, toes facing outwards.

He opened the window and inhaled the sweet smell of the night fragrant flowers and Jules' miraculous lemon tree that was so notoriously difficult to grow near the sea. The gardens of the château had become almost as famous as its hospitality. Bougainvillea tumbled and rioted over the garden sheds and boiler house disguising them charmingly. There was never a day in the year when something of beauty failed to captivate the eye.

It was late. His reminiscing had swallowed so much time but now his dreams were real. Apart from that dreadful high-tech communications room with its machines, Claude was content with all he had achieved. Climbing into bed his last words were as always, "Thank you, God. Thank you, Lisette."

Laura

CHAPTER EIGHTY-SEVEN

Laura stared moodily as she watched the last of the big vans move off. She wished she hadn't listened to her brother. She wished she'd gone back with him to London on Saturday after the wedding. Getting to know her family had been marvellous but she yearned for the city streets, the theatres and the bustle. She'd leave in the morning with her uncle, whether or not it was convenient for Charles.

Mrs Oz's voice had sounded strained on Sunday when Laura phoned. "Are you sure everything is OK?" Laura asked.

"Of course it is."

"How's Mum's cold?"

"She's still coughing a bit but she insists she's all right."

"Is Terry around, could I have a word with him?"

"He's not here," Mrs Oz said faintly.

"How do you mean, not there?" Laura questioned.

How could she spoil the poor girl's holiday by letting her speak to Terry? Time enough to break the news when Laura got home. "He's down at the stables," she lied.

"I'll see you on Thursday. Remind Terry that he's meeting me."

"I will sweetheart, have a good time."

"No problem. 'Bye."

The flat was quiet and messy. Clothes were

flung on the chairs, empty glasses had left rings on the table. Laura pushed the clothes into an untidy heap and ignored the rest.

"Laura! I thought you'd vanished. I phoned a couple of times yesterday but there was no reply," Nadia said.

"It's a long story - but I'm back now."

"Are you free tonight?"

"Yes."

"Good. I've arranged to meet three of my friends for dinner. How about if I call for you at the flat then we'll take a taxi together to the restaurant?"

It seemed strange to Laura, everyone jumping in and out of taxis as if they were the same price as buses.

"I'll look forward to that, what time?"

"Say seven? That OK?"

"Lovely, see you then."

She rooted through her case and chose a soft heather-coloured suit. It was badly creased but she could iron it later. Unpacking could wait too. She grabbed a pair of flat shoes, combed her hair, added some lipstick and left the flat. She had no plans - except to wander where the mood took her.

The store was hot and crowded. She slid gratefully into an empty seat in the restaurant. Her feet were aching. She unwrapped her sandwich and took a welcome bite. She hadn't noticed the time slipping by and she was hungry. She was pleased with the things she'd bought, particularly the featherweight mobile phone for her mother. It could be kept on the bed if necessary and the press-buttons would be simple for her to use. Laura wasn't so confident about the book she had selected for Terry, but he did love horses and it was a safe buy she supposed. She smiled as she thought of the cute satin sewing box with its lid in the shape of a face. Later on she would buy reels of cotton and needles and anything else she thought Mrs Oz would like. It was still only three o'clock, plenty of time to browse.

CHAPTER EIGHTY-EIGHT

Charles frowned. Of course - it was Laura's case. Damn, he could live without her at the moment. He poured a large dollop of Scotch into his last clean glass and wandered to the window. Another agonising day. No amount of number-crunching or file-searching had given him any hope of juggling accounts or moving funds. He should have stayed at the office but that would have caused suspicion. Normally he left before the office closed. He needed more time. Time to go over the files again, undisturbed by the ringing of the telephone and appointments with clients. That was it! He'd go back to the bank tonight, he had keys and there would be no one there to bother him. It was a perfect opportunity to search the computer for his uncle's client-accounts. Laura would just have to look after herself. Why the hell hadn't she stayed in the country? Wasn't his life complicated enough?

He heard the key turn in the lock.

"I'm back," said Laura.

"So I see," he said acidly. "I'm afraid I'm not free tonight so you'll have to amuse yourself."

"Welcome back Laura, nice to see you," Laura said sarcastically. "Don't worry about me, I'm going out with friends." Charles hadn't improved with age. Still, who cared? Nothing's changed, he's a nasty piece of work, always was. It was somewhere to stay and that's all she needed from him.

He must get his act together. It was stress that made him snap at her like that. Her friend hadn't been too impressed, he could tell. Laura hadn't half let her displeasure show, the door had rocked on its hinges when she left. Another half hour and then he could leave for the bank. The cleaners should be long gone by then - and the porter who checked them in and out.

"I'm sorry about my awful brother," Laura apologised.

"Don't give it a thought, maybe he had a tough day," Nadia said understandingly.

"Do me a favour - that's no excuse. Who are we meeting, anyone I know?"

"No, you don't know them. We get together once a month. This was arranged ages ago. There's no popping into the local here the way we do at home. The chances of finding three people free at the drop of a hat is remote. By the way, I tried to contact the girls today but without any luck. Apparently they're still away, although Fiona could be back by tomorrow. It would've been fun to get together, but I'll try her again tomorrow before I leave the office. How long are you staying?"

"Just till Thursday."

"So soon?"

"I'm grateful for my mother's small mercy. I still can't believe she suggested it all!"

The Lebanese restaurant was busy when they arrived, the waiters moving swiftly with their trays of food. The three girls were friendly when Nadia introduced Laura.

"What are you going to eat?" Nadia asked.

"I haven't a clue. This is all new to me. Maybe

you'd choose for me," she suggested to her friend.

"Why don't we order a lot of different dishes, and share?"

Everyone agreed. The attractive girl sitting opposite Laura took charge of the menus.

A large plate of crudités were placed on the table - black and green olives, tomatoes, and crunchy radishes. Laura followed the girls' example and dipped a radish into the pale spicy dip.

"Humus," Nadia said, "It's made of chick peas with garlic and oil, sesame and cayenne pepper."

As they picked at the appetisers the girls talked of the market rise that day and its effect on house prices. The waiter returned with puffy cakes of pitta bread, a dish of hot spicy lamb kebabs, deep fried fingers of aubergines and cold peppers in olive oil and garlic which he crowded onto the table.

Laura loved the unusual tastes, each one so different. They talked about the latest play which was to open the following week. They'd all bought tickets. Empty plates were whisked away and replaced by platters of lamb cooked with lemon, chicken garnished with peppers and chillies, a dish of crisply fried courgettes and something that looked like deep fried pears.

"You must try one of these," Louise, the commodities dealer, urged.

The pear-shaped objects were made of finely ground mincemeat, very spicy but delicious. Spearing small pieces with her fork Laura listened to the conversation. They lived in a world she knew nothing about. Fast and cut-throat, she decided. Apparently they all set their alarms for six thirty a.m.. By seven or seven fifteen, perfectly groomed, they were on their way by bus or tube. By eight fifteen they were ready for the day's action.

"But surely your offices wouldn't be open by then?" Laura ventured, innocently.

"My desk must be cleared by nine o'clock," Caroline explained - patronisingly?

"Faxes come in overnight and the mail arrives early." Nadia came to her rescue. Laura was beginning to feel like a blow-in from another planet. She wasn't going to risk being put down again. She sullenly picked her way through small forkfuls of food. Even it bit back she thought to herself.

"Do you like it?" Louise asked, as Laura tasted the sweet, hot Turkish coffee.

"It's passable," Laura said loftily. She learnt fast. Actually it was delicious but she had begun to feel the same way she had that night in Kildare when Terry's horsy friends had dismissed her as *the pretty little local girl*. Terry. Her heart gave a skip of joy. Just two more days and she'd be back with him. She shivered as she thought of his kisses, his strong tanned arms around her.

"... It's a drag I admit, but it's the best cheese shop in London. Who can *bear* those dreadful slabs of plastic that pass for cheese?" Caroline moaned.

Obviously only I can, Laura giggled inwardly. This wine was good, it took the hard edges off the three girls. Laura glanced at Nadia and wondered how she put up with all this, certainly *she* had no airs or graces.

"Now it's my turn to say sorry," Nadia apologised as they settled into the taxi. "They're not a bad lot really, but this is a cold city and there's always someone with an oiled shoe-horn waiting to step into your Charles Jourdan's."

"Have Fiona and Georgie changed like that? You haven't," Laura added hastily.

"We have the same *craic* we always did. But it takes all sorts and when you get to know the girls you met tonight, properly, they drop the act. That was for your benefit."

"I'm glad they talked so much, I pigged out on those fabulous spices and, boy, were they good!"

Nadia smiled in the darkness. How much Laura reminded her of herself when she'd first arrived in London - green as grass *and* a lot younger than Laura. She took it all as a matter of course now. She gave of her best and demanded the same. Good clothes, smart restaurants, taxis when it suited her and holidays in exotic places. That was all part of the hard work. The unsociable hours, the wild goose chases, being charming when she wanted to shriek at dithering house buyers, and the ever-present danger of attack by a stranger in an empty house. All their staff carried mobiles now. They telephoned the office when they entered a building and switched off only when the potential client had left. She'd earned her rewards.

"What are your plans for tomorrow?" she asked.

"None really. It's lovely to be free and just meander."

"How about tomorrow night, would you like to go to a film or the theatre?"

"I'd adore that. Just the two of us?"

"If that's what you fancy. What if Fiona's home?"

"Absolutely. I'd love to see her, that goes without saying."

"Let's say I meet you at the flat at six o'clock and we'll take it from there."

The taxi stopped at the flat. Laura offered to pay but Nadia shooed her away. "You can do the honours when I come home," she promised.

Charles was in bed asleep when Laura left in the morning. She'd half-heard him moving around in the early hours. She walked through Hyde Park until she reached Speaker's Corner. She hesitated then decided to walk down Oxford Street. If there were any attractive clothes in the shop windows she just might treat herself to something nice.

Several hours later she'd spent more than she'd intended and abandoned the over-heated shops in favour of a comfortable cinema seat. Later, with hardly enough time left to have a bath and blow-dry her hair, she held up an arm to attract a passing taxi.

CHAPTER EIGHTY-NINE

"Why didn't my idiot of a sister wake me?" Charles Bingham asked his shaving mirror. It had been eleven o'clock when he'd opened his eyes - washed out and no nearer to a solution. What day was it? Wednesday. What was it about Wednesday? Something was nidging. Terry Harvey, Argentina - of course. It all came back to him now. At this very moment he should be taking off, private jets usually left on time he'd heard. Cursing, he realised he'd forgotten to disconnect the phone again. It didn't matter now, Laura was out and Harvey would be long gone by the time she got back to the flat. He didn't want to, but he'd better do the decent thing and take her out for dinner tonight, she'd be gone tomorrow.

Charles could hear his uncle's angry voice as he passed his office. That in itself was surprising. The door opened and his uncle faced him. The blood in Charles' veins curdled and froze.

"Charles, come in here."

He could see the prison bars, hear the slam of the door closing for God knows how long. He couldn't take it, couldn't be locked up for years - he wasn't made that way.

His cousin avoided eye contact and stood behind his father, his expression inscrutable.

"Explain yourself," his uncle's face was forbidding.

"What do you mean?" Charles asked, playing for time.

"Lady Georgina, the missing money from the clients' accounts. You know bloody well what I mean, don't play games with me."

"May I sit down?" Charles asked.

"No," his uncle thundered, his face alarmingly purple with fury. "This is not a tea party. You have committed the gravest of offences, stealing clients' money, insider trading, betraying the bank's trust *and* jeopardising our good name."

"It was *borrowing,* not stealing," said Charles defensively.

"Stealing. Before you leave you will sign a document. If you should ever attempt to set one foot inside this bank again you'll be arrested. You are a despicable character, a thief, a cheat and stupid into the bargain. Now before you go ..."

"Do you mean you're not going to bring in the fraud squad?"

"You're damned right I'm not. It would ruin us, destroy our reputation. Don't think for a moment that you're going to get away with what you've done. Sign this document. Read it first," his uncle demanded.

...to return all the outstanding moneys owed by me, plus the interest accrued up until the time of settlement, immediately upon receipt of the legacy...

If he'd believed in any god, Charles would have thanked him for the mercy he'd shown. The pen wobbled in his hand as if it were made of rubber. His signature was almost unrecognisable. He was home free, unpunished. When his mother died he would inherit the estate. The document bound him to compensate his uncle in full. He couldn't care less, by then he'd be stinking rich anyway.

His cousin, who refused to look at him, witnessed the paper. His uncle's disgust didn't touch him, the one thing that scared him was the clause stating that he would never apply for any position which involved the handling of funds.

"For your father's sake I will spare you the disgrace of discussing this matter with anyone. Now clear your desk immediately and go."

Without a word Charles swaggered out of the room with a jaunty step. He stifled his instinct to shout for joy.

If the cheque from his mother hadn't arrived by the time he got home he'd ring the old trout and remind her.

He entered his office for the last time. An empty cardboard carton sat on his desk - waiting. He flung it to the ground. He pulled out drawer after drawer and threw their contents on the floor. He didn't need any of this stuff. And he certainly didn't need that stupid plant which he'd always hated. Bonus. A glint of malice shone in his eyes as he walked to the windowsill and grabbed the offensive object by its leaves. Like a dentist removing teeth, one at a time, he stripped the verdant leaves from their stem with his pliers. "He sacked me, he sacked me not. He fired me, he fired me not. I am upset, oh no I'm not! Goodbye, oh faithful rubber plant - and I hope that hurts like hell."

Charles eyed the stack of diskettes in their rack. Now *they* were something that could be useful. He popped them into his briefcase and slammed the door of his office with a resounding thud then made his way along the corridor.

Intrigue

"Charles." The sound of his uncle's voice behind made him start. "May I see the briefcase?"

"What for?" he demanded insolently.

"Give it to me."

The porter was walking towards them from the other end of the corridor. Charles was trapped between the two men like the filling in a human sandwich.

His uncle removed the diskettes from the briefcase. "These are the bank's property. You don't learn by your mistakes do you? More theft," he sighed. "Mr Reid, would you escort my nephew off the premises please."

He stood in the open doorway and watched the backs of the two men as they walked away from him, Mr Reid, the bank's porter, stiff and correct, and his nephew, cocky and strutting. What a career Charles had thrown away. Ironically it was the replacement of funds in Lady Georgina's account that had alerted their eagle-eyed accountant. Not that he condoned Charles' deception in any shape or form but, had the discovery been delayed, there was just the possibility that his nephew might have straightened out the whole mess. Sighing, he kicked the door shut with his foot and, in foul humour, began to answer his mail.

Now that he was free, and it was only twelve-thirty, Charles was at a loss as to what to do or where to go. He couldn't face the normal lunch-time banter of his colleagues and associates. They'd be tactful and sympathetic of course when they heard his news, but what they'd say behind his back was another thing. And then there was the question of his professional future.

"Lowndes Square," he said to the taxi driver.

"Right ho, guvner," the man replied starting the meter.

I'll have to be careful for a while. There'll be no pay cheque to draw on at the end of the month, Charles thought irritably, as the taxi stopped and started for the umpteenth time - the city traffic was murder at this time of the day. His euphoria was evaporating rapidly. Banking was the only thing he knew, would his uncle hold him to that document, or was it a spur of the moment threat? How *had* he found out? So swift was the blow it hadn't occurred to him to ask. Still, he was bloody lucky that he wasn't riding in a police van now instead of a taxi.

Dumping his briefcase in the tiny hallway he went into the living-room and threw open the windows. He looked around the trendy room, another miniature guillotine fell on his waiting head - the rent of this place- how would he pay that? His twice-yearly trust fund wouldn't keep him in taxis. He needed a drink. He'd forgotten he finished the bottle of Scotch last night, sherry would have to do. Charles stopped his restless conjecturing when the phone rang.

"Is that you Charles?" For a moment he couldn't place the voice.

"Hello, Mrs Oz. Are you looking for Laura?"

"Well, yes. Or you. Charles, your mother is not very well - in fact, she's very sick. Pneumonia, the doctor said, and they've taken her into hospital. I thought you and Laura should know."

"How bad is she?" Charles asked.

"Hard to say. They hope that the antibiotics should start working in a day or so but that's all I know."

"That's awful news," Charles said sincerely. It was awful news, that meant unless his cheque was already in the post he was penniless. "I'll tell Laura when she comes back. She left this morning before I was awake so I don't know when to expect her."

"Do you think she could ring me? I'll wait here at the house for her call."

"Very well Mrs Oz, goodbye."

She didn't bother to reply. There had been no - "Are you all right Mrs Oz? Can I do anything to help Mrs Oz? Which hospital is my mother in? Can I speak to the doctor?" Typical! Leave it to Laura.

CHAPTER NINETY

Luckily, Nadia was still in her office. Laura hated letting her down but she was in no mood for a theatre comedy, no matter how good the reviews.

"I hope you have better news when you get home. Keep in touch?" Laura promised Nadia she would phone her in a day or two and she rang off quickly. She wanted to go home immediately. Searching through the pages of the directory she reached for the pad and pencil beside her and scribbled down the phone number of the airport.

Doodling on the pad as she waited, she could see indentations from a previous page. Idly she held it level, *Al - rez, Argentina. T -rence Harvey.* What was his name doing there she wondered?

Terry's name brought a smile of pleasure to her face. It would be so good to see him standing at the exit of the customs hall waiting for her. Those gorgeous green eyes, his arms enveloping her in a bear hug, his lips - soft and warm. Several times since they'd been apart Laura had tried hard to conjure up an exact picture of him in her mind but couldn't. Now, all of a sudden, it was clear.

Mrs Oz had sounded really upset. There had been no further news from the hospital since she had spoken to Charles earlier and she cheered up considerably when Laura told her she'd be back later tonight.

"Will you tell Terry the flight arrives at nine

thirty so he can meet me?"

" I'll ..."

The phone went dead in her hand, they'd been cut off. Mrs Oz must have heard her, she was just about to answer. There was no point in ringing her back, she must go and pack right away.

"Charles, that you?" Laura called from the bedroom.

He came into the room, looking glum. "What news?" he asked, pushing aside her clothes and sitting on the bed.

"No change. They wouldn't give Mrs Oz much information because she's not a member of the family."

"Stupid woman," he said callously, "didn't she have the sense to say she was a relation?"

"That's unfair, she's had to cope with everything. Maybe lies don't spring easily to *her* lips."

"And what's that supposed to mean?" he asked belligerently.

"Put a sock in it Charles, and mind that parcel - it's a gift. By the way, why is Terry Harvey's name on the pad by the phone?"

"I didn't see any name on the pad."

"No, the page was torn out but I could still see the marks of the writing."

"How do I know? It could have been months ago. Anyway, it's none of your business, my pad is private."

"I wasn't thinking of having it published," Laura replied acidly. "Aren't you going to come to Kildare? After all, she's *your* mother too."

"I can't at the moment, too much pressure - the bank ..."

Anne Schulman

"Business as usual, you're always too busy to bother with us aren't you?"

"I'm here at the end of the phone if you need me. Give me a bell and keep me up to date."

"Yes, Milord." Laura glared at him.

The woman sitting beside her on the plane didn't speak. Instead, she opened a document case and spent the entire flight reading copious sheets of closely typed paper. Laura was quite content to lie back with her eyes closed and to let her mind drift. Since the wedding last Saturday Charles had returned to being his old obnoxious self. God, he was an unfeeling sod. He hadn't been at all pleased to see her when she'd arrived back from Gloucestershire. Annoyed, more like. How different her aunt and uncle had been from her mother's description. Warm and caring.

She still couldn't fathom what had prompted her mother to send her to the wedding. The papers that she'd signed were a nonsense, three or four days by post would have sufficed. Well, as she'd said to Terry, hers not to reason why, hers just to go and pack. It'd been a lovely break and, despite the fact that her mother was ill, it would be good to be home. It still niggled that Terry's name had appeared on that pad. Charles, with his usual lack of charm, had evaded her questions. She wondered what Argentina was like? Beautiful, she imagined. Not one of her worries, she'd never get there.

"Ladies and gentlemen ..." The announcement reminded them to extinguish their cigarettes and fasten their seat-belts for landing. The green fields were invisible in the dusk. Pity, she'd have loved to have seen those symmetrical blocks of colour rushing below her as the plane made its descent. Delving into her travelling bag she found her lipstick with its own little foldaway mirror. She'd bought two of them, one pink and the other a deep coral. Pulling her fringe into position and smoothing an eyebrow she clicked the mirror back into place with a pleasing snap. She loved the noise it made, so, with an eye on her silent seat-mate, she opened and closed it again.

The drone of engines stopped. Laura grabbed her jacket from the overhead locker and waited impatiently as the passengers moved slowly along the plane to the exit. Striding smartly along the electric walkway she found herself in the brightly lit baggage claims area. Several people were pulling trolleys from the waiting stacks. Following their lead she tugged one free and placed her travel bag in its basket - searching the overhead signs on each carousel for the London flight.

She walked through the green channel and steered the wayward trolley towards the smoked-glass doors which parted automatically as she crossed the mat. Her eyes scanned the crowd expectantly. Poor Terry, it would have been a rush for him. Escaping the crowds she leant on the handle of the trolley and waited. She could murder a cup of tea and a sandwich but, if she left her lookout position near the entrance doors, she might miss him.

She shifted from her left foot to her right. Forty-five minutes, he really was late. For a moment she wondered if he'd had an accident.

From her stance near the door she could see the reception desk, so it stood to reason that she could watch the door from the desk.

"Let me see if I have a message for you, Miss Bingham," the pretty girl said reaching below her counter. She sorted through the envelopes. "Barrett, Bell, Bingham. Ah! Here we are. Miss Laura Bingham? You're aren't due till tomorrow?"

"No, I took an earlier flight. My mother's been taken ill." Why was she explaining all this to a stranger? Through the thin paper she could feel the outline of a key. Puzzled, she tore open the envelope. It was a key and a note.

"Oh no! Oh Terry, how could you." She hadn't been aware that she had spoken out loud until the pretty receptionist asked if everything was all right. Nodding blindly, she pushed her trolley away from the desk and, tucking herself away in a corner, she read the note again. Tears poured unchecked over her pale cheeks and on to her jacket. He had gone. Not a phone call, not a letter just a brief note at an airport.

Range Rover in the long term car park ... an incredible offer I couldn't refuse ... will never forget you ... maybe sometime ...

In the quiet corner she lowered her head on to her hands which were clasping the trolley for support, and sobbed uncontrollably. She didn't care who saw her.

"Are you in trouble, my dear?" A woman's voice asked.

Laura looked at her through blurred eyes.

"Can I help you, get you something?"

Laura shook her head. Frowning, the kindly woman muttered, "If you're sure, then."

Intrigue

The oncoming car lights blurred into sunbursts of yellow as her tears kept falling. Her cheeks stung from wiping them against the nubbly material of her jacket. She could find no excuse for Terry's cruel departure.

As the house came into view she could see Mrs Oz peering anxiously through the window. As Laura stumbled towards the door it opened and she threw herself into Mrs Oz's arms, sobbing wildly.

"You poor child, I'm so sorry. Oh Laura, I wish I could have spared you all of this."

"Why did Terry go? What happened? Is there any news from the hospital?" Her questions tumbled jerkily over one another.

"Come on in, I'll make you a nice cup of tea."

How could tea help her broken heart? Laura wondered desperately.

"I'll phone the hospital in a minute," she said, picking up the cup with trembling hands. "Tell me what happened to my mother."

"She started running a temperature a couple of days ago but she wouldn't allow me to call the doctor. But when she got worse next day I was frightened and phoned him. I'm so sorry I obeyed her Laura, I should've called him in sooner."

"You know how stubborn she is, don't blame yourself. The important thing is that you called him in and now she's in good hands. I want to know about Terry, do you know what happened? He didn't even phone me - just left a note at the airport." Laura's face was wet with tears again.

Mrs Oz patted her arm sympathetically. She'd agonised for days about whether she should repeat the conversation that she'd overheard. Her loyalties were torn. She couldn't give a damn about Charles but she did owe a lot to Olivia Bingham - even if she was such an uncaring mother.

"I'm not too sure, Laura. He said he'd been offered a fabulous job in Ar.. Argentina."

The sound of the phone echoed through the quiet house. Neither of them expected it to be Charles. They looked at each other fearfully then Laura rose from her chair to answer it while Mrs Oz stood at the kitchen doorway, her heart thudding uncomfortably.

"I've got to go right away," Laura said, her face like chalk. "It's the hospital, she's taken a turn for the worse. Will you ring Charles?"

"When we get back," Mrs Oz said firmly. "I'm going with you." Her face showed none of the panic she was feeling.

Laura didn't argue, she was glad to have the support of Mrs Oz's company.

As they stood in the corridor with its smell of disinfectant a nurse approached. "Miss Bingham? I'm Sister Theresa. I'm sorry..." They both realised by the look on her face that they were too late. "I'm very sorry," she repeated, "your mother passed away about five minutes ago. It was very peaceful."

Laura clutched an envelope which the nurses had given her. It contained the key which her mother had always worn round her neck, also her watch and wedding ring. Laura's tears flowed unceasingly. She couldn't grasp the fact that her mother was dead. They left the hospital. She'd lost two people in one day, she grieved for them both, her mother and Terry.

"I'll stay in the house tonight, darling," Mrs Oz said kindly, her eyes suspiciously bright. She had to be strong for Laura.

"Thank you, but it's not necessary, honestly."

"You shouldn't be alone. It's been a terrible day for you. Sad for us both."

"Mrs Oz, I'm sorry for being so selfish, you must be hurting too."

Mrs Oz nodded and wiped her eyes with a little flowered handkerchief. "If only you'd been old enough to remember your mother before her accident. She was so vivacious, never still for a minute. It must have been hard for her - lying in that room year after year, no friends left, just the horses. I don't mean that *you* weren't a good daughter, you were. Patient too, staying with her when you should've had a life of your own - not like your brother." A bitter look crossed her face, now what would happen to Laura? Or to herself for that matter.

"I'm so sad that she died alone," Laura said, unshed tears glazing her eyes.

"You heard what the sister said, she wouldn't have known if there was anyone there or not." Mrs Oz sought desperately for something comforting to say.

"I suppose I'd better phone Charles," Laura sighed, dragging herself from the chair.

The phone kept ringing, but there was no reply. She'd try again in about an hour.

"There's no reply," she said dropping back into the chair. Mrs Oz had made a fresh pot of tea and poured them each another cup.

"What are you thinking about?" Mrs Oz

interrupted Laura's unhappy thoughts.

"I was thinking about Charles. They were almost strangers, weren't they? He and Mum, I mean. I was trying to remember how many times he came home since he finished school - very few." A tear splashed into her cup. "I noticed something odd tonight while I was waiting to book my ticket. Charles keeps a note-pad and pencil near the phone. I wrote the airport number on it and was just scribbling when I saw some pencil marks. They'd obviously come through from a torn-out page. When I held it up level with my eyes - you remember, the way we used to do when we used invisible ink - I saw Terry's name. Above it was some foreign name and the word 'Argentina'. He bit my head off when I asked him about..." Laura's voice trailed off as she stared at Mrs Oz. Her cheeks were flaming like beacons as she shifted uncomfortably on her chair.

"Mrs Oz? You *do* know something about this. I *know* you do, tell me, please," Laura begged.

The worry about being loyal no longer applied. Olivia didn't need her protection now. But what was best for Laura?

"Listen sweetheart, I'm not sure of all the details. When I was tidying your mother's room I couldn't help overhearing a conversation between her and Charles." Mrs Oz felt disloyal, but ploughed on. "Naturally, I couldn't hear what Charles was saying, but ... your mother was upset that you'd fallen for Terry and wanted him out of the way. That's why she packed you off to London."

"What happened then?" Laura's voice was as

cold as chipped ice.

"Charles must have got a job for him with someone he knew in Argentina. Your mother was angry because she had to pay him to do it. I'd left the room by then, but, God forgive me, I listened outside the door. She told him to make sure that Terry couldn't contact you – anyway, the next thing was Terry came and told me that he'd had the offer of a wonderful job in Argentina. Some man or other who had loads of polo ponies, he said, and since the stud here was closing down, it was too good an opportunity to miss. I'm *sure* he tried to phone you, Laura."

"He didn't succeed, did he?" Laura retorted acerbically. "Did he leave an address?"

"Not with me," Mrs. Oz replied miserably. The last thing in the world she wanted to do was upset Laura any more than she already was.

"I'm sure Charles would be delighted to sell it to me for a fee. Don't worry, I'm not going to ask him. What's the use? Terry didn't think enough of me, did he?"

"Of course he did, he thought the world of you. He asked after you every day when you were away."

"Yeah, then did a bunk to prove how much he cared. It's true what they say, everyone has their price and his was a job in Argentina." Her tears fell again and kept on falling. Mrs Oz put her arms around Laura and rocked her as she had when she was a baby.

"Would you mind if I rang Billy in the morning? I'm sure he'd want to come back for the funeral if he could," she said when Laura was calmer.

"Of course, ring him. Mrs Oz, will you phone Charles now? I don't think I could trust myself to speak to him."

"Right away," she said, stroking Laura's head.

"Where would I be without you?" Laura caught hold of her hand hugging it to her cheek. "You've always been so good to me." It was Mrs Oz who'd loved and cherished her for as long as she could remember. She was the one who had kissed her better when she fell, she and Billy. It was Mrs Oz who knew her secrets, all her longings. What a strain she and her mother had put on the poor woman, who had struggled to be fair to both of them.

"There's still no reply," Mrs Oz scowled disapprovingly. "Do you think he'll be at home at all tonight?"

Laura looked at her watch, it was almost one-thirty. "You must be worn out. Go back to the cottage and have a rest. I'll try him again in a while."

"I'd really be happier here in the house with you."

"I need to be alone, please don't worry - you look exhausted."

"It's been a long old day, and a sad one."

"Don't start me crying again. I'll see you in the morning - and thank you for everything. You're the best friend I could ever have."

Laura bolted the door securely and made her way up the stairs. Halfway up she stopped, remembering the packet they had given her in the hospital.

CHAPTER NINETY-ONE

Her mother's room was dank and cold, the shadows of the trees weaving eerie patterns on the wall. A shiver ran through her body as she looked at the empty bed that was bathed in moonlight. She reached for the light switch. Mrs Oz must have given the room a really good spring-clean but even so it still looked shabby and miserable. Laura forced herself to sit on the bed and phone Charles again. If he didn't answer this time she would wait until morning. As she sat with the receiver purring in her hand, a fresh bout of crying racked her body. She cried for herself, for her mother who'd never been able to love her, for Terry and the unswerving love she had felt for him.

She eyed the package in her hand. The key, it was hers now, or at least hers and Charles'. She walked over to the wardrobe and knelt on the floor. She took the key from the packet. Inserting it into the lock she opened the safe. Furtively, and half-expecting to hear her mother's voice, she pulled the contents out and spread them on the floor. The envelopes, documents and bank books were blurred, her sight was distorted from crying. She wiped the tears from her eyes with her sleeve and opened one of the little books, then the others. The amounts of money were astronomical, hundreds of thousands of pounds in each one. That couldn't be right. Blinking hard she looked again. There was no mistake. Rage began to boil inside her, driving away her tears. Apart from the money spent on the horses they'd been living like paupers. The house was falling down around them. She went over to her desk, found her calculator and then squatted on the floor again.

Punching in each total she totted them up. This was crazy. She did it again but the answer was the same. Two million, four hundred thousand and sixty-three pounds and twenty-five pence. She stared at the figure, her brain told her that she was mad, it had to be wrong. Look at the other things, then try again. By then she'd have come to her senses.

Her birth certificate was there with her mother's. In a long envelope were her father's papers. His birth and death certificates, his passport, old and battered, his will, simple and precise, leaving everything to his wife. His will... where was her mother's will? It must be here somewhere. She knew that Olivia had written one. Her mother's trust fund, what did that entail? She would have to contact her mother's new solicitors and have them explain it all.

The big package was there, the one the courier had delivered. She eased open the flap. More documents. On an envelope the same as their own, she read: *Last Will and Testament of Olivia Bingham*. It had been typed on their old typewriter because she recognised the solid top of the "e", and the "v" instead of "y". As Laura turned it over the flap sprang away, its glue had dried up with age. Looking guiltily towards her mother's bed she slid the sheet of paper out and opened it carefully. It was brief and to the point.

Intrigue

Apart from her jewellery and one hundred thousand pounds for Laura her mother had left everything to Charles. The house, the stud, her trust funds, the money in her bank accounts, everything. He would be worth millions. Her no-good brother, who never cared what happened to them. Who visited his mother only when forced to. He would get the lot. Laura's anger, which had abated, turned to white fury. She was almost twenty-one years old. When all her friends had left she'd been buried here with no life of her own, at her mother's beck and call all day and all night. She was often cold and even more often miserable. While Charles was living the life of Reilly in London, and who knows where else in the country, she'd been shivering here in her unheated bedroom. When Charles lost a packet at the races, Olivia had helped him. And worst of all, the two of them had plotted to get rid of the only person who had given her a feeling of self-worth - afraid that she might leave the crumbling mansion and her demanding mother.

Charles, everything was for Charles. He didn't deserve *any* of it. It should be her name on that will, and Charles could have the jewellery and her bequest. She wished it read differently. To mv *daughter, Laura* Bingham, instead of, To my *son, Charles* Bingham. Just interchange those four words and their fortunes would be reversed. *She* would be the one worth the millions and the comparatively small sum of money left to her would go to Charles instead. She would sell the house and the stud, settle a lump sum on Mrs Oz … Mrs Oz, after all those years of faithful service and caring, Mrs Oz wasn't even mentioned. Laura felt a flush rise to her face. How could her mother have been so despicable? If Charles sold the house, Mrs Oz would be homeless, they both would. Laura would look after Mrs Oz herself. She'd always felt that life was unjust but now a seething anger was screaming to get out. She flung the will aside and straightened her cramped legs. What would happen if she tore the will to shreds and threw it away? Would they share the proceeds of those iniquitous little bank books with their mocking totals? Or would Charles inherit everything regardless? On one of his rare visits he had hinted that when the old trout - as he liked to call his mother - popped off, *he* would be all right.

A tingling sensation gripped her. Getting awkwardly to her feet she crossed to her battered desk and started pulling out the drawers. Where was it? She positively knew it was there somewhere, she'd seen it only last week before she went away. Triumphantly she pulled the blank page clear of the drawer. There were two sheets, not one - the last two remaining sheets of their old stationery. Identical to the paper on which the will was written.

Laura climbed up into the attic. The ladder rocked precariously under her feet. There it was, the old typewriter, all covered in dust and cobwebs. In the half-gloom of the poorly-lit space something scampered across her foot and she screamed with fright, and almost dropped the heavy machine. She could hear a scraping noise but couldn't move, she was glued to the floor as if by adhesive. When her panic subsided she carried the ancient typewriter to the opening in the attic floor and took two tentative steps down the ladder. The weight of the machine was too much for one hand. She steadied herself and firmly pressed her legs and stomach against the rungs as she reached up.

"Please don't let me fall," she prayed aloud, swaying slightly under the weight. She set the typewriter in place on her old battered desk, dusted it thoroughly and then picked up the will and placed it beside the machine. She took a pen and a piece of scrap paper and began to practise the signatures. Her mother's was not too difficult, she'd seen it a million times, Seán O'Hagan's was a different matter. Poor old Seán, he was such a lovely man. Laura was so upset when he died and the firm closed down. Whenever he came to the house, Seán would produce a bar of something from his coat pocket. Once, when she was younger, he'd even brought her an ice cream, wrapped in wads of newspaper to prevent it melting. Seán had been the family solicitor as long as she could remember and probably for an age before that too. What would he have thought if he could see what she was doing now? She copied his name again and again just as he had scrawled it on the will. Laura had no idea where the clerks who'd worked for Seán had gone but she wasn't taking any risks, the signature had to be right. And *she* wouldn't leave any tell-tale signs of her scribbles on the blank paper for someone to find.

"Thanks Charles for the lesson you taught me - *I* won't press too hard or leave any evidence behind *me*."

Satisfied that she had the signatures off to a tee

she inserted the headed notepaper into the machine and began to type. With agonising slowness the words appeared on the paper. A replica of the will. She fed the paper from the typewriter into her hand and checked every word three times. It was perfect.

She picked up the old pen and shook the ink on to the blotter. Niggardly and stingy, her mother had refused to throw anything away - ever. "You never know when things may come in handy," she used to say.

"Thank you," Laura saluted the empty bed, then, feeling blasphemous, she looked away.

She waited until her hand stopped trembling then wrote her mother's signature in the correct place. There! It looked identical. Now for the difficult bit. Laura emptied away the blue ink and squirted water in and out of the old-fashioned barrel of the pen. She dried the gold nib and refilled the old Parker with black ink, testing it first. "Now, fingers crossed," she encouraged herself. She wrote with the same flourish that Seán O'Hagan had, dropped the pen on the table and all but collapsed in the chair. The second witness to the will had been Mrs Oz and her name could be added first thing in the morning - by Mrs Oz herself.

Laura checked it all again, word for word. She could find no fault and there were the two signatures, her mother's and "Seán O'Hagn's." Laura stared with horror at Seán's name, perfectly executed but missing the final "a". "You fool!" she chastised herself with a yell. How could she have missed out a letter? It had taken her two hours from start to finish, how could she begin again? She was utterly drained. She started to quake from sheer fatigue and the trauma of the day. Was there someone up there trying to tell her something or was she going plain mad? She needed a drink to calm her nerves but, if she had a drink, she might become even more careless. A cup of tea might revive her, Mrs Oz's cure-all. She sat at the table with a mug of hot sweet tea clasped between her hands and questioned her own sense of guilt and immorality. There wasn't a single mitigating factor. It was wrong. But there was nothing to be said for Charles either, and at the end of the day it was between the two of them. There was no contest. She came first by a mile. Leaving her half-filled cup on the table she dashed back to her mother's room and wound the last precious piece of paper into the typewriter.

"Pick the bones out of that, Charles Bingham," Laura said, as the first light of the new day shone through the window. "I'm only taking what is rightfully mine."

CHAPTER NINETY-TWO

Mrs Oz ushered Laura inside her little cottage and sat her down in the big cosy chair. "Did you manage to sleep darling?" She hardly needed to ask. Laura's face was ashen, the shadows under her eyes were as purple as the hills. Even her hair hung limp and dull.

"Not a wink," Laura said truthfully. Until this paper that was burning a hole in her bag was fully completed there would be no rest.

"You poor little thing, you stay put where you are and I'll make us both a good breakfast."

The rattle of plates woke her.

"There's a good girl, get some food inside you - it will make you feel a lot better."

"Mrs Oz, there's a paper that needs signing, would you mind?"

"God love you, of course I don't mind."

Mrs Oz added her signature to the others on the half-folded paper. It was touching to see that Laura was using that old pen of her mother's, tears clouded her eyes. Such a good girl Laura was, even in her hour of grief she didn't neglect her duty.

Laura put the paper in her bag and, at Mrs Oz's urging, attacked the plate of bacon, sausages and egg. The poor little thing must be starving.

Together they walked over to the house. The silence was almost eerie as they passed the stables.

"What happened to the rest of the horses?"

Laura had totally forgotten about them until now.

"Terry arranged for them to be sold to the Carroll Stud. He was pleased that they would take the stable lads too. He didn't want them to lose their jobs." Mrs Oz eyed Laura cautiously.

"Nice to think he cared about *someone*," Laura snapped.

"Don't think about anything now. You go straight to bed, I'll wake you later."

"I am jaded," Laura admitted, "but first I've got to ring Charles, then my uncle. You wanted to phone Billy too."

"Do you want me to make the call to Charles?" Mrs Oz frowned.

"No. I'll have to talk to the creep sometime, it might as well be now."

Laura wouldn't swear to it but Charles' cry when she broke the news to him sounded more like joy than sorrow. It was a kind of whoop.

"I presume you'll come over for the funeral?" Laura suggested sarcastically.

"What a silly question, of course I will, Sis," Charles answered in a sickly sweet voice. "I'll phone you back and let you know what time my flight arrives so you can meet me."

"Don't bother. There's a lot to do here. There's no way I could possibly manage to get to Dublin to collect you." He could find his own way home just as she'd had to do last night. The pain as she thought of Terry shot through her like an arrow. Pulling herself together she said, "Will you tell Uncle Anthony? He should know."

"Well actually … I … I won't see him today, I'm not going into the bank. Best if you contact him yourself." He had no intention of speaking to that man unless he was forced to. No doubt his uncle would be there fast enough when he heard of his sister-in-law's death, Charles thought smugly. But now, when probate was granted, he'd be able to afford to repay his uncle and then he would give him and his bank the finger.

Laura's uncle sounded genuinely sorry to hear her sad tidings. It wasn't possible for him to make the journey at the moment. "Especially now, as you're aware."

"Why's that?" Laura asked out of politeness, was there something she'd forgotten?

"Never mind, you have enough worries to cope with. I'll speak to you tomorrow. Laura please accept our deepest sympathies and if there is anything at all we can do, we're here. There'll always be a welcome here for *you,* you know that."

Why had her uncle stressed "you" like that? As opposed to Charles? She had to get that will resealed and back in the safe.

Mrs Oz was working in the kitchen. She blushed as Laura found her humming to herself. Billy was coming home for the funeral.

"I'm going to bed now, Mrs Oz. Will you wake me in a couple of hours?"

"Have a good sleep sweetheart, I'll wake you with a nice cup of tea."

Laura smiled. Mrs Oz should market her tea.

Last night Mrs Oz had insisted that she'd make all the funeral arrangements. "Leave it to me. You mustn't argue, Laura," she said firmly.

It was difficult to go back to her mother's room. Last night seemed so long ago. She put the will on her desk, opened the safe and took out the envelope. The new will was creased in exactly the same place as the original. She slipped the genuine will from its envelope and reassured herself again that they were, indeed, identical. She smeared just enough glue on a cotton bud, then closed the flap and smoothed it down. Good, it hadn't even puckered and there was no sign of glue anywhere on the back. She put it back into the big packet and placed it amongst the other documents. Then she re-locked the safe. Laura placed the key, her mother's wedding ring and watch in a fresh brown envelope. She lit a match and set fire to the original will. She held it over the empty wastepaper bin checking that it was thoroughly burnt, then crushed the remains of the charred sheet to a fine powder and opened the window. Laura watched as the ashes of the will wafted away on the breeze, lost forever. One more phone call and then she could rest.

The solicitor was courteous and kind. Certainly he would read the will, he still had several other papers belonging to her mother. Laura was not to worry, he would take care of everything. There was nothing more that she could do now but wait. She turned and looked at the bed, its pillows plumped, the sheets crisply laundered.

"It won't worry you now, Mum, but I earned every penny." Laura closed the door quietly as if not to disturb her mother and went to her own room where she cried herself to sleep.

CHAPTER NINETY-THREE

Charles wasn't really listening to Mrs Oz as they crunched over the gravel. The funeral had upset him more than he imagined it would. He'd never spent much time with the old girl but her death was the end of an era. Billy hadn't been overjoyed to see him again. Billy and Laura should have been brother and sister, they had more in common than he and Laura ever did.

"I'm glad it's over for Laura's sake, she looked so terrible yesterday when she came over to the cottage for me to sign the paper," Mrs Oz confided. "It was so early and the poor thing hadn't had a wink of sleep. Don't you think she looks very washed out?"

"Sorry Mrs Oz, I got distracted, what did you say?"

"I was saying, that when Laura came over to me to have her paper signed yesterday, she looked dreadful. Don't you think she's still very pale?"

"Yes she is, but she'll get over it."

Apart from her stinging greeting, Laura had barely said two words to him since he'd arrived. Mrs Oz hadn't been over-effusive either.

"Laura," Charles called up the stairs, "I'm here."

"How's the treachery business doing?" she mocked brushing past him.

For a moment he thought she'd flipped. "What do you mean?" Charles asked catching her arm.

"I *mean* - your two-faced employment agency.

What do you call it? *Wreck-a-life?*"

She was choked about losing Terry. "Just a minute, that was *not* my idea."

"Of course not. Mum made all the arrangements to send him to Argentina. After all, Charles, she had so many contacts there. She met so many people every week at the races or the polo matches."

Laura shrugged off his arm and marched to the kitchen.

"Which room am I using?" Charles asked.

"Sleep in the stables," she replied evenly, "horses seem to be your field of expertise."

His back was broad, he could take the flak, especially today. Especially now as he heard the crunch of car wheels behind him. That would be Peter Riordan, his mother's solicitor, spot on time.

Laura had been so intractable last night. He had wanted to search the safe for the will and to read it immediately but she'd refused point-blank.

"Peter Riordan will read it tomorrow after the funeral. He has more papers or trusts or something - I'm not sure what - so we'll wait for him. That's what Mum wanted and that's the way it will be."

Charles hadn't bothered to argue. Let her have her moment. Much good it would do her. Now his moment was approaching and his heart quickened. In a very short time he'd be a millionaire at least but, he suspected, it would be far more than that. His mother had spent very little except for the money she had lavished on the horses. He doubted that she'd touched her own trust money from her parents. Then there was all the profit from the stud - and that he *did* know about. His father's money had been wisely invested by Anthony Bingham - the only good thing he could find to say for his uncle. And then there was the house and the stud. The house might be falling apart but the land was worth a packet and the stud was in super condition. It could compete with any stud anywhere, Terry said. What bad timing that had been. Another few days and Laura could have had her precious Terry. Mind you he hadn't taken too much persuading to up and go - but that was her problem.

"Peter, how nice to see you. Thank you so much for coming," Charles said, in his best banking manner.

"Hello, Charles. My deepest sympathy on your untimely loss. It's very sad to lose a parent." Peter noticed that Charles didn't look at all sad. Poor Laura, so pale and wan. "Excuse me, I must go and pay my respects to your sister."

Charles wasn't going to offend the man who was about to make him so rich. On the flight coming over he had sorted out in his mind which of his so-called friends he would dump. The ones who had been *unavailable* once the news of his departure from the bank had leaked out. A few of them had hung round long enough to dish the dirt but, when they failed to get any information, they too were *booked up for months, old chap. Give you a bell when I'm free.* His bookmaker had chased him incessantly. His tailor was threatening court action. All this in less than a few days.

Now it would be a different story. For starters, if he handled his money cleverly he would never have to work again. Whatever happens, he thought, it won't be invested in the Bingham bank. His uncle could go hang himself - escorted off the premises, indeed!

"Charles, would you and Laura like to bring me all the relevant papers and we can proceed with reading the will?"

Together they went to their mother's room. "The key is in there," Laura said, handing him the sealed brown envelope.

Charles ripped it open. "Here, Laura, you can have the ring and the watch."

She stared as he opened the safe and gathered together the papers in his large hands. He may want these trinkets back when he sees what's inside the will, she thought to herself with satisfaction.

Despite the warmth of the day the dining-room was chilly, musty from lack of use.

"We will deal with the will first, then I'll answer any questions you may have to ask regarding the trusts etc." Taking his time, Peter Riordan perused the document.

"Get on with it," Charles pleaded silently.

"There are just two beneficiaries, Laura Bingham and Charles Bingham."

"Not Mrs Oz?" Laura asked innocently.

Why didn't she shut up and let him read the bloody thing.

"No, Laura, she's not mentioned."

"Right. We start with the usual statement, *Being of sound mind...* Here we are, *To my son Charles Rudolph Bingham, I bequeath the sum of one hundred thousand pounds and all my jewellery. Should he not have reached the age of majority at the time of my demise, I appoint*

Anne Schulman

*Anthony Bingham of The Bingham Merchant
Bank, London, England, to administer the
bequest. To my daughter, Laura Sarah Bingham, I
bequest all moneys accrued, and all lands,
properties and trusts owned by me. Should she not
have reached the age of majority…"*

"Just a minute, that's not correct. You'd better
read it again," Charles interrupted, frowning.
What sort of legal representative was he? Imagine
making such an obvious mistake.

"I can assure you there is no mistake, here, see
for yourself."

Charles snatched the will from Peter Riordan's
hand. His eyes scanned the page in a flash. This
was all wrong. He was the son, it was his
entitlement, his inheritance. Charles dropped the
paper on to the table too stunned to speak. In a
couple of dozen words his whole world had
crashed about him. At the bottom of the
document he recognised his mother's signature.
Seán O'Hagan and Loretta O'Sullivan had acted
as witnesses. It was dated Friday, the Thirteenth
of September, Nineteen Hundred and Eighty. In
his stupefied state he tried to recall who Loretta
O'Sullivan was. Mrs Oz - he'd forgotten that she
had another name.

"I'll explain everything to you now if you wish,
or do …"

"This is insane," Charles shouted, "I have
always been led to believe that I would inherit
the estate. Everything was to be left to *me*. After
my father died, my mother told me that I would
take his place. Everything, except a cash bequest
to Laura, would be mine."

Peter Riordan studied the enraged man facing

him. He had seen it all before. This was a sizeable estate and Charles Bingham's attitude had changed from hauteur to shock and now hostility was setting in. He waited for the onslaught of litigious threats that would surely follow.

"If you've been misled, I'm sorry. I can understand your disappointment, Mr Bingham, but in my experience people often change their minds. Usually the expectant beneficiary is the last to know of the changes, for obvious reasons. In case of point, a verbal promise made so long ago is worthless and not legally binding. This will, however, is."

Laura sat rigidly on the chair, her body taut as a violin string. She had not expected this to be easy and had steeled herself in advance. By clamping her two feet closely together, and pushing the tension to the balls of her feet, she was able to control her tremors. She pressed her arms tightly against her body, her clenched hands were hidden from sight on her knees. Unless it was strictly necessary she wouldn't speak, a quavering voice would surely betray her.

"I shall contest the will," Charles said. His voice caused a fresh assault of shudders to rock Laura's body.

What have I done? she asked herself, as she felt her self-control slipping. If she owned up now, maybe Charles would go easy on her. He might be content to let it go at that. What was the penalty for what she'd done? Peter Riordan's calm voice broke through her thoughts.

"You are, of course, free to contest the will, but I feel it my duty to warn you that you are unlikely to succeed. It can be a distressing and expensive procedure. Furthermore, everything appears to be in order so I would advise you to think long and hard before involving yourself in any such action."

Charles jumped to his feet, his chair crashed to the ground behind him. "I don't need your advice," he bellowed. "Why should you give a damn, you cold fish. It's *my* life that's in shreds."

A panel in the worn door splintered as it crashed shut. Laura was no longer able to hold herself together. She gave free rein to her pent-up emotions. Sobbing loudly she apologised and then cried again.

"This is so distressing for you, Laura," Peter Riordan said kindly, handing her a big white handkerchief. "I've seen more reactions like your brother's than you've had hot dinners."

"I'm sorry," she sobbed. "I feel such a fool."

He sat quietly, letting her crying fit work itself out of her system. Charles Bingham was, in his opinion, an arrogant bastard, but he couldn't allow his partiality for Laura to show. He'd always liked Laura and had been floored when she'd bounced into his office one day looking like something from a fashion magazine. What a change from the frumpy but pleasant girl she had been. In such a small town rumours abounded and the word was that she was doing a line with that English fellow who'd been brought over to manage the stud. Peter would have liked to ask her out but he didn't fancy his chances. Now he heard that the manager had gone to Venezuela or somewhere - but this wasn't the time to make his move. All he could do for now was to make himself indispensable. There at her beck and call should she need him, and she *would* need him. The estate was pretty straightforward, there was just a lot of it. Aside from her burgeoning beauty what a catch she'd be now for some likely lad. He knew it would amount to a fortune. Why shouldn't he throw his cap in the ring? After all he had a grandstand seat.

"Laura, may I make a suggestion?"

"Yes please do," she sniffed.

"We should abandon all discussions for a couple of days until you're feeling up to it. Then we can get together and I'll explain everything in detail. A couple of days here or there will make no difference. You've suffered such a shock that you're probably not able to think straight just now anyway."

Laura reached across and placed her hand lightly on his. "You are so understanding, Peter. And you're right, I don't think anything would sink in. Will you come and have a drink? I could do with one. I still have my brother to cope with."

"Don't let him intimidate you. If you have problems, let me know - any time."

Peter opened his wallet and took out a card. "I'll put my home number on this so you can contact me, day or night." He hesitated. Should he warn her that, if Charles showed any signs of violence, she must contact the police. It had happened before, but not very often. Maybe, in this instance, silence was golden. Laura was a sensible girl and he was probably being over-protective. Don't push it, he warned himself, there was more than one way to skin a cat. Lord, I'm full of clichés today, he groaned inwardly.

CHAPTER NINETY-FOUR

Alone in the kitchen mother and son stared at each other silently. Mrs Oz was the first to speak. "I can't believe it, glory be! After the hell she put that girl through, she finally did the right thing."

"I'm stunned myself," Billy said. He couldn't understand Olivia Bingham's change of heart.

"Of course one day I'll own the stud and the land," Charles had always boasted to Billy.

"It's the best thing that could've happened to him and I'm thrilled to bits for Laura. This place is worth a bob or two and Olivia must have made a fair few quid from the horses."

"I wouldn't be surprised," his mother agreed. "She certainly didn't spend it on the house!"

They sat lost in their own thoughts.

It was just like old times. Laura and Billy sat at the kitchen table watching Mrs Oz bustling about, humming and preparing the meal. The only difference was the silence upstairs. No ringing bell to disturb them.

"I know I keep staring at you," Billy laughed, "but you've turned into a real cracker. If I wasn't getting married I'd fancy you myself." Their easy relationship had picked up where it left off. Laura still adored her surrogate brother. He was a fine man and had lost nothing of his kind nature. Billy could make her laugh no matter how sad she felt. None of them said anything but they all breathed a sigh of relief when Charles left for the evening to go to the K Club to meet some friends.

Cursing and swearing Charles had stormed round the house after the reading of the will. He'd been positively rude to the few people who had come to offer their condolences. His ranting and raving had worn the three of them to a frazzle until finally Billy stepped in.

"You can't hold anyone here responsible for what's happened, so why not calm down," Billy reasoned. "Laura's no more to blame for your mother's decision than I am."

"Get stuffed. This is family business and nothing to do with the likes of you."

Laura leapt to Billy's defence. "How dare you speak to Billy like that ... *in my house,*" she added spitefully.

"Not *yet* it's not." They could see the pulse beating in his throat as he groped for words. "It'll be a different story when I contest the will, then you'll be out on your ear." How lame that sounded. Charles's frustration had robbed him of any power to come up with a devastating reply. If his sister was going to keep on blubbing all around the place then at least let it be him that caused it. Little hypocrite she was, she'd had as little time for their mother as he had. He was delighted that Terence Harvey had left her, let her weep about *that.*

"It's no wonder Terry accepted Alvirez's offer with such alacrity," Charles sneered. "He preferred to go and bury himself in the wilds than to fall into your clutches. He told me so himself when he asked me to find him another job, as far away from you as possible."

Anne Schulman

Mrs Oz pressed down on her son's shoulders as he tried to rise from his chair.

"That's a lie and you know it," she said angrily. "Don't bother to invent stories about what Terry Harvey said and didn't say. I was there and heard it all. You and your mother plotting and planning to get him away - and the fee you demanded from her for yourself. The reason he left was because he was told the stud was closing down and there'd be no future for him here any more. He was very upset to leave Laura. Because of her duty to *your* mother he realised that it would be impossible for her to live anywhere but here, he told me that himself." The latter part of her story she made up as she went along. She would do anything to remove the stricken look from Laura's face.

In all the years she had known Mrs Oz, Laura had never known her to be so angry or to speak so sharply.

"Is that true, Mrs Oz?" Laura asked. If it was true it would go a little way towards healing her wounds.

"Of course it's true, do you think I'd make up something that important?" She could confess her sin and pray for forgiveness later.

"Now that his lordship is out of the way and we can relax, I think we should discuss your future, Mam," Billy said.

"Would you like me to leave?" Laura asked querulously.

"To the woodshed my girl," Billy pointed dramatically towards the back door. "Don't be silly, Laura. In fact, this concerns you as much as it does us."

Billy and Mrs Oz had remained impassive when Laura told them the reason for Charles' irrational behaviour. "He expected to inherit everything, you see." Laura shook her head as if dumbfounded by the bombshell that had landed in her lap. This would be the one secret that she'd never share with Mrs Oz. It would go with her to the grave.

"I'm sorry that my mother didn't provide for you, but I most certainly will." Telling the truth was a lot easier than lying. "I promise you, no matter what happens, you won't have to worry about money."

"That's a wonderful gesture, thank you. What will you do? Will you stay here or sell up?" Billy asked.

"I'll get rid of all this as fast as I can," Laura said vehemently. "Peter Riordan says I have to sit tight until probate is granted. And don't forget that my dear brother is still screaming about contesting the will."

"Take no notice of him, he's all mouth," Billy laughed. He hoped, for Laura's sake, that Charles would forget the idea. Courts could hand out some weird decisions at times. "Anyway, what'll you do when it's all finished? Where will you go?"

"I thought about that last night. At first I thought I'd go and live in Dublin, but then I decided I wouldn't. There's no one there I know so what's the point? Then it came to me - London! If I lived there I'd have friends *and* a family - not counting Charles, if I ever see him again it'll be too soon. But most important of all, will you come with me, Mrs Oz? I couldn't live

Anne Schulman

my life without you."

"London? I've never been abroad, I mean, away from here not since I was... since I came to work here. London, my goodness," she floundered.

"Think how near you'll be to Billy and his wife. You'd have loads of free time and it's a wonderful city, so exciting. There'd be a million things for you to see and to do. *Please* Mrs Oz, say yes."

"It sounds a good idea, Mam. I'd love to be able to see you more often. And Laura's right, there are loads of things to do. Imagine, you could go to the Chelsea Flower Show..."

"You could join a gardening club," Laura interjected. They were never at a loss for a gift for her. An illustrated book of flowers sent Mrs Oz into raptures for weeks. Her own cottage was like an oasis in the desert, blooming, flourishing, nurtured with loving care and a riot of intoxicating colour.

"It's so sudden," Mrs Oz said, "London, of all places."

"Think about it, Mam, you don't have to decide this minute."

This was definitely the time for a cup of tea. Laura and Billy smiled knowingly at each other. When there was something to be thought about seriously some people walked, others sat quietly, but Mrs Oz automatically reached for her kettle.

CHAPTER NINETY-FIVE

Charles left the house at the crack of dawn. As a last spiteful gesture, he had taken the Range Rover. A curt note propped on the kitchen table informed Laura she could pick it up at Dublin Airport.

Despite the ferocious, tongue-lashing argument they'd had when Charles returned the previous night, Laura presumed that he'd abandoned the idea of contesting the will. The name, John Moloney, rang a bell. He had phoned to say that he would be late for dinner, but Charles had already left for the K Club. The name nipped at her brain all evening like a little midge.

"Who's John Moloney?" Laura asked her brother.

"Why?" Charles growled.

"No reason, the name rang a bell. He phoned..."

"I know, he told me."

"Will you tell Uncle Anthony I send my love and will ring him?"

"No, I won't. Pass your own messages," Charles snarled. He glared at Laura and shook his head. "God alone knows how you managed to turn my mother against me."

"I did nothing. You and she were hell-bent on destroying *my* happiness. I'll never forgive you for that."

"Shiver! Shiver!" Charles retorted, shaking his wrists at his sister. "And you, my dear sister?

You're a dull, boring country bumpkin. I suppose now that you have 'expectations' you'll take some lessons on how to become a *rich,* boring, country bumpkin instead."

"At least I'll be *rich,*" jibed Laura, *"very, very rich."*

"You bitch. Someday I'll find out how you managed to manipulate her. I hope your legacy brings you nothing but unhappiness."

"It won't, I assure you. If you'd been half decent I might have considered giving you some of it, but not now." If he had been half decent this would never have happened, she reminded herself.

Was there a chink in her armour? Charles wondered. He flashed a quick look at his sister's face. Before she could reply they heard Billy calling her.

"Your minder is calling you," Charles said, caustically.

"He's very kind to me, which is more than I can say for you."

"I'll bet. Think how many men will be good to you now, little Miss Money Bags, up for grabs. If you ever do find someone stupid enough to marry you, he can put you in the safe and sleep with your money."

Charles caught her by the wrist as she lashed out at him.

"Enjoy it Laura, while you can. You know, and I know, that estate was meant for me and I won't rest until I get what's rightfully mine, and mark my words - I *will* get it." His tone was icy calm and far more frightening than his temper.

Suddenly Laura remembered. John Moloney,

he and Charles had been in university together. Her brother had expressed his derision when John, armed with a law degree, had left the big-smoke to open a practice in Dublin. So that was why Charles had demanded a photocopy of the will. Obviously *he* must have persuaded Charles there was no point in trying to contest it.

"Thank you, John Moloney," Laura prayed silently.

CHAPTER NINETY-SIX

"Perhaps it would be easier all round if you both came over to London," Anthony Bingham suggested.

"Maybe so. I think that would be more satisfactory than all these phone calls," Peter Riordan replied. "I think it will do Laura good, quite frankly. It's lonely in that house. Mrs Oz is there during the day, of course, but I hate to think of her on her own at night."

"Tell you what, why don't we arrange for her to spend her birthday here. I'll round up my sons and my daughter-in-law, my wife will organise a restaurant and we'll celebrate. It would be a shame for her big day to go by without some sort of recognition."

Peter Riordan had planned to take Laura to dinner the night of her twenty-first but spending several days with her in London would be a real bonus. He took her to dinner or went to the house at least once a week. He was becoming more and more attracted to her. Peter was aware that she liked and trusted him but it was as plain as the nose on her face she was still grieving for Terence Harvey. In a weak moment she had told him the whole story. It confirmed his opinion of Charles Bingham and it hadn't made him think more kindly of Olivia Bingham either. He must phone Laura.

"Hello," Laura replied in a flat voice.

"Hello Laura, my, you sound a bit down."

Peter Riordan kept his voice chirpy.

"A bit I suppose. I hate this incessant rain," Laura moaned.

"How would you like to go to London with me next week?" Was that a slight gasp? "It was your uncle's suggestion," he added hastily.

"I thought for a moment you were propositioning me," Laura laughed.

"Strictly legit, I promise!"

"Any reason?"

"It will be just a couple of months now before probate is granted and he would like to tie up all the loose ends. It's much easier than phone calls and faxes."

"I think I'd like that very much. Anything to get out of this place. The only thing is, I don't like leaving Mrs Oz on her own," Laura said dubiously.

"Then why not take her along. I'm sure Billy would be thrilled to see her and she could spend a few days with him. Why not give Billy a ring and see what he says. Let me know in the morning what you decide and I'll make the bookings."

"It would be fun. I'll get in touch with Nadia, Fiona and Georgie and we can have a night out - you and four women!"

"I better get plenty of rest then, I'm going to need all my health and strength." He put down the receiver and made a note on his pad to mention Laura's friends to Anthony Bingham should he wish to include them in the birthday celebration. Peter vaguely remembered Georgina, a vivacious teenager with a zest for life. He knew Nadia well and, if his memory served him, Fiona was a tall, slim girl with curly black hair and a ready smile.

His day had brightened considerably, he could rearrange most of his appointments - there was nothing too urgent. Laura's uncle seemed a kindly man and Peter agreed with him that her twenty-first birthday should be marked. It wasn't till later that night that Peter realised that Anthony Bingham had made no mention of Charles. He wondered if her uncle was aware of the situation between brother and sister.

Laura heard the note of alarm in Billy's voice. "It's OK, Billy, everything's fine. I have a great idea and wanted to talk to you first."

"Sorry, Laura, I did get a fright," Billy said, his tone relaxed. "What's the idea?"

"I have to go to London next week and I was wondering if you would like me to persuade your Mam to go with me to visit you?"

"You don't need to ask! You know how often I've tried to persuade her and what she's like. I'd love her to meet Debbie. It's a great idea, so give it your best shot, Laura."

"I promise I will. How are things with you, Billy?"

"Terrific, mad busy. What's happening over there? Have you heard any more from Charles?"

"Not a word, thank goodness. Peter Riordan is looking after everything. He's great, Billy, hardly lets me think for myself. I don't know how I would have managed without him."

"Oh, yes?"

"Not like that, don't go jumping to conclusions. He's been a terrific friend and we have an odd dinner here and there but that's it."

"OK, if you say so," Billy said, disappointed. Peter Riordan was a nice guy and would be good for Laura. He wondered if she was still hung up on Harvey. "Anything happening about the house and all the rest?"

"Peter's cousin, Jill Riordan, is an estate agent and as soon as I can give the word she'll start advertising it. In the meantime she phoned to say that she might have a client of hers who'd be interested. She's explained to him that it won't be available for at least two more months but he's dead keen to see it. He's away at the moment but when he gets back she's going to phone me. We'll see what happens after that."

"I hope you sell it easily Laura. The sooner you're out of it the better. I wish you'd move in with Mam, I know it's a bit cramped but so what?"

"I'm fine, Billy, but thanks for worrying about me. I'll get your Mam to phone you tomorrow. She's over at the cottage and it's a shame to disturb her. Wish me luck," Laura laughed.

Mrs Oz drove a hard bargain. The more Laura thought about it the more she was convinced that she couldn't go to London and leave Mrs Oz alone. Throwing on a warm jacket and a woolly hat she crossed the path to the cottage.

"It's a filthy night," Laura said, warming her hands by the fire.

"I'm delighted to see you, but what brings you over?"

Laura wasn't sure now how to broach the subject. "How about a cup of your famous tea?" she asked, playing for time. "I might as well come straight out with it, I'm going to London next week and you're coming with me." Laura had failed to come up with a more subtle approach.

"Who said?" Mrs Oz demanded.

"I said."

"For what?"

"For a little break. I've never known you take a holiday and you could stay with Billy, meet Debbie and her parents and you'd have a great time."

"If you don't mind Laura, I'd prefer to wait till the wedding."

"Well, if you won't go then neither will I. I wouldn't stay here on my own without *you.*"

"That's blackmail."

"That's right!" Laura grinned.

"I'll have to think about it. Just listen to that rain."

"Don't change the subject."

"I'll think about it, I promise."

The little room was cosy and warm, it shone with a pride only love could bring. The chairs and the couch, with their starched antimacassars, were a bit big for the room. They had been chosen for comfort and were better than anything back at the house. Laura lay on the couch and stretched her legs. "It sort of hugs you, this settee, doesn't it?"

Mrs Oz smiled but she knew what Laura meant. She loved every inch of her dinky little home. Perhaps it was the contrast between the big house and this but it never failed to give her a thrill when she opened the door and walked inside. If only Laura would stay here during these cold winter nights.

Intrigue

"I suppose I should be getting back," Laura sighed.

"You can't go out in this, you'll catch your death of cold. At least wait until it stops raining."

"Just a little longer then." They could hear the rain beating against the windows.

In the bookcase against the wall Laura could see all Mrs Oz's gardening books, each one covered with a transparent film of plastic. Soft music was barely audible from the little radio beside Mrs Oz's chair. "What are you thinking about?" Laura asked.

"About whether I could go to London."

Laura snuggled deeply into the couch, at least Mrs Oz was considering it.

"Laura," the voice, though low, startled her.

"I must have nodded off," she said struggling to sit up. "I must go back to the house."

Mrs Oz smiled at the sleepy-eyed girl. "Have some breakfast first, we might as well eat here."

"Breakfast?" Laura asked, squinting at the closed curtains. She could hear the chirping of a bird and, over the curtain rail, a thin ribbon of light intruded into the darkened room.

"Have you given any more thought to the London idea?"

"I have. Did you sleep well?"

"Brilliantly, but what's that got to do with it?"

"Just this. If you sleep here until the end of the winter, at least, I'll go with you."

"More blackmail!"

"Exactly."

* * *

Laura held Mrs Oz's trembling hand in her own,

the roar of the jets had frightened her.

"We'll be in the air in a minute," Peter said, smiling at the cowering woman.

She relaxed her grip as the plane levelled off and even managed a wavering smile. By the time the stewardess had arrived with her trolley Mrs Oz was contentedly reading the in-flight magazine.

Billy's face was wreathed in smiles as he stood at the barrier, waving. Beside him a pretty girl with short wavy hair and a fresh complexion waited quietly. Laura could see her name on one of the cards held up by waiting drivers and recognised the bank's representative from her last trip. Mrs Oz hugged Laura and promised to keep in touch. She was deep in conversation with Billy's fiancée before they reached the end of the concourse.

Anthony Bingham greeted them warmly. He kissed his niece and enquired if they'd had a good flight. His secretary brought them some coffee and left with instructions that they were not to be disturbed. Laura listened attentively at first but after a while the figures and legal jargon merged in her brain like so many telephone numbers. She fidgeted nervously, dreading that at any time the door could open and her brother would enter the room. She felt trapped.

"Does that meet with your approval, Laura?" her uncle was asking.

"I'm sorry, I wandered off, does what meet with my approval?"

"Your trust fund, it's released tomorrow - your twenty-first birthday."

Laura had lost the gist of the conversation and

was embarrassed.

"Why don't we break for lunch?" Anthony Bingham suggested. His niece looked strained. He was used to dealing with figures and the legalities - it was probably all a bit much for Laura to grasp.

They adjourned to the boardroom where a light lunch was set out on the table. They helped themselves to cucumber mousse, a smoked fish quiche and a variety of interesting salads. Laura asked about her aunt, the newly-weds and her cousin Bertie. No sooner were the words out of her mouth than Bertie entered the room. He hugged Laura affectionately.

"I was just asking about you," she said smiling. How long before Charles appeared?

She put her fork down on her plate, her appetite had vanished.

"I think it best now if I leave the two of you together," Peter said. "I'll call back for you at four o'clock, Laura. How about tickets for a theatre tonight?"

"That would be lovely - a comedy maybe?"

"He's a very pleasant young man," her uncle observed after Peter had left, "sensible and straightforward. I think you're in good hands."

"Uncle Anthony, I have a favour to ask," Laura began nervously. "As you can imagine, Charles was very upset when Mum's will was read. We fought all the time he was in Kildare and I'd prefer if he didn't handle any of this." She waved a vague hand at the mountains of papers spread out on the desk.

Her uncle looked at her thoughtfully. "You didn't know that Charles had left the bank?" he asked.

Anne Schulman

Laura's amazed look answered his question.

"I can see that you know nothing of his departure from Bingham's." Her uncle's tone was frosty.

"What happened?" Laura demanded.

"As a member of the family I'll tell you, however it must remain confidential."

Laura nodded her head in agreement. Her uncle related the sordid details.

No wonder Charles was hysterical when he discovered the terms of the will.

"How will he repay you now?" she asked.

Her uncle shrugged. "Probably he never will. It's a small price to pay compared with the scandal that there might have been had the news leaked out." Anthony Bingham had been astounded to learn that Olivia had made Laura the beneficiary of her will. He had been certain that Charles could repay him from his inheritance when he'd let him off the hook. He was delighted that his niece had been so generously provided for, but ...

"I'll settle his debt." In a way she felt some responsibility. She had cheated him of his inheritance.

"That's a generous offer, Laura, but it's not necessary. The bank can stand the loss. Your brother is one of the things I wanted to discuss with you."

Laura blushed with shame as her uncle revealed the rough total of her inheritance. "That's not including the property, of course, you can probably add a half a million more for that."

A multi-millionairess, even after death duties.

"I can't take it in. It's ... it's ... I don't know what it is," Laura gasped. "All I can think of is how we lived in that freezing, shabby house and there were all those millions - just lying there."

"You must understand, Laura. That dreadful accident changed your mother. I'm not implying that she was in any way mentally disturbed, she just wasn't the same person after it happened. Her values had altered." I've said enough, Anthony Bingham cautioned himself, I mustn't impose my own opinions on Laura. Privately he thought his sister-in-law had been a cold fish. He'd been well aware of the worsening condition of the house - after visiting home Charles often remarked how shabby it had become. But when he himself had approached Olivia, and told her she could well afford to carry out the repairs and redecoration necessary, she had slammed down the phone. That was their last verbal contact. All their business from then on was conducted by post or through Charles.

"Laura, a word of warning. Charles may well try to borrow money from you. He has expensive tastes. He likes to gamble, to be seen at all the right places, live the good life and that takes a lot of money. Be careful, his needs are a bottomless pit."

"I can assure you, I want nothing to do with Charles. As you have taken me into your confidence, I'll tell you why I feel so bitter towards him," Laura faced her uncle across his paper-strewn desk and told him about Terry. "So now you understand."

"Will you try to contact him now?" her uncle asked. He was not easily shocked but Laura's tale had sickened him.

"No, never. Terence Harvey is history," she replied.

CHAPTER NINETY-SEVEN

The phone woke her from a deep sleep. "Happy birthday, Laura," Billy's voice sang.

"Billy, what a lovely surprise. How's your Mam?"

"She's right here beside me, waiting to say hello."

"Laura? Happy birthday darling, and many happy returns."

"Thank you, this is a lovely start to the day. How are you enjoying yourself?"

"It's wonderful to be with Billy. Debbie is such a nice girl, you'd like her, Laura. I have to go now. See you on Friday."

Within ten minutes the phone was ringing again.

"Nadia, I was just finishing breakfast and then I was going to give you a ring."

"Happy twenty-first," her friend said.

"You remembered!" Laura exclaimed, flattered.

"Of course I did, silly, did you forget *my* twenty-first?"

Laura laughed, this was getting better by the minute. "I'm dashing, how about lunch?"

"Do you mind if I bring Peter with me?"

"Course not. See you at the Lanesborough, one o'clock, OK?"

"I'm really looking forward to it." On her previous trip Laura had listened to Nadia and her friends discussing the hotel, built on the site of the old St George's Hospital at Hyde Park Corner.

"Happy birthday, you don't mind if I don't sing it?" Peter said, laughing.

Laura told him of her intended lunch. "I want to do some research for a client, would you mind if I opted out?"

"Whatever … I have to go to the bank, don't forget my trust fund matures today."

"I know - and you should really enjoy spending your money, it *is* your birthday - see you back at the hotel around six-thirty."

Laura stood in the doorway of the conservatory restaurant and looked for Nadia.

A voice called from behind and she turned around to see the rushing figure of her friend. Nadia hugged Laura and pushed a prettily wrapped packet into her hand. They followed the waiter to their table.

"It's gorgeous, so bright!" Laura said, admiring the room, which was modelled on the Brighton Pavilion.

"So, today you're an adult! Welcome to the clan," Nadia teased.

"Thank you, kind lady," Laura grinned.

"I'm delighted you're back so soon. Maybe now that your … now that you are free, you'll be able to visit more often. You said last night that you wanted to discuss something with me, I'm dead curious."

"Prepare yourself for a shock, I'm coming to live in London."

"Fantastic, oh Laura, I'm thrilled!" Nadia's face shone with delight.

"That's why I needed to see you, I'd like you to find me somewhere suitable to live."

"Of course I will. A flat? I suppose you'll want

to rent, property in London is expensive."

"I'd like to buy a house. Up till an hour ago I didn't know where, but I strolled around Wilton Crescent and that's where I'd like to be ..."

"Laura, sweetheart, they cost a *fortune*, those houses."

"I know they do, but there's something else you don't know. When my mother died she left everything to me, and it is a fortune, a great big one."

Nadia sat with her fork poised in mid-air. "You mean, she left the stud and everything to you and not Charles?"

"Exactly." Laura was coping well with her guilty feelings about the great inheritance although they floated accusingly across her mind at regular intervals.

"I'm floored," Nadia said, "I thought the blue-eyed boy would cop the lot. I'm sorry, Laura, I didn't mean to be so rude."

"Be my guest, except he's now the green-eyed monster."

"You're now a lady of means?"

"You could say that!"

"I'll certainly get on to it for you, but prepare yourself for a shock - price-wise."

The waiter removed their plates and produced a dessert menu.

"What's in those cups that everyone is ordering?" Laura asked him.

"Cappuccino brûlée, Madam."

"I adore coffee, what about you Nadia?"

"Why not? I can starve myself for two days."

Laura looked round the big dining-room with its domed-glass roof. Fountains splashed, and palms towered in their tubs shading hand-painted Chinese figures.

She loved the mineral water in the blue bottles and noticed there was one at almost every table. "People prefer not to drink at lunch-time these days," Nadia explained. "When mineral water became the fashion a lot of people sighed with relief."

The waiter placed the pretty china cups and saucers in front of them. "Oh look!" Laura exclaimed, "the spoon is made of biscuit."

"It's too pretty to eat!" Using their teaspoons they tapped the delicate layer of hardened caramel and spooned up some of the delicious coffee-cream.

"It's gorgeous!" Nadia said, "well spotted!"

Laura insisted on paying the bill. With a flourish she wrote a cheque in her new cheque-book and added a generous tip.

They walked through the long foyer making a detour through the Great Hall with its regency striped sofas and magnificent flower arrangements. In one corner of the room blinding arc-lights shone on the slender figure of a blonde woman whose face was familiar. Laura, puzzled for a moment, said, "It's Ivana Trump. I knew I recognised her." She was surrounded by cameras and journalists. They peeped inside the Library which served as a bar.

"It's almost like a room in a private house," Nadia remarked.

Laura strolled back to her hotel in Wilton Place. It was only a few hundred yards away. She was well wrapped up against the chill wind so she decided to keep on walking and make a circuit of the elegant crescent. She loved the tall, immaculate houses with their window boxes which were in flower, even at this time of the year. The houses were smaller than some of those in Lowndes Square …The thought of her brother sent a shiver through Laura. How did he propose to relieve her of her fortune? He was her only sibling. She presumed it would pass to him in the event of her death. She must check with her uncle about that, she would prefer to leave it to Billy. Mrs Oz would be well taken care of, the transfer of a generous sum was already in hand.

Laura found herself back at the hotel. The doorman smiled and opened the door for her. The big fire blazing in the hearth instantly shut out memories of the cold winter's afternoon. Laura adored the intimate atmosphere of what had been the home of the Bishop of Berkeley, the Berkeley Hotel. Her uncle had made the reservations there for them. He knew that Laura would enjoy a touch of luxury for a change. Tonight her uncle and aunt would be joining them at the hotel for dinner, a birthday celebration, her uncle had said. She was a little disappointed that neither Georgie nor Fiona had contacted her, but perhaps they were away. She'd left messages on their answering machines.

Taking the lift to the top floor she explored the gymnasium and the swimming-pool. If she lived in London she might join a health club but first she had to decide what work she wanted to do and what further training she might need. There were so many things to be decided, so much to sort out. She dreaded stripping the house. When she had suggested to Peter that she'd hire a load of skips and turf everything into them he had been almost apoplectic. "Are you nuts?" he had asked. "There's a lot of good furniture in the house, it only needs careful restoration."

Laura continued to work out her priorities as she dressed for dinner. Giving a last look in the mirror she was satisfied with her appearance. Her green silk overblouse, with its sophisticated pleating, flattered her fair colouring and relieved the severity of the black skirt, tights and shoes. Peter was waiting for her in front of the fire in the entrance hall and kissed her warmly on the cheek as he handed her his gift.

Laura smiled at him, he was so kind, she wished she could think of him as more than a friend.

"Leave it here for now," Peter said indicating the porter's desk, "you can open it later."

He led her along the corridor, stopped at a door and opened it politely as he ushered her in. Laura's heart skipped a beat. There in the pretty dining-room were her uncle and aunt but also Mrs Oz, Billy and Debbie, her cousins and Nadia, Georgie and Fiona. Laura put her hand to her mouth, but no sound would come out.

"Happy birthday!" they chorused.

Laura hugged her aunt and uncle warmly and thanked them. She had never experienced such love. She had no doubts about living in London after tonight.

CHAPTER NINETY-EIGHT

Charles Bingham looked with disgust at the sleeping figure beside him and sighed. How had he let himself in for this? Muriel Evans was not his type. Clinging and possessive she had reduced him to little better than a toy-boy.

The decor of the flat in a chi-chi terrace on the wrong side of Chelsea turned his stomach. Pink satin furniture! The carpets and curtains were pink and, worst of all, were the pink satin sheets to match. The lampshades were covered by chiffon scarves which were badly scorched by the bulbs when any breeze floated through the windows. In a fit of pique one day he had held her favourite tiger-striped scarf against the bulb, but she had replaced it with one in a violent shade of lavender.

The one saving grace was that she was generous, generous to a fault - and rich. She paid all the bills, bought him luxurious presents and he had money in his pocket but he was chained to her side, twenty-four hours a day.

With each passing week his anger grew. He raged inwardly about Laura, his mother, his uncle and his cousins, his fair-weather friends. Raged against the world. He tried to fathom out his mother's reason for her change of heart. She'd had no more affection for Laura than she'd had for himself, but she was a stickler for convention. By rights the estate was his. Half dozing his mind drifted back to the house and the funeral and the reading of the will. He could picture himself in his excited state walking over the gravel drive with Mrs Oz, Peter Riordan's car crunching to a halt, like the arrival of the Messiah. He could remember Mrs Oz's voice describing how terrible his sister looked that morning when she had gone to the cottage to get some paper signed. Then the cruel, punishing blow. Pulverising him to … He stopped dead in his thoughts. Why was Laura having papers signed? As far as he knew there were very few times that she would need a witness. He went through the possibilities in his mind. Something kept drawing him back like a piece of elastic - the will. She couldn't, she wouldn't, how could she? It couldn't be possible, Laura wouldn't have that kind of skill. The elastic snapped back, what skill would it need? To be able to forge signatures? To re-type the will? The paper was old, they'd had new stuff for ages and a new typewriter. He'd seen the upmarket letters that had arrived at the bank.

Muriel Evans stirred, "Good morning, darling," she said.

"Go back to sleep," Charles ordered sharply.

Throwing back the covers he padded to the wardrobe and pulled his briefcase from the top shelf. Taking it into his pink satin prison he placed it on a coffee table, squashing an arrangement of dried flowers. For a moment he couldn't remember the code for the lock. Finally snapping it open he took out the papers and crossed to the dining table. In disgust he threw the pink lace table mat to the floor and spread out the documents. He had to find a way out of this torture.

Anne Schulman

He compared his mother's signature on the will with those on other documents, but that proved nothing. As the years had passed his mother's writing had deteriorated. He had no way of checking Seán O'Hagan's scrawl, his name wasn't on any of the other papers. But the more he looked at the photocopy of the will the more sure he was. That's exactly what Laura had done. She had made another will. His mother hadn't had a change of heart, nothing had changed. That would also explain the unusual bequest to him of her jewellery. All that had been needed was for Laura to transpose their names and she became the beneficiary instead of him. Pacing up and down with excitement Charles tried to work out a plan.

"What about a cup of coffee?" Muriel asked tousle-haired and sleepy.

"Yes, make one," he said rudely. It didn't matter what he said to her, she never sulked.

"Answer the thing," he yelled down the burring receiver. Where was Mrs Oz? Was it possible that Laura was away or at the cottage? He groaned, there was no phone in the cottage. Every half hour he dialled, slamming the pink phone back on its cradle in disgust when there was no reply.

Muriel had never seen anyone so agitated. If she spoke, he just barked an answer. He'd squashed her beautiful flowers in his rage. Never mind. I can have them rearranged, she thought, picking up the mat and smoothing it.

"I have to go to Ireland for a couple of days," Charles announced the following morning.

"Lovely! I've always wanted to go there."

"Sorry, this is family business," he snapped.

It was a fruitless journey. Neither Laura nor Mrs Oz was at the house or at the cottage. His footsteps echoed in the empty buildings of the stud, the horses were long gone. He telephoned Peter Riordan's office hoping to get some information, but Peter was away. He was totally at a loss, there was nothing he could do but go back to London. Mrs Oz had to be back sometime.

CHAPTER NINETY-NINE

Laura sat in the back of the car. The moment she had heard Billy's voice fear had clutched her.

"It's Mam, she's had an accident."

"Oh no! Billy, what happened?"

"You know how independent she is, she climbed on a ladder to take down her suitcase for tomorrow and, as far as we can tell, the ladder slipped and she fell, crashing her head on the corner of the dressing table. She's in the local hospital now, but she's still unconscious."

Shaking and crying with fright Laura dialled Peter's room.

"I'll make all the arrangements for you to go to Norfolk. Just get dressed."

Within an hour her uncle had sent the bank's car and they were on the road. Peter sat quietly holding Laura's hand as she prayed that Mrs Oz would come round. There was little he could say to cheer her up, his presence was all he could offer.

Billy rushed to Laura when he saw her enter the hospital doors.

"No change," he said, his eyes reddened by dried tears.

In the little cubicle Laura gazed at Mrs Oz who was lying white-faced and still.

"Any change?" Billy asked the nurse, just as he had done five minutes ago.

"Not yet," she said sympathetically.

For two days Laura kept vigil at Mrs Oz's bedside. Eventually she fell asleep on the chair in exhaustion.

"There's no point in your making yourself ill too," Billy said. Mrs Oz had slipped into a coma, the doctor had told him, and there was no way of knowing when she would come out of it.

They hadn't spoken on the journey back to London or on the plane. Peter was feeling every bit of her anguish but couldn't find any way of comforting her.

"I'd give every penny due to me if I could arrive home and find Mrs Oz waiting there," Laura said, finally breaking her silence.

"I understand," Peter sympathised. "Laura, I hate your being in the house alone." He would like to have suggested the cottage but didn't have the heart.

A couple of weeks later Laura herself suggested that she should move away from the house. "I'll stay in a hotel, anywhere, but I can't bear being here any longer without Mrs Oz," she wept.

Her hair smelt sweet and it took all Peter's control not to kiss her on her trembling mouth. He held her instead like a child in his arms and allowed her to cry away her grief.

She stayed in a local hotel for a month. Jill Riordan had been as good as her word and had produced her client. He had pulled a rueful face when he saw the state of the house but shrewdly recognised the superb condition of the stud and the usefulness of the little cottage. Jill had taken Peter to one side and advised him it would be better if Laura had no part in the sale. "She's so upset she'll give it away at this stage."

"I agree wholeheartedly. He's ready to pay a deposit. I think it should be just a matter of weeks now before probate is complete."

Jill dropped the papers into the house at Easter. Laura stopped her work and glanced through the window as Jill's car drew up. She looked at the gorgeous, tanned girl who stayed in the car and, suddenly, Laura thought longingly of the companionship she would enjoy if she moved to London.

"You could do with a proper holiday, Laura. You've been through a tough time," Jill said sympathetically.

"I've never had a holiday, except in London," Laura admitted. She could afford to go anywhere she pleased now.

"There's a château in the South of France. It's absolutely gorgeous, I've been there myself. They'll look after you like a baby. It's very expensive but incredibly soothing. I can give you the address if you like."

"I think I'd like that very much, please send it to me. When all this is over I'll certainly consider it."

Peter Riordan read the letter with mixed feelings. Wonderful news for Laura but not for him. Probate had finally been granted, two months later than he had anticipated. His love for her was, he supposed, unselfish. She had faded to a shadow of her former self and he had taken two weeks leave from his firm to stay with her in the hotel when Billy had rung him with the dreadful news.

"I want you to break it to Laura," Billy had

begged. "Please don't leave her alone."

Within three hours they were on the plane to London. Peter had arranged a car to meet them at the airport and the next day Laura, sobbing and half-fainting with grief, stood in the protection of his arms at the graveside.

They left immediately after the funeral and returned to Ireland. Never had he witnessed such prolonged crying. It had lasted three days and, despite her protests, Peter had called in her doctor who immediately sedated her.

When he was reasonably satisfied that she was back on her feet Peter had returned to his office. Jill had found the address of the hotel in France that they had discussed. Laura promised that she would take the holiday when everything was complete.

He checked with Nadia in London, no suitable property had come on the market yet. "It's not a problem, Peter, Laura can stay with me for as long as she likes."

"Actually it would be better for her at the moment, she shouldn't be on her own. She's so low and she can't seem to shake it."

Anthony Bingham greeted the news that probate had been granted with relief. Peter seemed to think that the sooner Laura was able to begin a new life the better. Anthony and his wife were delighted that their niece was going to live near them and they were determined to give her the family support that Laura had never experienced.

CHAPTER ONE HUNDRED

As she stepped from the plane the force of the heat almost knocked her over. The light was blinding as she groped in her bag for her sunglasses. The air was different too, pungent. The babble of strange voices mingled with the smell of sun creams and perfumes as she stood near the barrier searching for the château's limousine driver.

Mademoiselle L. Bingham, she read. She introduced herself to the pleasant-faced man who was holding the sign.

"Welcome to France, *m'mselle,*" he said, relieving her of her cases.

As they drove along, Laura, unused to being on the right hand side of the road, hunched herself into a corner of the limousine and prepared to meet her end. Never had she seen anything like the speed of the cars that flashed past them.

Joseph always drove slowly if he sensed a passenger was nervous. He assured her it was quite safe and she flushed prettily, realising how foolish she must appear.

"Is there someone called Gabrielle O'Neill staying at the château?" she asked.

"Ah! *M'mselle* Gaby, you know her?"

"No, a friend of mine told me to introduce myself to her."

"She is one of our most favourite guests. You will like her very much, everybody does. I will find her for you myself, when you are ready."

Laura began to relax by the time they turned off the road to the château. The big black gates swung open and Joseph rolled down the windows. Laura craned her neck to see the gardens which Jill had raved about. She inhaled the sweet perfume of the flowers and shrubs lining the drive, was she imagining it or could she smell lemons?

Claude d'Albion waited for the limousine to draw up in front of the steps. Gabrielle had told him that M'mselle Bingham had been through some difficult times recently and to be sure to let her know when she arrived.

"She's very vulnerable, Gaby, she could do with a friendly face," Jill said when she'd phoned the château the previous night.

She reminded Gaby of the day they had stopped en route, the time they had passed through Kildare.

"Say no more, I'm your girl," Gaby said chirpily.

"Don't lead her into mischief, Gaby!" Jill laughed. "Bye for now."

Laura stepped from the car and smiled shyly at the dapper man approaching her.

"Welcome to the Château d'Albion, I am Claude d'Albion. If there is anything that we can do to make your stay a happy one, please don't hesitate to ask."

"Thank you, it is so beautiful here it would be difficult to be unhappy," she smiled.

Another lovely Irish girl, he thought. Try as he might he could not avoid taking his fleeting inventory of her dress. Everything stylish and expensive, he thought, but possibly lacking a soupçon of flair.

"A glass of champagne," Claude offered, taking Laura into the cool green and pink salon.

"What a lovely room!" Laura said, spinning in a slow circle. She was going to love it here. Jill Riordan was right, this was better than the doctor ordered.

Claudine closed the suitcase and stowed it away. Joining Laura at the window she pointed to a tall, attractive blonde lying stretched out on one of the sunbeds.

"That's M'mselle Gaby," she said. "If you would like, I will take you to meet her."

Laura dimpled, "I'd be grateful, if you wouldn't mind." Unaccountably, she felt gripped by shyness.

"Gabrielle, may I present Mademoiselle Bingham?"

Laura put two and two together and recognised Gabrielle. She was the laughing girl in Jill's car.

"Hi!" Gaby said, getting off her sunlounger and holding out a hand which almost as quickly she retracted. "Sorry, I'm plastered with gunge," she laughed.

"Gabrielle, are you properly covered with sun cream?" Claude frowned.

"Yes, *Daddy!*"

"And you, m'mselle, take care, the sun is strong today."

Laura bit back her natural instinct to mimic Gabrielle. "I'll be careful," she smiled.

"Plonk here," Gaby said, moving her wrap. "Take no notice of Claude, he means well. It's like having two fathers when he's around. How about a cold drink? I'm going to be as fat as a pig when I leave here, I haven't stopped eating since I arrived."

"You're as slim as a reed! Surely you don't have a problem with weight?"

"You're kidding. My nickname in school was *Flabby Gaby*. After another two days you'll be entitled to use it!"

"I have to diet like mad too! I should've been called *Lolloping Laura.*"

They lay in the sun laughing and talking. Laura felt the tension draining from her body. She liked this friendly girl, who reminded her of Nadia. This holiday was going to be all she'd hoped for - and more.

EPILOGUE

They stared at the red stain as it spread across the pink tablecloth.

Rachel made no sound as she fell forward, her glorious black hair fanning around her in a wavy arc.

As silently as he'd arrived the gunman vanished into the dark, his feet making no sound on the path. A slight smell of burnt powder hung in the air and then dissipated as if in a dream.

❋ ❋ ❋

Claude was the first to recover his voice. "Quickly, phone for an ambulance!" he shouted. His body shook, he was astonished to be alive. Thierry Thibault had not been the man hiding behind the black mask.

Gaby rose unsteadily from her chair and ran across the terrace into the pink and gold room. She picked up the telephone with trembling hands. So the cliché *was* true, her life *had* flashed before her eyes in those few frightening minutes.

Eduardo Conti steeled himself and placed his hand on Rachel Hunt's neck. The only pulse he could feel was his own, pounding rapidly. Frozen, he had waited for the bullet to lodge in his chest, Henri Ducroix's words echoing in his brain. *"You can't expect to get nine or ten million dollars without some worry."*

Intrigue

Laura Bingham saw the flash of light as the bullet exploded quietly from the silenced gun. She would take her punishment but how quickly Charles had found her. Jill and Peter Riordan would never have told him where she was nor would her family. Had he had her followed?

Rachel Hunt faced the muzzle of the gun. She felt hardly any pain as the bullet ploughed into her chest. The terrace was spinning and she could feel herself falling forward. "Roberto, he kept his word," she thought as her head hit the table.

❊ ❊ ❊

Daniel Hunt wiped the tears from his eyes as his investigator confirmed Rachel's death, his beautiful young wife. Hobbling uncomfortably on his stick he pressed a button on the tiny remote control and waited for the concealed door in the wall to open. Slowly he limped into the little room and sat in front of the bank of consoles. He flipped a switch on the one marked "Rachel." As the screen flickered into life he watched as Rachel's empty room came into view. The cameras scanned every inch of the bedroom. They never tired. Twenty-four hours a day they reported. No section of the room was hidden, no sound unrecorded. Rachel had questioned him about the diminutive black boxes on the ceiling. Clearly he could recall his answer. "Protection for your Canaletto," he'd said lightly.

From a drawer he removed the audio tape of Roberto's phone call, he'd played it a thousand times. Daniel too had noted Roberto Maroni's address and had given it to his investigator. The planted drugs had resulted in Maroni's arrest just as they'd planned. But it was Rachel's part in his mugging that had ripped him apart. He knew the words on the tape by heart … *"You just vanished and left me to deal with the police … your part in his downfall … when he hears what I have to say that will be the end of the lovely Mrs Hunt."* Those words haunted him by day and he dreamt of them at night. He'd been betrayed again. This time by his beloved Rachel.

"I'm sorry, Rachel," he wept, "but I couldn't allow you to live."

The End